The Urbana Free Library

To renew materials call
217-367-4057

DATE DUE	
AUG 10 2009	SEP 28 2009
SEP 24 2009	NOV 18 2009
OCT 17 2009	
JAN 19 2010	
NOV 29 2009	MAR 16 2012
FEB 09 2010	JUL 05 2012
JUN 01 2012	JUL 29 2012

Call Me Joe

Volume One

The Collected Short Works of Poul Anderson

Edited by Rick Katze and Lis Carey

NESFA Press
Post Office Box 809
Framingham, MA 01701
www.nesfa.org/press
2009

© 2008 by the Trigonier Trust
"Poul Anderson" © 2008 by Greg Bear
"Editor's Introduction" © 2008 by Rick Katze
Dust jacket illustration © 2008 by Bob Eggleton
Dust jacket design © 2008 by Alice N. S. Lewis

All rights reserved.

No part of this book may be reproduced in any form or by any electronic, magical or mechanical means including information storage and retrieval without permission in writing from the publisher, except by a reviewer, who may quote brief passages in a review.

FIRST EDITION, March 2009

ISBN-10: 1-886778-75-2
ISBN-13: 978-1-886778-75-7

Publication History

Editor's Introduction is original to this volume.
"Poul Anderson" by Greg Bear is original to this volume.
"Call Me Joe" first appeared in *Astounding Science Fiction,* April 1957.
"Prayer in War" appeared in *Staves,* 1993.
"Tomorrow's Children" first appeared in *Astounding Science Fiction,* March 1947.
"Kinnison's Band" appeared in *Primary Beams,* 2001.
"The Helping Hand" first appeared in *Astounding Science Fiction,* May 1950.
"Clausius' Chaos" first appeared in *Isaac Asimov's Science Fiction Magazine,* October 1980.
"Wildcat" first appeared in *The Magazine of Fantasy & Science Fiction,* November 1958.
"Journey's End" first appeared in *The Magazine of Fantasy & Science Fiction,* February 1957.
"Heinlein's Stories" first appeared in *Isaac Asimov's Science Fiction Magazine,* October 1980.
"Logic" first appeared in *Astounding Science Fiction,* July 1947.
"Time Patrol" first appeared in *The Magazine of Fantasy & Science Fiction,* May 1955.
"The First Love" appeared in appeared in *Staves,* 1993.
"The Double-Dyed Villains" first appeared in *Astounding Science Fiction* April 1949.
"To a Tavern Wench" appeared in appeared in *Staves,* 1993.
"The Immortal Game" first appeared in *The Magazine of Fantasy & Science Fiction,* February 1954.
"Upon the Occasion of Being Asked to Argue That Love and Marriage are Incompatible" appeared in *Staves,* 1993.
"Backwardness" first appeared in *The Magazine of Fantasy & Science Fiction,* March 1958.
"Haiku" appeared in *Staves,* 1993.
"Genius" first appeared in *Astounding Science Fiction* December, 1948
"There Will be Other Times" appeared in *Staves,* 1993.
"The Live Coward" first appeared in *Astounding Science Fiction,* June 1956.
"Ballade of an Artificial Satellite" first appeared in *The Magazine of Fantasy & Science Fiction,* October 1958.
"Time Lag" first appeared in *The Magazine of Fantasy & Science Fiction,* January 1961.
"The Man Who Came Early" first appeared in *The Magazine of Fantasy & Science Fiction,* June 1956.
"Autumn" appeared in *Staves,* 1993
"Turning Point" first appeared in *Worlds of If ,* May 1963.
"Honesty" appeared in *Staves,* 1993.
"The Alien Enemy" (as Michael Karageorge) first appeared in *Analog Science Fiction,* December, 1968.
"Eventide" appeared in *Staves,* 1993.
"Enough Rope" first appeared in *Astounding Science Fiction,* July 1953.
"The Sharing of Flesh" first appeared in *Galaxy Magazine,* December 1968.
"Barbarous Allen" first appeared in "The Zed", Winter 1953.
"Welcome" first appeared in *The Magazine of Fantasy & Science Fiction,* October 1960.
"Flight to Forever" first appeared in *Super Science Stories,* November 1950.
"Barnacle Bull" (as Winston P. Sanders) first appeared in *Analog Science Fiction,* September 1960.
"To Jack Williamson" appeared in *Staves,* 1993.
"Time Heals" first appeared in *Astounding Science Fiction,* October 1949.
"MacCannon" appeared in *Staves,* 1993.
"The Martian Crown Jewels" first appeared in *The Magazine of Fantasy & Science Fiction,* April 1959.
"Then Death Will Come" appeared in *Staves,* 1993.
"Prophecy" first appeared in *Astounding Science Fiction,* May 1949.
"Sea Burial" appeared in *Staves,* 1993.
"Einstein's Distress" first appeared in *Isaac Asimov's Science Fiction Magazine,* September 1980.
"Kings Who Die" first appeared in *Worlds of If ,* March 1962.
"Ochlan" appeared in *Staves,* 1993.
"Starfog" first appeared in *Analog Science Fiction,* August 1967.

Contents

Editor's Introduction 6
Poul Anderson by Greg Bear 7
Call Me Joe 11
Prayer in War 36
Tomorrow's Children 37
Kinnison's Band 57
The Helping Hand 58
Wildcat 77
Clausius' Chaos 100
Journey's End 101
Heinlein's Stories 107
Logic 108
Time Patrol 129
The First Love 156
The Double-dyed Villains 157
To a Tavern Wench 177
The Immortal Game 178
Upon the Occasion of Being Asked to Argue That Love and
    Marriage Are Incompatible 186
Backwardness 187
Haiku 195
Genius 196
There Will Be Other Times 222
The Live Coward 223
Ballade of an Artificial Satellite 240
Time Lag 241
The Man Who Came Early 266
Autumn 283
Turning Point 284
Honesty 294
The Alien Enemy 295
Eventide 307
Enough Rope 308
The Sharing of Flesh 329
Barbarous Allen 353
Welcome 354
Flight to Forever 360
Barnacle Bull 399
To Jack Williamson 411
Time Heals 412
MacCannon 425
The Martian Crown Jewels 426
Then Death Will Come 438
Prophecy 439
Sea Burial 444
Einstein's Distress 444
Kings Who Die 445
Ochlan 466
Starfog 467

Call Me Joe

Editor's Introduction

This is the first in a multi-volume collection of Poul Anderson stories. The stories are not in any discernible pattern. I hope to include at least one story from the Pulps in each volume. Future volumes will also contain selected portions of his non-fiction writing on science fiction topics.

In this volume you will find a selection of his earliest works from his first published story, "Tomorrow's Children", to "Genius". which discusses the dangers in social experimentation.

There are the stories of time travel. We meet, for the first time, Manse Everard in "Time Patrol". Poul wrote many stories about him. In "Wildcat" we are drilling for oil in prehistoric times to feed America's needs. "The Man Who Came Early" shows us just how far a modern soldier suddenly sent back in time to the era of the Vikings can progress. "A Connecticut Yankee in King Arthur's Court", it isn't. "Time Lag" explores war between two planets, separated by light years and without faster-than light drive.

The near future is represented by "Kings Who Die" showing the effects of war on society and the soldier who fight. There is "The Martian Crown Jewels" in which some priceless jewelry is stolen from an unmanned spaceship. A Martian detective, who bears a striking resemblance to a 19th century Earth detective who also appeared in "Time Patrol", solves the problem. "The Alien Enemy" examines the after effects on a colony invaded by an unknown enemy.

"The Double-Dyed Villains", "The Live Coward" and "Enough Rope" are three stories describing the adventures of Wing Alak. In his introduction to "The Double-Dyed Villains", in *Astounding Science Fiction* John W. Campbell noted that E. E. Smith described one way to run an empire, and that Poul Anderson described another.

We have the far future. The Hugo winning "The Sharing of Flesh" and "Starfog" both of which look at the reintegration of planets into a Galactic civilization after the collapse of empire.

Poul also wrote a huge amount of verse. A small but representative example will be found scattered throughout this volume.

Space considerations prevent a discussion of all the stories in this volume. You will find ideas and concepts in the stories that seem familiar and standard. That is because later writers incorporated the ideas that Poul articulated for the first time.

Rick Katze
November 2008

Poul Anderson
By Greg Bear

In 1962, at age ten, I came across Poul Anderson's novel *The High Crusade* in a navy station library in Kodiak, Alaska. The library was well-stocked with science fiction novels and anthologies from the 1950s and 60s, but I remember being bowled over by this lean, elegant, and funny tale, full of unexpected twists and turns.

I followed Poul's works with respect and admiration for years, but in 1970, his full range and brilliance became even more obvious when I read *The Broken Sword* and *Tau Zero* back to back. In 1972, I arranged to have Poul come south to speak at San Diego State College. When asked by a member of the audience (me) what it felt like to write a masterpiece like *Tau Zero*, he answered, from behind a wall of humility in which I could find no flaw, "Well, it was a good yarn, but really, just another story." Utterly charming.

The story-tellers we discover in our own golden age of literature fill special places in our lives. They become part of our growing bones and blood, and our gratitude is almost that of child for parent. Ultimately, I was privileged not just to be guided by Poul Anderson's fiction, but by the man and his family. I was brought into his life as with no other writer. He remains with me as a powerful presence, gentle and kindly, but also uniquely intelligent. His slightly veiled gaze, a paternal generosity of eyelids, seemed at once patient and friendly, but brows and lids could unpredictably vault to high and expressive arcs, revealing startled pale blue eyes. At rest, his face showed pleasantly bowed lips through which he delivered halting but well-formed speech, hands ascribing unbalanced curves in space. Hunched shoulders belied the strength of a man who fought in Society for Creative Anachronism tourneys; his face-folding smile, eyes almost disappearing, went perfectly with the slow rumble of his voice.

He had the gait of a wanderer who could go incredible distances—light years, really—without making a fuss.

Fine European beers were sipped on many afternoons of almost effortless conversation, punctuated by reflective moments of silence as we gathered our wits and reached for new words and fresh thoughts. Karen sat by him, symbiotic; doing embroidery, taking notes, planning trips to other lands for research, laughing and breaking into song at some fond memory of a convention or a filking festival; making sure that receipts were kept and novels were written to reflect the things learned on those journeys, for the tax man's critical gaze.

Poul's only enemy, I believe, was the tax man. But if a tax collector had dared show his face at the Anderson door in Orinda, he would have been treated with civility. He might not have been invited to stay or offered a beer, but I think he might have acknowledged having read Poul Anderson…and Poul might have thanked him and wondered what other bitter ironies the Norns had in store.

Poul was a modern skald, heir to the traditions of those who entertained weary Vikings centuries past. He could sing songs sad and happy with equal grace—crack a joke, spin out a yarn, create a wholly convincing world, with no apparent effort. He was an arch-libertarian, yet lived in the gentle and liberal climate of Orinda, near the People's Republic of Berkeley; reveled in physics and math, yet wrote raucous limericks and rollicking comedies; was a wizard at describing strange aliens, asteroids, and spaceships, yet deft at creating entertaining and convincing human characters…

Some writers you picture sweating and swearing as they plot and compose. Poul I see grinning. This is not to say that Poul's work is not serious, or that it came easily to him, or that he was not a master craftsman. He was just not the type to self-analyze or complain.

Poul's first story was published in 1947. His first major fantasy novel was THE BROKEN SWORD (1954); the first major science fiction novel, BRAIN WAVE, was published in the same year. (Daughter Astrid also arrived in 1954.) He has since earned more Nebulas, Hugos, and other awards than any mortal fireplace mantle can hold.

As with so many writers in the mid-twentieth century, Poul was mentored by John W. Campbell, Jr., editor of *Astounding Science Fiction,* later *Analog*. Poul was not averse to incorporating some of Campbell's ideas and storytelling prejudices, but more often than not, the result was original, more illustrative of Poul's talent than Campbell's philosophy. Their correspondence was long and fruitful. We still have a few letters to Campbell, but unfortunately, a peculiar sense of honor kept Poul from saving Campbell's replies.

His fiction emphasizes the trials, contradictions, and victories of the competent and thoughtful individual. The long and tortuous travels of characters in history fascinated Poul, and he earned a reputation for mastering tales of time travel and alternate realities. Both wings of Poul's eagle-span—the fantasy and the science fiction—seem to me superior in both spirit and discipline to most of the fiction of its day.

The Broken Sword's chilly portrait of the relationships between elves and men was published just as the long reign of Tolkien began in the United States, though no doubt Poul and Karen had already read *The Hobbit*. Poul derived his material from the same sources as Tolkien—the Northern myths, and of course Wagner. But his take was Nordic. The woods are deeper in the far north—darker and colder.

In *The High Crusade* (1960), Poul dropped a marauding spaceship filled with brutal, cocksure aliens into medieval England. Using his knowledge of both science and history to reverse all our expectations, he created a masterpiece of comic adventure. On his office wall hung an authentic-looking replica of a long sword. Lifting that sword was like reliving history, and brought deep respect for the men who lived and died with such weapons in hand.

He wrote of the Time Patrol; space merchant Nicholas van Rijn; Dominic Flandry of the Polesotechnic League, the furry, mimicking Teddy bears known as

Hokas (with good friend Gordon Dickson), and more; all series highly favored by connoisseurs.

Poul made many friends and (to my knowledge) few or no enemies. As a father and grandfather, he projected respect and humor. For Astrid he wrote and illustrated tales of a purple submarine, and for grandchildren Erik and Alexandra, handmade booklets, stories and poems/songs of zoos and sailors. He had a quiet and insightful wit, and a kindly tolerance for his headstrong son-in-law.

He loved to gather with friends and family to listen and talk. Among those friends was French anthropologist Francois Bordes, who wrote French science fiction under the pen name of Francis Carsac. Bordes was fond of teaching folks how to knap flints the old-fashioned way. Poul's friendship with Jack Vance led to the building of a famous houseboat (Frank Herbert was also an early participant in this project). Jerry Pournelle, another long-time friend, invited Poul to help him sail a boat down the coast from Puget Sound to Los Angeles; they never completed the journey, but were inspected by spyglassing orcas one morning.

Through the mid-1970s, as I was publishing more and more short fiction and writing my first novels, Poul and I corresponded. We swapped science and story ideas. I remember a good debate over whether or not ice would evaporate without ever becoming liquid, in the deep cold of Saturn's rings. Here I was, contending with a true master, so with sweat on my brow, wild-eyed, I pored over reference books and science texts, and finally quoted figures from tables in the *CRC Handbook*. Poul kindly conceded I had a point. Later, he told Astrid, when she asked about the science in my novels, that I could be relied upon to know my stuff. No higher praise!

In the early 1980s, Jerry Pournelle helped assemble the Citizens' Advisory Council on National Space Policy. Poul attended these meetings, and in 1983, I was invited to join this amazing group of writers, generals, scientists, astronauts, and politicians. To this day, the CACNSP meetings are the subject of legend and history. They taught me much of what I know about politics and Washington D.C., and were crucial to the writing of my novel, *Eon*.

In the 1980s, Poul helped me devise orbits for both *Eon* and *The Forge of God*. Karen helped with my history and Greek. Poul and Karen together provided expertise and imagination for many aspects of my work over the decades. I remember a lengthy discussion with Poul and his brother John about the science behind *Darwin's Radio*. They helped me hone my facts and arguments, invaluable when exploring deep and controversial topics.

There are so many tales of camping, hiking, visits to Denmark (and especially to Tivoli). Twenty years! Amazing for a true fan of Poul Anderson.

But in 2000, a cloud loomed. Poul was diagnosed with cancer. Despite strong hopes for a reversal, by early 2001, it was obvious he would not survive. Poul and Karen visited our home in Washington state and we held a farewell party, attended by many friends. Shortly after, I visited Poul and Karen in Orinda and shared a lovely summer lunch in the shade on the front lawn. The Orinda house was the scene of so many parties, visits, discussions, debates. This was the childhood home of my wife; Poul and Karen were still here. How could things change? It was impossible to believe that Poul wouldn't continue to travel and visit and write. But it was not to be. He went into Alta Bates hospital. I last spoke with him by phone. The diagnosis was final.

Astrid flew to Orinda.

In late July of 2001 we alerted people by email that Poul was fading fast. The result was amazing. Within a few hours, a thousand messages poured in from around the world, expressing how much Poul meant to readers and friends everywhere. During his last afternoon, Karen and Astrid read these messages to him as he sat up in bed, drinking a Carlsberg and having a small glass of Jubilaeum akvavit. Poul listened and smiled; it was confirmation of what we already knew. Amazing, and wonderful, this tribute.

And now, for his friends and his readers, for all who love him or will come to love him, NESFA Press is collecting his finest works. If you have yet to read Poul Anderson, you have many adventures and treats in store, with or without long swords, slide rules, or beer.

Skol!

CALL ME JOE

The wind came whooping out of eastern darkness, driving a lash of ammonia dust before it. In minutes, Edward Anglesey was blinded.

He clawed all four feet into the broken shards which were soil, hunched down and groped for his little smelter. The wind was an idiot bassoon in his skull. Something whipped across his back, drawing blood, a tree yanked up by the roots and spat a hundred miles. Lightning cracked, immensely far overhead where clouds boiled with night.

As if to reply, thunder toned in the ice mountains and a red gout of flame jumped and a hillside came booming down, spilling itself across the valley. The earth shivered.

Sodium explosion, thought Anglesey in the drumbeat noise. The fire and the lightning gave him enough illumination to find his apparatus. He picked up tools in muscular hands, his tail gripped the trough, and he battered his way to the tunnel and thus to his dugout.

It had walls and roof of water, frozen by sun-remoteness and compressed by tons of atmosphere jammed onto every square inch. Ventilated by a tiny smoke hole, a lamp of tree oil burning in hydrogen made a dull light for the single room.

Anglesey sprawled his slate-blue form on the floor, panting. It was no use to swear at the storm. These ammonia gales often came at sunset, and there was nothing to do but wait them out. He was tired, anyway.

It would be morning in five hours or so. He had hoped to cast an axhead, his first, this evening, but maybe it was better to do the job by daylight.

He pulled a dekapod body off a shelf and ate the meat raw, pausing for long gulps of liquid methane from a jug. Things would improve once he had proper tools; so far, everything had been painfully grubbed and hacked to shape with teeth, claws, chance icicles, and what detestably weak and crumbling fragments remained of the spaceship. Give him a few years and he'd be living as a man should.

He sighed, stretched, and lay down to sleep.

Somewhat more than one hundred and twelve thousand miles away, Edward Anglesey took off his helmet.

He looked around, blinking. After the Jovian surface, it was always a little unreal to find himself here again, in the clean, quiet orderliness of the control room.

His muscles ached. They shouldn't. He had not really been fighting a gale of several hundred miles an hour, under three gravities and a temperature of 140 absolute. He had been here, in the almost nonexistent pull of Jupiter V, breathing oxynitrogen. It was Joe who lived down there and filled his lungs with hydrogen and helium at a pressure which could still only be estimated, because it broke aneroids and deranged piezoelectrics.

Nevertheless, his body felt worn and beaten. Tension, no doubt—psychosomatics. After all, for a good many hours now he had, in a sense, been Joe, and Joe had been working hard.

With the helmet off, Anglesey held only a thread of identification. The esprojector was still tuned to Joe's brain but no longer focused on his own. Somewhere in the back of his mind, he knew an indescribable feeling of sleep. Now and then, vague forms or colors drifted in the soft black—dreams? Not impossible that Joe's brain should dream a little when Anglesey's mind wasn't using it.

A light flickered red on the esprojector panel, and a bell whined electronic fear. Anglesey cursed. Thin fingers danced over the controls of his chair, he slewed around and shot across to the bank of dials. Yes, there—K tube oscillating again! The circuit blew out. He wrenched the face plate off with one hand and fumbled in a drawer with the other.

Inside his mind, he could feel the contact with Joe fading. If he once lost it entirely, he wasn't sure he could regain it. And Joe was an investment of several million dollars and quite a few highly skilled man-years.

Anglesey pulled the offending K tube from its socket and threw it on the floor. Glass exploded. It eased his temper a bit, just enough so he could find a replacement, plug it in, switch on the current again. As the machine warmed up, once again amplifying, the Joeness in the back alleys of his brain strengthened.

Slowly, then, the man in the electric wheel chair rolled out of the room, into the hall. Let somebody else sweep up the broken tube. To hell with it. To hell with everybody.

Jan Cornelius had never been farther from Earth than some comfortable Lunar resort. He felt much put upon that the Psionics Corporation should tap him for a thirteen-month exile. The fact that he knew as much about esprojectors and their cranky innards as any other man alive was no excuse. Why send anyone at all? Who cared?

Obviously the Federation Science Authority did. It had seemingly given those bearded hermits a blank check on the taxpayer's account.

Thus did Cornelius grumble to himself, all the long hyperbolic path to Jupiter. Then the shifting accelerations of approach to its tiny inner satellite left him too wretched for further complaint. And when he finally, just prior to disembarkation, went up to the greenhouse for a look at Jupiter, he said not a word. Nobody does, the first time.

Arne Viken waited patiently while Cornelius stared. *It still gets me too,* he remembered. *By the throat. Sometimes I'm afraid to look.*

At length Cornelius turned around. He had a faintly Jovian appearance himself, being a large man with an imposing girth. "I had no idea," he whispered. "I never thought…I had seen pictures, but…"

Viken nodded. "Sure, Dr. Cornelius. Pictures don't convey it."

Where they stood, they could see the dark broken rock of the satellite, jumbled for a short way beyond the landing slip and then chopped off sheer. This moon was scarcely even a platform, it seemed, and cold constellations went streaming past it, around it. Jupiter lay across a fifth of that sky, softly ambrous, banded with colors, spotted with the shadows of planet-sized moons and with whirlwinds as broad as Earth. If there had been any gravity to speak of, Cornelius would have thought, instinctively, that the great planet was falling on him. As it was, he felt as if sucked upward, his hands were still sore where he had grabbed a rail to hold on.

"You live here…all alone…with this?" He spoke feebly.

"Oh, well, there are some fifty of us all told, pretty congenial," said Viken. "It's not so bad. You sign up for four-cycle hitches—four ship arrivals—and believe it or not, Dr. Cornelius, this is my third enlistment."

The newcomer forbore to inquire more deeply. There was something not quite understandable about the men on Jupiter V. They were mostly bearded, though otherwise careful to remain neat; their low-gravity movements were somehow dreamlike to watch; they hoarded their conversation, as if to stretch it through the year and a month between ships. Their monkish existence had changed them—or did they take what amounted to vows of poverty, chastity, and obedience because they had never felt quite at home on green Earth?

Thirteen months! Cornelius shuddered. It was going to be a long, cold wait, and the pay and bonuses accumulating for him were scant comfort now, four hundred and eighty million miles from the sun.

"Wonderful place to do research," continued Viken. "All the facilities, hand-picked colleagues, no distractions—and, of course…" He jerked his thumb at the planet and turned to leave.

Cornelius followed, wallowing awkwardly. "It is very interesting, no doubt," he puffed. "Fascinating. But really, Dr. Viken, to drag me way out here and make me spend a year-plus waiting for the next ship—to do a job which may take me a few weeks…"

"Are you sure it's that simple?" asked Viken gently. His face swiveled around, and there was something in his eyes that silenced Cornelius. "After all my time here, I've yet to see any problem, however complicated, which when you looked at it the right way didn't become still more complicated."

They went through the ship's air lock and the tube joining it to the station entrance. Nearly everything was underground. Rooms, laboratories, even halls, had a degree of luxuriousness—why, there was a fireplace with a real fire in the common room! God alone knew what *that* cost! Thinking of the huge chill emptiness where the king planet laired, and of his own year's sentence, Cornelius decided that such luxuries were, in truth, biological necessities.

Viken showed him to a pleasantly furnished chamber which would be his own. "We'll fetch your luggage soon, and unload your psionic stuff. Right now, everybody's either talking to the ship's crew or reading his mail."

Cornelius nodded absently and sat down. The chair, like all low-gee furniture, was a mere spidery skeleton, but it held his bulk comfortably enough. He felt in his tunic, hoping to bribe the other man into keeping him company for a while. "Cigar? I brought some from Amsterdam."

"Thanks." Viken accepted with disappointing casualness, crossed long, thin legs and blew grayish clouds.

"Ah…are you in charge here?"

"Not exactly. No one is. We do have one administrator, the cook, to handle what little work of that type may come up. Don't forget, this is a research station, first, last, and always."

"What is your field, then?"

Viken frowned. "Don't question anyone else so bluntly, Dr. Cornelius," he warned. "They'd rather spin the gossip out as long as possible with each newcomer. It's a rare treat to have someone whose every last conceivable reaction hasn't been—no, no apologies to me. 'S all right. I'm a physicist, specializing in the solid state at ultra-high pressures." He nodded at the wall. "Plenty of it to be observed—there!"

"I see." Cornelius smoked quietly for a while. Then: "I'm supposed to be the psionics expert, but, frankly, at present I've no idea why your machine should misbehave as reported."

"You mean those, uh, K tubes have a stable output on Earth?"

"And on Luna, Mars, Venus—everywhere, apparently, but here." Cornelius shrugged. "Of course, psibeams are always persnickety, and sometimes you get an unwanted feedback when—no. I'll get the facts before I theorize. Who are your psimen?"

"Just Anglesey, who's not a formally trained esman at all. But he took it up after he was crippled, and showed such a natural aptitude that he was shipped out here when he volunteered. It's so hard to get anyone for Jupiter V that we aren't fussy about degrees. At that, Ed seems to be operating Joe as well as a Ps.D. could."

"Ah, yes. Your pseudojovian. I'll have to examine that angle pretty carefully, too," said Cornelius. In spite of himself, he was getting interested. "Maybe the trouble comes from something in Joe's biochemistry. Who knows? I'll let you into a carefully guarded little secret, Dr. Viken: psionics is not an exact science."

"Neither is physics," grinned the other man. After a moment, he added more soberly: "Not my brand of physics, anyway. I hope to make it exact. That's why I'm here, you know. It's the reason we're all here."

Edward Anglesey was a bit of a shock the first time. He was a head, a pair of arms, and a disconcertingly intense blue stare. The rest of him was mere detail, enclosed in a wheeled machine.

"Biophysicist originally," Viken had told Cornelius. "Studying atmospheric spores at Earth Station when he was still a young man—accident, crushed him up, nothing below his chest will ever work again. Snappish type, you have to go slow with him."

Seated on a wisp of stool in the esprojector control room, Cornelius realized that Viken had been soft-pedaling the truth.

Anglesey ate as he talked, gracelessly, letting the chair's tentacles wipe up after him. "Got to," he explained. "This stupid place is officially on Earth time, GMT. Jupiter isn't. I've got to be here whenever Joe wakes, ready to take him over."

"Couldn't you have someone spell you?" asked Cornelius.

"Bah!" Anglesey stabbed a piece of prot and waggled it at the other man. Since it was native to him, he could spit out English, the common language of the station, with unmeasured ferocity. "Look here. You ever done therapeutic esping? Not just listening in, or even communication, but actual pedagogic control?"

"No, not I. It requires a certain natural talent, like yours." Cornelius smiled. His ingratiating little phrase was swallowed without being noticed by the scored face opposite him. "I take it you mean cases like, oh, re-educating the nervous system of a palsied child?"

"Yes, yes. Good enough example. Has anyone ever tried to suppress the child's personality, take him over in the most literal sense?"

"Good God, no!"

"Even as a scientific experiment?" Anglesey grinned. "Has any esprojector operative ever poured on the juice and swamped the child's brain with his own thoughts? Come on, Cornelius, I won't snitch on you."

"Well…it's out of my line, you understand." The psionicist looked carefully away, found a bland meter face and screwed his eyes to that. "I have, uh, heard something about…Well, yes, there were attempts made in some pathological cases to, uh, bull through…break down the patient's delusions by sheer force—"

"And it didn't work," said Anglesey. He laughed. "It *can't* work, not even on a child, let alone an adult with a fully developed personality. Why, it took a decade of refinement, didn't it, before the machine was debugged to the point where a psychiatrist could even 'listen in' without the normal variation between his pattern of thought and the patient's—without that variation setting up an interference scrambling the very thing he wanted to study. The machine has to make automatic compensations for the differences between individuals. We still can't bridge the differences between species.

"If someone else is willing to cooperate, you can very gently guide his thinking. And that's all. If you try to seize control of another brain, a brain with its own background of experience, its own ego, you risk your very sanity. The other brain will fight back instinctively. A fully developed, matured, hardened human personality is just too complex for outside control. It has too many resources, too much hell the subconscious can call to its defense if its integrity is threatened. Blazes, man, we can't even master our own minds, let alone anyone else's!"

Anglesey's cracked-voice tirade broke off. He sat brooding at the instrument panel, tapping the console of his mechanical mother.

"Well?" said Cornelius after a while.

He should not, perhaps, have spoken. But he found it hard to remain mute. There was too much silence—half a billion miles of it, from here to the sun. If you closed your mouth five minutes at a time, the silence began creeping in like fog.

"Well," gibed Anglesey. "So our pseudojovian, Joe, has a physically adult brain. The only reason I can control him is that his brain has never been given a chance to develop its own ego. I *am* Joe. From the moment he was 'born' into consciousness, I have been there. The psibeam sends me all his sense data and sends him back my motor-nerve impulses. Nevertheless, he has that excellent brain, and its cells are recording every trace of experience, even as yours and mine; his synapses have assumed the topography which is my 'personality pattern.'

"Anyone else, taking him over from me, would find it was like an attempt to oust me myself from my own brain. It couldn't be done. To be sure, he doubtless has only a rudimentary set of Anglesey-memories—I do not, for instance, repeat trigonometric theorems while controlling him—but he has enough to be, potentially, a distinct personality.

"As a matter of fact, whenever he wakes up from sleep—there's usually a lag of a few minutes, while I sense the change through my normal psi faculties and get the amplifying helmet adjusted—I have a bit of a struggle. I feel almost a…a resistance until I've brought his mental currents completely into phase with mine. Merely dreaming has been enough of a different experience to…" Anglesey didn't bother to finish the sentence.

"I see," murmured Cornelius. "Yes, it's clear enough. In fact, it's astonishing that you can have such total contact with a being of such alien metabolism."

"I won't for much longer," said the esman sarcastically, "unless you can correct whatever is burning out those K tubes. I don't have an unlimited supply of spares."

"I have some working hypotheses," said Cornelius, "but there's so little known about psibeam transmission—is the velocity infinite or merely very great, is the beam strength actually independent of distance? How about the possible effects of transmission—oh, through the degenerate matter in the Jovian core? Good Lord, a planet where water is a heavy mineral and hydrogen is a metal! What do we know?"

"We're supposed to find out," snapped Anglesey. "That's what this whole project is for. Knowledge. Bull!" Almost, he spat on the floor. "Apparently what little we have learned doesn't even get through to people. Hydrogen is still a gas where Joe lives. He'd have to dig down a few miles to reach the solid phase. And I'm expected to make a scientific analysis of Jovian conditions!"

Cornelius waited it out, letting Anglesey storm on while he himself turned over the problem of K-tube oscillation.

"They don't understand back on Earth. Even here they don't. Sometimes I think they refuse to understand. Joe's down there without much more than his bare hands. He, I, we started with no more knowledge than that he could probably eat the local life. He has to spend nearly all his time hunting for food. It's a miracle he's come as far as he has in these few weeks—made a shelter, grown familiar with the immediate region, begun on metallurgy, hydrurgy, whatever you want to call it. What more do they want me to do, for crying in the beer?"

"Yes, yes," mumbled Cornelius. "Yes, I…"

Anglesey raised his white bony face. Something filmed over in his eyes.

"What—" began Cornelius.

"Shut up!" Anglesey whipped the chair around, groped for the helmet, slapped it down over his skull. "Joe's waking. Get out of here."

"But if you'll let me work only while he sleeps, how can I—"

Anglesey snarled and threw a wrench at him. It was a feeble toss, even in low gee. Cornelius backed toward the door. Anglesey was tuning in the esprojector. Suddenly he jerked.

"Cornelius!"

"Whatisit?" The psionicist tried to run back, overdid it, and skidded in a heap to end up against the panel.

"K tube again." Anglesey yanked off the helmet. It must have hurt like blazes, having a mental squeal build up uncontrolled and amplified in your own brain, but he said merely: "Change it for me. Fast. And then get out and leave me alone. Joe didn't wake up of himself. Something crawled into the dugout with me—I'm in trouble down there!"

It had been a hard day's work, and Joe slept heavily. He did not wake until the hands closed on his throat.

For a moment then he knew only a crazy smothering wave of panic. He thought he was back on Earth Station, floating in null gee at the end of a cable while a thousand frosty stars haloed the planet before him. He thought the great I-beam had broken from its moorings and started toward him, slowly, but with all the inertia of its cold tons, spinning and shimmering in the Earthlight, and the only sound himself screaming and screaming in his helmet, trying to break from the cable, the beam nudged him ever so gently but it kept on moving. He moved with it; he was crushed against the station wall; nuzzled into it, his mangled suit frothed as it tried to seal its wounded self. There was blood mingled with the foam—his blood. *Joe roared.*

His convulsive reaction tore the hands off his neck and sent a black shape spinning across the dugout. It struck the wall, thunderously, and the lamp fell to the floor and went out.

Joe stood in darkness, breathing hard, aware in a vague fashion that the wind had died from a shriek to a low snarling while he slept.

The thing he had tossed away mumbled in pain and crawled along the wall. Joe felt through lightlessness after his club.

Something else scrabbled. The tunnel! They were coming through the tunnel! Joe groped blind to meet them. His heart drummed thickly and his nose drank an alien stench.

The thing that emerged, as Joe's hands closed on it, was only about half his size, but it had six monstrously taloned feet and a pair of three-fingered hands that reached after his eyes. Joe cursed, lifted it while it writhed, and dashed it to the floor. It screamed, and he heard bones splinter.

"Come on, then!" Joe arched his back and spat at them, like a tiger menaced by giant caterpillars.

They flowed through his tunnel and into the room, a dozen of them entered while he wrestled one that had curled itself around his shoulders and anchored its sinuous body with claws. They pulled at his legs, trying to crawl up on his back. He struck out with claws of his own, with his tail, rolled over and went down beneath a heap of them and stood up with the heap still clinging to him.

They swayed in darkness. The legged seething of them struck the dugout wall. It shivered, a rafter cracked, the roof came down. Anglesey stood in a pit, among broken ice plates, under the wan light of a sinking Ganymede.

He could see now that the monsters were black in color and that they had heads big enough to accommodate some brain, less than human but probably more than apes. There were a score of them or so, they struggled from beneath the wreckage and flowed at him with the same shrieking malice.

Why?

Baboon reaction, thought Anglesey somewhere in the back of himself. See the stranger, fear the stranger, hate the stranger, kill the stranger. His chest heaved, pumping air through a raw throat. He yanked a whole rafter to him, snapped it in half, and twirled the iron-hard wood.

The nearest creature got its head bashed in. The next had its back broken. The third was hurled with shattered ribs into a fourth, they went down together. Joe began to laugh. It was getting to be fun.

"Yee-ow! Ti-i-i-iger!" He ran across the icy ground, toward the pack. They scattered, howling. He hunted them until the last one had vanished into the forest.

Panting, Joe looked at the dead. He himself was bleeding, he ached, he was cold and hungry and his shelter had been wrecked—but he'd whipped them! He had a sudden impulse to beat his chest and howl. For a moment he hesitated. Why not? Anglesey threw back his head and bayed victory at the dim shield of Ganymede.

Thereafter he went to work. First build a fire, in the lee of the spaceship—which was little more by now than a hill of corrosion. The monster pack cried in darkness and the broken ground, they had not given up on him, they would return.

He tore a haunch off one of the slain and took a bite. Pretty good. Better yet if properly cooked. Heh! They'd made a big mistake in calling his attention to their existence! He finished breakfast while Ganymede slipped under the western ice mountains. It would be morning soon. The air was almost still, and a flock of pancake-shaped sky-skimmers, as Anglesey called them, went overhead, burnished copper color in the first pale dawn streaks.

Joe rummaged in the ruins of his hut until he had recovered the water-smelting equipment. It wasn't harmed. That was the first order of business, melt some ice and cast it in the molds of ax, knife, saw, hammer he had painfully prepared. Under Jovian conditions, methane was a liquid that you drank and water was a dense hard mineral. It would make good tools. Later on he would try alloying it with other materials.

Next—yes. To hell with the dugout, he could sleep in the open again for a while. Make a bow, set traps, be ready to massacre the black caterpillars when they attacked him again. There was a chasm not far from here, going down a long way toward the bitter cold of the metallic-hydrogen strata: a natural icebox, a place to store the several weeks' worth of meat his enemies would supply. This would give him leisure to—Oh, a hell of a lot!

Joe laughed exultantly and lay down to watch the sunrise.

It struck him afresh how lovely a place this was. See how the small brilliant spark of the sun swam up out of eastern fog banks colored dusky purple and veined with rose and gold; see how the light strengthened until the great hollow arch of the sky became one shout of radiance; see how the light spilled warm and living over a broad fair land, the million square miles of rustling low forests and wave-blinking lakes and feather-plumed hydrogen geysers; and see, see, see how the ice mountains of the west flashed like blued steel!

Anglesey drew the wild morning wind deep into his lungs and shouted with a boy's joy

"I'm not a biologist myself," said Viken carefully. "But maybe for that reason I can better give you the general picture. Then Lopez or Matsumoto can answer any questions of detail."

"Excellent." Cornelius nodded. "Why don't you assume I am totally ignorant of this project? I very nearly am, you know."

"If you wish," laughed Viken.

They stood in an outer office of the xenobiology section. No one else was around, for the station's clocks said 1730 GMT and there was only one shift. No point in having more, until Anglesey's half of the enterprise had actually begun gathering quantitative data.

The physicist bent over and took a paperweight off a desk. "One of the boys made this for fun," he said, "but it's a pretty good model of Joe. He stands about five feet tall at the head."

Cornelius turned the plastic image over in his hands. If you could imagine such a thing as a feline centaur with a thick prehensile tail…The torso was squat, long-armed, immensely muscular; the hairless head was round, wide-nosed, with big deep-set eyes and heavy jaws, but it was really quite a human face. The overall color was bluish gray.

"Male, I see," he remarked.

"Of course. Perhaps you don't understand. Joe is the complete pseudojovian—as far as we can tell, the final model, with all the bugs worked out. He's the answer to a research question that took fifty years to ask." Viken looked sidewise at Cornelius. "So you realize the importance of your job, don't you?"

"I'll do my best," said the psionicist. "But if…well, let's say that tube failure or something causes you to lose Joe before I've solved the oscillation problem. You do have other pseudos in reserve, don't you?"

"Oh, yes," said Viken moodily. "But the cost…We're not on an unlimited budget. We do go through a lot of money, because it's expensive to stand up and sneeze this far from Earth. But for that same reason our margin is slim."

He jammed hands in pockets and slouched toward the inner door, the laboratories, head down and talking in a low, hurried voice. "Perhaps you don't realize what a nightmare planet Jupiter is. Not just the surface gravity—a shade under three gees, what's that?—but the gravitational potential, ten times Earth's. The temperature. The pressure. Above all, the atmosphere, and the storms, and the darkness!

"When a spaceship goes down to the Jovian surface, it's a radio-controlled job; it leaks like a sieve, to equalize pressure, but otherwise it's the sturdiest, most utterly powerful model ever designed; it's loaded with every instrument, every servomechanism, every safety device the human mind has yet thought up to protect a million-dollar hunk of precision equipment.

"And what happens? Half the ships never reach the surface at all. A storm snatches them and throws them away, or they collide with a floating chunk of Ice Seven—small version of the Red Spot—or, so help me, what passes for a flock of *birds* rams one and stoves it in!

"As for the fifty per cent which do land, it's a one-way trip. We don't even try to bring them back. If the stresses coming down haven't sprung something, the corrosion has doomed them anyway. Hydrogen at Jovian pressure does funny things to metals.

"It cost a total of about five million dollars to set Joe, one pseudo, down there. Each pseudo to follow will cost, if we're lucky, a couple of million more."

Viken kicked open the door and led the way through. Beyond was a big room, low-ceilinged, coldly lit and murmurous with ventilators. It reminded Cornelius of a nucleonics lab; for a moment he wasn't sure why, then he recognized the intricacies of remote control, remote observation, walls enclosing forces which could destroy the entire moon.

"These are required by the pressure, of course," said Viken, pointing to a row of shields. "And the cold. And the hydrogen itself, as a minor hazard. We have units here duplicating conditions in the Jovian, uh, stratosphere. This is where the whole project really began."

"I've heard something about that. Didn't you scoop up airborne spores?"

"Not I." Viken chuckled. "Totti's crew did, about fifty years ago. Proved there was life on Jupiter. A life using liquid methane as its basic solvent, solid ammonia as a starting point for nitrate synthesis: the plants use solar energy to build unsaturated carbon compounds, releasing hydrogen; the animals eat the plants and reduce those compounds again to the saturated form. There is even an equivalent of combustion. The reactions involve complex enzymes and—well, it's out of my line."

"Jovian biochemistry is pretty well understood, then."

"Oh, yes. Even in Totti's day they had a highly developed biotic technology: Earth bacteria had already been synthesized and most gene structures pretty well mapped. The only reason it took so long to diagram Jovian life processes was the technical difficulty, high pressure and so on."

"When did you actually get a look at Jupiter's surface?"

"Gray managed that, about thirty years ago. Set a televisor ship down, a ship that lasted long enough to flash him quite a series of pictures. Since then, the technique has improved. We know that Jupiter is crawling with its own weird kind of life, probably more fertile than Earth. Extrapolating from the airborne micro-organisms, our team made trial syntheses of metazoans and—"

Viken sighed. "Damn it, if only there were intelligent native life! Think what they could tell us, Cornelius, the data, the—just think back how far we've gone since Lavoisier, with the low-pressure chemistry of Earth. Here's a chance to learn a high-pressure chemistry and physics at least as rich with possibilities!"

After a moment, Cornelius murmured slyly, "Are you certain there *aren't* any Jovians?"

"Oh, sure, there could be several billion of them." Viken shrugged. Cities, empires, anything you like. Jupiter has the surface area of a hundred Earths, and we've only seen maybe a dozen small regions. But we do know there aren't any Jovians using radio. Considering their atmosphere, it's unlikely they ever would invent it for themselves—imagine how thick a vacuum tube has to be, how strong a pump you need! So it was finally decided we'd better make our own Jovians."

Cornelius followed him through the lab into another room. This was less cluttered, it had a more finished appearance; the experimenter's haywire rig had yielded to the assured precision of an engineer.

Viken went over to one of the panels which lined the walls and looked at its gauges. "Beyond this lies another pseudo," he said. "Female, in this instance. She's at a pressure of two hundred atmospheres and a temperature of 194 absolute. There's a…an umbilical arrangement, I guess you'd call it, to keep her alive. She was grown to adulthood in this, uh, fetal stage—we patterned our Jovians after the terrestrial mammal. She's never been conscious, she won't ever be till she's 'born.' We have a total of twenty males and sixty females waiting here. We can count on about half reaching the surface. More can be created as required. It isn't the pseudos that are so expensive, it's their transportation. So Joe is down there alone till we're sure that his kind *can* survive."

"I take it you experimented with lower forms first," said Cornelius.

"Of course. It took twenty years, even with forced-catalysis techniques, to work from an artificial airborne spore to Joe. We've used the psibeam to control everything from pseudo insects on up. Interspecies control is possible, you know, if your puppet's nervous system is deliberately designed for it and isn't given a chance to grow into a pattern different from the esman's."

"And Joe is the first specimen who's given trouble?"

"Yes."

"Scratch one hypothesis." Cornelius sat down on a workbench, dangling thick legs and running a hand through thin sandy hair. "I thought maybe some physical effect of Jupiter was responsible. Now it looks as if the difficulty is with Joe himself."

"We've all suspected that much," said Viken. He struck a cigarette and sucked in his cheeks around the smoke. His eyes were gloomy. "Hard to see how. The biotics engineers tell me *Pseudocentaurus sapiens* has been more carefully designed than any product of natural evolution."

"Even the brain?"

"Yes. It's patterned directly on the human, to make psibeam control possible, but there are improvements—greater stability."

"There are still the psychological aspects, though," said Cornelius. "In spite of all our amplifiers and other fancy gadgets, psi is essentially a branch of psychology, even today—or maybe it's the other way around. Let's consider traumatic experiences. I take it the…the adult Jovian fetus has a rough trip going down?"

"The ship does," said Viken. "Not the pseudo itself, which is wrapped up in fluid just like you were before birth."

"Nevertheless," said Cornelius, "the two-hundred-atmospheres pressure here is not the same as whatever unthinkable pressure exists down on Jupiter. Could the change be injurious?"

Viken gave him a look of respect. "Not likely," he answered. "I told you the J ships are designed leaky. External pressure is transmitted to the uh, uterine mechanism through a series of diaphragms, in a gradual fashion. It takes hours to make the descent, you realize."

"Well, what happens next?" went on Cornelius. "The ship lands, the uterine mechanism opens, the umbilical connection disengages, and Joe is, shall we say, born. But he has an adult brain. He is not protected by the only half-developed infant brain from the shock of sudden awareness."

"We thought of that," said Viken. "Anglesey was on the psibeam, in phase with Joe, when the ship left this moon. So it wasn't really Joe who emerged, who perceived. Joe has never been much more than a biological waldo. He can only suffer mental shock to the extent that Ed does, because it *is* Ed down there!"

"As you will," said Cornelius. "Still, you didn't plan for a race of puppets, did you?"

"Oh, heavens, no," said Viken. "Out of the question. Once we know Joe is well established, we'll import a few more esmen and get him some assistance in the form of other pseudos. Eventually females will be sent down, and uncontrolled males, to be educated by the puppets. A new generation will be born normally—well, anyhow, the ultimate aim is a small civilization of Jovians. There will be hunters, miners, artisans, farmers, housewives, the works. They will support a few key members, a kind of priesthood. And that priesthood will be esp-controlled, as Joe is. It will exist solely to make instruments, take readings, perform experiments, and tell us what we want to know!"

Cornelius nodded. In a general way, this was the Jovian project as he had understood it. He could appreciate the importance of his own assignment.

Only, he still had no clue to the cause of that positive feedback in the K tubes. And what could he do about it?

His hands were still bruised. *Oh God,* he thought with a groan, for the hundredth time, *does it affect me that much? While Joe was fighting down there, did I really hammer my fists on metal up here?*

His eyes smoldered across the room, to the bench where Cornelius worked. He didn't like Cornelius, fat cigar-sucking slob, interminably talking and talking. He had about given up trying to be civil to the Earthworm.

The psionicist laid down a screwdriver and flexed cramped fingers. "*Whuff!*" He smiled. "I'm going to take a break."

The half-assembled esprojector made a gaunt backdrop for his wide soft body, where it squatted toad fashion on the bench. Anglesey detested the whole idea of anyone sharing this room, even for a few hours a day. Of late he had been demanding his meals brought here, left outside the door of his adjoining bedroom-bath. He had not gone beyond for quite some time now.

And why should I?

"Couldn't you hurry it up a little?" snapped Anglesey.

Cornelius flushed. "If you'd had an assembled spare machine, instead of loose parts—" he began. Shrugging, he took out a cigar stub and relit it carefully; his supply had to last a long time. Anglesey wondered if those stinking clouds were blown from his mouth of malicious purpose. *I don't like you, Mr. Earthman Cornelius, and it is doubtless quite mutual.*

"There was no obvious need for one, until the other esmen arrive," said Anglesey in a sullen voice. "And the testing instruments report this one in perfectly good order."

"Nevertheless," said Cornelius, "at irregular intervals it goes into wild oscillations which burn out the K tube. The problem is why. I'll have you try out this new machine as soon as it is ready, but, frankly, I don't believe the trouble lies in electronic failure at all—or even in unsuspected physical effects."

"Where, then?" Anglesey felt more at ease as the discussion grew purely technical.

"Well, look. What exactly is the K tube? It's the heart of the esprojector. It amplifies your natural psionic pulses, uses them to modulate the carrier wave, and shoots the whole beam down at Joe. It also picks up Joe's resonating impulses and amplifies them for your benefit. Everything else is auxiliary to the K tube."

"Spare me the lecture," snarled Anglesey.

"I was only rehearsing the obvious," said Cornelius, "because every now and then it is the obvious answer which is hardest to see. Maybe it isn't the K tube which is misbehaving. Maybe it is you."

"What?" The white face gaped at him. A dawning rage crept across its thin bones.

"Nothing personal intended," said Cornelius hastily. "But you know what a tricky beast the subconscious is. Suppose, just as a working hypothesis, that way down underneath, you don't *want* to be on Jupiter. I imagine it is a rather terrifying environment. Or there may be some obscure Freudian element involved. Or, quite simply and naturally, your subconscious may fail to understand that Joe's death does not entail your own."

"Um-m-m." *Mirabile dictu*, Anglesey remained calm. He rubbed his chin with one skeletal hand. "Can you be more explicit?"

"Only in a rough way," replied Cornelius. "Your conscious mind sends a motor impulse along the psibeam to Joe. Simultaneously, your subconscious mind, being scared of the whole business, emits the glandular-vascular-cardiac-visceral impulses associated with fear. These react on Joe, whose tension is transmitted back along the beam. Feeling Joe's somatic fear symptoms, your subconscious gets still more worried, thereby increasing the symptoms. Get it? It's exactly similar to ordinary neurasthenia, with this exception, that since there is a powerful amplifier, the K tube, involved, the oscillations can build up uncontrollably within a second or two. You should be thankful the tube does burn out—otherwise your brain might do so!"

For a moment Anglesey was quiet. Then he laughed. It was a hard, barbaric laughter. Cornelius started as it struck his eardrums.

"Nice idea," said the esman. "But I'm afraid it won't fit all the data. You see, I like it down there. I like being Joe."

He paused for a while, then continued in a dry impersonal tone; "Don't judge the environment from my notes. They're just idiotic things like estimates of wind velocity, temperature variations, mineral properties—insignificant. What I can't put in is how Jupiter looks through a Jovian's infrared-seeing eyes."

"Different, I should think," ventured Cornelius after a minute's clumsy silence.

"Yes and no. It's hard to put into language. Some of it I can't, because man hasn't got the concepts. But…oh, I can't describe it. Shakespeare himself couldn't. Just remember that everything about Jupiter which is cold and poisonous and gloomy to us is *right* for Joe."

Anglesey's tone grew remote, as if he spoke to himself. "Imagine walking under a glowing violet sky, where great flashing clouds sweep the earth with shadow and rain strides beneath them. Imagine walking on the slopes of a mountain like polished metal, with a clean red flame exploding above you and thunder laughing in the ground. Imagine a cool wild stream, and low trees with dark coppery flowers, and a waterfall—methanefall, whatever you like—leaping off a cliff, and the strong live wind shakes its mane full of rainbows! Imagine a whole forest, dark and breathing, and here and there you glimpse a pale-red wavering will-o'-the-wisp, which is the life radiation of some fleet, shy animal, and…and…"

Anglesey croaked into silence. He stared down at his clenched fists then he closed his eyes tight and tears ran out between the lids, "Imagine being *strong!*"

Suddenly he snatched up the helmet, crammed it on his head and twirled the control knobs. Joe had been sleeping, down in the night, but Joe was about to wake up and—roar under the four great moons till all the forest feared him?

Cornelius slipped quietly out of the room.

In the long brazen sunset light, beneath dusky cloud banks brooding storm, he strode up the hill slope with a sense of day's work done. Across his back, two woven baskets balanced each other, one laden with the pungent black fruit of the thorn tree and one with cable-thick creepers to be used as rope. The ax on his shoulder caught the waning sunlight and tossed it blindingly back.

It had not been hard labor, but weariness dragged at his mind and he did not relish the household chores yet to be performed, cooking and cleaning and all the rest. Why couldn't they hurry up and get him some helpers?

His eyes sought the sky resentfully. Moon Five was hidden; down here, at the bottom of the air ocean, you saw nothing but the sun and the four Galilean satellites. He wasn't even sure where Five was just now, in relation to himself. *Wait a minute, it's sunset here, but if I went out to the viewdome I'd see Jupiter in the last quarter, or would I, oh, hell, it only takes us half an Earth day to swing around the planet anyhow—*

Joe shook his head. After all this time, it was still damnably hard, now and then, to keep his thoughts straight. *I, the essential I, am up in heaven, riding Jupiter Five between cold stars. Remember that. Open your eyes, if you will, and see the dead control room superimposed on a living hillside.*

He didn't, though. Instead, he regarded the boulders strewn windblasted gray over the tough mossy vegetation of the slope. They were not much like Earth rocks, nor was the soil beneath his feet like terrestrial humus.

For a moment Anglesey speculated on the origin of the silicates, aluminates, and other stony compounds. Theoretically, all such materials should be inaccessibly locked in the Jovian core, down where the pressure got vast enough for atoms to buckle and collapse. Above the core should lie thousands of miles of allotropic ice, and then the metallic-hydrogen layer. There should not be complex minerals this far up, but there were.

Well, possibly Jupiter had formed according to theory, but had thereafter sucked enough cosmic dust, meteors, gases and vapors down its great throat of gravitation to form a crust several miles thick. Or more likely the theory was altogether wrong. What did they know, what *could* they know, the soft pale worms of Earth?

Anglesey stuck his—Joe's—fingers in his mouth and whistled. A baying sounded in the brush, and two midnight forms leaped toward him. He grinned and stroked their heads; training was progressing faster than he'd hoped, with these pups of the black caterpillar beasts he had taken. They would make guardians for him, herders, servants.

On the crest of the hill, Joe was building himself a home. He had logged off an acre of ground and erected a stockade. Within the grounds there now stood a lean-to for himself and his stores, a methane well, and the beginnings of a large, comfortable cabin.

But there was too much work for one being. Even with the half-intelligent caterpillars to help, and with cold storage for meat, most of his time would still go to hunting. The game wouldn't last forever either; he had to start agriculture within the next year or so—Jupiter year, twelve Earth years, thought Anglesey. There was the cabin to finish and furnish; he wanted to put a waterwheel, no, methanewheel, in the river to turn any of a dozen machines he had in mind, he wanted to experiment with alloyed ice and—

And, quite apart from his need of help, why should he remain alone, the single thinking creature on an entire planet? He was a male in this body, with male instincts—in the long run, his health was bound to suffer if he remained a hermit, and right now the whole project depended on Joe's health.

It wasn't right!

But I am not alone. There are fifty men on the satellite with me. I can talk to any of them, anytime I wish. It's only that I seldom wish it, these days. I would rather be Joe.

Nevertheless…I, the cripple, feel all the tiredness, anger, hurt, frustration, of that wonderful biological machine called Joe. The others don't understand. When the ammonia gale flays open his skin. It is I who bleed.

Joe lay down on the ground, sighing. Fangs flashed in the mouth of the black beast which humped over to lick his face. His belly growled with hunger, but he was too tired to fix a meal. Once he had the dogs trained…

Another pseudo would be so much more rewarding to educate.

He could almost see it, in the weary darkening of his brain. Down there, in the valley below the hill, fire and thunder as the ship came to rest. And the steel egg would crack open, the steel arms—already crumbling, puny work of worms!—lift out the shape within and lay it on the earth.

She would stir, shrieking in her first lungful of air looking about with blank mindless eyes. And Joe would come and carry her home. And he would feed her, care for her, show her how to walk—it wouldn't take long, an adult body would learn those things very fast. In a few weeks she would even be talking, be an individual, a soul.

Did you ever think, Edward Anglesey, in the days when you also walked, that your wife would be a gray four-legged monster?

Never mind that. The important thing was to get others of his kind down here female *and* male. The station's niggling little plan would have him wait two more Earth years, and then send him only another dummy like himself, a contemptible human mind looking through eyes which belonged rightfully to a Jovian. It was not to be tolerated.

If he weren't so tired…

Joe sat up. Sleep drained from him as the realization entered. *He* wasn't tired, not to speak of. Anglesey was. Anglesey, the human side of him, who for months had slept only in cat naps, whose rest had lately been interrupted by Cornelius—it was the human body which drooped, gave up, and sent wave after soft wave of sleep down the psibeam to Joe.

Somatic tension traveled skyward; Anglesey jerked awake.

He swore. As he sat there beneath the helmet, the vividness of Jupiter faded with his scattering concentration, as if it grew transparent; the steel prison which was his laboratory strengthened behind it. He was losing contact. Rapidly, with the skill of experience, he brought himself back into phase with the neural currents of the other brain. He willed sleepiness on Joe, exactly as a man wills it on himself.

And, like any other insomniac, he failed. The Joe body was too hungry. It got up and walked across the compound toward its shack.

The K tube went wild and blew itself out.

The night before the ships left, Viken and Cornelius sat up late. It was not truly a night, of course. In twelve hours the tiny moon was hurled clear around Jupiter, from darkness back to darkness, and there might well be a pallid little sun over its crags when the clocks said witches were abroad in Greenwich. But most of the personnel were asleep at this hour.

Viken scowled. "I don't like it," he said. "Too sudden a change of plans. Too big a gamble."

"You are only risking—how many?—three male and a dozen female pseudos," Cornelius replied.

"And fifteen J ships. All we have. If Anglesey's notion doesn't work, it will be months, a year or more, till we can have others built and resume aerial survey."

"But if it does work," said Cornelius, "you won't need any J ships, except to carry down more pseudos. You will be too busy evaluating data from the surface to piddle around in the upper atmosphere."

"Of course. But we never expected it so soon. We were going to bring more esmen out here, to operate some more pseudos—"

"But they aren't *needed*," said Cornelius. He struck a cigar to life and took a long pull on it, while his mind sought carefully for words. "Not for a while, anyhow. Joe has reached a point where, given help, he can leap several thousand years of history—he may even have a radio of sorts operating in the fairly near future, which would eliminate the necessity of much of your esping. But without help, he'll just have to mark time. And it's stupid to make a highly trained human esman perform manual labor, which is all that the other pseudos are needed for at this moment. Once the Jovian settlement is well established, certainly, then you can send down more puppets."

"The question is, though," persisted Viken, "can Anglesey himself educate all those pseudos at once? They'll be helpless as infants for days. It will be weeks before they really start thinking and acting for themselves. Can Joe take care of them meanwhile?"

"He has food and fuel stored for months ahead," said Cornelius. "As for what Joe's capabilities are—well, hm-m-m, we just have to take Anglesey's judgment. He has the only inside information."

"And once those Jovians do become personalities," worried Viken, "are they necessarily going to string along with Joe? Don't forget, the pseudos are not carbon copies of each other. The uncertainty principle assures each one a unique set of genes. If there is only one human mind on Jupiter, among all those aliens—"

"One *human* mind?" It was barely audible. Viken opened his mouth inquiringly. The other man hurried on.

"Oh, I'm sure Anglesey can continue to dominate them," said Cornelius. "His own personality is rather—tremendous."

Viken looked startled. "You really think so?"

The psionicist nodded. "Yes. I've seen more of him in the past weeks than anyone else. And my profession naturally orients me more toward a man's psychology than his body or his habits. You see a waspish cripple. I see a mind which has reacted to its physical handicaps by developing such a hellish energy, such an inhuman power of concentration, that it almost frightens me. Give that mind a sound body for its use and nothing is impossible to it."

"You may be right, at that," murmured Viken after a pause. "Not that it matters. The decision is taken, the rockets go down tomorrow. I hope it all works out."

He waited for another while. The whirring of ventilators in his little room seemed unnaturally loud, the colors of a girlie picture on the wall shockingly garish. Then he said slowly, "You've been rather close-mouthed yourself, Jan. When do you expect to finish your own esprojector and start making the tests?"

Cornelius looked around. The door stood open to an empty hallway, but he reached out and closed it before he answered with a slight grin, "It's been ready for the past few days. But don't tell anyone."

"How's that?" Viken started. The movement, in low gee, took him out of his chair and halfway across the table between the men. He shoved himself back and waited.

"I have been making meaningless, tinkering motions," said Cornelius, "but what I waited for was a highly emotional moment, a time when I can be sure Anglesey's entire attention will be focused on Joe. This business tomorrow is exactly what I need."

"*Why?*"

"You see, I have pretty well convinced myself that the trouble in the machine is psychological, not physical. I think that for some reason, buried in his subconscious, Anglesey doesn't want to experience Jupiter. A conflict of that type might well set a psionic-amplifier circuit oscillating."

"Hm-m-m." Viken rubbed his chin. "Could be. Lately Ed has been changing more and more. When he first came here, he was peppery enough, and he would at least play an occasional game of poker. Now he's pulled so far into his shell you can't even see him. I never thought of it before, but…yes, by God, Jupiter must be having some effect on him."

"Hm-m-m." Cornelius nodded. He did not elaborate—did not, for instance, mention that one altogether uncharacteristic episode when Anglesey had tried to describe what it was like to be a Jovian.

"Of course," said Viken thoughtfully, "the previous men were not affected especially. Nor was Ed at first, while he was still controlling lower-type pseudos. It's only since Joe went down to the surface that he's become so different."

"Yes, yes," said Cornelius hastily. "I've learned that much. But enough shop talk—"

"No. Wait a minute." Viken spoke in a low, hurried tone, looking past him. "For the first time, I'm starting to think clearly about this. Never really stopped to analyze it before, just accepted a bad situation. There *is* something peculiar about Joe. It can't very well involve his physical structure, or the environment, because lower forms didn't give this trouble. Could it be the fact that Joe is the first puppet in all history with a potentially human intelligence?"

We speculate in a vacuum," said Cornelius. "Tomorrow, maybe I can tell you. Now I know nothing."

Viken sat up straight. His pale eyes focused on the other man and stayed there, unblinking. "One minute," he said.

"Yes?" Cornelius shifted, half rising. "Quickly, please. It is past my bedtime."

"You know a good deal more than you've admitted," said Viken. "Don't you?"

"What makes you think that?"

"You aren't the most gifted liar in the universe. And then, you argued very strongly for Anglesey's scheme, this sending down the other pseudos. More strongly than a newcomer should."

"I told you, I want his attention focused elsewhere when—"

"Do you want it that badly?" snapped Viken.

Cornelius was still for a minute. Then he sighed and leaned back.

"All right," he said. "I shall have to trust your discretion. I wasn't sure, you see, how any of you old-time station personnel would react. So I didn't want to blabber out my speculations, which may be wrong. The confirmed facts, yes, I will tell them; but I don't wish to attack a man's religion with a mere theory."

Viken scowled. "What the devil do you mean?"

Cornelius puffed hard on his cigar; its tip waxed and waned like a miniature red demon star. "This Jupiter Five is more than a research station," he said gently. "It is a way of life, is it not? No one would come here for even one hitch unless the work was important to him. Those who re-enlist, they must find something in the work, something which Earth with all her riches cannot offer them. No?"

"Yes," answered Viken. It was almost a whisper. "I didn't think you would understand so well. But what of it?"

"Well, I don't want to tell you, unless I can prove it, that maybe this has all gone for nothing. Maybe you have wasted your lives and a lot of money, and will have to pack up and go home."

Viken's long face did not flicker a muscle. It seemed to have congealed. But he said calmly enough, "Why?"

"Consider Joe," said Cornelius. "His brain has as much capacity as any adult human's. It has been recording every sense datum that came to it, from the moment of 'birth'—making a record in itself, in its own cells, not merely in Anglesey's physical memory bank up here. Also, you know, a thought is a sense datum, too. And thoughts are not separated into neat little railway tracks; they form a continuous field. Every time Anglesey is in rapport with Joe, and thinks, the thought goes through Joe's synapses as well as his own—and every thought carries its own associations, and every associated memory is recorded. Like if Joe is building a hut, the shape of the logs might remind Anglesey of some geometric figure, which in turn would remind him of the Pythagorean theorem—"

"I get the idea," said Viken in a cautious way. "Given time, Joe's brain will have stored everything that ever was in Ed's."

"Correct. Now, a functioning nervous system with an engrammatic pattern of experience, in this case a *nonhuman* nervous system—isn't that a pretty good definition of a personality?"

"I suppose so, Good Lord!" Viken jumped. "You mean Joe is—taking over?"

"In a way. A subtle, automatic, unconscious way." Cornelius drew a deep breath and plunged into it. "The pseudojovian is so nearly perfect a life-form: your biologists engineered into it all the experience gained from nature's mistakes in designing *us*. At first, Joe was only a remote-controlled biological machine. Then Anglesey and Joe became two facets of a single personality. Then, oh, very slowly, the stronger, healthier body…more amplitude to its thoughts…do you see? Joe is becoming the dominant side. Like this business of sending down the other pseudos—Anglesey only thinks he has logical reasons for wanting it done. Actually, his 'reasons' are mere rationalizations for the instinctive desires of the Joe facet.

"Anglesey's subconscious must comprehend the situation, in a dim reactive way; it must feel his human ego gradually being submerged by the steamroller force of *Joe's* instincts and *Joe's* wishes. It tries to defend its own identity, and is swatted down by the superior force of Joe's own nascent subconscious.

"I put it crudely," he finished in an apologetic tone, "but it will account for that oscillation in the K tubes."

Viken nodded, slowly, like an old man. "Yes, I see it," he answered. "The alien environment down there…the different brain structure…Good God! Ed's being swallowed up in Joe! The puppet master is becoming the puppet!" He looked ill.

"Only speculation on my part," said Cornelius. All at once, he felt very tired. It was not pleasant to do this to Viken, whom he liked. "But you see the dilemma, no? If I am right, then any esman will gradually become a Jovian—a monster with two bodies, of which the human body is the unimportant auxiliary one. This means no esman will ever agree to control a pseudo—therefore, the end of your project."

He stood up. "I'm sorry, Arne. You made me tell you what I think, and now you will lie awake worrying, and I am maybe quite wrong and you worry for nothing."

"It's all right," mumbled Viken. "Maybe you're not wrong."

"I don't know." Cornelius drifted toward the door. "I am going to try to find some answers tomorrow. Good night."

The moon-shaking thunder of the rockets, crash, crash, crash, leaping from their cradles, was long past. Now the fleet glided on metal wings, with straining secondary ram-jets, through the rage of the Jovian sky.

As Cornelius opened the control-room door, he looked at his telltale board. Elsewhere a voice tolled the word to all the stations, *One ship wrecked, two ships wrecked,* but Anglesey would let no sound enter his presence when he wore the helmet. An obliging technician had haywired a panel of fifteen red and fifteen blue lights above Cornelius' esprojector, to keep him informed, too. Ostensibly, of course, they were only there for Anglesey's benefit, though the esman had insisted he wouldn't be looking at them.

Four of the red bulbs were dark and thus four blue ones would not shine for a safe landing. A whirlwind, a thunderbolt, a floating ice meteor, a flock of mantalike birds with flesh as dense and hard as iron—there could be a hundred things which had crumpled four ships and tossed them tattered across the poison forests.

Four ships, hell! Think of four living creatures, with an excellence of brain to rival your own, damned first to years in unconscious night and then, never awakening save for one uncomprehending instant, dashed in bloody splinters against an ice mountain. The wasteful callousness of it was a cold knot in Cornelius' belly. It had to be done, no doubt, if there was to be any thinking life on Jupiter at all; but then let it be done quickly and minimally, he thought, so that the next generation could be begotten by love and not by machines!

He closed the door behind him and waited for a breathless moment. Anglesey was a wheel chair and a coppery curve of helmet, facing the opposite wall. No movement, no awareness whatsoever. Good! It would be awkward, perhaps ruinous, if Anglesey learned of this most intimate peering. But he needn't, ever. He was blindfolded and ear-plugged by his own concentration.

Nevertheless, the psionicist moved his bulky form with care, across the room to the new esprojector. He did not much like his snooper's role, he would not have assumed it at all if he had seen any other hope. But neither did it make him feel especially guilty. If what he suspected was true, then Anglesey was all unawares being twisted into something not human; to spy on him might be to save him.

Gently, Cornelius activated the meters and started his tubes warming up. The oscilloscope built into Anglesey's machine gave him the other man's exact alpha rhythm; his basic biological clock. First you adjusted to that, then you discovered the subtler elements by feel, and when your set was fully in phase you could probe undetected and—

Find out what was wrong. Read Anglesey's tortured subconscious and see what there was on Jupiter that both drew and terrified him.

Five ships wrecked.

But it must be very nearly time for them to land. Maybe only five would be lost in all. Maybe ten would get through. Ten comrades for—Joe?

Cornelius sighed. He looked at the cripple, seated blind and deaf to the human world which had crippled him, and felt a pity and an anger. It wasn't fair, none of it was.

Not even to Joe. Joe wasn't any kind of soul-eating devil. He did not even realize, as yet, that he *was* Joe, that Anglesey was becoming a mere appendage. He hadn't asked to be created, and to withdraw his human counterpart from him would very likely be to destroy him.

Somehow, there were always penalties for everybody when men exceeded the decent limits.

Cornelius swore at himself, voicelessly. Work to do. He sat down and fitted the helmet on his own head. The carrier wave made a faint pulse, inaudible, the trembling of neurons low in his awareness. You couldn't describe it.

Reaching up, he turned to Anglesey's alpha. His own had a somewhat lower frequency, it was necessary to carry the signals through a heterodyning process. Still no reception. Well, of course he had to find the exact wave form, timbre was as basic to thought as to music. He adjusted the dials slowly, with enormous care.

Something flashed through his consciousness, a vision of clouds roiled in a violet-red sky, a wind that galloped across horizonless immensity—he lost it. His fingers shook as he turned back.

The psibeam between Joe and Anglesey broadened. It took Cornelius into the circuit. He looked through Joe's eyes, he stood on a hill and stared into the sky above the ice mountains, straining for sign of the first rocket; and simultaneously he was still Jan Cornelius, blurrily seeing the meters, probing about for emotions, symbols, any key to the locked terror in Anglesey's soul.

The terror rose up and struck him in the face.

Psionic detection is not a matter of passive listening in. Much as a radio receiver is necessarily also a weak transmitter, the nervous system in resonance with a source of psionic-spectrum energy is itself emitting. Normally, of course, this effect is unimportant; but when you pass the impulses, either way, through a set of heterodyning and amplifying units, with a high negative feedback…

In the early days, psionic psychotherapy vitiated itself because the amplified thoughts of one man, entering the brain of another, would combine with the latter's own neural cycles according to the ordinary vector laws. The result was that both men felt the new beat frequencies as a nightmarish fluttering of their very thoughts. An analyst, trained into self-control, could ignore it; his patient could not, and reacted violently.

But eventually the basic human wave timbres were measured, and psionic therapy resumed. The modern esprojector analyzed an incoming signal and shifted its characteristics over to the "listener's" pattern. The *really* different pulses of the transmitting brain, those which could not possibly be mapped onto the pattern of the receiving neurones—as an exponential signal cannot very practicably be mapped onto a sinusoid—those were filtered out.

Thus compensated, the other thought could be apprehended as comfortably as one's own. If the patient were on a psibeam circuit, a skilled operator could tune in without the patient being necessarily aware of it. The operator could either probe the other man's thoughts or implant thoughts of his own.

Cornelius' plan, an obvious one to any psionicist, had depended on this. He would receive from an unwitting Anglesey-Joe. If his theory was right and the esman's personality was being distorted into that of a monster, his thinking would be too alien to come through the filters. Cornelius would receive spottily or not at all. If his theory was wrong, and Anglesey was still Anglesey, he would receive only a normal human stream of consciousness and could probe for other troublemaking factors.

His brain roared!

What's happening to me?

For a moment, the interference which turned his thoughts to saw-toothed gibberish struck him down with panic. He gulped for breath, there in the Jovian wind, and his dreadful dogs sensed the alienness in him and whined.

Then, recognition, remembrance, and a blaze of anger so great that it left no room for fear. Joe filled his lungs and shouted it aloud, the hillside boomed with echoes:

"Get out of my mind!"

He felt Cornelius spiral down toward unconsciousness. The overwhelming force of his own mental blow had been too much. He laughed, it was more like a snarl, and eased the pressure.

Above him, between thunderous clouds, winked the first thin descending rocket flare.

Cornelius' mind groped back toward the light. It broke a watery surface, the man's mouth snapped after air and his hands reached for the dials, to turn his machine off and escape.

"Not so fast, you." Grimly, Joe drove home a command that locked Cornelius' muscles rigid. "I want to know the meaning of this. Hold still and let me look!" He smashed home an impulse which could be rendered, perhaps, as an incandescent question mark. Remembrance exploded in shards through the psionicist's forebrain.

"So. That's all there is? You thought I was afraid to come down here and be Joe, and wanted to know why? But I *told* you I wasn't!"

I should have believed, whispered Cornelius.

"Well, get out of the circuit, then." Joe continued growling it vocally. "And don't ever come back in the control room, understand? K tubes or no, I don't want to see you again. And I may be a cripple, but I can still take you apart cell by cell. Now sign off—leave me alone. The first ship will be landing in minutes."

You a cripple—you, Joe Anglesey?

"What?" The great gray being on the hill lifted his barbaric head as if to sudden trumpets. "What do you mean?"

Don't you understand? said the weak, dragging thought. *You know how the esprojector works. You know I could have probed Anglesey's mind in Anglesey's brain without making enough interference to be noticed. And I could not have probed a wholly nonhuman mind at all, nor could it have been aware of me. The filters would not have passed such a signal. Yet you felt me in the first fractional second. It can only mean a human mind in a nonhuman brain.*

You are not the half-corpse on Jupiter Five any longer. You're Joe—Joe Anglesey.

"Well, I'll be damned," said Joe. "You're right."

He turned Anglesey off, kicked Cornelius out of his mind with a single brutal impulse, and ran down the hill to meet the spaceship.

Cornelius woke up minutes afterward. His skull felt ready to split apart. He groped for the main switch before him, clashed it down, ripped the helmet off his head and threw it clanging on the floor. But it took a little while to gather the strength to do the same for Anglesey. The other man was not able to do anything for himself.

They sat outside sick bay and waited. It was a harshly lit barrenness of metal and plastic, smelling of antiseptics—down near the heart of the satellite, with miles of rock to hide the terrible face of Jupiter.

Only Viken and Cornelius were in that cramped little room. The rest of the station went about its business mechanically, filling in the time till it could learn what had happened. Beyond the door, three biotechnicians, who were also the station's medical staff, fought with death's angel for the thing which had been Edward Anglesey.

"Nine ships got down," said Viken dully. "Two males, seven females. It's enough to start a colony."

"It would be genetically desirable to have more," pointed out Cornelius. He kept his own voice low, in spite of its underlying cheerfulness. There was a certain awesome quality to all this.

"I still don't understand," said Viken.

"Oh, it's clear enough—now. I should have guessed it before, maybe. We had all the facts, it was only that we couldn't make the simple, obvious interpretation of them. No, we had to conjure up Frankenstein's monster."

"Well," Viken's words grated, "we have played Frankenstein, haven't we? Ed is dying in there."

"It depends on how you define death." Cornelius drew hard on his cigar, needing anything that might steady him. His tone grew purposely dry of emotion.

"Look here. Consider the data. Joe, now: a creature with a brain of human capacity, but without a mind—a perfect Lockean *tabula rasa* for Anglesey's psi-beam to write on. We deduced, correctly enough—if very belatedly—that when enough had been written, there would be a personality. But the question was, whose? Because, I suppose, of normal human fear of the unknown, we assumed that any personality in so alien a body had to be monstrous. Therefore it must be hostile to Anglesey, must be swamping him—"

The door opened. Both men jerked to their feet.

The chief surgeon shook his head. "No use. Typical deep-shock traumata, close to terminus now. If we had better facilities, maybe…"

"No," said Cornelius. "You cannot save a man who has decided not to live any more."

"I know." The doctor removed his mask. "I need a cigarette. Who's got one?" His hands shook a little as he accepted it from Viken.

"But how could he—decide—anything?" choked the physicist. "He's been unconscious ever since Jan pulled him away from that…that thing."

"It was decided before then," said Cornelius. "As a matter of fact that hulk in there on the operating table no longer has a mind. I know. I was there." He shuddered a little. A stiff shot of tranquilizer was all that held nightmare away from him. Later he would have to have that memory exorcised.

The doctor took a long drag of smoke, held it in his lungs a moment, and exhaled gustily. "I guess this winds up the project," he said. "We'll never get another esman."

"I'll say we won't." Viken's tone sounded rusty. "I'm going to smash that devil's engine myself."

"Hold on a minute!" exclaimed Cornelius. "Don't you understand? This isn't the end. It's the beginning!"

"I'd better get back," said the doctor. He stubbed out his cigarette and went through the door. It closed behind him with a deathlike quietness.

"What do you mean?" Viken said it as if erecting a barrier.

"*Won't* you understand?" roared Cornelius. "Joe has all Anglesey's habits, thoughts, memories, prejudices, interests. Oh, yes, the different body and the different environment—they do cause some changes, but no more than any man might undergo on Earth. If you were suddenly cured of a wasting disease, wouldn't you maybe get a little boisterous and rough? There is nothing abnormal in it. Nor is it abnormal to want to stay healthy—no? Do you see?"

Viken sat down. He spent a while without speaking.

Then, enormously slow and careful: "Do you mean Joe is Ed?"

"Or Ed is Joe. Whatever you like. He calls himself Joe now I think—as a symbol of freedom—but he is still himself. What *is* the ego but continuity of existence?

"He himself did not fully understand this. He only knew—he told me, and I should have believed him—that on Jupiter he was strong and happy. Why did the K tube oscillate? A hysterical symptom! Anglesey's subconscious was not afraid to stay on Jupiter—it was afraid to come back!

"And then, today, I listened in. By now, his whole self was focused on Joe. That is, the primary source of libido was Joe's virile body not Anglesey's sick one. This meant a different pattern of impulses—not too alien to pass the filters, but alien enough to set up interference. So he felt my presence. And he saw the truth just as I did.

"Do you know the last emotion I felt as Joe threw me out of his mind? Not anger any more. He plays rough, him, but all he had room to feel was joy.

"I *knew* how strong a personality Anglesey has! Whatever made me think an overgrown child brain like Joe's could override it? In there, the doctors—bah! They're trying to salvage a hulk which has been shed because it is useless!"

Cornelius stopped. His throat was quite raw from talking. He paced the floor, rolled cigar smoke around his mouth but did not draw it any farther in.

When a few minutes had passed, Viken said cautiously, "All right. You should know—as you said, you were there. But what do we do now?' How do we get in touch with Ed? Will he even be interested in contacting us?"

"Oh, yes, of course," said Cornelius. "He is still himself, remember. Now that he has none of the cripple's frustrations, he should be more amiable. When the novelty of his new friends wears off, he will want someone who can talk to him as an equal."

"And precisely who will operate another pseudo?" asked Viken sarcastically. "I'm quite happy with this skinny frame of mine, thank you!"

"Was Anglesey the only hopeless cripple on Earth?" asked Cornelius quietly.

Viken gaped at him.

"And there are aging men, too," went on the psionicist, half to himself. "Someday, my friend, when you and I feel the years close in, and so much we would like to learn—maybe we too would enjoy an extra lifetime in a Jovian body." He nodded at his cigar. "A hard, lusty, stormy kind of life, granted—dangerous, brawling, violent—but life as no human, perhaps, has lived it since the days of Elizabeth the First. Oh, yes, there will be small trouble finding Jovians."

He turned his head as the surgeon came out again.

"Well?" croaked Viken.

The doctor sat down. "It's finished," he said. They waited for a moment, awkwardly.

"Odd," said the doctor. He groped after a cigarette he didn't have. Silently, Viken offered him one. "Odd. I've seen these cases before. People who simply resign from life. This is the first one I ever saw that went out smiling—smiling all the time."

Prayer in War

Lord beyond eternity,
Fountainhead of mystery,
Why have You now set us free?

You, Who unto death were given,
By Yourself, that we be shriven,
See, Your world will soon lie riven.

After Easter, need we dread
Fire and ice when we are dead?
Hell indwells in us instead.

From our hearts we raise a tower
Wherein sullen monsters glower.
Save us from our hard-won power!

You Who raged within the sun
When no life had yet begun,
Will You let it be undone?

We have wrought such ghastly wonders,
Lightning at our beck, and thunders—
Help, before this poor earth sunders.

Lord beyond eternity,
Fountainhead of mystery,
Why have You now set us free?

Tomorrow's Children

On the world's loom
Weave the Norns doom,
Nor may they guide it nor change.
    —**Wagner**, *Siegfried*

Ten miles up, it hardly showed. Earth was a cloudy green and brown blur, the vast vault of the stratosphere reaching changelessly out to spatial infinities, and beyond the pulsing engine there was silence and serenity no man could ever touch. Looking down, Hugh Drummond could see the Mississippi gleaming like a drawn sword, and its slow curve matched the contours shown on his map. The hills, the sea, the sun and wind and rain, they didn't change. Not in less than a million slow-striding years, and human efforts flickered too briefly in the unending night for that.

Farther down, though, and especially where cities had been—The lone man in the solitary stratojet swore softly, bitterly, and his knuckles whitened on the controls. He was a big man, his gaunt rangy form sprawling awkwardly in the tiny pressure cabin, and he wasn't quite forty. But his dark hair was streaked with gray, in the shabby flying suit his shoulders stooped, and his long homely face was drawn into haggard lines. His eyes were black-rimmed and sunken with weariness, dark and dreadful in their intensity. He's seen too much, survived too much, until he began to look like most other people of the world. *Heir of the ages,* he thought dully.

Mechanically, he went through the motions of following his course. Natural landmarks were still there, and he had powerful binoculars to help him. But he didn't use them much. They showed too many broad shallow craters, their vitreous smoothness throwing back sunlight in the flat blank glitter of a snake's eye, the ground about them a churned and blasted desolation. And there were the worse regions of—deadness. Twisted dead trees, blowing sand, tumbled skeletons perhaps at night a baleful blue glow of fluorescence. The bombs had been nightmares, riding in on wings of fire and horror to shake the planet with the death blows of cities. But the radioactive dust was worse than any nightmare.

He passed over villages, even small towns. Some of them were deserted, the blowing colloidal dust, or plague, or economic breakdown making them untenable. Others still seemed to be living a feeble half-life. Especially in the Midwest, there was a pathetic struggle to return to an agricultural system, but the insects and blights—

Drummond shrugged. After nearly two years of this, over the scarred and maimed planet, he should be used to it. The United States had been lucky. Europe, now—

Der Untergang des Abendlandes, he thought grayly. *Spengler foresaw the collapse of a topheavy civilization. He didn't foresee atomic bombs, radioactive-dust bombs, bacteria bombs, blight bombs—the bombs, the senseless inanimate bombs flying like monster insects over the shivering world. So he didn't guess the extent of the collapse.*

Deliberately he pushed the thoughts out of his conscious mind. He didn't want to dwell on them. He'd lived with them two years, and that was two eternities too long. And anyway, he was nearly home now.

The capital of the United States was below him, and he sent the stratojet slanting down in a long thunderous dive toward the mountains. Not much of a capital, the little town huddled in a valley of the Cascades, but the waters of the Potomac had filled the grave of Washington. Strictly speaking, there was no capital. The officers of the government were scattered over the country, keeping in precarious touch by plane and radio, but Taylor, Oregon, came as close to being the nerve center as any other place.

He gave the signal again on his transmitter, knowing with a faint spine-crawling sensation of the rocket batteries trained on him from the green of those mountains. When one plane could carry the end of a city, all planes were under suspicion. Not that anyone outside was supposed to know that that innocuous little town was important. But you never could tell. The war wasn't officially over. It might never be, with sheer personal survival overriding the urgency of treaties.

A light-beam transmitter gave him a cautious: "O.K. Can you land in the street?"

It was a narrow, dusty track between two wooden rows of houses, but Drummond was a good pilot and this was a good jet. "Yeah," he said. His voice had grown unused to speech.

He cut speed in a spiral descent until he was gliding with only the faintest whisper of wind across his ship. Touching wheels to the street, he slammed on the brake and bounced to a halt.

Silence struck at him like a physical blow. The engine stilled, the sun beating down from a brassy blue sky on the drabness of rude "temporary" houses, the total-seeming desertion beneath the impassive mountains—Home! Hugh Drummond laughed, a short harsh bark with nothing of humor in it, and swung open the cockpit canopy.

There were actually quite a few people, he saw, peering from doorways and side streets. They looked fairly well fed and dressed, many in uniform, they seemed to have purpose and hope. But this, of course, was the capital of the United States of America, the world's most fortunate country.

"Get out—quick!"

The peremptory voice roused Drummond from the introspection into which those lonely months had driven him. He looked down at a gang of men in mechanics' outfits, led by a harassed-looking man in captain's uniform. "Oh—of course," he said slowly. "You want to hide the plane. And, naturally, a regular landing field would give you away."

"Hurry, get out, you infernal idiot! Anyone, *anyone* might come over and see—"

"They wouldn't get unnoticed by an efficient detection system, and you still have that," said Drummond, sliding his booted legs over the cockpit edge. "And anyway, there won't be any more raids. The war's over."

"Wish I could believe that, but who are you to say? Get a move on!"

The grease monkeys hustled the plane down the street. With an odd feeling of loneliness, Drummond watched it go. After all, it had been his home for—how long?

The machine was stopped before a false house whose whole front was swung aside. A concrete ramp let downward, and Drummond could see a cavernous immensity below. Light within it gleamed off silvery rows of aircraft.

"Pretty neat," he admitted. "Not that it matters any more. Probably it never did. Most of the hell came over on robot rockets. Oh, well." He fished his pipe from his jacket. Colonel's insignia glittered briefly as the garment flipped back.

"Oh...sorry, sir!" exclaimed the captain. I didn't know—"

" 'S O.K. I've gotten out of the habit of wearing a regular uniform. A lot of places I've been, an American wouldn't be very popular." Drummond stuffed tobacco into his briar, scowling. He hated to think how often he'd had to use the Colt at his hip, or even the machine guns in his plane, to save himself. He inhaled smoke gratefully. It seemed to drown out some of the bitter taste.

"General Robinson said to bring you to him when you arrived, sir," said the captain. "This way, please."

They went down the street, their boots scuffing up little acrid clouds of dust. Drummond looked sharply about him. He'd left very shortly after the two-month Ragnarok which had tapered off when the organization of both sides broke down too far to keep on making and sending the bombs, and maintaining order with famine and disease starting their ghastly ride over the homeland. At that time, the United States was a cityless, anarchic chaos, and he'd had only the briefest of radio exchanges since then, whenever he could get at a long-range set still in working order. They made remarkable progress meanwhile. How much, he didn't know, but the mere existence of something like a capital was sufficient proof.

Robinson—His lined face twisted into a frown. He didn't know the man. He'd been expecting to be received by the President, who had sent him and some others out. Unless the others had—No, he was the only one who had been in eastern Europe and western Asia. He was sure of that.

Two sentries guarded the entrance to what was obviously a converted general store. But there were no more stores. There was nothing to put in them. Drummond entered the cool dimness of an antechamber. The clatter of a typewriter, the WAC operating it—He gaped and blinked. That was—impossible. Typewriters, secretaries—hadn't they gone out with the whole world, two years ago? If the Dark Ages had returned to Earth, It didn't seem—*right*—that there should still be typewriters. It didn't fit, didn't—

He grew aware that the captain had opened the inner door for him. As he stepped in, he grew aware how tired he was. His arm weighed a ton as he saluted the man behind the desk.

"At ease, at ease," Robinson's voice was genial. Despite the five stars on his shoulders, he wore no tie or coat, and his round face was smiling. Still, he looked tough and competent underneath. To run things nowadays, he'd have to be.

"Sit down, Colonel Drummond." Robinson gestured to a chair near his and the aviator collapsed into it, shivering. His haunted eyes traversed the office. It was almost well enough outfitted to be a prewar place.

Prewar! A word like a sword, cutting across history with a brutality of murder, hazing everything in the past until it was a vague golden glow through drifting, red-shot black clouds. And—only two years. *Only two years!* Surely sanity was meaningless in a world of such nightmare inversions. Why, he could barely remember Barbara and the kids. Their faces were blotted out in a tide of other visages—starved faces, dead faces, human faces become beast-formed with want and pain and eating throttled hate. His grief was lost in the agony of a world, and in some ways he had become a machine himself.

"You look plenty tired," said Robinson.

"Yeah,…yes, sir—"

"Skip the formality. I don't go for it. We'll be working pretty close together, can't take time to be diplomatic."

"Uh-huh. I came over the North Pole, you know. Haven't slept since—Rough time. But, if I may ask, you—" Drummond hesitated.

"I? I suppose I'm president. Ex officio, pro tem, or something. Here, you need a drink." Robinson got a bottle and glasses from a drawer. The liquor gurgled out in a pungent stream. "Prewar Scotch. Till it gives out I'm laying off this modern hooch. *Gambai.*"

The fiery, smoky brew jolted Drummond to wakefulness. Its glow was pleasant in his empty stomach. He heard Robinson's voice with surrealistic sharpness:

"Yes, I'm at the head now. My predecessors made the mistake of sticking together, and of traveling a good deal in trying to pull the country back into shape. So I think the sickness got the President, and I know it got several others. Of course, there was no means of holding an election. The armed forces had almost the only organization left, so we had to run things. Berger was in charge, but he shot himself when he learned he'd breathed radiodust. Then the command fell to me. I've been lucky."

"I see." It didn't make much difference. A few dozen more deaths weren't much, when over half the world was gone. "Do you expect to—continue lucky?" A brutally blunt question, maybe, but words weren't bombs.

"I do." Robinson was firm about that. "We've learned by experience, learned a lot. We've scattered the army, broken it into small outposts at key points throughout the country. For quite a while, we stopped travel altogether except for absolute emergencies, and then with elaborate precautions. That smothered the epidemics. The microorganisms were bred to work in crowded areas, you know. They were almost immune to known medical techniques, but without hosts and carriers they died. I guess natural bacteria ate up most of them. We still take care in traveling, but we're fairly safe now."

"Did any of the others come back? There were a lot like me, sent out to see what really had happened to the world."

"One did from South America. Their situation is similar to ours, though they lacked our tight organization and have gone further toward anarchy. Nobody else returned but you."

It wasn't surprising. In fact, it was a cause for astonishment that anyone had come back. Drummond had volunteered after the bomb erasing St. Louis had taken his family, not expecting to survive and not caring much whether he did. Maybe that was why he had.

"You can take your time in writing a detailed report," said Robinson, "but in general, how are things over there?"

Drummond shrugged. "The war's over. Burned out. Europe has gone back to savagery. They were caught between America and Asia, and the bombs came both ways. Not many survivors, and they're starving animals. Russia, from what I saw, has managed something like you've done here, though they're worse off than we. Naturally, I couldn't find out much there. I didn't get to India or China, but in Russia I heard rumors—No, the world's gone too far into disintegration to carry on war."

"Then we can come out in the open," said Robinson softly. "We can really start rebuilding. I don't think there'll ever be another war, Drummond. I think the memory of this one will be carved too deeply on the race for us ever to forget."

"Can you shrug it off that easily?"

"No, no, of course not. Our culture hasn't lost its continuity, but it's had a terrific setback. We'll never wholly get over it. But—we're on our way up again."

The general rose, glancing at his watch. "Six o'clock. Come on, Drummond, let's get home."

"Home?"

"Yes, you'll stay with me. Man, you look like the original zombie. You'll need a month or more of sleeping between clean sheets, of home cooking and home atmosphere. My wife will be glad to have you; we see almost no new faces. And as long as we'll work together, I'd like to keep you handy. The shortage of competent men is terrific."

They went down the street, an aide following. Drummond was again conscious of the weariness aching in every bone and fiber of him. A home—after two years of ghost towns, of shattered chimneys above blood-dappled snow, of flimsy lean-tos housing starvation and death.

"Your plane will be mighty useful, too," said Robinson. "Those atomic-powered craft are scarcer than hens' teeth used to be." He chuckled hollowly, as at a rather grim joke. "Got you through close to two years of flying without needing fuel. Any other trouble?"

"Some, but there were enough spare parts." No need to tell of those frantic hours and days of slaving, of desperate improvisation with hunger and plague stalking him who stayed overlong. He'd had his troubles getting food, too, despite the plentiful supplies he'd started out with. He'd fought for scraps in the winters, beaten off howling maniacs who would have killed him for a bird he'd shot or a dead horse he'd scavenged. He hated that plundering, and would not have cared personally if they'd managed to destroy him. But he had a mission, and the mission was all he'd had left as a focal point for his life, so he'd clung to it with fanatic intensity.

And now the job was over, and he realized he couldn't rest. He didn't dare. Rest would give him time to remember. Maybe he could find surcease in the gigantic work of reconstruction. Maybe.

"Here we are," said Robinson.

Drummond blinked in new amazement. There was a car, camouflaged under brush, with a military chauffeur—*a car!* And in pretty fair shape, too.

"We've got a few oil wells going again, and a small patched-up refinery," explained the general. "It furnishes enough gas and oil for what traffic we have."

They got in the rear seat. The aide sat in front, a rifle ready. The car started down a mountain road.

"Where to?" asked Drummond a little dazedly.

Robinson smiled. "Personally," he said, "I'm almost the only lucky man on Earth. We had a summer cottage on Lake Taylor, a few miles from here. My wife was there when the war came, and stayed, and nobody came along till I brought the head offices here with me. Now I've got a home all to myself."

"Yeah. Yeah, you're lucky," said Drummond. He looked out the window, not seeing the sun-spattered woods. Presently he asked, his voice a little harsh: "How is the country really doing now?"

"For a while it was rough. Damn rough. When the cities went, our transportation, communication, and distribution systems broke down. In fact, our whole economy disintegrated, though not all at once. Then there was the dust and the plagues. People fled, and there was open fighting when overcrowded safe places refused to take in any more refugees. Police went with the cities, and the army couldn't do much patrolling. We were busy fighting the enemy troops that'd flown over the Pole to invade. We still haven't gotten them all. Bands are roaming the country, hungry and desperate outlaws, and there are plenty of Americans who turned to banditry when everything else failed. That's why we have this guard, though so far none have come this way.

"The insect and blight weapons just about wiped out our crops, and that winter everybody starved. We checked the pests with modern methods, though it was touch and go for a while, and next year got some food. Of course, with no distribution as yet, we failed to save a lot of people. And farming is still a tough proposition. We won't really have the bugs licked for a long time. If we had a research center as well equipped as those which produced the things—But we're gaining. We're gaining."

"Distribution—" Drummond rubbed his chin. "How about railroads? Horse-drawn vehicles?"

"We have some railroads going, but the enemy was as careful to dust most of ours as we were to dust theirs. As for horses, they were nearly all eaten that first winter. I know personally of only a dozen. They're on my place; I'm trying to breed enough to be of use, but"—Robinson smiled wryly—"by the time we've raised that many, the factories should have been going quite a spell."

"And so now—?"

"We're over the worst. Except for outlaws, we have the population fairly well controlled. The civilized people are fairly well fed, with some kind of housing. We have machine shops, small factories, and the like going, enough to keep our transportation and other mechanism 'level.' Presently we'll be able to expand these, begin actually increasing what we have. In another five years or so, I guess, we'll be integrated enough to drop martial law and hold a general election. A big job ahead, but a good one."

The car halted to let a cow lumber over the road, a calf trotting at her heels. She was gaunt and shaggy, and skittered nervously from the vehicle into the brush.

"Wild," explained Robinson. "Most of the real wildlife was killed off for food in the last two years, but a lot of farm animals escaped when their owners died or fled, and have run free ever since. They—" He noticed Drummond's fixed gaze. The pilot was looking at the calf. Its legs were half the normal length.

"Mutant," said the general. "You find a lot of such animals. Radiation from bomb or dusted areas. There are even a lot of human abnormal births." He scowled, worry clouding his eyes. "In fact, that's just about our worst problem. It—"

The car came out of the woods onto the shore of a small lake. It was a peaceful scene, the quiet waters like molten gold in the slanting sunlight, trees ringing the circumference and all about them the mountains. Under one huge pine stood a cottage, a woman on the porch.

It was like one summer with Barbara—Drummond cursed under his breath and followed Robinson toward the little building. It wasn't, it wasn't, it could never be. Not ever again. There were soldiers guarding this place from chance marauders, and—There was an odd-looking flower at his foot. A daisy, but huge and red and irregularly formed.

A squirrel chittered from a tree. Drummond saw that its face was so blunt as to be almost human.

Then he was on the porch, and Robinson was introducing him to "my wife Elaine." She was a nice-looking young woman with eyes that were sympathetic on Drummond's exhausted face. The aviator tried not to notice that she was pregnant.

He was led inside, and reveled in a hot bath. Afterward there was supper, but he was numb with sleep by then, and hardly noticed it when Robinson put him to bed.

Reaction set in, and for a week or so Drummond went about in a haze, not much good to himself or anyone else. But it was surprising what plenty of food and sleep could do, and one evening Robinson came home to find him scribbling on sheets of paper.

"Arranging my notes and so on," he explained. "I'll write out the complete report in a month, I guess."

"Good. But no hurry." Robinson settled tiredly into an armchair. "The rest of the world will keep. I'd rather you'd just work at this off and on, and join my staff for your main job."

"O.K. Only what'll I do?"

"Everything. Specialization is gone; too few surviving specialists and equipment. I think your chief task will be to head the census bureau."

"Eh?"

Robinson grinned lopsidedly. "You'll *be* the census bureau, except for what few assistants I can spare you." He leaned forward, said earnestly: "And it's one of the most important jobs there is. You'll do for this country what you did for central Eurasia, only in much greater detail. Drummond, we have to *know*."

He took a map from a desk drawer and spread it out. "Look, here's the United States. I've marked regions known to be uninhabitable in red." His fingers traced out the ugly splotches. "Too many of 'em, and doubtless there are others we haven't found yet. Now, the blue X's are army posts." They were sparsely scattered over the land, near the centers of population groupings. "Not enough of those. It's all we can do to control the more or less well-off, orderly people. Bandits, enemy troops, homeless refugees—they're still running wild, skulking in the backwoods and barrens, and raiding whenever they can. And they spread the plague. We won't really have it licked till everybody's settled down, and that'd be hard to enforce. Drummond, we don't even have enough soldiers to start a feudal system for protection. The plague spread like a prairie fire in those concentrations of men.

"We have to *know*. We have to know how many people survived—half the population, a third, a quarter, whatever it is. We have to know where they are, and how they're fixed for supplies, so we can start up an equitable distribution system. We have to find all the small-town shops and labs and libraries still standing, and rescue their priceless contents before looters or the weather beat us to it. We have to locate doctors and engineers and other professional men, and put them to work rebuilding. We have to find the outlaws and round them up. We—I could go on forever. Once we have all that information, we can set up a master plan for redistributing population, agriculture, industry, and the rest most efficiently, for getting the country back under civil authority and police, for opening regular transportation and communication channels—for getting the nation back on its feet."

"I see," nodded Drummond. "Hitherto, just surviving and hanging on to what was left has taken precedence. Now you're in a position to start expanding, *if* you know where and how much to expand."

"Exactly." Robinson rolled a cigarette, grimacing. "Not much tobacco left. What I have is perfectly foul. Lord, that war was crazy!"

"All wars are," said Drummond dispassionately, "but technology advanced to the point of giving us a knife to cut our throats with. Before that, we were just beating our heads against the wall. Robinson, we can't go back to the old ways. We've *got* to start on a new track—a track of sanity."

"Yes. And that brings up—" The other man looked toward the kitchen door. They could hear the cheerful rattle of dishes there, and smell mouth-watering cooking odors. He lowered his voice. "I might as well tell you this now, but don't let Elaine know. She…she shouldn't be worried. Drummond, did you see our horses?"

"The other day, yes. The colts—"

"Uh-huh. There've been five colts born of eleven mares in the last year. Two of them were so deformed they died in a week, another in a few months. One of the two left has cloven hoofs and almost no teeth. The last one looked normal—so far. One out of eleven, Drummond."

"Were those horses near a radioactive area?"

"They must have been. They were rounded up wherever found and brought here. The stallion was caught near the site of Portland, I know. But if he were the only one with mutated genes, it would hardly show in the first generation, would it? I understand nearly all mutations are Mendelian recessives. Even if there were one dominant, it would show in all the colts, but none of these looked alike."

"Hm-m-m—I don't know much about genetics, but I do know hard radiation, or rather the secondary charged particles it produces will cause mutation. Only mutants are rare, and tend to fall into certain patterns—"

"*Were* rare!" Suddenly Robinson was grim, something coldly frightened in his eyes. "Haven't you noticed the animals and plants? They're fewer than formerly, and…well, I've not kept count, but at least half those seen or killed have something wrong, internally or externally."

Drummond drew heavily on his pipe. He needed something to hang onto, in a new storm of insanity. Very quietly, he said:

"In my college biology course, they told me the vast majority of mutations are unfavorable. More ways of not doing something than of doing it. Radiation might sterilize an animal, or might produce several degrees of genetic change. You could have a mutation so violently lethal the possessor never gets born, or soon dies. You could have all kinds of more or less handicapping factors, or just random changes not making much difference one way or the other. Or in a few cases you might get something actually favorable, but you couldn't really say the possessor is a true member of the species. And favorable mutations themselves usually involve a price in the partial or total loss of some other function."

"Right." Robinson nodded heavily, "One of your jobs on the census will be to try and locate any and all who know genetics, and send them here. But your real task, which only you and I and a couple of others must know about, the job overriding all other considerations, will be to find the human mutants."

Drummond's throat was dry. "There've been a lot of them?" he whispered.

"Yes. But we don't know how many or where. We only know about those people who live near an army post, or have some other fairly regular intercourse with us, and they're only a few thousand all told. Among them, the birth rate has gone down to about half the prewar ratio. And over half the births they do have are abnormal."

"Over half—"

"Yeah. Of course, the violently different ones soon die, or are put in an institution we've set up in the Alleghenies. But what can we do with viable forms, if their parents still love them? A kid with deformed or missing or abortive organs, twisted internal structure, a tail, or something even worse…well, *it'll* have a tough time in life, but it can generally survive. And perpetuate itself—"

"And a normal-looking one might have some unnoticeable quirk, or a characteristic that won't show up for years. Or even a normal one might be carrying recessives, and pass them on—God!" The exclamation was half blasphemy, half prayer. "But how'd it happen? People weren't all near atom-hit areas."

"Maybe not, though a lot of survivors escaped from the outskirts. But there was that first year, with everybody on the move. One could pass near enough to a blasted region to be affected, without knowing it. And that damnable radiodust, blowing on the wind. It's got a long half-life. It'll be active for decades. Then, as in any collapsing culture, promiscuity was common. Still is. Oh, it'd spread itself, all right."

"I still don't see why it spread itself so much. Even here—"

"Well, I don't know why it shows up here. I suppose a lot of the local flora and fauna came in from elsewhere. This place is safe. The nearest dusted region is three hundred miles off, with mountains between. There must be many such islands of comparatively normal conditions. We have to find them too. But elsewhere—"

"Soup's on," announced Elaine, and went from the kitchen to the dining room with a loaded tray.

The men rose; Grayly, Drummond looked at Robinson and said tonelessly: "O.K. I'll get your information for you. We'll map mutation areas and safe areas, we'll check on our population and resources, we'll eventually get all the facts you want. But—what are you going to do then?"

"I wish I knew," said Robinson haggardly. "I wish I knew."

Winter lay heavily on the north, a vast gray sky seeming frozen solid over the rolling white plains. The last three winters had come early and stayed long. Dust, colloidal dust of the bombs, suspended in the atmosphere and cutting down the solar constant by a deadly percent or two. There had even been a few earthquakes, set off in geologically unstable parts of the world by bombs planted right. Half of California had been ruined when a sabotage bomb started the San Andreas Fault on a major slip. And that kicked up still more dust.

Fimbulwinter, thought Drummond bleakly. *The doom of the prophecy. But no, we're surviving. Though maybe not as men—*

Most people had gone south, and there overcrowding had made starvation and disease and internecine struggle the normal aspects of life. Those who'd stuck it out up here, and had luck with their pest-ridden crops, were better off.

Drummond's jet slid above the cratered black ruin of the Twin Cities. There was still enough radioactivity to melt the snow, and the pit was like a skull's empty eye socket. The man sighed, but he was becoming calloused to the sight of death. There was so much of it. Only the struggling agony of life mattered anymore.

He strained through the sinister twilight, swooping low over the unending fields. Burned-out hulks of farmhouses, bones of ghost towns, sere deadness of dusted land—but he'd heard travelers speak of a fairly powerful community up near the Canadian border, and it was up to him to find it.

A lot of things had been up to him in the last six months. He'd had to work out a means of search, and organize his few, overworked assistants into an efficient staff, and go out on the long hunt.

They hadn't covered the country. That was impossible. Their few planes had gone to areas chosen more or less at random, trying to get a cross section of conditions. They'd penetrated wildernesses of hill and plain and forest, establishing contact with scattered, still demoralized out-dwellers. On the whole, it was more laborious than anything else. Most were pathetically glad to see any symbol of law and order and the paradisical-seeming "old days." Now and then there was danger and trouble, when they encountered wary or sullen or outright hostile groups suspicious of a government they associated with disaster, and once there had even been a pitched battle with roving outlaws. But the work had gone ahead, and now the preliminaries were about over.

Preliminaries—It was a bigger job to find out exactly how matters stood than the entire country was capable of undertaking right now. But Drummond had enough facts for reliable extrapolation. He and his staff had collected most of the essential data and begun correlating it. By questioning, by observation, by seeking and finding, by any means that came to hand they'd filled their notebooks. And in the sketchy outlines of a Chinese drawing, and with the same stark realism, the truth was there.

Just this one more place, and I'll go home, thought Drummond for the—thousandth?—time. His brain was getting into a rut, treading the same terrible circle and finding no way out. *Robinson won't like what I tell him, but there it is.* And darkly, slowly: *Barbara, maybe it was best you and the kids went as you did. Quickly, cleanly, not even knowing it. This isn't much of a world. It'll never be our world again.*

He saw the place he sought, a huddle of buildings near the frozen shores of the Lake of the Woods, and his jet murmured toward the white ground. The stories he'd heard of this town weren't overly encouraging, but he supposed he'd get out all right. The others had his data anyway, so it didn't matter.

By the time he'd landed in the clearing just outside the village, using the jet's skis, most of the inhabitants were there waiting. In the gathering dusk they were a ragged and wild-looking bunch, clumsily dressed in whatever scraps of cloth and leather they had. The bearded, hard-eyed men were armed with clubs and knives and a few guns. As Drummond got out, he was careful to keep his hands away from his own automatics.

"Hello," he said. "I'm friendly."

"Y' better be," growled the big leader. "Who are you, where from, an' why?"

"First," lied Drummond smoothly, "I want to tell you I have another man with a plane who knows where I am. If I'm not back in a certain time, he'll come with bombs. But we don't intend any harm or interference. This is just a sort of social call. I'm Hugh Drummond of the United States Army."

They digested that slowly. Clearly, they weren't friendly to the government, but they stood in too much awe of aircraft and armament to be openly hostile. The leader spat. "How long you staying?"

"Just overnight, if you'll put me up. I'll pay for it." He held up a small pouch. "Tobacco."

Their eyes gleamed, and the leader said, "You'll stay with me. Come on."

Drummond gave him the bribe and went with the group. He didn't like to spend such priceless luxuries this freely, but the job was more important. And the boss seemed thawed a little by the fragrant brown flakes. He was sniffing them greedily.

"Been smoking bark an' grass," he confided. "Terrible."

"Worse than that," agreed Drummond. He turned up his jacket collar and shivered. The wind starting to blow was bitterly cold.

"Just what y' here for?" demanded someone else.

"Well, just to see how things stand. We've got the government started again, and are patching things up. But we have to know where folks are, what they need, and so on."

"Don't want nothing t' do with the gov'ment," muttered a woman. "They brung all this on us."

"Oh, come now. We didn't ask to be attacked." Mentally, Drummond crossed his fingers. He neither knew nor cared who was to blame. Both sides, letting mutual fear and friction mount to hysteria—In fact, he wasn't sure the United States hadn't sent out the first rockets on orders of some panicky or aggressive officials. Nobody was alive who admitted knowing.

"It's the jedgment o' God, for the sins o' our leaders," persisted the woman. "The plague, the fire-death, all that, ain't it foretold in the Bible? Ain't we living in the last days o' the world?"

"Maybe." Drummond was glad to stop before a long low cabin. Religious argument was touchy at best, and with a lot of people nowadays it was dynamite.

They entered the rudely furnished but fairly comfortable structure. A good many crowded in with them. For all their suspicion, they were curious, and an outsider in an aircraft was a blue-moon event these days.

Drummond's eyes flickered unobtrusively about the room, noticing details. Three women—that meant a return to concubinage. Only to be expected in a day of few men and strong-arm rule. Ornaments and utensils, tools and weapons of good quality—yes, that confirmed the stories. This wasn't exactly a bandit town, but it had waylaid travelers and raided other places when times were hard, and built up a sort of dominance of the surrounding country. That, too, was common.

There was a dog on the floor nursing a litter. Only three pups, and one of those was bald, one lacked ears, and one had more toes than it should. Among the wide-eyed children present, there were several two years old or less, and with almost no obvious exceptions, they were also different.

Drummond sighed heavily and sat down. In a way, this clinched it. He'd known for a long time, and finding mutation here, as far as any place from atomic destruction, was about the last evidence he needed.

He had to get on friendly terms, or he wouldn't find out much about things like population, food production, and whatever else there was to know. Forcing a smile to stiff lips, he took a flask from his jacket. "Prewar rye," he said. "Who wants a nip?"

"Do we!" The answer barked out in a dozen voices and words. The flask circulated, men pawing and cursing and grabbing to get at it. *Their homebrew must be pretty bad,* thought Drummond wryly.

The chief shouted an order, and one of his women got busy at the primitive stove. "Rustle you a mess o' chow," he said heartily. "An' my name's Sam Buckman."

"Pleased to meet you, Sam." Drummond squeezed the hairy paw hard. He had to show he wasn't a weakling, a conniving city slicker.

"What's it like, outside?" asked someone presently. "We ain't heard for so long—"

"You haven't missed much," said Drummond between bites.

The food was pretty good. Briefly, he sketched conditions. "You're better off than most," he finished.

"Yeah. Mebbe so." Sam Buckman scratched his tangled beard. "What I'd give f'r a razor blade—! It ain't easy, though. The first year we weren't no better off 'n anyone else. Me, I'm a farmer, I kept some ears o' corn an' a little wheat an' barley in my pockets all that winter, even though I was starving. A bunch o' hungry refugees plundered my place, but I got away an' drifted up here. Next year I took an empty farm here an' started over."

Drummond doubted that it had been abandoned, but said nothing. Sheer survival outweighed a lot of considerations.

"Others came an' settled here," said the leader reminiscently. "We farm together. We have to; one man couldn't live by himself, not with the bugs an' blight, an' the crops sproutin' into all new kinds, an' the outlaws aroun'. Not many up here, though we did beat off some enemy troops last winter." He glowed with pride at that, but Drummond wasn't particularly impressed. A handful of freezing starveling conscripts, lost and bewildered in a foreign enemy's land, with no hope of ever getting home, weren't formidable.

"Things getting better, though," said Buckman. "We're heading up." He scowled blackly, and a palpable chill crept into the room. "If 'twern't for the births—"

"Yes—the births. The new babies. Even the stock an' plants." It was an old man speaking, his eyes glazed with near madness. "It's the mark o' the beast. Satan is loose in the world—"

"Shut up!" Huge and bristling with wrath, Buckman launched himself out of his seat and grabbed the oldster by his scrawny throat. "Shut up 'r I'll bash y'r lying head in. Ain't no son o' mine being marked by the devil."

"Or mine—" "Or mine—" The rumble of voices ran about the cabin, sullen and afraid.

"It's God's judgment, I tell you!" The woman was shrilling again. "The end o' the world is near. Prepare f'r the second coming—"

"An' you shut up too, Mag Schmidt," snarled Buckman He stood bent over, gnarled arms swinging loose, hands flexing, little eyes darting red and wild about the room. "Shut y' trap an' keep it shut. I'm still boss here, an' if you don't like it you can get out. I still don't think that gunny-looking brat o' y'rs fell in the lake by accident."

The woman shrank back, lips tight. The room filled with crackling silence. One of the babies began to cry. It had two heads.

Slowly and heavily, Buckman turned to Drummond, who sat immobile against the wall. "You see?" he asked dully "You see how it is? Maybe it is the curse o' God. Maybe the world is ending. I dunno. I just know there's few enough babies, an' most o' them *de*formed. Will it go on? Will all our kids be monsters? Should we…kill these an' hope we get some human babies? What is it? What to do?"

Drummond rose. He felt a weight as of centuries on shoulders, the weariness, blank and absolute, of having seen that smoldering panic and heard that desperate appeal too often, too often.

"Don't kill them," he said. "That's the worst kind of murder, and anyway it'd do no good at all. It comes from the bombs, and you can't stop it. You'll go right on having such children so you might as well get used to it."

By atomic-powered stratojet it wasn't far from Minnesota to Oregon, and Drummond landed in Taylor about noon the next day. This time there was no hurry to get his machine under cover, and up on the mountain was a raw scar of earth where a new airfield was slowly being built. Men were getting over their terror of the sky. They had another fear to face now, and it was one from which there was no hiding.

Drummond walked slowly down the icy main street to the central office. It was numbingly cold, a still, relentless intensity of frost eating through clothes and flesh and bone. It wasn't much better inside. Heating systems were still poor improvisations.

"You're back!" Robinson met him in the antechamber suddenly galvanized with eagerness. He had grown thin and nervous, looking ten years older, but impatience blazed from him. "How is it? How is it?"

Drummond held up a bulky notebook. "All here," he said grimly. "All the facts we'll need. Not formally correlated yet, But the picture is simple enough."

Robinson laid an arm on his shoulder and steered him into the office. He felt the general's hand shaking, but he'd sat down and had a drink before business came up again.

"You've done a good job," said the leader warmly. "When the country's organized again, I'll see you get a medal for this. Your men in the other planes aren't in yet."

"No, they'll be gathering data for a long time. The job won't be finished for years. I've only got a general outline here, but it's enough. It's enough." Drummond's eyes were haunted again.

Robinson felt cold at meeting that too-steady gaze. He whispered shakily: "Is it—bad?"

"The worst. Physically, the country's recovering. But biologically, we've reached a crossroads and taken the wrong fork."

"What do you mean? *What do you mean?*"

Drummond let him have it then, straight and hard as a bayonet thrust. "The birth rate's a little over half the prewar," he said, "and about seventy-five per cent of all births are mutant, of which possibly two-thirds are viable and presumably fertile. Of course, that doesn't include late-maturing characteristics, or those undetectable by naked-eye observation, or the mutated recessive genes that must be carried by a lot of otherwise normal zygotes. And it's everywhere. There are no safe places."

"I see," said Robinson after a long time. He nodded, like a man struck a stunning blow and not yet fully aware of it. "I see. The reason—"

"Is obvious."

"Yes. People going through radioactive areas—"

"Why, no. That would only account for a few. But—"

"No matter. The fact's there, and that's enough. We have to decide what to do about it."

"And soon," Drummond's jaw set. "It's wrecking our culture. We at least preserved our historical continuity, but even that's going now. People are going crazy as birth after birth is monstrous. Fear of the unknown, striking at minds still stunned by the war and its immediate aftermath. Frustration of parenthood, perhaps the most basic instinct there is. It's leading to infanticide, desertion, despair, a cancer at the root of society. We've got to act."

"How? How?" Robinson stared numbly at his hands.

"I don't know. You're the leader. Maybe an educational campaign, though that hardly seems practicable. Maybe an acceleration of your program for reintegrating the country. Maybe—I don't know."

Drummond stuffed tobacco into his pipe. He was near the end of what he had, but would rather take a few good smokes than a lot of niggling puffs. "Of course," he said thoughtfully, "it's probably not the end of things. We won't know for a generation or more, but I rather imagine the mutants can grow into society. They'd better, for they'll outnumber the humans. The thing is, if we just let matters drift there's no telling where they'll go. The situation is unprecedented. We may end up in a culture of specialized variations, which would be very bad from an evolutionary standpoint. There may be fighting between mutant types, or with humans. Interbreeding may produce worse freaks, particularly when accumulated recessives start showing up. Robinson, if we want any say at all in what's going to happen in the next few centuries, we have to act quickly. Otherwise it'll snowball out of all control."

"Yes. Yes, we'll have to act fast. And hard." Robinson straightened in his chair. Decision firmed his countenance, but his eyes were staring. "We're mobilized," he said. "We have the men and the weapons and the organization. They won't be able to resist."

The ashy cold of Drummond's emotions stirred, but it was with a horrible wrenching of fear. "What are you getting at?" he snapped.

"Racial death. All mutants and their parents to be sterilized whenever and wherever detected."

"You're crazy!" Drummond sprang from his chair, grabbed Robinson's shoulders across the desk, and shook him. "You…why, it's impossible! You'll bring revolt, civil war, final collapse!"

"Not if we go about it right." There were little beads of sweat studding the general's forehead. "I don't like it any better than you, but it's got to be done or the human race is finished. Normal births a minority—" He surged to his feet, gasping. "I've thought a long time about this. Your facts only confirmed my suspicions. This tears it. Can't you see? Evolution has to proceed slowly. Life wasn't meant for such a storm of change. Unless we can save the true human stock, it'll be absorbed and differentiation will continue till humanity is a collection of freaks, probably intersterile. Or…there must be a lot of lethal recessives. In a large population, they can accumulate unnoticed till nearly everybody has them, and then start emerging all at once. That'd wipe us out. It's happened before, in rats and other species. If we eliminate mutant stock now, we can still save the race. It won't be cruel. We have sterilization techniques which are quick and painless, not upsetting the endocrine balance. But it's got to be done!" His voice rose to a raw scream, broke. "It's got to be done!"

Drummond slapped him, hard. He drew a shuddering breath, sat down, and began to cry, and somehow that was the most horrible sight of all. "You're crazy," said the aviator. "You've gone nuts and with brooding alone on this the last six months, without knowing or being able to act. You've lost all perspective.

"We can't use violence. In the first place, it would break our tottering, cracked culture irreparably, into a mad-dog finish fight. We'd not even win it. We're outnumbered and we couldn't hold down a continent, eventually a planet. And remember what we said once, about abandoning the old savage way of settling things, that never brings a real settlement at all? We'd throw away a lesson our noses were rubbed in not three years ago. We'd return to the beast—to ultimate extinction.

"And anyway," he went on very quietly, "it wouldn't do a bit of good. Mutants would still be born. The poison is everywhere. Normal parents will give birth to mutants, somewhere along the line. We just have to accept that fact, and live with it. The *new* human race will have to."

"I'm sorry." Robinson raised his face from his hands. It was a ghastly visage, gone white and old, but there was calm on it. "I—blew my top. You're right. I've been thinking of this, worrying and wondering, living and breathing it, lying awake nights, and when I finally sleep I dream of it. I…yes, I see your point. And you're right."

"It's O.K. You've been under a terrific strain. Three years with never a rest, and the responsibility for a nation, and now this— Sure, everybody's entitled to be a little crazy. We'll work out a solution, somehow."

"Yes, of course." Robinson poured out two stiff drinks and gulped his. He paced restlessly, and his tremendous ability came back in waves of strength and confidence. "Let me see—Eugenics, of course. If we work hard, we'll have the nation tightly organized inside of ten years. Then…well, I don't suppose we can keep the mutants from interbreeding, but certainly we can pass laws to protect humans and encourage their propagation. Since radical mutations would probably be intersterile anyway, and most mutants handicapped one way or another, a few generations should see humans completely dominant again."

Drummond scowled. He was worried. It wasn't like Robinson to be unreasonable. Somehow, the man had acquired a mental blind spot where this most ultimate of human problems was concerned. He said slowly, "That won't work either. First, it'd be hard to impose and enforce. Second, we'd be repeating the old *Herrenvolk* notion. Mutants are inferior, mutants must be kept in their place—to enforce that, especially on a majority, you'd need a full-fledged totalitarian state. Third, that wouldn't work either, for the rest of the world, with almost no exceptions, is under no such control and we'll be in no position to take over that control for a long time—generations. Before then, mutants will dominate everywhere over there, and if they resent the way we treat their kind here, we'd better run for cover."

"You assume a lot. How do you know those hundreds or thousands of diverse types will work together? They're less like each other than like humans, even. They could be played off against each other."

"Maybe. But *that* would be going back onto the old road of treachery and violence, the road to Hell. Conversely, if every not-quite-human is called a 'mutant,' like a separate class, he'll think he is, and act accordingly against the lumped-together 'humans'. No, the only way to sanity—to *survival*—is to abandon class prejudice and race hate altogether, and work as individuals. We're all…well, Earthlings, and sub-classification is deadly. We all have to live together, and might as well make the best of it."

"Yeah…yeah, that's right too."

"Anyway, I repeat that all such attempts would be useless. All Earth is infected with mutation. It will be for a long time. The purest human stock will still produce mutants."

"Y—yes, that's true. Our best bet seems to be to find all such stock and withdraw it into the few safe areas left. It'll mean a small human population, but a *human* one."

"I tell you, that's impossible," clipped Drummond. "There is no safe place. Not one."

Robinson stopped pacing and looked at him as at a physical antagonist. "That so?" he almost growled. "Why?"

Drummond told him, adding incredulously, "Surely you knew that. Your physicists must have measured the amount of it. Your doctors, your engineers, that geneticist I dug up for you. You obviously got a lot of this biological information you've been slinging at me from him. They *must* all have told you the same thing."

Robinson shook his head stubbornly. "It can't be. It's not reasonable. The concentration wouldn't be great enough."

"Why, you poor fool, you need only look around you. The plants, the animals—Haven't there been any births in Taylor?"

"No. This is still a man's town, though women are trickling in and several babies are on the way—" Robinson's face was suddenly twisted with desperation. "Elaine's is due any time now. She's in the hospital here. Don't you see, our other kid died of the plague. This one's all we have. We want him to grow up in a world free of want and fear, a world of peace and sanity where he can play and laugh and become a man, not a beast starving in a cave. You and I are on our way out. We're the old generation, the one that wrecked the world. It's up to us to build it again, and then retire from it to let our children have it. The future's theirs. We've got to make it ready for them."

Sudden insight held Drummond motionless for long seconds. Understanding came, and pity, and an odd gentleness that changed his sunken bony face. "Yes," he murmured, "yes, I see. That's why you're working with all that's in you to build a normal, healthy world. That's why you nearly went crazy when this threat appeared. That…that's why you can't, just can't comprehend—"

He took the other man's arm and guided him toward the door. "Come on," he said. "Let's go see how your wife's making out. Maybe we can get her some flowers on the way."

The silent cold bit at them as they went down the street. Snow crackled underfoot. It was already grimy with town smoke and dust, but overhead the sky was incredibly clean and blue. Breath smoked whitely from their mouths and nostrils. The sound of men at work rebuilding drifted faintly between the bulking mountains.

"We couldn't emigrate to another planet, could we?" asked Robinson, and answered himself: "No, we lack the organization and resources to settle them right now. We'll have to make out on Earth. A few safe spots—there *must* be others besides this one—to house the true humans till the mutation period is over. Yes, we can do it."

"There are no safe places," insisted Drummond. "Even if there were, the mutants would still outnumber us. Does your geneticist have any idea how this'll come out, biologically speaking?"

"He doesn't know. His specialty is still largely unknown. He can make an intelligent guess, and that's all."

"Yeah. Anyway, our problem is to learn to live with the mutants, to accept anyone as—Earthling—no matter how he looks, to quit thinking anything was ever settled by violence or connivance, to build a culture of individual sanity. Funny," mused Drummond, "how the impractical virtues, tolerance and sympathy and generosity, have become the fundamental necessities of simple survival.

I guess it was always true, but it took the death of half the world and the end of a biological era to make us see that simple little fact. The job's terrific. We've got half a million years of brutality and greed, superstition and prejudice, to lick in a few generations. If we fail, mankind is done. But we've got to try."

They found some flowers, potted in a house, and Robinson bought them with the last of his tobacco. By the time he reached the hospital, he was sweating. The sweat froze on his face as he walked.

The hospital was the town's biggest building, and fairly well equipped. A nurse met them as they entered.

"I was just going to send for you, General Robinson," she said. "The baby's on the way."

"How…is she?"

"Fine, so far. Just wait here, please."

Drummond sank into a chair and with haggard eyes watched Robinson's jerky pacing. *The poor guy. Why is it expectant fathers are supposed to be so funny? It's like laughing at a man on the rack. I know, Barbara, I know.*

"They have some anaesthetics," muttered the general. "They…Elaine never was very strong."

"She'll be all right." *It's afterward that worries me.*

"Yeah—Yeah—How long, though, how long?"

"Depends. Take it easy." With a wrench, Drummond made a sacrifice to a man he liked. He filled his pipe and handed it over. "Here, you need a smoke."

"Thanks." Robinson puffed raggedly.

The slow minutes passed, and Drummond wondered vaguely what he'd do when—it—happened. It didn't have to happen. But the chances were all against such an easy solution. He was no psychologist. Best just to let things happen as they would.

The waiting broke at last. A doctor came out, seeming an inscrutable high priest in his white garments. Robinson stood before him, motionless.

"You're a brave man," said the doctor. His face, as he removed the mask, was stern and set. "You'll need your courage."

"She—" It was hardly a human sound that croak.

"Your wife is doing well. But the baby—"

A nurse brought out the little wailing form. It was a boy. But his limbs were rubbery tentacles terminating in boneless digits.

Robinson looked, and something went out of him as he stood there. When he turned, his face was dead.

"You're lucky," said Drummond, and meant it. He'd seen too many other mutants. "After all, if he can use those hands he'll get along all right. He'll even have an advantage in certain types of work. It isn't a deformity, really. If there's nothing else, you've got a good kid."

"*If*? You can't tell with mutants."

"I know. But you've got guts, you and Elaine. You'll see this through, together." Briefly, Drummond felt an utter personal desolation. He went on, perhaps to cover that emptiness:

"I see why you didn't understand the problem. You *wouldn't*. It was a psychological block, suppressing a fact you didn't dare face. That boy is really the center of your life. You couldn't think the truth about him, so your subconscious just refused to let you think rationally on that subject at all.

"Now you know. Now you realize there's no safe place, not on all the planet. The tremendous incidence of mutant births in the first generation could have told you that alone. Most such new characteristics are recessive, which means both parents have to have it for it to show in the zygote. But genetic changes are random, except for a tendency to fall into roughly similar patterns. Four-leaved clovers, for instance. Think how vast the total number of such changes must be, to produce so many corresponding changes in a couple of years. Think how many, *many* recessives there must be, existing only in gene patterns till their mates show up. We'll just have to take our chances of something really deadly accumulating. We'd never know till too late."

"The dust—"

"Yeah. The radiodust. It's colloidal, and uncountable other radiocolloids were formed when the bombs went off, and ordinary dirt gets into unstable isotopic forms near the craters. And there are radiogases too, probably. The poison is all over the world by now, spread by wind and air currents. Colloids can be suspended indefinitely in the atmosphere.

"The concentration isn't too high for life, though a physicist told me he'd measured it as being very near the safe limit and there'll probably be a lot of cancer. But it's everywhere. Every breath we draw, every crumb we eat and drop we drink, every clod we walk on, the dust is there. It's in the stratosphere, clear on down to the surface, probably a good distance below. We could only escape by sealing ourselves in air-conditioned vaults and wearing spacesuits whenever we got out, and under present conditions that's impossible.

"Mutations were rare before, because a charged particle has to get pretty close to a gene and be moving fast before its electromagnetic effect causes physicochemical changes, and then that particular chromosome has to enter into reproduction. Now the charged particles, and the gamma rays producing still more, are everywhere. Even at the comparatively low concentration, the odds favor a given organism having so many cells changed that at least one will give rise to a mutant. There's even a good chance of like recessives meeting in the first generation, as we've seen. Nobody's safe, no place is free."

"The geneticist thinks some true humans will continue."

"A few, probably. After all, the radioactivity isn't too concentrated, and it's burning itself out. But it'll take fifty or hundred years for the process to drop to insignificance, and by then the pure stock will be way in the minority. And there'll still be all those unmatched recessives, waiting to show up."

"You were right. We should never have created science. It brought the twilight of the race."

"I never said that. The race brought its own destruction, through misuse of science. Our culture was scientific anyway, in all except its psychological basis. It's up to us to take that last and hardest step. If we do, the race may yet survive."

Drummond gave Robinson a push toward the inner door. "You're exhausted, beat up, ready to quit. Go on in and see Elaine. Give her my regards. Then take a long rest before going back to work. I still think you've got a good kid."

Mechanically, the *de facto* President of the United States left the room. Hugh Drummond stared after him a moment, then went out into the street.

Kinnison's Band

(To the tune of *McNamara's Band*)

My name is Kimball Kinnison, I lead the Lensman band.
Although we're few in number, our abilities are grand;
We play with stars and planets, catch comets in a net,
And use a supernova to light a cigarette.
  Chorus:
    All clear and on green, QX, QX!
    All clear and on green, QX, QX!
    All clear and on green, QX, QX!
    Sound it loudly, clearly, Brek-ke-ke-kex, QX!

I met with good old Worsel and he took my by the hand
And said, "How's civilization, and how does she stand?
It's the most distressing galaxy that ever you have seen;
Boskone is hanging everyone whose tentacles aren't green."
  Chorus

So Tregonsee got down to work, our fearless mental scout.
His X-ray eyes and ESP went peering all about
Behind all doors where he might spy a lurking zwilnik louse;
Especially the dressing room down at the burlesque house.
  Chorus

Then frigid-blooded, poison-breathing Nadreck came to town
And said we all should have a drink to wet our whistles down.
King's Ransom isn't aqua regia, which he drank with vim,
But all we Earthmen cooled our beers by standing them on him.
  Chorus

Then Mentor of Arisia, our good old college dean,
Who personally ground each Lens upon his Dean machine,
Decided we must learn much more, lest Civilization fall.
To lecture us, he first went out and hired a Cosmic 'All.
  Chorus

The Helping Hand

A mellow bell tone was followed by the flat voice of the bororeceptionist: "His Excellency Valka Vahino, Special Envoy from the League of Cundaloa to the Commonwealth of Sol."

The Earthlings rose politely as he entered. Despite the heavy gravity and dry chill air of terrestrial conditions, he moved with the flowing grace of his species, and many of the humans were struck anew by what a handsome people his race was.

People—yes, the folk of Cundaloa were humanoid enough, mentally and physically, to justify the term. Their differences were not important; they added a certain charm, the romance of alienness, to the comforting reassurance that there was no really basic strangeness.

Ralph Dalton let his eyes sweep over the ambassador. Valka Vahino was typical of his race—humanoid mammal, biped, with a face that was very manlike, differing only in its beauty of finely chiseled features, high cheekbones, great dark eyes. A little smaller, more slender than the Earthlings, with a noiseless, feline ease of movement. Long shining blue hair swept back from his high forehead to his slim shoulders, a sharp and pleasing contrast to the rich golden skin color. He was dressed in the ancient ceremonial garb of Luai on Cundaloa—shining silvery tunic, deep-purple cloak from which little sparks of glittering metal swirled like fugitive stars, gold-worked boots of soft leather. One slender six-fingered hand held the elaborately carved staff of office which was all the credentials his planet had given him.

He bowed, a single rippling movement which had nothing of servility in it, and said in excellent Terrestrial, which still retained some of the lilting, singing accent of his native tongue: "Peace on your houses! The Great House of Cundaloa sends greetings and many well-wishings to his brothers of Sol. His unworthy member Valka Vahino speaks for him in friendship."

Some of the Earthlings shifted stance, a little embarrassed. It did sound awkward in translation, thought Dalton. But the language of Cundaloa was one of the most beautiful sounds in the Galaxy.

He replied with an attempt at the same grave formality. "Greetings and welcome. The Commonwealth of Sol receives the representative of the League of

Cundaloa in all friendship. Ralph Dalton, Premier of the Commonwealth, speaking for the people of the Solar System."

He introduced the others then—cabinet ministers, technical advisers military staff members. It was an important assembly. Most of the power and influence in the Solar System was gathered here.

He finished: "This is an preliminary conference on the economic proposals recently made to your gov…to the Great House of Cundaloa. It has no legal standing. But it is being televised and I daresay the Solar Assembly will act on a basis of what is learned at these and similar hearings."

"I understand. It is a good idea." Vahino waited until the rest were seated before taking a chair.

There was a pause. Eyes kept going to the clock on the wall. Vahino had arrived punctually at the time set, but Skorrogan of Skontar was late, thought Dalton. Tactless, but then the manners of the Skontarans were notoriously bad. Not at all like the gentle deference of Cundaloa, which in no way indicated weakness.

There was aimless conversation of the "How do you like it here?" variety. Vahino, it developed, had visited the Solar System quite a few times in the past decade. Not surprising, in view of the increasingly close economic ties between his planet and the Commonwealth There were a great many Cundaloan students in Earthian universities, and before the war there had been a growing tourist traffic from Sol to Avalki. It would probably revive soon—especially if the devastation were repaired and—

"Oh, yes," smiled Vahino. "It is the ambition of all young *anamai,* men on Cundaloa, to come to earth, if only for a visit. It is not mere flattery to say that our admiration for you and your achievements is boundless."

"It's mutual," said Dalton. "Your culture, your art and music, your literature—all have a large following in the Solar System. Why, many men, and not just scholars, learn Luaian simply to read the *Dvanago-Epai* in the original. Cundaloan singers, from concert artists to nightclub entertainers, get more applause than any others." He grinned. "Your young men here have some difficulty keeping our terrestrial coeds off their necks. And your few young women here are besieged by invitations. I suppose only the fact that there cannot be issue has kept the number of marriages as small as it has been."

"But seriously," persisted Vahino, "we realize at home that your civilization sets the tone for the known Galaxy. It is not just that Solarian civilization is the most advanced technically, though that has, of course, much to do with it. *You* came to *us,* with your spaceships and atomic energy and medical science and all else—but, after all, we can learn that and go on with you from there. It is, however, such acts as…well, as your present offer of help: to rebuild ruined worlds light-years away, pouring your own skill and treasure into our homes, when we can offer you so little in return—it is that which makes you the leading race in the Galaxy."

"We have selfish motives, as you well know," said Dalton a little uncomfortably. "Many of them. There is, of course, simple humanitarianism. We could not let races very like our own know want when the Solar System and its colonies have more wealth than they know what to do with. But our own bloody history has taught us that such programs as this economic-aid plan redound to the benefit of the initiator. When we have built up Cundaloa and Skontar, got them producing again, modernized their backward industry, taught them our science—they will be able to trade with us. And our economy is still, after all these centuries, primarily mercantile. Then, too, we will have knitted them too closely together for a repetition of the disastrous war just ended. And they will be allies for us against some of the really alien and menacing cultures in the Galaxy, planets and systems and empires against which we may one day have to stand."

"Pray the High One that that day never comes," said Vahino soberly. "We have seen enough of war."

The bell sounded again, and the robot announced in its clear inhuman tones: "His Excellency Skorrogan Valthak's son, Duke of Kraakahaym, Special Envoy from the Empire of Skontar to the Commonwealth of Sol."

They got up again, a little more slowly this time, and Dalton saw the expressions of dislike on several faces, expressions which smoothed into noncommittal blankness as the newcomer entered. There was no denying that the Skontarans were not very popular in the Solar System just now, and·partly it was their own fault. But most of it they couldn't help.

The prevailing impression was that Skontar had been at fault in the war with Cundaloa. That was plainly an error. The misfortune was that the suns Skang and Avaiki, forming a system about half a lightyear apart, had a third companion which humans usually called Allan, after the captain of the first expedition to the system. And the planets of Allan were uninhabited.

When terrestrial technology came to Skontar and Cundaloa, its first result had been to unify both planets—ultimately—both systems into rival states which turned desirous eyes on the green new planets of Allan. Both had had colonies there, clashes had followed, ultimately the hideous five years' war which had wasted both systems and ended in a peace negotiated with terrestrial help. It had been simply another conflict of rival imperialisms, such as had been common enough in human history before the Great Peace and the formation of the Commonwealth. The terms of the treaty were as fair as possible, and both systems were exhausted. They would keep the peace now, especially when both were eagerly looking for Solarian help to rebuild.

Still—the average human liked the Cundaloans. It was almost a corollary that he should dislike the Skontarans and blame them for the trouble. But even before the war they had not been greatly admired. Their isolationism, their clinging to outmoded traditions, their harsh accent, their domineering manner, even their appearance told against them.

Dalton had had trouble persuading the Assembly to let him include Skontar in the invitation to economic-aid conferences. He had finally persuaded them that it was essential—not only would the resources of Skang be a material help in restoration, particularly their minerals, but the friendship of a potentially powerful and hitherto aloof empire could be gained.

The aid program was still no more then a proposal. The Assembly would have to make a law detailing who should be helped, and how and how much and then the law would have to be embodied in treaties with the planets concerned. The initial informal meeting here was only the first step. But—crucial.

Dalton bowed formally as the Skontaran entered. The envoy responded by stamping the butt of his huge spear against the floor, leaning the archaic weapon against the wall, and extending his holstered blaster handle first. Dalton took it gingerly and laid it on the desk. "Greeting and welcome," he began, since Skorrogan wasn't saying anything. "The Commonwealth—"

"Thank you." The voice was a hoarse bass, somehow metallic, and strongly accented. "The Valtam of the Empire of Skontar sends greetings to the Premier of Sol by Skorrogan Valthak's son, Duke of Kraakahaym."

He stood out in the room, seeming to fill it with his strong, forbidding presence. In spite of coming from a world of higher gravity and lower temperature, the Skontarans were a huge race, over two meters tall and so broad that they seemed stocky. They could be classed as humanoid, in that they were bipedal mammals, but there was not much resemblance beyond that. Under a wide, low forehead and looming eyebrow ridges, the eyes of Skorrogan were fierce and golden, hawk's eyes. His face was blunt-snouted, with a mouthful of fangs in the terrific jaws; his ears were blunt and set high on the massive skull. Short brown fur covered his muscular body to the end of the long restless tail, and a ruddy mane flared from his head and throat. In spite of the, to him, tropical temperature, he wore the furs and skins of state occasions at home, and the acrid reek of his sweat hung about him.

"You are late," said one of the ministers with thin politeness. "I trust you were not detained by any difficulties."

"No, I underestimated the time needed to get here," answered Skorrogan. "Please to excuse me." He did not sound at all sorry, but lowered his great bulk into the nearest chair and opened his portfolio. We have business now, my sirs?"

"Well…I suppose so." Dalton sat down at the head of the long conference table. "Though we are not too concerned with facts and figures at this preliminary discussion. We want simply to agree on general aims, matters of basic policy."

"Naturally, you will wish a full account of the available resources of Avaiki and Skang as well as the Allanian colonies," said Vahino in his soft voice. "The agriculture of Cundaloa, the mines of Skontar, will contribute much even at this early date, and, of course, in the end there must be economic self-sufficiency."

"It is a question of education, too," said Dalton. "We will send many experts, technical advisers, teachers—"

"And, of course, some question of military resources will arise—" began the Chief of Staff.

"Skontar have own army," snapped Skorrogan. "No need of talk there yet."

"Perhaps not," agreed the Minister of Finance mildly. He took out a cigarette and lit it.

"Please, sir!" For a moment Skorrogan's voice rose to a bull roar., "No smoke. You know Skontarans allergic to tobacco—"

"Sorry!" The Minister of Finance stubbed out the cylinder. His hand shook a little and he glared at the envoy. There had been little need for concern, the air-conditioning system swept the smoke away at once. And in any case—you don't shout at a cabinet minister. Especially when you come to ask him for help—

"There will be other systems involved," said Dalton hastily, trying with a sudden feeling of desperation to smooth over the unease and tension. "Not only the colonies of Sol. I imagine your two races will be expanding beyond your own triple system, and the resources made available by such colonization—"

"We will have to," said Skorrogan sourly. "After treaty rob us of all fourth planet—No matter. Please to excuse. Is bad enough to sit at same table with enemy without being reminded of how short time ago he *was* enemy."

This time the silence lasted a long while. And Dalton realized, with a sudden feeling almost of physical illness, that Skorrogan had damaged his own position beyond repair. Even if he suddenly woke up to what he was doing and tried to make amends—and who ever heard of a Skontaran noble apologizing for anything—it was too late. Too many millions of people, watching their telescreens, had seen his unpardonable arrogance. Too many important men, the leaders of Sol, were sitting in the same room with him, looking into his contemptuous eyes and smelling the sharp stink of unhuman sweat.

There would be no aid to Skontar.

With sunset, clouds piled up behind the dark line of cliffs which lay to the east of Geyrhaym, and a thin, chill wind blew down over the valley with whispers of winter. The first few snowflakes were borne on it, whirling across the deepening purplish sky, tinted pink by the last bloody light. There would be a blizzard before midnight.

The spaceship came down out of darkness and settled into her cradle. Beyond the little spaceport, the old town of Geyrhaym. lay wrapped in twilight, huddling together against the wind. Firelight glowed ruddily from the old peak-roofed houses, but the winding cobbled streets were like empty canyons, twisting up the hill on whose crest frowned the great castle of the old barons. The Valtam had taken it for his own use, and little Geyrhaym was now the capital of the Empire. For proud Skirnor and stately Thruvang were radioactive pits, and wild beasts howled in the burned ruins of the old palace.

Skorrogan Valthak's son shivered as he came out of the airlock and down the gangway. Skontar was a cold planet. Even for its own people it was cold. He wrapped his heavy fur cloak more tightly about him.

They were waiting near the bottom of the gangway, the high chiefs of Skontar. Under an impassive exterior, Skorrogan's belly muscles tightened. There might be death waiting in that silent, sullen group of men. Surely disgrace—and he couldn't answer—

The Valtam himself stood there, his white mane blowing in the bitter wind. His golden eyes seemed luminous in the twilight, hard and fierce, a deep sullen hate smoldering behind them. His oldest son, the heir apparent, Thordin, stood beside him. The last sunlight gleamed crimson on the head of his spear; it seemed to drip blood against the sky. And there were the other mighty men of Skang, counts of the provinces on Skontar and the other planets, and they all stood waiting for him. Behind them was a line of Imperial household guards, helmets and corselets shining in the dusk, faces in shadow, but hate and contempt like a living force radiating from them.

Skorrogan strode up to the Valtam, grounded his spear butt in salute, and inclined his head at just the proper degree. There was silence then, save for the whimpering wind. Drifting snow streamed across the field.

The Valtam spoke at last; without ceremonial greeting. It was like a deliberate slap in the face: "So you are back again."

"Yes, sire." Skorrogan tried to keep his voice stiff. It was difficult to do. He had no fear of death, but it was cruelly hard to bear this weight of failure. "As you know, I must regretfully report my mission unsuccessful."

"Indeed. We receive telecasts here," said the Valtam acidly.

"Sire, the Solarians are giving virtually unlimited aid to Cundaloa But they refused any help at all to Skontar. No credits, no technical advisers—nothing. And we can expect little trade and almost no visitors."

"I know," said Thordin. "And *you* were sent to get their help."

"I tried, sire. Skorrogan kept his voice expressionless. He had to say something—*but be forever damned if I'll plead!* "But the Solarians have an unreasonable prejudice against us, partly related to their wholly emotional bias toward Cundaloa and partly, I suppose, due to our being unlike them in so many ways."

"So they do," said the Valtam coldly. "But it was not great before. Surely the Mingonians, who are far less human then we, have received much good at Solarian hands. They got the same sort of help that Cundaloa will be getting and that we might have had.

"We desire nothing but good relations with the mightiest power in the Galaxy. We might have had more than that. I know, from firsthand reports, what the temper of the Commonwealth was. They were ready to help us, had we shown any cooperativeness at all. We could have rebuilt, and gone farther than that—" His voice trailed off into the keening wind.

After a moment he went on, and the fury that quivered in his voice was like a living force: "I sent you as my special delegate to get that generously offered help. You, whom I trusted, who I thought was aware of our cruel plight—Arrrgh!" He spat. "And you spent your whole time there being insulting, arrogant, boorish. You, on whom all the eyes of Sol were turned, made yourself the perfect embodiment of all the humans think worst in us. No wonder our request was refused! You're lucky Sol didn't declare war!"

"It may not be too late," said Thordin. "We could send another—"

"No." The Valtam lifted his head with the inbred iron pride of his race, the haughtiness of a culture where for all history face had been more important than life. "Skorrogan went as our accredited representative. If we repudiated him, apologized for—not for any overt act but for bad manners!—if we crawled before the Galaxy—no! It isn't worth that. We'll just have to do without Sol."

The snow was blowing thicker now, and the clouds were covering the sky. A few bright stars winked forth in the clear portions. But it was cold, cold.

"And what a price to pay for honor!" said Thordin wearily. "Our folk are starving—food from Sol could keep them alive. They have only rags to wear—Sol would send clothes. Our factories are devastated, are obsolete, our young men grow up in ignorance of Galactic civilization and technology—Sol would send us machines and engineers, help us rebuild. Sol would send teachers, and we could become great— Well, too late, too late." His eyes searched through the gloom, puzzled, hurt. Skorrogan had been his friend. "But why did you do it? Why did you do it?"

"I did my best," said Skorrogan stiffly. "If I was not fitted for the task, you should not have sent me."

"But you were," said Valtam. "You were our best diplomat. Your wiliness, your understanding of extra-Skontaran psychology, your personality—all were invaluable to our foreign relations. And then, on this simple and most tremendous mission—No more!" His voice rose to a shout against the rising wind. "No more will I trust you. Skontar will know you failed."

"Sire—" Skorrogan's voice shook suddenly. "Sire, I have taken words from you which from anyone else would have meant a death duel. If you have more to say, say it. Otherwise let me go."

"I cannot strip you of your hereditary titles and holdings, said the Valtam. "But your position in the imperial government is ended, and you are no longer to come to court or to any official function. Nor do I think you will have many friends left."

"Perhaps not," said Skorrogan. "I did what I did, and even if I could explain further, I would not after these insults. But if you ask my advice for the future of Skontar—"

"I don't," said the Valtam. "You have done enough harm already."

"…then consider three things." Skorrogan lifted his spear and pointed toward the remote glittering stars. "First, those suns out there. Second, certain new scientific and technological developments here at home—such as Dyrin's work on semantics. And last—look about you. Look at the houses your fathers built, look at the clothes you wear, listen, perhaps, to the language you speak. And then come back in fifty years or so and beg my pardon!"

He swirled his cloak about him, saluted the Valtam again, and went with long steps across the field and into the town. They looked after him with incomprehension and bitterness in their eyes.

There was hunger in the town. He could almost feel it behind the dark walls, the hunger of ragged and desperate folk crouched over their fires, and wondered whether they could survive the winter. Briefly he wondered how many would die—but he didn't dare follow the thought out.

He heard someone singing and paused. A wandering bard, begging his way from town to town, came down the street, his tattered cloak blowing fantastically about him. He plucked his harp with thin fingers, and his voice rose in an old ballad that held all the harsh ringing music, the great iron clamor of the old tongue, the language of Naarhaym on Skontar. Mentally, for a moment of wry amusement, Skorrogan rendered a few lines into Terrestrial:

> Wildly the winging
> War birds, flying
> wake the winter-dead
> wish for the sea-road.
> Sweetheart, they summon me,
> singing of flowers
> fair for the faring.
> Farewell, I love you.

It didn't work. It wasn't only that the metallic rhythm and hard barking syllables were lost, the intricate rhyme and alliteration, though that was part of it—but it just didn't make sense in Terrestrial. The concepts were lacking. How could you render, well, such a word as *vorkansraavin* as "faring" and hope to get more than a mutilated fragment of meaning? Psychologies were simply too different.

And there, perhaps, lay his answer to the high chiefs. But they wouldn't know. They couldn't. And he was alone, and winter was coming again.

Valka Vahino sat in his garden and let sunlight wash over his bare skin. It was not often, these days, that he got a chance to *aliacaui*—What was that old Terrestrial word? "Siesta"? But that was wrong. A resting Cundaloan didn't sleep in the afternoon. He sat or lay outdoors, with the sun soaking into his bones or a warm rain like a benediction over him, and he let his thoughts run free. Solarians called that daydreaming, but it wasn't, it was, well—they had no real word for it. Psychic recreation was a clumsy term, and the Solarians never understood.

Sometimes it seemed to Vahino that he had never rested, not in an eternity of years. The grinding urgencies of wartime duty, and then his hectic journeys to Sol—and since then, in the past three years, the Great House had appointed him official liaison man at the highest level, assuming that he understood the Solarians better than anyone else in the League.

Maybe he did. He'd spent a lot of time with them and liked them as a race and as individuals. But—by all the spirits, how they worked! How they drove themselves! As if demons were after them.

Well, there was no other way to rebuild, to reform the old obsolete methods and grasp the dazzling new wealth which only lay waiting to be created. But right now it was wonderfully soothing to lie in his garden, with the great golden flowers nodding about him and filling the summer air with their drowsy scent, with a few honey insects buzzing past and a new poem growing in his head.

The Solarians seemed to have some difficulty in understanding a whole race of poets. When even the meanest and stupidest Cundaloan could stretch out in the sun and make lyrics—well, every race has its own peculiar talents. Who could equal the gadgeteering genius which the humans possessed?

The great soaring, singing lines thundered in his head. He turned them over, fashioning them, shaping every syllable, and fitting the pattern together with a dawning delight. This one would be—good! It would be remembered, it would be sung a century hence, and they wouldn't forget Valka Vahino. He might even be remembered as a masterversemaker—*Alia Amaui cauianriho, valana, valana, vro!*

"Pardon, sir." The flat metal voice shook in his brain, he felt the delicate fabric of the poem tear and go swirling off into darkness and forgetfulness. For a moment there was only the pang of his loss; he realized dully that the interruption had broken a sequence which he would never quite recapture.

"Pardon, sir, but Mr. Lombard wishes to see you."

It was a sonic beam from the roboreceptionist which Lombard himself had given Vahino. The Cundaloan had felt the incongruity of installing its shining metal among the carved wood and old tapestries of his house, but he had not wanted to offend the donor—and the thing was useful.

Lombard, head of the Solarian reconstruction commission, the most important human in Avaikian System. Just now Vahino appreciated the courtesy of the man's coming to him rather than simply sending for him. Only—why did he have to come exactly at this moment?

"Tell Mr. Lombard I'll be there in a minute."

Vahino went in the back way and put on some clothes. Humans didn't have the completely casual attitude toward nakedness of Cundaloa. Then he went into the forehall. He had installed some chairs there for the benefit of Earthlings, who didn't like to squat on a woven mat—another incongruity. Lombard got up as Vahino entered.

The human was short and stocky, with a thick bush of gray hair above a seamed face. He had worked his way up from laborer through engineer to High Commissioner, and the marks of his struggle were still on him. He attacked work with what seemed almost a personal fury, and he could be harder than tool steel. But most of the time he was pleasant, he had an astonishing range of interests and knowledge, and of course, he had done miracles for the Avaikian System.

"Peace on your house, brother," said Vahino.

"How do you do," clipped the Solarian. As his host began to signal for servants, he went on hastily: "Please, none of your ritual hospitality. I appreciate it, but there just isn't time to sit and have a meal and talk cultural topics for three hours before getting down to business. I wish…well, you're a native here and I'm not, so I wish you'd personally pass the word around—tactfully, of course—to discontinue this sort of thing."

"But…they are among our oldest customs—"

"That's just it! Old—backward—delaying progress. I don't mean to be disparaging, Mr. Vahino. I wish we Solarians had some customs as charming as yours. But—not during working hours. Please."

"Well…I dare say you're right. It doesn't fit into the pattern of a modern industrial civilization. And that is what we are trying to build, of course." Vahino took a chair and offered his guest a cigarette. Smoking was one of Sol's characteristic vices, perhaps the most easily transmitted and certainly the most easily defensible. Vahino lit up with the enjoyment of the neophyte.

"Quite. Exactly. And that is really what I came here about, Mr. Vahino. I have no specific complaints, but there has accumulated a whole host of minor difficulties which only you Cundaloans can handle for yourselves. We Solarians can't and won't meddle in your internal affairs. But you must change some things, or we won't be able to help you at all."

Vahino had a general idea of what was coming. He'd been expecting it for some time, he thought grayly, and there was really nothing to be done about it. But he took another puff of smoke, let it trickle slowly out, and raised his eyebrows in polite inquiry. Then he remembered that Solarians weren't used to interpreting nuances of expression as part of a language, and said aloud, "Please say what you like. I realize no offense is meant, and none will be taken."

"Good." Lombard leaned forward, nervously clasping and unclasping his big work-scarred hands. "The plain fact is that your whole culture, your whole psychology, is unfitted to modern civilization. It can be changed, but the change will have to be drastic. You can do it—pass laws, put on propaganda campaigns, change the educational system, and so on. But it *must* be done.

"For instance, just this matter of the siesta. Right now, all through this time zone on the planet, hardly a wheel is turning, hardly a machine is tended, hardly a man is at his work. They're all lying in the sun making poems or humming songs or just drowsing. There's a whole civilization to be built, Vahino! There are plantations, mines, factories, cities abuilding—you just can't do it on a four-hour working day."

"No. But perhaps we haven't the energy of your race. You are a hyperthyroid species, you know."

"You'll just have to learn. Work doesn't have to be backbreaking. The whole aim of mechanizing your culture is to release you from physical labor and the uncertainty of dependence on the land. And a mechanical civilization can't be cluttered with as many old beliefs and rituals and customs and traditions as yours is. There just isn't time. Life is too short. And it's too incongruous. You're still like the Skontarans, lugging their silly spears around after they've lost all practical value."

"Tradition *makes* life—the meaning of life—"

"The machine culture has its own tradition. You'll learn. It has its own meaning, and I think that is the meaning of the future. If you insist on clinging to outworn habits, you'll never catch up with history. Why, your currency system—"

"It's practical"

"In its own field. But how can you trade with Sol if you base your credits on silver and Sol's are an abstract actuarial quantity? You'll have to convert to our system for purpose of trade—so you might as well change over at home, too. Similarly, you'll have to learn the metric system if you expect to use our machines or make sense to our scientists. You'll have to adopt…oh, everything!

"Why, your very society— No wonder you haven't exploited even the planets, of your own system when every man insists on being buried at his birthplace. It's a pretty sentiment, but it's no more than that, and you'll have to get rid of it if you're going to reach the stars.

"Even your religion…excuse me…but you must realize that it has many elements which modern science has flatly disproved."

"I'm an agnostic," said Vahino quietly. "But the religion of Mauiroa means a lot to many people."

"If the Great House will let us bring in some missionaries, we can convert them to, say, Neopantheism. Which I, for one, think has a lot more personal comfort and certainly more scientific truth than your mythology. If your people are to have faith at all, it must not conflict with facts which experience in a modern technology will soon make self-evident."

"Perhaps. And I suppose the system of familial bonds is too complex and rigid for modern industrial society… Yes, yes—there is more than a simple conversion of equipment involved."

"To be sure. There's a complete conversion of minds," said Lombard. And then, gently, "After all, you'll do it eventually. You were building spaceships and atomic-power plants right after Allan left. I'm simply suggesting that you speed up the process a little."

"And language—"

"Well, without indulging in chauvinism, I think all Cundaloans should be taught Solarian. They'll use it at some time or other in their lives. Certainly all your scientists and technicians will have to use it professionally. The languages of Laui and Muara and the rest are beautiful, but they just aren't suitable for scientific concepts. Why, the agglutination alone—Frankly, your philosophical books read to me like so much gibberish. Beautiful, but almost devoid of meaning. Your language lacks—*precision.*"

"Aracles and Vranamaui were always regarded as models of crystal thought," said Vahino wearily. "And I confess to not quite grasping your Kant and Russell and even Korzybski—but then, I lack training in such lines of thought. No doubt you are right. The younger generation will certainly agree with you.

"I'll speak to the Great House and may be able to get something done now. But in any case you won't have to wait many years. All our young men are striving to make themselves what you wish. It is the way to success."

"It is," said Lombard; and then, softly, "Sometimes I wish success didn't have so high a price. But you need only look at Skontar to see how necessary it is."

"Why—they've done wonders in the last three years. After the great famine they got back on their feet, they're rebuilding by themselves, they've even sent explorers looking for colonies out among the stars." Vahino smiled wryly. "I don't love our late enemies, but I must admire them."

"They have courage," admitted Lombard. "But what good is courage alone? They're struggling in a tangle of obsolescence. Already the overall production of Cundaloa is three times theirs. Their interstellar colonizing is no more than a feeble gesture of a few hundred individuals. Skontar can live, but it will always be a tenth-rate power. Before long it'll be a Cundaloan satellite state.

"And it's not that they lack resources, natural or otherwise. It's that, having virtually flung our offer of help back in our faces, they've taken themselves out of the main stream of Galactic civilization. Why, they're even trying to develop scientific concepts and devices we knew a hundred years ago, and are getting so far off the track that I'd laugh if it weren't so pathetic. Their language, like yours, just isn't adapted to scientific thought, and they're carrying chains of rusty tradition around. I've seen some of the spaceships they've designed themselves, for instance, instead of copying Solarian models, and they're ridiculous. Half a hundred different lines of approach, trying desperately to find the main line we took long ago. Spheres, ovoids, cubes—I hear someone even thinks he can build a tetrahedral spaceship!"

"It might just barely be possible," mused Vahino. "The Riemannian geometry on which the interstellar drive itself is based would permit—"

"No, no! Earth tried that sort of thing and found it didn't work. Only a crank—and, isolated, the scientists of Skontar are becoming a race of cranks—would think so.

"We humans were just fortunate, that's all. Even we had a long history before a culture arose with the mentality appropriate to a scientific civilization. Before that, technological progress was almost at a standstill. Afterward, we reached the stars. Other races can do it, but first they'll have to adopt the proper civilization, the proper mentality—and without our guidance, Skontar or any other planet isn't likely to evolve that mentality for many centuries to come.

"Which reminds me—" Lombard fumbled in a pocket. "I have a journal here, from one of the Skontaran philosophical societies. A certain amount of communication still does take place, you know; there's no official embargo on either side. It's just that Sol has given Skang up as a bad job. Anyway"—he fished out a magazine—"there's one of their philosophers, Dyrin, who's doing some new work on general semantics which seems to be arousing quite a furor. You read Skontaran, don't you?"

"Yes," said Vahino. "I was in military intelligence during the war. Let me see—" He leafed through the journal to the article and began translating aloud:

"The writer's previous papers show that the principle of nonelementalism is not itself altogether a universal, but must be subject to certain psychomathematical reservations arising from consideration of the *broganar*—that's a word I don't understand—field, which couples to electronic wave-nuclei and—"

"What is that jabberwocky?" exploded Lombard.

"I don't know," said Vahino helplessly. "The Skontaran mind is as alien to me as to you."

"Gibberish," said Lombard. "With the good old Skontaran to-hell-with-you dogmatism thrown in." He threw the magazine on the little bronze brazier, and fire licked at its thin pages. "Utter nonsense, as anyone with any knowledge of general semantics, or even an atom of common sense, can see." He smiled crookedly, a little sorrowfully and shook his head. "A race of cranks!"

* * *

"I wish you could spare me a few hours tomorrow," said Skorrogan.

"Well—I suppose so." Thordin XI, Valtam of the Empire of Skontar, nodded his thinly maned head. "Though next week would be a little more convenient."

"Tomorrow—please."

The note of urgency could not be denied. "All right," said Thordin. "But what will be going on?"

"I'd like to take you on a little jaunt over to Cundaloa."

"Why there, of all places? And why must it be tomorrow, of all times?"

"I'll tell you—then." Skorrogan inclined his head, still thickly maned though it was quite white now, and switched off his end of the telescreen.

Thordin smiled in some puzzlement. Skorrogan was an odd fellow in many ways. But…well…we *old men have to stick together. There is a new generation, and one after that, pressing on our heels.*

No doubt thirty-odd years of living in virtual ostracism had changed the old joyously confident Skorrogan. But it had, at least, not embittered him. When the slow success of Skontar had become so plain that his own failure could be forgotten, the circle of his friends had very gradually included him again. He still lived much alone, but he was no longer unwelcome wherever he went. Thordin, in particular, had discovered that their old friendship could be as alive as ever before, and he was often over to the Citadel of Kraakahaym, or Skorrogan to the palace. He had even offered the old noble a position back in the High Council, but it had been refused, and another ten years—or was it twenty?—had gone by with Skrogan fulfilling no more than his hereditary duties as duke. Until now, for the first time, something like a favor was being asked… *Yes,* he thought, *I'll go tomorrow. To blazes with work. Monarchs deserve holidays, too.*

Thordin got up from his chair and limped over to the broad window. The new endocrine treatments were doing wonders for his rheumatism, but their effect wasn't quite complete yet. He shivered a little as he looked at the wind-driven snow sweeping down over the valley. Winter was coming again.

The geologists said that Skontar was entering another glacial epoch. But it would never get there. In another decade or so the climate engineers would have perfected their techniques and the glaciers would be driven back into the north. But meanwhile it was cold and white outside, and a bitter wind hooted around the palace towers.

It would be summer in the southern hemisphere now, fields would be green, and smoke would rise from freeholders' cottages into a warm blue sky. Who had headed that scientific team?—Yes, Aesgayr Haasting's son. His work on agronomics and genetics had made it possible for a population of independent smallholders to produce enough food for the new scientific civilization. The old freeman, the backbone of Skontar in all her history, had not died out.

Other things had changed, of course. Thordin smiled wryly as he reflected just how much the Valtamate had changed in the last fifty years. It had been Dyrin's work in general semantics, so fundamental to all the sciences, which had led to the new psychosymbological techniques of government. Skontar was an empire in name only now. It had resolved the paradox of a libertarian state with a nonelective and efficient government. All to the good, of course, and really it was what past Skontaran history had been slowly and painfully evolving toward. But the new science had speeded up the process, compressed centuries of evolution into two brief generations. As physical and biological science had accelerated beyond belief—But it was odd that the arts, music, literature had hardly changed, that handicraft survived, that the old High Naarhaym was still spoken.

Well, so it went. Thordin turned back toward his desk. There was work to be done. Like that matter of the colony on Aesric's Planet— You couldn't expect to run several hundred thriving interstellar colonies without some trouble. But it was minor. The empire was safe. And it was growing.

They'd come a long way from that day of despair fifty years ago, and from the famine and pestilence and desolation which followed. A long way—Thordin wondered if even he realized just how far.

He picked up the microreader and glanced over the pages. His mind training came back to him and he *arrished* the material. He couldn't handle the new techniques as easily as those of the younger generation, trained in them from birth, but it was a wonderful help to *arrish*, complete the integration in his subconscious, and *indolate* the probabilities. He wondered how he had ever survived the old days of reasoning on a purely conscious level.

Thordin came out of the warp just outside Kraakahaym Citadel. Skorrogan had set the point of emergence there, rather than indoors, because he liked the view. It was majestic, thought the Valtam, but dizzying—a wild swoop of gaunt gray crags and wind-riven clouds down to the far green valley below. Above him loomed the old battlements, with the black-winged kraakar which had given the place its name hovering and cawing in the sky. The wind roared and boomed about him, driving dry white snow before it.

The guards raised their spears in salute. They were unarmed otherwise, and the vortex guns on the castle walls were corroding away. No need for weapons in the heart of an empire second only to Sol's dominions. Skorrogan stood waiting in the courtyard. Fifty years had not bent his back much or taken the fierce golden luster from his eyes. It seemed to Thordin today, though, that the old being wore an air of taut and inwardly blazing eagerness: he seemed somehow to be looking toward the end of a journey.

Skorrogan gave conventional greeting and invited him in. "Not now, thanks," said Thordin. "I really am very busy. I'd like to start the trip at once."

The duke murmured the usual formula of polite regret, but it was plain that he could hardly wait, that he could ill have stood an hour's dawdling indoors. "Then please come," he said. "My cruiser is all set to go."

It was cradled behind the looming building, a sleek little roboship with the bewildering outline of all tetrahedral craft. They entered and took their seats at the center, which, of course, looked directly out beyond the hull.

"Now," said Thordin, "perhaps you'll tell me why you want to go to Cundaloa today?"

Skorrogan gave him a sudden look in which an old pain stirred.

"Today," he said slowly, "it is exactly fifty years since I came back from Sol."

"Yes—?" Thordin was puzzled and vaguely uncomfortable. It wasn't like the taciturn old fellow to rake up that forgotten score.

"You probably don't remember," said Skorrogan, "but if you want to *vargan* it from your subconscious, you'll perceive that I said to them, then, that they could come back in fifty years and beg my pardon."

"So now you want to vindicate yourself." Thordin felt no surprise—it was typically Skontaran psychology—but he still wondered what there was to apologize for.

"I do. At that time I couldn't explain. Nobody would have listened, and in any case I was not perfectly sure myself that I had done right." Skorrogan smiled, and his thin hands set the controls. "Now I am. Time has justified me. And I will redeem what honor I lost then by showing you, today, that I didn't really fail.

"Instead, I succeeded. You see, I alienated the Solarians on purpose."

He pressed the main-drive stud, and the ship flashed through half a light-year of space. The great blue shield of Cundaloa rolled majestically before them, shining softly against a background of a million blazing stars.

Thordin sat quietly, letting the simple and tremendous statement filter through all the levels of his mind. His first emotional reaction was a vaguely surprised realization that, subconsciously, he had been expecting something like this. He hadn't ever really believed, deep down inside himself, that Skorrogan could be an incompetent.

Instead—no, not a traitor. But—what, then? What had he meant? Had he been mad, all these years, or—

"You haven't been to Cundaloa much since the war, have you?" asked Skorrogan.

"No—only three times, on hurried business. It's a prosperous system. Solar help put them on their feet again."

"Prosperous...yes, yes, they are." For a moment a smile tugged at the corners of Skorrogan's mouth, but it was a sad little smile, it was as if he were trying to cry but couldn't quite manage it. "A bustling, successful little system, with all of three colonies among the stars."

With a sudden angry gesture he slapped the short-range controls and the ship warped down to the surface. It landed in a corner of the great spaceport at Cundaloa City, and the robots about the cradle went to work, checking it in and throwing a protective forcedome about it.

"What—now?" whispered Thordin. He felt, suddenly, dimly afraid; he knew vaguely that he wouldn't like what he was going to see.

"Just a little stroll through the capital," said Skorrogan. "With perhaps a few side trips around the planet. I wanted us to come here unofficially, incognito, because that's the only way we'll ever see the real world, the day-to-day life of living beings which is so much more important and fundamental than any number of statistics and economic charts. I want to show you what I saved Skontar from." He smiled again, wryly. "I gave my life for my planet, Thordin. Fifty years of it, anyway—fifty years of loneliness and disgrace."

They emerged into the clamor of the great steel and concrete plain and crossed over the gates. There was a steady flow of beings in and out, a never-ending flux, the huge restless energy of Solarian civilization. A large proportion of the crowd was human, come to Avaiki on business or pleasure, and there were some representatives of other races. But the bulk of the throng was, naturally, native Cundaloans. Sometimes one had a little trouble telling them from the humans. After all, the two species looked much alike, and with the Cundaloans all wearing Solarian dress—

Thordin shook his head in some bewilderment at the roar of voices. "I can't understand," he shouted to Skorrogan. "I know Cundaloan, both Laui and Muara tongues, but—"

"Of course not," answered Skorrogan. "Most of them here are speaking Solarian. The native languages are dying out fast."

A plump Solarian in shrieking sports clothes was yelling at an impassive native storekeeper who stood outside his shop. "Hey, you boy, gimme him fella souvenir chop-chop—"

"Pidgin Solarian," grimaced Skorrogan. "It's on its way out, too, what with all young Cundaloans being taught the proper speech from the ground up. But tourists never learn." He scowled, and for a moment his hand shifted to his blaster.

But no—times changed. You did not wipe out someone who simply happened to be personally objectionable, not even on Skontar. Not any more.

The tourist turned and bumped him. "Oh, so sorry," he exclaimed, urbanely enough. "I should have looked where I was going."

"Is no matter," shrugged Skorrogan.

The Solarian dropped into a struggling and heavily accented High Naarhaym: "I really must apologize, though. May I buy you a drink?"

"No matter," said Skorragan, with a touch of grimness.

"What a Planet! Backward as…as Pluto! I'm going on to Skontar from here. I hope to get a business contract—you know how to do business, you Skontarans!"

Skorrogan snarled and swung away, fairly dragging Thordin with him. They had gone half a block down the motilator before the Valtam asked, "What happened to your manners? He was trying hard to be civil to us. Or do you just naturally hate humans?"

"I like most of them," said Skorrogan. "But not their tourists. Praise the Fate, we don't get many of that breed on Skontar. Their engineers and businessmen and students are all right. I'm glad that relations between Sol and Skang are close, so we can get many of that sort. But keep out the tourists!"

"Why?"

Skorrogan gestured violently at a flashing neon poster. "That's why."

He translated the Solarian:

SEE THE ANCIENT MAUIROA CEREMONIES!
COLORFUL! AUTHENTIC!

THE MAGIC OF OLD CUNDALOA!
AT THE TEMPLE OF THE HIGH ONE
ADMISSION REASONABLE

"The religion of Mauiroa meant something, once," said Skorrogan quietly. "It was a noble creed, even if it did have certain unscientific elements. Those could have been changed— But it's too late now. Most of the natives are either Neopantheists or unbelievers, and they perform the old ceremonies for money. For a show."

He grimaced. "Cundaloa hasn't lost all its picturesque old buildings and folkways and music and the rest of its culture. But it's become conscious that they are picturesque, which is worse."

"I don't quite see what you're so angry about," said Thordin. "Times have changed. But they have on Skontar, too."

"Not in this way. Look around you, man! You've never been in the Solar System, but you must have seen pictures from it. Surely you realize that this is a typical Solarian city—a little backward, maybe, but typical. You won't find a city in the Avaikian System which isn't essentially—*human*.

"You won't find significant art, literature, music here any more—just cheap imitations of Solarian products, or else an archaistic clinging to outmoded native traditions, romantic counterfeiting of the past. You won't find science that isn't essentially Solarian, you won't find machines basically different from Solarian, you'll find fewer homes every year which can be told from human houses. The old society is dead; only a few fragments remain now. The familial bond, the very basis of native culture, is gone, and marriage relations are as casual as on Earth itself. The old feeling for the land is gone. There are hardly any tribal farms left; the young men are all coming to the cities to earn a million credits. They eat the products of Solarian-type food factories, and you can only get native cuisine in a few expensive restaurants.

"There are no more handmade pots, no more handwoven cloths. They wear what the factories put out. There are no more bards chanting the old lays and making new ones. They look at the telescreen now. There are no more philosophers of the Araclean or Vranamauian schools, there are just second-rate commentaries on Aristotle versus Korzybski or the Russell theory of knowledge—"

Skorrogan's voice trailed off. Thordin said softly, after a moment, "I see what you're getting at. Cundaloa has made itself over into the Solarian pattern."

"Just so. It was inevitable from the moment they accepted help from Sol. They'd *have* to adopt Solar science, Solar economics, ultimately the whole Solar culture. Because that would be the only pattern which would make sense to the humans who were taking the lead in reconstruction. And, since that culture was obviously successful, Cundaloa adopted it. Now it's too late. They can never go back. They don't even want to go back.

"It's happened before, you know. I've studied the history of Sol. Back before the human race even reached the other planets of its system, there were many cultures, often radically different. But ultimately one of them the so-called Western society, became so overwhelmingly superior technologically that…well, no others could coexist with it. To compete, they had to adopt the very approach of the West. And when the West helped them from their backwardness, it necessarily helped them into a Western pattern. With the best intentions in the world, the West annihilated all other ways of life."

"And you wanted to save us from that?" asked Thordin. "I see your point, in a way. Yet I wonder if the sentimental value of old institutions was equal to some millions of lives lost, to a decade of sacrifice and suffering."

"It was more than sentiment!" said Skorrogan tensely. "Can't you see? Science is the future. To amount to anything, we *had* to become scientific. But was Solarian science the only way? Did we have to become second-rate humans to survive—or could we strike out on a new path, unhampered by the overwhelming helpfulness of a highly developed but essentially alien way of life? I thought we could. I thought we would have to.

"You see no nonhuman race will ever make a really successful human. The basic psychologies—metabolic rates, instincts, logical patterns, *everything*—are too different One race *can* think in terms of another's mentality, but never too well. You know how much trouble there's been in translating from one language to another. And all thought is in language, and language reflects the basic patterns of thought. The most precise, rigorous, highly thought out philosophy and science of one species will never quite make sense to another race. Because they are making somewhat different abstractions from the same great basic reality.

"I wanted to save us from becoming Sol's spiritual dependents. Skang was backward. It *had* to change its ways. But—why change them into a wholly alien pattern? Why not, instead, force them rapidly along the natural path of evolution—our own path?"

Skorrogan shrugged. "I did," he finished quietly. "It was a tremendous gamble, but it worked. We saved our own culture. It's *ours*. Forced by necessity to become scientific on our own, we developed our own approach.

"You know the result. Dyrin's semantics was developed—Solarian scientists would have laughed it to abortion. We developed the tetrahedral ship, which human engineers said was impossible, and now we can cross the Galaxy while an old-style craft goes from Sol to Alpha Centauri. We perfected the spacewarp, the psychosymbology of our own race—not valid for any other—the new agronomic system which preserved the freeholder who is basic to our culture—everything! In fifty years Cundaloa has been revolutionized, Skontar has revolutionized itself. There's a universe of difference.

"And we've therefore saved the intangibles which are our own, the art and handicrafts and essential folkways, music, language, literature, religion. The *élan* of our success is not only taking us to the stars, making us one of the great powers in the Galaxy, but it is producing a renaissance in those intangibles equaling any Golden Age in history.

"And all because we remained ourselves."

He fell into silence, and Thordin said nothing for a while. They had come into a quieter side street, an old quarter where most of the buildings antedated the coming of the Solarians, and many ancient-style native clothes were still to be seen. A party of human tourists was being guided through the district and had clustered about an open pottery booth.

"Well?" said Skorrogan after a while. "Well?"

"I don't know." Thordin rubbed his eyes, a gesture of confusion. "This all so new to me. Maybe you're right. Maybe not. I'll have to think a while about it."

"I've had fifty years to think about it," said Skorrogan bleakly. "I suppose you're entitled to a few minutes."

They drifted up to the booth. An old Cundaloan sat in it among a clutter of goods, brightly painted vases and bowls and cups. Native work. A woman was haggling over one of the items.

"Look at it," said Skorrogan to Thordin. "Have you ever seen the old work? This is cheap stuff made by the thousands for the tourist trade. The designs are corrupt, the workmanship's shoddy. But every loop and line in those designs had meaning once."

Their eyes fell on one vase standing beside the old boothkeeper, and even the unimpressionable Valtam drew a shaky breath. It glowed, that vase. It seemed almost alive; in a simple shining perfection of clean lines and long smooth curves, someone had poured all his love and longing into it. Perhaps he had thought: This will live when I am gone.

Skorrogan whistled. "That's an authentic old vase," he said. "At least a century old—a museum piece! How'd it get in this junk shop?"

The clustered humans edged a little away from the two giant Skontarans, and Skorrogan read their expressions with a wry inner amusement: They stand in some awe of us. Sol no longer hates Skontar; it admires us. It sends its young men to learn our science and language. But who cares about Cundaloa any more?

But the woman followed his eyes and saw the vase glowing beside the old vendor. She turned back to him: "How much?"

"No sell," said the Cundaloan. His voice was a dusty whisper, and he hugged his shabby mantle closer about him.

"You sell." She gave him a bright artificial smile. "I give you much money. I give you ten credits."

"No sell."

"I give you hundred credits. Sell!"

"This mine. Fambly have it since old days. No sell."

"Five hundred credits!" She waved the money before him.

He clutched the vase to his thin chest and looked up with dark liquid eyes in which the easy tears of the old were starting forth. "No sell. Go 'way. No sell *oamaui*."

"Come on," mumbled Thordin. He grabbed Skorrogan's arm and pulled him away. "Let's go. Let's get back to Skontar."

"So soon?"

"Yes. Yes. You were right, Skorrogan. You were right, and I am going to make public apology, and you are the greatest savior of history. But let's get home!"

They hurried down the street. Thordin was trying hard to forget the old Cundaloan's eyes. But he wondered if he ever would.

WILDCAT

It was raining again, hot and heavy out of a hidden sky, and the air stank with swamp. Herries could just see the tall derricks a mile away, under a floodlight glare, and hear their engines mutter. Further away, a bull brontosaur cried and thunder went through the night.

Herries' boots resounded hollowly on the dock. Beneath the slicker, his clothes lay sweat-soggy, the rain spilled off his hat and down his collar. He swore in a tired voice and stepped onto his gangplank.

Light from the shack on the barge glimmered off drenched wood. He saw the snaky neck just in time, as it reared over the gangplank rail and struck at him. He sprang back, grabbing for the Magnum carbine slung over one shoulder. The plesiosaur hissed monstrously and flipper-slapped the water. It was like a cannon going off.

Herries threw the gun to his shoulder and fired. The long sleek form took the bullet—somewhere—and screamed. The raw noise hurt the man's eardrums.

Feet thudded over the wharf. Two guards reached Herries and began to shoot into the dark water. The door of the shack opened and a figure stood back against its yellow oblong, a tommy gun stammering idiotically in his hands.

"Cut it out!" bawled Herries. "That's enough! Hold your fire!"

Silence fell. For a moment, only the ponderous rainfall had voice. Then the brontosaur bellowed again, remotely, and there were seethings and croakings in the water.

"He got away," said Herries. "Or more likely his pals are now stripping him clean. Blood smell." A dull anger lifted in him, he turned and grabbed the lapel of the nearest guard. "How often do I have to tell you characters, every gangway has to have a man near it with grenades?"

"Yes, sir. Sorry, sir." Herries was a large man, and the other face looked up at him, white and scared in the wan electric radiance. "I just went off to the head—"

"You'll stay here," said Herries. "I don't care if you explode. Our presence draws these critters, and you ought to know that by now. They've already snatched two men off this dock. They nearly got a third tonight—me. At the first suspicion of anything out there, you're to pull the pin on a grenade and drop it in the water, understand? One more dereliction like this, and you're fired—No." He stopped, grinning humorlessly. "That's not much of a punishment, is it? A week in hack on bread."

The other guard bristled. "Look here, Mr. Herries, we got our rights. The union—"

"Your precious union is a hundred million years in the future," snapped the engineer. "It was understood that this is a dangerous job, that we're subject to martial law, and that I can discipline anyone who steps out of line. Okay—remember it."

He turned his back and tramped across the gangplank to the barge deck. It boomed underfoot. The shack had been closed again, with the excitement over. He opened the door and stepped through, peeling off his slicker.

Four men were playing poker beneath an unshaded bulb. The room was small and cluttered, hazy with tobacco smoke and the Jurassic mist. A fifth man lay on one of the bunks, reading. The walls were gaudy with pinups.

Olson riffled the cards and looked up. "Close call, boss," he remarked, almost casually. "Want to sit in?"

"Not now," said Herries. He felt his big square face sagging with weariness. "I'm bushed." He nodded at Carver, who had just returned from a prospecting trip further north. "We lost one more derrick today."

"Huh?" said Carver. "What happened this time?"

"It turns out this is the mating season." Herries found a chair, sat down, and began to pull off his boots. "How they tell one season from another, I don't know—length of day, maybe—but anyhow the brontosaurs aren't shy of us any more—they're going nuts. Now they go gallyhooting around and trample down charged fences or anything else that happens to be in the way. They've smashed three rigs to date, and one man."

Carver raised an eyebrow in his chocolate-colored face. It was a rather sour standing joke here, how much better the Negroes looked than anyone else. A white man could be outdoors all his life in this clouded age and remain pasty. "Haven't you tried shooting them?" he asked.

"Ever tried to kill a brontosaur with a rifle?" snorted Herries. "We can mess 'em up a little with .50-caliber machine guns or a bazooka—just enough so they decide to get out of the neighborhood—but being less intelligent than a chicken, they take off in any old direction. Makes as much havoc as the original rampage." His left boot hit the floor with a sullen thud. "I've been begging for a couple of atomic howitzers but it has to go through channels...Channels!" Fury spurted in him. "Five hundred human beings stuck in this nightmare world and our requisitions have to go through channels!"

Olson began to deal the cards. Polansky gave the man in the bunk a chill glance. "You're the wheel, Symonds," he said. "Why the devil don't you goose the great Transtemporal Oil Company?"

"Nuts," said Carver. "The great benevolent all-wise United States Government is what counts. How about it, Symonds?"

You never got a rise out of Symonds, the human tape recorder; just a playback of the latest official line. Now he laid his book aside and sat up in his bunk. Herries noticed that the volume was Marcus Aurelius, in Latin yet.

Symonds looked at Carver through steel-rimmed glasses and said in a dusty tone: "I am only the comptroller and supply supervisor. In effect, a chief clerk. Mr. Herries is in charge of operations."

He was a small shriveled man, with thin gray hair above a thin gray face. Even here, he wore stiff-collared shirt and sober tie. One of the hardest things to take about him was the way his long nose waggled when he talked.

"In charge!" Herries spat expertly into a gobboon. "Sure, I direct the prospectors and the drillers and everybody else on down through the bull cook. But who handles the paperwork—all our reports and receipts and requests? You." He tossed his right boot on the floor. "I don't want the name of boss if I can't get the stuff to defend my own men."

Something bumped against the supervisors' barge; it quivered and the chips on the table rattled. Since there was no outcry from the dock guards, Herries ignored the matter. Some swimming giant. And except for the plesiosaurs and the non-malicious bumbling bronties, all the big dinosaurs encountered so far were fairly safe. They might step on you in an absent-minded way, but most of them were peaceful and you could outrun those which weren't. It was the smaller carnivores, about the size of a man, leaping out of brush or muck with a skullful of teeth, which had taken most of the personnel lost. Their reptile life was too diffuse: even mortally wounded by elephant gun or grenade launcher, they could rave about for hours. They were the reason for sleeping on barges tied up by this sodden coast, along the gulf which would some day be Oklahoma.

Symonds spoke in his tight little voice: "I send your recommendations in, of course. The project office passes on them."

"I'll say it does," muttered young Greenstein irreverently.

"Please do not blame me," insisted Symonds.

I wonder. Herries glowered at him. Symonds had an in of some kind. That was obvious. A man who was simply a glorified clerk would not be called to Washington, for unspecified conferences with unspecified people, as often as this one was. But what was he, then?

A favorite relative? No…in spite of high pay, this operation was no political plum. FBI? Scarcely…the security checks were all run in the future. A hack in the bureaucracy? That was more probable. Symonds was here to see that oil was pumped and dinosaurs chased away and the hideously fecund jungle kept beyond the fence according to the least comma in the latest directive from headquarters.

The small man continued: "It has been explained to you officially that the heavier weapons are all needed at home. The international situation is critical. You ought to be thankful you are safely back in the past."

"Heat, large economy-size alligators, and not a woman for a hundred million years," grunted Olson. "I'd rather be blown up. Who dealt this mess?"

"You did," said Polansky. "Gimme two, and make 'em good."

Herries stripped the clothes off his thick hairy body, went to the rear of the cabin, and entered the shower cubby. He left the door open, to listen in. A boss was always lonely. Maybe he should have married when he had the chance. But then he wouldn't be here. Except for Symonds, who was a widower and in any case more a government than company man, Thansoco had been hiring only young bachelors for operations in the field.

"It seems kinda funny to talk about the international situation," remarked Carver. "Hell, there won't be any international situation for several geological periods."

"The inertial effect makes simultaneity a valid approximational concept," declared Symonds pedantically. His habit of lecturing scientists and engineers on their professions had not endeared him to them. "If we spend a year in the past, we must necessarily return to our own era to find a year gone, since the main projector operates only at the point of its own existence which—"

"Oh, stow it," said Greenstein. "I read the orientation manual too." He waited until everyone had cards, then shoved a few chips forward and added: "druther spend my time a little nearer home. Say with Cleopatra."

"Impossible," Symonds told him. "Inertial effect again. In order to send a body into the past at all, the projector must energize it so much that the minimal time-distance we can cover becomes precisely the one we have covered to arrive here, one hundred and one million, three hundred twenty-seven thousand, et cetera, years."

"But why not time-hop into the future? You don't buck entropy in that direction. I mean, I suppose there is an inertial effect there, too, but it would be much smaller, so you could go into the future—"

"—about a hundred years at a hop, according to the handbook," supplied Polansky.

"So why don't they look at the twenty-first century?" asked Greenstein.

"I understand that that is classified information," Symonds said. His tone implied that Greenstein had skirted some unimaginably gross obscenity.

Herries put his head out of the shower. "Sure it's classified," he said. "They'd classify the wheel if they could. But use your reason and you'll see why travel into the future isn't practical. Suppose you jump a hundred years ahead. How do you get home to report what you've seen? The projector will yank you a hundred million years back, less the distance you went forward."

Symonds dove back into his book. Somehow, he gave an impression of lying there rigid with shock that men dared think after he had spoken the phrase of taboo.

"Uh…yes. I get it." Greenstein nodded. He had only been recruited a month ago, to replace a man drowned in a grass-veiled bog. Before then, like nearly all the world, he had had no idea time travel existed. So far he had been too busy to examine its implications.

To Herries it was an old, worn-thin story.

"I daresay they did send an expedition a hundred million years up, so it could come back to the same week as it left," he said. "Don't ask me what was found. Classified: Tip-top Secret, Burn Before Reading."

"You know, though," said Polansky in a thoughtful tone, "I been thinking some myself. Why are we here at all? I mean, oil is necessary to defense and all that, but it seems to me it'd make more sense for the U.S. Army to come through, cross the ocean, and establish itself where all the enemy nations are going to be. Then we'd have a gun pointed at their heads!"

"Nice theory," said Herries. "I've daydreamed myself. But there's only one main projector, to energize all the subsidiary ones. Building it took almost the whole world supply of certain rare earths. Its capacity is limited. If we started sending military units into the past, it'd be a slow and cumbersome operation—and not being a Security officer, I'm not required to kid myself that Moscow doesn't know we've got time travel. They've probably even given Washington a secret ultimatum: 'Start sending back war material in any quantity, and we'll hit you with everything we've got.' But evidently they don't feel strongly enough about our pumping oil on our own territory—or what will one day be our own territory—to make it a, uh, *casus belli*."

"Just as we don't feel their satellite base in the twentieth century is dangerous enough for us to fight about," said Greenstein, "but I suspect we're the reason they agreed to make the Moon a neutral zone. Same old standoff."

"I wonder how long it can last?" murmured Polansky.

"Not much longer," said Olson. "Read your history. I'll see you, Greenstein, boy, and raise you two."

Herries let the shower run about him. At least there was no shortage of hot water. Transoco had sent back a complete atomic pile. But civilization and war still ran on oil, he thought, and oil was desperately short up there.

Time, he reflected, was a paradoxical thing. The scientists had told him it was utterly rigid. Perhaps, though of course it would be a graveyard secret, the cloak-and-dagger boys had tested that theory the hard way, going back into the historical past (it could be done after all, Herries suspected, though by a roundabout route which consumed fabulous amounts of energy) in an attempt to head off the Bolshevik Revolution. It would have failed. Neither past nor future could be changed—-they could only be discovered. Some of Transoco's men had discovered death, an eon before they were born…But there would not be such a shortage of oil up in the future if Transoco had not gone back and drained it in the past. A self-causing future—

Primordial stuff, petroleum. Hoyle's idea seemed to be right, it had not been formed by rotting dinosaurs but was present from the beginning. It was the stuff which had stuck the planets together.

And, Herries thought, was sticking to him now. He reached for the soap.

Earth spun gloomily through hours, and morning crept over wide brown waters. There was no real day as men understood day—the heavens were a leaden sheet with dirty black rainclouds scudding below the permanent fog layers.

Herries was up early, for there was a shipment scheduled. He came out of the bosses' messhall and stood for a moment looking over the mud beach and the few square miles of cleared land, sleazy buildings and gaunt derricks inside an electric mesh fence. Automation replaced thousands of workers, so that five hundred men were enough to handle everything, but still the compound was the merest scratch and the jungle remained a terrifying black wall. Not that the trees were so utterly alien—besides the archaic grotesqueries, like ferns and mosses of gruesome size, there were cycad, redwood, and gingko, scattered prototypes of oak and willow and birch. But Herries missed wild flowers.

A working party with its machines was repairing the fence the brontosaur had smashed through yesterday, the well it had wrecked, the viciously persistent inroads of grass and vine. A caterpillar tractor hauled a string of loaded wagons across raw red earth. A helicopter buzzed overhead, on watch for dinosaurs. It was the only flying thing. There had been a nearby pterodactyl rookery, but the men had cleaned that out months ago. When you got right down to facts, the most sinister animal of all was man.

Greenstein joined Herries. The new assistant was tall, slender, with curly brown hair and the defenseless face of youth. Above boots and dungarees he wore a blue sports shirt; it offered a kind of defiance to this sullen world. "Smoke?" he invited.

"Thanks." Herries accepted the cigarette. His eyes still dwelt on the derricks. Their walking beams went up and down, up and down, like a joyless copulation. Perhaps a man could get used to the Jurassic rain forest and eventually see some dark beauty there, for it was at least life; but this field would always remain hideous, being dead and pumping up the death of men.

"How's it going, Sam?" he asked when the tobacco had soothed his palate.

"All right," said Greenstein. "I'm shaking down. But God, It's good to know today is mail call!"

They stepped off the porch and walked toward the transceiving station. Mud squelched under their feet. A tuft of something, too pale and fleshy to be grass, stood near Herries' path. The yard crew had better uproot that soon, or in a week it might claim the entire compound.

"Girl friend, I suppose," said the chief. "That does make a month into a hell of a long drought between letters."

Greenstein flushed and nodded earnestly. "We're going to get married when my two years here are up," he said.

"That's what most of 'em plan on. A lot of saved-up pay and valuable experience—sure, you're fixed for life." It was on Herries' tongue to add that the life might be a short one, but he suppressed the impulse.

Loneliness dragged at his nerves. There was no one waiting in the future for him. It was just as well, he told himself during the endless nights. Hard enough to sleep without worrying about some woman in the same age as the cobalt bomb.

"I've got her picture here, if you'd like to see it," offered Greenstein shyly.

His hand was already on his wallet. A tired grin slid up Herries' mouth. "Right next to your…er…heart, eh?" he murmured.

Greenstein blinked, threw back his head, and laughed. The field had not heard so merry a laugh in a long while. Nevertheless, he showed the other man a pleasant-faced, unspectacular girl.

Out in the swamp, something hooted and threshed about.

Impulsively, Herries asked: "How do you feel about this operation, Sam?"

"Huh? Why, it's…interesting work. And a good bunch of guys."

"Even Symonds?"

"Oh he means well."

"We could have more fun if he didn't bunk with us."

"He can't help being...old," said Greenstein.

Herries glanced at the boy. "You know," he said, "you're the first man in the Jurassic Period who's had a good word for Ephraim Symonds. I appreciate that. I'd better not say whether or not I share the sentiment, but I appreciate it."

His boots sludged ahead, growing heavier with each step. "You still haven't answered my first question," he resumed after a while. "I didn't ask if you enjoyed the work, I asked how you feel about it. Its purpose. We have the answers here to questions which science has been asking—will be asking—for centuries. And yet, except for a couple of under-equipped paleobiologists, who aren't allowed to publish their findings, we're doing nothing but rape the earth in an age before it has even conceived us."

Greenstein hesitated. Then, with a surprising dryness: "You're getting too psychoanalytic for me, I'm afreud."

Herries chuckled. The day seemed a little more alive, all at once. "*Touché!* Well, I'll rephrase Joe Polansky's question of last night. Do you think the atomic standoff in our home era—to which this operation is potentially rather important—is stable?"

Greenstein considered for a moment. "No," he admitted. "Deterrence is a stopgap till something better can be worked out."

"They've said as much since it first began. Nothing has been done. It's improbable that anything will be. Ole Olson describes the international situation as a case of the irresistibly evil force colliding with the immovably stupid object."

"Ole likes to use extreme language," said Greenstein. "So tell me, what else could our side do?"

"I wish to God I had an answer." Herries sighed. "Pardon me. We avoid politics here, as much as possible; we're escapists in several senses of the word. But frankly, I sound out new men. I was doing it to you. Because in spite of what Washington thinks, a Q clearance isn't all that a man needs to work here."

"Did I pass?" asked Greenstein, a bit too lightly.

"Sure. So far. You may wish you hadn't. The burning issue today is not whether to tolerate 'privileged neutralism,' or whatever the latest catchword is up there. It's: Did I get the armament I've been asking for?"

The transceiving station bulked ahead. It was a long corrugated-iron shed, but dwarfed by the tanks which gleamed behind it. Every one of those was filled, Herries knew. Today they would pump their crude oil into the future. Or rather, if you wanted to be exact, their small temporal unit would establish a contact and the gigantic main projector in the twentieth century would then "suck" the liquid toward itself. And in return the compound would get—food, tools, weapons, supplies, and mail. Herries prayed there would be at least one howitzer...and no VIP's. That Senator a few months ago!

For a moment, contemplating the naked ugliness of tanks and pumps and shed, Herries had a vision of this one place stretching through time. It would be abandoned some day, when the wells were exhausted, and rain and jungle would rapidly eat the last thin traces of man. Later would come the sea, and then it would be dry land again, a cold prairie scoured by glacial winds, and then it would grow warm and…on and on, a waste of years until the time projector was invented and the great machine stood on this spot. And afterward? Herries didn't like to think what might be here after that.

Symonds was already present. He popped rabbit-like out of the building, a coded manifest in one hand a pencil behind his ear: "Good morning, Mr. Herries," he said. His tone gave its usual impression of stiff self-importance.

" 'Morning. All set in there?" Herries went in to see for himself. A spatter of rain began to fall, noisy on the metal roof. The technicians were at their posts and reported clear. Outside, one by one, the rest of the men were drifting up. This was mail day, and little work would be done for the remainder of it.

Herries laid the sack of letters to the future inside the shed in its proper spot. His chronometer said one minute to go. "Stand by!" At the precise time, there was a dim whistle in the air and an obscure pulsing glow. Meters came to life. The pumps began to throb, driving crude oil through a pipe which faced open-ended into the shed. Nothing emerged that Herries could see. Good. Everything in order. The other end of the pipe was a hundred million years in the future. The mail sack vanished with a small puff, as air rushed in where it had waited. Herries went back outside.

"Ah…excuse me."

He turned around, with a jerkiness that told him his nerves were half unraveled. "Yes?" he snapped.

"May I see you a moment?" asked Symonds. "Alone?" And the pale eyes behind the glasses said it was not a request but an order.

Herries nodded curtly, swore at the men for hanging around idle when the return shipment wasn't due for hours, and led the way to a porch tacked onto one side of the transceiving station. There were some camp stools beneath it. Symonds hitched up his khakis as if they were a business suit and sat primly down, his thin hands flat on his knees.

"A special shipment is due today," Symonds said. "I was not permitted to discuss it until the last moment."

Herries curled his mouth. "Go tell Security that the Kremlin won't be built for a hundred million years. Maybe they haven't heard."

'What no one knew, no one could put into a letter home."

"The mail is censored anyway. Our friends and relatives think we're working somewhere in Asia." Herries spat into the mud and said: "And in another year the first lot of recruits are due home. Plan to shoot them as they emerge, so they can't possibly talk in their sleep?"

Symonds seemed too humorless even to recognize sarcasm. He pursed his lips and declared: "Some secrets need be kept for a few months only; but within that period, they *must* be kept."

"Okay, okay. Let's hear what's coming today."

"I am not allowed to tell you that. But about half the total tonnage will be crates marked Top Secret. These are to remain in the shed, guarded night and day by armed men." Symonds pulled a slip of paper from his jacket. "These men will be assigned to that duty, each one taking eight hours a week."

Herries glanced at the names. He did not know everyone here by sight, though he came close, but he recognized several of these. "Brave, discreet, and charter subscribers to National Review," he murmured. "Teacher's pets. All right. Though I'll have to curtail exploration correspondingly—either that, or else cut down on their guards and sacrifice a few extra lives."

"I think not. Let me continue. You will get these orders in the mail today, but I will prepare you for them now. A special house must be built for the crates, as rapidly as possible, and they must be moved there immediately upon its completion. I have the specifications in my office safe: essentially, it must be air-conditioned, burglar-proof, and strong enough to withstand all natural hazards."

"Whoa, there!" Herries stepped forward. "That's going to take reinforced concrete and—"

"Materials will be made available," said Symonds. He did not look at the other man but stared straight ahead of him, across the rain-smoky compound to the jungle. He had no expression on his pinched face, and the reflection of light off his glasses gave him a strangely blind look.

"But—Judas priest!" Herries threw his cigarette to the ground; it was swallowed in mud and running water. He felt the heat enfold him like a blanket. "There's the labor too, the machinery, and—How the devil am I expected to expand this operation if—"

"Expansion will be temporarily halted," cut in Symonds. "You will simply maintain current operations with skeleton crews. The majority of the labor force is to be reassigned to construction."

"*What?*"

"The compound fence must be extended and reinforced. A number of new storehouses are to be erected, to hold certain supplies which will presently be sent to us. Bunkhouse barges for an additional five hundred are required. This, of course, entails more sickbay, recreational, mess, laundry, and other facilities."

Herries stood dumbly, staring at him. Pale lightning flickered in the sky.

The worst of it was, Symond's didn't even bother to be arrogant. He spoke like a schoolmaster.

"Oh no!" whispered Herries after a long while. "They're not going to try to establish that Jurassic military base after all!"

"The purpose is classified."

"Yeah. Sure. Classified. Arise, ye duly cleared citizens of democracy and cast your ballot on issues whose nature is classified, that your leaders whose names and duties are classified may—Great. Hopping. Balls. Of. Muck." Herries swallowed: Vaguely, through his pulse, he felt his fingers tighten into fists."

"I'm going up," he said. "I'm going to protest personally in Washington."

"That is not permitted, Symonds said in a dry, clipped tone. "Read your contract. You are under martial law. Of course," and his tone was neither softer nor harder, "you may file a written recommendation."

Herries stood for a while. Out beyond the fence stood a bulldozer wrecked and abandoned. The vines had almost buried it and a few scuttering little marsupials lived there. Perhaps they were his own remote ancestors. He could take a .22 and go potshooting at them some day.

"I'm not permitted to know anything," he said at last. "But is curiosity allowed? An extra five hundred men aren't much. I suppose given a few airplanes and so on, a thousand of us could plant atomic bombs where enemy cities will be. Or could we? Can't locate them without astronomical studies first, and it's always clouded here. So it would be practical to booby trap only with mass-action weapons. A few husky cobalt bombs, say. But there are missiles available to deliver those in the twentieth century. So…what *is* the purpose?"

"You will learn the facts in due course," answered Symonds. "At present, the government has certain military necessities."

"Haw!" said Herries. He folded his arms and leaned against the roofpost. It sagged a bit…shoddy work, shoddy world, shoddy destiny. "Military horses' necks! I'd like to get one of those prawn-eyed brass hats down here, just for a week, to run his precious security check on a lovesick brontosaur. But I'll probably get another visit from Senator Lardhead, the one who took up two days of my time walking around asking about the possibilities of farming. *Farming!*"

"Senator Wien is from an agricultural state. Naturally he would be interested—"

"—in making sure that nobody here starts raising food and shipping it back home to bring grocery prices down to where people can afford an occasional steak. Sure. I'll bet it cost us a thousand man-hours to make his soil tests and tell him, yes, given the proper machinery this land could be farmed. Of course, maybe I do him an injustice. Senator Wien is also on the Military Affairs Committee, isn't he? He may have visited us in that capacity, and soon we'll all get a directive to start our own little Victory gardens."

"Your language is close to being subversive," declared Symonds out of prune-wrinkled lips. "Senator Wien is a famous statesman."

For a moment the legislator's face rose in Herries' memory; and it had been the oldest and most weary face he had ever known. Something had burned out in the man who had fought a decade for honorable peace; the knowledge that there was no peace and could be none became a kind of death, and Senator Wien dropped out of his Free World Union organization to arm his land for Ragnarok. Briefly, his anger fading, Herries pitied Senator Wien. And the President, and the Chief of Staff, and the Secretary of State, for their work must be like a nightmare where you strangled your mother and could not stop your hands. It was easier to fight dinosaurs.

He even pitied Symonds, until he asked if his request for an atomic weapon had finally been okayed, and Symonds replied, "Certainly not." Then he spat at the clerk's feet and walked out into the rain.

After the shipment and guards were seen to, Herries dismissed his men. There was an uneasy buzz among them at the abnormality of what had arrived; but today was mail day, after all, and they did not ponder it long. He would not make the announcement about the new orders until tomorrow. He got the magazines and newspapers to which he subscribed (no one up there "now" cared enough to write to him, though his parents had existed in a section of spacetime which ended only a year before he took this job) and wandered off to the boss barge to read a little.

The twentieth century looked still uglier than it had last month. The nations felt their pride and saw no way of retreat. The Middle Eastern war was taking a decisive turn which none of the great powers could afford. Herries wondered if he might not be cut off in the Jurassic. A single explosion could destroy the main projector. Five hundred womanless men in a world of reptiles—he'd take the future, cobalt bomb and all.

After lunch there was a quiet, Sunday kind of atmosphere, men lay on their bunks reading their letters over and over. Herries made his rounds, machines and kitchen and sickbay, inspecting.

"I guess we'll discharge O'Connor tomorrow," said Dr. Yamaguchi. "He can do light work with that Stader on his arm. Next time tell him to duck when a power shovel comes down."

"What kind of sick calls have you been getting?" asked the chief.

Yamaguchi shrugged. "Usual things, very minor. I'd never have thought this swamp country would be so healthful. I guess disease germs which can live on placental mammals haven't evolved yet."

Father Gonzales, one of the camp's three chaplains, buttonholed Herries as he came out. "Can you spare me a minute?" he said.

"Sure, padre. What is it?"

"About organizing some baseball teams. We need more recreation. This is not a good place for men to live."

"Sawbones was just telling me—"

"I know. No flu, no malaria, oh, yes. But man is more than a body."

"Sometimes I wonder," said Herries. "I've seen the latest headlines. The dinosaurs have more sense than we do."

"We have the capacity to do nearly all things," said Father Gonzales. "At present, I mean in the twentieth century, we seem to do evil very well. We can do as much good, given the chance."

"Who's denying us the chance?" asked Herries. "Just ourselves, H. Sapiens. Therefore I wonder if we really are able to do good."

"Don't confuse sinfulness with damnation," said the priest. "We have perhaps been unfortunate in our successes. And yet even our most menacing accomplishments have a kind of sublimity. The time projector, for example. If the minds able to shape such a thing in metal were only turned toward human problems, what could we not hope to do?"

"But that's my point," said Herries. "We don't do the high things. We do what's trivial and evil so consistently that I wonder if it isn't in our nature. Even this time travel business…more and more I'm coming to think there's something fundamentally unhealthy about it. As if it's an invention which only an ingrown mind would have made first."

"First?"

Herries looked up into the steaming sky. A foul wind met his face. "There are stars above those clouds," he said, "and most stars must have planets. I've not been told how the time projector works, but elementary differential calculus will show that travel into the past is equivalent to attaining, momentarily, an infinite velocity. In other words, the basic natural law which the projector uses is one which somehow goes beyond relativity theory. If a time projector is possible, so is a spaceship which can reach the stars in a matter of days, maybe of minutes or seconds. If we were sane, padre, we wouldn't have been so anxious for a little organic grease and the little military advantage involved, that the first thing we did was go back into the dead past after it. No, we'd have invented that spaceship first, and gone out to the stars where there's room to be free and to grow. The time projector would have come afterward, as a scientific research tool."

He stopped, embarrassed at himself and trying awkwardly to grin. "Excuse me. Sermons are more your province than mine."

"It was interesting," said Father Gonzales. "But you brood too much. So do a number of the men. Even if they have no close ties at home—it was wise to pick them for that—they are all of above-average intelligence, and aware of what the future is becoming. I'd like to shake them out of their oppression. If we could get some more sports equipment—"

"Sure. I'll see what I can do."

"Of course," said the priest, "the problem is basically philosophical. Don't laugh. You too were indulging in philosophy, and doubtless you think of yourself as an ordinary, unimaginative man. Your wildcatters may not have heard of Aristotle, but they are also thinking men in their way. My personal belief is that this heresy of a fixed, rigid time line lies at the root of their growing sorrowfulness, whether they know it or not."

"Heresy?" The engineer lifted thick sandy brows. "It's been proved. It's the basis of the theory which showed how to build a projector: that much I do know. How could we be here at all, if the Mesozoic were not just as real as the Cenozoic? But if all time is coexistent, then all time must be fixed—unalterable—because every instant is the unchanging past of some other instant."

"Perhaps so, from God's viewpoint," said Father Gonzales. "But we are mortal men. And we have free will. The fixed-time concept need not, logically, produce fatalism; after all, Herries, man's will is itself one of the links in the causal chain. I suspect that this irrational fatalism is an important reason why twentieth-century civilization is approaching suicide. If we think we know our future is unchangeable, if our every action is foreordained, if we are doomed already, what's the use of trying? Why go through all the pain of thought, of seeking an answer and struggling to make others accept it? But if we really believed in ourselves, we would look for a solution, and find one."

"Maybe," said Herries uncomfortably. "Well, give me a list of the equipment you want, and I'll put in an order for it the next time the mail goes out."

As he walked off, he wondered if the mail would ever go out again.

* * *

Passing the rec hall, he noticed a small crowd before it and veered to see what was going on. He could not let men gather to trade doubts and terrors, or the entire operation was threatened. *In plain English,* he told himself with a growing bitter honesty, *I can't permit them to think.*

But the sounds which met him, under the subtly alien rustle of forest leaves and the distant bawl of a thunder lizard, was only a guitar. Chords danced forth beneath expert fingers, and a young voice lilted:

…*I traveled this wide world over,*
A hundred miles or more,
But a saddle on a milk cow.
I never seen before!…

Looking over shoulders, Herries made out Greenstein, sprawled on a bench and singing. There were chuckles from the listeners, Well-deserved: the kid was good; Herries wished he could relax and simply enjoy the performance. Instead, he must note that they were finding it pleasant, and that swamp and war were alike forgotten for a valuable few minutes.

The song ended. Greenstein stood up and stretched. "Hi, boss," he said.

Hard, wind-beaten faces turned to Herries and a mumble of greeting went around the circle. He was well enough liked, he knew, insofar as a chief can be liked. But that is not much. A leader can inspire trust, loyalty, what have you, but he cannot be humanly liked, or he is no leader.

"That was good," said Herries. "I didn't know you played."

"I didn't bring this whangbox with me, since I had no idea where I was going till I got here," answered Greenstein. "Wrote home for it and it arrived today."

A heavy-muscled crewcut man said, "You ought to be on the entertainment committee." Herries recognized Worth, one of the professional patriots who would be standing guard on Symonds' crates; but not a bad sort, really, after you learned to ignore his rather tedious opinions.

Greenstein said an indelicate word. "I'm sick of committees," he went on. "We've gotten so much into the habit of being herded around—everybody in the twentieth century has—that we can't even have a little fun without first setting up a committee."

Worth looked offended but made no answer. It began to rain again, just a little.

"Go on now, anyway," said Joe Eagle Wing. "Let's not take ourselves so goddam serious. How about another song?"

"Not in the wet." Greenstein returned his guitar to its case. The group began to break up, some to the hall and some back toward their barges.

Herries lingered, unwilling to be left alone with himself. "About that committee," he said. "You might reconsider. It's probably true what you claim, but we're stuck with a situation. We've simply got to tell most of the boys, 'Now it is time to be happy,' or they never will be."

Greenstein frowned. "Maybe so. But hasn't anyone ever thought of making a fresh start? Of unlearning all those bad habits?"

"You can't do that within the context of an entire society's vices," said Herries. "And how're you going to get away?"

Greenstein gave him a long look. "How the devil did you ever get this job?" he asked. "You don't sound like a man who'd be cleared for a dishwashing assistantship."

Herries shrugged. "All my life, I've liked totalitarianism even less than what passes for democracy. I served in a couple of the minor wars and—No matter. Possibly I might not be given the post if I applied now. I've been here more than a year, and it's changed me some."

"It must," said Greenstein, flickering a glance at the jungle.

"How's things at home?" asked Herries, anxious for another subject.

The boy kindled. "Oh, terrific!" he said eagerly. "Miriam, my girl, you know, she's an artist, and she's gotten a commission to—"

The loudspeaker coughed and blared across the compound, into the strengthening rain: "Attention! Copter to ground, attention! Large biped dinosaur, about two miles away north-northeast, coming fast."

Herries cursed and broke into a run.

Greenstein paced him. Water sheeted where their boots struck. "What is it?" he called.

"I don't know…yet…but it might be…a really big…carnivore." Herries reached the headquarters shack and flung the door open. A panel of levers was set near his personal desk. He slapped one down and the "combat stations" siren skirled above the field. Herries went on, "I don't know why anything biped should make a beeline for us unless the smell of blood from the critter we drove off yesterday attracts it. The smaller carnivores are sure as hell drawn. The charged fence keeps them away—but I doubt if it would do much more than enrage a dinosaur—Follow me!"

Jeeps were already leaving their garage when Herries and Greenstein came out. Mud leaped up from their wheels and dripped back off the fenders. The rain fell harder, until the forest beyond the fence blurred; and the earth smoked with vapors. The helicopter hung above the derricks, like a skeleton vulture watching a skeleton army, and the alarm sirens filled the brown air with screaming.

"Can you drive one of these buggies?" asked Herries.

"I did in the Army," said Greenstein.

"Okay, we'll take the lead one. The main thing is to stop that beast before it gets in among the wells." Herries vaulted the right-hand door and planted himself on sopping plastic cushions. There was a .50-caliber machine gun mounted on the hood before him, and the microphone of a police car radio hung at the dash. Five jeeps followed as Greenstein swung into motion. The rest of the crew, ludicrous ants across those wide wet distances, went scurrying with their arms to defend the most vital installations.

The north gate opened and the cars splashed out beyond the fence. There was a strip several yards across, also kept cleared; then the jungle wall rose, black, brown, dull red and green and yellow. Here and there along the fence an occasional bone gleamed up out of the muck, some animal shot by a guard or killed by the voltage. Oddly enough, Herries irrelevantly remembered, such a corpse drew enough scavenging insects to clean it in a day, but it was usually ignored by the nasty man-sized hunter dinosaurs which still slunk and hopped and slithered in this neighborhood. Reptiles just did not go in for carrion. However, they followed the odor of blood...

"Further east," said the helicopter pilot's radio voice. "There. Stop. Face the woods. He's coming out in a minute. Good luck, boss. Next time gimme some bombs and I'll handle the bugger myself."

"We haven't been granted any heavy weapons." Herries licked lips which seemed rough. His pulse was thick. No one had ever faced a tyrannosaur before.

The jeeps drew into line, and for a moment only their windshield wipers had motion. Then undergrowth crashed, and the monster was upon them.

It was indeed a tyrannosaur, thought Herries in a blurred way. A close relative, at least. It blundered ahead with the overweighted, underwitted stiffness which paleontologists had predicted, and which had led some of them to believe that it must have been a gigantic, carrion-eating hyena! They forgot that, like the Cenozoic snake or crocodile, it was too dull to recognize dead meat as food; that the brontosaurs it preyed on were even more clumsy; and that sheer length of stride would carry it over the scarred earth at a respectable rate.

Herries saw a blunt head three man-heights above ground, and a tail ending fifteen yards away. Scales of an unfairly beautiful steel gray shimmered in the rain, which made small waterfalls off flanks and wrinkled neck and tiny useless forepaws. Teeth clashed in a mindless reflex, the ponderous belly wagged with each step, and Herries felt the vibration of tons coming down claw-footed. The beast paid no attention to the jeeps, but moved jerkily toward the fence. Sheer weight would drive it through the mesh.

"Get in front of him, Sam!" yelled the engineer.

He gripped the machine gun. It snarled on his behalf, and he saw how a sleet of bullets stitched a bloody seam across the white stomach. The tyrannosaur halted, weaving its head about. It made a hollow, coughing roar. Greenstein edged the jeep closer.

The others attacked from the sides. Tracer streams hosed across alligator tail and bird legs. A launched grenade burst with a little puff on the right thigh. It opened a red ulcer-like crater. The tyrannosaur swung slowly about toward one of the cars.

That jeep dodged aside. "Get in on him!" shouted Herries. Greenstein shifted gears and darted through a fountain of mud. Herries stole a glance. The boy was grinning. Well, it would be something to tell the grandchildren, all right!

His jeep fled past the tyrannosaur, whipped about on two wheels, and crouched under a hammer of rain. The reptile halted. Herries cut loose with his machine gun. The monster standing there, swaying a little, roaring and bleeding, was not entirely real. This had happened a hundred million years ago. Rain struck the hot gun barrel and sizzled off.

"From the sides again," rapped Herries into his microphone. "Two and Three on his right, Four and Five on his left. Six, go behind him and lob a grenade at the base of his tail."

The tyrannosaur began another awkward about face. The water in which it stood was tinged red.

"Aim for his eyes!" yelled Greenstein, and dashed recklessly toward the profile now presented him.

The grenade from behind exploded. With a sudden incredible speed, the tyrannosaur turned clear around. Herries had an instant's glimpse of the tail like a snake before him, then it struck.

He threw up an arm and felt glass bounce off it as the windshield shattered. The noise when metal gave way did not seem loud, but it went through his entire body. The jeep reeled on ahead. Instinct sent Herries to the floorboards. He felt a brutal impact as his car struck the dinosaur's left leg. It hooted far above him. He looked up and saw a foot with talons, raised and filling the sky. It came down. The hood crumpled at his back and the engine was ripped from the frame.

Then the tyrannosaur had gone on. Herries crawled up into the bucket seat. It was canted at a lunatic angle. "Sam," he croaked. "Sam, Sam."

Greenstein's head was brains and splinters, with half the lower jaw on his lap and a burst-out eyeball staring up from the seat beside him.

Herries climbed erect. He saw his torn-off machine gun lying in the mud. A hundred yards off, at the jungle edge, the tyrannosaur fought the jeeps. It made clumsy rushes, which they side-swerved, and they spat at it and gnawed at it. Herries thought in a dull, remote fashion: *This can go on forever. A man is easy to kill, one swipe of a tail and all his songs are a red smear in the rain. But a reptile dies hard, being less alive to start with. I can't see an end to this fight.*

The Number Four jeep rushed in. A man sprang from it and it darted back in reverse from the monster's charge. The man—"Stop that, you idiot," whispered Herries into a dead microphone, "stop it, you fool"—plunged between the huge legs. He moved sluggishly enough with clay on his boots, but he was impossibly fleet and beautiful under that jerking bulk. Herries recognized Worth. He carried a grenade in his hand. He pulled the pin and dodged claws for a moment. The flabby, bleeding stomach made a roof over his head. Jaws searched blindly above him. He hurled the grenade and ran. It exploded against the tyrannosaur's belly. The monster screamed. One foot rose and came down. The talons merely clipped Worth, but he went spinning, fell in the gumbo ten feet away and tried weakly to rise but couldn't.

The tyrannosaur staggered in the other direction, spilling its entrails. Its screams took on a ghastly human note. Somebody stopped and picked up Worth. Somebody else came to Herries and gabbled at him. The tyrannosaur stumbled in yards of gut, fell slowly, and struggled, entangling itself.

Even so, it was hard to kill. The cars battered it for half an hour as it lay there, and it hissed at them and beat the ground with its tail. Herries was not sure it had died when he and his men finally left. But the insects had long been busy, and a few of the bones already stood forth clean white.

The phone jangled on Herries' desk. He picked it up. "Yeh?"

"Yamaguchi in sick bay," said the voice. "Thought you'd want to know about Worth."

"Well?"

"Broken lumbar vertebra. He'll live, possibly without permanent paralysis, but he'll have to go back for treatment."

"And be held incommunicado a year, till his contract's up. I wonder how much of a patriot he'll be by that time."

"What?"

"Nothing. Can it wait till tomorrow? Everything's so disorganized right now, I'd hate to activate the projector."

"Oh yes. He's under sedation anyway." Yamaguchi paused. "And the man who died—"

"Sure. We'll ship him back too. The government will even supply a nice coffin. I'm sure his girl friend will appreciate that."

"Do you feel well?" asked Yamaguchi sharply.

"They were going to be married," said Herries. He took another pull from the fifth of bourbon on his desk. It was getting almost too dark to see the bottle. "Since patriotism nowadays…in the future, I mean…in our own home, sweet home…since patriotism is necessarily equated with necrophilia, in that the loyal citizen is expected to rejoice every time his government comes up with a newer gadget for mass-producing corpses…I am sure the young lady will just love to have a pretty coffin. So much nicer than a mere husband. I'm sure the coffin will be chrome plated."

"Wait a minute—"

"With tail fins."

"Look here," said the doctor, "you're acting like a case of combat fatigue. I know you've had a shock today. Come see me and I'll give you a tranquilizer."

"Thanks," said Herries. "I've got one." He took another swig and forced briskness into his tone. "We'll send 'em back tomorrow morning, then. Now don't bother me. I'm composing a letter to explain to the great white father that this wouldn't have happened if we'd been allowed one stinking little atomic howitzer. Not that I expect to get any results. It's policy that we aren't allowed heavy weapons down here, and who ever heard of facts affecting a policy? Why, facts might be un-American."

He hung up, put the bottle on his lap and his feet on the desk, lit a cigarette and stared out the window. Darkness came sneaking across the compound like smoke. The rain had stopped for a while, and lamps and windows threw broken yellow gleams off puddles, but somehow the gathering night so thick that each light seemed quite alone. There was no else in the headquarters shack this hour. Herries had not turned on his own lights.

To hell with it, he thought. *To hell with it.*

His cigarette tip waxed and waned as he puffed, like a small dying star. But the smoke didn't taste right when invisible. Or had he put away so many toasts to dead men that his tongue was numbed? He wasn't sure. It hardly mattered.

The phone shrilled again. He picked it up, fumble-handed in the murk. "Chief of operations," he said pleasantly. "To hell with *you.*"

"What?" Symonds' voice rattled a bare bit. Then: "I have been trying to find you. What are you doing there this late?"

"I'll give you three guesses. Playing pinochle? No. Carrying on a sordid affair with a lady iguanodon? No. None of your business? Right! *Give* that gentleman a box of see-gars."

"Look here, Mr. Herries," wasped Symonds, "this is no time for levity. I understand that Matthew Worth was seriously injured today. He was supposed to be on guard duty tonight—the secret shipment. This has disarranged all my plans."

"Tsk-tsk-tsk. My nose bleeds for you."

"The schedule of duties must be revised. According to my notes, Worth would have been on guard from midnight until 4 A.M. Since I do not know precisely what other jobs his fellows are assigned to, I cannot single any one of them out to replace him. Will you do so? Select a man who can then sleep later tomorrow morning?"

"Why?" asked Herries.

"Why? Because—because—"

"I know. Because Washington said so. Washington is afraid some nasty dinosaur from what is going to be Russia will sneak in and look at an unguarded crate and hurry home with the information. Sure, I'll do it. I just wanted to hear you sputter."

Herries thought he made out an indignant breath sucked past an upper plate. "Very good," said the clerk. "Make the necessary arrangements for tonight, and we will work out a new rotation of watches tomorrow."

Herries put the receiver back.

The list of tight-lipped, tight-minded types was somewhere in his desk, he knew vaguely. A copy, rather. Symonds had a copy, and no doubt there would be copies going to the Pentagon and the FBI and the Transoco personnel office and—Well, look at the list, compare it with the work schedule, see who wouldn't be doing anything of critical importance tomorrow forenoon, and put him on a bit of sentry-go. Simple.

Herries took another swig. He could resign, he thought. He could back out of the whole fantastically stupid, fantastically meaningless operation. He wasn't compelled to work. Of course, they could hold him for the rest of his contract. It would be a lonesome year. Or maybe not; maybe a few others would trickle in to keep him company. To be sure, he'd then be under surveillance the rest of his life. But who wasn't, in a century divided between two garrisons?

The trouble was, he thought, there was nothing a man could do about the situation. You could become a peace-at-any-cost pacifist and thereby, effectively, league yourself with the enemy; and the enemy had carried out too many cold massacres for any halfway sane man to stomach. Or you could fight back (thus becoming more and more like what you fought) and hazard planetary incineration against the possibility of a tolerable outcome. It only took one to make a quarrel, and the enemy had long ago elected himself that one. Now, it was probably too late to patch up the quarrel. Even if important men on both sides wished for a disengagement, what could they do against their own fanatics, vested interests, terrified common people…against the whole momentum of history?

Hell take it, thought Herries, *we may be damned but why must we be fools in the bargain?*

Somewhere a brontosaur hooted, witlessly plowing through a night swamp. *Well, I'd better—No!*

Herries stared at the end of his cigarette. It was almost scorching his fingers. At least, he thought, at least he could find out what he was supposed to condone. A look into those crates, which should have held the guns he had begged for, and perhaps some orchestral and scientific instruments…and instead held God knew what piece of Pentagonal-brained idiocy…a look would be more than a blow in Symonds' smug eye. It would be an assertion that he was Herries, a free man, whose existence had not yet been pointlessly spilled from a splintered skull. He, the individual, would know what the Team planned; and if it turned out to be a crime against reason, he could at the very least resign and sit out whatever followed.

Yes. By the dubious existence of divine mercy, yes.

Again a little rain, just a small warm touch on his face, like tears. Herries splashed to the transceiver building and stood quietly in the sudden flashlight glare. At last, out of blackness, the sentry's voice came: "Oh, it's you, sir."

"Uh-huh. You know Worth got hurt today? I'm taking his watch."

"What? But I thought—"

"Policy," said Herries.

The incantation seemed to suffice. The other man shuffled forth and laid his rifle in the engineer's hands. "And here's the glim," he added. "Nobody came by while I was on duty."

"What would you have done if somebody'd tried to get in?"

"Why, stopped them, of course."

"And if they didn't stop?"

The dim face under the dripping hat turned puzzledly toward Herries. The engineer sighed. "I'm sorry, Thornton. It's too late to raise philosophical questions. Run along to bed."

He stood in front of the door, smoking a damp cigarette, and watched the man trudge away. All the lights were out now, except overhead lamps here and there. They were brilliant, but remote; he stood in a pit of shadow and wondered what the phase of the Moon was and what kind of constellations the stars made nowadays.

He waited. There was time enough for his rebellion. Too much time, really. A man stood in rain, fog about his feet and a reptile smell in his nose, and he remembered anemones in springtime, strewn under trees still cold and leafless, with here and there a little snow between the roots. Or he remembered drinking beer in a New England country inn one fall day when the door stood open to red sumac and yellow beech and a far blue wandering sky. Or he remembered a man snatched under black Jurassic quagmires, a man stepped into red ruin, a man sitting in a jeep and bleeding brains down onto the picture of the girl he had planned to marry. And then he started wondering what the point of it all was, and decided that it was either without any point whatsoever or else had the purpose of obliterating anemones and quiet country inns, and he was forced to dissent somehow.

When Thornton's wet footsteps were lost in the dark, Herries unlocked the shed door and went through. It was smotheringly hot inside. Sweat sprang forth under his raincoat as he closed the door again and turned on his flashlight. Rain tapped loudly on the roof. The crates loomed over him, box upon box, many of them large enough to hold a dinosaur. It had taken a lot of power to ship all that tonnage into the past. No wonder taxes were high. And what might the stuff be? A herd of tanks, possibly…some knocked-down bombers…Lord knew what concept the men who lived in offices, insulated from the sky, would come up with. And Symonds had implied it was just a beginning; there would be more shipments when this had been stored out of the way, and more, and more.

Herries found a workbench and helped himself to tools. He would have to be careful; no sense in going to jail. He laid the flashlight on a handy barrel and stooped down by one of the crates. It was of strong wood, securely screwed together. But while that would make it harder to dismantle, it could be reassembled without leaving a trace. Maybe. Of course, it might be booby trapped. No telling how far the religion of secrecy could lead the office men.

Oh, well, if I'm blown up I haven't lost much. Herries peeled off his slicker. His shirt clung to his body. He squatted and began to work.

It went slowly. After taking off several boards, he saw a regular manufacturer's crate, open-slatted. Something within was wrapped in burlap. A single curved metal surface projected slightly. What the devil? Herries got a crowbar and pried one slat loose. The nails shrieked. He stooped rigid for a while, listening, but there was only the rain, grown more noisy. He reached in and fumbled with the padding… God, it was hot!

Only when he had freed the entire blade did he recognize what it was. And then his mind would not quite function; he gaped a long while before the word registered.

A plowshare.

"But they don't know what to do with the farm surpluses at home," he said aloud, inanely.

Like a stranger's, his hands began to repair what he had torn apart. He couldn't understand it. Nothing seemed altogether real any more. Of course, he thought in a dim way, theoretically anything might be in the other boxes, but he suspected more plows, tractors, discs, combines…why not bags of seeds…? *What were they planning to do?*

"Ah."

Herries whirled. The flashlight beam caught him like a spear.

He grabbed blindly for his rifle. A dry little voice behind the blaze said: "I would not recommend violence." Herries let the rifle fall. It thudded.

Symonds closed the shed door behind him and stepped forward in his mincing fashion, another shadow among bobbing misshapen shadows. He had simply flung on shirt and pants, but bands of night across them suggested necktie, vest, and coat.

"You see," he explained without passion, "all the guards were instructed *sub rosa* to notify me if there was anything unusual, even when it did not seem to warrant action on their part." He gestured at the crate. "Please continue reassembling it."

Herries crouched down again. There was a hollowness in him, his only wonder was how best to die. For if he were sent back to the twentieth century, surely, surely they would lock him up and lose the key, and the sunlessness of death was better than that. It was strange, he thought, how his fingers used the tools with untrembling skill.

Symonds stood behind him and held his light on the work. After a long while he asked primly, "Why did you break in like this?"

I could kill him, thought Herries. *He's unarmed. I could wring his scrawny neck between these two hands, and take a gun, and go into the swamp to live a few days… But it might be easier all around just to turn the rifle on myself.*

He sought words with care, for he must decide what to do, even though it seemed remote and scarcely important. "That's not an easy question to answer," he said.

"The significant ones never are."

Astonished, Herries jerked a glance upward and back. (And was the more surprised that he could still know surprise.) But the little man's face was in darkness. Herries saw only a wan blank glitter off the glasses.

He said, "Let's put it this way. There are limits even to the right of self-defense. If a killer attacks me, I can fight back with anything I've got. But I wouldn't be justified in grabbing some passing child for a shield."

"So you wished to make sure that nothing you would consider illegitimate was in those boxes?" asked Symonds academically.

"I don't know. What is illegitimate, these days? I was…I was disgusted. I liked Greenstein, and he died because Washington had decided we couldn't have bombs or atomic shells. I just didn't know how much more I could consent to. I had to find out."

"I see." The clerk nodded. "For your information, it is *all* agricultural equipment. Later shipments will include industrial and scientific material, a large reserve of canned food, and as much of the world's culture as it proves possible to microfilm."

Herries stopped working, turned around and rose. His knees would not hold him. He leaned against the crate and it was a minute before he could get out: "Why?"

Symonds did not respond at once. He reached forth a precise hand and took up the flashlight Herries had left on the barrel. Then he sat down there himself, with the two glowing tubes in his lap. The light from below ridged his face in shadows, and his glasses made blind circles. He said, as if ticking off the points of an agenda:

"You would have been informed of the facts in due course, when the next five hundred people arrive. Now you have brought on yourself the burden of knowing what you would otherwise have been ignorant of for months yet. I think it may safely be assumed that you will keep the secret and not be broken by it. At least, the assumption is necessary."

Herries heard his own breath harsh in his throat. "Who are these people?"

The papery half-seen countenance did not look at him, but into the pit-like reaches of the shed. "You have committed a common error," said Symonds, as if to a student. "You have assumed that because men are constrained by circumstances to act in certain ways, they must be evil or stupid. I assure you, Senator Wien and the few others responsible for this are neither. They must keep the truth even from those officials within the project whose reaction would be rage or panic instead of a sober attempt at salvage. Nor do they have unlimited powers. Therefore, rather than indulge in tantrums about the existing situation, they use it. The very compartmentalization of effort and knowledge enforced by Security helps conceal their purposes and mislead those who must be given some information."

Symonds paused. A little frown crossed his forehead, and he tapped an impatient fingernail on a flashlight casing. "Do not misunderstand," he went on. "Senator Wien and his associates have not forgotten their oaths of office, nor are they trying to play God. Their primary effort goes, as it must, to a straightforward dealing with the problems of the twentieth century. It is not they who are withholding the one significant datum—a datum which, incidentally, any informed person could reason out for himself if he cared to. It is properly constituted authority, using powers legally granted to stamp certain reports Top Secret. Of course, the Senator has used his considerable influence to bring about the present eventuality, but that is normal politics."

Herries growled: "Get to the point, damn you! What are you talking about?"

Symonds shook his thin gray head. "You are afraid to know, are you not?" he asked quietly.

"I—" Herries turned about, faced the crate and beat it with his fist. The parched voice in the night continued to punish him:

"You know that a time-projector can go into the future about a hundred years at a jump, but can only go pastward in jumps of approximately one hundred megayears. You have spoken of a simple way to explore certain sections of the historical past, in spite of this handicap, by making enough century hops forward before the one long hop backward. But can you tell me how to predict the historical future? Say, a century hence? Come, come, you are an intelligent man. Answer me."

"Yeah," said Herries. "I get the idea. Leave me alone."

"Team A, a group of well-equipped volunteers, went into the twenty-first century," pursued Symonds. "They recorded what they observed and placed the data in a chemically inert box within a large block of reinforced concrete erected at an agreed-on location: one which a previous expedition to circa 100,000,000 A.D. had confirmed would remain stable. I presume they also mixed radioactive materials of long half-life into the concrete, to aid in finding the site. Of course, the bracketing of time jumps is such that they cannot now get back to the twentieth century. But Team B went a full hundred-megayear jump into the future, excavated the data, and returned home."

Herries squared his body and faced back to the small man. He was drained, so weary that it was. all he could do to keep on his feet. "What did they find?" he asked. There was no tone in his voice or in him.

"There have actually been several expeditions to 100,000,000," said Symonds. "Energy requirements for a visit to 200,000,000—A.D. or B.C.—were considered prohibitive. But in 100,000,000 life is re-evolving on Earth. However, as yet the plants have not liberated enough oxygen for the atmosphere to be breathable. You see, oxygen reacts with exposed rock, so that if no biological processes exist to replace it continuously—But you have a better technical education than I."

"Okay," said Herries, flat and hard. "Earth was sterile for a long time in the future. Including the twenty-first century?"

"Yes. The radioactivity had died down enough so that Team A reported no danger to itself, but some of the longer-lived isotopes were still measurably present. By making differential measurements of abundance, Team A was able to estimate rather closely when the bombs had gone off."

"And?"

"Approximately one year from the twentieth-century base date we are presently using."

"One year...from now." Herries stared upward. Blackness met him. He heard the Jurassic rain on the iron roof, like drums.

"Possibly less," Symonds told him. "There is a factor of uncertainty. This project must be completed well within the safety margin before the war comes."

"The war comes," Herries repeated…"Does it have to come? Fixed time line or not, does it have to come? Couldn't the enemy leaders be shown the facts—couldn't our side, even, capitulate—"

"Every effort is being made," said Symonds like a machine. "Quite apart from the theory of rigid time, it seems unlikely that they will succeed. The situation is too unstable. One man, losing his head and pressing the wrong button, can write the end; and there are so many buttons. The very revelation of the truth, to a few chosen leaders or to the world public, would make some of them panicky. Who can tell what a man in panic will do? That is what I meant when I said that Senator Wien and his coworkers have not forgotten their oaths of office. They have no thought of taking refuge, they know they are old men. To the end, they will try to save the twentieth century. But they do not expect it; so they are also trying to save the human race."

Herries pushed up from the crate he had been leaning against. "Those five hundred who're coming," he whispered. "Women?"

"Yes. If there is still time to rescue a few more, after the ones you are preparing for have gone through, it will be done. But there will be at least a thousand young, healthy adults here, in the Jurassic. You face a difficult time, when the truth must be told them; you can see why the secret must be kept until then. It is quite possible that someone here will lose his head. That is why no heavy weapons have been sent: a single deranged person must not be able to destroy everyone. But *you* will recover. You must."

Herries jerked the door open and stared out into the roaring darkness. "But there are no traces of us…in the future," he said, hearing his voice high and hurt like a child's.

"How much trace do you expect would remain after geological eras?" answered Symonds. He was still the reproving schoolmaster; but he sat on the barrel and faced the great moving shadows in a corner. "It is assumed that you will remain here for several generations, until your numbers and resources have been expanded sufficiently. The Team A I spoke of will join you a century hence. It is also, I might add, composed of young men and women in equal numbers. But this planet in this age is not a good home. We trust that your descendants will perfect the spaceships we know to be possible, and take possession of the stars instead."

Herries leaned in the doorway, sagging with tiredness and the monstrous duty to survive. A gust of wind threw rain into his eyes. He heard dragons calling in the night.

"And you?" he said, for no good reason.

"I shall convey any final messages you may wish to send home," said the dried-out voice.

Neat little footsteps clicked across the floor until the clerk paused beside the engineer. There was silence, except for the rain.

"Surely I will deserve to go home," said Symonds.

And suddenly the breath whistled inward between teeth which had snapped together. He raised his hands, claw-fingered and screamed aloud: "You can let me go home *then!*"

He began running toward the supervisors' barge. The sound of him was soon lost. Herries stood for a time yet in the door.

Clausius' Chaos

Entropy, Shmentropy,
Rudolph J. Clausius
Proved universally
Chaos will show
Increase in processes
Thermodynamical.
Something that housekeepers
Already know.

Journey's End

—doctor bill & twinges in chest but must be all right maybe indigestion & dinner last night & wasn't audrey giving me the glad eye & how the hell is a guy to know & maybe i can try and find out & what a fool i can look if she doesn't—

—goddam idiot & they shouldn't let some people drive & oh all right so the examiner was pretty lenient with me i haven't had a bad accident yet & christ blood all over my blood let's face it i'm scared to drive but the buses are no damn good & straight up three paces & man in a green hat & judas i ran that red light—

In fifteen years a man got used to it, more or less. He could walk down the street and hold his own thoughts to himself while the surf of unvoiced voices was a nearly ignored mumble in his brain. Now and then, of course, you got something very bad, it stood up in your skull and shrieked at you.

Norman Kane, who had come here because he was in love with a girl he had never seen, got to the corner of University and Shattuck just when the light turned against him. He paused, fetching out a cigarette with nicotine-yellowed fingers while traffic slithered in front of his eyes.

It was an unfavorable time, four-thirty in the afternoon, homeward rush of nervous systems jangled with weariness and hating everything else on feet or wheels. Maybe he should have stayed in the bar down on San Pablo. It had been pleasantly cool and dim, the bartender's mind an amiable cud-chewing somnolence, and he could have suppressed awareness of the woman.

No, maybe not. When the city had scraped your nerves raw, they didn't have much resistance to the slime in some heads.

Odd, he reflected how often the outwardly polite ones were the foully twisted inside. They wouldn't dream of misbehaving in public, but just below the surface of consciousness…Better not think of it, better not remember. Berkeley was at least preferable to San Francisco or Oakland. The bigger the town, the more evil it seemed to hold, three centimeters under the frontal bone. New York was almost literally uninhabitable.

There was a young fellow waiting beside Kane. A girl came down the sidewalk, pretty, long yellow hair and a well-filled blouse. Kane focused idly on her: yes, she had an apartment of her own, which she had carefully picked for a tolerant superintendent. Lechery jumped in the young man's nerves. His eyes followed the girl, Cobean-style, and she walked on…simple harmonic motion.

Too bad. They could have enjoyed each other. Kane chuckled to himself. He had nothing against honest lust, anyhow not in his liberated conscious mind; he couldn't do much about a degree of subconscious puritanism. Lord, you can't be a telepath and remain any kind of prude. People's lives were their own business, If they didn't hurt anyone else too badly.

—*the trouble is,* he thought, *they hurt me. but i can't tell them that. they'd rip me apart and dance on the pieces. the government /the military / wouldn't like a man to be alive who could read secrets but their fear-inspired anger would be like a baby's tantrum beside the red blind amok of the common man (thoughtful husband considerate father good honest worker earnest patriot) whose inward sins were known. you can talk to a priest or a psychiatrist because it is only talk & he does not live your failings with you—*

The light changed and Kane started across. It was clear fall weather, not that this area had marked seasons, a cool sunny day with a small wind blowing up the street from the water. A few blocks ahead of him, the University campus was a splash of manicured green under brown hills.

—*flayed & burningburningburning moldering rotted flesh & the bones the white hard clean bones coming out gwtjklfmx—*

Kane stopped dead. Through the vertigo he felt how sweat was drenching into his shirt.

And it was such an ordinary-looking man!

"Hey, there, buster, wake up! Ya wanna get killed?"

Kane took a sharp hold on himself and finished the walk across the street. There was a bench at the bus stop and he sat down till the trembling was over.

Some thoughts were unendurable.

He had a trick of recovery. He went back to Father Schliemann. The priest's mind had been like a well, a deep well under sun-speckled trees, its surface brightened with a few gold-colored autumn leaves...but there was nothing bland about the water, it had a sharp mineral tang, a smell of the living earth. He had often fled to Father Schliemann, in those days of puberty when the telepathic power had first wakened in him. He had found good minds since then, happy minds, but never one so serene, none with so much strength under the gentleness.

"I don't want you hanging around that papist, boy, do you understand?" It was his father, the lean implacable man who always wore a black tie. "Next thing you know, you'll be worshiping graven images just like him."

"But they *aren't*—"

His ears could still ring with the cuff. "Go up to your room! I don't want to see you till tomorrow morning. And you'll have two more chapters of Deuteronomy memorized by then. Maybe that'll teach you the true Christian faith."

Kane grinned wryly and lit another cigarette from the end of the previous one. He knew he smoked too much. And drank—but not heavily. Drunk, he was defenseless before the horrible tides of thinking.

He had had to run away from home at the age of fourteen. The only other possibility was conflict ending with reform school. It had meant running away from Father Schliemann too, but how in hell's red fire could a sensitive adolescent dwell in the same house as his father's brain? Were the psychologists now admitting the possibility of a sadistic masochist? Kane *knew* the type existed.

Give thanks for this much mercy, that the extreme telepathic range was only a few hundred yards. And a mind-reading boy was not altogether helpless; he could evade officialdom and the worst horrors of the underworld. He could find a decent elderly couple at the far end of the continent and talk himself into adoption.

Kane shook himself and got up again. He threw the cigarette to the ground and stubbed it out with his heel. A thousand examples told him what obscure sexual symbolism was involved in that act, but what the deuce…it was also a practical thing. Guns are phallic too, but at times you need a gun.

Weapons: he could not help wincing as he recalled dodging the draft in 1949. He'd traveled enough to know this country was worth defending. But it hadn't been any trick at all to hoodwink a psychiatrist and get himself marked hopelessly psychoneurotic—which he would be after two years penned with frustrated men. There had been no choice, but he could not escape a sense of dishonor.

—*haven't we all sinned / everyone of us / is there a single human creature on earth without his burden of shame?*—

A man was coming out of the drugstore beside him. Idly, Kane probed his mind. You could go quite deeply into anyone's self if you cared to, in fact you couldn't help doing so. It was impossible merely to scan verbalized thinking: the organism is too closely integrated. Memory is not a passive filing cabinet, but a continuous process beneath the level of consciousness; in a way, you are always reliving your entire past. And the more emotionally charged the recollection is, the more powerfully it radiates.

The stranger's name was—no matter. His personality was as much an unchangeable signature as his fingerprints. Kane had gotten into the habit of thinking of people as such-and-such a multidimensional symbolic topography; the name was an arbitrary gabble.

The man was an assistant professor of English at the University. Age forty-two, married, three children, making payments on a house in Albany. Steady sober type, but convivial, popular with his colleagues, ready to help out most friends. He was thinking about tomorrow's lectures, with overtones of a movie he wanted to see and an undercurrent of fear that he might have cancer after all, in spite of what the doctor said.

Below, the list of his hidden crimes. As a boy: tormenting a cat, well-buried Oedipean hungers, masturbation, petty theft…the usual. Later: cheating on a few exams, that ludicrous fumbling attempt with a girl which came to nothing because he was too nervous, the time he crashed a cafeteria line and had been shoved away with a cold remark (and praises be, Jim who had seen that was now living in Chicago)…still later: wincing memories of a stomach uncontrollably rumbling at a formal dinner, that woman in his hotel room the night he got drunk at the convention, standing by and letting old Carver be fired because he didn't have the courage to protest to the dean…now: youngest child a nasty whining little snotnose, but you can't show anyone what you really think, reading

Rosamond Marshall when alone in his office, disturbing young breasts in tight sweaters, the petty spite of academic politics, giving Simonson an undeserved good grade because the boy was so beautiful, disgraceful sweating panic when at night he considered how death would annihilate his ego—

And what of it? This assistant professor was a good man, a kindly and honest man, his inwardness ought to be between him and the Recording Angel. Few of his thoughts had ever become deeds, or ever would. Let him bury them himself, let him be alone with them. Kane ceased focusing on him.

The telepath had grown tolerant. He expected little of anyone; nobody matched the mask except possibly Father Schliemann and a few others…and those were human too, with human failings; the difference was that they knew peace. It was the emotional overtones of guilt which made Kane wince. God knew he himself was no better. Worse maybe, but then his life had thrust him to it. If you had an ordinary human sex drive, for instance, but could not endure to cohabit with the thoughts of a woman, your life became one of fleeting encounters; there was no help for it, even if your austere boyhood training still protested.

"Pardon me, got a match?"

—lynn is dead / i still can't understand it that i will never see her again & eventually you learn how to go on in a chopped-off fashion but what do you do in the meantime how do you get through the nights alone—

"Sure." —*maybe that is the worst: sharing sorrow and unable to help & only able to give him a light for his cigarette*—

Kane put the matches back in his pocket and went on up University, pausing again at Oxford. A pair of large campus buildings jutted up to the left; others were visible ahead and to the right, through a screen of eucalyptus trees. Sunlight and shadow damascened the grass. From a passing student's mind he discovered where the library was. A good big library—perhaps it held a clue, buried somewhere in the periodical files. He had already arranged for permission to use the facilities: prominent young author doing research for his next novel.

Crossing wistfully named Oxford Street, Kane smiled to himself. Writing was really the only possible occupation: he could live in the country and be remote from the jammed urgency of his fellow men. And with such an understanding of the soul as was his, with any five minutes on a corner giving him a dozen stories, he made good money at it. The only drawback was the trouble of avoiding publicity, editorial summonses to New York, autographing parties, literary teas…he didn't like those. But you could remain faceless if you insisted.

They said nobody but his agent knew who B. Traven was. It had occurred, wildly, to Kane that Traven might be another like himself. He had gone on a long journey to find out…No. He was alone on earth, a singular and solitary mutant, except for—

It shivered in him, again he sat on the train. It had been three years ago, he was in the club car having a nightcap while the streamliner ran eastward through the Wyoming darkness. They passed a westbound train, not so elegant a one. His drink leaped from his hand to the floor and he sat for a moment in stinging blindness. That flicker of thought, brushing his mind and coming aflame with recognition and then borne away again…Damn it, damn it, he should have pulled the emergency cord and so should *she*. There should have halted both trains and stumbled through cinders and sagebrush and found each other's arms.

Too late. Three years yielded only a further emptiness. Somewhere in the land there was, or there had been, a young woman, and she was a telepath and the startled touch of her mind had been gentle. There had not been time to learn anything else. Since then he had given up on private detectives. (How could you tell them: "I'm looking for a girl who was on such-and-such a train the night of—"?) Personal ads in all the major papers had brought him nothing but a few crank letters. Probably she didn't read the personals; he'd never done so till his search began, there was too much unhappiness to be found in them if you understood humankind as well as he did.

Maybe this library here, some unnoticed item…but if there are two points in a finite space and one moves about so as to pass through every infinitesimal volume *dV*, it will encounter the other one in finite time *provided* that the other point is not moving too.

Kane shrugged and went along the curving way to the gatehouse. It was slightly uphill. There was a bored cop in the shelter, to make sure that only authorized cars were parked on campus. The progress paradox: a ton or so of steel, burning irreplaceable petroleum to shift one or two human bodies around, and doing the job so well that it becomes universal and chokes the cities which spawned it. A telepathic society would be more rational. When every little wound in the child's soul could be felt and healed…when the thick burden of guilt was laid down, because everyone knew that everyone else had done the same…when men could not kill because soldier and murderer felt the victim die…

—*adam & eve? you can't breed a healthy race out of two people. but if we had telepathic children/ & we would be bound to do so i think because the mutation is obviously recessive/ then we could study the heredity of it & the gift would be passed on to other blood-lines in logical distribution & every generation there would be more of our kind until we could come out openly & even the mindmates could be helped by our psychiatrists & priests & earth would be fair and clean and sane—*

There were students sitting on the grass, walking under the Portland Cement Romanesque of the buildings, calling and laughing and talking. The day was near an end. Now there would be dinner, a date, a show, maybe some beer at Robbie's or a drive up into the hills to neck and watch the lights below like trapped stars and the mighty constellation of the Bay Bridge…or perhaps, with a face-saving grumble about mid-terms, an evening of books, a world suddenly opened. It must be good to be young and mindmute. A dog trotted down the walk and Kane relaxed into the simple wordless pleasure of being a healthy and admired collie.

—*so perhaps it is better to be a dog than a man? no/ surely not/ for if a man knows more grief he also knows more joy & so it is to be a telepath: more easily hurt yes but/ god/ think of the mindmutes always locked away in aloneness and think of sharing not only a kiss but a soul with your beloved—*

The uphill trend grew steeper as he approached the library, but Kane was in fair shape and rather enjoyed the extra effort. At the foot of the stairs he paused for a quick cigarette before entering. A passing woman flicked eyes across him and he learned that he could also smoke in the lobby. Mind reading had its everyday uses. But it was good to stand here in the sunlight. He stretched, reaching out physically and mentally.

—*let's see now the integral of log* x *dx well make a substitution suppose we call* y *equal to log* x *then this is interesting i wonder who wrote that line about euclid has looked on beauty bare—*

Kane's cigarette fell from his mouth.

It seemed that the wild hammering of his heart must drown out the double thought that rivered in his brain, the thought of a physics student, a very ordinary young man save that he was quite wrapped up in the primitive satisfaction of hounding down a problem, and the other thought, the one that was listening in.

—*she—*

He stood with closed eyes, away on his feet, breathing as if he ran up a mountain. —*are You there? are You there?—*

—*not daring to believe: what do i feel?—*

—*i was the man on the train—*

—*& i was the woman—*

A shuddering togetherness.

"Hey! Hey, mister, is anything wrong?"

Almost Kane snarled. Her thought was so remote, on the very rim of indetectability, he could get nothing but subvocalized words, nothing of the self, and this busybody— "No, thank, I'm OK, just a, a little winded." —*where are You, where can i find You o my darling?—*

—*image of a large white building/ right over here & they call it dwinelle hall & i am sitting on the bench outside & please come quickly please be here i never thought this could become real—*

Kane broke into a run. For the first time in fifteen years, he was unaware of his human surroundings. There were startled looks, he didn't see them, he was running to her and she was running too.

—*my name is norman kane & i was not born to that name but took it from people who adopted me because i fled my father (horrible how mother died in darkness & he would not let her have drugs though it was cancer & he said drugs were sinful and pain was good for the soul & he really honestly believed that) & when the power first appeared i made slips and he beat me and said it was witchcraft & i have searched all my life since & i am a writer but only because i must live but it was not aliveness until this moment—*

—*o my poor kicked beloved/ i had it better/ in me the power grew more slowly and i learned to cover it & i am twenty years old & came here to study but what are books at this moment—*

He could see her now. She was not conventionally beautiful, but neither was she ugly, and there was kindness in her eyes and on her mouth.

—*what shall i call you? to me you will always be You but there must be a name for the mindmutes & i have a place in the country among old trees & such few people as live nearby are good folk/ as good as life will allow them to be—*

—then let me come there with you & never leave again—

They reached each other and stood a foot apart. There was no need for a kiss or even a handclasp…not yet. It was the minds which leaped out and enfolded and became one.

—I REMEMBER THAT AT THE AGE OF THREE I DRANK OUT OF THE TOILET BOWL / THERE WAS A PECULIAR FASCINATION TO IT & I USED TO STEAL LOOSE CHANGE FROM MY MOTHER THOUGH SHE HAD LITTLE ENOUGH TO CALL HER OWN SO I COULD SNEAK DOWN TO THE DRUGSTORE FOR ICE CREAM & I SQUIRMED OUT OF THE DRAFT & THESE ARE THE DIRTY EPISODES INVOLVING WOMEN—

—AS A CHILD I WAS NOT FOND OF MY GRANDMOTHER THOUGH SHE LOVED ME AND ONCE I PLAYED THE FOLLOWING FIENDISH TRICK ON HER & AT THE AGE OF SIXTEEN I MADE AN UTTER FOOL OF MYSELF IN THE FOLLOWING MANNER & I HAVE BEEN PHYSICALLY CHASTE CHIEFLY BECAUSE OF FEAR BUT MY VICARIOUS EXPERIENCES ARE NUMBERED IN THE THOUSANDS—

Eyes watched eyes with horror.

—*it is not that you have sinned for i know everyone has done the same or similar things or would if they had our gift & i know too that it is nothing serious or abnormal & of course you have decent instincts & are ashamed—*

—*just so / it is that you know what i have done & you know every last little wish & thought & buried uncleanness & in the top of my head i know it doesn't mean anything but down underneath is all which was drilled into me when i was just a baby & i will not admit to* ANYONE *else that such things exist in* ME—

A car whispered by, homeward bound. The trees talked in the light sunny wind.

A boy and girl went hand in hand.

The thought hung cold under the sky, a single thought in two minds.

—*get out. i hate your bloody guts.—*

Heinlein's Stories

Far-faring, star-faring,
Robert A. Heinlein, sir,
Please tell more stories of
Men who are strong
And of those well-endowed,
Ultradesirable
Women—the kind who make
Lazarus Long.

Logic

Brother bringeth
brother his bane,
and sons of sisters
break kinship's bonds
Never a man
spareth another.
Hard is the world.
Whoredom prevaileth.
Axe-time. sword-time,
—shields are cloven—
wind-time and wolf-time.
Ere the world waneth.
               —Elder Edda

He was nearly always alone, and even when others were near him, even when he was speaking with them, he seemed to be standing on the far side of an unbridgeable gulf. His only companion was a gaunt gray mongrel with a curiously shaped head and a savage disposition, and the two had traveled far over the empty countryside, the rolling plains and straggling woods and high bluffs several miles down the river. They were an uncanny sight, walking along a ridge against the blood-flaring sunset, the thin, ragged, big-headed boy, like a dwarf from the legends of an irretrievable past, and the shaggy, lumpish animal skulking at his heels.

Roderick Wayne saw them thus as he walked home along the river. They were trotting rapidly along the other side. He hailed them, and they stopped, and the boy stared curiously, almost wonderingly. Wayne knew that attitude, though Alaric was only a grotesque outline against the fantastically red sky. He knew that his son was looking and looking at him, as if trying to focus, as if trying to remember who the—stranger—was. And the old pain lay deep in him, though he called out loudly enough: "Come on over, Al!"

Wayne had had a hard day's work in the shop, and he was tired. Fixing machinery was a long jump down from teaching mathematics in Southvale College, but the whole world had fallen and men survived as best they could in its ruins. He was better off than most—couldn't complain.

Of old he had been wont to stroll along the river that traversed the campus, each evening after classes, smoking his pipe and swinging his cane, thinking perhaps of what Karen would have for supper or of the stark impersonal beauty of the latest development in quantum mechanics—two topics not as unrelated as one might suppose. The quiet summer evenings were not to be spent in worry or petty plans for the next day, there was always too much time for that. He simply walked along in his loose-jointed way, breathing tobacco smoke and the cool still air, watching the tall old trees mirror themselves in the river or the molten gold and copper of sunset. There would be a few students on the broad smooth lawns who would hail him in a friendly way, for Bugsy Wayne was well liked; otherwise only the river and himself and the evening star.

But that was sixteen or more years ago, and his memories of that time were dim by now, blurted in a tidal wave of savage, resistless events. The brief, the incredible nightmare of a war that wiped out every important city in the world in a couple of months—its protracted aftermath of disease, starvation, battle, work, woe, and the twisting of human destiny—it covered those earlier experiences, distorted them like rocks seen through a flowing stream. Now the campus stood in ruinous desolation, cattle staked out in the long grass, crumbling empty buildings staring with blind eyes at the shards of civilization.

After the cities went, and the deliberately spread diseases and blights shattered the world's culture into fratricidal savages fighting for the scraps, there was no more need of professors but a desperate shortage of mechanics and technicians. Southvale, by-passed by war, a college town in the agricultural Midwest, drew into itself a tight communistic dictatorship defending what it had with blood and death. It was cruel, that no-admission policy. There had been open battles with wandering starvelings. But the plagues were kept out, and they had saved enough food for most of them to survive even that first terrible winter after the war-strewn blights and insects had devoured the crops. But farm machinery had to be kept going. It had to be converted to horse, ox, and human power when gasoline gave out. So Wayne was assigned to the machine shop and, somewhat to his own surprise, turned out to be an excellent technician. His talents for robbing now useless tractors and automobiles in search of spare parts for the literally priceless food machines got his nickname changed to Cannibal, and he rose to general superintendent.

That was a long time ago, and conditions had improved since. The dictatorship was relaxed now, but Southvale still didn't need professors, and it had enough elementary teachers for its waning child population. So Wayne was still machine shop boss. In spite of which, he was only a very tired man in patched and greasy overalls, going home to supper, and his thoughts darkened as he saw his child.

Alaric Wayne crossed the ruinous bridge a few yards upriver and joined his father. They were an odd contrast, the man tall and stooped with grayed hair and a long, lined face; the boy small for his fourteen years, lean and ragged, his frail-looking body too short for his long legs, his head too big for both. Under ruffled brown hair his face was thin, almost intense in its straight-lined, delicately cut pensiveness, but his huge light-blue eyes were vacant and unfocused.

"Where've you been all day, son?" asked Wayne. He didn't really expect an answer, and got none. Alaric rarely spoke, didn't even seem to hear most questions. He was looking blankly ahead now, like a blind creature, but for all his gawky appearance moved with a certain grace.

Wayne's glance held only pity, his mind only an infinite weariness. *And this is the future. The war, loading air and earth with radioactive colloids, dust, which won't burn out for a century. Not enough radioactivity to be lethal to any but highly susceptible individuals—but enough to saturate our organisms and environment, enough to start an explosion of mutations in every living creature. This was man's decision, to sell his birthright, his racial existence, for the sovereign prerogatives of nations existing today only in name and memory. And what will come of it, nobody can know.*

They walked up a hill and onto the street. Grass had grown between paving blocks, and tumbledown houses stood vacantly in weed-covered lots. A little farther on, though, they came into the district still inhabited. The population had fallen to about half the prewar, through privation and battle as well as causes which had once been more usual. At first glance, Southvale had a human, almost medieval look. A horse-drawn wagon creaked by. Folk went down toward the market place in rude homespun clothes, carrying torches and clumsy lanterns. Candlelight shone warmly through the windows of tenanted houses.

Then one saw the dogs and horses and cattle more closely—and the children. And knew what an irrevocable step had been taken, knew that man would, in a racial sense, no longer be human.

A small pack of grimy urchins raced by, normal by the old standards, normal too in their shouting spite: "Mutie! Mutie! Yaaah, mu*tant!*" Alaric did not seem to notice them, but his dog bristled and growled. In the dusk the animal's high round head, hardly canine, seemed demoniac, and his eyes gleamed red.

Then another band of children went by, as dirty and tattered as the first, but—not human. Mutant. No two alike. A muzzled beast face. An extra finger or more, or a deficiency. Feet like toeless, horny-skinned hoofs. Twisted skeletons, grotesque limping gait. Pattering dwarfs. Acromegalic giants, seven feet tall at twelve years of age. A bearded six-year-old. Things even worse—

Not all were obviously deformed. Most mutations were, of course, unfavorable, but none in that group were cripplingly handicapped. Several looked entirely normal, and their internal differences had been discovered more or less accidentally. Probably many of the "human" children had some such variation, unsuspected, or a latent mutation that would show up later. Nor were all the deviations deformities. Extremely long legs or an abnormally high metabolism, for instance, had advantages as well as disadvantages.

Those were the two kinds of children in Southvale and, by report, the world. A third pitiful group hardly counted, that of hopelessly crippled mutants, born with some handicap of mind or body which usually killed them in a few years.

At first, the tide of abnormal births following the war had brought only horror and despair. Infanticide had run rampant, but today, there were asylums for unwanted children. People knew their child had about three chances in four of being mutant to a greater or lesser degree—but, after all, there *could* be a human, if not this time then next—or even a genuinely favorable mutation.

But Wayne had not seen or heard of any such, and doubted that he ever would. There were so many ways of not doing something, and even an unquestionably good characteristic seemed to involve some loss elsewhere. Like the Martin kid, with his eagle-keen eyes and total deafness.

He waved to that boy, running along with the mutant band, and got an answer. The rest ignored him. Mutants were shy of humans, often resentful and suspicious. And one could hardly blame them. This first generation had been hounded unmercifully by the normal children as it grew up, and had had to endure a lot of abuse and discrimination on the part of adults. No wonder they drew together, and said little to anyone except their fellows. Today, with most of their persecutors grown up, the mutants were a majority among the children, but they still had nothing to do with humans of their generation beyond a few fights. The older ones generally realized that *they* would inherit the earth, and were content to wait. Old age and death were their allies.

But Alaric— The old uncertain pain stirred in Wayne. He didn't know. Certainly the boy was mutant; an X-ray, taken when the town machine had recently been put back into service, had shown his internal organs to be reversed in position. And apparently the mutation involved moronic traits, for he spoke so little and so poorly, had flunked out of elementary school, and seemed wholly remote from the world outside him. But—well, the kid read omnivorously, and at tremendous speed if he wasn't just idly turning pages. He tinkered with apparatus Wayne had salvaged from the abandoned college labs, though there seemed to be no particular purpose to his actions. And every now and then he made some remark which might be queerly significant—unless, of course, that was only his parents' wishful thinking.

Well, Alaric was all they had now. Little Ike, born before the war, had died of hunger the first winter. Since Al's birth they'd had no more children. The radioactivity seemed to have a slow sterilizing effect on many people.

Karen met them at the door. The mere sight of her blond vivacity lifted Wayne's spirits. "Hello, gentlemen," she said. "Guess what?"

"I wouldn't know," answered Wayne.

"Government jet was here today. We're going to get regular air service."

"No kidding!"

"Honest Injun, I have it straight from the pilot, a colonel no less. I was down by the port, on the way to market, about noon, when it landed, and of course forced my way into the conversation."

"You wouldn't have to," said Wayne admiringly.

"Flatterer! Anyway, he was informing the mayor officially, and a few passersby like myself threw in their two bits' worth."

"Hm-m-m." Wayne entered the house. "Of course, I knew the government was starting an airline, but I never thought we'd get a place on it even if we do have a cleared area euphemistically termed an airport."

"Anyway, think of it. We'll get clothes, fuel, machinery, food—no, I suppose we'll be shipping that ourselves. Apropos which, soup's on."

It was a good meal, plain ingredients but imaginative preparation. Wayne attacked it vigorously, but his mind was restless. "Funny," he mused, "how our culture overreached itself. It grew top-heavy and collapsed in a war so great we had to start almost over again. But we had some machines and enough knowledge to rebuild without too many intervening steps. Our railroads and highways, for instance, are gone, but now we're replacing them with a national airline. We'll likewise go later directly from foot and horseback to private planes."

"And we won't be isolated any more, contacting the outside maybe four times a year. We'll be part of the world again."

"Mm-m-m—what's left of it, and that isn't much. Europe and most of Asia, they tell me, are too far gone to make intercourse worthwhile or even possible. The southern parts of this country and the greater part of Latin America are still pretty savage. Most people who survived the war migrated there later, to escape cold and hunger. Result—overcrowding, more famine, fighting and general lawlessness. Those who stuck it out here in the north and stayed alive came out better in the end."

"It'll be a curious new culture," said Karen thoughtfully. "Scattered towns and villages, connected by airlines so fast that cities probably won't need to grow up again. Stretches of wild country between, and—well, it'll be strange."

"Certainly that. But we can hardly extrapolate at this stage of the game. Look, we here in Southvale, and a lot of similarly circumstanced places, have been able to relax for some ten years now. Blights and bugs and plagues pretty well licked, outlaws rounded up or gone into remote areas—Well, we've been back on our feet that long. Since then, the process of re-integrating the country has gone ahead pretty steadily. We're no longer isolated, as you said. With the government center in Oregon as a sort of central exchange, we've been able to trade some of the things we have for what we need, and now this regular airline service will be the way to a national economy. Martial law was…ah…undeclared nine years ago, and the formal unification of the United States, Canada, and Alaska carried out then. You and I helped elect Drummond to President last time, when the poll plane came around."

"I know a little of that already, O omniscient one. What is all this leading up to?"

"Simply that in spite of all which has been accomplished, there's still a long ways to go… South of us is anarchic barbarism. We have precarious contact with some towns in Latin America, Russia, China, Australia, and South Africa, otherwise we're an island of, shall I say, civilization in a planetary sea of savagery and desolation. What will come of that? Or still more important—what will come of the mutants?"

Karen's eyes were haggard as they searched Alaric's unheeding face. "Perhaps at last—the superman," she whispered.

"Not at all probable, clear. You read the official book explaining this thing. Since most mutations are recessive, though they do tend to follow certain patterns, there must have been an incredible totality of altered genes for so many to find their mates and show up in the first generation. Even after the radioactivity is gone, there'll be all those unmatched genes, waiting for a complement to become manifest. For several centuries, there'll be no way to tell what sort of children any couple will have, unless the geneticists figure out some system we don't even suspect at present. Even then, the mutated genes would still be there; we couldn't do anything about that. God only knows what the end result will be—but it won't be human."

"There may be other senses of that word."

"There will be, inevitably. But they won't be today's."

"Still—if all the favorable characteristics showed up in one individual, he'd be a superman."

"You assume no unfavorable ones, possibly linked, will appear. And the odds against it are unguessable. Anyway, what is a superman? Is he a bulletproof organism of a thousand horsepower? Is he a macrocephalic dwarf talking in calculus? I suppose you mean a godlike being, a greatly refined and improved human. I grant you, a few minor changes in human physique would be desirable though not at all necessary. But any semanticist will tell you Homo sapiens are a million miles from realizing his full mental capacities. He needs training right now, not evolution."

"In any case," finished Wayne grayly. "we're arguing a dead issue. Homo sapiens have committed race suicide. The mutants will *be* man."

"Yes—I suppose so. What do you think of the steak?"

Wayne settled down in his easy-chair after supper. Tobacco and newspapers were not being produced, and the government was still taking all the radios made in its new or revived factories. But he had a vast library, his own books and those he had salvaged from the college, and most of them were timeless. He opened a well-thumbed little volume and glanced at lines he knew by heart.

> *For a' that an a' that,*
> *It's comin' yet for a' that.*
> *When men to men, the whole world o'er,*
> *Shall brothers be for a' that.*

I wonder. How often I've wondered! And even if Burns was right, will the plowman's common sense apply to non-humanness? Let's see what another has to say—

> *And we, that now make merry in the Room*
> *They left, and Summer dresses in new bloom,*
> *Ourselves must we beneath the Couch of Earth*
> *Descend—ourselves to make a Couch—for whom?*

His gaze descended to Alaric. The boy sprawled on the floor in a litter of open books. His eyes darted from one to another, skipping crazily, their blankness become a weird blue flicker. The books—*Theory of Functions, Nuclear Mechanics,*

Handbook of Chemistry and Physics, Principles of Psychology, Rocket Engineering, Biochemistry. None of it could be skimmed through, or alternated that way. The greatest genius of history couldn't do it. And a senseless jumble like that—No, Alaric was just turning pages. He must be—a moron?

Well, I'm tired. Might as well go to bed. Tomorrow's Sunday—good thing we can take holidays again, and sleep late.

There were a good fifty men in Richard Hammer's gang, and about ten women equally gaunt and furtive and dangerous. They moved slowly along the riverbank, cursing the rocks they stumbled on, but in a ferocious whisper. Overhead a half moon gave vague light from a cloudy sky. The river sped on its way, moonlight shimmering fitfully off its darkness, and an uncertain wind ghosted through soughing trees. Somewhere a dog howled, and a wild cow bellowed alarm for her calf—descendants of domestic animals that ran free when their masters fled or died. And most savage of all the creatures moving through that night were the humans who had likewise been thrust back into wildness.

"Dick! How much longer, Dick?"

Hammer turned at the low call and scowled back at the uncertain shapes of his followers. "Shut up," he growled. "No talkin' on march."

"I'll talk when I please." The voice was louder.

Hammer hunched his great shoulders and thrust his battered hairy face aggressively into the moonlight. "I'm still boss," he said quietly. "Anytime you wanta fight me for the job, go ahead."

He had their only remaining firearm, a rifle slung over his back and a belt of a few cartridges, but with knife and club, fists and feet and teeth he was also the deadliest battler in the gang. That was all which had kept him alive, those unending dreadful years of feud and famine and hopeless drifting, for no gang-man was ever safe and a boss, with his own jealous subordinates to watch as well as outsiders, least of all.

"O.K., O.K.," yielded the other man sullenly. "Only I'm tired an' hungry, we been goin' so long—"

"Not much farther," promised Hammer. "I rec'nize this territory. Come on—an' quiet!"

They moved ahead, stumbling, half asleep with weariness and the terrible gnawing void in their bellies was all that kept them going. It had been a long journey, hundreds of miles of devastated southland, and it was hard, bitterly hard to pass these comparatively rich farms without lifting more than a few chickens or ears of corn. But Hammer was insistent on secrecy, and he had dominated them long enough for most of them to give in more or less automatically. He had not yet chosen to reveal his plans, but this far into "enemy" country they must involve fighting.

The moon was lowering when Hammer called a halt. They had topped a high ridge overlooking a darker mass some two miles off, a town, "You can sleep now," said the chief. "We'll attack shortly before sunrise. We'll take the place an' then—food! Houses! Women! Likker! An'—more."

The gang was too tired then to care about anything but sleep. They stretched on the ground, lank animal figures in clumsy garments of leather and ragged homespun, carrying knives and clubs, axes, even spears and bows. Hammer squatted motionless, a great bearded gorilla of a man, his massive face turned toward the sleeping town. A pair of his lieutenants, lean young men with something hard and deadly in their impassive countenances, joined him.

"O.K., Dick, what's the idea?" muttered one. "We don't just go tearin' in; if that was all, there're towns closer to where we came from. What're you cookin' now?"

"Plenty," said Hammer: "Now don't get noisy, an' I'll explain. My notion'll give us more'n a few days' food an' rest an' celebration. It'll give us—home."

"Home!" whispered the other outlaw. His cold eyes took on an odd remote look. "Home! The word tastes queer. I ain't spoke it so long—"

"I useta live here, before the war," said Hammer softly and tonelessly. "When things blew up, though, I was in the army. The plagues hit my unit, an' those who didn't die the first week went over the hill. I headed south, figgerin' the country'd busted up an' I'd better go where it'd be warm. Only too many other people got the same idea."

"You've told us that much before."

"I know, I know, but—anybody who lived through it can't forget it. I still see those men dyin'—the plague eatin' 'em. Well, we fought for food. Separate gangs attacked when they met. Until at last there were few enough left an' things picked up a little. So I j'ined the village an' tried farmin'."

The dog howled again, closer. There was an eerie quavering in that cry, something never voiced before the mutations began. "That mutt," growled one of the gang-men, "will wake the whole muckin' town."

"Nah, this place has been peaceful too long," said Hammer." You can see that. No guards nowhere. Why, there're sep'rate farms. *We* had to fight other men, an' then when we finally settled down, it was the bugs an' blights, an' at last the floods washed our land from under us an' we had to take to gang life again. Then I remembered my ol' home town Southvale. Nice farmin' land, not too bad weather, an' judgin' by reports an' rumors about this region, settled down, a'most rich. So I thought I'd come back—"Hammer's teeth gleamed white under the moon.

"Well, you always did love t'hear y'rself talk. Now suppose you say what your deal is."

"Just this. The town's cut off from outside by ordinary means. Once we hold it, we can easy take care o' the outlyin' farms an' villages. *But*—you can see the gov'ments's been here. Few bugs in the crops, so somebody must'a been sprayin'. A jet overhead yesterday. An' so on."

They stirred uneasily. One muttered, "'We don't want no truck with the gov'ment. They'll hang us f'r this."

"If they can! They're really not so strong. They ain't got aroun' to the South at all, 'cept f'r one or two visits. Way I figger it there's only one gov'ment center to speak of, this town out in Oregon we heard about. We can find out 'zac'ly from the people we catch. They'll tell!

"Now look. The gov'ment must deal with Southvale, one way 'r 'nother. There ain't enough cars 'r roads, they must use planes. That means one'll land in Southvale, sooner 'r later. The pilot steps out—an' we've got us a plane. I ain't forgot how to fly. A few o' us 'r maybe we can ferry a lot, fly to Oregon an' land at night near the house o' some big shot, the President even, whoever he is. The plane's pilot'll tell us what we need to know. Those jets just whisper along, an' anyway nobody expects air attack any more. We'll be just another incomin' plane if they do spot us.

"We capture our big shot, an' find out from him where the atom bombs're kept. There must be some stockpiled near the city, an' our man'll make a front f'r us to get at 'em. If he ain't scared f'r himself, he's got a family. We set the bombs an' clear out. The city blows. No more gov'ment worth mentionin'. With what we've taken from the arsenals, we'll hold Southvale an' all this territory. We'll be bosses, owners—kings! Maybe later we c'n go on an' conquer more land. There'll be no gov'ment t' stop us."

He stood up. His eyes caught the moonlight in a darkly splendid vision of power and destiny, for he was not, in his own estimate, a robber. Hardened by pain and sorrow and the long bitter fight to stay alive, he was more of a conqueror, with the grandiose dreams and at least something of the driving energy and transcendent genius of an Alexander or a Napoleon. He genuinely hoped to improve the lot of his own people, and as for others—well, "stranger" and "enemy" had been synonymous too long for him to give that side of it much thought now.

"No more hunger," he breathed. "No more cold an' wet, no more hidin' an' runnin' from a stronger gang, no more walkin' an' walkin' an' never gettin' nowheres. Our kids won't die before they're weaned, they'll grow up as God meant they should, free an' happy an' safe. We c'n build our own future, boys—I seem t' see it now, a tall city reachin' f'r the sun."

His lieutenants stirred uneasily. After some ten years of association they recognized their chief's strange moods but could not fathom them. His enormous ambitions were beyond the scope of minds focused purely on the daily struggle for life, they were awed and half afraid. But even his legion of enemies and rivals acknowledged Hammer's skill and audacity and luck. This might work.

Their own ideas of a future went little beyond a house and a harem, But to smash the government was a cause worth giving life for. They associated it with the disaster, and thus with all their woes. And it was their enemy. It would kill them, or at least lock them up, for deeds done when life depended on ruthless action. It would certainly never permit them to hold this green and lovely land.

Unless—unless!

The dog had been snuffling around the outlaw camp, a vague misshapen shadow in the fleeting moonlight. Now he howled once more and trotted down the ridge toward the dark silent mass of the town.

Alaric Wayne woke up at the sound of scratching. For a moment he lay in bed, mind still clouded with sleep. Moonlight streamed through the window to shimmer off the tumbled heaps of books and apparatus littering the room. Outside, the world was a black and white fantasy of bulking shadow, dreaming off into the remote star-torched sky.

Full wakefulness came. Alaric slid out of bed, went to the window, and leaned against the screen. It was his dog, scratching to get in. And—excited. He raised the screen and the animal jumped clumsily over the sill.

The dog whined, pulled at Alaric's leg, sniffed toward the south and shivered. The boy's great light eyes seemed to deepen and brighten, flash cold in the pouring moonlight; shadow-masked; his thin face was not discernible, but its habitual blankness slid into tight lines.

He had to—think!

The dog was warning him of danger from the south. But, though the mutation shaping the canine brain had given it abnormal intelligence, he was still a dog, not qualitatively different from the rest of his species, not able to understand or reason above an elementary level. Three years before, Alaric had spotted qualities in the pup by certain signs, and raised and trained it, and there was a curious half-rapport between them, a mutual understanding. They had co-operated earlier, on their long hikes, to hunt or to avoid the wild dog packs, but now—

There was danger. Men outside town, to the south with hostile intentions. That was all the dog had been able to gather. It would have been enough for any normal human, as a basis of action. But Alaric wasn't normal.

He stood shivering with effort, clenching his hands to his forehead as if to prevent a physical disintegration of his frantically groping brain. What did it mean? What to do?

Danger—danger was clear enough, and primitive instinct revealed the action one must take. One ran from the packs of human boys when they intended to commit mayhem on a mutant, and hid. One skirted the spoor of wild dogs or the bears beginning to spread since hunting fell off. Only in this case—slowly, reluctantly, fighting itself, his shuddering mind spewed out the conclusion—in this case, one couldn't run. If the town went, so did all safety.

Think—*think!* There was danger, it couldn't be run from—what to do? His mind groped in fog and chaos. It could grasp at nothing. Disjointed logic chains clanked insanely in his skull.

Reason did not supply the answer, but instinct came, the instinct which would have surged to the fore under the pressure of immediate peril, and now finally broke through the swirling storm of a mind trying to think.

Why—it was so simple. Alaric relaxed, eyes widening with the sheer delightful simplicity of it. It was, really, as obvious as—why, it had all the primitive elementariness of the three-body problem. If you couldn't run from danger—you fought it!

Fighting—destruction—yes, something to destroy, but he would only have the newly reclaimed powerhouse available—

He scrambled into his clothes with frantic speed. A glance at stars and moon told him, without his thinking about it, how long to sunrise. Not long—and in his own way he knew the enemy would attack just before dawn. He had to hurry!

He vaulted out the window and ran down the silent street, the dog following. All the town's electrical and electronic equipment was stored at the powerhouse.

It would be quite a while before the whole community had electricity again, but meanwhile the plant ran several important machines, charged storage batteries, and performed other essential services.

The building stood beside the river, the only lit windows in town besides the police station glowing from its dark bulk. After the war there had been no time, supplies, or parts to spare for the generators, and they had been plundered to repair the vital farm equipment, but recently the government had delivered what was necessary to get the water turbines going again. It had occasioned a formal celebration in Southvale—another step up the ladder, after that long fall down.

Alaric beat on the door, yelling wordlessly. There came the sound of a scraping chair and the maddeningly slow shuffle of feet. Alaric jittered on the steps, gasping. No time, no time!

The door creaked open and the night watchman blinked myopically at Alaric. He was an old man, and hadn't gotten new glasses since the war. "Who're you?" he asked. "And what do you want at this hour?"

Alaric brushed by unheedingly and made for the storeroom. He knew what he needed and what he must do with it, but the job was long and time was growing so desperately short.

"Here…hey, you!" The watchman hobbled after him, shaking with indignation. "You crazy mutie, what do you think you're doing—?"

Alaric shook loose the clutching hand and gestured to his dog. The mongrel snarled and bristled, and the watchman stumbled back, white-faced. "Help!" It was a high old man's yell. "Help, burglar—"

Somehow words came, more instinctive than reasoned. "Shut up," said Alaric, "or dog kill you." He meant it.

The animal added emphasis with a bass growl and a vicious snap of fangs. His head reeling, his heart seeming to burst his ribs, the watchman sank into a chair and the dog sat down to watch him.

The storeroom door was locked. Alaric grabbed a heavy wrench and beat down a panel. Tumbling into the storeroom, he grabbed for what he needed. Wire—meters—electronic tubes—batteries—*hurry, hurry!*

Dragging it out into the main room before the great droning generators, he squatted down, a tatterdemalion gnome, eyes like blued metal, face tautened into a savagery of concentration, and got to work. Through a visual blur, the guard stared in uncomprehending terror. The dog watched him steadily, with sullen malevolent hope that he would try something. It was embittering, to hate all the world save one being, because only that being understood—

False dawn glimmered wanly over the land, touching houses and fields with wandering ghost fingers, glittering briefly off the swift-flowing river before deeper darkness returned. Hammer's gang woke with the instant animal alertness of their kind, and stirred in the fog-drifting twilight. Their scant clothes were heavy with dew, they were cold and hungry—how hungry!—and they looked down at the moveless mass of their goal with smoldering savage yearning.

"Fair is the land," whispered Hammer, "more fair 'n land's ever been. The fields 're green t' harvest an' the fog runs white over a river like a polished knife—

an' it's our land, our home." His voice rose in hard snapping command: "Joe, take twenty men an' circle north. Come in by the main road, postin' men at the edge o' town an' the bridge over the river, then wait in the main square. Buck, take your fifteen, circle west, an' come in the same time as Joe, postin' men outside town an' in that big buildin' halfway down Fifth Street—that's the machine shop, as I recall, an' I *hope* you c'n still read street signs. Then join Joe. The rest follow me straight no'th. Go as quiet as you can, slug 'r kill anyone you meet, an' be ready f'r a fight but don't start one. O.K.!"

The two other groups filed down the hill and vanished into misty dusk. Hammer waited awhile. He had previously divided the gang into bands assigned to his lieutenants, reserving the best men for the group immediately under him. He spoke to them, softly but with metallic rapidity:

"Accordin' t' what I remember o' Southvale, an' to what I seen elsewhere, they don't expect nothin' like this. There've been no bandits here f'r a long time, an' anyway they'd never think a gang had the skill and self-control t' sneak through the fat lands farther south. So there'll be no patrol, just a few cops on their beats—an' too sleepy this time t' give us much trouble. An' nearly all the weapons 're gonna be in the police station—which is what we're gonna capture. With guns, we'll control the town. But f'r the love of life, don't start shootin' till I say to. There may be armed citizens, an' they c'n raise hell with us 'nless we handle 'em right."

A low mutter of assent ran along that line of haggard, bearded, fierce-eyed men. Knives and axes glittered in the first dim dawn-flush, bows were strung and spears hefted. But there was no restlessness, no uncontrollable lust to be off and into battle. They had learned patience the hard way, the last sixteen years. They waited.

Timing wasn't easy to judge, but Hammer had developed a sense for it which had enabled him to pull several coups in the past and served him now. When he figured the other groups were near the outskirts of town, he raised his hand in signal, slipped the safety catch on his gun, and started down the hill at a rapid trot.

The white mists rolled over the ground, but they needed nothing to muffle the soft pad of their feet, most bare and all trained in quietness. Grass whispered under their pace, a staked-out cow lowed, and a rooster greeted the first banners of day. Otherwise there was silence, and the town dreamed on in the cool twilight.

They came onto the cracked pavement of the road, and it was strange to be going on concrete again. They passed an outer zone of deserted houses. As Hammer had noticed elsewhere, Southvale had drawn into a compact defensive mass during the black years and not grown out of it since. As long as there were no fortified outposts, such an arrangement was easy to overrun. Still, the outlaws were enormously outnumbered, and had to counter-balance the disadvantage by the cold ruthlessness of direct action. Hammer stopped at the edge of habitation, told off half a dozen men to patrol the area, and led the rest on to the middle of town. They went more slowly now, senses strainingly alert, every nerve and muscle taut with the expectancy of danger.

Hoofs clattered from a side street. Hammer gestured to a bowman, who grinned and bent his weapon. A mounted policeman came into view a few blocks down. He wasn't impressive, he had no sign of office except gun and tarnished badge, he was sleepy and eager to report to the station and then get home. His wife would have breakfast ready—

The bow twanged, a great bass throb of music in the silent misty street. The policeman pitched out of his saddle, the arrow through his breast, the astonishment on his face so ridiculous that a couple of gangmen guffawed. Hammer cursed; the horse had reared, screamed, and then galloped on down the street. The clattering echoes beat at the walls of the house like alarm-crying sentries.

A man stuck his head out the window of a dwelling. He was drowsy, but he saw the unkempt band outside and yelled—a choked gurgle it was, drowned in an arrow's blood-track before it had been properly born.

"Snagtooth an' Mex, get in that house an' silence anyone else!" rapped Hammer. "You five"—he swept an arm in an unconsciously imperial gesture—"take care o' anyone else here who heard. The rest *come on!*"

They ran down the street, disregarding noise but not making much anyway. The town had changed considerably, but Hammer remembered the layout. The police station, he thought briefly and wryly, he knew very well—just about every Saturday night, in the old days.

They burst onto that block and raced for the station. There it was, the same square and solid structure, dingy now with years, the trimmings gone, but there were horses hitched before it and the door stood ajar—

Through the door! The desk sergeant and a couple of men gaped blankly down the muzzle of Hammer's gun, their minds refusing to comprehend, their hands rising by stunned automatism. Others of the gang poured down the short halls, into every room. There came yells, the clatter of feet, the brief sharp bark of a gun and the racket of combat.

Hoofs pounded outside. A gun cracked, and one of Hammer's men standing guard at the door, fell. Hammer himself jumped to the window, smashed the glass of it with his rifle butt, and shot at the half-dozen or so mounted police outside—returning from their beats, no doubt, and alarmed at what they saw.

He had little opportunity to practice. Shells were too scarce. His first shot went wild, the second hit a horse, the third was as ineffectual as the first. But the police did retreat. They weren't such good shots either, though a couple of slugs whined viciously close, through the window and thudding into the wall beyond.

"Here, Dick!" His men were returning from the interior of the building, and they bore firearms, bore them as they would something holy and infinitely beautiful, for these were the way to a life worth living. "Here—shootin' weapons!"

Hammer grabbed a submachine gun and cut loose. The troopers scattered, leaving their dead, and fled down the streets. And there were those other two bands entering—Hammer laughed for sheer joy.

"We got the whole station," reported one of his men. "Bob got it in the leg, an' I see they plugged Little Jack an' Tony. But the place is ours!"

"Yeah. Lock up these cops, take what weapons an' horses you need, an' ride aroun' town, Herd ever'body down into the main square in the center o' town. Be careful, there'll be some trouble an' killin', but we don't have to be on the receivin' end o' any o' it. Mart, Rog, an' One-Ear, hold the station here an' look after our wounded, Sambo an' Putzy, follow me. I'm goin' t' the square now to—take possession!"

There was noise in the street, running and stamping feet, shouts and oaths and screams. Now and then laughter or gunfire. Roderick Wayne gasped out of sleep, sweating. What a dream! Nightmare recollection of the black years—
No dream!
There was a tremendous kicking and beating on the door, and a voice bawling in some uncouth accent: "Open up in there! Open up in the name o' the law!"
More' laughter, like wolves baying. Someone yelling. A cry that choked off into silence. Wayne jumped out of bed. Even then he was dimly surprised to find he wasn't shaking and gibbering in blind panic. "Get Al, Karen," he said. "Stay inside, in a back room. I've got to look into this."
He stopped in the living room to get his rifle. It was only a souvenir now, few cartridges left, but he had killed men with it in the black years. *And must I go through that again? No—please not!*
Wood split and crashed, and a man leaped into the house over the fallen door. Wayne saw the pistol and dropped his own unloaded rifle. He remembered such ragged figures, the shaggy wolf-eyed men whose weapons were all too ready. The outlaws had returned.
"Smart," nodded the gangman. " 'Nother see 'n' I'd'a scragged you. Outside."
"What...is...this?" Wayne's lips were stiff.
"Get out!"
Wayne went obliquely, praying he could draw the bandit out of the house. "If it's loot you want," he said, fighting to keep his voice level, "I'll show you where the silver is."
Another gangman entered. He had abandoned his unaccustomed gun for his old ax. "Ever'body out o' here?" he asked.
"I just got in," said the first. "I'll search it myself. Find y'r own house." He turned on Wayne and slammed him in the stomach with one fist, "Scram, you—down t' the main square!"
Retching, Wayne staggered back, and outside mostly by chance. Sick and dizzy, head roaring like his collapsing world, he leaned against the wall.
"Rod!"
He turned, unbelieving. Karen had just come around the side of the house, pale but outwardly composed. "Are you all right, Rod?" she whispered.
"Yeah...yeah...but you...how—?"
"I heard them talking and slipped out a window. But Rod—Al's gone."
"Gone!" Briefly, new dismay shook Wayne. Al—whatever the mutant was, Al was his son. Then relief came, realization. "He must have sneaked out, too. He's

all right. He knows how to run and hide—all mutant kids learn that." His mind added grayly: *And in the next generation all human kids will have to learn it.*

"But us—Rod, what is this?"

Wayne shrugged and started down the street. "Town's apparently captured," he said.

"Outlaws—we have to run, Rod! Have to get away!"

"Not much use, I'm afraid. This is the work of a well-disciplined group under a smart leader. They must have come up from the south, resisting the temptation to plunder on the way. They took us by complete flat-footed surprise, overpowered the police—I recognized Ed Haley's pistol in that bandit's hand—and are now rounding us up in quite a methodical fashion. I wasn't just shoved out, I was ordered to report to the square. That suggests they're guarding all ways out. Anyway, we can't flee right now."

They had fallen in with a group of citizens moving with the dumb blank obedience of stunned minds toward the square under outlaw guard, The gang was having little trouble. They went from house to house, forcing the inhabitants into the street. The work went fast.

There was fighting now and then, short and sharp, ending in blow of club or knife or bullet. A couple of families with guns stood off the invaders. Wayne saw fire arrows shot into the roofs of those houses.

He shuddered and bent his head to Karen's ear. "We do have to get out as soon as we can," he muttered. "*If* we can. They're disciplined now, and wholly merciless. Once we're completely rounded up, the discipline will break but the ruthlessness stay in such an orgy of looting and drinking, burning and rape and murder, as has always followed barbarian conquests."

"They can't stay long," she answered desperately. "The government…this is on the air route—"

"That's what I can't figure out. They must know they can't remain, so why did they come here in the first place? Why not raid the lands closer to home? Well—we'll have to see, that's all."

The—herd—of citizens entered the square and walked toward the little memorial in its center with the queer blind shuffle that cattle in a stockyard chute have. There were other outlaw guards posted around the square and on the memorial, weapons ready. The monument was a granite shaft with a stone bench on each side, and seated there—

Wayne did not remember the bearded giant, but Karen caught a sudden gasp of recognition. "It…it…Rod, it's Hammer. Richard Hammer!"

"Eh?"

"Don't you recall—the mechanic at the service station—we always used to get our gas there, and once when I smashed a fender on the car he fixed it so you wouldn't notice—"

The chief heard them. There weren't many people in the square yet, and the early sun struck dazzling off Karen's hair. "Why, it's Miz' Wayne." he said. "Howdy Miz' Wayne."

"H-h-hello," faltered Karen.

"Lookin' purtier 'n ever, too. Wayne, you had all the luck."

The mathematician shouldered his way forward, suddenly weak with a dreadful clawing fear. "Hammer—what is this?" he got out.

"I'm takin' over Southvale. Meet y'r new boss."

"You—" Wayne swallowed. He choked down the panic rising in him and said in a level, toneless voice: "I gather you've become chief of this band and led it back here for a raid. But—you must know you can't get away with it. We're on an airline route. The government will know."

Hammer smiled wearily. "I've figgered all that out. I intend to stay here. I'm gatherin' all the folks t' tell 'em t' be good, because we don't mind killin'. But if y're really interested—" He sketched his further plans.

"You're crazy—it's not possible."

"A lot o' less possible things have happened. If you all, not too far no'th, felt safe, what about the gov'ment 'way out in Oregon? We'll do it!"

"But even if you can—Hammer, do you realize the government is the only link left with our past, our civilization? You'd throw man back a thousand years."

"So what? Wayne, don't you nor anybody else hand me none o' that crap 'bout law an' order an' humanity. You're fifteen years too late. You an' your kind made us outlaws, drivin' us away when we came starvin' to you, houndin' us south an' then in your fat smugness forgettin' about us. It's been hard, Wayne, battle an' death an' hunger all those years. We had t' get hard ourselves, t' stay alive."

"You could have stuck it out in the north as we did, and raised your own food free from most bandits."

"Free only because so many people like us went south. Nor were most o' us farmers, with land an' equipment an' experience. Anyway you did drive us out when you were strong. I ain't blamin' you. You had t' live. But it's our turn now, so shut up." Hammer's eaglesque eyes swung to Karen, he smiled. It was a winter-cold smile, warmth and humor had died long ago in him. "You, I'll be seein' more of," he said. "It's been so long—"

The square was well filled with people now, and more were arriving and being herded into side streets and buildings. Some were still numb. Some wept or prayed or implored or tried to ingratiate themselves, some cursed and threatened, some retreated into impassive silence. But—prisoners all. Captured, impotent, legitimate prey.

Hammer turned as an outlaw galloped up, thrusting his horse through the crowd without regard for their safety. "What is it?" asked the chief, not anxiously. His victory was too tremendously evident.

"I dunno—some trouble down by the river," said the gangman. "About half Joe's detail ain't showed up yet."

"Hm-m-m? Musta found some likker."

"Yeah—Hey—*What's that?*"

Hammer turned. He couldn't see much sitting down. Huge and shaggy and ablaze with the arrogance of his triumph, he sprang lithely onto the bench and looked north along the street. He grinned, then laughed, then shouted with humorless mirth. "Lamp that, boys. Some crazy mutie—*look* at him!"

Wayne was so placed that he could also see down that street. His heart staggered, for a black instant he couldn't believe, refused to comprehend, then—

"*Alaric.*"

The boy was coming down the street, walking slowly and carrying an object, a fantastic wire-tangled grotesquerie of electronic surrealism, thrown together in the wildest haste and with no recognizable design. A wire led from it to a reel of cable mounted on a mule's back, and the cable snaked behind, along the road—it must go clear to the powerhouse!

How had Al done it? That cable was sacrosanct, reserved for electrifying the airport. That apparatus, the invaluable parts in it—how had he gotten them? How—why? *Why*! What mad vagary of a reasonless brain had prompted him to go thus on this darkest of mornings? What—

"Come on, kid," shouted Hammer boisterously. "Whatcha got?"

Alaric came closer. His delicately cast features were set in concentration, his strange light eyes flashing like glacial ice, not a human gleam. He lifted his device and twirled a pair of dials.

"May be a weapon," said a bandit uneasily and raised his rifle.

"Not…Alaric—" It was a hoarse cry from Wayne's throat, and he made a clumsy lunge for the outlaw. Hammer swept one long arm in a careless blow and sent him crashing to the ground.

The gang-man squeezed the trigger on his rifle but never completed the motion. He was dead before that. Wayne, sprawled on his back, looking up through a whirling fog of grief and horror and hopeless defeat, saw the man's body explode.

It went up in a white burst of steam, a crash of rending bone and tissue and a brief glare of incandescence. The rifle flying from him glowed cherry red, blowing up as its cartridges detonated. Before the fragments had fallen, *something* had swept the outer edges of the square, and where the guards had stood were steam-clouded heaps of charred bone and shredded flesh.

The crowd yelled, a single beast cry half of terror, half of surging death-lusting triumph, and swept down on the remaining gangmen. Most were too demoralized to resist. Others struggled, and got a few townspeople before they were trampled under.

Hammer roared, the bellow of a pain-crazed bull, as the mob raged toward him. A horse reared as its outlaw rider was yanked from the saddle. Two slugging blows, and Hammer had cleared a way to the mount. He sprang upon its back, howling, and the attackers fell away from his insane charge.

Almost, he made it. He was on the edge of the square when a man whose brother had been killed made a long jump and grabbed the horse's bridle—grabbed it, and hung on till a dozen men held the gang boss secured.

Only one or two outlaws escaped. The rest, with the town in no mood for trials, were hanged that afternoon. Hammer asked not to be blindfolded, and they granted him that much. To the end, he stood looking out over the sun-glittering river, the rolling tree-clad hills, and the fair broad land green to harvest.

Wayne took no part in the executions. He had other things to think about.

After the celebrations, the unending parades and parties and speeches, the reorganization and the defense tightening, there was a rather grim conference in

Wayne's house. He and Karen were there, seated together before the fire, and Alaric sat opposite them, nervous and bewildered. A government representative was present, a lean man who looked older than he was, Robert Boyd by name and roving presidential agent by profession. In the corner, shadow-cloaked and unnoticed, squatted the shaggy troll-shape of the dog, his sullen eyes brooding redly on the others.

"You've heard the official account," said Wayne, "Alaric, a mutant *idiot savant*, invented and built a weapon to defeat the outlaws. He's been much made of, and nobody pays any attention to Pop Hanson—he's the powerhouse watchman, and was rather rudely treated. One must make allowance for the eccentricity of genius, or so they say."

"Well, one must," nodded Boyd.

"Hardly. If so many of our people hadn't died, I'd say this was a good thing. It taught us not to be complacent and careless. More important, it at least indicated that mutants can serve society as talented members." Wayne's eyes were haggard. "Only, you see, Al didn't behave like a genius. He acted like a low-grade moron."

"Inventing that—"

"Yes, going all around Robin Hood's barn, committing violence and theft, working like a slave, risking his neck, all to build that weapon and use it. But he told me his dog warned him hours ahead of time. Certainly he was at the powerhouse early. Don't you see, we could have been ready for the outlaws, we could have stood them off, driven their ill-armed force away with no loss to us *if Alaric had merely gone to the police with that warning.*"

Thunderstruck, Boyd swung his, eyes to meet the blue vacancy of Alaric's. "Why …why didn't you?"

The boy stared, slowly focusing his vision and mind, face twisted with effort. He…his father had told him the day before…what was it now? Yes—"I … didn't …think of it," he fumbled.

"You didn't think of it. It just never occurred to you." Dazed, Boyd turned to Wayne. "As long as you said it yourself, I agree—*idiot savant.*"

"No." Karen spoke very quietly. "No, not in any ordinary sense. Such a person is feeble-minded in all but one respect, where he is brilliant. I used to teach school and know a little psychology. Yesterday I gave Al some special tests I'd worked out. Science, mechanical skill, comprehension—in too many respects he's a genius,"

"I give up. What *is* he, then?"

"A mutant," said Karen.

"And…this weapon—?"

"Alaric tried to tell me, but we couldn't understand each other," said Wayne. "And the thing itself burned out very quickly in use. It's just fused junk now. From what I could gather, though, and by deduction on that basis, I think it projected an intense beam of an inconceivably complex wave form to which one or more important organic compounds in the body resonate, They disintegrated, releasing their binding forces. Or perhaps it was body colloids that were destroyed, releasing terrific surface energies, I'm just as glad I don't know. There are too many weapons in the world."

"Mm-m-m—officially I can't agree with you, but privately I do. Anyway, the inventor is still here—the genius."

"It takes more than genius," said Wayne. "It just isn't possible for any human being to sit down and figure such a thing out in detail. All the facts are available, in handbooks and texts and papers—quantum mechanics, circuit characteristics, physical constants. But even if he knew exactly what he was after, the greatest genius in the world would have to spend months or years in analytical thought, then more time in putting all those facts together into the pattern he was after. And even then he wouldn't know it all. There'd be a near infinitude of small factors interacting on each other, that he couldn't allow for. He'd have to build a model and experiment with it, the empirical process known to engineers as getting the bugs out.

"In his incoherent way, Alaric told me his only difficulty was to figure out what to do to meet the danger. All he could think of was to make some kind of weapon. But he hardly spent a second working out the details of that devil's engine, and his first model was as nearly perfect as his inadequate tools and materials permitted. He *knew* how to make it."

With a shuddering effort, Boyd relaxed. He couldn't look at that small, big-headed figure in the armchair. The ancient human dread of the unknown was too strong in him. He asked slowly:

"What's the answer, then?"

"Karen and I think we've figured it out, and what little Al can tell us seems to confirm our idea. But I'll have to explain it in a roundabout way. Tell me, how does a person think?"

"Think? Why…well…by logic. He follows a logical track—"

"Exactly! A track. He thinks in chains of logic, if under that we include everything from math to emotional experience. Premise to conclusion. One thing leads to another, one at a time.

"Physics and math have been able to make their great strides because they deal, actually, with the simplest concepts, which are artificially simplified still further. Newton's three laws of motion, for instance, assume that no force beyond the one set being considered is acting on a body in question; and the members of this set can be considered one at a time. We never really observe that. There is always friction, gravitation, or some other disturbing influence. Even in space there are externals. What saves physics is that these externals are usually negligibly small.

"Take a particular case. You know the two-body problem in astronomy? Given two bodies of known mass and distance from each other, and the laws of motion and gravitation, to find their position at any past or future time. Well, it's mathematically simple. It was solved a long time ago, because there are only two interacting bodies, But the three-body problem is quite another story. Right away, with three interactions, it becomes so complex that as far as I know there's never been any general solution, and only a few special ones. As for the *n*-body problem—!

"Now in the biological sciences, including psychology and sociology, you can't simplify. You have to consider the whole. A living organism is an incredibly complex set of interactions, beginning, probably, on the subatomic level and going on up to the universal environment, from which the organism cannot be separated either, acting on and being acted on by that all the time. You *can't* apply our single-track analysis methods to such a case. The result is, of course, that those sciences are almost purely empirical, sociology hardly deserving the name. If, to use an illustration that's been used before, I want to tackle the three-body problem, I can and will start with the special case where one of them has zero mass. But suppose I were making an analysis of the influence of Pan-Asiatic policies on American domestic affairs before the war. I could certainly not ignore the converse case, or the existence of other countries, I'd have to consider them all at once—which no existing math can do. Any results I got would be qualitative, nonmathematical, inexact."

"I think I see," nodded Boyd. "Of course, people can think of two or more things at once."

"That's different," said Karen. "That's a case of divided attention, each branch of the mind following its single track. It's normal enough, though carried to extremes it becomes schizophrenia."

"You get what I'm driving at," went on Wayne. "Our subhuman and human ancestors didn't need to see the world as a whole. They were only concerned with their immediate surroundings and events. So we never evolved the ability to consider an entire entity. Alaric is a mutant—"

"Some different brain structure," said Karen quietly. "The reversed internal organs may or may not be a linked characteristic. The X-rays showed no brain difference. They hardly would, as it's probably a very subtle matter of cellular or colloidal integration."

"Al didn't have to think, in our ordinary sense of the word, of how to make a weapon," added Wayne. "His extensive knowledge of scientific principles and data co-ordinated in his mind to show him that …well, if my guess is right, that the colloids of human bodies are resonant to a particular wave form. And at once he knew all the factors he'd need to generate that wave. It wasn't reason, as we reason, though it was thought—to him, thought on a very elementary, almost intuitive level. Yet he wasn't able to think of telling anybody."

"I see," answered Boyd. "Humans think in chains. *He* thinks in networks."

"Yes, that's about the size of it."

"Do you think…we…can ever do that?"

"Hm-m-m—I don't know. Since intelligence seems to depend on upbringing among normal humans, whereas genius and feeble-mindedness seem more independent of environment, and are hereditary, one might argue that they are both mutations, in the individual or an ancestor. Some people, such as Nikola Tesla, seem to have had a degree of network-thought ability, and the fact that Al is the son of a mathematician, who does deal with complexities, is suggestive. After all, no observed mutation has ever created a totally new characteristic. It would have to create a whole new set of genes for that. A mutation is a greater or less modification of an existing characteristic.

"The point I'm making is that humans naturally think in straight lines, but some sort of network, total-considering logic has been developed. The semanticists have their nonelementalistic principle. In math, we only add in special cases, the rest of the time we integrate, and we have our generalized calculi of vectors and tensors and the like. *But*—it doesn't come naturally. It's been worked out slowly and painfully, through many centuries. To Al, it's the natural way to think; but, as like most mutations it involves a loss elsewhere, the simple straightforward logic of humans is unnatural to him and since he is just a kid, and probably not a genius anyway—merely an ordinary network thinker—he hasn't seen the principles of that logic, any more than a human his age sees the principle of nonelementalism. I'd say, offhand, that both types of mind can learn the other type of thought, but not comprehend or apply it on its higher levels."

"There's another thing," put in Karen. Her eyes held a light which hadn't been there for a long time. "Rod just said it. Al should be able, with the proper training, to learn logic, at least enough to understand and communicate. His kind of thought is not adapted to the simple problems of life, but he can be taught to handle those, as we teach human children to think in terms of abstractions. Maybe...maybe, then, he can teach us something."

Boyd nodded again. "It's certainly worth the attempt," he said. "We have psychiatrists and other specialists at the capital. If we'd known before that you're a mathematician, Wayne, we'd have asked you there, to join the science center with which President Drummond hopes to rebuild our culture on a basis of genuine sanity. Consider yourself invited as of now. And if we and Alaric can come to understand each other—why, Wayne, you may even get your biological and sociological math. Then we may be able to pull ourselves out of this planetary mess."

"I hope so." murmured Wayne. "I certainly hope so, And thanks, Boyd." He smiled tiredly, crookedly. "By the way, Karen, you have your superman there. The greatest genius, in his way, that the world ever saw—and if he hadn't had some kind of protective civilization to grow up in and, now, to teach him the elements of thought, he'd never have lived. I'm afraid this particular kind of superman just isn't a survivor type."

"No," whispered Karen, "nor human. But he's our son."

Time Patrol

-1-

MEN WANTED—21-40, pref. single, mil. or tech. exp., good physique, for high-pay work with foreign travel. Engineering Studies Co., 305 E. 45, 9-12 & 2-6.

"The work is, you understand, somewhat unusual," said Mr. Gordon. "And confidential. I trust you can keep a secret?"

"Normally," said Manse Everard. "Depends on what the secret is, of course."

Mr. Gordon smiled. It was a curious smile, a closed curve of his lips which was not quite like any Everard had seen before. He spoke easy colloquial General American, and wore an undistinguished business suit, but there was a foreignness over him which was more than dark complexion, beardless cheeks, and the incongruity of Mongolian eyes above a thin Caucasian nose. It was hard to place.

"We're not spies, if that's what you're thinking," he said.

Everard grinned. "Sorry. Please don't think I've gone as hysterical as the rest of the country. I've never had access to confidential data anyway. But your ad mentioned overseas operations, and the way things are—I'd like to keep my passport, you understand."

He was a big man, with blocky shoulders and a slightly battered face under crew-cut brown hair. His papers lay before him: Army discharge, the record of work in several places as a mechanical engineer. Mr. Gordon had seemed barely to glance at them.

The office was ordinary, a desk and a couple of chairs, a filing cabinet, and a door leading off in the rear. A window opened on the banging traffic of New York, six stories down.

"Independent spirit," said the man behind the desk. "I like that. So many of them come cringing in, as if they'd be grateful for a kick. Of course, with your background you aren't desperate yet. You can still get work, even in…ah, I believe the current term is a rolling readjustment."

"I was interested," said Everard. "I've worked abroad, as you can see, and would like to travel again. But frankly, I still don't have the faintest idea what your outfit does."

"We do a good many things," said Mr. Gordon. "Let me see…you've been in combat. France and Germany." Everard blinked; his papers had included a record of medals, but he'd have sworn the man hadn't had time to read them. "Um…would you mind grasping those knobs on the arms of your chair? Thank you. Now, how do you react to physical danger?"

Everard bristled. "Look here—"

Mr. Gordon's eyes flicked to an instrument on his desk: it was merely a box with an indicator needle and a couple of dials. "Never mind. What are your views on internationalism?"

"Say, now—"

"Communism? Fascism? Women? Your personal ambitions?…That's all. You don't have to answer."

"What the devil is this, anyway?" snapped Everard.

"A bit of psychological testing. Forget it. I've no interest in your opinions except as they reflect basic emotional orientation." Mr. Gordon leaned back, making a bridge of his fingers. "Very promising so far. Now, here's the set up. We're doing work which is, as I've told you, highly confidential. We…ah…we're planning to spring a surprise on our competitors." He chuckled. "Go ahead and report me to the FBI if you wish. We've already been investigated and have a clean bill of health. You'll find that we really do carry on worldwide financial and engineering operations. But there's another aspect of the job, and that's the one we want men for. I'll pay you one hundred dollars to go in the back room and take a set of tests. It'll last about three hours. If you don't pass, that's the end of it. If you do, we'll sign you on, tell you the facts, and start you training. Are you game?"

Everard hesitated. He had a feeling of being rushed. There was more to this enterprise than an office and one bland stranger. Still…

Decision. "I'll sign on *after* you've told me what it's all about."

"As you wish," shrugged Mr. Cordon. "Suit yourself. The tests will say whether you're going to or not, you know. We use some very advanced techniques."

That, at least, was entirely true. Everard knew a little something about modem psychology: encephalographs, association tests, the Minnesota profile. He did not recognize any of the hooded machines that hummed and blinked around him. The questions which the assistant—a white-skinned, completely hairless man of indeterminate age, with a heavy accent and no facial expression—fired at him seemed irrelevant to anything. And what was the metal cap he was supposed to wear on his head? Into what did the wires from it lead?

He stole glances at the meter faces, but the letters and numerals were like nothing he had seen before. Not English, French, Russian, Greek, Chinese, anything belonging to A.D. 1954. Perhaps he was already beginning to realize the truth, even then.

A curious self-knowledge grew in him as the tests proceeded. Manson Emmert Everard, age thirty, onetime lieutenant in the U.S. Army Engineers; design and production experience in America, Sweden, Arabia; still a bachelor, though with increasingly wistful thoughts about his married friends; no current girl, no close ties of any kind; a bit of a bibliophile; a dogged poker player; fondness for sailboats and horses and rifles; a camper and fisherman on his vacations. He had known it all, of course, but only as isolated shards of fact. It was peculiar, this sudden sensing of himself as an integrated organism, this realization that each characteristic was a single inevitable facet of an overall pattern.

He came out exhausted and wringing wet. Mr. Gordon offered him a cigarette and swept eyes rapidly over a series of coded sheets which the assistant gave him. Now and then he muttered a phrase: "…Zeth-20 cortical…undifferentiated evaluation here…psychic reaction to antitoxin…weakness in central coordination …" He had slipped into an accent, a lilt and a treatment of vowels which were like nothing Everard had heard in a long experience of the ways in which the English language can be mangled.

It was half an hour before he looked up again. Everard was getting restless, a faint anger stirring at this cavalier treatment, but interest kept him sitting quietly. Mr. Gordon flashed improbably white teeth in a broad, satisfied grin. "Ah. At last. Do you know, I've had to reject twenty-four candidates already? But you'll do. You'll definitely do."

"Do for what?" Everard leaned forward, conscious of his pulse picking up.

"The Patrol: You're going to be a kind of policeman."

"Yeah? Where?"

"Everywhere. And everywhen. Brace yourself, this is going to be a shock.

"You see, our company, while legitimate enough, is only a front and a source of funds. Our real business is patrolling time."

-2-

The Academy was in the American West. It was also in the Oligocene period, a warm age of forests and grasslands when man's ratty ancestors scuttled away from the tread of giant mammals. It had been built a thousand years ago; it would be maintained for half a million—long enough to graduate as many as the Time Patrol would require—and then be carefully demolished so that no trace would remain. Later the glaciers would come, and there would be men, and in the year 19352 A.D. (the 7841st year of the Morennian Triumph), these men would find a way to travel through time and return to the Oligocene to establish the Academy.

It was a complex of long, low buildings, smooth curves and shifting colors, spreading over a greensward between enormous ancient trees. Beyond it, hills and woods rolled off to a great brown river, and at night you could sometimes hear the bellowing of titanotheres or the distant squall of a sabertooth.

Everard stepped out of the time shuttle—a big, featureless metal box—with a dryness in his throat. It felt like his first day in the Army, twelve years ago—or fifteen to twenty million years in the future, if you preferred—lonely and helpless, and wishing desperately for some honorable way to go home. It was a small comfort to see the other shuttles, discharging a total of fifty-odd young men and women. The recruits moved slowly together, forming an awkward clump. They didn't speak at first, but stood staring at each other. Everard recognized a Hoover collar and a bowler; the styles of dress and hairdo moved up through 1954 and on. Where was she from, the girl with the iridescent, close-fitting culottes and the green lipstick and the fantastically waved yellow hair? No—when?

A man of about twenty-five happened to stand beside him: obviously British, from the threadbare tweeds and the long, thin face. He seemed to be hiding a truculent bitterness under his mannered exterior. "Hello," said Everard. "Might as well get acquainted." He gave his name and origin.

"Charles Whitcomb, London, 1947," said the other shyly. "I was just demobbed—R.A.F.—and this looked like a good chance. Now I wonder."

"It may be," said Everard, thinking of the salary. Fifteen thousand a year to start with! How did they figure years, though? Must be in terms of one's actual duration-sense.

A man strolled in their direction. He was a slender young fellow in a skin-tight gray uniform with a deep-blue cloak which seemed to twinkle, as if it had stars sewn in. His face was pleasant, smiling, and he spoke genially with a neutral accent: "Hello, there! Welcome to the Academy. I take it you all know English?" Everard noticed a man in the shabby remnants of a German uniform, and a Hindu, and others who were probably from several foreign countries.

"We'll use English, then, till you've all learned Temporal." The man lounged easily, hands on his hips. "My name is Dard Kelm. I was born in—let me see—9573 Christian reckoning, but I've made a specialty of your period. Which, by the way, extends from 1850 to 2000, though you're all from some in-between years. I'm your official wailing wall, if something goes wrong.

"This place is run along different lines from what you've probably been expecting. We don't turn out men en masse, so the elaborate discipline of a classroom or an army is not required. Each of you will have individual as well as general instruction. We don't need to punish failure in studies, because the preliminary tests have guaranteed there won't be any and made the chance of failure on the job small. Each of you has a high maturity rating in terms of your particular cultures. However, the variation in aptitudes means that if we're to develop each individual to the fullest, there must be personal guidance.

"There's little formality here beyond normal courtesy. You'll have chances for recreation as well as study. We never expect more of you than you can give. I might add that the hunting and fishing are still pretty good even in this neighborhood, and if you fly just a few hundred miles they're fantastic.

"Now, if there aren't any questions, please follow me and I'll get you settled."

Dard Kelm demonstrated the gadgets in a typical room. They were the sort you would have expected by, say, A.D. 2000: unobtrusive furniture readily adjusted to a perfect fit, refresher cabinets, screens which could draw on a huge library of recorded sight and sound for entertainment. Nothing too advanced, as yet. Each cadet had his own room in the "dormitory" building; meals were in a central refectory, but arrangements could be made for private parties. Everard felt the tension easing within him.

A welcoming banquet was held. The courses were familiar but the silent machines which rolled up to serve them were not. There was wine, beer, an ample supply of tobacco. Maybe something had been slipped into the food, for Everard felt as euphoric as the others. He ended up beating out boogie on a piano while half a dozen people made the air hideous with attempts at song.

Only Charles Whitcomb held back, sipping a moody glass over in a corner by himself. Dard Kelm was tactful and did not try to force him into joining.

Everard decided he was going to like it. But the work and the organization and the purpose were still shadows.

"Time travel was discovered at a period when the Chorite Heresiarchy was breaking up," said Kelm, in the lecture hall. "You'll study the details later; for now, take my word that it was a turbulent age, when commercial and genetic rivalry was a tooth-and-claw matter between giant combines; anything went, and the various governments were pawns in a galactic game. The time effect was the by-product of a search for a means of instantaneous transportation, which some of you will realize requires infinitely discontinuous functions for its mathematical description…as does travel into the past. I won't go into the theory of it—you'll get some of that in the physics classes—but merely state that it involves the concept of infinite-valued relationships in a continuum of 4N dimensions, where N is the total number of particles in the universe.

"Naturally, the group which discovered this, the Nine, were aware of the possibilities. Not only commercial-trading, mining, and other enterprises you can readily imagine—but the chance of striking a deathblow at their enemies. You see, time is variable; the past can be changed—"

"Question!" It was the girl from 1972, Elizabeth Gray, who was a rising young physicist in her own period.

"Yes?" said Kelm politely.

"I think you're describing a logically impossible situation. I'll grant the possibility of time travel, seeing that we're here, but an event cannot both *have* happened and *not* happened. That's self-contradictory."

"Only if you insist on a logic which is not Aleph-sub-Aleph-valued," said Kelm. "What happens is like this: suppose I went back in time and prevented your father from meeting your mother. You would never have been born. That portion of universal history would read differently; it would always have been different, though I would retain memory of the 'original' state of affairs."

"Well, how about doing the same to yourself?" asked Elizabeth. "Would you cease existing?"

"No, because I would belong to the section of history prior to my own intervention. Let's apply it to you. If you went back to, I would guess, 1946, and worked to prevent your parents' marriage in 1947, you would still have existed in that year; you would not go out of existence just because you had influenced events. The same would apply even if you had only been in 1946 one microsecond before shooting the man who would otherwise have become your father."

"But then I'd exist without—without an origin!" she protested. "I'd have life, and memories, and…everything…though *nothing* had produced them."

Kelm shrugged. "What of it? You insist that the causal law, or strictly speaking the conservation-of-energy law, involve only continuous functions. Actually, discontinuity is entirely possible."

He laughed and leaned on the lectern. "Of course, there are impossibilities," he said. "You could not be your own mother, for instance, because of sheer genetics. If you went back and married your former father, the children would be different, none of them you, because each would have only half your chromosomes."

Clearing his throat: "Let's not stray from the subject. You'll learn the details in other classes. I'm only giving you a general background. To continue: the Nine saw the possibility of going back in time and preventing their enemies from ever having gotten started, even from ever being born. But then the Danellians appeared."

For the first time, his casual, half-humorous air dropped, and he stood there as a man in the presence of the unknowable. He spoke quietly: "The Danellians are part of the future—-our future, more than a million years ahead of me. Man has evolved into something…impossible to describe. You'll probably never meet a Danellian. If you ever should, it will be…rather a shock. They aren't malignant—nor benevolent—they are as far beyond anything we can know or feel as we are beyond those insectivores who are going to be our ancestors. It isn't good to meet that sort of thing face to face.

"They were simply concerned with protecting their own existence. Time travel was old when they emerged, there had been uncountable opportunities for the foolish and the greedy and the mad to go back and turn history inside out. They did not wish to forbid the travel—it was part of the complex which had led to them—but they had to regulate it. The Nine were prevented from carrying out their schemes. And the Patrol was set up to police the time lanes.

"Your work will be mostly within your own eras, unless you graduate to unattached status. You will live, on the whole, ordinary lives, family and friends as usual; the secret part of those lives will have the satisfactions of good pay, protection, occasional vacations in some very interesting places, supremely worthwhile work. But you will always be on call. Sometimes you will help time travelers who have gotten into difficulties, one way or another. Sometimes you will work on missions, the apprehension of would-be political or military or economic conquistadors. Sometimes the Patrol will accept damage as done, and work instead to set up counteracting influences in later periods which will swing history back to the desired track.

"I wish all of you luck."

The first part of instruction was physical and psychological. Everard had never realized how his own life had crippled him, in body and mind; he was only half the man he could be. It came hard, but in the end it was a joy to feel the utterly controlled power of muscles, the emotions which had grown deeper for being disciplined, the swiftness and precision of conscious thought.

Somewhere along the line he was thoroughly conditioned against revealing anything about the Patrol, even hinting at its existence, to any unauthorized person. It was simply impossible for him to do so, under any influence; as impossible as jumping to the moon. He also learned the ins and outs of his twentieth-century public *persona*.

Temporal, the artificial language with which Patrolmen from all ages could communicate without being understood by strangers, was a miracle of logically organized expressiveness.

He thought he knew something about combat, but he had to learn the tricks and the weapons of fifty thousand years, all the way from a Bronze Age rapier to a cyclic blast which could annihilate a continent. Returned to his own era, he would be given a limited arsenal, but he might be called into other periods and overt anachronism was rarely permissible.

There was the study of history, science, arts and philosophies, fine details of dialect and mannerism. These last were only for the 1850-2000 period; if he had occasion to go elsewhere he would pick up special instruction from a hypnotic conditioner. It was such machines that made it possible to complete his training in three months.

He learned the organization of the Patrol. Up "ahead" lay the mystery which was Danellian civilization, but there was little direct contact with it. The Patrol was set up in semimilitary fashion, with ranks, though without special formalities. History was divided into milieus, with a head office located in a major city for a selected twenty-year period (disguised by some ostensible activity such as commerce) and various branch offices. For his time, there were three milieus: the Western world, headquarters in London; Russia, in Moscow; Asia, in Peiping; each in the easygoing years 1890-1910, when concealment was less difficult than in later decades, when there were smaller offices such as Gordon's. An ordinary attached agent lived as usual in his own time, often with an authentic job. Communication between years was by tiny robot shuttles or by courier, with automatic shunts to keep such messages from piling up at one instant.

The entire organization was so vast that he could not really appreciate the fact. He had entered something new and exciting, that was all he truly grasped with all layers of consciousness…as yet.

He found his instructors friendly, ready to gab. The grizzled veteran who taught him to handle spaceships had fought in the Martian war of 3890. "You boys catch on fairly quick," he said. "It's hell, though, teaching pre-industrial people. We've quit even trying to give them more than the rudiments. Had a Roman here once—Caesar's time—fairly bright boy, too, but he never got it through his head that a machine can't be treated like a horse. As for the Babylonians, time travel just wasn't in their world-picture. We had to give them a battle-of-the-gods routine."

"What routine are you giving us?" asked Whitcomb. The spaceman regarded him narrowly. "The truth," he said at last. "As much of it as you can take."

"How did you get into this job?"

"Oh…I was shot up off Jupiter. Not much left of me. They picked me up, built me a new body—since none of my people were alive, and I was presumed dead, there didn't seem much point in going back home. No fun living under the Guidance Corps. So I took this position here. Good company, easy living, and furloughs in a lot of eras." The spaceman grinned. "Wait till you've been to the decadent stage of the Third Matriarchy! You don't know what fun is."

Everard said nothing. He was too captured by the spectacle of Earth, rolling enormous against the stars.

He made friends with his fellow cadets. They were a congenial bunch—naturally, with the same type being picked for Patrollers, bold and intelligent minds. There were a couple of romances. No *Portrait of Jenny* stuff; marriage was entirely possible, with the couple picking some year in which to set up housekeeping. He himself liked the girls, but kept his head.

Oddly, it was the silent and morose Whitcomb with whom he struck up the closest friendship. There was something appealing about the Englishman; he was so cultured, such a thoroughly good fellow, and still somehow lost.

They were out riding one day, on horses whose remote ancestors scampered before their gigantic descendants. Everard had a rifle, in the hope of bagging a shovel-tusker he had seen. Both wore Academy uniform, light grays which were cool and silky under the hot yellow sun.

"I wonder we're allowed to hunt," remarked the American. "Suppose I shoot a sabertooth—in Asia, I suppose—which was originally slated to eat one of those prehuman insectivores. Won't that change the whole future?"

"No," said Whitcomb. He had progressed faster in studying the theory of time travel. "You see, it's rather as if the continuum were a mesh of tough rubber bands. It isn't easy to distort it; the tendency is always for it to snap back to its, uh, 'former' shape. One individual insectivore doesn't matter, it's the total genetic pool of their species which led to man.

"Likewise, if I killed a sheep in the Middle Ages, I wouldn't wipe out all its later descendants, maybe all the sheep there were by 1940. Rather, those would still be there, unchanged down to their very genes in spite of a different ancestry, because over so long a period of time all the sheep, or men, are descendants of all the earlier sheep or men. Compensation, don't you see; somewhere along the line, some other ancestor supplies the genes you thought you had eliminated.

"In the same way…oh, suppose I went back and prevented Booth from killing Lincoln. Unless I took very elaborate precautions, it would probably happen that someone else did the shooting and Booth got blamed anyway.

"That resilience of time is the reason travel is permitted at all. If you want to change things, you have to go about it just right and work very hard, usually."

His mouth twisted. "Indoctrination! We're told again and again that if we interfere, there's going to be punishment for us. I'm not allowed to go back and shoot that ruddy bastard Hitler in his cradle. I'm supposed to let him grow up as he did, and start the war, and kill my girl."

Everard rode quietly for a while. The only noise was the squeak of saddle leather and the rustle of long grass. "Oh," he said at last. "I'm sorry. Want to talk about it?"

"Yes. I do. But there isn't much. She was in the W.A.A.F.—Mary Nelson—we were going to get married after the war. She was in London in '44. November seventeenth, I'll never forget that date. The V-bombs got her. She'd gone over to a neighbor's house in Streatham—was on furlough, you see, staying with her mother. That house was blown up; her own home wasn't scratched."

Whitcomb's cheeks were bloodless. He stared emptily before him. "It's going to be jolly hard not to…not to go back, just a few years, and see her at the very least. Only see her again …No! I don't dare."

Everard laid a hand on the man's shoulder, awkwardly, and they rode on in silence.

The class moved ahead, each at his own pace, but there was enough compensation so that all graduated together: a brief ceremony followed by a huge party and many maudlin arrangements for later reunions. Then each went back to the same year he had come from: the same hour.

Everard accepted Gordon's congratulations, got a list of contemporary agents (several of them holding jobs in places like military intelligence), and returned to his apartment. Later he might find work arranged for him in some sensitive listening post, but his present assignment—for income-tax purposes, "special consultant to Engineering Studies CO."—was only to read a dozen papers a day for the indications of time travel he had been taught to spot, and hold himself ready for a call.

As it happened, he made his own first job.

-3-

It was a peculiar feeling to read the headlines and know, more or less, what was coming next. It took the edge off, but added a sadness, for this was a tragic era. He could sympathize with Whitcomb's desire to go back and change history.

Only, of course, one man was too limited. He could not change it for the better, except by some freak; most likely he would bungle everything. Go back and kill Hitler and the Japanese and Soviet leaders—maybe someone shrewder would take their place. Maybe atomic energy would lie fallow, and the glorious flowering of the Venusian Renaissance never happen. The devil we know…

He looked out of his window. Lights flamed against a hectic sky; the street crawled with automobiles and a hurrying, faceless crowd; he could not see the towers of Manhattan from here, but he knew they reared arrogant toward the clouds. And it was all one swirl on a river that swept from the peaceful prehuman landscape where he had been to the unimaginable Danellian future. How many billions and trillions of human creatures lived, laughed, wept, worked, hoped, and died in its currents!

Well …He sighed, stoked his pipe, and turned back. A long walk had not made him less restless; his mind and body were impatient for something to do. But it was late and…He went over to the bookshelf, picked out a volume more or less at random, and started to read. It was a collection of Victorian and Edwardian stories.

A passing reference struck him. Something about a tragedy at Addleton and the singular contents of an ancient British barrow. Nothing more. Hm. Time travel? He smiled to himself.

Still…

No, he thought. *This is crazy.*

It wouldn't do any harm to check up, though. The incident was mentioned as occurring in the year 1894, in England. He could get out back files of the London *Times.* Nothing else to do…Probably that was why he was stuck with his dull newspaper assignment: so that his mind, grown nervous from boredom, would prowl into every conceivable corner.

He was on the steps of the public library as it opened.

The account was there, dated June 25, 1894, and several days following. Addleton was a village in Kent, distinguished chiefly by a Jacobean estate belonging to Lord Wyndham and a barrow of unknown age. The nobleman, an enthusiastic amateur archaeologist, had been excavating it, together with one James Rotherhithe, an expert from the British Museum who happened to be a relative. Lord Wyndham had uncovered a rather meager burial chamber: a few artifacts nearly rusted and rotted away, bones of men and horses. There was also a chest in surprisingly good condition, containing ingots of an unknown metal presumed to be a lead or silver alloy. He fell deathly ill, with symptoms of a peculiarly lethal poisoning; Rotherhithe, who had barely looked into the casket, was not affected, and circumstantial evidence suggested that he had slipped the nobleman a dose of some obscure Asiatic concoction. Scotland Yard arrested the man when Lord Wyndham died, on the twenty-fifth. Rotherhithe's family engaged the services of a well-known private detective, who was able to show, by most ingenious reasoning, followed by tests on animals, that the accused was innocent and that a "deadly emanation" from the chest was responsible. Box and contents had been thrown into the English Channel. Congratulations all around. Fade-out to happy ending.

Everard sat quietly in the long, hushed room. The story didn't tell enough. But it was highly suggestive, to say the least.

Then why hadn't the Victorian office of the Patrol investigated? Or had they? Probably. They wouldn't advertise their results, of course.

Still, he'd better send a memorandum.

Returning to his apartment, he took one of the little message shuttles given him, laid a report in it, and set the control studs for the London office, June 25, 1894. When he pushed the final button the box vanished with a small whoosh of air rushing in where it had been.

It returned in a few minutes. Everard opened it and took out a sheet of foolscap covered with neat typing—yes, the typewriter had been invented by then, of course. He scanned it with the swiftness he had learned.

> Dear Sir:
>
> In reply to yrs. of September 6, 1954, beg to acknowledge receipt and would commend your diligence. The affair has only just begun at this end, and we are much occupied at present with preventing assassination of Her Majesty, as well as with the Balkan Question, the

deplorable opium trade with China, &c. While we can, of course, settle current business and then return to this, it is well to avoid *curiosa* such as being in two places at once, which might be noticed. Would therefore much appreciate it if you and some qualified British agent would come to our assistance. Unless we hear otherwise, we shall expect you at 14-B, Old Osborne Road, on June 26, 1894, at 12 midnight. Believe me, Sir, yr. humble & obt. svt.,

J. Mainwethering

There followed a note of the spatio-temporal coordinates, incongruous under all that floridness.

Everard called up Gordon, got an okay, and arranged to pick up a time hopper at the "company's" warehouse. Then he shot a note to Charlie Whitcomb in 1947, got a one-word reply—"Surely"—and went off to get his machine.

It was reminiscent of a motorcycle without wheels or kickstand. There were two saddles and an antigravity propulsion unit. Everard set the dials for Whitcomb's era, touched the main button, and found himself in another warehouse.

London, 1947. He sat for a moment, reflecting that at this instant he himself, seven years younger, was attending college back in the States. Then Whitcomb shouldered past the watchman and took his hand. "Good to see you again, old chap," he said. His haggard face lit up in the curiously charming smile which Everard had come to know. "And so Victoria, eh?"

"Reckon so. Jump on." Everard reset. This time he would emerge in an office. A very private inner office.

It blinked into existence around him. There was an unexpectedly heavy effect to the oak furniture, the thick carpet, the flaring gas mantles. Electric lights were available, but Dalhousie & Roberts was a solid, conservative import house. Mainwethering himself got out of a chair and came to greet them: a large and pompous man with bushy side whiskers and a monocle. But he had also an air of strength, and an Oxford accent so cultivated that Everard could hardly understand it.

"Good evening, gentlemen. Pleasant journey, I trust? Oh, yes...sorry...you gentlemen are new to the business, eh, what? Always a bit disconcerting at first. I remember how shocked I was on a visit to the twenty-first century. Not British at all...Only a *res naturae*, though, only another facet of an always surprising universe, eh? You must excuse my lack of hospitality, but we really are frightfully busy. Fanatic German up in 1917 learned the time-travel secret from an unwary anthropologist, stole a machine, has come to London to assassinate Her Majesty. We're having the devil's own time finding him."

"Will you?" asked Whitcomb.

"Oh, yes. But deuced hard work, gentlemen, especially when we must operate secretly. I'd like to engage a private inquiry agent, but the only worthwhile one is entirely too clever. He operates on the principle that when one has eliminated the impossible, whatever remains, however improbable, must be the truth. And time trafficking may not be too improbable for him."

"I'll bet he's the same man who's working on the Addleton case, or will be tomorrow," said Everard. "That isn't important; we know he'll prove Rotherhithe's innocence. What matters is the strong probability that there's been hanky-panky going on back in ancient British times."

"Saxon, you mean," corrected Whitcomb, who had checked on the data himself. "Good many people confuse British and Saxons."

"Almost as many as confuse Saxons and Jutes," said Mainwethering blandly. "Kent was invaded from Jutland, I understand…Ah. Hm. Clothes here, gentlemen. And funds. And papers, all prepared for you. I sometimes think you field agents don't appreciate how much work we have to do in the offices for even the smallest operation. Haw! Pardon. Have you a plan of campaign?"

Mainwethering looked mournful. "If the barrow incident has gotten into a famous piece of literature as you say, we will be getting a hundred memoranda about it. Yours happened to come first. Two others have arrived since, from 1923 and 1960. Dear me, how I wish I were allowed a robot secretary!"

Everard struggled with the awkward suit. It fitted him well enough, his measurements were on file in this office, but he hadn't appreciated the relative comfort of his own fashions before. Damn that waistcoat! "Look here," he said, "this business may be quite harmless. In fact, since we're here now, it must have *been* harmless. Eh?"

"As of now," said Mainwethering. "But consider. You two gentlemen go back to Jutish times and find the marauder. But you fail. Perhaps he shoots you before you can shoot him; perhaps he waylays those we send after you. Then he goes on to establish an industrial revolution or whatever he's after. History changes. You, being back there before the change-point, still exist…if only as cadavers…but we up here have never been. This conversation never took place. As Horace puts it—"

"Never mind!" Whitcomb laughed. "We'll investigate the barrow first, in this year, then pop back here and decide what's next." He bent over and began transferring equipment from a twentieth-century suitcase to a Gladstonian monstrosity of flowered cloth. A couple of guns, some physical and chemical apparatus which his own age had not invented, a tiny radio with which to call up the office in case of trouble.

Mainwethering consulted his Bradshaw. "You can get the 8:23 out of Charing Cross tomorrow morning," he said. "Allow half an hour to get from here to the station."

"Okay." Everard and Whitcomb remounted their hopper and vanished. Mainwethering sighed, yawned, left instructions with his clerk, and went home. At 7:45 A.M. the clerk was there when the hopper materialized.

-4-

This was the first moment that the reality of time travel struck home to Everard. He had known it with the top of his mind, been duly impressed, but it was, for his emotions, merely exotic. Now, clopping through a London he did not know in a hansom cab (not a tourist-trap anachronism, but a working machine, dusty and battered), smelling an air which held more smoke than a twentieth-century city but no gasoline fumes, seeing the crowds which milled past—gentlemen in bowlers and top hats, sooty navvies, long-skirted women, and not actors but real, talking, perspiring, laughing and somber human beings off on real business—it hit him with full force that he was *here*. At this moment his mother had not been born, his grandparents were young couples just getting settled to harness, Grover Cleveland was President of the United States and Victoria was Queen of England, Kipling was writing and the last Indian uprisings in America yet to come…It was like a blow on the head.

Whitcomb took it more calmly, but his eyes were never still as he watched this day of England's glory. "I begin to understand," he murmured. "They never have agreed whether this was a period of unnatural, stuffy convention and thinly veneered brutality, or the last flower of Western civilization before it started going to seed. Just seeing these people makes me realize; it was everything they have said about it, good and bad, because it wasn't a simple thing happening to everyone, but millions of individual lives."

"Sure," said Everard. "That must be true of every age."

The train was almost familiar, not very different from the carriages of British railways anno 1954, which gave Whitcomb occasion for sardonic remarks about inviolable traditions. In a couple of hours it let them off at a sleepy village station among carefully tended flower gardens, where they engaged a buggy to drive them to the Wyndham estate.

A polite constable admitted them after a few questions. They were passing themselves off as archaeologists, Everard from America and Whitcomb from Australia, who had been quite anxious to meet Lord Wyndham and were shocked by his tragic end. Mainwethering, who seemed to have tentacles everywhere, had supplied them with letters of introduction from a well-known authority at the British Museum. The inspector from Scotland Yard agreed to let them look at the barrow—"The case is solved, gentlemen, there are no more clues, even if my colleague does not agree, hah, hah!" The private agent smiled sourly and watched them with a narrow eye as they approached the mound; he was tall, thin, hawk-faced, and accompanied by a burly, mustached fellow with a limp who seemed a kind of amanuensis.

The barrow was long and high, covered with grass save where a raw scar showed excavation to the funeral chamber. This had been lined with rough-hewn timbers but had long ago collapsed; fragments of what had been wood still lay on the dirt. "The newspapers mentioned something about a metal casket," said Everard. "I wonder if we might have a look at it too?"

The inspector nodded agreeably and led them off to an outbuilding where the major finds were laid forth on a table. Except for the box, they were only fragments of corroded metal and crumbled bone.

"Hm," said Whitcomb. His gaze was thoughtful on the sleek, bare face of the small chest. It shimmered bluely, some time-proof alloy yet to be discovered. "Most unusual. Not primitive at all. You'd almost think it had been machined, eh?"

Everard approached it warily. He had a pretty good idea of what was inside, and all the caution about such matters natural to a citizen of the *soi-disant* Atomic

Age. Pulling a counter out of his bag, he aimed it at the box. Its needle wavered, not much but...

"Interesting item there," said the inspector. "May I ask what it is?"

"An experimental electroscope," lied Everard. Carefully, he threw back the lid and held the counter above the box.

God! There was enough radioactivity inside to kill a man in a day! He had just a glimpse of heavy, dull-shining ingots before he slammed the lid down again. "Be careful with that stuff," he said shakily. Praise heaven, whoever carried that devil's load had come from an age when they knew how to block off radiation!

The private detective had come up behind them, noiselessly. A hunter's look grew on his keen face. "So you recognized the contents, sir?" he asked, quietly.

"Yes. I think so." Everard remembered that Becquerel would not discover radioactivity for almost two years; even X rays were still more than a year in the future. He had to be cautious. "That is...in Indian territory I've heard stories about an ore like this which is poisonous—"

"*Most* interesting." The detective began to stuff a big-bowled pipe. "Like mercury vapor, what?"

"So Rotherhithe placed that box in the grave, did he?" muttered the inspector.

"Don't be ridiculous!" snapped the detective. "I have three lines of conclusive proof that Rotherhithe is entirely innocent. What puzzled me was the actual cause of his lordship's death. But if, as this gentleman says, there happened to be a deadly poison buried in that mound...to discourage grave-robbers? I wonder, though, how the old Saxons came by an American mineral. Perhaps there is something to these theories about early Phoenician voyages across the Atlantic. I have done a little research on a notion of mine that there are Chaldean elements in the Cornish language, and this seems to bear me out."

Everard felt guilty about what he was doing to the science of archaeology. Oh, well, this box was going to be dumped in the Channel and forgotten. He and Whitcomb made an excuse to leave as soon as possible.

On the way back to London, when they were safely alone in their compartment, the Englishman took out a moldering fragment of wood. "Slipped this into my pocket at the barrow," he said. "It'll help us date the thing. Hand me that radiocarbon counter, will you?" He popped the wood into the device, turned some knobs, and read off the answer. "One thousand, four hundred and thirty years, plus or minus about ten. The mound went up around...um...A.D. 464, then, when the Jutes were just getting established in Kent."

"If those ingots are still that hellish after so long," murmured Everard, "I wonder what they were like originally? Hard to see how you could have that much activity with such a long half-life, but then, up in the future they can do things with the atom my period hasn't dreamed of."

Turning in their report to Mainwethering, they spent a day sight-seeing while he sent messages across time and activated the great machine of the Patrol. Everard was interested in Victorian London, almost captivated in spite of the grime and poverty. Whitcomb got a faraway look in his eyes. "I'd like to have lived here," he said.

"Yeah? With their medicine and dentistry?"

"And no bombs falling." Whitcomb's answer held a defiance.

Mainwethering had arrangements made when they returned to his office. Puffing a cigar, he strode up and down, pudgy hands clasped behind his tailcoat, and rattled off the story.

"Metal been identified with high probability. Isotopic fuel from around the thirtieth century. Checkup reveals that a merchant from the Ing Empire was visiting year 2987 to barter his raw materials for their synthrope, secret of which had been lost in the Interregnum. Naturally, he took precautions, tried to pass himself off as a trader from the Saturnian System, but nevertheless disappeared. So did his time shuttle. Presumably someone in 2987 found out what he was and murdered him for his machine. Patrol notified, but no trace of machine. Finally recovered from fifth-century England by two Patrolmen named, haw! Everard and Whitcomb."

"If we've already succeeded, why bother?" The American grinned.

Mainwethering looked shocked. "But my dear fellow! You have not already succeeded. The job is yet to do, in terms of your and my duration-sense. And please do not take success for granted merely because history records it. Time is not rigid; man has free will. If you fail, history will change and will not ever have recorded your success; I will not have told you about it. That is undoubtedly what happened, if I may use the term 'happened,' in the few cases where the Patrol has a record of failure. Those cases are still being worked on, and if success is achieved at last, history will be changed and there will 'always' have been success. *Tempus non nascitur, fit,* if I may indulge in a slight parody."

"All right, all right, I was only joking," said Everard. "Let's get going. *Tempus fugit.*" He added an extra "g" with malice aforethought, and Mainwethering winced.

It turned out that even the Patrol knew little about the dark period when the Romans had left Britain, the Romano-British civilization was crumbling, and the English were moving in. It had never seemed an important one. The office at London, A.D. 1000, sent up what material it had, together with suits of clothes that would get by. Everard and Whitcomb spent an hour unconscious under the hypnotic educators, to emerge with fluency in Latin and in several Saxon and Jutish dialects, and with a fair knowledge of the mores.

The clothes were awkward: trousers, shirts, and coats of rough wool, leather cloaks, an interminable collection of thongs and laces. Long flaxen wigs covered modern haircuts; a clean shave would pass unnoticed, even in the fifth century. Whitcomb carried an ax, Everard a sword, both made to measure of high-carbon steel, but put more reliance on the little twenty-sixth-century sonic stun guns stuck under their coats. Armor had not been included, but the time hopper had a pair of motorcycle crash helmets in one saddlebag: these would not attract much attention in an age of homemade equipment, and were a good deal stronger and more comfortable than the real thing. They also stowed away a picnic lunch and some earthenware jugs full of good Victorian ale.

"Excellent." Mainwethering pulled a watch out of his pocket and consulted it. "I shall expect you back here at…shall we say four o'clock? I will have some armed guards on hand, in case you have a prisoner along, and we can go out to tea afterward." He shook their hands. "Good hunting!"

Everard swung onto the time hopper, set the controls for A.D. 464 at Addleton Barrow, a summer midnight, and threw the switch.

-5-

There was a full moon. Under it, the land lay big and lonely, with a darkness of forest blocking out the horizon. Somewhere a wolf howled. The mound was there yet; they had come late.

Rising on the antigravity unit, they peered across a dense, shadowy wood. A thorp lay about a mile from the barrow, one hall of hewn timber and a cluster of smaller buildings around a courtyard. In the drenching moonlight, it was very quiet.

"Cultivated fields," observed Whitcomb. His voice was hushed in the stillness. "The Jutes and Saxons were mostly yeomen, you know, who came here looking for land. Imagine the Britons were pretty well cleared out of this area some years ago."

"We've got to find out about that burial," said Everard. "Shall we go back and locate the moment the grave was made? No, it might be safer to inquire now, at a later date when whatever excitement there was has died down. Say tomorrow morning."

Whitcomb nodded, and Everard brought the hopper down into the concealment of a thicket and jumped up five hours. The sun was blinding in the northeast, dew glistened on the long grass, and the birds were making an unholy racket. Dismounting, the agents sent the hopper shooting up at fantastic velocity, to hover ten miles aboveground and come to them when called on a midget radio unit built into their helmets.

They approached the thorp openly, whacking off the savage-looking dogs which came snarling at them with the flat of sword and ax. Entering the courtyard, they found it unpaved but richly carpeted with mud and manure. A couple of naked, tow-headed children gaped at them from a hut of earth and wattles. A girl who was sitting outside milking a scrubby little cow let out a small shriek; a thick-built, low-browed farmhand swilling the pigs grabbed for a spear. Wrinkling his nose, Everard wished that some of the "Noble Nordic" enthusiasts of his century could visit this one.

A gray-bearded man with an ax in his hand appeared in the hall entrance. Like everyone else of this period, he was several inches shorter than the twentieth-century average. He studied them warily before wishing them good morning.

Everard smiled politely. "I hight Uffa Hundingsson, and my brother is Knubbi," he said. "We are merchants from Jutland, come hither to trade at Canterbury." (He gave it the present name. Cant-wara-byrig.) "Wandering from the place where our ship is beached, we lost our way, and after fumbling about all night found your home."

"I hight Wulfnoth, son of Aelfred," said the yeoman. "Enter and break your fast with us."

The hall was big and dim and smoky, full of a chattering crowd: Wulfnoth's children, their spouses and children, dependent carls and *their* wives and children and grandchildren. Breakfast consisted of great wooden trenchers of half-cooked pork, washed down by horns of thin sour beer. It was not hard to get a conversation going; these people were as gossipy as isolated yokels anywhere. The trouble was with inventing plausible accounts of what was going on in Jutland. Once or twice, Wulfnoth, who was no fool, caught them in some mistake, but Everard said firmly: "You have heard a falsehood. News takes strange forms when it crosses the sea." He was surprised to learn how much contact there still was with the old countries. But the talk of weather and crops was not very different from the kind he knew in the twentieth-century Middle West.

Only later was he able to slip in a question about the barrow. Wulfnoth frowned, and his plump, toothless wife hastily made a protective sign toward a rude wooden idol. "It is not good to speak of such things," muttered the Jute. "I would the wizard had not been buried on my land. But he was close to my father, who died last year and would hear of naught else."

"Wizard?" Whitcomb pricked up his ears. "What tale is this?"

'Well, you may as well know," grumbled Wulfnoth. "He was a stranger hight Stane, who appeared in Canterbury some six years ago. He must have been from far away, for he spoke not the English or British tongues, but King Hengist guested him and eftsoons he learned. He gave the king strange but goodly gifts, and was a crafty redesman, on whom the king came more and more to lean. None dared cross him, for he had a wand which threw thunderbolts and had been seen to cleave rocks and once, in battle with the Britons, burn men down. There are those who thought he was Woden, but that cannot be since he died."

"Ah, so." Everard felt a tingle of eagerness. "And what did he whilst yet he lived?"

"Oh…he gave the king wise redes, as I have said. It was his thought that we of Kent should cease thrusting back the Britons and calling in ever more of our kinsmen from the old country; rather, we should make peace with the natives. He thought that with our strength and their Roman learning, we could together shape a mighty realm. He may have been right, though I for one see little use in all these books and baths, to say naught of that weird cross-god they have…Well, anyhow, he was slain by unknowns three years ago, and buried here with sacrifices and such of his possessions as his foes had not reaved. We give him an offering twice a year, and I must say his ghost has not made trouble for us. But still am I somewhat uneasy about it."

"Three years, eh?" breathed Whitcomb. "I see…"

It took a good hour to break away, and Wulfnoth insisted on sending a boy along to guide them to the river. Everard, who didn't feel like walking that far, grinned and called down the hopper. As he and Whitcomb mounted it, he said gravely to the bulging-eyed lad: "Know that thou hast guested Woden and Thunor, who will hereafter guard thy folk from harm." Then he jumped three years back in time.

"Now comes the rough part," he said, peering out of the thicket at the nighted thorp. The mound was not there now, the wizard Stane was still alive. "It's easy enough to put on a magic show for a kid, but we've got to extract this character from the middle of a big, tough town where he's the king's right-hand man. *And he has a blast-ray.*"

"Apparently we succeeded—or will succeed," said Whitcomb.

"Nope. It's not irrevocable, you know. If we fail, Wulfnoth will be telling us a different story three years from now, probably that Stane is there—he may kill us twice! And England, pulled out of the Dark Ages into a neoclassical culture, won't evolve into anything you'd recognize by 1894...I wonder what Stane's game is."

He lifted the hopper and sent it through the sky toward Canterbury. A night wind whistled darkly past his face. Presently the town loomed near, and he grounded in a copse. The moon was white on the half-ruined Roman walls of ancient Durovernum, dappled black on the newer earth and wood of the Jutish repairs. Nobody would get in after sunset.

Again the hopper brought them to daytime—near noon—and was sent skywards. His breakfast, two hours ago and three years in the future, felt soggy as Everard led the way onto a crumbling Roman road and toward the city. There was a goodly traffic, mostly farmers driving creaky oxcarts of produce in to market. A pair of vicious-looking guards halted them at the gate and demanded their business. This time they were the agents of a trader on Thanet who had sent them to interview various artisans here. The hoodlums looked surly till Whitcomb slipped them a couple of Roman coins; then the spears went down and they were waved past.

The city brawled and bustled around them, though again it was the ripe smell which impressed Everard most. Among the jostling Jutes, he spotted an occasional Romano-Briton, disdainfully picking a way through the muck and pulling his shabby tunic clear of contact with these savages. It would have been funny if it weren't pathetic.

There was an extraordinarily dirty inn filling the moss-grown ruins of what had been a rich man's town house. Everard and Whitcomb found that their money was of high value here where trade was principally in kind. By standing a few rounds of drinks, they got all the information they wanted. King Hengist's hall was near the middle of town...not really a hall, an old building which had been deplorably prettied up under the direction of that outlander Stane...not that our good and doughty king is any pantywaist, don't get me wrong, stranger...why, only last month...oh, yes, Stane! He lived in the house right next to it. Strange fellow, some said he was a god...he certainly had an eye for the girls...Yes, they said he was behind all this peace-talk with the Britons. More and more of those slickers coming in every day, it's getting so an honest man can't let a little blood without...Of course, Stane is very wise, I wouldn't say anything against him, understand, after all, he can throw lightning...

"So what do we do?" asked Whitcomb, back in their own room. "Go on in and arrest him?"

"No, I doubt if that's possible," said Everard cautiously. "I've got a sort of a plan, but it depends on guessing what he really intends. Let's see if we can't get an audience." As he got off the straw tick which served for a bed, he was scratching. "Damn! What this period needs isn't literacy but flea powder!"

The house had been carefully renovated, its white, porticoed facade almost painfully clean against the grubbiness around it. Two guards lounged on the stairs, and snapped to alertness as the agents approached. Everard fed them money and a story about being a visitor who had news that would surely interest the great wizard. "Tell him, 'Man from tomorrow.' 'Tis a password. Got it?"

"It makes not sense," complained the guard.

"Passwords need not make sense," said Everard with hauteur.

The Jute clanked off, shaking his head dolefully. All these newfangled notions!

"Are you sure this is wise?" asked Whitcomb. "He'll be on the alert now, you know."

"I also know a VIP isn't going to waste time on just any stranger. This business is urgent, man! So far, he hasn't accomplished anything permanent, not even enough to become a lasting legend. But if Hengist should make a genuine union with the Britons…"

The guard returned, grunted something, and led them up the stairs and across the peristyle. Beyond was the atrium, a good-sized room where modern bearskin rugs jarred with chipped marble and faded mosaics. A man stood waiting before a rude wooden couch. As they entered, he raised his hand, and Everard saw the slim barrel of a thirtieth-century blast-ray.

"Keep your hands in sight and well away from your sides," said the man gently. "Otherwise I shall belike have to smite you with a thunderbolt."

Whitcomb sucked in a sharp, dismayed breath, but Everard had been rather expecting this. Even so, there was a cold knot in his stomach.

The wizard Stane was a small man, dressed in a fine embroidered tunic which must have come from some British villa. His body was lithe, his head large, with a face of rather engaging ugliness under a shock of black hair. A grin of tension bent his lips.

"Search them, Eadgar," he ordered. "Take out aught they may bear in their clothing."

The Jute's frisking was clumsy, but he found the stunners and tossed them to the floor. "Thou mayst go," said Stane.

"Is there no danger from them, my lord?" asked the soldier.

Stane grinned wider. "With this in my hand? Nay, go." Eadgar shambled out.

At least we still have sword and ax, thought Everard. *But they're not much use with that thing looking at us.*

"So you come from tomorrow," murmured Stane. A sudden film of sweat glistened on his forehead. "I wondered about that. Speak you the later English tongue?"

Whitcomb opened his mouth, but Everard, improvising with his life at wager, beat him to the draw. "What tongue mean you?"

"Thus-wise." Stane broke into an English which had a peculiar accent but was recognizable to twentieth-century ears: "Ih want know where an' when y're from, what y'r 'tentions 'r, an' all else. Gimme d' facts 'r Ih'll burn y' doon."

Everard shook his head. "Nay," he answered in Jutish. "I understand you not." Whitcomb threw him a glance and then subsided, ready to follow the American's lead. Everard's mind raced; under the brassiness of desperation, he knew that death waited for his first mistake. "In our day we talked thus…" And he reeled off a paragraph of Mexican-Spanish chatter, garbling it as much as he dared.

"So…a Latin tongue!" Stane's eyes glittered. The blaster shook in his hand. *"When* be you from?"

"The twentieth century after Christ, and our land hight Lyonesse. It lies across the western ocean—"

"America!" It was a gasp. 'Was it ever called America?"

"No. I wot not what you speak of."

Stane shuddered uncontrollably. Mastering himself: "Know you the Roman tongue?"

Everard nodded.

Stane laughed nervously. 'Then let us speak that. If you know how sick I am of this local hog language…" His Latin was a little broken, obviously he had picked it up in this century, but fluent enough. He waved the blaster. "Pardon my discourtesy. But I have to be careful."

"Naturally," said Everard. "Ah…my name is Mencius, and my friend is Iuvenalis. We came from the future, as you have guessed; we are historians, and time travel has just been invented."

"Properly speaking, I am Rozher Schtein, from the year 2987. Have you… heard of me?"

'Who else?" said Everard. "We came back looking for this mysterious Stane who seemed to be one of the crucial figures of history. We suspected he might have been a time traveler, *peregrinator temporis,* that is. Now we know."

"Three years," Schtein began pacing feverishly, the blaster swinging in his hand; but he was too far off for a sudden leap. "Three years I have been here. If you knew how often I have lain awake, wondering if I would succeed…Tell me, is your world united?"

"The world and the planets," said Everard. "They have been for a long time." Inwardly, he shivered. His life hung on his ability to guess what Schtein's plans were.

"And you are a free people?"

'We are. That is to say, the Emperor presides, but the Senate makes the laws and it is elected by the people."

There was an almost holy look on the gnomish face, transfiguring it. "As I dreamed," whispered Schtein. "Thank you."

"So you came back from your period to…create history?"

"No," said Schtein. "To change it."

Words tumbled out of him, as if he had wished to speak and dared not for many years: "I was a historian too. By chance I met a man who claimed to be a merchant from the Saturnian moons, but since I had lived there once, I saw through the fraud. Investigating, I learned the truth. He was a time traveler from the very far future.

"You must understand, the age I lived in was a terrible one, and as a psychographic historian I realized that the war, poverty, and tyranny which cursed us were not due to any innate evil in man, but to simple cause and effect. Machine technology had risen in a world divided against itself, and war grew to be an ever larger and more destructive enterprise. There had been periods of peace, even fairly long ones; but the disease was too deep-rooted, conflict was a part of our very civilization. My family had been wiped out in a Venusian raid, I had nothing to lose. I took the time machine after…disposing…of its owner.

"The great mistake, I thought, had been made back in the Dark Ages. Rome had united a vast empire in peace, and out of peace justice can always arise. But Rome exhausted herself in the effort, and was now falling apart. The barbarians coming in were vigorous, they could do much, but they were quickly corrupted.

"But here is England. It has been isolated from the rotting fabric of Roman society. The Germanics are entering, filthy oafs but strong and willing to learn. In my history, they simply wiped out British civilization and then, being intellectually helpless, were swallowed up by the new—and evil—civilization called Western. I want to see something better happen.

"It hasn't been easy. You would be surprised how hard it is to survive in a different age until you know your way around, even if you have modern weapons and interesting gifts for the king. But I have Hengist's respect now, and increasingly more of the confidence of the Britons. I can unite the two people in a mutual war on the Picts. England will be one kingdom, with Saxon strength and Roman learning, powerful enough to stand off all invaders. Christianity is inevitable, of course, but I will see to it that it is the right kind of Christianity, one which will educate and civilize men without shackling their minds.

"Eventually England will be in a position to start taking over on the Continent. Finally, one world. I will stay here long enough to get the anti-Pictish union started, then vanish with a promise to return later. If I reappear at, say, fifty-year intervals for the next several centuries, I will be a legend, a god, who can make sure they stay on the right track."

"I have read much about St. Stanius," said Everard slowly.

"And I won!" cried Schtein. "I gave peace to the world." Tears were on his cheeks.

Everard moved closer. Schtein pointed the blast-ray at his belly, not yet quite trusting him. Everard circled casually, and Schtein swiveled to keep him covered. But the man was too agitated by the seeming proof of his own success to remember Whitcomb. Everard threw a look over his shoulder at the Englishman.

Whitcomb hurled his ax. Everard dove for the floor. Schtein screamed, and the blast-ray sizzled. The ax had cloven his shoulder. Whitcomb sprang, getting a grip on his gun hand. Schtein howled, struggling to force the blaster around. Everard jumped up to help. There was a moment of confusion.

Then the blaster went off again and Schtein was suddenly a dead weight in their arms. Blood drenched their coats from the hideous opening in his chest.

The two guards came running in. Everard snatched his stunner off the floor and thumbed the ratchet up to full intensity. A flung spear grazed his arm. He fired twice, and the burly forms crashed. They'd be out for hours.

Crouching a moment, Everard listened. A feminine scream sounded from the inner chambers, but no one was entering at the door. "I guess we've carried it off," he panted.

"Yes." Whitcomb looked dully at the corpse sprawled before him. It seemed pathetically small.

"I didn't mean for him to die," said Everard. "But time is…tough. It was written, I suppose."

"Better this way than a Patrol court and the exile planet," said Whitcomb.

"Technically, at least, he was a thief and a murderer," said Everard. "But it was a great dream he had."

"And we upset it."

"History might have upset it. Probably would have. One man just isn't powerful enough, or wise enough. I think most human misery is due to well-meaning fanatics like him."

"So we just fold our hands and take what comes."

"Think of all your friends, up in 1947. They'd never even have existed."

Whitcomb took off his cloak and tried to wipe the blood from his clothes.

"Let's get going," said Everard. He trotted through the rear portal. A frightened concubine watched him with large eyes.

He had to blast the lock off an inner door. The room beyond held an Ing-model time shuttle, a few boxes with weapons and supplies, some books. Everard loaded it all into the machine except the fuel chest. That had to be left, so that up in the future he would learn of this and come back to stop the man who would be God.

"Suppose you take this to the warehouse in 1894," he said. "I'll ride our hopper back and meet you at the office."

Whitcomb gave him a long stare. The man's face was drawn. Even as Everard watched him, it stiffened with resolution.

"All right, old chap," said the Englishman. He smiled, almost wistfully, and clasped Everard's hand. "So long. Good luck."

Everard stared after him as he entered the great steel cylinder. That was an odd thing to say, when they'd be having tea up in 1894 in a couple of hours.

Worry nagged him as he went out of the building and mingled with the crowd. Charlie was a peculiar cuss. Well…

No one interfered with him as he left the city and entered the thicket beyond. He called the time hopper back down and, in spite of the need for haste lest someone come to see what kind of bird had landed, cracked a jug of ale. He needed it badly. Then he took a last look at Old England and jumped up to 1894.

Mainwethering and his guards were there as promised. The officer looked alarmed at the sight of one man arriving with blood clotting across his garments, but Everard gave him a reassuring report.

It took a while to wash up, change clothes, and deliver a full account to the secretary. By then, Whitcomb should have arrived in a hansom, but there was no sign of him. Mainwethering called the warehouse on the radio, and turned back with a frown. "He hasn't come yet," he said. "Could something have gone wrong?"

"Hardly. Those machines are foolproof." Everard gnawed his lip. "I don't know what the matter is. Maybe he misunderstood and went up to 1947 instead."

An exchange of notes revealed that Whitcomb had not reported in at that end either. Everard and Mainwethering went out for their tea. There was still no trace of Whitcomb when they got back.

"I had best inform the field agency," said Mainwethering. "Eh, what? They should be able to find him."

"No. Wait." Everard stood for a moment, thinking. The idea had been germinating in him for some time. It was dreadful.

"Have you a notion?"

"Yes. Sort of." Everard began shucking his Victorian suit. His hands trembled. "Get my twentieth-century clothes, will you? I may be able to find him by myself."

"The Patrol will want a preliminary report of your idea and intentions," reminded Mainwethering.

"To hell with the Patrol," said Everard.

-6-

London, 1944. The early winter night had fallen, and a thin cold wind blew down streets which were gulfs of darkness. Somewhere came the *crump* of an explosion, and a fire was burning, great red banners flapping above the roofs.

Everard left his hopper on the sidewalk—nobody was out when the V-bombs were falling—and groped slowly through the murk. November seventeenth; his trained memory had called up the date for him. Mary Nelson had died this day.

He found a public phone booth on the corner and looked in the directory. There were a lot of Nelsons, but only one Mary listed for the Streatham area. That would be the mother, of course. He had to guess that the daughter would have the same first name. Nor did he know the time at which the bomb had struck, but there were ways to learn that.

Fire and thunder roared at him as he came out. He flung himself on his belly while glass whistled where he had been. November seventeenth, 1944. The younger Manse Everard, lieutenant in the United States Army Engineers, was somewhere across the Channel, near the German guns. He couldn't recall exactly where, just then, and did not stop to make the effort. It didn't matter. He knew he was going to survive *that* danger.

The new blaze was a-dance behind him as he ran for his machine. He jumped aboard and took off into the air. High above London, he saw only a vast darkness spotted with flame. *Walpurgisnacht*, and all hell let loose on earth!

He remembered Streatham well, a dreary stretch of brick inhabited by little clerks and greengrocers and mechanics, the very petite bourgeoisie who had stood up and fought the power which conquered Europe to a standstill. There had been a girl living there, back in 1943…Eventually she married someone else.

Skimming low, he tried to find the address. A volcano erupted not far off. His mount staggered in the air, he almost lost his seat. Hurrying toward the place, he saw a house tumbled and smashed and flaming. It was only three blocks from the Nelson home. He was too late.

No! He checked the time—just ten-thirty—and jumped back two hours. It was still night, but the slain house stood solid in the gloom. For a second he wanted to warn those inside. But no. All over the world, people were dying. He was not Schtein, to take history on his shoulders.

He grinned wryly, dismounted, and walked through the gate. He was not a damned Danellian either. He knocked on the door, and it opened. A middle-aged woman looked at him through the murk, and he realized it was odd to see an American in civilian clothes here.

"Excuse me," he said. "Do you know Miss Mary Nelson?"

"Why, yes." Hesitation. "She lives nearby. She's coming over soon. Are you a friend?"

Everard nodded. "She sent me here with a message for you, Mrs…ah…"

"Enderby."

"Oh, yes, Mrs. Enderby. I'm terribly forgetful. Look, Miss Nelson wanted me to say she's very sorry but she can't come. However, she wants you and your entire family over at ten-thirty."

"All of us, sir? But the children—"

"By all means, the children too. Every one of you. She has a very special surprise arranged, something she can only show you then. All of you have to be there."

'Well,…all right, sir, if she says so."

"All of you at ten-thirty, without fail. I'll see you then, Mrs. Enderby." Everard nodded and walked back to the street.

He had done what he could. Next was the Nelson house. He rode his hopper three blocks down, parked it in the gloom of an alley, and walked up to the house. He was guilty too now, as guilty as Schtein. He wondered what the exile planet was like.

There was no sign of the Ing shuttle, and it was too big to conceal. So Charlie hadn't arrived yet. He'd have to play it by ear till then.

As he knocked on the door, he wondered what his saving of the Enderby family would mean. Those children would grow up, have children of their own: quite insignificant middle-class Englishmen, no doubt, but somewhere in the centuries to come an important man would be born or fail to be born. Of course, time was not very flexible. Except in rare cases, the precise ancestry didn't matter, only the broad pool of human genes and human society did. Still, this might be one of those rare cases.

A young woman opened the door for him. She was a pretty little girl, not spectacular but nice looking in her trim uniform. "Miss Nelson?"

"Yes?"

"My name is Everard. I'm a friend of Charlie Whitcomb. May I come in? I have a rather surprising bit of news for you."

"I was about to go out." she said apologetically.

"No, you weren't." Wrong line; she was stiffening with indignation. "Sorry. Please, may I explain?"

She led him into a drab and cluttered parlor. "Won't you sit down, Mr. Everard? Please don't talk too loudly. The family are all asleep. They get up early."

Everard made himself comfortable. Mary perched on the edge of the sofa, watching him with large eyes. He wondered if Wulfnoth and Eadgar were among her ancestors. Yes...undoubtedly they were, after all these centuries. Maybe Schtein was too.

"Are you in the Air Force?" she asked. "Is that how you met Charlie?"

"No. I'm in Intelligence, which is the reason for this mufti. May I ask when you last saw him?"

"Oh, weeks ago. He's stationed in France just now. I hope this war will soon be over. So silly of them to keep on when they must know they're finished, isn't it?" She cocked her head curiously. "But what is this news you have?"

"I'll come to it in a moment." He began to ramble as much as he dared, talking of conditions across the Channel. It was strange to sit conversing with a ghost. And his conditioning prevented him from telling the truth. He wanted to, but when he tried his tongue froze up on him.

"...and what it costs to get a bottle of red-ink ordinaire—"

"Please," she interrupted impatiently. 'Would you mind coming to the point? I do have an engagement for tonight."

"Oh, sorry. Very sorry, I'm sure. You see, it's this way—"

A knock at the door saved him. "Excuse me," she murmured, and went out past the blackout drapes to open it. Everard padded after her.

She stepped back with a small shriek. *"Charlie!"*

Whitcomb pressed her to him, heedless of the blood still wet on his Jutish clothes. Everard came into the hall. The Englishman stared with a kind of horror. "You..."

He snatched for his stunner, but Everard's was already out. "Don't be a fool," said the American. "I'm your friend. I want to help you. What crazy scheme did you have, anyway?"

"I...keep her here...keep her from going to—"

"And do you think *they* haven't got means of spotting you?" Everard slipped into Temporal, the only possible language in Mary's frightened presence. "When I left Mainwethering, he was getting damn suspicious. Unless we do this right, every unit of the Patrol is going to be alerted. The error will be rectified, probably by killing her. You'll go to exile."

"I..." Whitcomb gulped. His face was a mask of fear. "You...would you let her go ahead and die?"

"No. But this has to be done more carefully."

"We'll escape...find some period away from everything...go back to the dinosaur age, if we must."

Mary slipped free of him. Her mouth was pulled open, ready to scream. "Shut up!" said Everard to her. "Your life is in danger, and we're trying to save you. If you don't trust me, trust Charlie."

Turning back to the man, he went on in Temporal: "Look, fellow, there isn't any place or any time you can hide in. Mary Nelson died tonight. That's history. She wasn't around in 1947. That's history. I've already got myself in Dutch: the family she was going to visit will be out of their home when the bomb hits it. If you try to run away with her, you'll be found. It's pure luck that a Patrol unit hasn't already arrived."

Whitcomb fought for steadiness. "Suppose I jump up to 1948 with her. How do you know she hasn't suddenly reappeared in 1948? Maybe that's history too."

"Man, you *can't*. Try it. Go on, tell her you're going to hop her four years into the future."

Whitcomb groaned. "A giveaway—and I'm conditioned—"

"Yeh. You have barely enough latitude to appear this way before her, but talking to her, you'll have to lie out of it because you can't help yourself. Anyway, how would you explain her? If she stays Mary Nelson, she's a deserter from the W.A.A.F. If she takes another name, where's her birth certificate, her school record, her ration book, any of those bits of paper these twentieth-century governments worship so devoutly? It's hopeless, son."

'Then what can we do?"

"Face the Patrol and slug it out. Wait here a minute." There was a cold calm over Everard, no time to be afraid or to wonder at his own behavior.

Returning to the street, he located his hopper and set it to emerge five years in the future, at high noon in Piccadilly Circus. He slapped down the main switch, saw the machine vanish, and went back inside. Mary was in Whitcomb's arms, shuddering and weeping. The poor, damned babes in the woods!

"Okay." Everard led them back to the parlor and sat down with his gun ready. "Now we wait some more."

It didn't take long. A hopper appeared, with two men in Patrol gray aboard. There were weapons in their hands. Everard cut them down with a low-powered stun beam. "Help me to tie 'em up, Charlie," he said.

Mary huddled voiceless in a corner.

When the men awoke, Everard stood over them with a bleak smile. "What are we charged with, boys?" he asked in Temporal.

"I think you know," said one of the prisoners calmly. "The main office had us trace you. Checking up next week, we found that you had evacuated a family scheduled to be bombed. Whitcomb's record suggested you had then come here, to help him save this woman who was supposed to die tonight. Better let us go or it will be worse for you."

"I have not changed history," said Everard. "The Danellians are still up there, aren't they?"

"Yes, of course, but—"

"How did you know the Enderby family was supposed to die?"

"Their house was struck, and they said they had only left it because—"

"Ah, but the point is they did leave it. That's written. Now it's you who wants to change the past."

"But this woman here—"

"Are you sure there wasn't a Mary Nelson who, let us say, settled in London in 1850 and died of old age about 1900?"

The lean face grinned. "'You're trying hard, aren't you? It won't work. You can't fight the entire Patrol."

"Can't I, though? I can leave you here to be found by the Enderbys. I've set my hopper to emerge in public at an instant known only to myself. What's that going to do to history?"

"The Patrol will take corrective measures…as you did back in the fifth century."

"Perhaps! I can make it a lot easier for them, though, if they'll hear my appeal. I want a Danellian."

"What?"

"You heard me," said Everard. "If necessary, I'll mount that hopper of yours and ride a million years up. I'll point out to them personally how much simpler it'll be if they give us a break."

That will not be necessary.

Everard spun around with a gasp. The stunner fell from his hand.

He could not look at the shape which blazed before his eyes. There was a dry sobbing in his throat as he backed away.

Your appeal has been considered, said the soundless voice. *It was known and weighed ages before you were born. But you were still a necessary link in the chain of time. If you had failed tonight, there would not be mercy.*

To us, it was a matter of record that one Charles and Mary Whitcomb lived in Victoria's England. It was also a matter of record that Mary Nelson died with the family she was visiting in 1944, and that Charles Whitcomb had lived a bachelor and finally been killed on active duty with the Patrol, The discrepancy was noted, and as the smallest paradox is a dangerous weakness in the space-time fabric, it had to be rectified by eliminating one or the other fact from ever having existed. You have decided which it will be.

Everard knew, somewhere in his shaking brain, that the Patrolmen were suddenly free. He knew that his hopper had been…was being…would be snatched invisibly away the instant it materialized. He knew that history now read: W.A.A.F. Mary Nelson missing, presumed killed by bomb near the home of the Enderby family, who had all been at her house when their own was destroyed; Charles Whitcomb disappearing in 1947, presumed accidentally drowned. He knew that Mary was given the truth, conditioned against ever revealing it, and sent back with Charlie to 1850. He knew they would make their middle-class way through life, never feeling quite at home in Victoria's reign, that Charlie would often have wistful thoughts of what he had been in the Patrol…and then turn to his wife and children and decide it had not been such a great sacrifice after all.

That much he knew, and then the Danellian was gone. As the whirling darkness in his head subsided and he looked with clearing eyes at the two Patrolmen, he did not know what his own destiny was.

"Come on," said the first man. "Let's get out of here before somebody wakes up. We'll give you a lift back your year. 1954, isn't it?"

"And then what?" asked Everard.

The Patrolman shrugged. Under his casual manner lay the shock which had seized him in the Danellian's presence. "Report to your sector chief. You've shown yourself obviously unfit for steady work."

"So…just cashiered, huh?"

"You needn't be so dramatic. Did you think this case was the only one of its kind in a million years of Patrol work? There's a regular procedure for it.

"You'll want more training, of course. Your type of personality goes best with Unattached status—any age, any place, wherever and whenever you may be needed. I think you'll like it."

Everard climbed weakly aboard the hopper. And when he got off again, a decade had passed.

The First Love
By Olaf Haraldsson

From my hill I followed
The faring, when on horseback,
Lightly did the lovely
Let herself be outborne;
And her shiny eyes
Did all my joy bereave me.
Known it is, to no one
Naught of sorrows happen.

Formerly in fairness,
Filled with golden blossoms,
Trees stood green and trembling
Tall above the jarldom.
Soon their leaves grew sallow,
Silently, in Russia.
Only gold now garlands
Ingigerdha's forehead.

The Double-Dyed Villains

The Premier of Luan was speaking, and over the planet his face glared into telescreens and his voice rang its anger. Before the Administration Building milled a crowd that screamed itself hoarse before the enormously magnified image on the wall, screamed and cheered and surged like a living wave against the tight-held lines of the Palanthian Guard. There was mob violence in the air, a dog would have bristled at the stink of adrenalin and sensed the tension which crackled under the waves of explosive sound. The tautness seemed somehow to be transmitted over the screens, and watchers on the other side of the world raved at the image.

The Premier was young and dynamic and utterly sure of himself. There was steel in his tones, and his hard handsome face was vibrant with a deep inward, strength. He was, thought Wing Alak, quite a superior type.

In spite of being in the capital of the planet, Alak preferred sitting alone in his hotel room and watching the telescreen to joining the mob that yelled its hosannahs in the streets. He sat back with a drink in one hand and a cigarette in the other, physically relaxed as the speech shouted at him:

"...not only a matter of material gain, but of sacred Luanian honor. Lhing was ours, ours by right of our own blood and sweat and treasure, and the incredible betrayal of the League in giving it to Marhal as a political bribe shall not be permitted to succeed. We will fight for our rights and honor—if need be, we will fight the Patrol itself—fight and win!"

The cheers rose fifty stories to rattle the windows of Alak's room. Overhead rushed a squadron of navy speedsters, their gravitic drives noiseless but the thunder of cloven air rolling in their wake, and each of them carried bombs which could wipe out a city. Alak's thoughts turned to a more potent menace, the monster cruisers and battleships orbiting about Luan—yes, the situation was getting out of hand. He wondered, suddenly and grimly, if it might not have gone too far to be remedied.

"...we will not fight alone. The whole Galaxy waits only one bold leader to rise and throw off the yoke of the League. For four hundred years we have groaned under the most corrupt and cynical tyranny ever to rise in all man's tortured history. The League government remains in power only by such an unbelievable network of intrigue, bribery, threat, terror, betrayal, and appeal to all the worst elements of society that the like has never before been imagined. This is not mere oratory, people of Luan, it is sober truth which we have slowly and painfully learned over generations. Your government has carefully compiled a list of corrupt and terroristic acts of the Patrol which include every violation of every moral law existing on every planet in the universe, and each of these accusations has been verified in every detail. The Marhalian thievery is a minor matter in that list— but Luan has had enough!"

Wing Alak puffed on his cigarette in nervous breaths. It was, he reflected bleakly, not exaggerated more than political oratory required, and the anger of Luan's Tranis Voal had its counterpart on more planets than he cared to think about.

The speech paused for cheers, and the door chime sounded in Alak's room. He turned in his seat, scowling, to face the viewplate. It showed him a hard, unfamiliar face, and his hand stole toward his tunic pocket. Then he thought: *No, you fool! Force is the most useless possible course—here!*

He rose, pressing the admittance button, and he felt his spine crawl as four men entered. They were obviously secret agents—only what did police want with a harmless commercial traveler from Maxlan IV?

"Wing Alak of Sol III," declared one of the men, "you are under arrest for conspiracy against the state."

"There…must be some mistake." Alak licked his lips with just the right amount of nervousness, but his stomach was turning over with the magnitude of this catastrophe. "I am Gol Duhonitar of Maxlan IV—here, my papers."

The detective took them and put them in a pocket. "Forged identity papers are important evidence," he said tonelessly.

"I tell you, they're genuine, you can see the Patrol stamp and the League secretary for Maxlan has his signature—"

"Sure. Doesn't prove a thing. Search him, Gammal."

Voal's voice roared from the telescreen: "As of today, Luan has officially seceded from the Galactic League and war has been declared on Marhal. And let the Patrol's criminals dare try to stop us!"

Thokan looked across the table at his visitor, and then back at the notes heaped before him. "Just what does this mean?" he asked slowly.

The newcomer, a Sirian like himself, shrugged. "Let's not waste time" he said. "You want to win the coming system-wide election. Here are fifty thousand League credits, good anywhere in the civilized Galaxy, as a retainer. There are a million more waiting if you lose."

Thokan half rose, then settled back. His tendrils hung limply. "Lose?" he whispered.

"Yes. We don't want you as Director of this system. But we have nothing against you personally, and would rather pay you to conduct a losing campaign than spend even more money corrupting the electorate and otherwise fighting you. If you really try, you can win an honest election. But we are determined that Ruhoc shall continue as Director, and, to put it melodramatically, we will stop at nothing to insure your defeat."

Strickenly, Thokan looked into the visitor's bleak eyes: "But you said you were from the Patrol!"

"I am."

"The Patrol—" Thokan's voice rose. "But Cosmos! The Patrol is the law-enforcement agency of the *League*!"

"That's right. And, friend, you don't know what a really dirty campaign is like till you've seen the Patrol in action. However, we don't want to ruin your reputation and your private business and the honesty of a lot of officials connected with elections. We would much prefer simply to pay you to stop campaigning so effectively."

"But—Oh, no—But *why?*"

"You are an honest being, too honest and too set in your views—including a belief in the League constitution's clause that the Patrol should stay out of local politics—for us. Ruhoc is a scoundrel, yes, but he is open to suggestions if they are, shall I say, subsidized. Also, under him the present corruption and hopeless inefficiency of the Sirian military forces will continue."

"I know—it's one of the major points in my campaign—Cosmos, you race-traitor, do you want the Centaurians simply to come in and take us over?" Thokan snarled into the Patrolman's impassive face. "Have they bribed the Patrol? Do they really run the League? You incredible villain, I—"

"You have your choice." The voice was pitiless. "Think it over. My orders are simply to spend what is necessary to win Ruhoc the election. How I spend it is a matter of indifference to me."

As the policeman approached him, Alak drew a deep breath and let one hand, hanging by his side, squeeze the bulb in that tunic pocket. The situation was suddenly desperate, and his act was of ultimate emergency.

The sphere of brain-stunning supersonic vibrations emitted by the bulb was so heterodyned that most of Alak's body, including his head, was not affected. But otherwise it had a range of some meters, and the detective dropped as if poleaxed. They'd be out for some minutes, but there was no time to lose, not an instant of the fleeing seconds. Alak grabbed his cloak, reversing it to show a dark blue color quite unlike the gray he had been seen wearing. He put its cowl over his red hair, shading his thin sharp features, and went out the door. The change should help some when his description was broadcast. It had better help, he thought grimly. He was the only Patrolman on a planet that had just proclaimed its intentions of killing Patrolmen on sight.

Hurry, hurry!

He went down the nearest gravity shaft and out the lobby into the street. Voal's speech had just ended, and the crowds were howling themselves hoarse. Alak mingled with them. Luan having been colonized largely by Baltravians, who in turn were descendants of Terrestrials, he was physically inconspicuous, but his Solarian accent was not healthy at the moment. Sol was notoriously the instigator and leader of the Galactic League.

The street telescreens were showing a parade of the Palanthian Guard, rank upon brilliantly uniformed rank of the system's crack troops, and the brassy rhythm of their bands pulsed in the veins and shrieked in the head. *Beat, beat, beat,* yelling bugles and rolling drums and the heart-stopping slam of a thousand boots landing simultaneously on the pavement. Swing and crash and tramp, aircraft snarling overhead with their sides afire in the sun, banners flying and trumpets roaring and the long wild charge of heroes to vengeance and glory. All Luan went crazy and shouted for blood.

Alak reflected tautly that the danger to Marhal was no less threatening other systems. The Luanian battle fleet could get to Sol, say, in three weeks, and if Voal suspected just how strong the Patrol really was—or wasn't—

Alak had seen the dead planets swinging on their lonely way. Their seas mourned on ashen beaches, and the ash blew inland on whining winds, in over the dusty plains. Their suns were a dim angry copper-red, smoldering in skies of scudding dust and ash. Only the wind and the dust stirred, only the empty heavens and the barren seas had voice. At night there might still be an evil blue glow of radioactivity, roiling in the ash storms or glimmering out of the fused craters. Here and there the wind might briefly uncover crumbling skeletons of once sentient creatures, with only dust now stirring in their hollow skulls, with the storms piping through their ribs. A few snags of broken buildings still stood, and now and then there were acid rains sluicing out of the birdless skies. But no life stirred anywhere. War had passed by, and returned to the remotely shining stars.

He made his way through the jammed avenue into a quieter side street. Any moment, now, he could expect the hunt to start. He went with careful casualness over to a parked private car, a fast little ground-air job. He had a Patrol key, which would open any ordinary magnetolock, and with it he let himself into the vehicle and got started. Car stealing was a minor offense compared to what he was wanted for.

As he drove, he scowled in thought. That Voal's police had known him for what he was indicated that the leader's interests and spy system reached well beyond the local stars. He must have agents on Maxlan IV, which lay seventy lightyears from Luan's sun. If he had known the name of the Patrol's agent, it would indicate that he knew a lot more about the Patrol itself, and this supposition was supported by Voal's mention of fully verified cases of League perfidy. Though it was no secret that the Patrol used corrupt methods, the details were carefully suppressed wherever possible.

What was more to the immediate point, the police must have followed all Alak's movements. So now his underworld contacts must be arrested, leaving Alak stranded and alone on Luan. And a League agent who had associated himself with some of the worst crooks on the planet could expect no particular mercy.

Headquarters underestimated the danger, thought Alak. *They took this to be just another obscure squabble between frontier systems, and now Luan turns out to be a highly organized, magnificently armed power spoiling for a fight. I suppose slip-ups are bound to occur in trying to co-ordinate a million stars and this is one of the mistakes—and I'm in the middle of it.*

He drove aimlessly, trying to collect his thoughts. Six weeks of careful work in the Luanian underworld were shot. His bribes and promises had been getting a program of sabotage under way which should have thrown plenty of sand in the gears of the war machine. He was on the point of contacting ambitious officers who were ready to overthrow the elected government and establish their own dictatorship—one amenable to the Patrol as long as it had free access to the public treasury. Only—Cosmos, he'd been finding it too easy! The police had been stringing him along, giving him enough rope to hang himself several times over and now—

Wing Alak licked his lips. A lot of Patrolmen got killed on the job, and it looked as if he would be another name on the list, and he personally much preferred being a live coward to a dead hero. He did not have a single lethal weapon, and he was alone on a planet out to get him. It didn't look good.

The hall was old, a long dim structure of gray stone, where only the leaping ruddy flames broke the chill dusk and where the hollow echoes were like voices of the dead centuries which had stirred bloodily here. Many a council had been held in the great chamber, the results being announced with screaming war-horns and the clash of arms and armor, but perhaps none so dark as the secret meeting tonight.

The twelve earls of Mordh were seated at the head of the huge ancient table. Red firelight seemed to splash them with blood, throwing their grim bony faces into eerie visibility against the sliding misshapen shadows. Outside the windows, the mighty autumn wind flung sleet and rain at the castle walls and roared about its towers.

Dorlok, who had called the meeting, spoke first. His deep voice was low, and the storm snarled over and around its rumble: "To me, at least, the situation has become intolerable. When so-called honor clashes with basic instincts—and just how much honor does our dead king have left?—there is only one choice if we wish to remain sane. The king must go."

Yorm sprang out of his seat. The light gleamed bloodily on his slitted yellow eyes. Three of his fists were clenched, the fourth half drew his dagger from its sheath. "Treason!" he gasped.

"As you like." Dorlok's scarred face twisted in a snarl. "Yet I would say that we have a higher duty than our oath to the king. As earls of Mordh, which now rules the entire planet and thus our entire species, we are pledged to preserve the integrity of our race and traditions. This the king, corrupted by the she-devil Franna, has lost. He is no longer a warrior, he is a drinker and idler in his palace—the swords of Mordh rust, the people cry for battle, and *he* sits under the complete dominion of his mistress. This won't be the first time a king has been deposed—and we will be driving her off the throne rather than him."

More than half of the earls nodded their heads in dark agreement. Valtan murmured: "I wonder if she is of this planet at all? Could she not be some devilish robot invented by the Patrol's unholy agents? Her very nature is alien to all we know."

"No, no, my agents have checked very carefully on her background," said Dorlok. "She is the daughter of a Mordhan spaceman who sold her on Sol III after he had run up a great gambling debt—sold her to a man of the very Patrol which seeks to destroy slavery, or says it does! Franna was educated in the Solar System, apparently with the ultimate object of becoming the king's mistress. I have reason to believe plastic surgery was used to make her the most beautiful of our race, and certainly her education in the arts of love—At any rate, she did come back here, enslaved the king, and now for ten years has run the country—the planet—the system! And—undoubtedly on behalf of the cursed Patrol!"

"It was an evil day that the Galactic explorers landed here," said Valtan glumly.

"To date, yes," answered Yorm. "Of course, it was more or less accidental. If they had known we are a carnivorous people to whom combat is a psychological necessity, they would probably have left us in our feudal state. As it was, the introduction of Galactic technology soon enabled Mordh to subjugate the rest of the planet." His yellow eyes flamed. "And now…now we could go out and fight on a more glorious scale than the old heroes dreamed…go out conquering among the stars!"

"Except that Franna holds the king slothful while we eat our hearts in tameness and kill ourselves in silly little private duels for lack of better occupation," said Valtan. "But we are sworn by our honor to obey the king. What to do? What to do?"

"Kill her," snarled another.

"Little use—the king would know who had done that, and have us all slain—and soon the Patrol would find some other agent of control," said Dorlok. "No, the king must go, too."

Yorm shook his head. "I won't do it. No one in my family ever broke his word and I won't be the first."

"It is a hard choice—" mused Valtan.

In the end, seven of the great earls of Mordh were prepared to assassinate the king. The others held back but Dorlok had, before calling this meeting, sworn them to secrecy about it. They would not help in the killing, but they would not hinder it and be glad enough to see it done.

Dorlok swept his cloak about him.

"I'll let you know my arrangements tomorrow," he said.

He went to a certain remote room in the castle and let himself in with a special key. *She* was waiting, and his heart turned over at her loveliness.

"Well?" she asked.

His voice was thick as he gave her the names of the rebellious earls. She nodded gravely. "I'll see that they are arrested tonight," she said. "They'll have their choice—exile to the second planet or suicide."

Dorlok sat down, burying his head in two brawny hands, the other two hanging limp in his lap. "Now I'm forever damned," he groaned. "I really, deep inside, believe in what I told them when I was provoking them. Those 'weak links' were actually the hope of Mordh. And I've sold them—for you." He lifted desperate eyes. "And I'm even betraying my lord the king, with you," he said hopelessly. "I love you—and I curse the day I saw you."

Franna stroked his mane. "Poor Dorlok," she murmured softly. "Poor, helpless, honest warrior."

* * *

Alak abandoned his car in an alley near the spaceport and set out on foot through the dark tangle of narrow streets and passageways which was the Old City. The decayed district clustered on the west side of the port and its warehouses, and had become the hangout of most of the city's criminal elements. It was not wise to go alone after dark through its dreary huddle, and twilight was beginning to creep over the capital. But Alak had no choice—and he had become used to such thieves' quarters.

Presently he located Yamen's tavern and slipped cautiously past the photoelectric doors. The place was crowded as usual with the sweepings of space, including a good many nonhumans from remote planets, and he was grateful for the dim light and the fog of smoke. There was a live show performing on a tiny stage, but even its nudity was no recommendation and Alak did not regret having to sit with his back to it in order to watch the door. He sat at a small table in a dark corner and slipped a coin in the vendor for beer. When it arrived from the chute it was warm and thin, but it was at least alcoholic. He sipped it and sat gloomily waiting for something to happen.

That didn't take long. A Rassalan slithered into the chair opposite him. The reptile's beadly glittering eyes searched under the man's cowl. "Hello," he said. "You might buy me a drink. Wouldn't snub an old friend, would you?"

"Hardly, when the old friend would let out a squawk as to my identity if I did," said Alak wryly. He set the vendor for the acrid and ultimately poisonous vurzin to which he knew the Rassalan was addicted, and put in the coin. "How are things, Slinh?" he asked.

"So-so." The little dragonlike creature shrugged his leathery wings. "But the sivva-peddling racket is getting unsafe. Voal's narcotics squad is cracking down. I can't complain—made my share on this planet—but I'm about to leave Luan." His black passionless eyes studied Alak's foxy face. "I suppose you are, too."

"Why so?" asked the Solarian cautiously.

"Look Sarb Duman—I might as well stick to the alias you've been giving around here, though the police have been broadcasting a certain other name for the past half hour or more—let's be sensible. When an unknown with apparently limitless resources starts organizing the crooks of a planet for something big whose nature he won't reveal exactly, a being who's seen something of the Galaxy begins to have suspicions. When the police suddenly pick up all this stranger's contacts and start televising 'Wanted' notices for him with a different name and occupation appended—well, any high-grade moron can guess the story." Slinh sipped his drink, adding smugly, "I consider myself a step above moron. Seems I have just now heard rumors of arrests in the army, too. Seems there has been a revolutionary tendency—Could the mysterious stranger have any connection?"

"Could be," said Alak. He didn't inquire into the nature of the so quickly spreading rumors, or how they had got started. Someday the Patrol must investigate the evidence hinting at some race in the Galaxy which had not chosen to reveal its telepathic abilities but to use them instead for private advantage. At the moment there was more urgent business.

"I might have a little trouble leaving this planet," said Alak. "You might, too."

"I can always find a hiding place and go into hibernation for a few years till they forget about me," said Slinh. "But a human at large might have difficulties even staying alive. I doubt if any Luanian crooks would help a"—he lowered his hissing voice—"Patrolman now that there's a war on. In such times, the mob hysteria officially known as patriotism infects all classes of society."

"True. But illogical. Patrolmen are more tolerant toward lawbreakers than local police."

Slinh shook his scaly head in some bewilderment. "I never could figure out the Patrol," he said. "Even its members of my own race I can't understand. Officially it exists to coordinate the systems of the Galactic League and to enforce the laws of the central authority. But after a while I quit paying attention to the stories of fabulous raids and arrests by Patrolmen and began watching for myself and speaking to eyewitnesses. And y'know, I have not been able to verify one case of the Patrol acting directly against a crook. The best they ever do is give the local police some technical advice, and that's rare. I'm beginning to suspect that the stories of the huge Patrol battle fleet are deliberate lies and the stereographs of it fakes—that though the Patrol makes big claims, it's never yet really arrested a criminal. In fact"—Slinh's claws tightened about his glass—"it seems one of the most corrupt organizations in the Galaxy. Voal's speech today was—true! I know of more cases where it's made alliance with crooks, or supported crooked governments, or engaged in crooked political deals, that I could easily count. Like in this case here—first the Patrol on the feeblest 'right of discovery' excuse, awards Lhing to the Marhalian System—Lhing, that was a Luanian development from the first—and then it seeks to overthrow the democratically elected Luanian government and set up some kind of revolutionary junta that's sure to empty the public coffers before running for a distant planet. I don't blame Luan for seceding from the League!"

"You could turn me in," said Alak. "There must be a reward."

"Not I," said Slinh. He grinned evilly. "The police don't approve of sivva or those who sell it. Also, what's Luan to me? They could blow up the planet for all I care—once I'm off it. And finally—it's barely possible we could make a deal."

Alak ordered another beer and vurzin. "Pray continue," he said. "You interest me strangely."

Despite his purpose, despite the knowledge he had and the implacable hostility which seethed within him, Sharr felt a stirring of awe as he entered the cathedral. The long nave loomed before him, a dusky immensity lit with the wonderful chromatic sunlight that streamed through the stained-glass windows; the vaulted ceiling was lost in a twilight of height through which fluttered white birds like living benedictions; the heavy languor of incense was in the cool dark air, and music breathed invisible beauty about him from—somewhere. Here, he thought, was peace and security, rest for the weary and hope for the grieving—

Aye, the peace and security of death, the resting from duty, and a false cold-bloodedly manufactured hope which destroyed souls. The magnificent shell of the cathedral covered a cosmic rottenness that—

The archbishop stood waiting for him near the great altar, resplendent in the dazzling robes of the new church. He was of this planet, Crios, but tall and impressive, with the cold wisdom of the Galaxy behind his eyes—the upper clergy of the new god were all Crians educated on League planets. Sharr was acutely conscious of his own shabby dress and his own ignorance of the cynical science that made miracles to order. No wonder all Crios was turning from the old faith to this lying devil who called himself a new god.

"Greeting, my son," said the archbishop sonorously. "I was told by my angel you were coming hither and—"

"I am not your son," said Sharr flatly, "and I happen to know that your 'angel' is a creature from the stars who has to live in a tank but has the unholy power to read men's thoughts—"

"That is blasphemy," said the archbishop mildly, "but since you have been misled all your life, even to the extent of becoming a high priest of the false god, you will be forgiven this time."

"Oh, I know your artificial thunderbolts—you must have some, all your other miracles are artificial—could smite me where I stand," said Sharr wearily. "No matter. My knowledge will not die with me."

The archbishop's eyes narrowed. Sharr hurried on: "When the strangers first came from beyond the stars, they brought a great hope to Crios. They cured us of many ancient ills, they gave us machines which produced more abundantly than slaves ever could…oh, yes, all the nations of Crios were glad to unify and join their Galactic League as a whole planet. But now I see all this was but the mask of the Evil Ones."

"In what way?" asked the other. "Before, there was only one faith on Crios. Now all gods can compete equally. If the stronger—that is, the truer—gods drive the weaker from the hearts of the people, what harm? Rather it is good. If your god is true, let him produce miracles such as ours."

"Let us not mince words," said Sharr. "There is no one here but us. All Crios rejoiced at the possession of spaceships, for now we could bring the true faith to other worlds, saving countless souls from the Evil Ones. But no sooner had we begun organizing a great crusade than *you* appeared—and your sly words and your false miracles and your machine-made magnificence turn more and more Crian hearts to the god in which you yourselves do not believe."

"How do you know we don't?"

"Few Crians have been to space, and most of those who went have returned as traitors like yourself," said Sharr. *I* went to see what power this Galactic lord of yours has elsewhere. I had my own ship and I used my own eyes. I saw that no other world had ever heard of him. I saw machines doing the same sort of things which you do here, seemingly by the power of your god, to impress the ignorant—building your churches overnight, scattering gold from nowhere, turning one metal into another; I saw creatures of horrible aspect which read minds—Oh, I began to see what your god really was. When I came back, I did a little investigation, I had my spies here and there—I know you for the cold-blooded liars you are."

"Why should we lie? What is the point in preaching a false religion?"

"Power, glory—I can think of many reasons, but my personal belief is that you are agents of the Evil Ones, sent to destroy the great Crian crusade before it got started. Had all of this planet been pure in faith, the All-Father would have aided us and we would have swept the Galaxy before us into his fold—now we must first get rid of the false Galactic lord and then slowly, by prayer and repentance, win back our worthiness."

The archbishop smiled, a curiously chilling smile. "And how will you go about it?" he asked softly.

"I have taken care that all priests of the true faith know what I do," said Sharr. "It won't help you to kill me. We will tell the truth to the people. We have prepared machines which will duplicate a number of your miracles." Sharr lifted a clenched fist and his voice shook with triumph: "I came, really, to warn you—if you're wise, you will leave this planet at once!"

The expected dismay did not appear. The archbishop said calmly and implacably: "You might be better off doing that. Surely you don't think we didn't foresee this?"

With a sense of dawning horror, Sharr stood in the singing gloom while the white birds circled far overhead. He heard the steady, relentless voice continue:

"I doubt if your machines will work. You never heard of an inhibitor field, but we have our projectors ready to generate one over the whole planet if need be. But it will not stop certain other devices we have had in preparation. If you blaspheme against the Galactic lord, major miracles will be in order. The lord himself might appear, ten kilometers tall with lightning blazing around him. Can your god do that?"

"Then"–Sharr spoke out of a dry, constricted throat–"you admit it is true–?"

"If you like," said the archbishop cheerfully. "But try to get anyone to believe that."

Slinh had a room—more accurately, a den—in one of the old abandoned sewers under the city. The little stony niche was dank and slimy and vile-smelling, but it was at least fairly safe from the police who were rounding up all aliens. Wing Alak sat hunched on the floor and cursed the day he was born.

"This hideout may be saving my life," he grumbled, "but I wonder if life is worth saving on such terms."

The little reptile coiled before him leered complacently. "It's all I can offer the great Patrolman," he gibed. His eyes glistened in the dim glow of the radiant heater that was his sole article of furniture. "If you don't like it—"

"Never mind, never mind." Alak tried to get down another mouthful of the fishy mess the Rassalan called food but decided it involved too great a risk of losing what he already had eaten. "Now about this deal you offered to make—we have to act fast. Already we're too late to prevent the war but it'll take the Luanian battle fleet a few days to get started for Marhal, or the Marhalians a few days to get to us. In that time we have to stop the war. Once battle is joined, it'll be pretty hopeless before several million have been killed."

"Never mind the pious platitudes," said Slinh coldly. "A being who makes deals with sivva peddlers can't afford to moralize. The point is that I'm running a terrific risk in helping you and will expect a commensurate reward."

"Such as—?"

"How about a million League credits? That's a good round number."

"Done." Alak reached for his checkbook. "Only I'll give you my personal check. Then if I'm killed and you escape"—he grinned in the sullen red light—"it'll do you no good, because I haven't near that much in my account. But if we both survive, the Patrol will transfer a million to me and you'll get 'em."

"How do I know you won't welsh?"

"You don't. But if you think back, you may recall that the Patrol has that much honor. Not that we have any notions about the sacredness of oaths—I've committed perjury often enough when the occasion called for it—but we don't want to antagonize allies such as yourself. You, for instance, get around. You have contacts. We may have other jobs for you in the future."

"I may be a sivva runner," said Slinh contemptuously, "but I haven't yet sunk to being a Patrolman." He took the check and laid it carefully in the purse worn about his neck. "Very well. Now I've given you a hideout, but you can't stay here long. So I'll help you along further in case you can find a way for us both to get off this planet."

"If I complete my job, we both will," replied Alak. "If I don't, it'll be too bad—for me at any rate." He looked into the dripping gloom of the tunnel. The light was like blood on his thin pale face.

Slinh shivered. "You're crazy as well as a crook," he said. "Two hunted, weaponless beings against an armed system—Starfire, even stereofilms don't indulge in that kind of trash any more." He huddled closer to the heater. "Why doesn't your glorious Patrol just bring its great battle fleet over here and tell the Luanians there'll be peace or else? What kind of policeman is it that makes deals with criminals and skulks in old sewers?"

Alak ignored the complaint. Presently he stirred, holding cold hands over the red glow. "Voal is officially only premier of Luan and its colonies on other planets," he said. "But he has influence enough to swing events as he wishes."

"Unfortunately, he believes in what he says. You can't bribe him."

"No, maybe not. Unless the price was sufficiently high—Look, he's married. He has two little children and I don't think those pictures of him playing with them are all posed."

"If you're thinking what I'm thinking—" began Slinh. "Anyway, the secret service guards—"

Alak took the vibrosphere out of his pocket. "I fooled them with this once," he said. "It's a secret Patrol weapon and it may fool them again. It has to!" Briefly, he explained its operation. Then he went on, his voice rising with excitement:

"Voal has a private estate in the country, about fifty kilometers from here. His family should be there—and you can carry a three-year-old child—"

They sneaked out of the tunnel after dark, emerging in a narrow alley of the Old City. Crouching back into the shadows, they strained their senses—no, no vigilance beyond routine patrols and the tension that lay like a shroud over the whole planet, the expectation of death from the skies. The whole capital huddled under its force dome, waiting for the hammer blows of hyperatomic bombs and gravity snatchers, the silent murder of radiodust and biotoxin and all the synthetic hell which could lay waste a world in hours. Whether or not the enemy bombardments could penetrate that shield was an open question—it was the business of the navy to see that the matter was never decided, by going to Marhal and blowing the system open before the Marhalians took off for Luan.

Alak and Slinh went along the darkened walks. Not many beings were abroad, though the taverns shook with an unnatural hysterical merriment. It was no trick to find a parked ground-air car and appropriate it with the help of Alak's key. The difficulty would lie in escaping from the city.

The Patrolman sent the car whispering into the sky toward the dimly glowing force-field. In moments, the call screen was buzzing and blinking an angry red. Alak switched over to the police band, keeping his face cowled and shadowed. An indignant helmeted head glared out of the screen at him.

"Where do you think you're going?" demanded the policeman.

"Officer, I've got to get out of the city," said Alak. "My wife and children—"

"The screen isn't lowered for any civilian in wartime. One second without protection and—Now get back on the ground where you belong."

"Be reasonable, officer. If the Marhalians were within ten lightyears you'd be alerted. I…I wasn't expecting war. I left my family up at North Pole Resort—that's no place for them to be in wartime. They'll recall my wife anyway, she's an electronician—"

"How many times must I—"

"Of course, I could take it up with my old friend Jeron Kovals," said Alak, naming the city police chief, "but I didn't think he'd want to be bothered—"

"Well, there's a lot of military and government traffic tonight. Wait till the next official car comes along, then you can go out with it."

"Thanks," Alak snapped off the screen and let his body relax, muscle by muscle. It was as much as he'd dared hope for. But if his theft was discovered while he waited—

It wasn't. The stolen car slipped past the lowered force-dome together with a long sleek black flier bearing several stars. Alak took a direct north course until the city was behind the horizon, then opened the car up and swung in a screaming arc for the Premier's estate.

Nighted countryside slipped beneath him. The numbers representing position co-ordinates changed on the car's dashboard. He let the autopilot take over, and studied the landscape below.

"Mostly agricultural," he said.

"But…wait, there's a pretty big region of forested hills. We'll hide there."

"If we escape to hide," said Slinh gloomily.

When they were within a kilometer of Voal's home, Alak halted the car and hung motionless on its gravity beams. "They'd detect a metal object coming any closer," he said. "I'll wait here for you, Slinh."

Wordlessly, the reptile opened the door. His leathery wings flapped and the night swallowed him.

The servants were wakened by a shout and the sound of falling bodies. A blaster roared in the dark. Someone screamed and there was heard a beating of wings out the nursery window.

When order of a sort was restored, it was found that—something—had come into the room, rendering several guards unconscious on the way; one, who had had a brief glimpse at which he had fired, swore it was a devil complete with tail and bat wings. Be that as it may, Alia, youngest daughter of the Premier of Luan, was missing, and a note addressed to her father lay on the floor.

He read it with his cheeks whitening:

> Bring ten thousand League credits in unmarked bills tomorrow night at 0100 hours to that island in the Mortha River lying one hundred and three kilometers due south-southwest of your country house. Do not tell police or make any attempt to use tracer beams or otherwise trail us, or you will not see your child again.

The Zordoch of the Branna Kai was dead, and over the whole planet Cromman and such other planets of the system as had been colonized, there was mourning; for the hereditary chief of the most powerful of the clans had been well loved.

Duwan stood at the window and looked out over the great estate of his fathers. Torches bobbed through the dusk, a long ceremonial procession approached the castle with the slowness of ancient ritual. The weird skirl of pipes and the rolling thunder of drums rose in the evening, breaking in a surf of sound against the high stone walls, surf that sent its broken spindrift up to the ears of Duiwan. He savored the sound, hungrily.

The Zordoch of the Branna Kai was dead; and the chiefs of the clans were coming with their immemorial ceremonies to give the crown to his eldest son.

A slave entered, genuflecting before the tall arrogant figure, purple-robed and turbaned, that stood before the window. "Your pardon, lord," he said fearfully, "but a stranger desires admittance."

"Eh?" Duwan scowled. The castle was closed to all but the slowly approaching chiefs. The old rituals were not to be disturbed nor did Duwan wish distraction in his greatest of hours. He snarled his gathering anger: "I'll have the warders' heads for this."

"Sire," mumbled the slave "he did not come in by the gates. He landed on the roof in an airship. He is not of Cromman, but from some strange world—"

"Hm-m-m?" Duwan pricked up his ears, and an ominous tingle ran along his spine. He could not imagine a Galactic having much interest in as newly discovered and backward a system as this. Later, of course, after a progressive had held the Zordochy for a few years—but now—"Send him in."

The stranger came so quickly that Duwan suspected he had been on the way while the slave went ahead to get permission. The Crommanite recognized him as terrestrial, though he did not have the look of a Solarian—probably some colonist. What was more to the point, he wore the blue uniform of the League Patrol.

The human bowed formally. "Your pardon," he said, "but I am on an urgent mission." He glanced out the window at the approaching torches. "In fact, I am almost too late."

"That is true," replied Duwan coldly. "I must ask you to leave before the chiefs reach the castle's gates."

"My business can be accomplished in less time. I am, as you see, a representative of the Patrol—here are my credentials, if you wish to see them."

Duwan barely glanced at the papers. "I am familiar with the like," he said. "After all, Cromman has been in the League for almost a century now, though we have had little outside contact." He felt, somehow, irritated at the compulsion, that he must explain the fact: "When we were introduced to spaceships and the like, we naturally wished to develop our own planet and its sisters first before venturing into other worlds. Also, most of the Zordochs were conservatives. But a newer generation of leaders is arising—I myself, as you see, am about to become head of the most influential clan—and we will see some changes now."

"That is what I came about," said the Patrolman. "It may seem strange, but I will make it short: I bear a most urgent request from Galactic headquarters that you refuse the crown when it is offered you tonight and direct that it be given to your younger brother Kian."

For a moment the sheer barefaced effrontery of it held Duwan paralyzed. Then the black rage that made him grab for his sword was throttled by a grim control, and when he spoke his voice was unnaturally level: "You must be mad."

"Perfectly sane, I assure you. But hurry, please, the procession will be here soon."

"But what imaginable reason—Why, Kian is more hopelessly conservative than even my father—And the League constitution specifically forbids interference in the internal affairs of member planets—" Duwan shook his head, slowly, slowly. "I can't comprehend it."

"The Patrol recognizes no laws save those of its own making—otherwise there is only immediate necessity," said the human cynically. "I will tell you why we wish this later, if you desire, but there is no time now. You must agree at once."

"Why…you are just crazy—" The rage came again, bitter in Duwan's throat: "If you try to impose your will forcibly on Cromman, you'll find that our boast of being a warrior race is not idle."

"There is no question of force. It is not necessary." The Patrolman reached into his portfolio. "You traveled quite a bit through the Galaxy some years ago. And the moral code of Cromman is stern and inflexible. Those two facts are sufficient."

With a horrible feeling of having stepped over the edge of the world, Duwan watched him extract a bundle of stereofilms, psychographs, and other material from his case. "When the chiefs arrive with the crown" said the Patrolman smugly, "I will explain that, while the League does not wish to meddle, it feels it to be a duty to warn its member planets against making mistakes. And the coronation of a Zordoch who had been guilty of, shall we say, moral turpitude in the fleshpots of the Galaxy, would be a definite mistake."

"But—" With a feeling of physical illness, Duwan looked at the pictures. "But…by the Spirit, I was young then—"

"So you were. But will that matter to Cromman?"

"I…I'll deny—"

"Stereofilms could be faked, yes, but not psychographic recordings, and there are plenty of scientists on Cromman who know that. Also we could produce a Crommanite or two who had been with you—"

"But—Oh, no!—Why, one of those Crommanites was a Patrolman who…who *took* me to that place—"

"Certainly. In fact, just between us—and I shall deny it on oath if you repeat it in public—the Patrol maintains that house and others like it and makes a point of persuading as many influential and potentially influential beings as possible to have a fling there. The records we get are often useful later on."

Duwan reached for his sword. The Patrolman said evenly: "If I fail to report back, this evidence will be made public. I think you will be wiser to refuse the Zordochy for reasons of…well, ill health. Then this information can safely gather dust in the Patrol's secret files."

For a long, long moment Duwan stared at the sword. The tears blurring his eyes seemed like a film of rust across the bright steel. Then he clashed it back into its sheath.

"I have no choice," he said. "But when the League breaks its own laws, and employs the filthiest blackmailers to do the job, then justice is dead in the Galaxy."

Three days later, Alak's agreed code call went over the Luanian telescreens. Slinh received it and lifted the stolen car into the air. "Now be quiet," he told the dirty, tear-faced child with him. "We're going back to Daddy." He added to himself "Of course, it's possible that Daddy had Alak drugged or tortured to give the signal. That's what I'd have tried. But if so, it's only what the Patrolman deserves for leaving me in charge of this brat."

For fear of its radiations revealing his hidden car to searchers—metal detectors were dangerous enough—Slinh had only turned the televisor on for a few seconds at the agreed hours. Now, as he listened to the newscasts, a dawning amazement held him motionless. "Marhal has offered compromise—Premier Voal in secret conference—Secession from League being reconsidered—"

Holy Galaxy! Had Alak really pulled it off? If a crook like that Patrolman, hunted and alone, could overturn a planet—

Slinh set his vehicle down on the lawn of the Premier's city residence. The force dome was down and only a few military craft were in sight. Peace—

Tranis Voal stood before the house with his arm about his wife's shoulders. There were no other officials in sight, with the possible exception of Alak. The Patrolman stood to one side, his hair like coppery fire in the sun, the look of a fox who has just raided a chicken coop on his sharp face; but there was somehow a loneliness over him. Though he was the conqueror he was still one man against a world.

Slinh led the child outside. Voal uttered a queer little choking cry and fell on his knees before her. When he looked up, tears gleamed in his eyes and ran down his haggard cheeks. "She's all right," he choked. "She's all right—"

"Of course she's all right," said Alak impatiently. "Now that your government has gone too far toward peace to back down, I don't mind telling you that no matter what your attitude would have been, she wouldn't have been harmed. Patrolmen may have no scruples, but we aren't fiends." He added slowly, somewhat bitterly, "Only a completely honest man, a fanatic or a fool, can be really fiendish."

Slinh tugged at Alak's sleeve. "Now will you tell me just what happened?" he hissed.

"What I hoped for," said Alak. "After you left me on the island and took the kid into hiding, I just waited. That night Voal showed up with the money."

"Hm-m-m—so you also got a little personal profit out of it," said the Rassalan slyly.

"I didn't want his money, I didn't take it," said Alak wearily. "The ransom demand was simply a device to make him think a gang of ordinary kidnapers had taken the girl. If he'd known it was the hated and untrustworthy Patrolman who had her, he'd probably have been out of his head with fear and loathing, have brought all the cops on the planet down on me, and…well, this way I got him alone and I had a club over his head. I told him the Patrol couldn't weigh the life of one child against several million, perhaps billion, and that we'd kill the kid if he didn't listen to reason. He did. I came here with him, secretly, and used him as my puppet. With his emergency powers, he was able to stop the scheduled assault on Marhal and swing the government toward conciliation. A truce has been declared, and a League mediator is on the way."

Voal came over. The wrath that had ravaged his face still smoldered sullenly in his eyes. "Now that I have her back," he said, "how do you know I'll continue to follow your dictates?"

"I've come to know you in the last few days," answered Alak coolly. "One thing I've found out is that, unlike me, you're a perfectly honest man, and you want to do what you think is right. That makes it possible for me to take an oath of secrecy from you and reveal something which will—I hope—change your attitude on this whole matter."

"That will have to be something extraordinary," said Voal icily.

"It is. If we could find a private place—?"

Slinh looked wistfully after the two men as they entered the house. He'd give a lot to eavesdrop on that conference. He had a shrewd suspicion that the greatest secret in the Galaxy was about to be revealed—which could have been useful to him.

They were in Voal's study before Alak said: "I want to get over that barrier of hostility to me you still have. I think you're objective enough to have seen in the last few days that the Patrol has no desire to oppress Luan or discriminate against it. Our job is to keep the peace, no more and no less, but that involves a paradox which we have only been able to resolve by methods unknown to policemen of any other kind. You can't forgive my murderousness toward your child—but I repeat that there never was any. We would not have harmed her under any circumstances. But we had to make you think otherwise till my job was done."

"I can stand it myself," said Voal grimly. "But what my wife went through—"

"That was tough, wasn't it?" Suddenly the bitterness was alive and corrosive on Alak's face. Contempt twisted his thin lips. "Yes, that was really rugged, all three days of it. Have you ever thought how many *millions* of mothers this holy war of yours would have left without any prospect of getting their children back?"

Voal looked away from his bleak eyes and, for lack of better occupation, began to fumble with bottles and glasses. Alak accepted his drink but went on speaking:

"The basic secret of the League Patrol—and I want your solemn oath you will never breathe a word of it to anyone—" he waited till Voal gave agreement, "is this: The Patrol may under no circumstances take life. We may not kill."

He paused to let it sink in, then added; "We have a few impressive-looking battleships to show the Galaxy and overawe planets when necessary, but they have never fought and never will. The rest of the mighty fleet is—nonexistent! Faked pictures and cooked news stories! Patrolmen may have occasion to carry lethal weapons, but if they ever use them it means mnemonic erasure and discharge from the service. We encourage fiction about the blazing guns of the Patrol—we write quite a bit ourselves and call it news releases—but it has absolutely no basis in fact."

He smiled. "So, though we might kidnap your daughter, we would certainly never kill her," he finished.

Voal sat down. His knees seemed suddenly to have failed him. But he looked up, it was with an expression that Alak found immensely cheering. He spoke slowly: "I can see why a reputation as formidable fighters would be a great asset to you—but why stop there? Why can't you stand up and fight honestly? Why have you, instead, built up a record of such incredible villainy that the worst criminals of the Galaxy could not equal it?"

Alak relaxed into a chair and sipped his cocktail. "It's a long story," he said. "It goes right back to the beginning of interstellar travel."

He searched for words a moment, then began: "After about three centuries of intercourse between the stars, it became plain that an uncoordinated Galactic civilization would inevitably destroy itself. Consider the problems in their most elementary form. Today there are over a million civilized stars, with a population running up over ten to the fifteenth, and exploration adds new ones almost daily. Even if that population were completely uniform, the sheer complexity of administrative detail is inconceivable—why, if all government services from legislators to postmen added up to only one percent of the total, and no government has ever been that efficient, that would be some ten to the thirteenth individual beings in government! Robocomputers help some, but not much. You run a system with a population of about two and a half billion, and you know yourself what a job that is.

"And then the population is not uniform, but fantastically diverse. We are mammals, warm-blooded, oxygen breathing—but there are intelligent reptiles, birds, fish, cephalopods, and creatures Earth never heard of, among the oxygen breathers alone—there are halogen breathers covering as wide a range, there are eaters of raw energy, there are creatures from worlds almost next to a sun and creatures from worlds where oxygen falls as snow. Reconciling all their needs and wants—

"The minds and the histories of the races differ so much that no intelligence could ever imagine them all. Could you think the way the communal race-mind of Sturvel's Planet does? Do you have the cold emotions of a Vergan arthropod or the passionate temper of a Goldran? And individuals within the races usually differ as much as, say, humans do, if not more. And histories are utterly unlike. We try to bring the benefits of civilization to all races not obviously unfit—but often we can't tell till too late. Or even…well, take the case of us humans. Sol has been at peace for centuries. But humans colonizing out among the stars forget their traditions until barbarians like Luanians and Marhalians go to war!"

"That hurt," said Voal very quietly. "But maybe I deserved it."

Alak looked expectantly at his empty glass. Voal refilled it and the Patrolman drank deep. Then he said:

"And technology has advanced to a point where armed conflict, such as was at first inevitable and raged between the stars, is death for one side and ruin for another unless the victor manages completely to wipe out his foe in the first attack. In those three unorganized centuries, some hundreds of planets were simply sterilized, or even destroyed. Whole intelligent races were wiped out almost overnight. Sol and a few allies managed to suppress piracy, but no conceivable group short of an overwhelming majority of all planets—and with the diversity I just mentioned such unanimity is impossible—could ever have imposed order on the Galaxy.

"Yet—such order was a necessity of survival.

"One way, the 'safest' in a short-term sense, would have been for a powerful system, say Sol, to conquer just as many stars as it needed for an empire to defend itself against all comers, without conquering too many to administer. Such a procedure would have involved the permanent establishment of totalitarian militarism, the murder or reduction to peonage of all other races within the imperial bounds, and the ultimate decadence and disintegration which statism inevitably produces.

"But a saner way was found. The Galactic League was formed, to arbitrate and co-ordinate the activities of the different systems as far as possible. Slowly, over some four centuries, all planets were brought in as members, until today a newly discovered system automatically joins. The League carries on many projects, but its major function is the maintenance of interstellar order. And to do that job, as well as to carry out any League mandates, the Patrol exists."

With a flash of defiance, Voal challenged: "Yes, and how does the Patrol do it? With thievery, bribery, lies, blackmail, meddlesome interference—Why don't you stand up openly for the right and fight for it honestly?"

"With what?" asked Alak wearily. "Oh, I suppose we could maintain a huge battle fleet and crush any disobedient systems. But how trustful would that leave the others? How long before we had to wipe out another aggrieved world? Don't forget—when you fight on a planetary scale, you fight women and children and innocent males who had nothing whatsoever to do with the trouble. You kill a billion civilians to get at a few leaders. How long before the injustice of it raised an alliance against us which we couldn't beat? Who would stay in a tyrannical League when he could destroy it?

"As it is, the Galaxy is at peace. Eighty or ninety percent of all planets know the League is their friend and have nothing but praise for the Patrol that protects them. When trouble arises, we quietly settle it, and the Galaxy goes on its unknowing way. Those something times ten to the fifteenth beings are free to live their lives out without fear of racial extinction."

"Peace can be bought too dearly at times. Peace without honor—"

"Honor!" Alak sprang from his chair. His red hair blazed about the suddenly angry face. He paced before Voal with a cold and bitter glare.

"Honor!" he sneered. "Another catchword. I get so sick of those unctuous phrases—Don't you realize that deliberate scoundrels do little harm, but that the evil wrought by sincere fools is incalculable?

"Murder breeds its like. For psychological reasons, it is better to prohibit Patrolmen completely from killing than to set up legalistic limits. But if we can't use force, we have to use any other means that comes in handy. And I, for one, would rather break any number of arbitrary laws and moral rules, and wreck a handful of lives of idiots who think with a blaster, than see a planet go up in flames or…or see one baby killed in a war it never even heard about!"

He calmed down. For a while he continued pacing, then he sat down and said conversationally:

"Let me give you a few examples from recent cases of Patrol methods. Needless to say, this is strictly confidential. All the Galaxy knows is that there is peace—but we had to use every form of perfidy and betrayal to maintain it."

He thought a moment, then began: "Sirius and Alpha Centauri fought a war just before the founding of the League which nearly ruined both. They've managed to reconstruct since, but there is an undying hatred between them. League or no League they mean to be at each other's throats the first chance they get.

"Well, no matter what methods we use to hold the Centaurians in check. But on Sirius the government has become so hopelessly corrupt, the military force so graft-ridden and inefficient, that action is out of the question.

"Now a vigorous young reformer rose; honest, capable, popular, all set to win an election which would sweep the rascally incumbents out and bring good government to Sirius for the first time in three centuries. And—the Patrol bribed him to throw the election. He wouldn't take the money, but he did as we said because otherwise, as he knew, we'd make it the dirtiest election in even Sirian history, ruin his business and reputation and family life, and defeat him.

"Why? Because, of course, the first thing he'd have done if elected would have been to get the military in trim. Which would have meant the murder of several hundred million Centaurians—unless they struck first. Sure, we don't like crooked government either—but it costs a lot less in lives, suffering, natural resources, and even money than war.

"Then there was the matter of an obscure barbarian system whose people are carnivorous and have a psychological need of combat. Imagine them loose in the Galaxy! We have to hold them in check for several generations until sublimation can be achieved. Fortunately, they are under an absolute monarch. A native woman whom *we* had educated managed to become his mistress and completely dominate him. And when the great nobles showed signs of revolt, she seduced one of them to act as her agent provocateur and smoke out the rebellious ones.

"Immoral? Sure. But two or three centuries hence, even the natives will thank us for it. Meanwhile, the Galaxy is safe from them

"A somewhat similar case was a race by nature so fanatically religious that they were all set to go crusading among the stars with all the weapons of modern science. We wrecked that scheme by introducing a phony religion with esoteric scientific 'miracles' and priests who were Patrolmen trained in psychotechnology—a religion that preaches peace and tolerance. A dirty trick to play on a trusting people, but it saved their neighbors—and also themselves, since otherwise their extinction might have been necessary.

"We really hit a moral bottom in the matter of another primitive and backward system. Its people are divided into clans whose hereditary chiefs have absolute authority. When one of the crown princes took a tour through the Galaxy, our agents managed to guide him into one of the pleasure houses we maintain here and there. And we got records. Recently this being succeeded to the chiefship of the most influential clan. We were pretty sure, from study of his psychographs, that before long he would want to throw off the League 'yoke' and go off on a spree of conquest—it's a race of warriors with a contempt for all outsiders. So—the Patrol used those old records to blackmail him into refusing the job in favor of a safely conservative brother.

"Finally we come to your present case. Marhal was ready to fight for the rich prize of Lhing, and the League arbitrator, underestimating the determination of Luan, awarded the whole planet to them. That was enough to swing an election so that a pro-League government came into power there. I was sent here to check on your reactions, and soon saw a serious mistake had been made. War seemed inevitable. I tried the scoundrelly procedure of fomenting sabotage and revolution. After all, that damage would have been negligible compared to the cost of even a short war."

"The cost to Marhal," said Voal grimly.

"Maybe. But after all, I had to think of the whole Galaxy, not Luan. Sometimes someone must suffer a little lest someone else suffer a lot more. At any rate, my scheme failed. I resorted to alliance with a dope smuggler—he ruins a very few lives, while war takes them by the millions—and to kidnapping. I threatened and bluffed until you had backed up so far that mediation was possible.

"Well, that's all, then. The League commission is on its way. They'll have some other fat plum to give Luan in place of Lhing—which I suppose will make trouble elsewhere for the Patrol to settle. Your government will have to go out of power after such an about-face—you're rejoining the League, of course—but I daresay you'll soon get back in. And you have been entrusted with a secret which could split the Galaxy wide open."

"I'll keep it," said Voal. He smiled faintly. "From what I know of your methods—I'd better!" For a moment he hesitated, then: "And thanks. I was a fool. All Luan was populated by hysterical fools." He soon grimaced. "Only I still wonder if that isn't better than being a rogue."

"Take your choice," shrugged Wing Alak. "As long as the Galaxy keeps going I don't care. That's my job."

To a Tavern Wench

Vineleaf, O my vineleaf, now pour the hoarded sunshine out
From bottles where it lay in a dream of summers lost
To the sunsets wrought by frost
All throughout the vineyards where grapes have swollen purple
And well nigh sweet as kisses that from boy to girl were tossed
When their lightfoot pathways crossed—
Nor count the cost!
Aldebaran is not so red within the Hyades
As in the heartside claret heartward flowing;
Nor gold or whiteness quivers across the winter seas
Like that which gleams where chardonnay is glowing.
Drink, before our time shall come for going.

Once again the vinters have wrought their humble miracle,
To give us in communion a year that long has past
On an autumn stormwind's blast.
Here there is remembrance of vineyards flaming scarlet,
As vivid as your spirit, which must also go at last
To wherever it is cast,
And oh, how fast!
Then taste that summer once again which dreams within the cup
Of sun-gold wings upon a hawk at hover
No higher in the sky than our hearts went winging up,
And dance your way through music to discover,
Wine-renewed, that I remain your lover.

The Immortal Game

The first trumpet sounded far and clear and brazen cold, and Rogard the Bishop stirred to wakefulness with it. Lifting his eyes, he looked through the suddenly rustling, murmuring line of soldiers, out across the broad plain of Cinnabar and the frontier, and over to the realm of Leukas.

Away there, across the somehow unreal red-and-black distances of the steppe, he saw sunlight flash on armor and caught the remote wild flutter of lifted banners. *So it is war,* he thought. *So we must fight again.*

Again? He pulled his mind from the frightening dimness of that word. Had they ever fought before?

On his left, Sir Ocher laughed aloud and clanged down the vizard on his gay young face. It gave him a strange, inhuman look, he was suddenly a featureless thing of shining metal and nodding plumes, and the steel echoed in his voice: "Ha, a fight! Praise God, Bishop, for I had begun to fear I would rust here forever."

Slowly, Rogard's mind brought forth wonder. "Were you sitting and thinking—before now?" he asked.

"Why—" Sudden puzzlement in the reckless tones: "I think I was... Was I?" Fear turning into defiance: "Who cares? I've got some Leukans to kill!" Ocher reared in his horse till the great metallic wings thundered.

On Rogard's right, Flambard the King stood, tall in crown and robes. He lifted an arm to shade his eyes against the blazing sunlight. "They are sending Diomes, the royal guardsman, first," he murmured. "A good man." The coolness of his tone was not matched by the other hand, its nervous plucking at his beard.

Rogard turned back, facing over the lines of Cinnabar to the frontier. Diomes, the Leukan King's own soldier, was running. The long spear flashed in his hand, his shield and helmet threw back the relentless light in a furious dazzle, and Rogard thought he could hear the clashing of iron. Then that noise was drowned in the trumpets and drums and yells from the ranks of Cinnabar, and he had only his eyes.

Diomes leaped two squares before coming to a halt on the frontier. He stopped then, stamping and thrusting against the Barrier which suddenly held him, and cried challenge. A muttering rose among the cuirassed soldiers of Cinnabar, and spears lifted before the flowing banners.

King Flambard's voice was shrill as he leaned forward and touched his own guardsman with his scepter. "Go, Carlon! Go to stop him!"

"Aye, sire." Carlon's stocky form bowed, and then he wheeled about and ran, holding his spear aloft, until he reached the frontier. Now he and DIOMES stood face to face snarling at each other across the Barrier, and for a sick moment Rogard wondered what those two had done, once in an evil and forgotten year, that there should be such hate between them.

"Let me go, sire!" Ocher's voice rang eerily from the slit-eyed mask of his helmet. The winged horse stamped on the hard red ground, and the long lance swept a flashing arc. "Let me go next."

"No, no, Sir Ocher." It was a woman's voice. "Not yet. There'll be enough for you and me to do, later in this day."

Looking beyond Flambard, the Bishop saw his Queen, Evyan the Fair, and there was something within him which stumbled and broke into fire. Very tall and lovely was the gray-eyed Queen of Cinnabar, where she stood in armor and looked out at the growing battle. Her sun-browned young face was coifed in steel, but one rebellious lock blew forth in the wind, and she brushed at it with a gauntleted hand while the other drew her sword snaking from its sheath. "Now may God strengthen our arms," she said, and her voice was low and sweet. Rogard drew his cope tighter about him and turned his mitered head away with a sigh. But there was a bitter envy in him for Columbard, the Queen's Bishop of Cinnabar.

Drums thumped from the LEUKAN ranks, and another soldier ran forth. Rogard sucked his breath hissingly in, for this man came till he stood on DIOMES' right. And the newcomer's face was sharp and pale with fear. There was no Barrier between him and Carlon.

"To his death," muttered Flambard between his teeth. "They sent that fellow to his death."

Carlon snarled and advanced on the LEUKAN. He had little choice—if he waited, he would be slain, and his king had not commanded him to wait. He leaped, his spear gleamed, and the LEUKAN soldier toppled and lay emptily sprawled in the black square.

"First blood!" cried Evyan, lifting her sword and hurling sunbeams from it.

"First blood for us!"

Aye, so, thought Rogard bleakly, *but King* MIKILLATI *had a reason for sacrificing that man. Maybe we should have let Carlon die. Carlon the bold, Carlon the strong, Carlon the lover of laughter. Maybe we should have let him die.*

And now the Barrier was down for Bishop ASATOR of LEUKAS, and he came gliding down the red squares, high and cold in his glistening white robes, until he stood on the frontier. Rogard thought he could see ASATOR's eyes as they swept over Cinnabar. The LEUKAN Bishop was poised to rush in with his great mace should Flambard, for safety, seek to change with Earl Ferric as the Law permitted.

Law?

There was no time to wonder what the Law was, or why it must be obeyed or what had gone before this moment of battle. Queen Evyan had turned and shouted to the soldier Raddic, guardsman of her own Knight Sir Cupran: Go! Halt him!" And Raddic cast her his own look of love, and ran, ponderous in his mail, up to the frontier. There he and ASATOR stood, no Barrier between them if either used a flanking move.

Good! Oh, good, my Queen! thought Rogard wildly. For even if ASATOR did not withdraw, but slew Raddic, he would be in Raddic's square, and his threat would be against a wall of spears. *He will retreat, he will retreat—*

Iron roared as ASATOR'S mace crashed through helm and skull and felled Raddic the guardsman.

Evyan screamed, once only. "And I sent him! I sent him!" Then she began to run.

"Lady!" Rogard hurled himself against the Barrier. He could not move, he was chained here in his square, locked and barred by a Law he did not understand, while his lady ran toward death. "O Evyan, Evyan!"

Straight as a flying javelin ran the Queen of Cinnabar. Turning, straining after her, Rogard saw her leap the frontier and come to a halt by the Barrier which marked the left-hand bound of the kingdoms, beyond which lay only dimness to the frightful edge of the world. There she wheeled to face the dismayed ranks of LEUKAS, and her cry drifted back like the shriek of a stooping hawk: "MIKILLATI! Defend yourself!"

The thunder-crack of cheering from Cinnabar drowned all answer but Rogard saw, at the very limits of his sight, how hastily King MIKILLATI stepped from the line of her attack, into the stronghold of Bishop ASATOR. Now, thought Rogard fiercely, now the white-robed ruler could never see shelter from one of his Earls. Evyan had stolen his greatest shield.

"Hola, my Queen!" With a sob of laughter, Ocher struck spurs into his horse. Wings threshed, blowing Rogard's cape about him, as the Knight hurtled over the head of his own guardsman and came to rest two squares in front of the Bishop. Rogard fought down his own anger; he had wanted to be the one to follow Evyan. But Ocher was a better choice.

Oh, much better! Rogard gasped as his flittering eyes took in the broad battlefield. In the next leap, Ocher could cut down DIOMES, and then between them he and Evyan could trap MIKILLATI!

Briefly, that puzzlement nagged at the Bishop. Why should men die to catch someone else's King? What was there in the Law that said Kings should strive for mastery of the world and—

"Guard yourself, Queen!" Sir MERKON, King's Knight of LEUKAS, sprang in a move like Ocher's. Rogard's breath rattled in his throat with bitterness, and he thought there must be tears in Evyan's bright eyes. Slowly, then, the Queen withdrew two squares along the edge, until she stood in front of Earl Ferric's guardsman. It was still a good place to attack from, but not what the other had been.

BOAN, guardsman of the LEUKAN Queen DOLORA, moved one square forward, so that he protected great DIOMES from Ocher. Ocher snarled and sprang in front of Evyan, so that he stood between her and the frontier: clearing the way for her, and throwing his own protection over Carlon.

MERKON jumped likewise, landing to face Ocher with the frontier between them. Rogard clenched his mace and vision blurred for him; the LEUKANS were closing in on Evyan.

"Ulfar!" cried the King's Bishop. "Ulfar, can you help her?"

The stout old yeoman who was guardsman of the Queen's Bishop nodded wordlessly and ran one square forward. His spear menaced Bishop ASATOR, who growled at him—no Barrier between those two now!

MERKON of LEUKAS made another soaring leap, landing three squares in front of Rogard. "Guard yourself!" the voice belled from his faceless helmet. "Guard yourself, O Queen!"

No time now to let Ulfar slay ASATOR. Evyan's great eyes looked wildly about her; then, with swift decision, she stepped between MERKON and Ocher. Oh, a lovely move! Out of the fury in his breast, Rogard laughed.

The guardsman of the LEUKAN King's Knight clanked two squares ahead, lifting his spear against Ocher. It must have taken boldness thus to stand before Evyan herself; but the Queen of Cinnabar saw that if she cut him down, the Queen of LEUKAS could slay her. "Get free, Ocher!" she cried. "Get away!" Ocher cursed and leaped from danger, landing in front of Rogard's guardsman.

The King's Bishop bit his lip and tried to halt the trembling in his limbs. How the sun blazed! Its light was a cataract of dry white fire over the barren red and black squares. It hung immobile, enormous in the vague sky, and men gasped in their armor. The noise of bugles and iron, hoofs and wings and stamping feet, was loud under the small wind that blew across the world. There had never been anything but this meaningless war, there would never be aught else, and when Rogard tried to think beyond the moment when the fight had begun, or the moment when it would end, there was only an abyss of darkness.

Earl RAFAEON of LEUKAS took one ponderous step toward his King, a towering figure of iron readying for combat. Evyan whooped. "Ulfar!" she yelled. "Ulfar, your chance!"

Columbard's guardsman laughed aloud. Raising his spear, he stepped over into the square held by ASATOR. The white-robed Bishop lifted his mace, futile and feeble, and then he rolled in the dust at Ulfar's feet. The men of Cinnabar howled and clanged sword on shield.

Rogard held aloof from triumph. ASATOR, he thought grimly, had been expendable anyway. King MIKILLATI had something else in mind.

It was like a blow when he saw Earl RAFAEON's guardsman run forward two squares and shout to Evyan to guard herself. Raging, the Queen of Cinnabar withdrew a square to her rearward. Rogard saw sickly how unprotected King Flambard was now, the soldiers scattered over the field and the hosts of LEUKAS marshaling. But Queen DOLORA, he thought with a wild clutching hope, Queen DOLORA, her tall cold beauty was just as open to a strong attack.

The soldier who had driven Evyan back took a leap across the frontier. "Guard yourself, O Queen!" he cried again. He was a small, hard-bitten, unkempt warrior in dusty helm and corselet. Evyan cursed, a bouncing soldierly oath, and moved one square forward to put a Barrier between her and him. He grinned impudently in his beard.

It is ill for us, it is a bootless and evil day. Rogard tried once more to get out of his square and go to Evyan's aid, but his will would not carry him. The Barrier held, invisible and uncrossable, and the Law held, the cruel and senseless Law which said a man must stand by and watch his lady be slain, and he railed at the bitterness of it and lapsed into a gray waiting.

Trumpets lifted brazen throats, drums boomed, and Queen DOLORA of LEUKAS stalked forth into battle. She came high and white and icily fair, her face chiseled and immobile in its haughtiness under the crowned helmet, and stood two squares in front of her husband, looming over Carlon. Behind her, her own Bishop SORKAS poised in his stronghold, hefting his mace in armored hands. Carlon of Cinnabar spat at DOLORA's feet, and she looked at him from cool blue eyes and then looked away. The hot dry wind did not ruffle her long pale hair; she was like a statue, standing there and waiting.

"Ocher," said Evyan softly, "out of my way."

"I like not retreat, my lady," he answered in a thin tone.

"Nor I," said Evyan. "But I must have an escape route open. We will fight again.

Slowly, Ocher withdrew, back to his own home. Evyan chuckled once, and a wry grin twisted her young face.

Rogard was looking at her so tautly that he did not see what was happening until a great shout of iron slammed his head around. Then he saw Bishop SORKAS, standing in Carlon's square with a bloodied mace in his hands, and Carlon lay dead at his feet.

Carlon, your hands are empty, life has slipped from them and there is an unending darkness, risen in you who loved the world. Goodnight, my Carlon, goodnight.

"Madame—" Bishop SORKAS spoke quietly, bowing a little, and there was a smile on his crafty face. "I regret, madame, that—ah—"

"Yes. I must leave you." Evyan shook her head, as if she had been struck, and moved a square backwards and sideways. Then, turning, she threw the glance of an eagle down the black squares to LEUKAS' Earl ARACLES. He looked away nervously as if he would crouch behind the three soldiers who warded him. Evyan drew a deep breath sobbing into her lungs.

Sir THEUTAS, DOLORA's Knight, sprang from his stronghold, to place himself between Evyan and the Earl. Rogard wondered dully if he meant to kill Ulfar the soldier; he could do it now. Ulfar looked at the Knight who sat crouched, and hefted his spear and waited for his own weird.

"Rogard!"

The Bishop leaped, and for a moment there was fire-streaked darkness before his eyes.

"Rogard, to me! To me, and help sweep them from the world!"

Evyan's voice.

She stood in her scarred and dinted armor, holding her sword aloft, and on that smitten field she was laughing with a new-born hope. Rogard could not shout his reply. There were no words. But he raised his mace and ran.

The black squares slid beneath his feet, footfalls pounding, jarring his teeth, muscles stretching with a resurgent glory and all the world singing. At the frontier, he stopped, knowing it was Evyan's will though he could not have said how he knew. Then he faced about, and with clearing eyes looked back over that field of iron and ruin. Save for one soldier and a knight, Cinnabar was now cleared of LEUKAN forces, Evyan was safe, a counterblow was readying like the first whistle of hurricane. Before him were the proud banners of LEUKAS—now to throw them into the dust! Now to ride with Evyan into the home of MIKILLATI!

"Go to it, sir," rumbled Ulfar, standing on the Bishop's right and looking boldly at the white Knight who could slay him. "Give 'em hell from us."

Wings beat in the sky, and THEUTAS soared down to land on Rogard's left. In the hot light, the blued metal of his armor was like running water. His horse snorted, curveting and flapping its wings; he sat it easily, the lance swaying in his grasp, the blank helmet turned to Flambard. One more such leap, reckoned Rogard wildly, and he would be able to assail the King of Cinnabar. Or—no—a single spring from here and he would spit Evyan on his lance.

And there is a Barrier between us!

"Watch yourself, Queen!" the arrogant LEUKAN voice boomed hollow out of the steel mask.

"Indeed I will, Sir Knight!" There was only laughter in Evyan's tone. Lightly, then, she sped up the row of black squares. She brushed by Rogard, smiling at him as she ran, and he tried to smile back but his face was stiffened. Evyan, Evyan, she was plunging alone into her enemy's homeland!

Iron belled and clamored. The white guardsman in her path toppled and sank at her feet. One fist lifted strengthlessly, and a dying shrillness was in the dust: "Curse you, curse you, MIKILLATI, curse you for a stupid fool, leaving me here to be slain—no, no, no—"

Evyan bestrode the body and laughed again in the very face of Earl ARACLES. He cowered back, licking his lips—he could not move against her, but she could annihilate him in one more step. Beside Rogard, Ulfar whooped, and the trumpets of Cinnabar howled in the rear.

Now the great attack was launched! Rogard cast a fleeting glance at Bishop SORKAS. The lean white-coped form was gliding forth, mace swinging loose in one hand, and there was a little sleepy smile on the pale face. No dismay—? SORKAS halted, facing Rogard, and smiled a little wider, skinning his teeth without humor." You can kill me if you wish," he said softly. "But do you?"

For a moment Rogard wavered. To smash that head—!

"Rogard! Rogard, to me!"

Evyan's cry jerked the King's Bishop around. He saw now what her plan was, and it dazzled him so that he forgot all else. LEUKAS *is ours!*

Swiftly he ran. DIOMES and BOAN howled at him as he went between them, brushing impotent spears against the Barriers. He passed Queen DOLORA, and her lovely face was as if cast in steel, and her eyes followed him as he charged over the plain of LEUKAS. Then there was no time for thinking, Earl RAFAEON loomed before him, and he jumped the last boundary into the enemy's heartland.

The Earl lifted a meaningless ax. The Law read death for him, and Rogard brushed aside the feeble stroke. The blow of his mace shocked in his own body, slamming his jaws together. RAFAEON crumpled, falling slowly, his armor loud as he struck the ground. Briefly, his fingers clawed at the iron-hard black earth, and then he lay still.

They have slain Raddic and Carlon—we have three guardsmen, a Bishop and an Earl—Now we need only be butchers! Evyan, Evyan, warrior Queen, this is your victory!

DIOMES of LEUKAS roared and jumped across the frontier. Futile, futile, he was doomed to darkness. Evyan's lithe form moved up against ARACLES, her sword flamed and the Earl crashed at her feet. Her voice was another leaping brand: "Defend yourself, King!"

Turning, Rogard grew aware that MIKILLATI himself had been right beside him. There was a Barrier between the two men—but MIKILLATI had to retreat from Evyan, and he took one step forward and sideways. Peering into his face, Rogard felt a sudden coldness. There was no defeat there, it was craft and knowledge and an unbending steel will—*what was* LEUKAS *planning?*

Evyan tossed her head, and the wind fluttered the lock of hair like a rebel banner. "We have them, Rogard!" she cried.

Far and faint, through the noise and confusion of battle, Cinnabar's bugles sounded the command of her King. Peering into the haze, Rogard saw that Flambard was taking precautions. Sir THEUTAS was still a menace, where he stood beside SORKAS. Sir Cupran of Cinnabar flew heavily over to land in front of the Queen's Earl's guardsman, covering the route THEUTAS must follow to endanger Flambard.

Wise, but—Rogard looked again at MIKILLATI's chill white face, and it was as if a breath of cold blew through him. Suddenly he wondered why they fought. For victory, yes, for mastery over the world—but when the battle had been won, what then?

He couldn't think past that moment. His mind recoiled in horror he could not name. In that instant he knew icily that this was not the first war in the world, there had been others before, and there would be others again. Victory is death.

But Evyan, glorious Evyan, she could not die. She would reign over all the world and—

Steel blazed in Cinnabar. MERKON of LEUKAS came surging forth, one tigerish leap which brought him down on Ocher's guardsman. The soldier screamed, once, as he fell under the trampling, tearing hoofs, but it was lost in the shout of the LEUKAN Knight: "Defend yourself, Flambard! Defend yourself!"

Rogard gasped. It was like a blow in the belly. He had stood triumphant over the world, and now all in one swoop it was brought toppling about him. THEUTAS shook his lance, SORKAS his mace, DIOMES raised a bull's bellow—somehow, incredibly somehow, the warriors of LEUKAS had entered Cinnabar and were thundering at the King's own citadel.

"No, no—" Looking down the long empty row of squares, Rogard saw that Evyan was weeping. He wanted to run to her, hold her close and shield her against the falling world, but the Barriers were around him. He could not stir from his square, he could only watch.

Flambard cursed lividly and retreated into his Queen's home. His men gave a shout and clashed their arms—there was still a chance!

No, not while the Law bound men, thought Rogard, not while the Barriers held. Victory was ashen, and victory and defeat alike were darkness.

Beyond her thinly smiling husband, Queen DOLORA swept forward. Evyan cried out as the tall white woman halted before Rogard's terrified guardsman, turned to face Flambard where he crouched, and called to him: "Defend yourself, King!"

"No—no—you fool!" Rogard reached out, trying to break the Barrier, clawing at MIKILLATI. "Can't you see, none of us can win, it's death for us all if the war ends. Call her back!"

MIKILLATI ignored him. He seemed to be waiting.

And Ocher of Cinnabar raised a huge shout of laughter. It belled over the plain, dancing joyous mirth and men lifted weary heads and turned to the young Knight where he sat in his own stronghold, for there was youth and triumph and glory in his laughing. Swiftly, then, a blur of steel, he sprang, and his winged horse rushed out of the sky on DOLORA herself. She turned to meet him, lifting her sword, and he knocked it from her hand and stabbed with his own lance. Slowly, too haughty to scream, the white Queen sank under his horse's hoofs.

And MIKILLATI smiled.

"I see," nodded the visitor "Individual computers, each controlling its own robot piece by a tight beam, and all the computers on a given side linked to form a sort of group-mind constrained to obey the rules of chess and make the best possible moves. Very nice. And it's a pretty cute notion of yours, making the robots look like medieval armies." His glance studied the tiny figures where they moved on the oversize board, under one glaring floodlight.

"Oh, that's pure frippery," said the scientist. "This is really a serious research project in multiple computer-linkages. By letting them play game after game, I'm getting some valuable data."

It's a lovely setup," said the visitor admiringly. "Do you realize that in this particular contest the two sides are reproducing one of the great classic games?"

"Why, no. Is that a fact?"

"Yes. It was a match between Anderssen and Kieseritsky back in—I forget the year, but it was quite some time ago. Chess books often refer to it as the Immortal Game…So your computers must share many of the properties of a human brain."

"Well, they're complex things, all right," admitted the scientist. "Not all their characteristics are known yet. Sometimes my chessmen surprise even me."

"Hm." The visitor stooped over the board. "Notice how they're limping around inside their squares, waving their arms, batting at each other with their weapons?" He paused, then murmured slowly: "I wonder—I wonder if your computers may not have consciousness. If they might not have—minds."

"Don't get fantastic," snorted the scientist.

"But how do you know?" persisted the visitor. "Look, your feedback arrangement is closely analogous to a human nervous system. How do you know that your individual computers, even if they are constrained by the group linkage, don't have individual personalities? How do you know that their electronic senses don't interpret the game as, oh, as an interplay of free will and necessity; how do you know they don't receive the data of the moves as their own equivalent of blood, sweat and tears?" He shuttered a little.

"Nonsense," grunted the scientist. "They're only robots."

"Now—Hey! Look there! Look at that move!"

Bishop SORKAS took one step ahead, into the black square adjoining Flambard's. He bowed and smiled. "The war is ended," he said.

Slowly, very slowly, Flambard looked about him. SORKAS, MERKON, THEUTAS, they were crouched to leap on him wherever he turned; his own men raged helpless against the Barriers; there was no place for him to go.

He bowed his head. "I surrender," he whispered.

Rogard looked across the red and black to Evyan. Their eyes met, and they stretched out their arms to each other.

"Checkmate," said the scientist. "That game's over."

He crossed the room to the switchboard and turned off the computers.

Upon the Occasion of Being Asked to Argue That Love and Marriage are Incompatible

Love is no lady, but a wench with wings,
Fickle and fleet, the child of wind and sky,
Cool as a fall where tumbling waters ring,
Brazen as sunlight and like moonlight shy.
Love is a hawk no man may hope to tame.
She is not chased, but hers is the attack.
Love is no bride who meekly leads her name,
Nor, being winged, lies always on her back.
How shall you cage the river or the gale?
How shall you pluck and lifelong keep alive
Blossoms in bowls where air is walled and stale?
Love comes to whom she will, not those who strive,
Therefore, my sweet, be in no haste to marry,
So it may be that Love will deign to tarry.

Backwardness

As a small boy he wanted to be a rocket pilot—and what boy didn't in those days?—but learned early that he lacked the aptitudes. Later he decided on psychology, and even took a bachelor's degree cum laude. Then one thing led to another, and Joe Husting ended up as a confidence man. It wasn't such a bad life; it had challenge and variety as he hunted in New York, and the spoils of a big killing were devoured in Florida, Greenland Resort, or Luna City.

The bar was empty of prospects just now, but he dawdled over his beer and felt no hurry. Spring had reached in and touched even the East Forties. The door stood open to a mild breeze, the long room was cool and dim, a few other men lazed over midafternoon drinks and the TV was tuned low. Idly, through cigarette smoke, Joe Husting watched the program.

The Galactics, of course. Their giant spaceship flashed in the screen against wet brown fields a hundred miles from here. Copter view…now we pan to a close-up, inside the ring of UN guards, and then back to the sightseers in their thousands. The announcer was talking about how the captain of the ship was at this moment in conference with the Secretary-General, and the crewmen were at liberty on Earth. "They are friendly, folks. I repeat, they are friendly. They will do no harm. They have already exchanged their cargo of U-235 for billions of our own dollars, and they plan to spend those dollars like any friendly tourist. But both the UN Secretariat and the President of the United States have asked us all to remember that these people come from the stars. They have been civilized for a million years. They have powers we haven't dreamed of. Anyone who harms a Galactic can ruin the greatest—"

Husting's mind wandered off. A big thing, yes, maybe the biggest thing in all history. Earth a member planet of the Galactic Federation! All the stars open to us! It was good to be alive in this year when anything could happen…hm. To start with, you could have some rhinestones put in fancy settings and peddle them as gen-yu-wine Tardenoisian sacred flame-rocks, but that was only the beginning—

He grew aware that the muted swish of electrocars and hammering of shoes in the street had intensified. From several blocks away came a positive roar of excitement. What the devil? He left his beer and sauntered to the door and looked out. A shabby man was hurrying toward the crowd. Husting buttonholed him. "What's going on, pal?"

"Ain't yuh heard? Galactics! Half a dozen of 'em. Landed in duh street uptown, some kinda flying belt dey got, and went inna Macy's and bought a million bucks' wortha stuff! Now dey're strolling down dis-a-way. Lemme go!"

Husting stood for a while, drawing hard on his cigarette. There was a tingle along his spine. Wanderers from the stars, a million-year-old civilization embracing the whole Milky Way! For him actually to see the high ones, maybe even talk to them…it would be something to tell his grandchildren about if he ever had any.

He waited, though, till the outer edge of the throng was on him, then pushed with skill and ruthlessness. It took a few sweaty minutes to reach the barrier.

An invisible force-field, holding off New York's myriads—wise precaution. You could be trampled to death by the best-intentioned mob.

There were seven crewmen from the Galactic ship. They were tall, powerful, as handsome as expected: a mixed breed, with dark hair and full lips and thin aristocratic noses. In a million years you'd expect all the human races to blend into one. They wore shimmering blue tunics and buskins, webby metallic belts in which starlike points of light glittered—and jewelry! My God, they must have bought all the gaudiest junk jewelry Macy's had to offer, and hung it on muscular necks and thick wrists. Mink and ermine burdened their shoulders, a young fortune in fur. One of them was carefully counting the money he had left, enough to choke an elephant. The others beamed affably into Earth's milling folk.

Joe Husting hunched his narrow frame against the pressure that was about to flatten him on the force screen. He licked suddenly dry lips, and his heart hammered. Was it possible—could it really happen that he, insignificant he, might speak to the gods from the stars?

Elsewhere in the huge building, politicians, specialists, and vips buzzed like angry bees. They should have been conferring with their opposite numbers from the Galactic mission—clearly, the sole proper way to meet the unprecedented is to set up committees and spend six months deciding on an agenda. But the Secretary-General of the United Nations owned certain prerogatives, and this time he had used them. A private face-to-face conference with Captain Hurdgo could accomplish more in half an hour than the councils of the world in a year.

He leaned forward and offered a box of cigars. "I don't know if I should," he added. "Perhaps tobacco doesn't suit your metabolism?"

"My what?" asked the visitor pleasantly. He was a big man, running a little to fat, with distinguished gray at the temples. It was not so odd that the Galactics should shave their chins and cut their hair in the manner of civilized Earth. That was the most convenient style.

"I mean, we smoke this weed, but it may poison you," said Larson. "After all, you're from another planet."

"Oh, that's OK," replied Hurdgo. "Same plants grow on every Earth-like planet, just like the same people and animals. Not much difference. Thanks." He took a cigar and rolled it between his fingers. "Smells nice."

"To me, that is the most astonishing thing about it all. I never expected evolution to work identically throughout the universe. *Why?*"

"Well, it just does." Captain Hurdgo bit the end off his cigar and spat it out onto the carpet. "Not on different-type planets from this, of course, but on Earth-type it's all the same."

"But why? I mean, what process—it can't be coincidence!"

Hurdgo shrugged. "I don't know. I'm just a practical spaceman. Never worried about it." He put the cigar in his mouth and touched the bezel of an ornate finger ring to it. Smoke followed the brief, intense spark.

"That's a…a most ingenious development," said Larson. Humility, yes, there was the line for a simple Earthman to take. Earth had come late into the cosmos and might as well admit the fact.

"A what?"

"Your ring. That lighter."

"Oh, that. Yep. Little atomic-energy gizmo inside." Hurdgo waved a magnanimous hand. "We'll send some people to show you how to make our stuff. Lend you machinery till you can start your own factories. We'll bring you up to date."

"It—you're incredibly generous," said Larson, happy and incredulous.

"Not much trouble to us, and we can trade with you once you're all set up. The more planets, the better for us."

"But…excuse me, sir, but I bear a heavy responsibility. We have to know the legal requirements for membership in the Galactic Federation. We don't know anything about your laws, your customs, your—"

"Nothing much to tell," said Hurdgo. "Every planet can pretty well take care of itself. How the hell you think we could police fifty million Earth-type planets? If you got a gripe, you can take it to the, uh, I dunno what the word would be in English. A board of experts with a computer that handles these things. They'll charge you for the service—no Galactic taxes, you just pay for what you get, and out of the profits they finance free services like this mission of mine."

"I see," nodded Larson. "A Coordinating Council."

"Yeh, I guess that's it."

The Secretary-General shook his head in bewilderment. He had sometimes wondered what civilization would come to be, a million years hence. Now he knew, and it staggered him. An ultimate simplicity, superman disdaining the whole cumbersome apparatus of interstellar government, freed of all restraints save the superman morality, free to think his giant thoughts between the stars!

Hurdgo looked out the window to the arrogant towers of New York. "Biggest city I ever saw," he remarked, "and I seen a lot of planets. I don't see how you run it. Must be complicated."

"It is, sir." Larson smiled wryly. Of course the Galactics would long ago have passed the stage of needing such a human ant hill. They would have forgotten the skills required to govern one, just as Larson's people had forgotten how to chip flint.

"Well, let's get down to business." Hurdgo sucked on his cigar and smacked his lips. "Here's how it works. We found out a big while back that we can't go letting any new planet bust its way into space with no warning to anybody. Too much danger. So we set up detectors all over the Galaxy. When they spot the, uh, what-you-call-'ems—vibrations, yes, that's it, vibrations—the vibrations of a new star drive, they alert the, uh, Coordinating Council and it sends out a ship to contact the new people and tell 'em the score."

"Ah, indeed. I suspected as much. We have just invented a faster-than-light engine…very primitive, of course, compared to yours. It was being tested when—"

"Uh-huh. So me and my boys are supposed to give you the once-over and see if you're all right. Don't want warlike peoples running around loose, you know. Too much danger."

"I assure you—"

"Yes, yes, pal, it's OK. You got a good strong world setup and the computer says you've stopped making war." Hurdgo frowned. "I got to admit, you got some funny habits. I don't really understand everything you do…you seem to think funny, not like any other planet I ever heard of. But it's all right. Everybody to his own ways. You get a clean bill of health."

"Suppose…" Larson spoke very slowly. "Just suppose we had not been…approved—what then? Would you have reformed us?"

"Reformed? Huh? What d'you mean? We'd have sent a police ship and blown every planet in this system to smithereens. Can't have people running loose who might start a war."

Sweat formed under Larson's arms and trickled down his ribs. His mouth felt dry. *Whole planets—*

But in a million years you would learn to think *sub specie aeternitatis*. Five billion warlike Earthlings could annihilate fifty billion peaceful Galactics before they were overcome. It was not for him to judge a superman.

"Hello, there!"

Husting had to yell to be heard above the racket. But the nearest of the spacemen looked at him and smiled.

"Hi," he said.

Incredible! He had greeted little Joe Husting as a friend. Why—? Wait a minute! Perhaps the sheer brass of it had pleased him. Perhaps no one else had dared speak first to the strangers. And when you only said, "Yes, sir," to a man, even to a Galactic, you removed him—you might actually make him feel lonely.

"Uh, like it here?" Husting cursed his tongue, that its glibness should have failed him at this moment of all moments.

"Sure, sure. Biggest city I ever seen. And *draxna,* look at what I got!" The spaceman lifted a necklace of red glass sparklers. "Won't their eyes just bug out when I get home!"

Someone shoved Husting against the barrier so the wind went from him. He gasped and tried to squirm free.

"Say, cut that out. You're hurting the poor guy." One of the Galactics touched a stud on his belt. Gently but inexorably, the field widened, pushing the crowd back…and somehow, somehow Husting was inside it with the seven from the stars.

"You OK, pal?" Anxious hands lifted him to his feet.

"I, yeah, sure. Sure, I'm fine!" Husting stood up and grinned at the envious faces ringing him in. "Thanks a lot."

"Glad to help you. My name's Gilgrath. Call me Gil." Strong fingers squeezed Husting's shoulder. "And this here is Bronni, and here's Col, and Jordo, and—"

"Pleased to meet you," whispered Husting inadequately. "I'm Joe."

"Say, this is all right!" said Gil enthusiastically. "I was wondering what was wrong with you folks."

"Wrong?" Husting shook a dazed head, wondering if They were peering into his mind and reading thoughts of which he himself was unaware. Vague memories came back, grave-eyed Anubis weighing the heart of a man.

"You know," said Gil. "Stand-offish, like."

"Yeh," added Bronni. "Every other new planet we been to, everybody was coming up and saying hello and buying us drinks and—"

"Parties," reminded Jordo.

"Yeh. Man, remember that wing-ding on Alphaz? Remember those girls?" Col rolled his eyes lickerishly.

"You got a lot of good-looking girls here in New York," complained Gil. "But we got orders not to offend nobody. Say, do you think one of those girls would mind if I said hello to her?"

Husting was scarcely able to think; it was the reflex of many years which now spoke for him, rapidly: "You have us all wrong. We're just scared to talk to you. We thought maybe you didn't want to be bothered."

"And *we* thought *you*— Say!" Gil slapped his thigh and broke into a guffaw. "Now ain't that something? They don't want to bother us and we don't want to bother them!"

"I'll be *rixt!*" bellowed Col. "Well, what do you know about that?"

"Hey, in that case—" began Jordo.

"Wait, wait!" Husting waved his hands. It was still habit which guided him; his mind was only slowly getting back into gear. "Let me get this straight. You want to do the town, right?"

"We sure do," said Col. "It's mighty lonesome out in space."

"Well, look," chattered Husting, "you'll never be free of all these crowds, reporters—" (A flashbulb, the tenth or twelfth in these few minutes, dazzled his eyes.) "You won't be able to let yourselves go while everybody knows you're Galactics."

"On Alphaz—" protested Bronni.

"This isn't Alphaz. Now I've got an idea. Listen." Seven dark heads bent down to hear an urgent whisper. "Can you get us away from here? Fly off invisible or something?"

"Sure," said Gil. "Hey, how'd you know we can do that?"

"Never mind. OK, we'll sneak off to my apartment and send out for some Earth-style clothes for you, and then—"

John Joseph O'Reilly, Cardinal Archbishop of New York, had friends in high places as well as in low. He thought it no shame to pull wires and arrange an interview with the chaplain of the spaceship. What he could learn might be of vital importance to the Faith. The priest from the stars arrived, light-screened to evade the curious, and was received in the living room.

Visible again, Thyrkna proved to be a stocky white-haired man in the usual blue-kirtled uniform. He smiled and shook hands in quite an ordinary manner. At least, thought O'Reilly, these Galactics had during a million years conquered overweening Pride.

"It is an honor to meet you," he said.

"Thanks," nodded Thyrkna. He looked around the room.

"Nice place you got."

"Please be seated. May I offer you a drink?"

"Don't mind if I do."

O'Reilly set forth glasses and a bottle. In a modest way, the Cardinal was a connoisseur, and had chosen the Chambertin-Clos carefully. He tasted the ritual few drops. Whatever minor saint, if any, was concerned with these things had been gracious; the wine was superb. He filled his guest's glass and then his own.

"Welcome to Earth," he smiled.

"Thanks." The Galactic tossed his drink off at one gulp. "Aaah! That goes good."

The Cardinal winced, but poured again. You couldn't expect another civilization to have the same tastes. Chinese liked aged eggs while despising cheese…

He sat down and crossed his legs. "I'm not sure what title to use," he said diffidently.

"Title? What's that?"

"I mean, what does your flock call you?"

"My *flock*? Oh, you mean the boys on board? Plain Thyrkna. That's good enough for me." The visitor finished his second glass and belched. Well, so would a cultivated Eskimo.

"I understand there was some difficulty in conveying my request," said O'Reilly. "Apparently you did not know what our word *chaplain* means."

"We don't know every word in your lingo," admitted Thyrkna. "It works like this. When we come in toward a new planet, we pick up its radio, see?"

"Oh, yes. Such of it as gets through the ionosphere."

Thyrkna blinked. "Huh? I don't know all the *de*-tails. You'll have to talk to one of our tech…technicians. Anyway, we got a machine that analyzes the different languages, figures 'em out. Does it in just a few hours, too. Then it puts us all to sleep and teaches us the languages. When we wake up, we're ready to come down and talk."

The Cardinal laughed. "Pardon me, sir. Frankly, I was wondering why the people of your incredibly high civilization should use our worst street dialects. Now I see the reason. I am afraid our programs are not on a very high level. They aim at mass taste, the lowest common denominator—and please excuse my metaphors. Naturally you— But I assure you, we aren't all that bad. We have hopes for the future. This electronic educator of yours, for instance…what it could do to raise the cultural level of the average man surpasses imagination."

Thyrkna looked a trifle dazed. "I never seen anybody what talks like you Earthlings. Don't you ever run out of breath?"

O'Reilly felt himself reproved. Among the Great Galactics, a silence must be as meaningful as a hundred words, and there were a million years of dignity behind them. "I'm sorry," he said.

"Oh, it's all right. I suppose a lot of our ways must look just as funny to you." Thyrkna picked up the bottle and poured himself another glassful.

"What I asked you here for…there are many wonderful things you can tell me, but I would like to put you some religious questions."

"Sure, go ahead," said Thyrkna amiably.

"My Church has long speculated about this eventuality. The fact that you, too, are human, albeit more advanced than we, is a miraculous revelation of God's will. But I would like to know something about the precise form of your belief in Him."

"What do you mean?" Thyrkna sounded confused. "I'm a, uh, quartermaster. It's part of my job to kill the rabbits—we can't afford the space for cattle on board a ship. I feed the gods, that's all."

"The *gods!*" The Cardinal's glass crashed on the floor.

"By the way, what's the names of your top gods?" inquired Thyrkna. "Be a good idea to kill them a cow or two, as long as we're here on their planet. Don't wanna take chances on bad luck."

"But…you…*heathen*—"

Thyrkna looked at the clock. "Say, do you have TV?" he asked. "It's almost time for *John's Other Life.* You got some real good TV on this planet."

By the dawn's early light, Joe Husting opened a bleary eye and wished he hadn't. The apartment was a mess. What happened, anyway?'

Oh, yeah…those girls they picked up…but had they really emptied all those bottles lying on the floor?

He groaned and hung onto his head lest it split open. Why had he mixed scotch and stout?

Thunder lanced through his eardrums. He turned on the sofa and saw Gil emerging from the bedroom. The spaceman was thumping his chest and booming out a song learned last night. *"Oh, roly poly—"*

"Cut it out, will you?" groaned Husting.

"Huh? Man, you've had it, ain't you?" Gil clicked his tongue sympathetically. "Here, just a minute." He took a vial from his belt. "Take a few drops of this. It'll fix you up."

Somehow Husting got it down. There was a moment of fire and pinwheels, then—

–he was whole again. It was as if he had just slept ten hours without touching alcohol for the past week.

Gil returned to the bedroom and started pummeling his companions awake. Husting sat by the window, thinking hard. That hangover cure was worth a hundred million if he could only get the exclusive rights. But no, the technical envoys would show Earth how to make it, along with star ships and invisibility screens and so on. Maybe, though, he could hit the Galactics for what they had with them, and peddle it for a hundred dollars a drop before the full-dress mission arrived.

Bronni came in, full of cheer. "Say, you're all right, Joe," he trumpeted. "Ain't had such a good time since I was on Alphaz. What's next, old pal, old pal, old pal?" A meaty hand landed stunningly between Husting's shoulder blades.

"I'll see what I can do," said the Earthman cautiously. "But I'm busy, you know. Got some big deals cooking."

"I know," said Bronni. He winked. "Smart fellow like you. How the *hell* did you talk that bouncer around? I thought sure he was gonna call the cops."

"Oh, I buttered him up and slipped him a ten-spot. Wasn't hard."

"Man!" Bronni whistled in admiration. "I never heard anybody sling the words like you was doing."

Gil herded the others out and said he wanted breakfast. Husting led them all to the elevator and out into the street. He was rather short-spoken, having much to think about. They were in a ham-and-eggery before he said:

"You spacemen must be pretty smart. Smarter than average, right?"

"Right," said Jordo. He winked at the approaching waitress.

"Lotta things a spaceman's got to know," said Col. "The ships do just about run themselves, but still, you can't let just any knucklehead into the crew."

"I see," murmured Husting. "I thought so."

A college education helps the understanding, especially when one is not too blinkered by preconceptions.

Consider one example: Sir Isaac Newton discovered *(a)* the three laws of motion, *(b)* the law of gravitation, *(c)* the differential calculus, *(d)* the elements of spectroscopy, *(e)* a good deal about acoustics, and *(f)* miscellaneous, besides finding time to serve in half a dozen official and honorary positions. A single man! And for a genius, he was not too exceptional; most gifted Earthmen have contributed to several fields.

And yet…such supreme intellect is not necessary. The most fundamental advances, fire- and tool-making, language and clothing and social organization, were made by apish dimbulbs. It simply took a long time between discoveries.

Given a million years, much can happen. Newton founded modern physics in one lifespan. A hundred less talented men, over a thousand-year period, could slowly and painfully have accomplished the same thing.

The IQ of Earth humanity averages about 100. Our highest geniuses may have rated 200; our lowest morons, as stupid as possible without needing institutional care, may go down to 60. It is only some freak of mutation which has made the Earthman so intelligent; he never actually needed all that brain.

Now if the Galactic average was around IQ 75, with their very brightest boys going up to, say, 150—

The waitress yipped and jumped into the air. Bronni grinned shamelessly as she turned to confront him.

Joe Husting pacified her. After breakfast he took the Galactic emissaries out and sold them the Brooklyn Bridge.

HAIKU

1.

Stars across fairness,
    Drift of dandelion seeds—
        What, springtime again?

2.

Cherry blossoms white—
    Sunset colorless, breath-quick—
        Stars hastening, cold.

3.

In snowfall of stars
    Those we see red are not old—
        An early winter.

4.

This high summer's day—
    Beneath it, a winter night
        Amid the same stars.

5.

While shadows lengthen
    A dandelion and bee
        Exchange tomorrows.

Genius

"The experiment has been going on for almost fifteen hundred years," said Heym, "and it's just starting to get under way. You *can't* discontinue it now."

"Can and will," replied Goram, "if the situation seems to justify it. That's what I'm going to find out."

"But—one planet! One primitive planet! What sort of monsters do you think live there? I tell you, they're people, as human as I—" Heym paused. He had meant to add—"and you," but couldn't quite bring himself to it. Goram seemed less than human, an atavistic remnant of screaming past ages, an ape in uniform. "—as I am," finished Heym.

The hesitation seemed lost on Goram. The marshal stood regarding the psychologist out of sullen little black eyes, blocky form faintly stooped, long arms dangling, prognathous jaw thrust ahead of the broad flat-nosed countenance. The fluorotubes gleamed down on his shining shaven bullet skull. The black gold-braided uniform fitted him closely, a military neatness and precision that was in its way the most primitive characteristic of all.

He said in his hoarse bass: "So are the rebels. So are the barbarians and pirates. So are the serfs and slaves and criminals and insane. But it's necessary to suppress all of them. If Station Seventeen represents a menace, it must be suppressed."

"But what conceivable danger—One barbarian planet—under constant surveillance throughout its history! If that can menace an empire of a hundred thousand star systems, we're not safe from anything!"

"We aren't. For three thousand years of history, the Empire has been in danger. You have to live with it, as we soldiers do, to realize how ultimately unstable the stablest power in history really is. Oh, we can smash the peripheral barbarians. We can hold the Taranians and the Comi and Magellanics in check." The marshal's heavy-ridged eyes swept contemptuously up and down the scientist's long weedy form. "I'm in no danger from you. I could break you with my bare hands. But a dozen viruses of Antaric plague, entering my body and multiplying, would paralyze me in agony and rot the flesh off my bones and probably empty this ship of life."

The office quivered, ever so faintly. The muffled throb of the great engines was vibrant in its walls and floor and ceiling, in the huge ribs and plates of the hull, in guns that could incinerate a continent and the nerves and bones of the two thousand men manning that planetoidal mass. Monstrously the ship drove through a night of mind-cracking empty distances, outpacing light in her furious subdimensional quasivelocity, impregnable and invincible and inhuman in her arrogance. And a dozen blind half-living protein molecules could kill her.

Heym nodded stiffly. "I know what you mean," he said. "After all"—deliberate snobbery edging his voice—"applied psychological science is the basis of the Empire. Military power is only one tool for—us."

"As you will. But I am not a researcher's tool, I belong to practical men, and they have decided this mission. If I report Station Seventeen potentially dangerous, they will order me to destroy it. If I decide it is already dangerous, I have the authority to order it destroyed myself."

Heym kept his gaunt face impassive, but for a moment he felt physically ill. He looked across the sparsely furnished office at the marshal's squat simian form, he saw the barely suppressed triumph-smile in the heavy coarse visage, and a wave of sick revulsion swept over him.

He thought wearily: *Fifteen hundred years...patience, work, worry, heartbreak, and triumph and a gathering dawn...generation after generation, watching from the skies, learning, pouring their whole lives into the mighty project—As if I didn't know the danger, the fear which is the foundation and the reason for the Empire...and here we have the first glimmerings of what may be a way out of the rattrap which history has become...and it's now all dependent on him! On the whim of a two-legged animal which will strike out in blind fear to destroy whatever it doesn't understand...or even understanding, will destroy just for the satisfaction of venting an inferiority complex, of watching better men squirm in pain.*

Calmness came, a steadiness and an icy calculation. After all, he thought, he was a psychologist and Goram was a soldier. It should be possible for him to handle the creature, talk him over, deftly convince him that he himself wanted what Heym wanted and had in fact thought of it himself and had to argue the scientist into agreement.

Yet—slow, easy, careful. He, Sars Heym, was a research man, not a practicing psychotechnician. He wasn't necessarily able to handle the blind brutal irrationality of man, any more than a physicist was ordinarily capable of solving an engineering problem. And so much depended on the outcome that...that—

Briefly, he sagged beneath the burden of responsibility. The load seemed for a dizzying instant too much to bear—unfair, unfair, to load one man with the weight of all the future. For Station Seventeen was the key to the next phase of history—of that Heym was certain. The history of man, his evolution—the whole universe seemed to open vertiginously before him, and he stood alone with the cosmos blazing on his shoulders.

He shook himself, as if to get rid of a clinging burden, and with a convulsive effort forced coolness on himself. Detached argument—well, he had used that often enough at Sol without convincing anyone who mattered. He could still use it on Goram, but not for itself, only as a means of flattery by appealing to reason—among other means.

Intolerable, to have to play sycophant to this—atavist—but there was too much at stake for pride to count.

"I understand your position, of course," said Heym, "even if I do not agree. I am sure that a glance at our records will convince you there is no danger."

"I'm not interested in records," rasped the marshal. "I could have had all that transvised to me at Sol if I wanted to see it. But that's the psychologists' department. I want to make a personal inspection."

"Very well. Though we could just as well have transvised the scenes revealed on the spy devices from our headquarters to Sol."

"I'm not interested in telescreen images either. I want to land on the planet, see its people with my own eyes, hear them talk, watch them at work and play. There's a *feel* to a race you can only get by direct observation." Goram's bulldog face thrust aggressively forward. "Oh, I know your fancy theories don't include that—you just watch from afar and write it all down in mathematical symbols nobody can read without twenty years of study. But I'm a practical man, I've dealt with enough barbarians to have an instinct for them."

Superstition! thought Heym bitterly. *Typical primitive mind reaction—magnifying his own ignorant guesses and impulses into an "instinct": No doubt he also believes hair turns gray from fear and drowned men always float face down. Behold the "practical man"!*

It was surprisingly hard to lie, after a lifetime's training in the honesty of science and the monastic community of observers at the station. But he said calmly enough: "Well, that's very interesting, Marshal Goram. We've often noticed curious talents—precognition, telepathy, telekinesis, and the rest, appearing sporadically among people who have some use for them, but we've never been able to pin them down. It's as if they were phenomena inaccessible to the ordinary scientific method. I see your point."

And I flatter myself that's good flattery—not too obviously in agreement, but still hinting that he's some kind of superman.

"Haven't you ever landed at all?" asked Goram.

"Oh, yes, fairly often—usually invisible, of course, but now and then making an open and even spectacular appearance to test the effects of seemingly supernatural manifestations. However, we can generally see quite enough through the strategically planted recording televisors and other spy devices."

"You think," grunted Goram. "But a planet is mighty big, I tell you. How do you know what they're cooking up in places your gadgets don't see?"

Heym was unable to keep all the weariness and disgust out of his voice. "Because history is a unity," he said. "The whole can be inferred from the part, since the part belongs to the whole. Why should the only unwarlike people in the Galaxy suddenly start building weapons?"

"Oh, we don't fear their military power—yet," replied Goram. "I should think you, as a psychologist, would know what sort of a danger Station Seventeen represents—a danger that can wreck civilization. They can become *a disrupting factor*—the worst in all history."

"Progress *is* disruption."

"Maybe. But the Empire is based on stasis. It's sacrificed progress for—survival."

"True—but here we may have a clue to controlled progress, safe advancement. Even stasis isn't safe, as we well know. It's a poor makeshift, intended to keep civilization alive while something else is worked out. Well—we're working it out at Station Seventeen."

Coram grunted again, but remained silent.

Valgor's Star lay a good hundred parsecs from Sol, not far from the Empire's border though sufficiently within the garrisoned marches to be protected from barbarian raids. The early researchers, looking for an uninhabited Earth-like planet, had found the obscure G0-type sun far off the regular space lanes; an ancient planetographic expedition had stopped briefly there, recording that the third world was practically terrestrial, but this whole galactic sector was so isolated and unprofitable that there had been no further visits, and the old report lay for centuries in the Imperial files before the Psychotechnic Foundation resurrected it. The remoteness and unknownness were assets in any such project, and the fact that there were no aborigines requiring troublesome and costly extermination and eradication of all traces had been decisive.

At an easy cruising speed, the battleship used three days going from Sol to Valgor's Star. Sars Heym spent most of that time getting on the right side of Tamman Goram. It involved listening to endless dreary reminiscing of border warfare and the consummate ability required to rise from simple conscript to Imperial Marshal, but the price was small if it could save Station Seventeen.

"Nobody appreciates the border garrisons who hasn't served in them," declared Goram, "but I tell you, if it weren't for them the Empire wouldn't last a year. The barbarians would sweep in, the rival empires would gobble up all they could hold and go to war over the spoils, the Spirit alone knows what the Magellanics would do—but it wouldn't be pleasant—and the whole structure would disintegrate—three thousand years of stability might as well never have been!"

A high official would be used to open flattery. Heym disagreed just enough to seem sincerely to agree on all important points. "We couldn't do without the border patrols," he said, "but it's like any organism, requiring all its parts to live—we couldn't dispense with internal police either, and certainly not with the psychotechnicians who *are* the government."

"Spirit-damned bureaucrats," snorted Goram. "Theoreticians—what do they know of real life? Why, d'you know, I saw three stellar systems lost once to the barbarians because we didn't have enough power to stand them off. There was a horde of them, a dozen allied suns, and we had only three garrisoned planets. For months we begged—wrote to Antares and Sirius and Sol itself *begging* for a single Nova-class battleship. Just one, and we could have beaten off their fleet and carried the war to them. But no, it was 'under consideration' or 'deferred for more urgent use'—three suns and a hundred thousand men lost because some soft-bellied psychotechnician mislaid a file."

"Robot-checked files don't get mislaid," said Heym softly. "I have friends in administration, and I've seen them weep at some of the decisions they had to make. It isn't easy to abandon an army to its fate—and yet the power that could have saved them is needed elsewhere, to drive off a larger invasion or to impress the Taranians or to take a star cluster of strategic value. The Empire has sacrificed a lot for sheer survival. Humanness in government is only one thing lost."

"The rules! How can a general in the field keep track of every ship and turn in forms in quadruplicate on their condition?"

"He can't. Probably a million units a year are lost in recording. And yet, the vast majority of such forms *are* filled out and *do* get to the appropriate center, are recorded in electronic code and put on instantly accessible file, mathematically coordinated with all other relevant information. When Grand Strategy wants an overall picture of the military situation, it has one right there. Military planning would be impossible otherwise.

"And it isn't only in the military field," argued Heym. "After all, you know the Empire isn't interested in further expansion. It wants to keep civilization alive on the planets where it exists, and keep the nonhuman imperia out. Ever since the Founder, our military policy has been basically defensive—because we can't handle more than we have. The border is always in a state of war and flux, but the Empire is at peace, inside the marches.

"Yet—how long would the Empire last, even assuming no hostile powers outside, without the most rigid form of psychotechnocratic government? There are roughly three times ten to the fourteenth power humans in the Solarian Empire. The nonhuman aborigines have been pretty thoroughly exterminated, assimilated as helots, or otherwise rendered harmless, but there are still all those humans, with all the terrific variations and conflicting desires inherent in man and intensified by radically different planetary and consequently social environments. Can you imagine a situation where three hundred trillion humans went their own uncoordinated ways—with atomic energy, biotoxic weapons, and interstellar spaceships to back up their conflicting demands?"

"Yes, I can," said Goram, "because after all it has happened—for nearly a thousand years before the Empire, there was virtual anarchy. And"—he leaned forward, the hard black glitter of his eyes nailing Heym—"that's why we can't take chances, with this experiment of yours or anything else—anything at all. In the anarchic centuries, with a much smaller population, there was horror—many planets were blasted back to savagery, or wiped out altogether. Have you seen the dead worlds? Black cinders floating in space, some still radioactive, battlegrounds of the ancient wars. The human barbarians beyond the Imperial borders are remnants of that age—some of them have spaceships, even a technology matching our own, but they think only of destruction—if they ever got past the marches, they'd blast and loot and fight till nothing was left. Not to mention the nonhuman border barbarians, or the rival empires always watching their chance, or the Magellanics sweeping in every century or so with weapons such as we never imagined. Just let any disrupting factor shake the strength and unity of the Empire and see how long it could last."

"I realize that," said Heym coldly. "After all, I *am* a psychologist. I know fully what a desperate need the establishment of the Empire filled. But I also know that it's a dead end—its purpose of ultimate satisfied stasis cannot be realized in a basically dynamic cosmos. Actually, Imperial totalitarianism is simply the result of Imperial ignorance of a better way. We can only find that better way through research, and the project at Station Seventeen is the most promising of all the Foundation's work. Unless we find some way out of our dilemma, the Empire is doomed—sooner or later, something will happen and we'll go under."

Goram's eyes narrowed. "That's near lese majesty," he murmured.

Heym laughed, and gave the marshal a carefully gauged you-and-I-know-better-don't-we look. "The Imperium is tolerant of local gods," he said, "but the divinity of the Emperor must be acknowledged and is taught in all schools. Why? Because a state church, with the temporal ruler as the material incarnation of the Spirit, is another hold on the imagination of the people, another guarantee of subservience. So are local garrisons, political indoctrination, state control of commerce and travel, careful psychotechnic preparation and supervision of amusements, rigid limitation of birth but complete sexual freedom as an outlet, early selection and training of all promising children for government service—with unlimited opportunities for advancement *within* the established framework—and every other thing we can possibly control. If you stop to think about it—the Empire is founded on mediocrity."

"That's as may be," muttered Goram, "but in that case a planet full of geniuses becomes doubly dangerous."

Heym went over to the wall of the officers' lounge and touched a button. The telescreen sprang to life with a simulacrum of the outside view. An uncounted host of stars blazed against the infinite blackness, a swarming magnificent arrogance of unwinking hard jewels strewn across the impassive face of eternity. The Milky Way foamed around the sky, the misty nebulae and star clusters wheeled their remote godlike way around heaven, and the other galaxies flashed mysterious signals across the light-years and the centuries. As ever, the psychologist felt dwarfed and awed and numbed by the stupendous impact.

"It was a great dream," he whispered. "There never was a higher dream than man's conquest of the universe—and yet like so many visions it overleaped itself and shattered to bits on the rocks of reality—in this case, simple arithmetic defeated us. How to reconcile and coordinate a hundred thousand stars except by absolutism, by deliberate statism—by chaining ourselves to our own achievements? What other answer is there?"

He turned around to Goram. The soldier sat unmoving, face stone-hard, like a primitive idol. "We're looking for a new way," said Heym. "We think we're finding it, at Station Seventeen. It's the first hope in four thousand years."

The planet might almost have been Earth, a great blue spheroid swinging majestically against the incredible spatial sky with a softly shining moon for companion. Auroras wavered over the ice-capped poles, and cloud masses blurred the greenish-brown continents. They were storms, those clouds, snow and rain and wind blowing out of a living heaven over broad fair fields and haughty mountains, and looking down from the sterile steel environment of the ship, remembering the world city sprawling over Earth and the cold hard mechanized pattern of all Imperial life, Heym felt a brief wistfulness. All at once, he envied his experimental animals, down there on the green young planet. Even if they were to be destroyed, they had been more fortunate than their masters.

But they wouldn't be destroyed. They mustn't be.

"Where is your observation post?" asked Goram.

"On an asteroid well away from here and rendered invisible."

"Why not on the satellite? It'd be a lot closer."

"Yes, but distance doesn't mean anything to a transvisor. Also, if—when—the colonists learn the means of interplanetary travel, we'd have had to move off the Moon, while we can remain hidden indefinitely on the invisible planetoid."

"I'd say 'if' rather than 'when'," amended Goram grimly. "It was your report that the inhabitants were experimenting with rockets that alarmed the rulers enough to order me here to see if it weren't best simply to sterilize the planet."

"I've told you before, there's no need for alarm," protested Heym. "What if the people do have a few rocketships? They have no reason to do more than visit the other worlds of this system, which aren't habitable—certainly no reason to colonize, with their own planet still practically uninhabited. The present population is estimated at only some eight hundred million."

"Nevertheless, as soon as they have a whole system to move about in they'll be dangerous. It'll no longer be possible to keep track of everything of importance they may do. They'll be stimulated by this success to perfect an interstellar drive—and even you will agree that that cannot be permitted. That engine may be developed without our knowledge, on some remote world of this system—and once even a few of them are running loose between the stars we'll have no further control—and the results may well be catastrophic! Imagine a pure-bred line of geniuses allied with the barbarians!"

"I tell you, they're not warlike. They haven't had a single war in all their history."

"Well, then they'll try to innovate within the Empire, which would be just as bad if not worse. Certainly they won't be satisfied with the status quo—yet that status quo means survival to us."

"They can be co-ordinated. Good Spirit, we have plenty of geniuses in the Galaxy today! We couldn't do without them. They are the very ones who run the Empire. Advancement is on a strict merit basis simply because we *must* have the best brains of mankind for the gigantic job of maintaining the social order."

"Sure—everyone's strictly brought up to accept the Empire, to identify its survival with its own. We have plenty of tame geniuses. But these are wild—a planetful of undomesticated intellects! If they can't be tamed, they must be killed."

"They can be," insisted Heym. "Rather, they can become the leaders to get us out of status quo safely—if not directly, then indirectly through knowledge gained by observing them. Already administrative techniques have been improved, within the last five hundred or so years, because by watching unhampered intellect at work we have been able to derive more accurate psychomathematical expressions for the action of logic as a factor in society, A group in the Psychotechnic Foundation is working out a new theory of cerebration which may become the basis of a system of mind training doubling the efficiency of logical processes—just as semantic training has already increased mind power by applying it more effectively. But in order to develop and test that theory, as well as every other psychological research project, we must have empirical data such as the observation stations, above all Seventeen, furnish us. Without such new basic information, science comes to a standstill."

"I've heard it all before," said Goram wearily. "Now I want to go down there and look."

"Very well. I'll come along, of course. Do you wish to take anyone else?"

"Do I need to?"

"No, it's perfectly safe."

"Then I won't. Meet me at Lifeboat Forty in half an hour." Goram tramped off to give such orders as might be needed.

Heym stood for a while, chain smoking and looking out the visiplate at the silently rolling planet. Like an ominous moon, the warship swung in an orbit just beyond the atmosphere. For all its titanic mass, it was insignificant against the bulk of a world. Yet in guns and bombs and death-mists, gravitational beams and long-range disintegrators and mass-conversion torpedoes, in coagulative radiations and colloid-resonant generators, in the thousand hells man had made through all his tormented existence, lay the power to rip life off that surface and blanket the shuddering continents in smoke and flame and leave the blackened planet one great tomb under the indifferent stars.

No—no, that was wrong. The power did not lie in the ship, it was inert metal and will-less electronic intellect, a cosmic splinter that without man would spin darkly into eternity. The will, and hence the power, to destroy lay in men—in one man. One gorilla in uniform. One caveman holding a marshal's baton. One pulsing mass of colloidal tissue, ultimately unstable, not even knowing its own desire.

Heym scowled and drew heavily on his cigarette. Goram had been soothed into comparative geniality, but his frantic notion of death as panacea was as strong as ever. The creature wasn't even consistent—one moment talking philosophy of history as if he had brains, the next snarling his mindlessly destructive xenophobia. There was something wrong about Goram—*though it might only be my own ignorance of practical psychology,* thought Heym. *As a research man I'm used to dealing with only one factor at a time. A situation in life is really too complex for me—I don't have enough rules of thumb. I wish I'd brought a practicing technician along, say Kharva or Junn—they'd soon analyze the mental mechanism of our marshal and push the appropriate buttons.*

The old sickening fear fell anew on him. What if, after all he should fail—what if fifteen hundred years of work were to be sponged out at the arbitrary whim of a superstition-ridden military moron? *If I fail, the Empire fails with me—I know it.*

And it isn't fair! I should have been told what I was being recalled to Sol for. I should have had a chance to prepare my arguments better. I should have been allowed to take a practical psycho along—but no, they obviously couldn't permit me to do that or I'd have had everything my own way.

But couldn't they see? Can't they understand? Or has the worship of statism penetrated so deep that it's like an instinct, a blind need for which everything else must be sacrificed?

He turned and went heavily toward his cabin to make ready.

Screened by an invisibility field, the lifeboat spiraled down toward the surface. Goram let the robopilot handle the vessel, and spent most of his time peering through a field-penetrating visiscope.

"Not much sign of habitation," he said.

"No, I told you the population was still small," replied Heym. After all, only a few thousand were planted originally and the struggle for existence was as hard as with any savages for the first few centuries. Only lately has the population really begun growing."

"And you say they have cities now—machines—civilization? It's hard to believe."

"Yes, it is. The whole result has been a triumphant confirmation of the psychotechnic theory of history, but nevertheless the sheer spectacular character of the success has awed us. I can understand it's a little frightening. One naturally thinks a race which can go from naked savages to mechanized civilization in fifteen hundred years is somehow demonic. Yet they're humans, fully as human as anyone else in the Galaxy, the same old Earthly stock as all men. They've simply enjoyed the advantage of freedom from stupidity."

"How many stations are there?"

"About a hundred—planetary colonies, with colonists in ignorance of their own origin, where various special conditions are maintained. Different environments, for instance, or special human stocks. The progress of history is being observed on all of them, secretly, and invaluable data on mass-psychologic processes are thereby gained. But Seventeen has been by far the most fruitful."

Goram wrinkled his low forehead. With concealed distaste, Heym thought how very like an ape he looked—throwback, atavist, cunning in his own narrow field but otherwise barely above moron level—typical militarist, the biped beast who had ridden mankind's back like some nightmarish vampire through all history—except on the one planet of Valgor's Star—

"I don't quite see the point," admitted the marshal. "Why spend all that time and money on creating artificial conditions that you'd never meet in real life?"

"It's the scientific method," said Heym, wondering at what elementary level he would have to begin his explanation. How stupid could one be and hold a marshal's position? "The real world is an interaction of uncounted factors, constantly changing in relation to themselves and each other, far too vast and complex to be understood in its entirety. In order to find casual relationships, the scientist has to perform experiments in which he varies only one factor at a time, observing its effect—and, of course, running control experiments at the same time. From these data he infers similar relationships in the real world. By means of theoretical analysis of observed facts he can proceed to predict new phenomena—if these predictions are borne out by further observation, the theory is probably—though never certainly—right, and can be used as a guide in understanding and controlling the events of the real world."

In spite of himself, Heym was warming up to his subject. After all, it was his whole life. He went on in a gathering rush of words:

"All the evidence shows that reality is not object but process. You yourself are not the same object as an instant ago—physicochemical-psychological changes, the very change of entropy which is 'time,' are all continuous. They are rapid in the case of an organism, slow in the case of a rock, say, but always continuous. The object is an abstraction, a set of constant characteristics of a process—more or less constant, I should say, since nothing is permanent, change, process, is always continuous. The grammatical distinction between noun and verb has misled us to think there is a corresponding distinction between what an object is and what it does—completely false, as a moment's reflection will show."

"Hm-m-m" Gorman looked out the visiscope. The boat was sweeping over a broad plain, yellow with ripening grain. A few primitive villages, houses built of stone and wood and brick, were scattered over the great landscape, a peaceful scene, reminiscent of civilization's dawn. "The planet *looks* backward enough," grunted Goram dubiously.

"It is," said Heym eagerly. "I assure you it is."

"Well…you were saying—" Goram didn't look at all sure of what Heym had been saying. "Get to the point."

"Civilization—history, if you will —is a process like all else." resumed the scientist. "A nation is not a concrete object, a giant man, a god or All-Father to whom one owes fanatical loyalty and unquestioning obedience. How much misery could have been prevented if men had seen that simple, common sense fact! A nation is part of a culture, and a culture is an interaction of certain peoples with themselves, their neighbors, and their 'natural' environment over a space-time region. When the process has lost its distinctive characteristics, its continuity of development, we say the culture is dead, but that is only a convenient figure of speech. Actually causality is indefinitely extended. We are still influenced by events that occurred in prehistoric ages.

"The early students of culture were struck by the similarity of development of different civilizations, as if man went along one inevitable historic path. And in a way he did—because one thing leads to another. The expanding units of culture clash, there are ever fiercer wars, old fears and grudges intensify, economic breakdowns increase the misery, finally, and usually unwittingly and even unwillingly, one nation overcomes all others to protect itself and founds a 'universal state' which brings a certain peace of exhaustion but eventually decays and collapses of its own weaknesses or under the impact of alien invaders. That's exactly what happened to mankind as a whole, when he exploded into the Galaxy—only this time the fearful scale and resources of the wars all but shattered the civilization;

and the Solarian Empire, the passive rigidity solving the problems of the time of troubles by force, has lasted immensely longer than most preceding universal states, because its rulers have enough knowledge of mass-psychologic processes to have a certain control over them and all the power of a hundred thousand planetary systems to back their decisions."

Goram looked a little dazed. "I still don't see what this has to do with the Foundation and its stations," he complained.

"Simply this," said Heym, "that though history is a natural process, like anything else, it is peculiarly hard to understand and hence almost impossible to control. This is not only because of the very complex character of the interactions but because we ourselves are concerned in it—the observer is part of the phenomenon. And also, it had long been impossible to conduct controlled experiments in history and thus separate out causal factors and observe their unhindered working. On the basis of thousands of years of history as revealed—usually quite incompletely—by records and by archeology, and of extrapolations from individual and mob psychological knowledge, and whatever other data were available, the scientists of the period preceding the Empire worked out a semi-mathematical theory of history which gave some idea of the nature of the processes involved—causal factors and the manner of their action. This theory made possible qualitative predictions of the behavior of masses of men under certain conditions. Thus the early emperors knew what factors to vary in order to control their provinces. They could tell whether a certain measure might, say, precipitate a revolt, or just what phrasing to use in proclamations for the desired effect. If you want a man to do something for you, you don't usually slap him in the face—it's much more effective to appeal to his vanity or his prejudices, best of all to convince him it's what he himself wants to do. But once in a while, a face slapping becomes necessary. Why, even today the barbarians are held at bay more by subtle psychological and economic pressures dividing them against each other and putting them in awe of us than by actual military might."

An ocean rolled beneath the boat, gray and green, shaking its white mane out on the restless horizon. "Swing northeast," said Heym. "The planet's greatest city lies that way, on a large island."

"Good. A city's a good place to observe a people. Can we go around incognito?"

"Naturally. I know the language well enough to pass for a traveler from some other part of the world, There's a lot of intercourse between continents. The cities are quite cosmopolitan."

"Well—go on. You've still not explained why the station and all this rigmarole of secrecy."

"I was laying the background," said Heym, unable to keep all the tiredness out of his voice. *Can I really talk this moron over? Can anyone? Reason is wasted on an ape.* "It's really very simple. The crude psychotechnology available made it possible for the early emperors to conquer most of the human-inhabited Galaxy, hold it together, and reach an uneasy truce with the Taranian and Comi Empires. Our military might can hold off the barbarians and the Magellanic raiders, and have sufficient power left over to police the three hundred trillion citizens.

"Yet our science is primitive. On that vast scale, it can only deal with the simplest possible situations. It's all we can do to keep the Empire stable. If it should develop on the colossal scale of which it is capable and with all the unpredictable eraticism of the free human mind, It would simply run away from us. We have trouble enough keeping industry and commerce flowing smoothly when we know exactly how it should work. If we permitted free invention and progress, there'd be an industrial revolution every year—there is never a large proportion of discoverers, but with the present population the number would be immense. Our carefully evolved techniques of control would become obsolete, there'd be economic anarchy, conflict, suffering, individuals rising to power outside the present social framework and threatening the co-ordinating authority—with planet-smashing power to back both sides and all our enemies on the watch for a moment's instability.

"That's only one example. It applies to any field. Science, philosophy—we can control known religions, channel the impulses to safe directions—but a new religion, rousing discontent, containing unknown elements—a billion fanatics going to war—No! We have to keep status quo, which we understand, at the cost of an uncontrollable advance into the unknown.

"The Empire really exists only to simplify the psychotechnic problem of co-ordination. Enforcement of population stability—good, we don't have to worry about controlling trillions of new births, there's no land hunger. Stable industry, ossified physical science, state religion, totalitarian control of the entire life span—good, we know exactly what we're dealing with and our decisions will be obeyed—imagine the situation if three hundred trillion people were free to do exactly as they pleased in the Galaxy! Subjugation of nonhuman aborigines, or outright extermination—good, we only have to deal with human-type minds and needs, which are complex enough, not with a million or a trillion psychologies and past histories as wildly different as the planets of origin. Heym shrugged "Why go on? You know as well as I do that the Empire is only an answer to a problem of survival—not a good answer, but the best our limited knowledge can make."

"Hah!" Goram's exclamation was triumphant. "And you want to turn a world of unpredictable geniuses loose in that!"

"If I thought for an instant there was any danger of this people's becoming a disrupting factor, I'd be the very first to advocate sterilization," said Heym. "After all I want to live, too. But there's nothing to fear. Instead, there is—hope."

"What hope?" snorted Goram, "Personally, I can't see what you want, anyway. For three thousand years, we've kept man satisfied. Who'd want to change it?"

Heym bit back his temper. "Aside from the fact that the contentment is like death," he said, "history shows that universal states don't endure forever. Sooner or later, we'll face something that will overwhelm us. Unless we've evolved ourselves. But safe evolution is only possible when we know enough psychotechnics to keep the process orderly and peaceful—when our science is really quantitative.

The Stations, and especially Seventeen, are giving us the information we must have to develop such a science."

The island lay a few kilometers north of the great northern continent. A warm stream in the ocean made the climate equable, so that the land lay green in the gray immensity of sea, but polar air swept south with fog and rain and snow, storms roaring over the horizon and the sun stabbing bright lances down through a mightily stooping sky of restless clouds and galloping winds. Heym thought that the stimulating weather had as much to do as the favorable location along the northern trade routes with the islanders' leadership in the planet's civilization.

Many villages lay in the fields and valleys and on the edges of the forest that still filled the interior, but there was only one city, on an estuary not far from the southern coast. From the air, it was not impressive to one who had seen the world cities of Sol and Sirius and Antares, a sprawling collection of primitive, often thatch-roofed, dwellings that could hardly have housed more than a million, the narrow cobbled streets crowded with pedestrians and animal-drawn vehicles, the harbor where a few steam- or oil-driven vessels were all but lost in the throng of wind-powered ships, the almost prehistoric airport—but the place had the character, subtle and unmistakable, of a city, a community knowing of more than its own horizon inclosed and influencing events beyond the bounds of sight.

"Can we land without being detected?" inquired Goram.

Heym laughed. "An odd question for a military man to ask. This boat is so well screened that the finest instruments of the Imperial navy would have trouble locating us. Oh, yes, we observers have been landing from time to time all through the station's history."

"I must say the place *looks* backward enough," said Coram dubiously. "The existence of cities is certainly evidence of crude transportation."

"Well"—honesty forced Heym to argue—"not necessarily. The city, that is, the multi-purpose community, is one criterion of whether a society is civilized or merely barbaric, in the technical anthropological sense. It's true that cities as definite centers disappeared on Earth after the Atomic Revolution, but that was simply because such closely spaced buildings were no longer necessary. In the sense of close relation to the rest of mankind and of resultant co-ordination, Earth's people kept right on having cities. And today the older planets of the Empire have become so heavily populated that the crowded structures are reappearing—in effect, the whole world becomes one vast city. But I will agree that the particular stage of city evolution existing here on Seventeen is primitive."

Goram set the boat down in a vacant field outside the community's limits. "What now?" he asked

"Well, I suppose you'll want to spend a time just walking around the place." Heym fumbled in a bag. "I brought the proper equipment, clothes and money of the local type. Planetary type, that is—since a universal coinage was established at the same time as a common language was adopted for international use and nobody cares what sort of dress you wear." He unfolded the brief summer garments, shorts and sandals and tunic of bleached and woven plant fiber. Funny thing," he mused, "how man has always made a virtue of necessity. The lands threatened with foreign invasion came to glorify militarism and war. The people who had to work hard considered idleness disgraceful. Dwellers in a northern climate, who had to wear clothes, made nudity immoral. But our colonists here are free of that need for compensation and self-justification You can work, think, marry, eat, dress, whatever you want to do, just as you please, and if you aren't stepping on someone else's toes too hard nobody cares. Which indicates that intolerance is characteristic of stupidity, while the true intellectual is naturally inclined to live and let live."

Goram struggled awkwardly and distastefully into the archaic garments. "How about weapons?" he asked.

"No need to carry them. No one does, except in places where wild animals might be dangerous. In fact, arms are about the only thing in which the colonists' inventiveness has lagged. They never got past the bow and arrow. Aside from a few man-to-man duels in the early stages of their history, and now abandoned, they've never fought each other."

"Impossible! Man is a fighting animal."

Heym tried to find a reply which was not to obviously a slap at the whole military profession. "There's been war on all our other colonies," he said slowly, "and, of course, through all human history—yet there's never been any real, logical reason for it. In fact, at one stage of prehistoric man, the late Neolithic, war seems to have been unknown—at least, no weapons were found buried with the men of that time. And your whole professional aim today is to maintain peace within the Empire, isn't it?

"It takes only one to make a quarrel unless the other lacks all spirit to resist—and a people like these are obviously spirited, in fifteen hundred years they've explored their whole planet. But suppose neither side wants to fight. Whenever two tribes met, in the history of Station Seventeen, they were all too intelligent to suffer from xenophobia or other non-logical motivations to murder, and certainly they had no logical reason to fight. So they didn't. It was as simple as that."

Goram snorted, whether in disbelief or contempt Heym didn't know. "Let's go," he said.

They stepped out of the boat and its invisibility screen into the field. Tall breeze-rippled grass tickled their bare legs, and the wind in their faces had the leashless wild exuberance and the heady scent of green growing life brought over the many kilometers of field and forest across which it had rushed—incredible, that pulsing warm vitality after the tanked sterility of the ship, of the Empire. And up in the blue cloud-fleeced sky a bird was singing, rising higher and ever higher toward the sun, drunk with wind and light.

The two men walked across the field to a road that led cityward. It was a narrow rutted brown track in the earth, and Goram snorted again. They walked along it. On a hill to the right stood a farm, a solid, substantial, contented-looking cluster of low tile-roofed stone buildings amid the open fields, and ahead on the horizon was the straggling misty line of the city. Otherwise they were alone.

"Are all your colonies this wild?" asked Goram.

"Just about," said Heym, "though the environments are often radically different—everything from a planet that's barely habitable desert to one that's all jungle and swamp. That way, we can isolate the effects of environment. We even have one world equipped with complex robot-run cities, to see how untutored humans will react. There are three control stations, Earth-like planets where ordinary human types were left, and from them we're getting valuable information on the path which terrestrial history actually took, we can test basic anthropological hypotheses and so on. Then there are a number of planets where different human types are planted—different races, different intelligence levels, and so on, to isolate the effects of heredity and see if there is any correlation of civilization with, say, physiology. But only here on Seventeen, populated exclusively by geniuses, has progress been rapid. All the other colonies are still in the stone ages or even lower, though there have been some unique responses made to severe environmental stimuli."

"And you mean you just dumped your subjects down on all these worlds?"

"Crudely put, yes. For instance, before colonizing Seventeen we—that is, the Foundation—spent several generations breeding a pure genius strain of man. On Imperial orders, the Galaxy's best brains were bred, and genetic control and selection were applied, until a stock had been developed whose members had only genius in the intellectual part of their heredity. Barring mutation or accident, both negligible, the people here and their children can only be geniuses. Then the few thousand adult end-products, who had naturally not been told what was in store for them, were seized and put under the action of memory erasers which left them able to walk and eat and little else. Then a couple of hundred were planted in each climatic region of this planet, near strategically placed invisible spy devices, and the observers sat back on their asteroid to see what would happen. That was fifteen hundred-odd years ago, but even in the forty or so years I've been in charge the change here has been very noticeable. In fact, on choosing the proper psychomathematical quantities to represent the various types of progress and plotting them against time, almost perfect exponential curves were obtained."

"Sure. All progress, scientific progress anyway, is exponential."

"Oh, no—quite the contrary. There are only a few sudden, brilliant, and—brief—periods of expansion in human history; long dreary dark ages intervene, and even the times of expansion are irregular. Nor has there ever been any real social progress made today as in the stone ages, law is based on force, though most of our force is the subtler psychotechnic kind—and even it is not essentially different from the taboo or priestcraft holding earlier cultures in check. I tell you, only on Seventeen has scientific progress been continuous, and only on Seventeen has there been any real social progress at all."

Goram scowled. "So on that exponential advance, you can expect them to work out interplanetary travel in a matter of years," he said. "They'll know the principles of the star drive in a few more generations, and invent a faster-than-light engine almost at once. No—they aren't safe!"

* * *

It was strange to walk through the narrow twisting streets and among the high archaic facades of a city which belonged to the almost forgotten past. To Goram, who must have visited uncivilized planets often, it could not be as queer as to Heym, and, also, the military mind would be too unimaginative to appreciate the situation. But even though Heym had spent the better part of his life watching this culture, it never failed to waken in him a dim feeling of dreamlike unreality.

Mere picturesqueness counted for a little, though the place was colorful enough. Along those cobbled ways went the traffic of a world. There were fantastic-looking beasts, variations of the horned ungulate genus which the colonists had early tamed to ride and load with their burdens, and still more exotic pets; and steering cautiously between them came trucks and passenger vehicles which for all their crudeness of material and principle had a cleanness of design, all the taut inherent beauty of the machine, that only Imperial mechanisms matched. More significant were the people.

There was nothing marking them out as obviously different. Many physical types were in evidence here, from the tall fair islanders to the stocky arctic dwellers or the sunburned southern folk; and costumes varied accordingly, though even strangers tended to wear some form of the light local summer dress. If perhaps a tendency toward higher foreheads and more clean-cut features than the Galactic average existed, it was not striking, and there was as wide deviation from it as could be found anywhere. The long hair of both sexes and the full beards worn by many men screened any intellectuality of appearance behind a hirsute veil associated with the peripheral barbarians.

No—the difference from any other world in the Galaxy was real and unmistakable, but it wasn't physical. It was in the clear air of the city, where all chimneys were smokeless, and in the clean-swept streets. It was in the orderliness of traffic, easy movement without jostling and confusion. It was in the clean bodies and soft voices of the people, in the casually accepted equality of the sexes even at this primitive level of technology. It was negative, in the absence of slums and jails, and positive, in the presence of parks and schools and hospitals. There were no weapons or uniforms in sight, but many in the street carried books or wore chemical-stained smocks. There were no ranting orators, but a large group sat on the grass of one park and listened to a lecture on ornithology. Laughter was quiet, but there was more of it than Heym had heard elsewhere in the Empire.

Goram muttered once: "I seem to hear quite a few languages here."

"Oh, yes," replied Heym. "Each region naturally developed its own tongue and generally sticks to it for sentimental reasons and also because the thoughts of a people are best expressed in the speech they themselves developed. But as soon as contact between the lands became common, an international language was worked out and learned by all concerned. In fact, only about fifty years ago a completely new world language was adopted, one correct according to the newly established principles of semantics. That's more than the Empire has yet done. We can talk Terrestrial safely enough, it'll pass for some local dialect, and I can do the talking for both of us with the natives."

"Still"—Goram scowled—"I don't like it. Everybody here has a higher I.Q. than myself—that's not right for a bunch of barbarians. I feel as if everyone was looking at me."

"Most of them observe us, yes, geniuses being naturally observant," said Heym. "But we aren't conspicuous in any way. Our men have often been on the planet in person without attracting attention."

"Didn't you say you'd appeared openly?"

"Yes—a few times, some centuries back, we made the most awe inspiring possible descents, coming down through the air on gravibeams in luminous clothes and performing seeming miracles. You see, even the primitive tribes had shown no signs of organized religion beyond the usual magic rites which they soon outgrew. We wanted to see if god-worship couldn't be induced." Heym smiled wryly. "But after the generation which had actually seen us, there was no sign of our manifestation. I suppose the young, being of independent mind, simply refused to believe their elders' wild stories. Not that the people are without religious sense. There is a high proportion of unbelievers, but there is also a large philosophical and even devotional literature. But nobody founds a school of thought, rather everybody reaches his own conclusions."

"I don't see how progress is possible then."

You wouldn't, thought Heym contemptuously, but he only smiled and said, "Apparently it is."

An aircraft roared low overhead, and a wagon driver fought to control his suddenly panicky animals. Goram said: "The biggest paradox here is the anachronism. Sail ships and oilburners docked side by side, animal power in the same street with chemical engines, stone and wood houses with efficient smoke precipitators—how come?"

"It's partly a matter of the extremely rapid progress," declared Heym, "A new invention appears before the economy has become geared to it. There won't be many machines until mass-production factories are set up to produce them in quantity, and that will have to wait till mechanical knowledge is sufficiently advanced to develop factories almost entirely automatic—for few if any geniuses could stand to work on an assembly line all day. Meanwhile, the people are in no hurry to advance their standard of living. Already they have sufficient food, clothing, and other necessities for all, as well as abundant free time—why strain themselves to go beyond that? This isn't the first time a brilliantly creative civilization has existed without interest in material progress; I might cite the Hellenic phase of the ancient Classical culture on Earth as another case."

Goram, who had obviously heard nothing and cared less about Hellenic culture, was silent for a while, then at last a blurted protest: "But they're working on rockets!"

"Oh, yes—but there's a difference: between exploration and exploitation. The social system here is unique, and doesn't lend itself to imperialism. The Empire doesn't have to fear Station Seventeen."

"I've told you before I'm not worried about their military power," snarled Goram.

Heym fell silent, for he felt the sudden sickening fear that the marshal might, without reason or provocation, decide to annihilate the colony—destroy it out of pure spite, pique with the psychologists and, their dominion over the soldiers, vent for a gathering wrath at the subconscious, frantically denied realization of his own basic inferiority to these barbarians. If he killed them, it would be proof, the militarists' twisted proof, that he was superior after all.

With a growing desperation, Heym looked around at the people—the fortunate children of an open sky, quiet, glad, urbane, and strong with the unconquerable strength of intelligence. Here was truly Homo sapiens, man the wise—man who had plucked fire from the mouth of a volcano, far back in the lost ages of the ice, and started on a long journey into darkness. He had come far since then, but he had ended in a blind alley. Only here, on this one insignificant world of the countless millions swarming around the stars, only here was the old quest being renewed, the path of hope being trodden. Elsewhere lay only the sorry road of empire and death. Where the path of Station Seventeen led, Heym could not imagine. Unguessably far it went, out beyond the glittering stars his mind reeled at thought of the infinities open to mankind if he took the right turning.

The psychologist said, with desperation raw in his voice "Goram—Marshal Goram—surely you can see the experiment is harmless. More than that, it's the most beneficial thing that has yet happened in all human history. Good Spirit, here's hope for the Empire! A race which can progress as this has done can show us the way."

"The Empire," said Goram tightly, "isn't interested in progress. It's only interested in survival."

"But—this is the way to survive. Every civilization—yes, every species—that quit advancing has become extinct."

"I'm a practical man," snapped Goram. "I'm not interested in crackpot schemes to save the universe."

"What's so practical about clinging to a system that in all history has consistently failed to work?" When the officer's face remained cold and shut, Heym said with forced persuasiveness, "After all, in physical science the planet is still centuries behind us. In fact, strangely enough, though their advance in that branch of knowledge has been as extremely rapid as you can see, they have shown a proportionately greater concentration on biological and sociological work. I don't know why, unless it is that genius is less afraid than mediocrity to study subjects which strike close to home. On Earth, astronomy, the most remote science, was the oldest, and psychiatry and sociology the youngest, but here all the sciences have got off to an even start. The mere absence of war is enough to show how far ahead of us these people are, and I could list any amount of supporting evidence. Their social system has achieved the miracle of combining progressiveness and stability. Just give the Foundation a chance to learn from them—or even, if they do work out an interstellar drive, give them a chance to teach us themselves, They're the most reasonable race in the universe—they'll be on the side of civilization, and even while overhauling it they'll be better able to preserve it than we ourselves."

"Let a bunch of barbarians take over the holy throne?" muttered Goram.

Heym closed his mouth, and gathering determination tightened his gaunt face. He looked around the pulsing city, and a vast tenderness and pity welled up in him—poor geniuses, poor helpless unwitting supermen—and answering it came a steely implacable resolve.

There was too much at stake to let his own personal fate matter. Certainly a mindlessly destructive atavist could not be allowed to block history. He would keep trying, he'd do his best to talk Goram over, because the alternative was fantastically risky for the station and against all his own training and principles—including elementary self-preservation.

But if he failed, if Goram remained obdurate, then he'd have to apply the same primitive methods as the soldier. Goram would have to die.

Rain clouds came out of the west with sunset, thunder rolling over the sky and a cool wet wind blowing from the sea. Goram and Heym finished a primitive but satisfying meal in a small restaurant and the psychologist said: "We'd better look for a place to stay tonight. Will you be in this city tomorrow?"

"Don't know," answered Goram curtly. He had been silent and withdrawn during the day's tour of the metropolis. "I have to think over what I've seen today. It may be enough basis for a decision, or I may want to see more of the planet."

"I'll pay the score," offered Heym. He fought to keep his voice and face blank. "And I'll ask the waiter to recommend a tavern."

He followed the man toward the kitchen. "Please," he said in the common tongue, "I wish to pay the check."

"Very well," answered the native. He was a tall young fellow with the faintly weary eyes of a scholar—probably a student, thought Heym, doing his stint here and getting his education free. He took the few coins casually.

"And—is there a place to stay overnight near here?"

"Right down the street. Stranger, I take it?"

"Yes. From Caralla on business. Oh—one other thing." It was a tremendous effort to meet that steady gaze. Heym was aware of his own clumsiness as he blurted the request: "I…uh…I've lost my knife and I need it to prepare some handicraft samples for display tomorrow. The stores are all closed now. I wonder if you have an extra one in the kitchen I could buy."

"Why—" The native paused. For a vertiginous instant, Heym thought he was going to ask questions, and he braced himself as if to meet a physical impact. But on a world where crime was virtually unknown and lying hardly ever went beyond the usual polite social fibs, even so crude a fiction could get by. "Yes, I suppose we have," said the waiter. "Here, I'll get one."

"No…I'll come along…save you the trouble…choose one for my purpose if…uh…if you have several you can spare." Heym stuck close to the waiter's heels.

The kitchen was spotlessly clean, though it seemed incredible that cooking should still be done with fire. Heym chose a small sharp knife, wrapped it in a rag, and slipped it into his pocket. The waiter and chef refused his money. "Plenty where this one came from—a pleasure to help out a visitor."

"What were you out there for?" asked Goram.

Heym licked stiff lips. "The waiter was new here himself and went to ask the cook about hotels."

The first raindrops were falling as the two came out into the street. Lightning forked vividly overhead. Goram shuddered in the raw damp chill. "Foul place," he muttered. "No weather control, not even a roof for the city—uncivilized."

Heym made no reply, though he tried to unlock his jaws. The blade in his pocket seemed to have the weight of a world. He looked down from his stringy height at the soldier's squat massiveness. *I've never killed,* he thought dully. *I've never even fought, physically or mentally. I'm no match for him. It'll have to be a sneak thrust from behind.*

They entered the hotel. The clerk was reading a journal whose pages seemed purely mathematical symbols. He was probably a scientist of some kind in his main job. There was, luckily for Goram, no register to sign, the clerk merely nodded them casually toward their room.

"No system here," muttered Goram. "How can they keep track of anybody without registry?"

"They don't," said Heym. "And they don't have to."

The room was large and airy and well furnished. "I've slept in worse, places," said the soldier grudgingly. He flopped into a chair. "But it's the first place where the hired help reads technical journals that I've seen."

"The social order here is unique," Heym repeated himself. "The colonists evolved through families, clans, tribes, kingdoms, and republics in a matter of centuries. Finally the most advanced countries worked out the present system, which was universally adopted when planetary government was established."

"What is it?"

"Well, it's a kind of democratic socialism—really the only logical form of government for a race of geniuses, at least until robots are developed. You see, the race needs an advanced civilization, with its technical advantages, in order to give the brilliant minds contact with each other and resources to carry out and propagate their ideas. Yet no high-grade mind should be put to the myriad routine and menial tasks essential to running a civilization, everything from garbage collection to government. The present set-up is a compromise, in which everyone puts in a small proportion of his time at those jobs. He can do manual work, or teach, or run a public-service enterprise like a farm or restaurant—whatever he wishes. And he can work steadily at it for a few years and then have all his needs taken care of for the rest of his life, or else put in a few hours a day, two or three, over a longer period of time. The result is that needs and a social surplus are available for all, as well as education, health services, entertainment, or whatever else is considered desirable. The planet could, in fact, do without money, but it's more convenient to pay in cash than fill out credit slips.

"Incidentally, that's probably one reason there's no great interest in providing more material goods for all—it would mean that everyone would have to put in more time in the mines and factories and less on his chosen work. Which is apparently a price that genius is unwilling to pay. I don't think there'll be any great progress in applied science until the research project established some time back perfects the robots it's set for a goal."

"Uh-huh," muttered Goram.

"And just let them expand into the Galaxy and find we have such robots—left unproduced since the Imperial populace has to be kept busy—and see what they'll do. They'd be able to wreck the whole set-up, just by inventing and distributing, and they'll know it."

"Can't you credit them with being smart enough to see the reasons for maintaining the status quo?" asked Heym desperately. "They don't want the barbarians on their necks any more than we do. They'll help us maintain the Empire until they have developed a way to change conditions safely."

"Maybe." Goram's mouth was tight. "Still, they'll hold the balance of power which is something no group except the Imperium can be permitted to do. Spirit! How do you even know they'll be on our side? They may decide their best advantage lies with our rivals. Or they may be irritated with our having used them so cavalierly all these centuries."

"They won't hold grudges," said Heym. "A genius doesn't."

"How do you know?" Goram sprang out of his chair and paced the floor. His voice rose almost to a shout. "You've said all along that the genius is naturally peaceful and tolerant and unselfish and every other of the milk-and-water virtues. Yet, your own history is against you all the way. Every great military leader has been a genius. There've been sadistic geniuses, and bigoted geniuses, and criminal geniuses—yes, insane geniuses! Why, every one of the hundred billion or so important men in the Imperial government is a genius—on our side—and more than half the barbarian chiefs are known to have genius intellect." He swung a red and twisted face on the psychologist. "How do you know this is a planet of saints? Answer me that!"

Thunder roared in the fulgurous sky, rolling and booming between the rain-running streets. The single dim electric bulb in the room flickered. Wind whined around the corners of the building.

Heym took out a cigarette pack with fingers that shook. He held it out to Goram, who shook his heavy bullet head in angry refusal. The psychologist took time to bring one of the cylinders into his mouth and puff it into lighting. He drew smoke deeply into his lungs, fighting for steadiness.

It was his last real chance to convince Goram. If this failed, he'd just have to try to murder the soldier. If that attempt miscarried—oh, Spirit, then Station Seventeen and the Empire were doomed. But if he succeeded, well, he might be able to convince the Imperial police that it had been an accident, a runaway animal or something of the sort, or they might send him to the disintegration chamber for murder. In any case, there would be a faint hope that the next inspector would be a reasonable man.

He said slowly; "To explain the theory of historical progress, I'd have to give you a fairly long lecture."

Goram sprawled back into his chair, crude and strong and arrogant. His little black eyes were drills, boring into the psychologist's soul. "I'm listening," he snapped.

"'Well"—Heym walked up and down the floor, hands clasped behind his back—"it's evident from a study of history that all progress is due to gifted individuals. Always, in every field, the talented or otherwise fortunate few have led and the mass has dumbly followed. A republic is the only form of state which even pretends to offer self-government, and as soon as the population becomes any size at all the people are again led by the nose, their rulers struggling for power with money and such means of mass hypnotism as news services and other propaganda machines. And all republics become dictatorships, in fact if not in name, within a few centuries at most. As for art and science and religion and the other creative fields, it is still more obviously the few who lead.

"The ordinary man is just plain stupid. Perhaps proper mind training could lift him above himself, but it's never been tried. Meanwhile he remains immensely conservative, only occasional outbreaks of mindless hysteria engineered by some special group stirring him out of his routine. He follows, or rather he accepts what the creative or dominant minority does, but it is haltingly and unwillingly.

"Yet it is society as a whole which *does*. History is a mass action process. Gifted individuals start it off, but it is the huge mass of the social group which actually accomplishes the process. A new invention or a new land to colonize or a new philosophy or any other innovation would have no significance unless everybody eventually adopted or exploited or otherwise made use of it. And society as a whole is conservative, or perhaps I should say preservative. Civilization is ninety-nine percent habit, the use of past discoveries or the influence of past events. Against the immense conservatism of mankind in the mass, and in comparison to the tremendous accumulation of past accomplishment, the achievement of the individual genius or the small group is almost insignificant. It is not surprising that progress is slow and irregular and liable to stagnation or violent setbacks. The surprising thing is really that any event of significance can happen at all."

Heym paused. Thunder snarled in the sky and the rain drummed on the windowpane with cold restless fingers. Goram stirred impatiently. "What are you leading up to?" he muttered.

"Simply this." Heym's hand fell into his pocket and closed on the smooth hard handle of the knife. Goram slumped in his chair, head lowered, staring sullenly at the floor. If the blade were driven in now, right into that bull neck, a paralyzing blow and then a swift slash across the jugular—

The intensity of the hatred welling up in him shocked Heym. He should be above the brutal level of his enemy. Yet—to see his blood spurt!

Steady—steady—That move of desperation might not be necessary.

"Two factors control the individual in society," said Heym, and the detached calm of his voice was vaguely surprising to him. "They are only arbitrarily separable, being aspects of the same thing, but it's convenient to take them up in turn.

"There is first the simple weight of social pressure. We all want to be approved by our fellows, within reasonable limits at least. The mores of the society, whatever they may be, are those of the individual. Only a psychopath would disregard them completely. Not only does society apply force on the nonconformist, but mere disapproval can be devastating. It takes a really brave—and somewhat neurotic—individual to be different in any important respect. Many have paid with their lives for innovating. So a genius will be hampered in making original contributions, and they are adopted only slowly. It usually takes a new idea many generations to become accepted. The astonishing rate of growth of science, back in the days when free research was permitted and even encouraged, indicates how rapid progress can be when there are no barriers.

"And, of course, this social pressure usually forces conformity even on reluctant individuals. A scientist may be naturally peaceful, for instance, but he will hardly ever refuse to engage in war research when so directed.

"The second hold of the mass on the individual is subtler and more effective. It is the mental conditioning induced by growing up in a society where certain conditions of living and rules of thought are accepted. A 'born' pacifist, growing up in a warlike culture, will generally accept war as part of the natural order of things. A man who might have been a complete skeptic in a science-based society will nearly always accept the gods of a theocracy if he has been brought up to believe in them. He may even become a priest and direct his logical talents toward elaborating the accepted theology—and help in the persecution of unbelievers. And so on. I needn't go into detail. The power of social conditioning is unbelievable—combined with social pressure, it is almost insuperable.

"And—this is the important point—the rules and assumptions of a society are accepted and enforced by the mass—the overwhelming majority, shortsighted, conservative, hating and fearing all that is new and strange, wishing only to remain in whatever basic condition it has known from birth. The genius is forced into the straight-jacket of the mediocre man's and the moron's mentality. That he can expand any distance at all beyond his prison is a tribute to the supreme power of the high intellect."

Heym looked out at the empty street. Rain blew wildly across its darkened surface. Lightning glared blindingly, almost in his eyes. His voice rose over the shattering thunder: "The Solarian Empire is nothing but the triumph of stupidity over intelligence. If every man could think for himself, we wouldn't need an empire."

"Watch yourself," muttered Goram. "The ruling class has a certain latitude of speech, but don't overstep it." And more loudly: "What does this mean in the case of Station Seventeen?"

"Why, it's a triumphant confirmation of the historical theory I was just explaining," said Heym. "We've isolated pure genius from mediocrity and left it free to work out its own destiny. The result has even exceeded our predictions.

"Most of man's history has been spent in the stone ages, because the savage is even more superstitious and conservative than the civilized man, whose culture does have a certain momentum. But the people of this planet had invented metallurgy and writing within a thousand years of the colony's establishment. The essential difference was that there was progress made each generation, rather than every hundred or thousand generations. Every mind is creative, and every individual is willing to accept the ideas and work of every other.

"No doubt there are aggressive and conservative and selfish people born. But on this world the weight of social conditioning and social pressure is away from those tendencies, they don't get a chance to develop themselves.

"Man's brain is physically not qualitatively different from that of the other higher mammals. It has no feature not found in the brain of an ape, say. But the quantitative difference, in the relatively immense forebrain, leads to a qualitative difference of mental *type*. Man is sharply differentiated from the other animals by the power to make indefinite orders of abstraction. Hence progress is possible for him.

"It seems"—Heym's voice rose over the whistle of wind—"that genius shows a similar qualitative distinction, due to quantitative difference, from mere human intelligence. The genius is basically a distinct type, just as the moron is on the other end of the scale. And here—on Seventeen—the new type has been set free."

He turned around from the window. The voice of the storm seemed remote, lost in the tremendous silence that suddenly filled the room. Goram sat motionless, staring at the floor, and the slow seconds ticked away before he spoke.

"I don't know—" he murmured. "I don't know—"

Defeat and despair and a binding hatred rose into Heym's throat, tasting of vomit. *You don't know!* His mind screamed the thought, it seemed incredible that Goram should sprawl there, not moving, not hearing. *No, you don't know. Your sort never does, never has known anything but his own witless bestial desires, its own self-righteous rationalization of impulses that should have died with Smilodon. You'll destroy Seventeen, in spite of all reason, in sheer perversity—and you'll say you did it for the good of the Empire!*

The knife seemed to spring of its own accord into his hand. He was lunging forward before he realized it. He saw the blade gleam down as if another man were wielding it. The blow shocked back into his muscles and for an instant his mind wavered, it wasn't real—*what am I doing?*

No time to lose. Goram twisted around in his seat, yelling, grabbing for Heym. The knife was deep in his neck. Heym yanked at it—pull it loose, stick it in the throat, kill—

Something struck him from behind. The world shattered in a burst of stars, he crashed to the floor and rolled over. Through a haze of dizzy pain he saw men bending over Goram—men of the planet, rescuers for the monster who would annihilate them.

Words tumbled from the hotel clerk, anxious, shaken: "Are you hurt? Did you—Still, lie still, here comes a doctor—"

Pain curled Goram's lips back from his teeth, but he muttered reply: "No... I'm all right...flesh wound—"

The doctor bent over his bloody form. "Deep," he said, "but it missed the important veins. Here I'll just pull it out—"

"Go ahead," whispered Goram. I've taken worse than this, though…I never expected it here."

Heym lay on the floor while they worked over the soldier. His ringing, whirling head throbbed toward steadiness, and slowly, with so tremendous an impact that it overloaded his nerves and entered his consciousness without emotional shock, the realization grew.

Goram had spoken to the natives—in their own language.

A man bent over the psychologist "Are you all right?" he asked. "I'm sorry I had to hit you so hard. Here—drink this,"

Heym forced the liquid down his throat. It coursed fierily through his veins, he sat up with an arm supporting him about his waist and held his head in his hands.

Someone else spoke, the voice seemed to come from across an abyss: "Did he hear?"

"I'm afraid so." Goram, his neck bandaged, spoke painfully. A rueful smile crossed his ugly face "The excitement was too much for me, or I would have kept silent. This is going to be—inconvenient."

The men of the planet helped Heym into a chair. He began to revive, and looked dazedly across at the man he had tried to kill. The others stood around the chairs, tall bearded men in barbaric dress, watching him with alertness and a strange pity.

"Yes," said Tamman Goram very quietly, "the assistant Grand Marshal of the Solarian Empire is a native of Station Seventeen."

"Who else?" whispered Heym. "How and why? I tried to kill you because I thought you meant to order the planet sterilized."

"It was an act," said Goram. "I meant to concede at last that the station was harmless and could be safely left to the Foundation's observers. Coming from one who had apparently been strongly inclined to the opposite view, the statement would have been doubly convincing to Imperial officialdom. It was a powerful and suspicious minister who ordered the investigation, and I went to soothe his feelings. His successor will be one of our men, who will see that Station Seventeen drops into safe obscurity as an unimportant and generally unsuccessful experiment conducted by a few harmless cranks."

"But…aren't you…weren't you—"

"Oh, yes. My history is perfectly genuine. I was planted as an obscure recruit in the border guards many years ago, and since then my rise has been strictly in accord with Imperial principles. All our men in the Empire will bear the most searching investigation. Sometimes they come from families which have lived several generations on Imperial planets. Our program of replacing key personnel with our men is planned centuries ahead of time, and succeeds by the simple fact that on the average, over long periods of time, they are so much more capable than anyone else."

"How long—?"

"About five hundred years. You underestimated the capabilities of your experimental animals." Goram rested for a moment, then asked, "If human intelligence is qualitatively different from animal intelligence, and genius is different from ordinary reasoning power—then tell me, what about the equivalent of geniuses in a world where the average man is a genius by the usual standards?"

"Pure genius strains kept right on evolving, more rapidly indeed than can be explained on any other basis than the existence of an orthogenetic factor in evolution. Super genius—give it a different name, call it transcendence, since it is a different quality—has capabilities which the ordinary mind can no more than comprehend than pure instinct can comprehend logic.

"Your spectacular god-revelations were not forgotten, they were treated discreetly. Later, when a theory of evolution was developed, it seemed strange that man, though obviously an animal, should have no apparent phylogenesis. The stories of the 'gods,' the theories of evolution and astronomy—we began to suspect the truth. With that suspicion, it was not hard for a transcendent to spot your masquerading psychologists. Kidnapping, questioning under drugs developed by psychiatry, and release of the prisoner with memory of his experience removed told us the rest. Later, disguised as other prisoners, with their knowledge, and his own intelligence to fill the gaps, one transcendent after another made his way to the observation asteroid—thence out into the Galaxy, where a little spying was sufficient to reveal the principles of the interstellar drive and the other mechanisms of the Empire."

Heym murmured: "The whole planet has been—acting?"

"Yes." Goram chuckled. "Rather fun for all concerned. You'd be surprised at the installations we have, out of spy-machine range. As soon as they are old enough to carry out the deception, our children are told the truth. It has actually made little difference to our lives except for those few million who are out in the Galaxy taking it over."

"Taking…it…over?" Heym's mind seemed to be turning over slowly, infinitely slowly and wearily.

"Of course." A strange blend of sternness and sympathy overlay Goram's harsh features. "One planet obviously cannot fight the Galaxy, nor do we wish to. Yet we cannot permit it to menace us. The only answer is—annexation."

"And…then?"

"I'm sorry." Goram's voice came slowly, implacably, "but I'm afraid you overrated the good intentions of the pure genius strain. After all, Homo intelligens can no more be expected to serve Homo sapiens than early man to serve the apes.

"We're taking over barbarians and Empire alike. After that, the Galaxy will do as we wish. Oh, we won't be hard masters. Man may never know that he is being ruled from outside, and he will enter a period of peace and contentment such as he has never imagined.

"As for you—"

Heym realized with vague shock that he had not even wondered or cared what was to become of him personally.

"You are sympathetic to us—but your loyalty is to the Empire. You have thought of us only in relation to our usefulness to the Imperium. Perhaps we could trust you to keep our secret, perhaps not. We can't take the risk. You might even release the truth inadvertently. Nor can we erase your memory of this—it would leave traces that an expert psychiatrist could detect, and all high officials undergo regular psychoanalytic checkups.

"I'll just have to report you as accidentally killed on the planet." Goram smiled. "I don't think you'll find life exile on this world, out of sight of the observers, uncongenial. And we might as well see about making your successor one of our men. It was about ready for that."

He added thoughtfully: "In fact, the Galaxy may be ready for a new Solarian Emperor."

There Will Be Other Times

There will be other times, my comrades, there will be
A day of trumpets. This we must believe.
Now when all flags guide corpses to the sea
And ships lie hollow on a smoking shore,
Broken of bone, and windy shadows weave
A dark about tall windows turning whore
To feed gashed children, I must say that more
Days shall remain then hobnailed victors thieve.
And if our iron's broken, there's still ore—
Stones of our sharded cities lying free
To sharpen it; and if you should perceive
Rust and the dimness in us, do it silently.

The Live Coward

The fugitive ship was pursued for ten light-years. Then, snapping in and out of subspace drive with a reckless disregard of nearby suns and tracer-blocking dust clouds, it shook the Patrol cruiser.

The search that followed was not so frantic as the danger might seem to warrant. Haste would have done no good; there are a million planetary systems affiliated with the League, and their territory includes several million more too backward for membership. Even a small planet is such a wilderness of mountains, valleys, plains, forests, oceans, icefields, cities, and loneliness—much of it often quite unexplored—that it was hopeless to ransack them meter by meter for a single man. The Patrol knew that Varris' boat had a range of three hundred parsecs, and in the course of months and man-years of investigation it was pretty well established that he had not refueled at any registered depot. But a sphere two thousand light-years across can hold a lot of stars.

The Patrol offered a substantial reward for information leading to the arrest of Samel Varris, human, from the planet Caldon (No. so-and-so in the Pilots' Manual), wanted for the crime of inciting to war. It circulated its appeal as widely as possible. It warned all agents to keep an eye or a feeler or a telepathic organ out for a man potentially still capable of exploding a billion living entities into radioactive gas. Then it waited.

A year went by.

Captain Jakor Thymal of the trading ship *Ganash*, operating out of Sireen in the primitive Spiral Cluster area, brought the news. He had seen Varris, even spoken to the fellow. There was no doubt of it. Only one hitch: Varris had taken refuge with the king of Thunsba, a barbarous state in the southern hemisphere of a world known to the Galactics—such few as had ever heard of it—as Rylin's Planet. He had gotten citizenship and taken the oath of service as a royal guardsman. Loyalty between master and man was a powerful element in Thunsban morality. The king would not give up Varris without a fight.

Of course, axes and arrows were of small use against flamers. Perhaps Varris could be taken alive, but the patrol would kill him without whiffing very many Thunsban. Captain Thymal settled complacently back to wait for confirmation of his report and the blood money. Nothing ever occurred to him but that the elimination of Varris would be the simplest of routine operations.

Like hell!

Wing Alak eased his flitter close to the planet. It hung in cloudy splendor against a curtain of hard, needle-shape spatial stars, the Cluster sky. He sat gloomily listening to the click and mutter of instruments as Drogs checked surface conditions.

"Quite terrestroid," said the Galmathian. His antennae lifted in puzzlement above the round, snouted face and the small black eyes. Why did you bother testing? It's listed in the Manual."

"I have a nasty suspicious mind," said Alak. "Also an unhappy one. He was a thin, medium-tall human with the very white skin that often goes with flaming red hair. His Patrol uniform was as dandified as regulations allowed.

Drogs hitched three meters of green, eight-legged body across the cabin. His burly arms reached out to pick up the maps in three-fingered hands "Yes…here's the Thunsba kingdom and the capital city…what's it called? …Wainabog. I suppose our quarry is still there; Thymal swore he didn't alarm him. He sighed. "Now I have to spend an hour at the telescope and identify which place is what. And you can sit like my wife on an egg thinking beautiful thoughts!"

"The only beautiful concept I have right now is that all of a sudden the Prime Directive was repealed."

"No chance of that, I'm afraid…not till a less bloodthirsty race than yours gets the leadership of the League."

"Less? You mean more, don't you? 'Under no circumstances whatsoever may the Patrol or any unit thereof kill any intelligent being.' If you do—" Alak made a rather horrible gesture. "Is that blood-thirsty?"

"Quite. Only a race with as gory a past as the Terrans would go to such extremes of reaction. And only as naturally ferocious a species could think of making such a commandment the Patrol's great top secret…and bluffing with threats of planetwide slaughter, or using any kind of chicanery to achieve its ends. Now a Galmathian will run down a farstak in his native woods and jump on its back and make a nice lunch while it's still running…but he wouldn't be able to imagine cold-bloodedly sterilizing an entire world, so he doesn't have to ban himself from honest killing even in self-defense." Drogs' caterpillar body hunched itself over the telescope.

"Get thee behind me, Satan…and don't push!" Alak returned murkily to his thoughts. His brain was hypnotically stuffed with all the information three generations of traders had gathered about Thunsba. None of it looked hopeful.

The king was—well, if not an absolute monarch, pretty close to being one, simply because the law had set him over the commons. Like many warlike barbarians, the Thunsbans had a quasi-religious reverence for the letter of the law, if not always for its spirit. The Patrol had run head-on into two items of the code: (a) the king would not yield up a loyal guardsman to an enemy, but would fight to the death instead; (b) if the king fought, so would the whole male population, unmoved by threats to themselves or their mates and cubs. Death before dishonor! Their religion, which they seemed quite fervent about, promised a roisterous heaven to all who fell in a good cause, and suitably gruesome hell for oath-breakers.

Hm-m-m…there was a powerful ecclesiastical organization, and piety had not stopped a good deal of conflict between church and throne. Maybe he could work through the priesthood somehow.

The outworld traders who came to swap various manufactured articles for the furs and spices of Ryfin's Planet had not influenced the local cultures much. Perhaps they had inspired a few wars and heresies, but on the whole the autochthones were content to live in the ways of their fathers. The main effect of trading had been a loss of superstitious awe—the strangers were mighty, but they were known to be mortal. Alak doubted that even the whole Patrol fleet could bullyrag them into yielding on so touchy a point as Varris' surrender.

"What I can't understand," said Drogs, "is why we don't just swoop down and give the city a blanket of sleep-gas." This mission had been ordered in such tearing haste that he had been given only the most nominal briefing; and on the way here, he had followed his racial practice of somnolence—his body could actually "store" many days' worth of sleep.

His free hand gestured around the flitter. It was not a large boat, but it was well equipped, not only with weapons—for bluffing—but with its own machine shop and laboratory.

"Metabolic difference," said Alak. "Every anaesthetic known to us is poisonous to them, and their own knockout chemicals would kill Varris. Stun beams are just as bad—supersonics will scramble a Ryfinnian's brain like an egg. I imagine Varris picked this world for a bolthole just on that account."

"But he didn't know we wouldn't simply come down and shoot up the den."

"He could make a pretty shrewd guess. It's a secret that we never kill, but no secret that we're reluctant to hurt innocent bystanders." Alak scowled. "There are still a hundred million people on Caldon who'd rise—bloodily—against the new government if he came back to them. Whether he succeeded or not, it'd be a genocidal affair and a big loss of face to the Patrol."

"Hm-m-m…he can't get far from this world without more fuel; his tanks must be nearly dry. So why don't we blockade this planet and make sure he never has a chance to buy fuel?"

"Blockades aren't that reliable," said Alak. Drogs had never been involved in naval operation, only in surface work. "We could destroy his own boat easily enough, but word that he's alive is bound to leak back to Caldon now. There'd be attempt after attempt to run the blockade, and get him out. Sooner or later, one would succeed. We're badly handicapped by not being allowed to shoot to hit. No, damn it, we've got to lift him, and fast!"

His eyes traveled wistfully to the biochemical shelves. There was a potent drug included, a nembutal derivative, hypnite. A small intramuscular injection could knock Varris out; he would awaken into a confused, passive state, and remain thus for hours, following any lead he was given. Much useful information about his conspiracy could be extracted. Later, this drug and other techniques would be used to rehabilitate his twisted psyche, but that was a job for the specialists at Main Base.

Alak felt more handcuffed than ever before in his pragmatist life. The blaster at his waist could incinerate a squad of Thunsban knights—but their anachronistic weapons weren't so ridiculous when he wasn't allowed to use the blaster.

"Hurry it up," he said on a harsh note. "Let's get moving—and don't ask me where!"

A landing field had been made for the traders just outside the walls of Wainabog. Those bulked thick and gray, studded with turrets and men-at-arms, over a blue landscape of rolling fields and distant hills. Here and there Alak saw thatch-roofed hamlets; two kilometers from the town was a smaller community, also fortified, a single great tower in its middle crowned with a golden X. It must be the place mentioned in the trader narratives. Grimmoch Abbey, was that the name?

It was not too bad a mistranslation to speak of abbeys, monks, knights, and kings. Culturally and technologically, Thunsba was fairly close to medieval Europe.

Several peasants and townsfolk stood gaping at the flitter as Alak emerged. Others were on their way. He swept his gaze around the field and saw another spaceboat some distance off—must be Varris', yes, he remembered the description now. A dozen liveried halberdiers guarded it.

Carefully ignoring the drab-clad commons, Alak waited for the official greeters. Those came out in a rattle of plate armor, mounted on yellow-furred animals with horns and shoulder humps. A band of crossbowmen trotted in their wake and a herald wearing a scarlet robe blew his trumpet in their van. They pulled up with streaming banners and thunderous hoofs; lances dipped courteously, but eyes had a watchful stare behind the snouted visors of their helmets.

The herald rode forth and looked down at Alak, who was clad in his brightest dress uniform. "Greeting to you, stranger, from our lord Morlach, King of all Thunsba and Defender of the West. Our lord Morlach bids you come sup and sleep with him." The herald drew a sword and extended it hilt first. Alak ran hastily through his lessons and rubbed his forehead against the handle.

They were quite humanoid on Ryfin's Planet—disturbingly so, if you hadn't seen as many species as Alak. It was not the pale-blue skin or the violet hair or the short tails which made the difference: always, in a case like this, the effect was of a subtler wrongness. Noses a shade too long, faces a trifle too square, knees and elbows held at a peculiar angle—they looked like cartoon figures brought to life. And they had a scent of their own, a sharp mustardy odor. Alak didn't mind, knowing full well that he looked and smelled as odd to them, but he had seen young recruits get weird neuroses after a few months on a planet of "humanoids to six points of classification."

He replied gravely in the Thunsban tongue: "My lord Morlach has my thanks and duty. I hight Wing Alak, and am not a trader but an envoy of the traders' king, sent hither on a mission most delicate. I pray the right to see my lord Morlach as soon as he grant."

There was more ceremony, and a number of slaves were fetched to carry Alak's impressive burden of gifts. Then he was offered a mount, but declined—the traders had warned him of this little joke, where you put an outworlder on a beast that goes frantic at alien smells. With proper haughtiness he demanded a sedan chair, which was an uncomfortable and seasick thing to ride but had more dignity. The knights of Wainabog enclosed him and he was borne through the gates and the cobbled avenues to the fortresslike palace.

Inside, he did not find the rude splendor he had expected, but a more subtle magnificence, really beautiful furnishings. Thunsba might throw its garbage out in the streets, but had excellent artistic taste. There were a hundred nobles in the royal audience chamber, a rainbow of robes, moving about and talking with boisterous gestures. Servants scurried around offering trays of food and liquor. A small orchestra was playing: the saw-toothed music hurt Alak's ears. A number of monks, in gray robes and with hoods across their faces, stood unspeaking along the walls, near the motionless men-at-arms.

Alak advanced under gleaming pikes and knelt before the king. Morlach was burly, middle-aged, and long-bearded, wearing a coronet and holding a naked sword on his lap. At his left, the place of honor—most of this species were left-handed—sat an older "man," clean-shaven, hook-nosed, bleakfaced, in yellow robe and a tall bejeweled hat marked with a golden X.

"My duty to you, puissant lord Morlach. Far have I, unworthy Wing Alak of Terra, come to behold your majesty before whom the nations tremble. From my king unto you, I bear a message and these poor gifts."

The poor gifts made quite a heap, all the way from clothes and ornaments of lustrous synthetic to flashlights and swords of manganese steel. Ryfin's Planet couldn't legally be given modern tools and weapons—not at their present social stage of war and feudalism—but there was no ban on lesser conveniences which they couldn't reproduce anyhow.

"Well met, Sir Wing Alak. Come, be seated at my right. Morlach's voice rose, and the buzzing voices, already lowered in curiosity, stopped at once. "Be it known to all men, Sir Wing Alak is in truth my guest, most holy and inviolable, and all injuries to him, save in lawful duel, are harms to me and my house which the Allshaper bids me avenge."

The nobles crowded closer. It was not a very formal court, as such things go. One of them came to the front as Alak mounted the high seat. The Patrolman felt a tingle along his back and a primitive stirring in his scalp.

Samel Varris.

The refugee war lord was dressed like the other aristocrats, a gaudy robe of puffed and slashed velvet, hung with ropes of jewels. Alak guessed correctly that a royal guardsman ranked very high indeed, possessing his own lands and retinue. Varris was a big dark man with arrogant features and shrewd eyes. Recognition kindled in him, and he strode forward and made an ironic bow.

"Ah Sir Wing Alak" he said in Thunsban. "I had not awaited the honor of your calling on me yourself."

King Morlach huffed and laid a ring hand on his sword. "I knew not you twain were acquainted."

Alak covered an empty feeling with his smoothest manner. "Yes, my lord, Varris and I have jousted erenow. Indeed my mission hither concerns him."

"Came you to fetch him away?" It was a snarl, and the nobility of Wainabog reached for their dagger.

"I know not what he has told you, my lord—"

"He came hither because foemen had overwhelmed his own kingdom and sought his life. Noble gifts did he bring me, not least of them one of the flame-weapons you folk are so niggardly with, and he gave wise redes by which we hurled back the armies of Rachanstog and wrung tribute out of their ruler." Morlach glared from lowered brows. "Know then, Sir Wing Alak, that though you are my guest and I may not harm you, Sir Varris has taken oath as my guardsman and served right loyally. For this I have given him gold and a broad fief. The honor of my house is sacred…if you demand he be returned to his foes, I must ask that you leave at once and when we meet it shall be the worse for you."

Alak pursed his lips to whistle, but thought better of it. Handing out a blaster—! It was unimportant in itself, the firearm would be useless once its charge was spent, but as measure of Varris' contempt for Galactic law—

"My lord," he said hastily, "I cannot deny I had such a request. But it was never the intent of my king or myself to insult your majesty. The request will not be made of you."

"Let there be peace," said the high priest on Morlach's left. His tone was not as unctuous as the words: here was a fighter, in his own way, more intelligent and more dangerous than the brawling warriors around him. "In the name of the Allshaper, we are met in fellowship. Let not black thoughts give to the Evil an entering wedge."

Morlach swore.

"In truth, my lord, I bear this envoy no ill will," smiled Varris. "I vouch that he is knightly, and wishes but to serve his king as well as I seek to serve yourself. If my holy lord abbot"—the title was nearly equivalent—"calls peace on this hall, then I for one will abide by it."

"Yes…a sniveling shavechin to whine peace when treachery rises," growled Morlach. "You have enough good lands which should be mine, Abbot Gulmanan—keep your greasy fingers off my soul, at least!"

"What my lord says to me is of no consequence," answered the cleric thinly. "But if he speaks against the Temple, he blasphemes the Allshaper."

"Hell freeze you, I'm a pious man!" roared Morlach. "I make the sacrifices—for the Allshaper, though not for his fat-gutted Temple that would push me off my own throne!"

Gulmanan flushed purple, but checked himself a bit, narrow lips together and made a bridge of his bony fingers. "This is not the time or place to question where the ghostly and the worldly authorities have their proper bounds," he said. "I shall sacrifice for your soul, my lord, and pray you be led out of error."

Morlach snorted and called for a beaker of wine. Alak sat inconspicuously till the king's temper had abated. Then he began to speak of increased trade possibilities.

He had not the slightest power to make treaties, but he wanted to be sure he wasn't kicked out of Wainabog yet.

Heavily dosed with anti-allergen, Alak was able to eat enough of the king's food to cement his status as guest. But Drogs brought him a case of iron rations when the Galmathian came to attend his "master" in the assigned palace apartment.

The human sat moodily by the window, looking out at the glorious night sky of clotted stars and two moons. There was a fragrant garden beneath him, under the bleak castle walls. Somewhere a drunken band of nobles was singing—he had left the feast early and it was still carousing on. A few candles lit the tapestried dankness of the room; they were perfumed, but not being a Ryfinnian he did not enjoy the odor of mercaptan.

"If we got several thousand husky Patrolmen" he said "and put them in armor, and equipped them with clubs we might slug our way in and out of this place. Right now I can't think of anything else."

"Well, why don't we?" Drogs hunched over a burbling water pipe, cheerfully immune to worry.

"It lacks finesse. Nor is it guaranteed—these Thunsbans are pretty hefty too, they might overpower our men. If we used tanks or something to make ourselves invincible it'd be just our luck to have some gallant fathead of a knight get squashed under the treads. Finally, with the trouble at Sannanton going on, the Patrol can't spare so large a force—and by the time they can, it might well be too late. Those unprintable traders must have told half the League that Varris has been found. We can look for a rescue attempt from Caldon within a week."

"Hm-m-m…according to your account, the local church is at loggerheads with the king. Maybe it can be persuaded to do our work for us. Nothing in the Prime Directive forbids letting entities murder each other."

"No—I'm afraid the Temple priests are only allowed to fight in self-defense, and these people never break a law." Alak rubbed his chin. "You may have the germ of an idea there, though. I'll have to—"

The gong outside the door was struck. Drogs humped across the floor and opened it.

Varris came in, at the head of half a dozen warriors. Their drawn blades gleamed against flickering shadow.

Alak's blaster snaked out. Varris grinned and lifted his hand. "Don't be so impetuous," he advised. "These boys are only precautionary. I just wanted to talk."

Alak took out a cigarette and puffed it into lighting. "Go on, then," he invited tonelessly.

"I'd like to point out a few things, that's all." Varris was speaking Terran; the guards waited stolidly, not understanding, their eyes restless. "I wanted to say I'm a patient man, but there's a limit to how much persecution I'll stand for."

"Persecution! Who ordered the massacres at New Venus?"

Fanaticism smoldered in Varris' eyes, but he answered quietly: "I was the legitimately chosen dictator. Under Caldonian law, I was within my rights. It was the

Patrol which engineered the revolution. It's the Patrol which now maintains a hated colonialism over my planet."

"Yes—until such time as those hellhounds you call people have had a little sense beaten into them. If you hadn't been stopped, there'd be more than one totally dead world by now." Alak's smile was wintry. "You'll comprehend that for yourself, once we've normalized your psyche."

"You can't cleanly execute a man. Varris paced tiger-fashion. "You have to take and twist him till everything that was holy to him has become evil and everything he despised is good. I'll not let that happen to me."

"You're stuck here," said Alak. "I know your boat is almost out of fuel. Incidentally, in case you get ideas, mine is quite thoroughly booby trapped. All I need do is holler for reinforcements. Why not surrender now and save me the trouble?"

Varris grinned. "Nice try, friend, but I'm not that stupid. If the Patrol could have sent more than you to arrest me, It would have done so. I'm staying here and gambling that a rescue party from Caldon will arrive before your ships get around to it. The odds are in my favor."

His finger stabbed out. "Look here! By choice, I'd have my men cut you down where you stand—you and that slimy little monster. I can't, because I have to live up to the local code of honor; they'd throw me out if I broke the least of their silly laws. But I can maintain a large enough bodyguard to prevent you from kidnapping me, as you've doubtless thought of doing."

"I had given the matter some small consideration," nodded Alak.

"There's one other thing I can do, too. I can fight a duel with you. A duel to the death—they haven't any other kind."

"Well, I'm a pretty good shot."

"They won't allow modern weapons. The challenged party has the choice, but it's got to be swords or axes or bows or something provided for in their law." Varris laughed. "I've spent a lot of time this past year, practicing with just such arms. And I went in for fencing at home. How much training have you had?"

Alak shrugged. Not being even faintly a romantic, he had never taken much interest in archaic sports.

"I'm good at thinking up nasty tricks," he said. "Suppose I chose to fight you with clubs, only I had a switchblade concealed in mine."

"I've seen that kind of thing pulled," said Varris calmly. "Poison is illegal, but gimmicks of the kind you mention are accepted. However, the weapons must be identical. You'd have to get me with your switchblade the first try—and I don't think you could—or I'd see what was going on and do the same. I assure you, the prospect doesn't frighten me at all.

"I'll give you a few days here to see how hopeless your problem is. If you turn your flitter's guns on the city, or on me…well, I have guns, too. If you aren't out of the kingdom in a week—or if you begin to act suspiciously before that time—I'll duel you."

"I'm a peaceable man," said Alak. "It takes two to make a duel."

"Not here, it doesn't. If I insult you before witnesses, and you don't challenge me, you lose knightly rank and are whipped out of the country. It's a long walk to the border, with a bull whip lashing you all the way. You wouldn't make it alive."

"All right," sighed Alak. "What do you want of me?"

"I want to be let alone."

"So do the people you were going to make war on last year."

"Good night." Varris turned and went out the door. His men followed him.

Alak stood for a while in silence. Beyond the walls, he could hear the night wind of Ryfin's Planet. Somehow, it was a foreign wind, it had another sound from the rushing air of Terra. Blowing through different trees, across an unearthly land—

"Have you any plan at all?" murmured Drogs.

"I had one." Alak clasped nervous hands behind his back.

"He doesn't *know* I won't bushwhack him, or summon a force of gunners, or something lethal like that. I was figuring on a bluff—but it seems he has called me. He wants to be sure of taking at least one Patrolman to hell with him."

"You could study the local *code duello*," suggested Drogs. "You could let him kill you in a way which looked like a technical foul. Then the king would boot him out and I could arrest him with the help of a stun beam."

"Thanks," said Alak. "Your devotion to duty is really touching."

"I remember a Terran proverb," said Drogs. Galmathian humor can be quite heavy at times. " 'The craven dies a thousand deaths, the hero dies but once.' "

"Yeh. But you see, I'm a craven from way back. I much prefer a thousand synthetic deaths to one genuine case. As far as I'm concerned, the live coward has it all over the dead hero—" Alak stopped. His jaw fell down and then snapped up again. He flopped into a chair and cocked his feet up on the windowsill and ran a hand through his ruddy hair.

Drogs returned to the water pipe and smoked imperturbably. He knew the signs. If the Patrol may not kill, it is allowed to do anything else—and sublimated murder can be most fascinatingly fiendish.

In spite of his claims to ambassadorial rank, Alak found himself rating low—his only retinue was one ugly nonhumanoid. But that could be useful. With their faintly contemptuous indifference, the nobles of Wainabog didn't care where he was.

He went, the next afternoon, to Grimmoch Abbey.

An audience with Gulmanan was quickly granted. Alak crossed a paved courtyard, strolled by a temple where the hooded monks were holding an oddly impressive service and entered a room in the great central tower. It was a large room, furnished with austere design but lavish materials gold and silver and gems and brocades. One wall was covered by bookshelves, illuminated folios, many of them secular. The abbot sat stiffly on a carved throne of rare woods. Alak made the required prostration and was invited to sit down.

The old eyes were thoughtful, watching him. "What brought you here, my cub?"

"I am a stranger, holy one," said the human. "I understand little of your faith, and considered it shame that I did not know more."

"We have not yet brought any outworlder to the Way," said the abbot gravely. "Except, of course, Sir Varris, and I am afraid his devotions smack more of expediency than conviction."

"Let me at least hear what you believe," asked the Patrolman with all the earnestness he could summon in daylight.

Gulmanan smiled, creasing his gaunt blue face. "I have a suspicion that you are not merely seeking the Way," he replied. "Belike there is some more temporal question in your mind."

"Well—" They exchanged grins. You couldn't run a corporation as big as this abbey without considerable hardheadedness.

Nevertheless, Alak persisted in his queries. It took an hour to learn what he wanted to know.

Thunsba was monotheistic. The theology was subtle and complex, the ritual emotionally satisfying, the commandments flexible enough to accommodate ordinary fleshly weaknesses. Nobody doubted the essential truth of the religion; but its Temple was another matter.

As in medieval Europe, the church was a powerful organization, international, the guardian of learning and the gradual civilizer of a barbarous race. It had no secular clergy—every priest was a monk of some degree, inhabiting a large or small monastery. Each of these was ruled by one officer—Gulmanan in this case—responsible to the central Council in Augnachar city; but distances being great and communications slow, this supreme authority was mostly background.

The clergy were celibate and utterly divorced from the civil regime, with their own laws and courts and punishments. Each detail of their lives, down to dress and diet, was minutely prescribed by an unbreakable code—there were no special dispensations. Entering the church, if you were approved, was only a matter of taking vows; getting out was not so easy, requiring a Council decree. A monk owned nothing; any property he might have had before entering reverted to his heirs, any marriage he might have made was automatically annulled. Even Gulmanan could not call the clothes he wore or the lands he ruled his own: it all belonged to the corporation, the abbey. And the abbey was rich; for centuries, titled Thunsbans had given it land or money.

Naturally there was conflict between church and king. Both sought power, both claimed overlapping prerogatives, both insisted that theirs was the final authority. Some kings had had abbots murdered or imprisoned, some had gone weakly to Canossa. Morlach was in between, snarling at the Temple but not quite daring to lay violent hands on it.

"…I see." Alak bowed his head. "Thank you, holy one."

"I trust your questions are all answered?" The voice was dry.

"Well now…there are some matters of business—" Alak sat for a moment, weighing the other. Gulmanan seemed thoroughly honest; a direct bribe would only be an insult. But honesty is more malleable than one might think—

"Yes? Speak without fear, my cub. No words of yours shall pass these walls."

Alak plunged into it: "As you know, my task is to remove Sir Varris to his own realm for punishment of many evil deeds."

"He has claimed his cause was righteous," said Gulmanan noncommittally.

"And so he believes. But in the name of that cause he was prepared to slay more folk than dwell on this entire world."

"I wondered about that—"

Alak drew a long breath and then spoke fast. "The Temple is eternal, is it not? Of course. Then it must look centuries ahead. It must not let one man, whose merits are doubtful at best, stand in the way of an advancement which could mean saving thousands of souls."

"I am old," said Gulmanan in a parched tone "My life has not been as cloistered as I might have wished. If you are proposing that you and I could work together to mutual advantage, say so."

Alak made a sketchy explanation. "And the lands would be yours," he finished.

"Also the trouble, my cub," said the abbot. "We already have enough clashes with King Morlach."

"This would not be a serious one. The law would be on our side."

"Nevertheless, the honor of the Temple may not be compromised."

"In plain words, you want more than I've offered."

"Yes," said Gulmanan bluntly.

Alak waited. Sweat studded his body. What could he do if an impossible demand was made?

The seamed blue face grew wistful. "Your race knows much," said the abbot. "Our peasants wear out their lives struggling against a miserly soil and seasonal insect hordes. Are there ways to better their lot?"

"Is that all? Certainly there are. Helping folks to progress when they wish to is one of our chief policies. My…king would be only too glad to lend you some technicians—farmwrights?—and show you how."

"Also…it is pure greed on my part. But sometimes at night, looking up at the stars, trying to understand what the traders have said—that this broad fair world of ours is but a mote spinning through vastness beyond comprehension—it has been an anguish in me that I do not know how that is." Now it was Gulmanan who leaned forward and shivered. "Would it be possible to…to translate a few of your books on this science astronomic into Thunsban?"

Alak regarded himself as a case-hardened cynic. In the line of duty, he had often and cheerfully broken the most solemn oaths with an audible snap. But this was one promise he meant to keep though the sky fell down.

On the way back, he stopped at his flitter, where Drogs was hiding from a gape-mouthed citizenry, and put the Galmathian to work in the machine shop.

* * *

A human simply could not eat very much of this planet's food; he would die in agony. Varris had taken care to have a food-synthesizer aboard his boat, and ate well that night of special dishes. He did not invite Alak to join him, and the Patrolman munched gloomily on what his service imagined to be an adequate, nutritious diet.

After supper, the nobles repaired to a central hall, with a fireplace at either end waging hopeless war on the evening chill, for serious drinking. Alak, ignored by most, sauntered through the crowd till he got to Varris. The fugitive was conversing with several barons; from his throne, King Morlach listened interestedly. Varris was increasing his prestige by explaining some principles of games theory which ought to guarantee success in the next war.

"…And thus, my gentles, it is not that one must seek a certain victory, for there is no certainty in battle, but must so distribute his forces as to have the greatest *likelihood* of winning—"

"Hogwash!" snapped Alak. The Thunsban phrase he used was more pungent.

Varris raised his brows. "Said you something?" he asked.

"I did." Alak slouched forward, wearing his most insolent expression. "I said it is nonsense you speak."

"You disagree, then, sir?" inquired a native.

"Not exactly," said the Patrolman. "It is not worth disagreeing with so lunkheaded a swine as this baseborn Varris."

His prey remained impassive. There was no tone in the voice: "I trust you will retract your statement, sir."

"Yes, perhaps I should," agreed Alak. "It was too mild. Actually, of course, as is obvious from a single glance at his bloated face, Sir Varris is a muckeating sack of lip-wagging flatulence whose habits I will not even try to describe since they would make a barnyard blush."

Silence hit the hall. The flames roared up the chimneys. King Morlach scowled and breathed heavily, but could not legally interfere. His warriors dropped hands to their knives.

"What's your purpose?" muttered Varris in Terran.

"Naturally," said Alak in Thunsban, "if Sir Varris does not dispute my assertions, there is no argument."

The Caldonian sighed. "I will dispute them on your body tomorrow morning," he answered.

Alak's foxy face broke into a delighted grin. "Do I understand that I am being challenged?" he asked.

"You do, sir. I invite you to a duel."

"Very well." Alak looked around. Every eye in the place was welded to him. "My lords, you bear witness that I have been summoned to fight Sir Varris. If I mistake me not, the choice of weapons and ground is mine."

"Within the laws of single combat," rumbled Morlach venomously. "None of your outworld sorceries."

"Indeed not." Alak bowed. "I choose to fight with my own swords, which are lighter than your claymores but I assure you, quite deadly if one does not wear armor. Sir Varris may, of course, have first choice of the pair. The duel will take place just outside the main gate of Grimmoch Abbey."

There was nothing unusual about that. A badly wounded contestant could be taken into the monks, who were also the local surgeons. In such a case, he was allowed to recover after which a return engagement was fought. In the logical belief that enmities should not be permitted to fester, the Thunsban law said that no duel was officially over till one party had been killed. It was the use of light swords that caused interest.

"Very good," said Varris in a frosty voice. He was taking it well; only Alak could guess what worries—*what trap is being set?*—lay behind those eyes. "At dawn tomorrow, then."

"Absolutely not," said Alak firmly. He never got up before noon if he could help it. "Am I to lose my good sleep on account of you? We will meet at the time of Third Sacrifice." He bowed grandly. "Good night, my lord and gentles."

Back in his apartment, he went through the window and, with the help of his small antigrav unit, over the wall and out to his boat. Varris might try to assassinate him as he slept.

Or would the Caldonian simply rely on being a better swordsman? Alak knew that was the case. This might be his last night alive.

A mid-afternoon sun threw long streamers of light across blue turf and the walls of Grimmoch Abbey. There was a hundred-meter square cleared before the gate; beyond that, a crowd of lords and ladies stood talking, drinking, and betting on the outcome. King Morlach watched ominously from a portable throne—he would not thank the man who did away with the useful Sir Varris. Just inside the gateway, Abbot Gulmanan and a dozen monks waited like stone saints.

Trumpets blew, and Alak and Varris stepped forth. Both wore light shirts and trousers, nothing else. An official frisked them ceremoniously for concealed weapons and armor. The noble appointed Master of Death trod out and recited the code. Then he took a cushion on which the rapiers were laid, tested each, and extended them to Varris.

The outlaw smiled humorlessly and selected one. Alak got the other. The Master of Death directed them to opposite corners of the field.

Alak's blade felt light and supple in his fingers. His vision and hearing were unnaturally clear, it was as if every grass blade stood out sharp before him. Perhaps his brain was storing data while it still could. Varris, one hundred forty meters off, loomed like a giant.

"And now, let the Allshaper defend the right!"

Another trumpet flourish. The duel was on.

Varris walked out, not hurrying. Alak went to meet him. They crossed blades and stood for a moment, eyes thrusting at eyes.

"Why are you doing this?" asked the refugee in Terran. "If you have some idiotic hope of killing me, you might as well forget it. I was a fencing champion at home."

"These shivs are gimmicked," said Alak with a rather forced grin. "I'll let you figure out how."

"I suppose you know the penalty for using poison is burning at the stake—" For a moment, there was a querulous whine in the voice. "Why can't you leave me alone? What business was it ever of yours?"

"Keeping the peace is my business," said Alak. "That's what I get paid for, anyhow."

Varris snarled. His blade whipped out. Alak parried just in time. There was a thin steel ringing in the air.

Varris danced gracefully, aggressively, a cold intent on his face. Alak made wild slashes, handling his rapier like a broadsword. Contempt crossed Varris' mouth. He parried a blow, riposted, and Alak felt pain sting his shoulder. The crowd whooped.

Just one cut! Just one cut before he gets me through the heart! Alak felt his chest grow warm and wet. A flesh wound, no more. He remembered that he'd forgotten to thumb the concealed button in his hilt, and did so with a curse.

Varris' weapon was a blur before his eyes. He felt another light stab. Varris was playing with him! Coldly, he retreated, to the jeers of the audience, while he rallied his wits.

The thing to do...what the devil did you call it, riposte, slash, *en avant*? Varris came close as Alak halted. The Patrolman thrust for his left arm. Varris blocked that one. Somehow, Alak slewed his blade around and pinked the outlaw in the chest.

Now—God help me, I have to survive the next few seconds! The enemy steel lunged for his throat. He slapped it down, clumsily, in bare time. His thigh was furrowed. Varris sprang back to get room. Alak did the same.

Watching, he saw the Caldonian's eyes begin helplessly rolling. The rapier wavered. Alak, deciding he had to make this look good, ran up and skewered Varris in the biceps—a harmless cut, but it bled with satisfactory enthusiasm. Varris dropped his sword and tottered. Alak got out of the way just as the big body fell.

The nobles were screaming. King Morlach roared. The Master of Death rushed out to shove Alak aside. "It is not lawful to smite a fallen man," he said.

"I...assure you...no such intention—" Alak sat down and let the planet revolve around him.

Abbot Gulmanan and the monks stooped over Varris, examining with skilled fingers. Presently the old priest looked up and said in a low voice that somehow cut through the noise: "He is not badly hurt. He should be quite well tomorrow. Perhaps he simply fainted."

"At a few scratches like that?" bawled Morlach. "Master check that red-haired infidel's blade! I suspect poison!"

Alak pressed the retracting button and handed over his sword. While it was being inspected, Varris was borne inside the abbey and its gate closed on him. The Master of Death looked at both weapons, bowed to the king, and said puzzledly:

"There is no sign of poison, my lord. And after all, Sir Varris had first choice of glaives...and these two are identical, as far as I can see...and did not the holy one say he is not really injured?"

Alak swayed erect. "Jussa better man, tha's all," he mumbled. "I won fair an' square. Lemme go get m' hurts dressed—I'll see y' all in the morning—"

He made it to his boat, and Drogs had a bottle of Scotch ready.

It took will power to be at the palace when the court convened—not that Alak was especially weakened, but the Thunsbans started their day at a hideous hour. In this case early rising was necessary, because he didn't know when the climax of his plot would be on him.

He got a mixed welcome, on the one hand respect for having overcome the great Sir Varris—at least in the first round—on the other hand, a certain doubt as to whether he had done it fairly. King Morlach gave him a surly greeting, but not openly hostile; he must be waiting for the doctors' verdict.

Alak found a congenial earl and spent his time swapping dirty jokes. It is always astonishing how many of the classics are to be found among all mammalian species. This is less an argument for the prehistoric Galactic Empire than for the parallelism of great minds.

Shortly before noon, Abbot Gulmanan entered. Several hooded monks followed him, bearing weapons—most unusual—and surrounding one who was unarmed. The priest lifted his hand to the king, and the room grew very quiet.

"Well," snapped Morlach, "what brings you hither?"

"I thought it best to report personally on the outcome of the duel, my lord," said Gulmanan. "It was…surprising."

"Mean you Sir Varris is dead?" Morlach's eyes flared. He could not fight his own guest, but it would be easy enough to have one of his guardsmen insult Wing Alak.

"No, my lord. He is in good health, his wounds are negligible. But—somehow the grace of the Allshaper fell on him." The abbot made a pious gesture; as he saw Alak, one eyelid dropped.

"What mean you?" Morlack dithered and clutched his sword.

"Only this. As he regained consciousness, I offered him ghostly counsel, as I always do to hurt men. I spoke of the virtues of the Temple, of sanctity, of the dedicated life. Half in jest, I mentioned the possibility that he might wish to renounce this evil world and enter the Temple as a brother. My lord, you can imagine my astonishment when he agreed…nay, he insisted on deeding all his lands and treasure to the abbey and taking the vows at once." Gulmanan rolled his eyes heavenward. "Indeed, a miracle!"

"*What?*" It was a shriek from the king.

The monk who was under guard suddenly tore off his hood. Varris' face glared out. "Help!" he croaked. "Help, my lord! I've been betrayed—"

"There are a dozen brothers who witnessed your acts and will swear to them by the mightiest oaths," said the abbot sternly. "Be still, Brother Varris. If the Evil has reentered your soul, I shall have to set you heavy penances."

"Witchcraft!" It whispered terribly down the long hall.

"All men know that witchcraft has no power inside the walls of a sacred abbey," warned Gulmanan. "Speak no heresies."

Varris looked wildly about at the spears and axes that ringed him in. "I was drugged, my lord," he gasped. "I remember what I did, yes, but I had no will of my own—I followed this old devil's words—" He saw Alak and snarled. *"Hypnite!"*

The Patrolman stepped forth and bowed to the king. "Your majesty," he said, "Sir Varris-that-was had first choice of blades. But if you wish to inspect them again, I have them here."

It had been easy enough, after all: two swords with retractable hypodermic needles, only they wouldn't do you any good unless you knew of them and knew where to press. The flitter's machine shop could turn one out in a couple of hours.

Alak handed them to the king from beneath his cloak. Morlach stared at the metal, called for a pair of gauntlets, and broke the blades in his hands. The mechanism lay blatant before him.

"Do you see?" cried Varris. "Do you see the poisoned darts? Burn that rogue alive!"

Morlach smiled grimly. "It shall be done," he said.

Alak grinned, and inwardly his muscles tightened. This was the tricky point. If he couldn't carry it off, it meant a pretty agonizing death. "My Lord," he answered, "that were unjust. The weapons are identical, and Sir Varris-that-was had first choice. It is permitted to use concealed extra parts, and not to warn of them."

"Poison—" began Morlach.

"But this was not poison. Does not Varris stand hale before you all?"

"Yes—" Morlach scratched his head. "But when the next engagement is fought, *I* shall provide the swords."

"A monk," said Gulmanan, "may not have private quarrels. This novice is to be returned to his cell for fasting and prayer."

"A monk may be released from his vows under certain conditions," argued Morlach. "I shall see to it that he is."

"Now hold!" shouted Wing Alak in his best Shakespearean manner. "My lord, I have won the duel. It were unlawful to speak of renewing it—for who can fight a dead man?"

"Won it?" Varris wrestled with the sturdy monks gripping his arms. "Here I stand, alive, ready to take you on again any minute—"

"My lord king," said Alak, "I crave leave to state my case."

The royal brow knotted, but: "Do so," clipped Morlach.

"Very well." Alak cleared his throat. "First, then, I fought lawfully. Granted, there was a needle in each sword of which Sir Varris had not been warned, but that is allowable under the code. It might be said that I poisoned him, but that is a canard, for as you all see he stands here unharmed. The drug I used has only a temporary effect and thus is not, by definition, a poison. Therefore, it was a lawful and just combat."

Morlach nodded reluctantly. "But not a completed battle," he said.

"Oh, it was, my lord. What is the proper termination of a duel? Is it not that one party die as the direct result of the other's craft and skill?"

"Yes…of course—"

"Then I say that Varris, though not poisoned, died as an immediate consequence of my wounding him. *He is now dead!* For mark you, he has taken vows as a monk—he did this because of the drug I administered. Those oaths may not be wholly irrevocable, but they are binding on him until such time as the Council releases him from them. And…a monk owns no property. His worldly goods revert to his heirs. His wife becomes a widow. He is beyond all civil jurisdiction. He is, in short, *legally dead!*"

"But I stand here!" shouted Varris.

"The law is sacred," declared Alak blandly. "I insist that the law be obeyed. And by every legal definition, you are dead. You are no longer Sir Varris of Wainabog, but Brother Varris of Grimmoch—a quite different person. If this fact be not admitted, then the whole structure of Thunsban society must topple, for it rests on the total separation of civil and ecclesiastical law." Alak made a flourishing bow. "Accordingly, my lord, I am the winner of the duel."

Morlach sat for a long while. His mind must be writhing in his skull, hunting for a way out of the impasse, but there was none.

"I concede it," he said at last, thickly. "Sir Wing Alak, you are the victor. You are also my guest, and I may not harm you…but you have till sunset to be gone from Thunsba forever." His gaze shifted to Varris. "Be not afraid. I shall send to the Council and have you absolved of your vows."

"That you may do, lord," said Gulmanan. "Of course, until that decree is passed, Brother Varris must remain a monk, living as all monks do. The law does not allow of exceptions."

"True," grumbled the king. "A few weeks only…be patient."

"Monks," said Gulmanan, "are not permitted to pamper themselves with special food. You shall eat the good bread of Thunsba, Brother Varris, and meditate on—"

"I'll die!" gasped the outlaw.

"Quite probably you will depart erelong for a better world," smiled the abbot. "But I may not set the law aside—To be sure, I *could* send you on a special errand, if you are willing to go. An errand to the king of the Galactics, from whom I have requested certain books. Sir Wing Alak will gladly transport you."

Morlach sat unstirring. Nobody dared move in all the court. Then something slumped in Varris. Mutely, he nodded. The armed brethren escorted him out toward the spacefield.

Wing Alak bade the king polite thanks for hospitality and followed them. Otherwise he spoke no word until his prisoner was safely fettered and his boat safely space-borne, with Drogs at the control panel and himself puffing on a good cigar.

Then: "Cheer up, old fellow," he urged. "It won't be so bad. You'll feel a lot better once our psychiatrists have rubbed out those kill-compulsions."

Varris gave him a bloodshot glare. "I suppose you think you're a great hero," he said.

"Lord deliver me, no!" Alak opened a cupboard and took forth the bottle of Scotch. "I'm quite willing to let you have that title. It was your big mistake, you realize. A hero should never tangle with an intelligent coward."

Ballade of an Artificial Satellite

Thence they sailed far to the southward along the land, and came to a ness; the land lay upon the right; there were long and sandy strands. They rowed to land, and found there upon the ness the keel of a ship, and called the place Keelness, and the strands they called Wonderstrands for it took long to sail by them. —Thorfinn Karlsefni's voyage to Vinland, as related in the saga of Erik the Red

One inland summer I walked through rye,
a wind at my heels that smelled of rain
and harried white clouds through a whistling sky
where the great sun stalked and shook his mane
and roared so brightly across the grain
it burned and shimmered like alien sands.
Ten years old, I saw down a lane
the thunderous light on Wonderstrands.

In ages before the world ran dry,
what might the mapless not contain?
Atlantis gleamed like a dream to die,
Avalon lay under faerie reign.
Cibola guarded a golden plain,
Tir-nan-Og was fair-locked Fand's,
sober men saw from a gull's-road wain
the thunderous light on Wonderstrands.

Such clanging countries in cloudland lie;
but men grew weary and they grew sane
and they grew grow—and so did I—
and knew Tartessus was only Spain.
No galleons call at Taprobane
(Ceylon, with English); no queenly hands
wear gold from Punt; nor sees the Dane
the thunderous light on Wonderstrands.

Ahoy, Prince Andros Horizon's-bane!
They always wait, the elven lands.
An evening planet gives again
the thunderous light on Wonderstrands.

Time Lag

522 Anno Coloniae Conditae:

Elva was on her way back, within sight of home, when the raid came.

For nineteen thirty-hour days, riding in high forests where sunlight slanted through leaves, across ridges where grass and the first red lampflowers rippled under springtime winds, sleeping by night beneath the sky or in the hut of some woodsdweller—-once, even, in a nest of Alfavala, where the wild little folk twittered in the dark and their eyes glowed at her—she had been gone. Her original departure was reluctant. Her husband of two years, her child of one, the lake and fields and chimney smoke at dusk which were now hers also, these were still too marvelous to leave.

But the Freeholder of Tervola had duties as well as rights. Once each season, he or his representative must ride circuit. Up into the mountains, through woods and deep dales, across the Lakeland as far as The Troll and then following the Swiftsmoke River south again, the route ran which Karlavi's fathers had traveled for nearly two centuries. Whether on hailu-back in spring, summer, through the scarlet and gold of fall, or by motorsled when snow had covered all trails, the Freeholder went out into his lands. Isolated farm clans, forest rangers on patrol duty, hunters and trappers and timber cruisers, brought their disputes to him as magistrate, their troubles to him as leader. Even the flitting Alfavala had learned to wait by the paths, the sick and injured trusting he could heal them, those with more complex problems struggling to put them into human words.

This year, however, Karlavi and his bailiffs were much preoccupied with a new dam across the Oulu. The old one had broken last spring, after a winter of unusually heavy snowfall, and 2000 hectares of bottom land were drowned. The engineers at Yuvaskula, the only city on Vaynamo, had developed a new construction process well adapted to such situations. Karlavi wanted to use this.

"But blast it all," he said, "I'll need every skilled man I have, including myself. The job has got to be finished before the ground dries, so the ferroplast can bond with the soil. And you know what the labor shortage is like around here."

"Who will ride circuit, then?" asked Elva.

"That's what I don't know." Karlavi ran a hand through his straight brown hair. He was a typical Vaynamoan, tall, light-complexioned, with high cheekbones and oblique blue eyes. He wore the working clothes usual to the Tervola district, leather breeches, mukluks, a mackinaw in the tartan of his family. There was nothing romantic about his appearance. Nevertheless, Elva's heart turned over when he looked at her. Even after two years.

He got out his pipe and tamped it with nervous motions. "Somebody must," he said. "Somebody with enough technical education to use a medikit and discuss people's difficulties intelligently. And with authority. We're more tradition-minded hereabouts than they are at Ruuyalka, dear. Our people wouldn't accept the judgment of just anyone. How could a servant or tenant dare settle an argument between two pioneers? It must be me, or a bailiff, or—" His voice trailed off.

Elva caught the implication. "No!" she exclaimed. "I can't! I mean …that is—"

"You're my wife," said Karlavi slowly. "That alone gives you the right, by well-established custom. Especially since you're the daughter of the Magnate of Ruuyalka. Almost equivalent to me in prestige, even if you do come from the other end of the continent, where they're fishers and marine farmers instead of woodsfolk." His grin flashed. "I doubt if you've yet learned what awful snobs the free yeomen of Tervola are."

"But Hauki, I can't leave him."

"Hauki will be spoiled rotten in your absence by an adoring nanny and a villageful of tenant wives. Otherwise he'll do fine." Karlavi dismissed the thought of their son with a wry gesture. "I'm the one who'll get lonesome. Abominably so."

"Oh, darling," said Elva, utterly melted.

A few days later she rode forth.

And it had been an experience to remember. The easy, rocking motion of the six-legged hailu, the mindless leisure of kilometer after kilometer—where, however, the body, skin and muscle and blood and all ancient instinct, gained an aliveness such as she had never before felt—the silence of mountains with sunlit ice on their shoulders, then birdsong in the woods and a river brawling; the rough warm hospitality when she stayed overnight with some pioneer, the eldritch welcome at the Alfa nest—she was now glad she had encountered those things, and she hoped to know them again, often.

There had been no danger. The last violence between humans on Vaynamo (apart from occasional fist fights, caused mostly by sheer exuberance and rarely doing any harm) lay a hundred years in the past. As for storms, landslides, flood, wild animals, she had the unobtrusive attendance of Huiva and a dozen other "tame" Alfavala. Even these, the intellectual pick of their species, who had chosen to serve man in a doglike fashion rather than keep to the forests, could only speak a few words and handle the simplest tools. But their long ears, flat nostrils, feathery antennae, every fine green hair on every small body, were always aquiver. This was their planet, they had evolved here, and they were more animal than rational beings. Their senses and reflexes kept her safer than an armored aircraft might.

All the same, the absence of Karlavi and Hauki grew sharper each day. When finally she came to the edge of cleared land, high on the slopes of Hornback Fell, and saw Tervola below, a blindness that stung descended momentarily on her eyes.

Huiva guided his hailu alongside her. He pointed down the mountain with his tail. "Home," he chattered. "Food tonight. Snug bed."

"Yes." Elva blinked hard. *What sort of crybaby am I, anyhow?* she asked herself, half in anger. *I'm the Magnate's daughter and the Freeholder's wife, I have a University degree and a pistol-shooting medal, as a girl I sailed through hurricanes and skindove into grottos where fangfish laired, as a woman I brought a son into the world …I will not bawl!*

"Yes," she said. "Let's hurry."

She thumped heels on the hailu's ribs and started downhill at a gallop. Her long yellow hair was braided, but a lock of it broke loose, fluttering behind her. Hoofs rang on stone. Ahead stretched grainfields and pastures, still wet from winter but their shy green deepening toward summer hues, on down to the great metallic sheet of Lake Rovaniemi and then across the valley to the opposite horizon where the High Mikkela reared into a sky as tall and blue as itself. Down by the lake clustered the village, the dear red tile of roofs, the curve of a processing plant, a road lined with trees leading to the Freeholder's mansion. There, old handhewn timbers glowed with sun; the many windows flung the light dazzlingly back to her.

She was halfway down the slope when Huiva screamed. She had learned to react fast. Thinly scattered across all Vaynamo, men could easily die from the unforeseen. Reining in, Elva snatched loose the gun at her waist. "What is it?"

Huiva cowered on his mount. One hand pointed skyward.

At first Elva could not understand. An aircraft descending above the lake… what was so odd about that? How else did Huiva expect the inhabitants of settlements hundreds of kilometers apart to visit each other?—And then she registered the shape. And then, realizing the distance, she knew the size of the thing.

It came down swiftly, quiet in its shimmer of drive fields, a cigar shape which gleamed. Elva holstered her pistol again and took forth her binoculars. Now she could see how the sleekness was interrupted with turrets and boat housings, cargo locks, viewports. An emblem was on the armored prow, a gauntleted hand grasping a planetary orb. Nothing she had ever heard of. But—

Her heart thumped, so loudly that she could almost not hear the Alfavala's squeals of terror. "A spaceship," she breathed. A spaceship, do you know that word? Like the ships my ancestors came in, long ago…Oh, bother! A big aircraft, Huiva. Come on!"

She whipped her hailu back into gallop. The first spaceship to arrive at Vaynamo in, in, how long? More than a hundred years. And it was landing here! At her own Tervola!

The vessel grounded just beyond the village. Its enormous mass settled deeply into the plowland. Housings opened and auxiliary aircraft darted forth, to hover and swoop. They were of a curious design, larger and blunter than the fliers built on Vaynamo. The people, running toward the marvel, surged back as hatches gaped, gangways extruded, armored cars beetled down to the ground.

Elva had not yet reached the village when the strangers opened fire.

There were no hostile ships, not even an orbital fortress. To depart, the seven craft from Chertkoi simply made rendezvous beyond the atmosphere, held a short gleeful conference by radio, and accelerated outward. Captain Bors Golyev, commanding the flotilla, stood on the bridge of the *Askol* and watched the others. The light of the yellow sun lay incandescent on their flanks. Beyond reached blackness and the many stars.

His gaze wandered off among constellations which the parallax of fifteen light-years had not much altered. The galaxy was so big, he thought, so unimaginably enormous…Sedes Regis was an L scrawled across heaven. Tradition claimed Old Sol lay in that direction, a thousand parsecs away. But no one on Chertkoi was certain any longer. Golyev shrugged. Who cared?

"Gravitational field suitable for agoric drive, sir," intoned the pilot.

Golyev looked in the sternward screen. The planet called Vaynamo had dwindled, but remained a vivid shield, barred with cloud and blazoned with continents, the overall color a cool blue-green. He thought of ocherous Chertkoi, and the other planets of its system, which were not even habitable. Vaynamo was the most beautiful color he had ever seen. The two small moons were also visible, like drops of liquid gold.

Automatically, his astronaut's eye checked the claims of the instruments. Was Vaynamo really far enough away for the ships to go safely into agoric? Not quite, he thought—no, wait, he'd forgotten that the planet had a five percent greater diameter than Chertkoi. "Very good," he said, and gave the necessary orders to his subordinate captains. A deep hum filled air and metal and bones. There was a momentary sense of falling, as the agoratron went into action. And then the stars began to change color and crawl weirdly across the visual field.

"All's well, sir," said the pilot. The chief engineer confirmed it over the intercom.

"Very good," repeated Golyev. He yawned and stretched elaborately. "I'm tired! That was quite a little fight we had at that last village, and I've gotten no sleep since. I'll be in my cabin. Call me if anything seems amiss."

"Yes, sir." The pilot smothered a knowing leer.

Golyev walked down the corridor, his feet slamming its metal under internal pseudogravity. Once or twice he met a crewman and accepted a salute as casually as it was given. The men of the Interplanetary Corporation didn't need to stand on ceremony. They were tried spacemen and fighters, every one of them. If they chose to wear sloppy uniforms, to lounge about off duty cracking jokes or cracking a bottle, to treat their officers as friends rather than tyrants—so much the better. This wasn't the nice-nelly Surface Transport Corporation, or the spit-and-polish Chemical Synthesis Trust, but IP, explorer and conqueror. The ship was clean and the guns were ready. What more did you want?

Pravoyats, the captain's batman, stood outside the cabin door. He nursed a scratched cheek and a black eye. One hand rested broodingly on his sidearm. "Trouble?" inquired Golyev.

"Trouble ain't the word, sir."

"You didn't hurt her, did you?" asked Golyev sharply.

"No, sir, I heard your orders all right. Never laid a finger on her in anger. But she sure did on me. Finally I wrassled her down and gave her a whiff of sleepy gas. She'd'a torn the cabin apart otherwise. She's prob'ly come out of it by now, but I'd rather not go in again to see, captain."

Golyev laughed. He was a big man, looming over Pravoyats, who was no midget. Otherwise he was a normal patron-class Chertkoian, powerfully built, with comparatively short legs and strutting gait, his features dark, snubnosed, bearded, carrying more than his share of old scars. He wore a plain green tunic, pants tucked into soft boots, at hip, his only sign of rank a crimson star at his throat. "I'll take care of all that from here on," he said.

"Yes, sir." Despite his wounds, the batman looked a shade envious. "Uh, you want the prod? I tell you, she's a troublemaker."

"No."

"Electric shocks don't leave any scars, captain."

"I know. Be on your way, Pravoyats." Golyev opened the door, went through, and closed it behind him again.

The girl had been seated on his bunk. She stood up with a gasp. A looker, for certain. The Vaynamoan women generally seemed handsome; this one was beautiful, tall and slim, delicate face and straight nose lightly dusted with freckles. But her mouth was wide and strong, her skin suntanned, and she wore a coarse, colorful riding habit. Her exoticism was the most exciting thing: yellow hair, slant blue eyes, who'd ever heard of the like?

The tranquilizing after-effects of the gas—or else plain nervous exhaustion—kept her from attacking him. She backed against the wall and shivered. Her misery touched Golyev a little. He'd seen unhappiness elsewhere, on Imfan and Novagal and Chertkoi itself, and hadn't been bothered thereby. People who were too weak to defend themselves must expect to be made booty of. It was different, though, when someone as good-looking as this was so woebegone.

He paused on the opposite side of his desk from her, gave a soft salute, and smiled. "What's your name, my dear?"

She drew a shaken breath. After trying several times, she managed to speak. "I didn't think…anyone…understood my language."

"A few of us do. The hypnopede, you know." Evidently she did not know. He thought a short, dry lecture might soothe her. "An invention made a few decades ago on our planet. Suppose another person and I have no language in common. We can be given a drug to accelerate our nervous systems, and then the machine flashes images on a screen and analyzes the sounds uttered by the other person. What it hears is transferred to me and impressed on the speech center of my brain, electronically. As the vocabulary grows, a computer in the machine figures out the structure of the whole language—semantics, grammar, and so on—and orders my own learning accordingly. That way, a few short, daily sessions make me fluent."

She touched her lips with a tongue that seemed equally parched. "I heard once …of some experiments at the University," she whispered. "They never got far. No reason for such a machine. Only one language on Vaynamo."

"And on Chertkoi. But we've already subjugated two other planets, one of 'em divided into hundreds of language groups. And we expect there'll be others." Golyev opened a drawer, took out a bottle and two glasses. "Care for brandy?"

He poured. "I'm Bors Golyev, an astronautical executive of the Interplanetary Corporation, commanding this scout force," he said. "Who are you?"

She didn't answer. He reached a glass toward her. "Come, now," he said, "I'm not such a bad fellow. Here, drink. To our better acquaintance."

With a convulsive movement, she struck the glass from his hand. It bounced on the floor. "Almighty Creator! No!" she yelled. "You murdered my husband!"

She stumbled to a chair, fell down in it, rested head in arms on the desk and began to weep. The spilled brandy crept across the floor toward her.

Golyev groaned. Why did he always get cases like this? Glebs Narov, now, had clapped hands on the jolliest tawny wench you could imagine, when they conquered Marsya on Imfan: delighted to be liberated from her own drab culture.

Well, he could kick this female back down among the other prisoners. But he didn't want to. He seated himself across from her, lit a cigar out of the box on his desk, and held his own glass to the light. Ruby smoldered within.

"I'm sorry," he said. "How was I to know? What's done is done. There wouldn't have been so many casualties if they'd been sensible and given up. We shot a few to prove we meant business, but then called on the rest over a loudspeaker, to yield. They didn't. For that matter, you were riding a six-legged animal out of the fields, I'm told. You came busting right *into* the fight. Why didn't you ride the other way and hide out till we left?"

"My husband was there," she said after a silence. When she raised her face, he saw it gone cold and stiff. "And our child."

"Oh? Uh, maybe we picked up the kid, at least. If you'd like to go see—"

"No," she said, toneless and yet somehow with a dim returning pride. "I got Hauki away. I rode straight to the mansion and got him. Then one of your fireguns hit the roof and the house began to burn. I told Huiva to take the baby—never mind where. I said I'd follow if I could. But Karlavi was out there, fighting. I went back to the barricade. He had been killed just a few seconds before. His face was all bloody. Then your cars broke through the barricade and someone caught me. But you don't have Hauki. Or Karlavi!"

As if drained by the effort of speech, she slumped and stared into a corner, empty-eyed.

"Well," said Golyev, not quite comfortably, "your people had been warned." She didn't seem to hear him. "You never got the message? But it was telecast over your whole planet. After our first non-secret landing. That was several days ago. Were you out in the woods or something? —Yes, we scouted telescopically, and made clandestine landings, and caught a few citizens to interrogate. But when we understood the situation, more or less, we landed openly in, uh, your city. Yuvaskula, is that the name? We seized it without too much damage, captured some officials of the planetary government, claimed the planet for IP and called on all citizens to cooperate. But they wouldn't! Why, one ambush alone cost us fifty good men. What could we do? We had to teach a lesson. We announced we'd punish a few random villages. That's more humane than bombarding from space with cobalt missiles. Isn't it? But I suppose your people didn't really believe us, the way they came swarming when we landed. Trying to parley with us first, and then trying to resist us with hunting rifles! What would you expect to happen?"

His voice seemed to fall into an echoless well.

He loosened his collar, which felt a trifle tight, took a deep drag on his cigar and refilled his glass. "Of course, I don't expect you to see our side of it at once," he said reasonably. "You've been jogging along, isolated, for centuries, haven't you? Hardly a spaceship has touched at your planet since it was first colonized. You have none of your own, except a couple of interplanetary boats which hardly ever get used. That's what your President told me, and I believe him. Why should you go outsystem? You have everything you can use, right on your own world. The nearest sun to yours with an oxygen atmosphere planet is three parsecs off. Even with a very high-powered agoratron, you'd need ten years to get there, another decade to get back. A whole generation! Sure, the time-contraction effect would keep you young—ship's time for the voyage would only be a few weeks, or less—but all your friends would be middle-aged when you came home. Believe me, it's lonely being a spaceman."

He drank. A pleasant burning went down his throat. "No wonder men spread so slowly into space, and each colony is so isolated," he said. "Chertkoi is a mere name in your archives. And yet it's only fifteen light-years from Vaynamo. You can see our sun on any clear night. A reddish one. You call it Gamma Navarchi. Fifteen little light-years, and yet there's been no contact between our two planets for four centuries or more!

"So why now? Well, that's a long story. Let's just say Chertkoi isn't as friendly a world as Vaynamo. You'll see that for yourself. We, our ancestors, we came up the hard way, we had to struggle for everything. And now there are four billion of us! That was the census figure when I left. It'll probably be five billion when I get home. We have to have more resources. Our economy is grinding to a halt. And we can't afford economic dislocation. Not on as thin a margin as Chertkoi allows us. First we went back to the other planets of our system and worked them as much as practicable. Then we started re-exploring the nearer stars. So far we've found two useful planets. Yours is the third. You know what your population is? Ten million, your President claimed. Ten million people for a whole world of forests, plains, hills, oceans … why, your least continent has more natural resources than all Chertkoi. And you've stabilized at that population. You don't want more people!"

Golyev struck the desk with a thumb. "If you think ten million stagnant agriculturists have a right to monopolize all that room and wealth, when four billion Chertkoians live on the verge of starvation," he said indignantly, "you can think again."

She stirred. Not looking at him, her tone small and very distant, she said, "It's our planet, to do with as we please. If you want to breed like maggots, you must take the consequences."

Anger flushed the last sympathy from Golyev. He ground out his cigar in the ashwell and tossed off his brandy. "Never mind moralizing, he said. I'm no martyr. I became a spaceman because it's fun."

He got up and walked around the desk to her.

538 A.C.C.

When she couldn't stand the apartment any more, Elva went out on the balcony and looked across Dirzh until that view became unendurable in its turn.

From this height, the city had a certain grandeur. On every side it stretched horizonward, immense gray blocks among which rose an occasional spire shining with steel and glass. Eastward at the very edge of vision it ended before some mine pits, whose scaffolding and chimneys did not entirely cage off a glimpse of primordial painted desert. Between the buildings went a network of elevated trafficways, some carrying robofreight, others pullulating with gray-clad clients on foot. Overhead, against a purple-black sky and the planet's single huge moon, nearly full tonight, flitted the firefly aircars of executives, engineers, military techs, and others in the patron class. A few stars were visible, but the fever-flash of neon drowned most of them. Even by full red-tinged daylight, Elva could never see all the way downward. A fog of dust, smoke, fumes and vapors hid the bottom of the artificial mountains. She could only imagine the underground, caves and tunnels where workers of the lowest category were bred to spend their lives tending machines, and where a criminal class slunk about in armed packs.

It was rarely warm on Chertkoi, summer or winter. As the night wind gusted, Elva drew more tightly around her a mantle of genuine fur from Novagal. Bors wasn't stingy about clothes or jewels. But then, he liked to take her out in public places, where she could be admired and he envied. For the first few months she had refused to leave the apartment. He hadn't made an issue of it, only waited. In the end she gave in. Nowadays she looked forward eagerly to such times; they took her away from these walls. But of late there had been no celebrations. Bors was working too hard.

The moon Drogoi climbed higher, reddened by the hidden sun and the lower atmosphere of the city. At the zenith it would be pale copper. Once Elva had fancied the markings on it formed a death's head. They didn't really; that had just been her horror of everything Chertkoian. But she had never shaken off the impression.

She hunted among the constellations, knowing that if she found Vaynamo's sun it would hurt, but unable to stop. The air was too thick tonight, though, with an odor of acid and rotten eggs. She remembered riding out along Lake Rovaniemi, soon after her marriage. Karlavi was along: no one else, for you didn't need a bodyguard on Vaynamo. The two moons climbed fast. Their light made a trembling double bridge on the water. Trees rustled the air smelled green, something sang with a liquid plangency far off among moon-dappled shadows.

"But that's beautiful!" she whispered. "Yonder songbird. We haven't anything like it in Ruuyalka."

Karlavi chuckled. "No bird at all. The Alfavala name—well, who can pronounce that? We humans say 'yanno.' A little pseudomammal, a terrible pest. Roots up tubers. For a while we thought we'd have to wipe out the species."

"But they sing so sweetly."

"True. Also, the Alfavala would be hurt. Insofar as they have anything like a religion, the yanno seems to be part of it, locally. Important to them somehow, at least." Unspoken was the law under which she and he had both been raised: The green dwarfs are barely where man was two or three million years ago on Old Earth, but they are the real natives of Vaynamo, and if we share their planet we're bound to respect them and help them.

Once Elva had tried to explain the idea to Bors Golyev. He couldn't understand at all. If the abos occupied land men might use, why not hunt them off it? They'd make good, crafty game, wouldn't they?

"Can anything be done about the yanno?" she asked Karlavi.

"For several generations, we fooled around with electric fences and so on. But just a few years ago, I consulted Paaska Ecological Institute and found they'd developed a wholly new approach to such problems. They can now tailor a dominant mutant gene which produces a strong distaste for Vitamin C. I suppose you know Vitamin C isn't part of native biochemistry, but occurs only in plants of Terrestrial origin. We released the mutants to breed, and every season there are fewer yanno that'll touch our crops. In another five years there'll be too few to matter."

"And they'll still sing for us." She edged her hailu closer to his. Their knees touched. He leaned over and kissed her.

Elva shivered. *I'd better go in,* she thought.

The light switched on automatically as she re-entered the living room. At least artificial illumination on Chertkoi was like home. Dwelling under different suns had not yet changed human eyes. Though in other respects, man's colonies had drifted far apart indeed…The apartment had three cramped rooms, which was considered luxurious. When five billion people, more every day, grubbed their living from a planet as bleak as this, even the wealthy must do without things that were the natural right of the poorest Vaynamoan—spaciousness, trees, grass beneath bare feet, your own house and an open sky. Of course, Chertkoi had very sophisticated amusements to offer in exchange, everything from multisensory films to live combats.

Belgoya pattered in from her offside cubicle. Elva wondered if the maidservant ever slept. "Does the mistress wish anything, please?"

"No." Elva sat down. She ought to be used to the gravity by now, she thought. How long had she been here? A year, more or less. She hadn't kept track of time, especially when they used an unfamiliar calendar. Denser than Vaynamo, Chertkoi exerted a ten percent greater surface pull; but that wasn't enough to matter, when you were in good physical condition. Yet she was always tired.

"No, I don't want anything." She leaned back on the couch and rubbed her eyes. The haze outside had made them sting.

"A cup of stim, perhaps, if the mistress please?" The girl bowed some more, absurdly doll-like in her uniform.

"No!" Elva shouted. "Go away!"

"I beg your pardon. I am a worm. I implore your magnanimity." Terrified, the maid crawled backward out of the room on her belly.

Elva lit a cigarette. She hadn't smoked on Vaynamo, but since coming here she'd take it up, become a chain-smoker like most Chertkoians who could afford it. You needed something to do with your hands. The servility of clients toward patrons no longer shocked her, but rather made her think of them as faintly slimy. To be sure, one could see the reasons. Belgoya, for instance, could be fired any time and sent back to the street level. Down there were a million eager applicants for her position. Elva forgot her and reached after the teleshow dials. Something must be on, loud and full of action, something to watch, something to do with her evening.

The door opened. Elva turned about, tense with expectation. So Bors was home. And alone. If he'd brought a friend along, she would have had to go into the sleeping cubicle and merely listen. Upper-class Chertkoians didn't like women intruding on their conversation. But Bors alone meant she would have someone to talk to.

He came in, his tread showing he was also tired. He skimmed his hat into a corner and dropped his cloak on the floor. Belgoya crept forth to pick them up. As he sat down, she was there with a drink and a cigar.

Elva waited. She knew his moods. When the blunt, bearded face had lost some of its hardness, she donned a smile and stretched herself along the couch, leaning on one elbow. "You've been working yourself to death," she scolded.

He sighed. "Yeh. But the end's in view. Another week, and all the damn paperwork will be cleared up."

"You hope. One of your bureaucrats will probably invent nineteen more forms to fill out in quadruplicate."

"Probably."

"We never had that trouble at home. The planetary government was only a coordinating body with strictly limited powers. Why won't you people even consider establishing something similar?"

"You know the reasons. Five billion of them. You've got room to be an individual on Vaynamo." Golyev finished his drink and held the glass out for a refill. "By all chaos! I'm tempted to desert when we get there."

Elva lifted her brows. "That's a thought," she purred.

"Oh, you know it's impossible," he said, returning to his usual humorlessness. "Quite apart from the fact I'd be one enemy alien on an entire planet—"

"Not necessarily."

"—All right, even if I got naturalized (and who wants to become a clodhopper?) I'd have only thirty years till the Third Expedition came. I don't want to be a client in my old age. Or worse, see my children made clients."

Elva lit a second cigarette from the stub of the first. She drew in the smoke hard enough to hollow her cheeks.

But it's fine to launch the Second Expedition and make clients of others, she thought. *The First, that captured me and a thousand more (What's become of them? How many are dead, how many found useless and sent lobotomized to the mines, how many are still being pumped dry of information?) …that was a mere scouting trip. The Second will have fifty warships, and try to force surrender. At the very least, it will flatten all possible defenses, destroy all imaginable war potential, bring back a whole herd of slaves. And then the Third, a thousand ships or more, will bring the final conquest, the garrisons, the overseers and entrepreneurs and colonists. But that won't be for forty-five years or better from tonight. A man on Vaynamo…Hauki…a man who survives the coming of the Second Expedition will have thirty-odd years left in which to be free. But will he dare have children?*

"I'll settle down there after the Third Expedition, I think," Golyev admitted. "From what I saw of the planet last time, I believe I'd like it. And the opportunities are unlimited. A whole world waiting to be properly developed!"

"I could show you a great many chances you'd otherwise overlook," insinuated Elva.

Golyev shifted position. "Let's not go into that again," he said. "You know I can't take you along."

"You're the fleet commander, aren't you?"

"Yes, I will be, but curse it, can't you understand? The IP is not like any other corporation. We use men who think and act on their own, not planet-hugging morons like what's-her-name—" he jerked a thumb at Belgoya, who lowered her eyes meekly and continued mixing him a third drink. "Men of patron status, younger sons of executives and engineers. The officers can't have special privileges. It'd ruin morale."

Elva fluttered her lashes. "Not that much. Really."

"My oldest boy's promised to take care of you. He's not such a bad fellow as you seem to think. You only have to go along with his whims. I'll see you again, in thirty years."

"When I'm gray and wrinkled. Why not kick me out in the street and be done?"

"You know why," he said ferociously. "You're the first woman I could ever talk to. No, I'm not bored with you! But—"

"If you really cared for me—"

"What kind of idiot do you take me for? I know you're planning to sneak away to your own people, once we've landed."

Elva tossed her head, haughtily. "Well! If you believe that of me, there's nothing more to say."

"Aw, now, sweetling, don't take that attitude." He reached out a hand to lay on her arm. She withdrew to the far end of the couch. He looked baffled.

"Another thing," he argued. "If you care about your planet at all, as I suppose you do, even if you've now seen what a bunch of petrified mudsuckers they are …remember, what we'll have to do there won't be pretty."

"First you call me a traitor," she flared, "and now you say I'm gutless!"

"Hoy, wait a minute—"

"Go on, beat me. I can't stop you. You're brave enough for that."

"I never—"

In the end, he yielded.

553 A.C.C

The Missile which landed on Yuvaskula had a ten-kilometer radius of total destruction. Thus most of the city went up in one radioactive fire-gout. In a way, the thought of men and women and little children with pet kittens, incinerated, made a trifle less pain in Elva than knowing the Old Town was gone: the cabin raised by the first men to land on Vaynamo, the ancient church of St. Yarvi with its stained-glass windows and gilded bell tower, the Museum of Art where she went as a girl on entranced visits, the University where she studied and where she met Karlavi—*I'm a true daughter of Vaynamo,* she thought with remorse. *Whatever is traditional, full of memories, whatever has been looked at and been done by all the generations before me, I hold dear. The Chertkoians don't care. They haven't any past worth remembering.*

Flames painted the northern sky red, even at this distance, as she walked among the plastishelters of the advanced base. She had flown within a hundred kilometers, using an aircar borrowed from the flagship, then landed to avoid possible missiles and hitched a ride here on a supply truck. The Chertkoian enlisted men aboard had been delighted until she showed them her pass, signed by Commander Golyev himself. Then they became cringingly respectful.

The pass was only supposed to let her move freely about in the rear areas, and she'd had enough trouble wheedling it from Bors. But no one thereafter looked closely at it. She herself was so unused to the concept of war that she didn't stop to wonder at such lax security measures. Had she done so, she would have realized Chertkoi had never developed anything better, never having faced an enemy of comparable strength. Vaynamo certainly wasn't, even though the planet was proving a hard-shelled opponent, with every farmhouse a potential arsenal and every forest road a possible death trap. Guerrilla fighters hindered the movements of an invader with armor, atomic artillery, complete control of air and space; they could not stop him.

Elva drew her dark mantle more tightly about her and crouched under a gun emplacement. A sentry went by, his helmet square against the beloved familiar face of a moon his rifle aslant across the stars. She didn't want needless questioning. For a moment the distant blaze sprang higher, unrestful ruddy light touched her, she was afraid she had been observed. But the man continued his round.

From the air she had seen that the fire was mostly a burning forest, kindled from Yuvaskula. Those wooden houses not blown apart by the missile stood unharmed in the whitest glow. Some process must have been developed at one of the research institutes, for indurating timber, since she left…How Bors would laugh if she told him. An industry which turned out a bare minimum of vehicles, farm machinery, tools, chemicals; a science which developed fireproofing techniques and traced out ecological chains; a population which deliberately held itself static, so as to preserve its old customs and laws—presuming to make war on Chertkoi!

Even so, he was too experienced a fighter to dismiss any foe as weak without careful examination. He had been excited enough about one thing to mention it to Elva—a prisoner taken in a skirmish near Yuvaskula, when he still hoped to capture the city intact: an officer, who cracked just enough under interrogation to indicate he knew something important. But Golyev couldn't wait around for the inquisitors to finish their work. He must go out the very next day to oversee the battle for Lempo Machine Tool Works, and Elva knew he wouldn't return soon. The plant had been constructed underground as an economy measure, and to preserve the green parkscape above. Now its concrete warrens proved highly defensible, and were being bitterly contested. The Chertkoians meant to seize it, so they could be sure of demolishing everything. They would not leave Vaynamo any nucleus of industry. After all, the planet would have thirty-odd years to recover and rearm itself against the Third Expedition.

Left alone by Bors, Elva took an aircar and slipped off to the advanced base.

She recognized the plastishelter she wanted by its Intelligence insignia. The guard outside aimed a rifle at her. "Halt!" His boyish voice cracked over with nervousness. More than one sentry had been found in the morning with his throat cut.

"It's all right," she told him. "I'm to see the prisoner Ivalo."

"The gooze officer?" He flashed a pencil-thin beam across her face. "But you're a—uh—"

"A Vaynamoan myself. Of course. There are a few of us along, you know. Prisoners taken last time, who've enlisted in your cause as guides and spies. You must have heard of me. I'm Elva, Commander Golyev's lady."

"Oh. Yes, mistress. Sure I have."

"Here's my pass."

He squinted at it uneasily. "But, uh, may I ask what, uh, what *you* figure to do? I've got strict orders—"

Elva gave him her most confidential smile. "My own patron had the idea. The prisoner is withholding valuable information. He has been treated roughly, but resisted. Now, all at once, we'll take the pressure off. An attractive woman of his own race …"

"I get it. Maybe he will crack. I dunno, though, mistress. These slant-eyed towheads are mean animals—begging your pardon! Go right on in. Holler if he gets rough or, or anything."

The door was unlocked for her. Elva went on through, into a hemicylindrical room so low that she must stoop. A lighting tube switched on, showing a pallet laid across the floor.

Captain Ivalo was gray at the temples, but still tough and supple. His face had gone haggard, sunken eyes and a stubble of beard; his garments were torn and filthy. When he looked up, coming awake, he was too exhausted to show much surprise. "What now?" he said in dull Chertkoian. "What are you going to try next?"

Elva answered in Vaynamoan (oh, God, it was a year and a half, her own time, nearly seventeen years cosmic time, since she had uttered a word to anyone from her planet): "Be quiet. I beg you. We mustn't be suspected."

He sat up. "Who are you?" he snapped. His own Vaynamoan accent was faintly pedantic; he must be a teacher or scientist in that peacetime life which now seemed so distant. "A collaborator? I understand there are some. Every barrel must hold a few rotten apples, I suppose."

She sat down on the floor near him, hugged her knees and stared at the curving wall. "I don't know what to call myself," she said tonelessly. "I'm with them, yes. But they captured me the last time."

He whistled, a soft note. One hand reached out, not altogether steady, and stopped short of touching her. "I was young then," he said. "But I remember. Do I know your family?"

"Maybe. I'm Elva, daughter of Byarmo, the Magnate of Ruuyalka. My husband was Karlavi, the Freeholder of Tervola." Suddenly she couldn't stay controlled. She grasped his arm so hard that her nails drew blood. "Do you know what became of my son? His name was Hauki. I got him away, in care of an Alfa servant. Hauki, Karlavi's son, Freeholder of Tervola. Do you know?"

He disengaged himself as gently as possible and shook his head. "I'm sorry. I've heard of both places, but only as names. I'm from the Aakinen Islands myself."

Her head drooped.

"Ivalo is my name," he said clumsily.

"I know."

"What?"

"Listen." She raised her eyes to him. They were quite dry. "I've been told you have important information."

He bridled. "If you think—"

"No. Please listen. Here." She fumbled in a pocket of her gown. At last her fingers closed on the vial. She held it out to him. "An antiseptic. But the label says it's very poisonous if taken internally. I brought it for you."

He stared at her for a long while.

"It's all I can do," she mumbled, looking away again.

He took the bottle and turned it over and over in his hands. The night grew silent around them.

Finally he asked, "Won't you suffer for this?"

"Not too much."

"Wait…If you could get in here, you can surely escape completely. Our troops can't be far off. Or any farmer hereabouts will hide you."

She shook her head. "No. I'll stay with them. Maybe I can help in some other small way. What else has there been to keep me alive, but the hope of—It wouldn't be any better, living here, if we're all conquered. There's to be a final attack, three decades hence. Do you know that?"

"Yes. Our side takes prisoners too, and quizzes them. The first episode puzzled us. Many thought it had only been a raid by—what's the word?—by pirates. But now we know they really do intend to take our planet away."

"You must have developed some good linguists," she said, seeking impersonality. "To be able to talk with your prisoners. Of course, you yourself, after capture, could be educated by the hypnopede."

"The what?"

"The language-teaching machine."

"Oh, yes, the enemy do have them, don't they? But we do too. After the first raid, those who thought there was a danger the aliens might come back set about developing such machines. I knew Chertkoian weeks before my own capture."

"I wish I could help you escape," she said dully. But I don't know how. That bottle is all I can do. Isn't it?"

"Yes." He regarded the thing with a fascination.

"My patron—Golyev himself—said his men would rip you open to get your knowledge. So I thought—"

"You're very kind." Ivalo grimaced, as if he had tasted something foul. "But your act may turn out pointless. I don't know anything useful. I wasn't even sworn to secrecy about what I do know. Why've I held out, then? Don't ask me. Stubbornness. Anger. Or just hating to admit that my people—our people, damn it!—that they could be so weak and foolish."

"What?" Her glance jerked up to him.

"They could win the war at a stroke," he said. "They won't. They'd rather die, and let their children be enslaved by the Third Expedition."

"What do you mean?" She crouched to hands and knees, bowstring-tense.

He shrugged. "I told you, a number of people of Vaynamo took the previous invasion at its word, that it was the vanguard of a conquering army. There was no official action. How could there be, with a government as feeble as ours? But some of the research biologists—"

"Not a plague!"

"Yes. Mutated from the local coryzoid virus. Incubation period, approximately one month, during which time it's contagious. Vaccination is still effective two weeks after exposure, so all our people could be safeguarded. But the Chertkoians would take the disease back with them. Estimated deaths, ninety percent of the race."

"But—"

"That's where the government did step in," he said with bitterness. "The information was suppressed. The virus cultures were destroyed. The theory was, even to save ourselves we couldn't do such a thing."

Elva felt the tautness leave her. She sagged. She had seen small children on Chertkoi too.

"They're right, of course," she said wearily.

"Perhaps. Perhaps. And yet we'll be overrun and butchered or reduced to serfdom. Won't we? Our forests will be cut down, our mines gutted, our poor Alfavala exterminated…To hell with it." Ivalo gazed at the poison vial. "I don't have any scientific data, I'm not a virologist. It can't do any military harm to tell the Chertkoians. But I've seen what they've done to us. I would give them the sickness."

"I wouldn't." Elva bit her lip.

He regarded her for a long time. "Won't you escape? Never mind being a planetary heroine. There's nothing you can do. The invaders will go home when they've wrecked all our industry. They won't come again for thirty years. You can be free most of your life."

"You forget," she said, "that if I leave with them, and come back, the time for me will only have been one or two years." She sighed. "I can't help make ready for the next battle. I'm just a woman. Untrained. While maybe …oh, if nothing else, there'll be more Vaynamoan prisoners brought to Chertkoi. I have a tiny bit of influence. Maybe I can help them."

Ivalo considered the poison. "I was about to use this anyway," he muttered. "I didn't think staying alive was worth the trouble. But now—if you can—No." He gave the vial back to her. "I thank you, my lady."

"I have an idea," she said, with a hint of color in her voice. "Go ahead and tell them what you know. Pretend I talked you into it. Then I might be able to get you exchanged. It's barely possible."

"Oh, perhaps," he said, not believing. "I'll try."

She rose to go. "If you are set free," she stammered, "will you make a visit to Tervola? Will you find Hauki. Karlavi's son, and tell him you saw me? If he's alive."

569 A.C.C.:

Dirzh had changed while the ships were away, The evolution continued after their return. The city grew bigger, smokier, uglier. More people each year dropped from client status, went underground and joined the gangs. Occasionally, these days, the noise and vibration of pitched battles down in the tunnels could be detected up on patron level. The desert could no longer be seen, even from the highest towers, only the abandoned mine and the slag mountains, in process of conversion to tenements. The carcinogenic murkiness crept upward until it could be smelled on the most elite balconies. Teleshows got noisier and nakeder, to compete with live performances, which offering more elaborate bloodlettings than old-fashioned combats. The news from space was of a revolt suppressed on Novagal, resulting in such an acute labor shortage that workers were drafted from Imfan and shipped thither.

Only when you looked at the zenith was there no apparent change. The daylight sky was still cold purplish-blue, with an occasional yellow dustcloud. At night there will still the stars, and a skull.

And yet, thought Elva, you wouldn't need a large telescope to see the Third Expedition fleet in orbit—eleven hundred spacecraft, the unarmed ones loaded with troops and equipment, nearly the whole strength of Chertkoi marshaling to conquer Vaynamo. Campaigning across interstellar distances wasn't easy. You couldn't send home for supplies or reinforcements. You broke the enemy or he broke you. Fleet Admiral Bors Golyev did not intend to be broken.

He did not even plan to go home with news of a successful operation or a successful raid. The Third Expedition was to be final. And he must allow for the Vaynamoans having had a generation in which to recuperate. He'd smashed their heavy industry, but if they were really determined, they could have rebuilt. No doubt a space fleet of some kind would be waiting to oppose him.

He knew it couldn't be of comparable power. Ten million people, forced to recreate all their mines and furnaces and factories before they could lay the keel of a single boat, had no possibility of matching the concerted efforts of six and a half billion whose world had been continuously industrialized for centuries, and who could draw on the resources of two subject planets. Sheer mathematics ruled it out. But the ten million could accomplish something: and nuclear-fusion missiles were to some degree an equalizer. Therefore Bors Golyev asked for so much strength that the greatest conceivable enemy force would be swamped. And he got it.

Elva leaned on the balcony rail. A chill wind fluttered her gown around her, so that the rainbow hues rippled and ran into each other. She had to admit that the fabric was lovely. Bors tried hard to please her. (Though why must he mention the price?) He was so childishly happy himself, at his accomplishments, at his new eminence, at the eight-room apartment which he now rated on the very heights of the Lebedan Tower.

"Not that we'll be here long," he had said, after they first explored its intricacies. "My son Nivko has done good work in the home office. That's how come I got this command; experience alone wasn't enough. Of course, he'll expect me to help along his sons...But anyhow, the Third Expedition can go even sooner than I'd hoped. Just a few months, and we're on our way."

"We?" murmured Elva.

"You do want to come, don't you?"

"The last voyage, you weren't so eager."

"Uh, yes. I did have a deuce of a time, too, getting you aboard. But this'll be different. First, I've got so much rank I'm beyond criticism, even beyond jealousy. And second, well, you count too. You're not any picked-up native female. You're Elva! The girl who on her own hook got that fellow Ivalo to confess."

She turned her head slightly, regarding him sideways from droop-lidded blue eyes. Under the ruddy sun, her hair turned to raw gold. "I should think the news would have alarmed them, here on Chertkoi," she said. "Being told that they nearly brought their own extinction about. I wonder that they dare launch another attack."

Golyev grinned. "You should have heard the ruckus. Some Directors did vote to keep hands off Vaynamo. Others wanted to sterilize the whole planet with cobalt missiles. But I talked 'em around. Once we've beaten the fleet and occupied the planet, its whole population will be hostage for good behavior. We'll make examples of the first few goozes who give us trouble of any sort. Then they'll know we mean what we say when we announce our policy. At the first suspicion of plague among us, we'll lay waste a continent. If the suspicion is confirmed, we'll bombard the whole works. No, there won't be any bug warfare."

"I know. I've heard your line of reasoning before. About five hundred times, in fact."

"Destruction! Am I really that much of a bore?" He came up behind her and laid his hands on her shoulders. "I don't mean to be. Honest. I'm not used to talking to women, that's all."

"And I'm not used to being shut away like a prize fish, except when you want to exhibit me," she said sharply.

He kissed her neck. His whiskers tickled. "It'll be different on Vaynamo. When we're settled down. I'll be governor of the planet. The Directorate has as good as promised me. Then I can do as I want. And so can you."

"I doubt that. Why should I believe anything you say? When I told you I'd made Ivalo talk by promising you would exchange him, you wouldn't keep the promise. She tried to wriggle free, but his grip was too strong. She contented herself with going rigid. "Now, when I tell you the prisoners we brought back this time are to be treated like human beings, you whine about your damned Directorate—"

"But the Directorate makes policy!"

"You're the Fleet Admiral, as you never lose a chance to remind me. You can certainly bring pressure to bear. You can insist the Vaynamoans be taken out of those kennels and given honorable detention—"

"Awww, now." His lips nibbled along her cheek. She turned her head away and continued:

"—and you can get what you insist on. They're your own prisoners, aren't they? I've listened enough to you, and your dreary officers when you brought them home. I've read books, hundreds of books. What else have I got to do, day after day and week after week?"

"But I'm busy! I'd like to take you out, honest, but—"

"So I understand the power structure on Chertkoi just as well as you do, Bors Golyev. If not better. If you don't know how to use your influence, then slough off some of that conceit, sit down and listen while I tell you how."

"Well, uh, I never denied, sweetling, you've given me some useful advice from time to time."

"So listen to me. I say all the Vaynamoans you hold are to be given decent quarters, recreation, and respect. What did you capture them for, if not to get some use out of them? And the proper use is not to titillate yourself by kicking them around. A dog would serve that purpose better.

"Furthermore, the fleet has to carry them back to Vaynamo. All of them."

"What? You don't know what you're talking about! The logistics is tough enough without—"

"I do so know what I'm talking about. Which is more than I can say for you. You want guides, intermediaries, puppet leaders, don't you? Not by the score, a few cowards and traitors, as you have hitherto. You need hundreds. Well, there they are, right in your hands."

"And hating my guts."

"Give them reasonable living conditions and they won't Not quite so much, anyhow. Then bring them back home—a generation after they left, all their friends aged or dead, everything altered once you've conquered the planet. And let me deal with them. You'll get helpers."

"Uh, well, uh, I'll think about it."

"You'll do something about it!" She eased her body leaning back against the rubbery muscles of his chest Her face turned upward, with a slow smile. "You're good at doing things, Bors."

"Oh, Elva—"

Later: "You know one thing I want to do? As soon as I'm well established in the governorship? I want to marry you. Properly and openly. Let 'em be shocked. I won't care. I want to be your husband, and the father of your kids, Elva. How's that sound? Mistress Governor General Elva Golyev of Vaynamo Planetary Province. Never thought you'd get that far in life, did you?"

584 A.C.C.:

As they neared the end of the journey, he sent her to his cabin. An escape suit—an armored cylinder with propulsors, air regenerator, food and water supplies, which she could enter in sixty seconds—occupied most of the room. "Not that I expect any trouble," he said. "But if something should happen…I hope you can make it down to the surface. He paused. The officers on the bridge moved quietly about their tasks; the engines droned; the distorted stars of near-light velocity framed his hard brown face. There was a thin sheen of sweat on his skin; not fear but an effort to say something.

"I love you, you know," he finished. Quickly, he turned back to his duties. Elva went below.

Clad in a spaceman's uniform, seated on the bunk, enclosed in toning metal, she felt the inward wrench as the agoratron went off and speed was converted back to atomic mass. The cabin's private viewscreen showed stars in their proper constellations again, needle-sharp against blackness. Vaynamo was tiny and blue, still several hundred thousand kilometers remote. Elva ran fingers through her hair. The scalp beneath felt tight, and her lips were dry. A person couldn't help being afraid, she thought. Just a little afraid.

She called up the memory of Karlavi's land, where he had now lain for sixty-two years. Reeds whispered along the shores of Rovaniemi, the wind made a rippling in long grass, and it was time again for the lampflowers to blow, all down the valley. Dreamlike at the edge of vision, the snowpeaks of the High Mikkela floated in an utter blue.

I'm coming back, Karlavi, she thought.

In her screen, the nearer vessels were glinting toys, plunging through emptiness. The further ones were not visible at this low magnification. Only the senses of radar, gravpulse, and less familiar creations, analyzed by whirling electrons in a computer bank, gave any approach to reality. But she could listen in on the main intercom line to the bridge if she chose, and hear those data spoken. She flipped the switch. Nothing yet, only routine reports. Had the planet's disc grown a trifle?

Have I been wrong all the time? she thought. Her heart stopped for a second.

Then: "Alert! Condition red! Alert! Condition red! Objects detected, approaching nine-thirty o'clock, fifteen degrees high. Neutrino emissions indicate nuclear engines."

"Alert! Condition yellow! Quiescent object detected in orbit about target planet, two-thirty o'clock, ten degrees low, circa 75,000 kilometers distant. Extremely massive. Repeat, quiescent. Low level of nuclear activity, but at bolometric temperature of ambient space. Possibly an abandoned space fortress, except for being so massive."

"Detected objects identified as space craft. Approaching with average radial velocity of 250 KPS. No evident deceleration. Number very large, estimated at five thousand. All units small, about the mass of our scoutboats."

The gabble went on until Golyev's voice cut through: "Attention! Fleet Admiral to bridge of all units. Now hear this." Sardonically: "The opposition is making a good try. Instead of building any real ships—they could only have constructed a few at best—they've turned out thousands of manned warboats. Their plan is obviously to cut through our formation, relying on speed, and release tracking torps in quantity. Stand by to repel. We have enough detectors, antimissiles, negafields, to overwhelm them in this department too. Once past us, the boats will need hours to decelerate and come back within decent shooting range. By that time we should be in orbit around the planet. Be alert for possible emergencies, of course. But I only expect standard operations will be necessary. Good shooting!"

Elva strained close to her screen. All at once she saw the Vaynamoan fleet, sparks, but a horde of them, twinkling among the stars. Closer! Her fingers strained against each other. *They must have some plan,* she told herself. *If I'm blown up in five minutes—I was hoping I'd get down to you, Karlavi. But if I don't, goodbye, goodbye.*

The fleets neared each other: on the one side, ponderous dreadnaughts, cruisers, auxiliary warcraft, escorting swarms of transport and engineer ships; on the opposite side, needle-thin boats whose sole armor was velocity. The guns of Chertkoi swung about, hoping for a lucky hit. At such speeds it was improbable. The fleets would interpenetrate and pass in a fractional second. The Vaynamoans could not be blasted until they came to grips near their home world. However, if a nuclear shell should find its mark now—what a blaze in heaven!

The flagship staggered.

"Engine room to bridge. What's happened?"

"Bridge to engine room. Gimme some power there! What in all destruction—?"

"*Sharyats* to *Askol*. *Sharyats* to *Askol*. Am thrown off course. Accelerating. What's going on?"

"Look out!"

"*Fodorev* to *Zuevots*! Look alive, you bloody fool! You'll ram us!"

Cushioned by the internal field, Elva felt only the minutest fraction of that immense velocity change. Even so a wave of sickness went through her. She clutched at the bunk stanchion. The desk ripped from a loose mooring and crashed into the wall, which buckled. The deck split open underfoot. A roar went through the entire hull, ribs groaned as they bent, plates screamed as they sheared. A girder snapped in twain and spat sharp fragments among a gun turret crew. A section broke apart, air gushed out, a hundred men died before the sealing bulkheads could close.

After a moment, the stabilizing energies regained interior control. The images on Elva's screen steadied. She drew a shaken lungful of air and watched. Out of formation, the *Askol* plunged within a kilometer of her sister ship the *Zuevots*—just when that cyclopean hull smashed into the cruiser *Fodorev*. Fire sheeted as accumulator banks were shorted. The two giants crumpled, glowed white at the point of impact, fused, and spun off in a lunatic waltz. Men and supplies pinwheeled from the cracks gaping in them. Two gun turrets wrapped their long barrels around each other like intertwining snakes. Then the whole mess struck a third vessel. Steel chunks exploded into space.

Through the noise and the human screaming, Golyev's voice blasted. "Pipe down there! Belay that! By Creation, I'll shoot the next man who whimpers! The enemy will be here in a minute. All stations, by the numbers, report."

A measure of discipline returned. These were fighting men. Instruments fingered outward, the remaining computers whirred, minds made deductive leaps, gunners returned to their posts. The Vaynamoan fleet passed through, and the universe exploded in brief pyrotechnics. Many a Chertkoian ship died then, its defenses too battered, its defenders too stunned to ward off the tracking torpedoes. But others fought back, saved themselves, and saw their enemies vanish in the distance.

Still they tumbled off course, their engines helpless to free them. Elva heard a physicist's clipped tones give the deduction from his readings. The entire fleet had been caught in a cone of gravitational force emanating from that massive object detected in orbit. Like a maelstrom of astronomical dimensions, it had snatched them from their paths. Those closest and in the most intense field strength—a fourth of the armada—had been wrecked by sheer deceleration. Now the force was drawing them down the vortex of itself.

"But that's impossible!" wailed the *Askol's* chief engineer. "A gravity attractor beam of that magnitude ...Admiral, it can't be done! The power requirements would burn out any generator in a microsecond!"

"It's being done," said Golyev harshly. "Maybe they figured out a new way to feed energy into a space distorter. Now, where are those figures on intensity? And my slide rule ...Yeh. The whole fleet will soon be in a field so powerful that—Well, we won't let it happen. Stand by to hit that generator with everything we've got."

"But sir ...we must have—I don't know how many ships—close enough to it now to be within total destruction radius."

"Tough on them. Stand by. Gunnery Control, fire when ready."

And then, whispered, even though that particular line was private and none else in the ship would hear: "Elva. Are you all right down there? Elva!"

Her hands had eased their trembling enough for her to light a cigarette. She didn't speak. Let him worry. It might reduce his efficiency.

Her screen did not happen to face the vortex source and thus did not show its destruction by the nuclear barrage. Not that that could have registered. The instant explosion of sun-center ferocity transcended any sense, human or electronic. Down on Vaynamo surface, in broad daylight, they must have turned dazzled eyes from that brilliance. Anyone within a thousand kilometers of those warheads died, no matter how much steel and force field he had interposed. Twoscore Chertkoian ships were suddenly manned by corpses. Those further in were fused to lumps. Still further in, they ceased to exist save as gas at millions of degrees temperature. The vessels already crashed on the giant station were turned into unstable isotopes, their very atoms dying.

But the station itself vanished. And Vaynamo had only the capacity to build one such monster. The Chertkoian ships were free again.

"Admiral to all captains!" cried Golyev. "Admiral to all captains. Let the reports wait. Clear the lines. I want every man in the fleet to hear me. Stand by for message.

"Now hear this. This is Supreme Commander Bors Golyev. We just took a rough blow, boys. The enemy had an unsuspected weapon, and cost us a lot of casualties. But we've destroyed the thing. I repeat, we blew it out of the cosmos. And I say, well done! I say also, we still have a hundred times the strength of the enemy, and he's shot his bolt. We're going on in. We're going to—"

"Alert! Condition red! Enemy boats returning. Enemy boats returning. Radial velocity circa 50 KPS, but acceleration circa 100 G."

"*What?*"

Elva herself saw the Vaynamoan shooting stars come back into sight.

Golyev tried hard to shout down the panic of his officers. Would they stop running around like old women? The enemy had developed something else, some method of accelerating at unheard-of rates under gravitational thrust. But not by witchcraft! It would be an internal-stress compensator developed to ultimate efficiency, plus an adaptation of whatever principle was used in the attractor vortex. Or it could be a breakthrough, a totally new principle, maybe something intermediate between the agoratron and the ordinary interplanetary drive…"Never mind what, you morons! They're still only a flock of splinters! Kill them!"

But the armada was roiling about in blind confusion. The detectors had given mere seconds of warning, which were lost in understanding that the warning was correct and in frantically seeking to rally men already shaken. Then the splinter fleet was in among the Chertkoians. It braked its furious relative velocity with a near-instantaneous quickness for which the Chertkoian gunners and gun computers had never been prepared. However, the Vaynamoan gunners were ready. And even a boat can carry torpedoes which will annihilate a battleship.

In a thousand fiery bursts, the armada died.

Not all of it. Unarmed craft were spared, if they would surrender. Vaynamoan boarding parties freed such of their countrymen as they found. The *Askol,* under Golyev's personal command, stood off its attackers and move doggedly outward toward regions where it could use the agoratron to escape. The captain of a prize revealed that over a hundred Vaynamoans were aboard the flagship. So the attempt to blow it up was abandoned. Instead, a large number of boats shot dummy missiles, which kept the defense fully occupied. Meanwhile a companion force lay alongside, cut its way through the armor, and sent men in.

The Chertkoian crew resisted But they were grossly outnumbered and outgunned. Most died, under bullets and grenades, gas and flamethrowers. Certain holdouts, who fortified an apartment, were welded in from the outside and left to starve or capitulate, whichever they chose. Even so, the *Askol* was so big that the boarding party took several hours to gain full possession.

The door opened. Elva stood up.

At first the half-dozen men who entered seemed foreign. In a minute—she was too tired and dazed to think clearly—she understood why. They were all in blue jackets and trousers, a uniform. She had never seen two Vaynamoans dressed exactly alike. *But of course they would be,* she thought in a vague fashion. *We had to build a navy, didn't we?*

And they remained her own people: fair skin, straight hair, high cheekbones, tilted light eyes which gleamed all the brighter through the soot of battle. And, yes, they still walked like Vaynamoans, the swinging freeman's gait and the head held high, such as she had not seen for …for how long? So their clothes didn't matter, nor even the guns in their hands.

Slowly, through the ringing in her ears, she realized that the combat noise had stopped.

A young man in the lead took a step in her direction, "My lady—" he began.

"Is that her for certain?" asked someone else, less gently. "Not a collaborator?"

A new man pushed his through the squad. He was grizzled, pale from lack of sun, wearing a sleazy prisoner's coverall. But a smile touched his lips, and his bow to Elva was deep.

"This is indeed my lady of Tervola," he said. To her: "When these men released me, up in Section Fourteen, I told them we'd probably find you here. I am so glad."

She needed a while to recognize him. "Oh. Yes." Her head felt heavy. It was all she could do to nod. "Captain Ivalo. I hope you're all right."

"I am, thanks to you, my lady. Someday we'll know how many hundreds are alive and sane—and here!—because of you."

The squad leader made another step forward, sheathed his machine pistol and lifted both hands toward her. He was a well-knit, good-looking man, blond of hair, a little older than she: in his mid-thirties, perhaps. He tried to speak, but no words came out, and then Ivalo drew him back.

"In a moment," said the ex-captive. "Let's first take care of the unpleasant business."

The leader hesitated, then, with a grimace, agreed. Two men shoved forward Bors Golyev. The admiral dripped blood from a dozen wounds and stumbled in his weariness. But when he saw Elva, he seemed to regain himself. "You weren't hurt," he breathed, as if the words were holy. "I was so afraid …"

Ivalo said like steel: "I've explained the facts of this case to the squad officer here, as well as his immediate superior. I'm sure you'll join us in our wish not to be inhumane, my lady. And yet a criminal trial in the regular courts would publicize matters best forgotten and could only give him a limited punishment. So we, here and now, under the conditions of war and in view of your high services—"

The squad officer interrupted. He was white about the nostrils. "Anything you order, my lady," he said. "You pass the sentence. We'll execute it at once."

"Elva," whispered Golyev.

She stared at him, remembering fire and enslavements and a certain man dead on a barricade. But everything seemed distant, not quite real.

"There's been too much suffering already," she said.

She pondered a few seconds. "Just take him out and shoot him."

The officer looked relieved. He led his men forth. Golyev started to speak, but was hustled away too fast.

Ivalo remained in the cabin. "My lady—" He began, slow and awkward.

"Yes?" As her weariness overwhelmed her, Elva sat down again on the bunk. She fumbled for a cigarette. There was no emotion in her, only a dull wish for sleep.

"I've wondered…Don't answer this if you don't want to. You've been through so much."

"That's all right," she said mechanically. "The trouble is over now, isn't it? I mean, we mustn't let the past obsess us."

"Of course. Uh, they tell me Vaynamo hasn't changed much. The defense effort was bound to affect society somewhat, but they've tried to minimize that, and succeeded. Our culture has a built-in stability, you know, a negative feedback. To be sure, we must still take action about the home planet of those devils. Liberate their slave worlds and make certain they can't ever try afresh. But that shouldn't be difficult.

"As for you, I inquired very carefully on your behalf. Tervola remains in your family. The land and the people are as you remember."

She closed her eyes, feeling the first thaw within herself. "Now I can sleep," she told him.

Remembering, she looked up with a touch of startlement. "But you had a question for me, Ivalo?"

"Yes. All this time, I couldn't help wondering. Why you stayed with the enemy. You could have escaped. Did you know all the time how great a service you were going to do?"

Her own smile was astonishing to her. "Well, I knew I couldn't be much use on Vaynamo," she said. "Could I? There was a chance I could help on Chertkoi. But I wasn't being brave. The worst had already happened to me. Now I need only wait …a matter of months only, my time …and everything bad would be over. Whereas, well, if I'd escaped from the Second Expedition, I'd have lived most of my life in the shadow of the Third. Please don't make a fuss about me. I was actually an awful coward."

His jaw dropped. "You mean you knew we'd win? But you couldn't have! Everything pointed the other way!"

The nightmare was fading more rapidly than she had dared hope. She shook her head, still smiling, not triumphant but glad to speak the knowledge which had kept her alive. "You're being unfair to our people. As unfair as the Chertkoians were. They thought that because we preferred social stability and room to breathe, we must be stagnant. They forgot you can have bigger adventures in, well, in the spirit, than in all the physical universe. We really did have a very powerful science and technology. It was oriented toward life, toward beautifying and improving instead of exploiting nature. But it wasn't less virile for that. Was it?"

"But we had no industry to speak of. We don't even now."

"I wasn't counting on our factories, I said, but on our science. When you told me about that horrible virus weapon being suppressed, you confirmed my hopes. We aren't saints. Our government wouldn't have been quite so quick to get rid of the plague—would at least have tried to bluff with it—if there weren't something better in prospect. Wouldn't they?

"I couldn't even guess what our scientists might develop, given two generations which the enemy did not have. I did think they would probably have to use physics rather than biology. And why not? You can't have an advanced chemical, medical, genetic, ecological technology without knowing all the physics there is to know. Can you? Quantum theory explains mutations. But it also explains atomic reactions, or whatever they used in those new machines.

"Oh, yes, Ivalo, I felt sure we'd win. All I had to do myself was work to get us prisoners—especially me, to be quite honest—get us there at the victory."

He looked at her with awe. Somehow that brought back the heaviness in her. *After all,* she thought..*sixty-two years. Tervola abides. But who will know me? I am going to be so much alone.*

Boots rang on metal. The young squad leader stepped back in. "That's that," he said. His bleakness vanished and he edged closer to Elva, softly, almost timidly.

"I trust," said Ivalo with a rich, growing pleasure in his voice, "that my lady will permit me to visit her from time to time."

"I hope you will," she murmured.

"We temporal castaways are bound to be disoriented for a while," he said. "We must help each other. You, for example, may have some trouble adjusting to the fact that your son Hauki, the Freeholder of Tervola—"

"Hauki!" She sprang to her feet. The cabin blurred around her.

"—is now a vigorous elderly man who looks back on a most successful life," said Ivalo. "Which includes the begetting of Karlavi here." Her grandson's strong hands closed about her own. "Who in turn," finished Ivalo, "is the recent father of a bouncing baby boy named Hauki. And all your people are waiting to welcome you home."

The Man Who Came Early

Yes, when a man grows old he has heard so much that is strange there's little more can surprise him. They say the king in Miklagard has a beast of gold before his high seat, which stands up and roars. I have it from Eilif Eiriksson, who served in the guard down there and he is a steady fellow when not drunk. He has also seen the Greek fire used, it burns on water.

So, priest, I am not unwilling to believe what you say about the White Christ. I have been in England and France myself, and seen how the folks prosper. He must be a very powerful god to ward so many realms…and did you say that everyone who is baptized will be given a white robe? I would like to have one. They mildew, of course, in this cursed wet Iceland weather, but a small sacrifice to the house elves should—No sacrifices? Come now! I'll give up horseflesh if I must, my teeth not being what they were, but every sensible man knows how much trouble the elves make if they're not fed.

…Well, let's have another cup and talk about it. How do you like the beer? It's my own brew, you know. The cups I got in England, many years back. I was a young man then…time goes, time goes. Afterward I came back and inherited this, my father's steading, and have not left it since. Well enough to go in viking as a youth, but grown older you see where the real wealth lies: here, in the land and the cattle.

Stoke up the fires, Hjalti. It's growing cold. Sometimes I think the winters are colder than when I was a boy. Thorbrand of the Salmondale says so, but he believes the gods are angry because so many are turning from them. You'll have trouble winning Thorbrand over, priest. A stubborn man. Myself I am open-minded, and willing to listen at least.

…Now then. There is one point on which I must correct you. The end of the world is not coming in two years. This I know.

And if you ask me how I know, that's a very long tale, and in some ways a terrible one. Glad I am to be old, and safely in the earth before that great tomorrow comes. It will be an eldritch time before the frost giants march…oh, very well, before the angel blows his battle horn. One reason I hearken to your preaching is that I know the White Christ will conquer Thor. I know Iceland is going to be Christian erelong, and it seems best to range myself on the winning side.

No, I've had no visions. This is a happening of five years ago, which my own household and neighbors can swear to. They mostly did not believe what the stranger told; I do, more or less, if only because I don't think a liar could wreak so much harm. I loved my daughter, priest, and after it was over I made a good marriage for her. She did not naysay it, but now she sits out on the ness-farm with her husband and never a word to me; and I hear he is ill pleased with her silence and moodiness, and spends his nights with an Irish concubine. For this I cannot blame him, but it grieves me.

Well, I've drunk enough to tell the whole truth now and whether you believe it or not makes no odds to me. Here…you, girls!…fill these cups again for I'll have a dry throat before I finish the telling.

It begins, then, on a day in early summer, five years ago. At that time, my wife Ragnhild and I had only two unwed children still living with us: our youngest son Helgi of seventeen winters, and our daughter Thorgunna, of eighteen. The girl, being fair, had already had suitors. But she refused them, and I am not a man who would compel his daughter. As for Helgi, he was ever a lively one, good with his hands but a breakneck youth. He is now serving in the guard of King Olaf of Norway. Besides these, of course, we had about ten housefolk—two Irish thralls, two girls to help with the women's work, and half a dozen hired carles. This is not a small steading.

You have not seen how my land lies. About two miles to the west is the bay; the thorps at Reykjavik are about five miles south. The land rises toward the Long Jökull so that my acres are hilly; but it's good hayland, and there is often drift-wood on the beach. I've built a shed down there for it as well as a boathouse.

There had been a storm the night before, so Helgi and I were going down to look for drift. You, coming from Norway, do not know how precious wood is to us Icelanders who have only a few scrubby trees and must bring all our timber from abroad. Back there men have often been burned in their houses by their foes, but we count that the worst of deeds, through it's not unknown.

I was on good terms with my neighbors so we took only hand weapons. I my ax, Helgi a sword, and the two carles we had with us bore spears. It was a day washed clean by the night's fury, and the sun fell bright on long wet grass. I saw my garth lying rich around its courtyard, sleek cows and sheep, smoke rising from the roof hole of the hall, and knew I'd not done so ill in my lifetime. My son Helgi's hair fluttered in the low west wind as we left the steading behind a ridge and neared the water. Strange how well I remember all which happened that day, somehow it was a sharper day than most.

When we came down to the strand, the sea was beating heavy, white and gray out to the world's edge. A few gulls flew screaming above us, frightened off a cod washed up onto the shore. I saw there was a litter of no few sticks, even a baulk of timber…from some ship carrying it that broke up during the night, I suppose. That was a useful find, though, as a careful man, I would later sacrifice to be sure the owner's ghost wouldn't plague me.

We had fallen to and were dragging the baulk toward the shed when Helgi cried out. I ran for my ax as I looked the way he pointed. We had no feuds then, but there are always outlaws.

This one seemed harmless, though. Indeed, as he stumbled nearer across the black sand I thought him quite unarmed and wondered what had happened. He was a big man and strangely clad—he wore coat and breeches and shoes like anyone else, but they were of peculiar cut and he bound his trousers with leggings rather than thongs. Nor had I ever seen a helmet like his: it was almost square, and came down to cover his neck, but it had no nose guard; it was held in place by a leather strap. And this you may not believe, but it was not metal, yet had been cast in one piece!

He broke into a staggering run as he neared, and flapped his arms and croaked something. The tongue was none I had ever heard, and I have heard many; it was like dogs barking. I saw that he was clean-shaven and his black hair cropped short, and thought he might be French. Otherwise he was a young man, and good-looking, with blue eyes and regular features. From his skin I judged that he spent much time indoors yet he had a fine manly build.

"Could he have been shipwrecked?" asked Helgi.

"His clothes are dry and unstained," I said, "nor has he been wandering long, for there's no stubble on his chin. Yet I've heard of no strangers guesting hereabouts."

We lowered our weapons, and he came up to us and stood gasping. I saw that his coat and the shirt behind was fastened with bonelike buttons rather than laces, and were of heavy weave. About his neck he had fastened a strip of cloth tucked into his coat. These garments were all in brownish hues. His shoes were of a sort new to me, very well cobbled. Here and there on his coat were bits of brass, and he had three broken stripes on each sleeve; also a black band with white letters, the same letters being on his helmet. Those were not runes, but Roman letters—thus: MP. He wore a broad belt, with a small clublike thing of metal in a sheath at the hip and also a real club.

"I think he must be a warlock," muttered my carle Sigurd. "Why else all those tokens?"

"They may only be ornament, or to ward against witchcraft," I soothed him. Then, to the stranger. "I hight Ospak Ulfsson of Hillstead. What is your errand?"

He stood with his chest heaving and a wildness in his eyes. He must have run a long way. Then he moaned and sat down and covered his face.

"If he's sick, best we get him to the house," said Helgi. His eyes gleamed—we see so few new faces here.

"No...no..." The stranger looked up. "Let me rest a moment—"

He spoke the Norse tongue readily enough, though with a thick accent not easy to follow and with many foreign words I did not understand.

The other carle, Grim, hefted his spear. "Have Vikings landed?" he asked.

"When did Vikings ever come to Iceland?" I snorted. "It's the other way around."

The newcomer shook his head, as if it had been struck. He got shakily to his feet. "What happened?" he said. "What happened to the city?"

"What city?" I asked reasonably.

"Reykjavik!" he groaned. "Where is it?"

"Five miles south, the way you came—unless you mean the bay itself," I said.

"No! There was only a beach, and a few wretched huts, and—"

"Best not let Hjalmar Broadnose hear you call his thorp that," I counseled.

"But there was a city!" he cried. Wildness lay in his eyes. "I was crossing the street, it was a storm, and there was a crash and then I stood on the beach and the city was gone!"

"He's mad," said Sigurd, backing away. "Be careful...if he starts to foam at the mouth, it means he's going berserk."

"Who are you?" babbled the stranger. "What are you doing in those clothes? Why the spears?"

"Somehow," said Helgi, "he does not sound crazed—only frightened and bewildered. Something evil has happened to him."

"I'm not staying near a man under a curse!" yelped Sigurd, and started to run away.

"Come back!" I bawled. "Stand where you are or I'll cleave your louse-bitten head!"

That stopped him, for he had no kin who would avenge him; but he would not come closer. Meanwhile the stranger had calmed down to the point where he could at least talk evenly.

"Was it the *aitchbomb*?" he asked. "Has the war started?"

He used that word often, *aitchbomb*, so I know it now, though unsure of what it means. It seems to be a kind of Greek fire. As for the war, I knew not which war he meant, and told him so.

"There was a great thunderstorm last night," I added. "And you say you were out in one too. Perhaps Thor's hammer knocked you from your place to here."

"But where is here?" he replied. His voice was more dulled than otherwise, now that the first terror had lifted.

"I told you. This is Hillstead, which is on Iceland."

"But that's where I was!" he mumbled. "Reykjavik...what happened? Did the *aitchbomb* destroy everything while I was unconscious?"

"Nothing has been destroyed," I said.

"Perhaps he means the fire at Olafsvik last month," said Helgi.

"No, no, no!" He buried his face in his hands. After a while he looked up and said. "See here. I am Sergeant Gerald Roberts of the United States Army base on Iceland. I was in Reykjavik and got struck by lightning or something. Suddenly I was standing on the beach, and got frightened and ran. That's all. Now, can you tell me how to get back to the base?"

Those were more or less his words, priest. Of course, we did not grasp half of it, and made him repeat it several times and explain the words. Even then we did not understand, except that he was from some country called the United States of America, which he said lies beyond Greenland to the west, and that he and some others were on Iceland to help our folk against their enemies. Now this I did not consider a lie—more a mistake or imagining. Grim would have cut him down for thinking us stupid enough to swallow that tale, but I could see that he meant it.

Trying to explain it to us cooled him off. "Look here," he said, in too reasonable a tone for a feverish man, "perhaps we can get at the truth from your side. Has there been no war you know of? Nothing which—well, look here. My country's men first came to Iceland to guard it against the Germans…now it is the Russians, but then it was the Germans. When was that?"

Helgi shook his head. "That never happened that I know of," he said. "Who are these Russians?" He found out later that Gardariki was meant. "Unless," he said, "the old warlocks—"

"He means the Irish monks," I explained. "There were a few living here when the Norsemen came, but they were driven out. That was, hm, somewhat over a hundred years ago, Did your folk ever help the monks?"

"I never heard of them!" he said. His breath sobbed in his throat. "You…didn't you Icelanders come from Norway?"

"Yes, about a hundred years ago," I answered patiently. "After King Harald Fairhair took all the Norse lands and—"

"A hundred years ago!" he whispered. I saw whiteness creep up under his skin "What year is this?"

We gaped at him. "Well, it's the second year after the great salmon catch," I tried.

"What year after Christ, I mean?" It was a hoarse prayer

"Oh, so you are a Christian? Hm, let me think…I talked with a bishop in England once, we were holding him for ransom, and he said…let me see…I think he said this Christ man lived a thousand years ago, or maybe a little less."

"A thousand—" He shook his head; and then something went out of him, he stood with glassy eyes—yes, I have seen glass, I told you I am a traveled man—he stood thus, and when we led him toward the garth he went like a small child.

You can see for yourself, priest, that my wife Ragnhild is still good to look upon even in eld, and Thorgunna took after her. She was—is tall and slim, with a dragon's hoard of golden hair. She being a maiden then, it flowed loose over her shoulders. She had great blue eyes and a small heart-shaped face and very red lips. Withal she was a merry one, and kind-hearted, so that all men loved her. Sverri Snorrason went in voking when she refused and was slain, but no one had the wit to see that she was unlucky.

We led this Gerald Samsson—when I asked, he said his father was named Sam—we led him home, leaving Sigurd and Grim to finish gathering the driftwood. There are some who would not have a Christian in their house, for fear of witchcraft, but I am a broad-minded man and Helgi of course was wild for anything new. Our guest stumbled like a blind man over the fields, but seemed to wake up as we entered the yard. His eyes went around the buildings that enclosed it from the stables and sheds to the smokehouse, the brewery, the kitchen, the bathhouse, the god-shrine, and thence to the hall. And Thorgunna was standing in the doorway.

Their gazes locked for a moment, and I saw her color but thought little of it then. Our shoes rang on the flagging as we crossed the yard and kicked the dogs aside. My two thralls paused in cleaning out the stables to gawp, until I got them back to work with the remark that a man good for naught else was always a pleasing sacrifice. That's one useful practice you Christians lack; I've never made a human offering myself, but you know not how helpful is the fact that I could do so.

We entered the hall and I told the folk Gerald's name and how we had found him. Ragnhild set her maids hopping, to stoke up the fire in the middle trench and fetch beer while I led Gerald to the high seat and sat down by him. Thorgunna brought us the filled horns.

Gerald tasted the brew and made a face. I felt somewhat offended, for my beer is reckoned good, and asked him if there was aught wrong. He laughed with a harsh note and said no, but he was used to beer that foamed and was not sour.

"And where might they make such?" I wondered testily.

"Everywhere. Iceland, too—no…" He stared emptily before him. "Let's say… in Vinland."

"Where is Vinland?" I asked.

"The country to the west whence I came. I thought you knew…wait a bit." He shook his head. "Maybe I can find out—have you heard of a man named Leif Eiriksson?"

"No," I said. Since then it has struck me that this was one proof of his tale, for Leif Eiriksson is now a well-known chief; and I also take more seriously those tales of land seen by Bjarni Herjulfsson.

"His father, maybe—Eirik the Red?" asked Gerald.

"Oh yes," I said. "If you mean the Norseman who came hither because of a manslaughter, and left Iceland in turn for the same reason, and has now settled with other folk in Greenland."

"Then this is…a little before Leif's voyage," he muttered. "The late tenth century."

"See here," demanded Helgi, "we've been patient with you, but this is no time for riddles. We save those for feasts and drinking bouts. Can you not say plainly whence you come and how you got here?"

Gerald covered his face, shaking.

"Let the man alone, Helgi," said Thorgunna. "Can you not see he's troubled?"

He raised his head and gave her the look of a hurt dog that someone has patted. It was dim in the hall, enough light coming in by the loft windows so no candles were lit, but not enough to see well by. Nevertheless, I marked a reddening in both their faces.

Gerald drew a long breath and fumbled about; his clothes were made with pockets. He brought out a small parchment box and from it took a little white stick that he put in his mouth. Then he took out another box, and a wooden stick from it which burst into flame when scratched. With the fire he kindled the stick in his mouth, and sucked in the smoke.

We all stared. "Is that a Christian rite?" asked Helgi.

"No…not just so." A wry, disappointed smile twisted his lips. "I'd have thought you'd be more surprised, even terrified."

"It's something new," I admitted, "but we're a sober folk on Iceland. Those fire sticks could be useful. Did you come to trade in them?"

"Hardly." He sighed. The smoke he breathed in seemed to steady him, which was odd, because the smoke in the hall had made him cough and water at the eyes. "The truth is…something you will not believe. I can scarce believe it myself."

We waited. Thorgunna stood leaning forward, her lips parted.

"That lightning bolt—" Gerald nodded wearily. "I was out in the storm, and somehow the lightning must have struck me in just the right way, a way that happens only once in many thousands of times. It threw me back into the past."

Those were his words, priest. I did not understand, and told him so.

"It's hard to see," he agreed. "God give that I'm only dreaming. But if this is a dream, I must endure till I wake up…well, look. I was born one thousand, nine hundred and thirty-two years after Christ, in a land to the west which you have not yet found. In the twenty-third year of my life, I was in Iceland as part of my country's army. The lightning struck me, and now…now it is less than one thousand years after Christ, and yet I am here—almost a thousand years before I was born, I am here!"

We sat very still. I signed myself with the Hammer and took a long pull from my horn. One of the maids whimpered, and Ragnhild whispered so fiercely I could hear. "Be still. The poor fellow's out of his head. There's no harm in him."

I agreed with her, though less sure of the last part of it. The gods can speak through a madman, and the gods are not always to be trusted. Or he could turn berserker or he could be under a heavy curse that would also touch us.

He sat staring before him, and I caught a few fleas and cracked them while I thought about it. Gerald noticed and asked with some horror if we had many fleas here.

"Why, of course," said Thorgunna. "Have you none?"

"No." He smiled crookedly. "Not yet."

"Ah," she sighed, "you must be sick."

She was a level-headed girl. I saw her thought, and so did Ragnhild and Helgi. Clearly, a man so sick that he had no fleas could be expected to rave. There was still some worry about whether we might catch the illness, but I deemed it unlikely; his trouble was all in the head, perhaps from a blow he had taken. In any case, the matter was come down to earth now, something we could deal with.

As a godi, a chief who holds sacrifices it behooved me not to turn a stranger out. Moreover, if he could fetch in many of those little fire-kindling sticks, a profitable trade might be built up. So I said Gerald should go to bed. He protested, but we manhandled him into the shut-bed and there he lay tired and was soon asleep. Thorgunna said she would take care of him.

The next day I decided to sacrifice a horse, both because of the timber we had found and to take away any curse there might be on Gerald. Furthermore, the beast I had picked was old and useless, and we were short of fresh meat. Gerald had spent the day lounging moodily around the garth, but when I came in to supper I found him and my daughter laughing.

"You seem to be on the road to health," I said.

"Oh yes. It...could be worse for me." He sat down at my side as the carles set up the trestle table and the maids brought in the food. "I was ever much taken with the age of the vikings, and I have some skills."

"Well," I said, "if you've no home, we can keep you here for a while."

"I can work," he said eagerly. "I'll be worth my pay."

Now I knew he was from a far land, because what chief would work on any land but his own, and for hire at that? Yet he had the easy manner of the highborn, and had clearly eaten well all his life. I overlooked that he had made no gifts; after all, he was shipwrecked.

"Maybe you can get passage back to your United States," said Helgi. "We could hire a ship. I'm fain to see that realm."

"No," said Gerald bleakly. "There is no such place. Not yet."

"So you still hold to that idea you came from tomorrow? grunted Sigurd. "Crazy notion. Pass the pork."

"I do," said Gerald. There was a calm on him now. "And I can prove it."

"I don't see how you speak our tongue, if you come from so far away," I said. I would not call a man a liar to his face, unless we were swapping brags in a friendly way, but...

"They speak otherwise in my land and time," he replied, "but it happens that in Iceland the tongue changed little since the old days, and I learned it when I came there."

"If you are a Christian," I said, "you must bear with us while we sacrifice tonight."

"I've naught against that," he said. "I fear I never was a very good Christian. I'd like to watch. How is it done?"

I told him how I would smite the horse with a hammer before the god, and cut his throat, and sprinkle the blood about with willow twigs; thereafter we would butcher the carcass and feast. He said hastily: "There's my chance to prove what I am. I have a weapon that will kill the horse with...with a flash of lightning."

What is it? I wondered. We all crowded around while he took the metal club out of his sheath and showed it to us. I had my doubts; it looked well enough for hitting a man, perhaps, but had no edge, though a wondrously skillful smith had forged it. "Well, we can try," I said.

He showed us what else he had in his pockets. There were some coins of remarkable roundness and sharpness, a small key, a stick with lead in it for writing, a flat purse holding many bits of marked paper; when he told us solemnly that some of this paper was money, even Thorgunna had to laugh. Best of all was a knife whose blade folded into the handle. When he saw me admiring that, he gave it to me, which was well done for a shipwrecked man. I said I would give him clothes and a good ax, as well as lodging for as long as needful.

No, I don't have the knife now. You shall hear why. It's a pity, for it was a good knife, though rather small.

What were you ere the war arrow went out in your land?" asked Helgi. "A merchant?"

"No," said Gerald. "I was an…engineer…that is I was learning how to be one. That's a man who builds things, bridges and roads and tools…more than just an artisan. So I think my knowledge could be of great value here." I saw a fever in his eyes. "Yes, give me time and I'll be a king!"

"We have no king in Iceland," I grunted. "Our forefathers came hither to get away from kings. Now we meet at the Things to try suits and pass new laws, but each man must get his own redress as best he can."

"But suppose the man in the wrong won't yield?" he asked.

"Then there can be a fine feud," said Helgi, and went on to relate with sparkling eyes some of the killings there had lately been. Gerald looked unhappy and fingered his gun. That is what he called his fire-spitting club.

"Your clothing is rich," said Thorgunna softly. "Your folk must own broad acres at home."

"No," he said, "our…our king gives every man in the army clothes like these. As for my family, we owned no land, we rented our home in a building where many other families also dwelt."

I am not purse-proud, but it seemed to me he had not been honest, a landless man sharing my high seat like a chief. Thorgunna covered my huffiness by saying. "You will gain a farm later."

After dark we went out to the shrine. The carles had built a fire before it, and as I opened the door the wooden Odin appeared to leap forth. Gerald muttered to my daughter that it was a clumsy bit of carving, and since my father had made it I was still more angry with him. Some folks have no understanding of the fine arts.

Nevertheless, I let him help me lead the horse forth to the altar stone. I took the blood-bowl in my hands and said he could now slay the beast if he would. He drew his gun, put the end behind the horse's ear, and squeezed. There was a crack, and the beast quivered and dropped with a hole blown through its skull, wasting the brains—a clumsy weapon. I caught a whiff of smell, sharp and bitter like that around a volcano. We all jumped, one of the women screamed, and Gerald looked proud. I gathered my wits and finished the rest of the sacrifice as usual. Gerald did not like having blood sprinkled over him, but then, of course, he was a Christian. Nor would he take more than a little of the soup and flesh.

Afterward Helgi questioned him about the gun, and he said it could kill a man at bowshot distance but there was no witchcraft in it, only use of some tricks we did not know as yet. Having heard of the Greek fire, I believed him. A gun could be useful in a fight, as indeed I was to learn, but it did not seem very practical—iron costing what it does, and months of forging needed for each one.

I worried more about the man himself.

And the next morning I found him telling Thorgunna a great deal of foolishness about his home, buildings tall as mountains and wagons that flew or went without horses. He said there were eight or nine thousand thousands of folk in his city, a burgh called New Jorvik or the like. I enjoy a good brag as well as the next man, but this was too much and I told him gruffly to come along and help me get in some strayed cattle.

* * *

After a day scrambling around the hills I knew well enough that Gerald could scarce tell a cow's prow from her stern. We almost had the strays once, but he ran stupidly across their path and turned them so the work was all to do again. I asked him with strained courtesy if he could milk, shear, wield scythe or flail, and he said no, he had never lived on a farm.

"That's a pity," I remarked, "for everyone on Iceland does, unless he be outlawed."

He flushed at my tone. "I can do enough else," he answered. "Give me some tools and I'll show you metalwork well done."

That brightened me, for truth to tell, none of our household was a very gifted smith. "That's an honorable trade," I said, "and you can be of great help. I have a broken sword and several bent spearheads to be mended, and it were no bad idea to shoe all the horses." His admission that he did know how to put on a shoe was not very dampening to me then.

We had returned home as we talked, and Thorgunna came angrily forward. "That's no way to treat a guest, father!" she said. "Making him work like a carle, indeed!"

Gerald smiled. "I'll be glad to work," he said. "I need a…a stake…something to start me afresh. Also, I want to repay a little of your kindness."

That made me mild toward him, and I said it was not his fault they had different customs in the United States. On the morrow he could begin work in the smithy, and I would pay him, yet he would be treated as an equal, since craftsmen are valued. This earned him black looks from the housefolk.

That evening he entertained us well with stories of his home; true or not, they made good listening. However, he had no real polish, being unable to compose even two lines of verse. They must be a raw and backward lot in the United States. He said his task in the army had been to keep order among the troops. Helgi said this was unheard-of, and he must be a brave man who would offend so many men, but Gerald said folk obeyed him out of fear of the king. When he added that the term of a levy in the United States was two years, and that men could be called to war even in harvest time, I said he was well out of a country with so ruthless and powerful a king.

"No," he answered wistfully, "we are a free folk, who say what we please."

"But it seems you may not do as you please," said Helgi.

"Well," he said, "we may not murder a man just because he offends us."

"Not even if he has slain your own kin?" asked Helgi.

"No. It is for the…the king to take vengeance on behalf of us all."

I chuckled. "Your yarns are good," I said, "but there you've hit a snag. How could the king even keep track of all the murders, let alone avenge them? Why, the man wouldn't even have time to beget an heir!"

He could say no more for all the laughter that followed.

The next day Gerald went to the smithy, with a thrall to pump the bellows for him. I was gone that day and night, down to Reykjavik to dicker with Hjalmar Broadnose about some sheep. I invited him back for an overnight stay, and we rode into the garth with his son Ketill, a red-haired sulky youth of twenty winters who had been refused by Thorgunna.

I found Gerald sitting gloomily on a bench in the hall. He wore the clothes I had given him, his own having been spoiled by ash and sparks—what had he awaited, the fool? He was talking in a low voice with my daughter.

"Well," I said as I entered, "how went it?"

My man Grim snickered. "He has ruined two spearheads, but we put out the fire he started ere the whole smithy burned."

"How's this?" I cried. "I thought you said you were a smith."

Gerald stood up, defiantly. "I worked with other tools, and better ones, at home," he replied. "You do it differently here."

It seemed he had built up the fire too hot; his hammer had struck everywhere but the place it should; he had wrecked the temper of the steel through not knowing when to quench it. Smithcraft takes years to learn, of course, but he should have admitted he was not even an apprentice.

"Well," I snapped, "what can you do, then, to earn your bread?" It irked me to be made a fool of before Hjalmar and Ketill, whom I had told about the stranger.

"Odin alone knows," said Grim. "I took him with me to ride after your goats, and never have I seen a worse horseman. I asked him if he could even spin or weave, and he said no."

"That was no question to ask a man!" flared Thorgunna. "He should have slain you for it!"

"He should indeed," laughed Grim. "But let me carry on the tale. I thought we would also repair your bridge over the foss. Well, he can just barely handle a saw, but he nearly took his own foot off with the adz."

"We don't use those tools, I tell you!" Gerald doubled his fists and looked close to tears.

I motioned my guests to sit down. "I don't suppose you can butcher a hog or smoke it either," I said.

"No." I could scarce hear him.

"Well, then, man…what can you do?"

"I—" He could get no words out.

"You were a warrior," said Thorgunna.

"Yes—that I was!" he said, his face kindling.

"Small use in Iceland when you have no other skills," I grumbled, "but perhaps, if you can get passage to the eastlands, some king will take you in his guard." Myself I doubted it, for a guardsman needs manners that will do credit to his master; but I had not the heart to say so.

Ketill Hjalmarsson had plainly not liked the way Thorgunna stood close to Gerald and spoke for him. Now he sneered and said: "I might even doubt your skill in fighting."

"That I have been trained for," said Gerald grimly.

"Will you wrestle with me, then?" asked Ketill.

"Gladly!" spat Gerald.

Priest, what is a man to think? As I grow older, I find life to be less and less the good-and-evil, black-and-white thing you say it is; we are all of us some hue of gray. This useless fellow, this spiritless lout who could even be asked if he did women's work and not lift ax, went out in the yard with Ketill Hjalmarsson and threw him three times running. There was some trick he had of grabbing the clothes as Ketill charged…I called a stop when the youth was nearing murderous rage, praised them both, and filled the beer-horns. But Ketill brooded sullenly on the bench all evening.

Gerald said something about making a gun like his own. It would have to be bigger, a cannon he called it, and could sink ships and scatter armies. He would need the help of smiths and also various stuffs. Charcoal was easy, and sulfur could be found in the volcano country, I suppose, but what is this saltpeter?

Also, being suspicious by now, I questioned him closely as to how he would make such a thing. Did he know just how to mix the powder? No, he admitted. What size would the gun have to be? When he told me—at least as long as a man—I laughed and asked him how a piece that size could be cast or bored, even if we could scrape together that much iron. This he did not know either.

"You haven't the tools to make the tools to make the tools," he said. I don't know what he meant by that. "God help me I can't run through a thousand years of history all by myself."

He took out the last of his little smoke sticks and lit it. Helgi had tried a puff earlier and gotten sick, though he remained a friend of Gerald's. Now my son proposed to take a boat in the morning and go up to Ice Fjord, where I had some money outstanding I wanted to collect. Hjalmar and Ketill said they would come along for the trip, and Thorgunna pleaded so hard that I let her come along too.

"An ill thing," muttered Sigurd. "All men know the landtrolls like not a woman aboard a ship. It's unlucky."

"How did your father ever bring women to this island?" I grinned.

Now I wish I had listened to him. He was not a clever man, but he often knew whereof he spoke.

At this time I owned a half share in a ship that went to Norway, bartering wadmal for timber. It was a profitable business until she ran afoul of vikings during the disorders while Olaf Tryggvason was overthrowing Jarl Haakon there. Some men will do anything to make a living—thieves, cutthroats, they ought to be hanged, the worthless robbers pouncing on honest merchantmen. Had they any courage or honesty they would go to Ireland, which is full of plunder.

Well, anyhow, the ship was abroad, but we had three boats and took one of these. Besides myself, Thorgunna, and Helgi, Hjalmar and Ketill went along, with Grim and Gerald. I saw how the stranger winced at the cold water as we launched her, and afterward took off his shoes and stockings to let his feet dry. He had been surprised to learn we had a bathhouse—did he think us savages?—but still, he was dainty as a woman and soon moved upwind of our feet.

There was a favoring breeze, so we raised mast and sail. Gerald tried to help, but of course did not know one line from another and got them tangled. Grim snarled at him and Ketill laughed nastily. But erelong we were under way, and he came and sat by me where I had the steering oar.

He had plainly lain long awake thinking, and now he ventured timidly: "In my land they have…will have a rig and rudder which are better than this. With them, you can criss-cross against the wind."

"Ah, so now our skilled sailor must give us redes!" sneered Ketill.

"Be still" said Thorgunna sharply. "Let Gerald speak!"

He gave her a sly look of thanks, and I was not unwilling to listen. "This is something which could easily be made," he said. "I've used such boats myself, and know them well. First, then, the sail should not be square and hung from a yardarm, but three-cornered, with the third corner lashed to a yard swiveling from the mast. Then, your steering oar is in the wrong place—there should be a rudder in the middle of the stern, guided by a bar." He was eager now, tracing the plan with his fingernail on Thorgunna's cloak. "With these two things, and a deep keel—going down to about the height of a man for a boat this size—a ship can move across the path of the wind…so. And another sail can be hung between the mast and the prow."

Well, priest, I must say the idea had its merits, and were it not for fear of bad luck—for everything of his was unlucky—I might even now play with it. But there are clear drawbacks, which I pointed out to him in a reasonable way.

"First and worst," I said, "this rudder and deep keel would make it all but impossible to beach the ship or sail up a shallow river. Perhaps they have many harbors where you hail from but here a craft must take what landings she can find, and must be speedily launched if there should be an attack. Second, this mast of yours would be hard to unstep when the wind dropped and oars came out. Third, the sail is the wrong shape to stretch as an awning when one must sleep at sea."

"The ship could lie out, and you could go to land in a small boat," he said. "Also, you could build cabins aboard for shelter."

"The cabins would get in the way of the oars," I said, "unless the ship were hopelessly broad-beamed or unless the oarsmen sat below a deck like the galley slaves of Miklagard; and free men would not endure rowing in such foulness."

"Must you have oars?" he asked like a very child.

Laughter barked along the hull. Even the gulls hovering to starboard, where the shore rose darkly, mewed their scorn. "Do they also have tame winds in the place whence you came?" snorted Hjalmar. "What happens if you're becalmed—for days, maybe, with provisions running out—"

"You could build a ship big enough to carry many weeks' provisions," said Gerald.

"If you have the wealth of a king, you could," said Helgi. "And such a king's ship, lying helpless on a flat sea, would be swarmed by every viking from here to Jomsborg. As for leaving the ship out on the water while you make camp, what would you have for shelter, or for defense if you should be trapped there?"

Gerald slumped. Thorgunna said to him gently: "Some folks have no heart to try anything new. I think it's a grand idea."

He smiled at her, a weary smile, and plucked up the will to say something about a means for finding north even in cloudy weather—he said there were stones which always pointed north when hung by a string. I told him kindly that I would be most interested if he could find me some of this stone; or if he knew where it was to be had, I could ask a trader to fetch me a piece. But this he did not know, and fell silent. Ketill opened his mouth, but got such an edged look from Thorgunna that he shut it again; his looks declared plainly enough what a liar he thought Gerald to be.

The wind turned contrary after a while, so we lowered the mast and took to the oars. Gerald was strong and willing, though clumsy; however, his hands were so soft that erelong they bled. I offered to let him rest, but he kept doggedly at the work.

Watching him sway back and forth, under the dreary creak of the tholes, the shaft red and wet where he gripped it, I thought much about him. He had done everything wrong which a man could do—thus I imagined then, not knowing the future—and I did not like the way Thorgunna's eyes strayed to him and rested there. He was no man for my daughter, landless and penniless and helpless. Yet I could not keep from liking him. Whether his tale was true or only a madness, I felt he was honest about it; and surely there was something strange about the way he had come. I noticed the cuts on his chin from my razor; he had said he was not used to our kind of shaving and would grow a beard. He had tried hard. I wondered how well I would have done, landing alone in this witch country of his dreams, with a gap of forever between me and my home.

Perhaps that same misery was what had turned Thorgunna's heart. Women are a kittle breed, priest, and you who leave them alone belike understand them as well as I who have slept with half a hundred in six different lands. I do not think they even understand themselves. Birth and life and death, those are the great mysteries, which none will ever fathom, and a woman is closer to them than a man.

The ill wind stiffened, the sea grew iron gray and choppy under low leaden clouds, and our headway was poor. At sunset we could row no more, but must pull in to a small unpeopled bay and make camp as well as could be on the strand.

We had brought firewood along, and tinder. Gerald, though staggering with weariness, made himself useful, his little sticks kindling the blaze more easily than flint and steel. Thorgunna set herself to cook our supper. We were not warded by the boat from a lean, whining wind; her cloak fluttered like wings and her hair blew wild above the streaming flames. It was the time of light nights, the sky a dim dusky blue, the sea a wrinkled metal sheet and the land like something risen out of dream-mists. We men huddled in our cloaks, holding numbed hands to the fire and saying little.

I felt some cheer was needed, and ordered a cask of my best and strongest ale broached. An evil Norn made me do that, but no man escapes his weird. Our bellies seemed all the emptier now when our noses drank in the sputter of a spitted joint, and the ale went swiftly to our heads. I remember declaiming the death song of Ragnar Hairybreeks for no other reason than that I felt like declaiming it.

Thorgunna came to stand over Gerald where he slumped. I saw how her fingers brushed his hair, ever so lightly, and Ketill Hjalmarsson did too. "Have they no verses in your land?" she asked.

"Not like yours," he said, looking up. Neither of them looked away again. "We sing rather than chant. I wish I had my guitar here—that's a kind of harp."

"Ah, an Irish bard!" said Hjalmar Broadnose.

I remember strangely well how Gerald smiled and what he said in his own tongue, though I know not the meaning: *"Only on me mither's side, begorra."* I suppose it was magic.

"Well, sing for us," asked Thorgunna.

"Let me think," he said. "I shall have to put it in Norse words for you." After a little while, staring up at her through the windy night, he began a song. It had a tune I liked, thus:

> *From this valley they tell me you're leaving,*
> *I shall miss your bright eyes and sweet smile*
> *You will carry the sunshine with you,*
> *That has brightened my life all the while…*

I don't remember the rest, except that it was not quite decent.

When he had finished, Hjalmar and Grim went over to see if the meat was done. I saw a glimmering of tears in my daughter's eyes. "That was a lovely thing," she said.

Ketill sat upright. The flames splashed his face with wild, running hues. There was a rawness in his tone: "Yes, we've found what this fellow can do: sit about and make pretty songs for the girls. Keep him for that, Ospak."

Thorgunna whitened, and Helgi clapped hand to sword. I saw how Gerald's face darkened, and his voice was thick: "That was no way to talk. Take it back."

Ketill stood up. "No," he said, "I'll ask no pardon of an idler living off honest yeomen."

He was raging, but he had sense enough to shift the insult from my family to Gerald alone. Otherwise he and his father would have had the four of us to deal with. As it was Gerald stood up too, fists knotted at his sides, and said. "Will you step away from here and settle this?"

"Gladly!" Ketill turned and walked a few yards down the beach, taking his shield from the boat. Gerald followed. Thorgunna stood with stricken face, then picked up his ax and ran after him.

"Are you going weaponless?" she shrieked.

Gerald stopped, looking dazed. "I don't want that," he mumbled. "Fists—"

Ketill puffed himself up and drew sword. "No doubt you're used to fighting like thralls in your land," he said. "So if you'll crave my pardon, I'll let this matter rest."

Gerald stood with drooped shoulders. He stared at Thorgunna as if he were blind, as if asking her what to do. She handed him the ax.

"So you want me to kill him?" he whispered.

"Yes," she answered.

Then I knew she loved him, for otherwise why should she have cared if he disgraced himself?

Helgi brought him his helmet. He put it on, took the ax, and went forward.

"Ill is this," said Hjalmar to me. "Do you stand by the stranger, Ospak?"

"No," I said. "He's no kin or oath-brother of mine. This is not my quarrel."

"That's good," said Hjalmar. "I'd not like to fight with you, my friend. You were ever a good neighbor."

We went forth together and staked out the ground. Thorgunna told me to lend Gerald my sword, so he could use a shield too, but the man looked oddly at me and said he would rather have the ax. They squared away before each other, he and Ketill, and began fighting.

This was no holmgang, with rules and a fixed order of blows and first blood meaning victory. There was death between those two. Ketill rushed in with the sword whistling in his hand. Gerald sprang back, wielding the ax awkwardly. It bounced off Ketill's shield. The youth grinned and cut at Gerald's legs. I saw blood well forth and stain the ripped breeches.

It was murder from the beginning. Gerald had never used an ax before. Once he even struck with the flat of it. He would have been hewed down at once had Ketill's sword not been blunted on his helmet and had he not been quick on his feet. As it was, he was soon lurching with a dozen wounds.

"Stop the fight!" Thorgunna cried aloud and ran forth. Helgi caught her arms and forced her back, where she struggled and kicked till Grim must help. I saw grief on my son's face but a malicious grin on the carle's.

Gerald turned to look. Ketill's blade came down and slashed his left hand. He dropped the ax. Ketill snarled and readied to finish him. Gerald drew his gun. It made a flash and a barking noise. Ketill fell, twitched for a moment, and was quiet. His lower jaw was blown off and the back of his head gone.

There came a long stillness, where only the wind and the sea had voice.

Then Hjalmar trod forth, his face working but a cold steadiness over him. He knelt and closed his son's eyes, as token that the right of vengeance was his. Rising, he said. "That was an evil deed. For that you shall be outlawed."

"It wasn't magic," said Gerald in a numb tone. "It was like a…a bow. I had no choice. I didn't want to fight with more than my fists."

I trod between them and said the Thing must decide this matter, but that I hoped Hjalmar would take weregild for Ketill.

"But I killed him to save my own life!" protested Gerald.

"Nevertheless, weregild must be paid, if Ketill's kin will take it," I explained. "Because of the weapon, I think it will be doubled, but that is for the Thing to judge."

Hjalmar had many other sons, and it was not as if Gerald belonged to a family at odds with his own, so I felt he would agree. However, he laughed coldly and asked where a man lacking wealth would find the silver.

Thorgunna stepped up with a wintry calm and said we would pay it. I opened my mouth, but when I saw her eyes I nodded. "Yes, we will," I said, "in order to keep the peace."

"Then you make this quarrel your own?" asked Hjalmar.

"No," I answered. "This man is no blood of my own. But if I choose to make him a gift of money to use as he wishes, what of it?"

Hjalmar smiled. There was sorrow crinkled around his eyes, but he looked on me with old comradeship.

"Erelong this man may be your son-in-law," he said. "I know the signs, Ospak. Then indeed he will be of your folk. Even helping him now in his need will range you on his side."

"And so?" asked Helgi, most softly.

"And so, while I value your friendship, I have sons who will take the death of their brother ill. They'll want revenge on Gerald Samsson, if only for the sake of their good names, and thus our two houses will be sundered and one manslaying will lead to another. It has happened often enough erenow." Hjalmar sighed. "I myself wish peace with you, Ospak, but if you take this killer's side it must be otherwise."

I thought for a moment, thought of Helgi lying with his skull cloven, of my other sons on their garths drawn to battle because of a man they had never seen, I thought of having to wear byrnies every time we went down for driftwood and never knowing when we went to bed whether we would wake to find the house ringed in by spearmen.

"Yes," I said, "you are right, Hjalmar. I withdraw my offer. Let this be a matter between you and him alone."

We gripped hands on it.

Thorgunna gave a small cry and fled into Gerald's arms. He held her close. "What does this mean?" he asked slowly.

"I cannot keep you any longer," I said, "but belike some crofter will give you a roof. Hjalmar is a law-abiding man and will not harm you until the Thing has outlawed you. That will not be before midsummer. Perhaps you can get passage out of Iceland ere then."

"A useless one like me?" he replied bitterly.

Thorgunna whirled free and blazed that I was a coward and a perjurer and all else evil. I let her have it out, then laid my hands on her shoulders.

"It is for the house," I said. "The house and the blood, which are holy. Men die and women weep, but while the kindred live our names are remembered. Can you ask a score of men to die for your own hankerings?"

Long did she stand, and to this day I know not what her answer would have been. It was Gerald who spoke.

"No," he said. "I suppose you have right, Ospak…the right of your time, which is not mine." He took my hand, and Helgi's. His lips brushed Thorgunna's cheek. Then he turned and walked out into the darkness.

I heard later that he went to earth with Thorvald Hallsson, the crofter of Humpback Fell, and did not tell his host what had happened. He must have hoped to go unnoticed until he could arrange passage to the eastlands somehow. But of course word spread. I remember his brag that in the United States men had means to talk from one end of the land to another. So he must have looked down on us, sitting on our lonely garths, and not know how fast word could get around. Thorvald's son Hrolf went to Brand Sealskin-boots to talk about some matter and of course mentioned the stranger, and soon all the western island had the tale.

Now if Gerald had known he must give notice of a manslaying at the first garth he found, he would have been safe at least till the Thing met, for Hjalmar and his sons are sober men who would not kill a man still under the protection of the law. But as it was, his keeping the matter secret made him a murderer and therefore at once an outlaw. Hjalmar and his kin rode up to Humpback Fell and haled him forth. He shot his way past them with the *gun* and fled into the hills. They followed him, having several hurts and one more death to avenge. I wonder if Gerald thought the strangeness of his weapon would unnerve us. He may not have known that every man dies when his time comes, neither sooner nor later, so that fear of death is useless.

At the end, when they had him trapped, his weapon gave out on him. Then he took up a dead man's sword and defended himself so valiantly that Ulf Hjalmarsson has limped ever since. It was well done, as even his foes admitted; they are an eldritch race in the United States, but they do not lack manhood.

When he was slain, his body was brought back. For fear of the ghost, he having perhaps been a warlock, it was burned, and all he had owned was laid in the fire with him. That was where I lost the knife he had given me. The barrow stands out on the moor north of here, and folk shun it, though the ghost has not walked. Now, with so much else happening, he is slowly being forgotten.

And that is the tale, priest, as I saw it and heard it. Most men think Gerald Samsson was crazy, but I myself believe he did come from out of time, and that his doom was that no man may ripen a field before harvest season. Yet I look into the future, a thousand years hence, when they fly through the air and ride in horseless wagons and smash whole cities with one blow. I think of this Iceland then, and of the young United States men there to help defend us in a year when the end of the world hovers close. Perhaps some of them, walking about on the heaths, will see that barrow and wonder what ancient warrior lies buried there, and they may even wish they had lived long ago in his time when men were free.

Autumn

Slowly the moon
Slides aloft.
Keen is its edge,
Cutting the dark.
Stars and frost,
As still as the dead,
Warn of another
Waning year.

Turning Point

"Please, mister, could I have a cracker for my oontatherium?"

Not exactly the words you would expect at an instant when history changes course and the universe can never again be what it was. *The die is cast; In this sign conquer; It is not fit that you should sit here any longer; We hold these truths to be self-evident; The Italian navigator has landed in the New World; Dear God, the thing works!*—no man with any imagination can recall those, or others like them, and not have a coldness run along his spine. But as for what little Mierna first said to us, on that island half a thousand light-years from home...

The star is catalogued AGC 4256836, a K_2 dwarf in Cassiopeia. Our ship was making a standard preliminary survey of that region, and had come upon mystery enough—how easily Earthsiders forget that every planet is a complete world!—but nothing extraordinary in this fantastic cosmos. The Traders had noted places that seemed worth further investigation; so had the Federals; the lists were not quite identical.

After a year, vessel and men were equally jaded. We needed a set-down, to spend a few weeks refitting and recuperating before the long swing homeward. There is an art to finding such a spot. You visit whatever nearby suns look suitable. If you come on a planet whose gross physical characteristics are terrestroid, you check the biological details—very, very carefully, but since the operation is largely automated it goes pretty fast—and make contact with the autochthons, if any. Primitives are preferred. That's not because of military danger, as some think. The Federals insist that the natives have no objection to strangers camping on their land, while the Traders don't see how anyone, civilized or not, that hasn't discovered atomic energy, can be a menace. It's only that primitives are less apt to ask complicated questions and otherwise make a nuisance of themselves. Spacemen rejoice that worlds with machine civilizations are rare.

Well, Joril looked ideal. The second planet of that sun, with more water than Earth, it offered a mild climate everywhere. The biochemistry was so like our own that we could eat native foods, and there didn't seem to be any germs that UX_2 couldn't handle. Seas, forests, meadows made us feel right at home, yet the countless differences from Earth lent a fairyland glamour. The indigenes were savages, that is, they depended on hunting, fishing, and gathering for their whole food supply. So we assumed there were thousands of little cultures and picked the one that appeared most advanced: not that aerial observation indicated much difference.

Those people lived in neat, exquisitely decorated villages along the western seaboard of the largest continent, with woods and hills behind them. Contact went smoothly. Our semanticians had a good deal of trouble with the language, but the villagers started picking up English right away. Their hospitality was lavish whenever we called on them, but they stayed out of our camp except for the conducted tours we gave and other such invitations. With one vast, happy sigh, we settled down.

But from the first there were certain disturbing symptoms. Granted they had humanlike throats and palates, we hadn't expected the autochthons to speak flawless English within a couple of weeks. Every one of them. Obviously they could have learned still faster if we'd taught them systematically. We followed the usual practice and christened the planet "Joril" after what we thought was the local word for "earth"—and then found that "Joril" meant "Earth," capitalized, and the people had an excellent heliocentric astronomy. Though they were too polite to press themselves on us, they weren't merely accepting us as something inexplicable; curiosity was afire in them, and given half a chance they *did* ask the most complicated questions.

Once the initial rush of establishing ourselves was over and we had time to think, it became plain that we'd stumbled on something worth much further study. First we needed to check on some other areas and make sure this Dannicar culture wasn't a freak. After all, the neolithic Mayas had been good astronomers; the ferro-agricultural Greeks had developed a high and sophisticated philosophy. Looking over the maps we'd made from orbit, Captain Barlow chose a large island about 700 kilometers due west. A gravboat was outfitted and five men went aboard.

Pilot: Jacques Lejeune. Engineer: me. Federal militechnic representative: Commander Ernest Baldinger, Space Force of the Solar Peace Authority. Federal civil government representative: Walter Vaughan. Trader agent: Don Haraszthy. He and Vaughan were the principals, but the rest of us were skilled in the multiple jobs of planetography. You have to be, on a foreign world months from home or help.

We made the aerial crossing soon after sunrise, so we'd have a full eighteen hours of daylight. I remember how beautiful the ocean looked below us, like one great bowl of metal, silver where the sun struck, cobalt and green copper beyond. Then the island came over the world's edge, darkly forested, crimson-splashed by stands of gigantic red blossoms. Lejeune picked out an open spot in the woods, about two kilometers from a village that stood on a wide bay, and landed us with a whoop and a holler. He's a fireball pilot.

"Well—" Haraszthy rose to his sheer two meters and stretched till his joints cracked. He was burly to match that height, and his hook-nosed face carried the marks of old battles. Most Traders are tough, pragmatic extroverts; they have to be, just as Federal civils have to be the opposite. It makes for conflict, though. "Let's hike."

"Not so fast," Vaughan said: a thin young man with an intense gaze. "That tribe has never seen or heard of our kind. If they noticed us land, they may be in a panic."

"So we go jolly them out of it," Haraszthy shrugged.

"Our whole party? Are you serious?" Commander Baldinger asked. He reflected a bit. "Yes, I suppose you are. But I'm responsible now. Lejeune and Cathcart, stand by here. We others will proceed to the village."

"Just like that?" Vaughan protested.

"You know a better way?" Haraszthy answered.

"As a matter of fact—" But nobody listened. The government operates on some elaborate theories, and Vaughan was still too new in Survey to understand how often theory has to give way. We were impatient to go outside, and I regretted not being sent along to town. Of course, someone had to stay, ready to pull out our emissaries if serious trouble developed.

We emerged into long "grass" and a breeze that smelled of nothing so much as cinnamon. Trees rustled overhead against a deep blue sky; the reddish sunlight spilled across purple wild flowers and bronze-colored insectoid wings. I drew a savoring breath before going around with Lejeune to make sure our landing gear was properly set. We were all lightly clad; Baldinger carried a blast rifle and Haraszthy a radiocom big enough to contact Dannicar, but both seemed ludicrously inappropriate.

"I envy the Jorillians," I remarked.

"In a way," Lejeune said. "Though perhaps their environment is too good. What stimulus have they to advance further?"

"Why should they want to?"

"They don't, consciously, my old. But every intelligent race is descended from animals that once had a hard struggle to survive, so hard they were forced to evolve brains. There is an instinct for adventure, even in the gentlest herbivorous beings, and sooner or later it must find expression—"

"Holy jumping Judas!"

Haraszthy's yell brought Lejeune and me bounding back to that side, of the ship. For a moment my reason wobbled. Then I decided the sight wasn't really so strange…here.

A girl was emerging from the woods. She was about the equivalent of a Terrestrial five-year-old, I estimated. Less than a meter tall (the Jorillians average more short and slender than we), she had the big head of her species to make her look still more elfin. Long blondish hair, round ears, delicate features that were quite humanoid except for the high forehead and huge violet eyes added to the charm. Her brow-skinned body was clad only in a white loincloth. One four-fingered hand waved cheerily at us. The other carried a leash. And at the opposite end of that leash was a grasshopper the size of a hippopotamus.

No, not a grasshopper, I saw as she danced toward us. The head looked similar, but the four walking legs were short and stout, the several others mere boneless appendages. The gaudy hide was skin, not chitin. I saw that the creature breathed with lungs, too. Nonetheless it was a startling monster; and it drooled.

"Insular genus," Vaughan said. "Undoubtedly harmless, or she wouldn't—But a child, coming so casually—!"

Baldinger grinned and lowered his rifle. "What the hell," he said, "to a kid everything's equally wonderful. This is a break for our side. She'll give us a good recommendation to her elders."

The little girl (damn it, I will call her that) walked to within a meter of Haraszthy, turned those big eyes up and up till they met his piratical face, and trilled with an irresistible smile:

"Please, mister, could I have a cracker for my oontatherium?"

I don't quite remember the next few minutes. They were confused. Eventually we found ourselves, the whole five, walking down a sun-speckled woodland path. The girl skipped beside us, chattering like a xylophone. The monster lumbered behind, chewing messily on what we had given it. When the light struck those compound eyes I thought of a jewel chest.

"My name is Mierna," the girl said, "and my father makes things out of wood, I don't know what that's called in English, please tell me, oh, carpentry, thank you, you're a nice man. My father thinks a lot. My mother makes songs. They are very pretty songs. She sent me out to get some sweet grass for a borning couch, because her assistant wife is going to born a baby soon, but when I saw you come down just the way Pengwil told, I knew I should say hello instead and take you to Taori. That's our village. We have *twenty-five houses.* And sheds and a Thinking Hall that's bigger than the one in Riru. Pengwil said crackers are awful tasty, Could I have one too?"

Haraszthy obliged in a numb fashion. Vaughan shook himself and fairly snapped, "How do you know our language?"

"Why, everybody does in Taori. Since Pengwil came and taught us. That was three days ago. We've been hoping and hoping you would come. They'll be so jealous in Riru! But we'll let them visit if they ask us nicely."

"Pengwil...a Dannicarian name, all right," Baldinger muttered. "But they never heard of this island till I showed them our map. And they couldn't cross the ocean in those dugouts of theirs! It's against the prevailing winds, and square sails—"

"Oh, Pengwil's boat can sail right into the wind," Mierna laughed. "I saw him myself, he took everybody for rides, and now my father's making a boat like that too, only better."

"Why did Pengwil come here?" Vaughan asked.

"To see what there was. He's from a place called Folat. They have such funny names in Dannicar, and they dress funny too, don't they, mister?"

"Folat...yes, I remember, a community a ways north of our camp," Baldinger said.

"But savages don't strike off into an unknown ocean for, for curiosity," I stammered.

"These do," Haraszthy grunted. I could almost see the relays clicking in his blocky head. There were tremendous commercial possibilities here, foods and textiles and especially the dazzling artwork. In exchange—

"No!" Vaughan exclaimed. "I know what you're thinking, Trader Haraszthy, and you are not going to bring machines here."

The big man bridled. "Says who?"

"Says me, by virtue of the authority vested in me. And I'm sure the Council will confirm my decision." In that soft air Vaughan was sweating. "We don't dare!"

"What's a Council?" Mierna asked. A shade of trouble crossed her face. She edged close to the bulk of her animal.

In spite of everything, I had to pat her head and murmur, "Nothing you need worry about, sweetheart." To get her mind, and my own, off vague fears: "Why do you call this fellow an oontatherium? That can't be his real name."

"Oh, no." She forgot her worries at once. "He's a *yao* and his real name is, well, it means Big-Feet-Buggy-Eyes-Top-Man-Underneath-And-Over. That's what I named him. He's mine and he's lovely." She tugged at an antenna. The monster actually purred. "But Pengwil told us about something called an *oont* you have at your home, that's hairy and scary and carries things and drools like a *yao,* so I thought that would be a nice English name. Isn't it?"

"Very," I said weakly.

"What is this *oont* business?" Vaughan demanded.

Haraszthy ran a hand through his hair. "Well," he said, "you know I like Kipling, and I read some of his poems to some natives one night at a party. The one about the *oont,* the camel, yeah, I guess that must have been among 'em. They sure enjoyed Kipling."

"And had the poem letter-perfect after one hearing, and passed it unchanged up and down the coast, and now it's crossed the sea and taken hold," Vaughan choked.

"Who explained that *therium* is a root meaning 'mammal'?" I asked. Nobody knew, but doubtless one of our naturalists had casually mentioned it. So five-year-old Mierna had gotten the term from a wandering sailor and applied it with absolute correctness: never mind feelers and insectoidal eyes, the *yao* was a true mammal.

After a while we emerged in a cleared strip fronting on the bay. Against its glitter stood the village, peak-roofed houses of wood and thatch, a different style from Dannicar's but every bit as pleasant and well-kept. Outrigger canoes were drawn up on the beach, where fishnets hung to dry. Anchored some way beyond was another boat. The curved, gaily painted hull, twin steering oars, mat sails and leather tackle were like nothing on our poor overmechanized Earth; but she was sloop-rigged, and evidently a deep keel made it impossible to run her ashore.

"I thought so," Baldinger said in an uneven voice. "Pengwil went ahead and invented tacking. That's an efficient design. He could cross the water in a week or less."

"He invented navigation too," Lejeune pointed out.

The villagers, who had not seen us descend, now dropped their occupations—cooking, cleaning, weaving, potting, the numberless jobs of the primitive—to come on the run. All were dressed as simply as Mierna. Despite large heads, which were not grotesquely big, odd hands and ears, slightly different body proportions, the women were good to look on: too good, after a year's celibacy. The beardless long-haired men were likewise handsome, and both sexes were graceful as cats.

They didn't shout or crowd. Only one exuberant horn sounded, down on the beach. Mierna ran to a grizzled male, seized him by the hand, and tugged him forward. "This is my father," she crowed. "Isn't he wonderful? And he thinks a lot. The name he's using right now, that's Sarato. I liked his last name better."

"One wearies of the same word," Sarato laughed. "Welcome, Earthfolk. You do us great…*lula*…pardon, I lack the term. You raise us high by this visit." His handshake—Pengwil must have told him about that custom—was hard, and his eyes met ours respectfully but unawed.

The Dannicarian communities turned what little government they needed over to specialists, chosen on the basis of some tests we hadn't yet comprehended. But these people didn't seem to draw even that much class distinction. We were introduced to everybody by occupation: hunter, fisher, musician, prophet (I think that is what *nonalo* means), and so on. There was the same absence of taboo here as we had noticed in Dannicar, but an equally elaborate code of manners—which they realized we could not be expected to observe.

Pengwil, a strongly built youth in the tunic of his own culture, greeted us. It was no coincidence that he'd arrived at the same spot as we. Taori lay almost exactly west of his home area, and had the best anchorage on these shores. He was bursting with desire to show off his boat. I obliged him, swimming out and climbing aboard. "A fine job," I said with entire honesty. "I have a suggestion, though. For sailing along coasts, you don't need a fixed keel." I described a centerboard. "Then you can ground her."

"Yes, Sarato thought of that after he had seen my work. He has started one of such pattern already. He wants to do away with the steering oars also, and have a flat piece of wood turn at the back end. Is that right?"

"Yes," I said after a strangled moment.

"It seemed so to me." Pengwil smiled. "The push of water can be split in two parts like the push of air. Your Mister Ishihara told me about splitting and rejoining forces. That was what gave me the idea for a boat like this."

We swam back and put our clothes on again. The village was abustle, preparing a feast for us. Pengwil joined them. I stayed behind, walking the beach, too restless to sit. Staring out across the waters and breathing an ocean smell that was almost like Earth's, I thought strange thoughts. They were broken off by Mierna. She skipped toward me, dragging a small wagon.

"Hello, Mister Cathcart!" she cried. "I have to gather seaweed for flavor. Do you want to help me?"

"Sure," I said.

She made a face. "I'm glad to be here. Father and Kuaya and a lot of the others, they're asking Mister Lejeune about ma-the-*matics*. I'm not old enough to like functions. I'd like to hear Mister Haraszthy tell about Earth, but he's talking alone in a house with his friends. Will you tell me about Earth? Can I go there someday?"

I mumbled something. She began to bundle leafy strands that had washed ashore. "I didn't used to like this job," she said. "I had to go back and forth so many times. They wouldn't let me use my oontatherium because he gets buckety when his feet are wet. I told them I could make him shoes, but they said no. Now it's fun anyway, with this, this, what do you call it?"

"A wagon. You haven't had such a thing before?"

"No, never, just drags with runners. Pengwil told us about wheels. He saw the Earthfolk use them. Carpenter Huanna started putting wheels on the drags right away. We only have a few so far."

I looked at the device, carved in wood and bone, a frieze of processional figures around the sides: The wheels weren't simply attached to axles. With permission, I took the cover off one and saw a ring of hard-shelled spherical nuts. As far as I knew, nobody had explained ball bearings to Pengwil.

"I've been thinking and thinking," Mierna said. "If we made a great big wagon, then an oontatherium could pull it couldn't he? Only we have to have a good way for tying the oontatherium on, so he doesn't get hurt and you can guide him. I've thinked…thought of a real nice way." She stooped and drew lines in the sand. The harness ought to work.

With a full load, we went back among the houses. I lost myself in admiration of the carved pillars and panels. Sarato emerged from Lejeune's discussion of group theory (the natives had already developed that, so the talk was a mere comparison of approaches) to show me his obsidian-edged tools. He said the coast dwellers traded inland for the material, and spoke of getting steel from us. Or might we be so incredibly kind as to explain how metal was taken from the earth?

The banquet, music, dances, pantomimes, conversation, all was as gorgeous as expected, or more so. I trust the happy-pills we humans took kept us from making too grim an impression. But we disappointed our hosts by declining an offer to spend the night. They guided us back by torch-glow, singing the whole distance, on a twelve-tone scale with some of the damnedest harmony I have ever come across. When we reached the boat they turned homeward again. Mierna was at the tail of the parade. She stood a long time in the coppery light of the single great moon, waving to us.

Baldinger set out glasses and a bottle of Irish. "Okay," he said. "Those pills have worn off by now, but we need an equivalent."

"Hoo, yes!" Haraszthy grabbed the bottle.

"I wonder what their wine will be like, when they invent that?" Lejeune mused.

"Be still!" Vaughan said. "They aren't going to."

We stared at him. He sat shivering with tension, under the cold fluoroluminance in that bleak little cabin.

"What the devil do you mean?" Haraszthy demanded at last. "If they can make wine half as well as they do everything else, it'll go for ten credits a liter on Earth."

"Don't you understand?" Vaughan cried. "We can't deal with them. We have to get off this planet and—Oh, God, why did we have to find the damned thing?" He groped for a glass.

"Well," I sighed, "we always knew, those of us who bothered to think about the question, that someday we were bound to meet a race like this. Man…what is man that thou art mindful of him?"

"This is probably an older star than Sol," Baldinger nodded. "Less massive, so it stays longer on the main sequence."

"There needn't be much difference in planetary age," I said. "A million years, half a million, whatever the figure is, hell, that doesn't mean a thing in astronomy or geology. In the development of an intelligent race, though—"

"But they're *savages!*" Haraszthy protested.

"Most of the races we've found are," I reminded him. "Man was too, for most of his existence. Civilization is a freak. It doesn't come natural. Started on Earth, I'm told, because the Middle East dried out as the glaciers receded and something had to be done for a living when the game got scarce. And scientific, machine civilization, that's a still more unusual accident. Why should the Jorillians have gone beyond an Upper Paleolithic technology? They never needed to."

"Why do they have the brains they do, if they're in the stone age?" Haraszthy argued.

"Why did we, in our own stone age?" I countered. "It wasn't necessary for survival. Java man, Peking man, and the low-browed rest, they'd been doing all right. But evidently evolution, intraspecies competition, sexual selection…whatever increases intelligence in the first place continues to force it upward, if some new factor like machinery doesn't interfere. A bright Jorillian has more prestige, rises higher in life, gets more mates and children, and so it goes. But this is an easy environment, at least in the present geological epoch. The natives don't even seem to have wars, which would stimulate technology. Thus far they've had little occasion to use those tremendous minds for anything but art, philosophy, and social experimentation."

"What is their average IQ?" Lejeune whispered.

"Meaningless," Vaughan said dully. "Beyond 180 or so, the scale breaks down. How can you measure an intelligence so much greater than your own?"

There was a stillness. I heard the forest sough in the night around us.

"Yes," Baldinger ruminated, "I always realized that our betters must exist. Didn't expect we'd run into them in my own lifetime, however. Not in this microscopic sliver of the galaxy that we've explored. And…well, I always imagined the Elders having machines, science, space travel."

"They will," I said.

"If we go away—" Lejeune began.

"Too late," I said. "We've already given them this shiny new toy, science. If we abandon them, they'll come looking for us in a couple of hundred years. At most."

Haraszthy's fist crashed on the table. "Why leave?" he roared. "What the hell are you scared of? I doubt the population of this whole planet is ten million. There are fifteen billion humans in the Solar System and the colonies! So a Jorillian can outthink me. So what? Plenty of guys can do that already, and it don't bother me as long as we can do business."

Baldinger shook his head. His face might have been cast in iron. "Matters aren't that simple. The question is what race is going to dominate this arm of the galaxy."

"Is it so horrible if the Jorillians do?" Lejeune asked softly.

"Perhaps not. They seem pretty decent. But—" Baldinger straightened in his chair. "I'm not going to be anybody's domestic animal. I want my planet to decide her own destiny."

That was the unalterable fact. We sat weighing it for a long and wordless time.

The hypothetical superbeings had always seemed comfortably far off. We hadn't encountered them, or they us. Therefore they couldn't live anywhere near. Therefore they probably never would interfere in the affairs of this remote galactic fringe where we dwell. But a planet only months distant from Earth; a species whose average member was a genius and whose geniuses were not understandable by us: bursting from their world, swarming through space, vigorous, eager, jumping in a decade to accomplishments that would take us a century—if we ever succeeded—how could they help but destroy our painfully built civilization? We'd scrap it ourselves, as the primitives of our old days had scrapped their own rich cultures in the overwhelming face of Western society. Our sons would laugh at our shoddy triumphs, go forth to join the high Jorillian adventure, and come back spirit-broken by failure, to build some feeble imitation of an alien way of life and fester in their hopelessness. And so would every other thinking species, unless the Jorillians were merciful enough to leave them alone.

Which the Jorillians probably would be. But who wants that kind of mercy?

I looked upon horror. Only Vaughan had the courage to voice the thing:

"There are planets under technological blockade, you know. Cultures too dangerous to allow modern weapons, let alone spaceships. Joril can be interdicted."

"They'll invent the stuff for themselves, now they've gotten the idea," Baldinger said.

Vaughan's mouth twitched downward. "Not if the only two regions that have seen us are destroyed."

"Good God!" Haraszthy leaped to his feet.

"Sit down!" Baldinger rapped.

Haraszthy spoke an obscenity. His face was ablaze. The rest of us sat in a chill sweat.

"You've called *me* unscrupulous," the Trader snarled. "Take that suggestion back to the hell it came from, Vaughan, or I'll kick out your brains."

I thought of nuclear fire vomiting skyward, and a wisp of gas that had been Mierna, and said, "No."

"The alternative," Vaughan said, staring at the bulkhead across from him, "is to do nothing until the sterilization of the entire planet has become necessary."

Lejeune shook his head in anguish. "Wrong, wrong, wrong. There can be too great a price for survival."

"But for our children's survival? Their liberty? Their pride and—"

"What sort of pride can they take in themselves, once they know the truth?" Haraszthy interrupted. He reached down grabbed Vaughan's shirt front, and hauled the man up by sheer strength. His broken features glared three centimeters from the Federal's. "I'll tell you what we're going to do," he said. "We're going to trade, and teach, and xenologize, and fraternize, the same as with any other people whose salt we've eaten. And take our chances like men!"

"Let him go," Baldinger commanded. Haraszthy knotted a fist. "If you strike him, I'll brig you and prefer charges at home. Let him go, I said!"

Haraszthy opened his grasp. Vaughan tumbled to the deck. Haraszthy sat down, buried his head in his hands, and struggled not to sob.

Baldinger refilled our glasses. "Well, gentlemen," he said, "it looks like an impasse. We're damned if we do and damned if we don't, and I lay odds no Jorillian talks in such tired clichés."

"They could give us so much," Lejeune pleaded.

"Give!" Vaughan climbed erect and stood trembling before us. "That's p-p-precisely the trouble. They'd give it! If they could, even. It wouldn't be ours. We probably couldn't understand their work, or use it, or…It wouldn't be ours, I say!"

Haraszthy stiffened. He sat like stone for an entire minute before he raised his face and whooped aloud.

"*Why not?*"

Blessed be whisky. I actually slept a few hours before dawn. But the light, stealing in through the ports, woke me then and I couldn't get back to sleep. At last I rose, took the drop-shaft down, and went outside.

The land lay still. Stars were paling, but the east held as yet only a rush of ruddiness. Through the cool air I heard the first bird-flutings from the dark forest mass around me. I kicked off my shoes and went barefoot in bare grass.

Somehow it was not surprising that Mierna should come at that moment, leading her oontatherium. She let go the leash and ran to me. "Hi, Mister Cathcart! I hoped a lot somebody would be up. I haven't had any breakfast."

"We'll have to see about that." I swung her in the air till she squealed. "And then maybe take a little flyaround in this boat. Would you like that?"

"Oooh!" Her eyes grew round. I set her down. She needed a while longer before she dared ask, "Clear to Earth?"

"No, not that far, I'm afraid. Earth is quite a ways off."

"Maybe someday? Please?"

"Someday, I'm quite sure, my dear. And not so terribly long until then, either."

"I'm going to Earth, I'm going to Earth, I'm going to Earth." She hugged the oontatherium. "Will you miss me awfully, Big-Feet-Buggy-Eyes-Top-Man-Underneath-And-Over? Don't drool so sad. Maybe you can come too. Can he, Mister Cathcart? He's a very nice oontatherium, honest he is, and he does so love crackers."

"Well, perhaps, perhaps not," I said. "But you'll go, if you wish. I promise you. Anybody on this whole planet who wants to will go to Earth."

As most of them will. I'm certain our idea will be accepted by the Council. The only possible one. If you can't lick 'em...get 'em to jine you.

I rumpled Mierna's hair. *In a way, sweetheart, what a dirty trick to play on you! Take you straight from the wilderness to a huge and complicated civilization. Dazzle you with all the tricks and gadgets and ideas we have, not because we're better but simply because we've been at it a little longer than you. Scatter your ten million among our fifteen billion. Of course you'll fall for it. You can't help yourselves. When you realize what's happening, you won't be able to stop, you'll be hooked. I don't think you'll even be able to resent it.*

You'll be assimilated, Mierna. You'll become an Earth girl. Naturally, you'll grow up to be one of our leaders. You'll contribute tremendous things to our civilization, and be rewarded accordingly. But the whole point is, it will be our civilization. Mine...and yours.

I wonder if you'll ever miss the forest, though, and the little houses by the bay, and the boats and songs and old, old stories, yes, and your darling oontatherium. I know the empty planet will miss you, Mierna. So will I.

"Come on," I said. "Let's go build us that breakfast."

Honesty

In other times I played the troubadour,
Or thought I did, like any lovesick youth,
And for my Lady's sake let fancy soar
On flashing-feathered wings above dull truth.
By foam-born Venus foamily I swore
That in my love of her was naught uncouth,
But 'twas her heart and soul I did adore,
Those beauties which we know defy time's tooth.

The devil now may have such dreary bliss!
Your mortal self is what has made me blest,
Your shining eyes, deep riches of your hair
The springtime drunkenness within your kiss,
The lovely upward surging of your breast,
Soft skin, round hip, slim leg—those things are fair.

The Alien Enemy

Winter darkness falls early on Rotterdam. When my flitter had parked, I walked to a parapet and saw light in star clusters, nebulae, comet tails, filling the spaces of the city. Windows were blinking out in the offices, where towers lifted row on row from the waterfront. But vehicles swarmed, signs danced, shops beckoned, the pavements made a luminous web as far inland as I could see—it appeared to flicker with the ground traffic that counted endless rosaries along it—and the harbor and canals interwove a softer sheen. I was too high to make out people through all that gloom and glow. They were melted into a mere humanity, and their voices came to me as the distant surf of machines.

Up here was less illumination, just some tubes around the lanes and walkways, a fluorescent door to the elevator head, and whatever spilled down from the beacon. So although the air was raw and damp in my nostrils, forcing my hands into tunic pockets, I could look past the electric star which marks this building, out to a few of the real stars. Orion was aloft and the Charles Wain stood on its head over the Pole. I shivered and wished the Ministry of Extraterrestrial Affairs had picked some other place for a centrum, an island farther south where the constellations bloom after dark like flowers.

But even the Directorate has to make compromises. The desirable places on Earth filled up long ago, and then the less desirable, and then the undesirable, until the only clear horizons left are on the mountain roofs, the icecaps, the stone-and-sand deserts, whatever is still worse to make a living from than the bottom of a megalopolis. The bureaucrats I work for did not do so badly; the Low Countries complex has much to recommend it. They control a lot of wealth and are correspondingly influential.

Anyway, I don't have to live in Rotterdam, except a few days at a time, reporting in or getting briefed. Otherwise I mostly spend my furloughs at one or another resort, as expensive and exclusive as possible. Thus I needn't observe what man has inflicted on this planet his mother while I was gone. Spaceman's pay accumulates wonderfully on the long hauls, years or decades in a stretch. I can afford whatever I want on Earth: even clean air, trees, a brook to drink from, a deer to glimpse, unlighted nights when I take a girl out and show her the stars I have visited.

Let me see, I thought, once this is over with here, where should I go? Hitherto I've avoided places where Cumae is visible. But why, really? Hm...catalogued HR 6806, 33.25 light-years distant, K_2 dwarf of luminosity 0.62 Sol...yes, I'll want a small telescope as well as some large brags for the girl...

One star detached itself and whirred toward me. Startled, I realized that this must be Tom Brenner coming. Suddenly I was in no more mood to brag about what I had done at Cumae than I was on first returning. I didn't want to confront him, especially alone. If I hurried, I could be inside before he set down. I could await him together with d'Indre, impregnable in the apparatus of government.

But no. I had seen too much—we had both seen too much, he and I, and all those men and women and children for whom he must speak tonight—on the high plains of his planet. In our very separate ways, we had both known the terror of the alien enemy. I could never be totally an official to him. So I stayed by the parapet, waiting. The breath came out of me like smoke and the cold crept inside.

On Sibylla it was always hot. Cumae glowers half again as great in the sky of that world as Sol does on Earth, and pours down nearly twice the energy. Those wavelengths are poor in ultraviolet but rich in infrared. The sunlight is orange-tinted, not actually furnace color though it feels that way.

I asked Brenner why the colonists didn't move upward. Peaks shouldered above the horizon. Their snows were doubly bright against the purplish heaven, doubly beautiful against the gray-green bushland that stretched around us, murmurous and resinous under a dry wind. I saw that timberline, or whatever passed for it, reached almost to the tops. The dark, slightly iridescent hues suggested denser growth than here. Yonder must be a well-watered country, fertile in soil, and cool, cool.

"Not enough air," he said. He spoke English, with a faint American twang remaining after generations. They were chiefly Americans who went to Sibylla. "We're about as high on this massif as we can go."

"But...oh, yes," I recalled. "The pressure gradient's steeper than on Earth. Your planet's got fifty percent more diameter, a third more surface gravity."

"And less air to start with." Brenner cleared his throat. I recognized the preliminary to a speech.

"We leave the lowlands be because they're too hot, not because of too thick an atmosphere," he said. "Remember, this is a metal-poor globe, lowish density in spite of its mass. So it didn't outgas as much as it might have, in the beginning. Also, on account of the slow rotation, it don't have any magnetic field worth mentioning. Cumae may not be the liveliest star in the universe, but it does spit plenty protons and photons and stuff to thin out an atmosphere that hasn't got a magnetic field to hide behind. We get a pretty strong radiation background too for the same reason; gives medical problems, and it'd be worse higher up. Furthermore, when you got an extra ought-point-three gee on you, and manual labor to do, you need lots of oxygen. So the long and the short of it is, we can't colonize the real heights." He cocked his head at me. "Didn't they brief you ay-tall, son?"

I looked back at him hard, feeling I rated more respect as the first officer of an exploratory ship. His leathery features crinkled in a slow grin. The President of Sibylla was no more formal than the rest of his ten thousand people.

He wore the usual archaic kilts, blouse, boots, sun helmet set rakishly on his grizzled head, machete at hip. But my uniform was less neat than his garb, ten minutes after we had left the buggy by the roadside and started climbing. The gravity didn't bother me; we use rougher accelerations on a craft like the *Bering*. I was aware of my flesh and bones dragging downward, nothing worse. The heat, though, the booming and thrusting wind, the scanted lungfuls I breathed, dryness afire in nose and throat, malignant grab of branches and slither of sandy soil, something faintly intoxicant about the plant odors, had entered me. I was sweat-drenched, dusty, a-gasp and a-tremble, and gladder than I should be of a chance to rest.

I decided not to stand on the dignity I didn't have. Besides, I thought, we were men together in the face of the not human. It had killed, it could kill again, it could smite Earth herself. I felt lonelier in that wide grim landscape than ever between the stars.

"They gave us what information was available," I said. "But it was simultaneously too ample—for one head to contain—and too little—for the totality of a world. Hard for us to guess what's significant and what's incidental. And you've been isolated from us for nearly two centuries. Nothing but a thread of laser contact, with a third of each century needed to cross the distance between. Our fleet took longer still, of course; the big ships aren't meant to go above one gee, so they need a year to approach light speed and another year to decelerate. Inboard time at minimum tau factor isn't negligible either. We experienced several months in covering those parsecs. And we were wondering the whole way if we'd arrive to find the aliens had returned—arrive to find you dead here and a trap set for us. Under the circumstances, sir, we were bound to forget some of what we'd learned."

"Well, yes, I reckon you would at that," Brenner said. "Getting back to why we've settled this Devil's Meadows district, I can tell you we haven't got any better place, and most are not as good. Sibylla is not Earth and never will be."

"But you have colonized the polar regions, haven't you? The original expedition team suggested it, and my briefing said—"

"We abandoned them a spell back. They do have higher air pressure and lower background count, at a reasonable average temperature. But that's only an average. Don't you forget, the rotation period is locked to two-thirds of the year, we being so close to the sun. Sixty-five Earthdays of light are tolerable, though it gets too hot toward evening for us to work. We can grow crops, sort of, with lamps to help through the sixty-five-day night. But at the poles, a thirty-seven-degree axial tilt, the seasons are too flinkin' extreme. What with everything else they had going against them, our poor little terrestrial plants kept dying off there. We haven't the industry or the resources to practice greenhouse agriculture on the needful scale." Brenner shrugged. "Finally we gave up and everybody moved equatorward."

I glanced down the crater slope. The road from Jimstown was dirt, a track nearly lost to sight, rutted, overgrown in places, little used since the destruction of New Washington. But traffic had never been heavy along it; no community on Sibylla was ever more than an overgrown village, and most were less. Tiny at this remove stood Brenner's buggy. The lank horse sniffed discouragedly at the brush it could not eat.

We might have taken a flitter from one of the relief ships. But that would have meant waiting until it could be unloaded and fetched down from orbit. Besides, I had wanted some feel of what Sibylla and its people were really like.

I was getting it.

High hopes, two hundred years ago. People who were going to an uncrowded unplundered world, a whole new world, and this time build things right. They understood there would be hardships, danger, strangeness, on a planet for which our kind of life is not really fitted. But there would be nothing that men had not encountered and overcome elsewhere. The explorers had made certain of that beforehand.

Economics was a stronger motive than decency for being sure. The Directorate takes a bit of political pressure off itself with each colony it establishes, but does not really solve any physical problems at home; and the cost of sending the big ships is fantastic. The aim is to make Earth's people look up through the dust and smoke and say, "Well, at, least somebody's doing all right out there, and maybe we'll be picked to go in the next emigration, if we stay in favor with the authorities meanwhile." Failures would be very, very upsetting. Only the news of outright attack had justified organizing the Colonial Fleet to evacuate the Sibyllans.

The investment in them was so huge. Their ancestors came with tools, machinery, chemicals, seeds, suspended-frozen animal embryos, scientific gear…the basics. Of course, they brought a full stock of technical references too. As population expanded, they would build fusion power stations, they would replace the native life forms in ever larger areas with terrene species, they would at last create Paradise. To judge from their laser reports, they had been following out the plan. It was going slowly, because Sibylla was uncommonly hostile, but it was going.

Now—the reasons why they had not rebuilt were plain to see. The lean ships that appeared in the sky, sixty-eight years ago, bombing and flaming, had knocked the foundations out from under the colony. Too much plant was wrecked, too many lives were lost, too few resources were left. For a lifetime, the people could merely hang on, keep their economy stumbling along at a seventeenth- or eighteenth-century level, cling to the hope that we would answer their appeal. And all the while they knew fear.

I looked again at Tom Brenner. Before he was born, the enemy aliens had destroyed from pole to pole. In days—Earth-days—their fleet had departed back into unknownness. At any instant they might return, and not be content with blowing his toy towns off the map. I wondered how deep the weariness went that I read upon him. Yet he stood straight, and he had a squinty-eyed grin, and two of his children had survived to adulthood and one grandchild was alive and healthy.

"Come on," I said in a harshened voice. "Let's get this finished."

We didn't stop till we mounted the rim and looked down into the fused black bowl where New Washington had been. A few skeletons of buildings jutted from the edges, but only a few, their frameworks grotesquely twisted. I estimated that the blast had released fifty megatons.

The star became a taxi. It glided to a halt across the deck from me and balanced while the stocky figure climbed out. I wondered how he paid it. They had told me the Sibyllans were interned on a military reservation while the Director and his cabinet decided what to do about them. Well, when d'Indre demanded a live conference with the old man, perhaps the colonel had taken pity and slipped him some munits so he could arrive like a citizen, not a consignment.

The taxi took off. Brenner started toward the door. At home he had walked with a rolling, ursine gait. Here he flowstepped, light and easy as an Earthdweller on Mars. His cloak flapped loose, his singlet was open on the broad hairy chest. The unaccustomed cold didn't seem to bother him, rather he savored it.

I moved to intercept him. "Good evening," I said.

Shadows barred our faces. He leaned forward to peer at me. The cigar dropped from his jaws. "Holy hopping Judas—Nick Simić!" He shook his head in bewilderment. But you, your ship, you stayed behind."

"Your settlement was out of touch with astronautics," I said. My tone was sharper than intended; I really wanted to gentle the shock for him. "The Colonial Fleet accelerates at one gee. But in an exploratory vessel like the *Bering*, we're selected professionals; and the motors have a lot less mass to act on. We load ourselves with gravanol and crank her up as high as ten gees. In five or six weeks we're close to light speed and can ease off. I've been home for a year."

"You, uh, didn't stay long on Sibylla then."

"Long enough."

"Well." He straightened. The remembered chuckle sounded in his throat. "Quite a surprise, son, quite a surprise. But pleasant." He thrust out his hand. I took it. His clasp was firm. "And how are your shipmates?"

"Very well, thank you, the last I saw. The *Bering* has left again. Further study of the Delta Eridani System. The third planet looks promising, but its ecology is peculiar and—" I realized I was chattering to avoid speaking truth. "I stayed," I said, "since I was in charge of our investigation on the ground and drafted our report. Citizen d'Indre wanted me for a consultant when you arrived."

"I'm sorry if you missed going on account of us."

"No matter. I'm in line for a command of my own." That was true, but I said it merely to cheer him a little. "How are your people doing?"

"Okay to date." Brenner didn't seem in need of consolation, now that he had gotten over his surprise. I don't suppose anyone grew old on Sibylla who couldn't land on his feet when the floor caved in. He drew a breath and gave that straight-in-the-eye look which he had once described as Horsetrader's Honest Expression Number Three. " 'Course," he said, "we wonder a wee bit why we're held incommunicado and till when."

"That has to be decided," I said. "What happens tonight could be pivotal."

"Don't the proles know we're here?"

"Nothing except rumors. Your story has to be handled like fulminate. You can't imagine how restless those billions there are." My hand swept an arc around the city. It growled and grumbled. "The original news, nonhuman vessels attacking Sibylla, was let out with infinite care, and only because it couldn't be suppressed. Considering that they seemed to have faster-than-light travel, and something like gravity control, the way you told it, the photographs you transmitted—Panic can bring riot, insurrection." I paused. "So can rage."

"Um. Yeh." The lines deepened around Brenner's mouth, but somehow he kept his tone easy. "Well, what say we get on with it?…Oh, almost forgot." He stooped to pick up the cigar. "Soldier gave me some o' these. Friendly taste. No tobacco on our planet, you recall. We'd everything we could do to raise enough food to keep alive."

My gullet tightened. "Put that thing away!" I exclaimed. "Over the side with it! Don't you understand who we're about to see? Jules d'Indre, Minister of Extraterrestrial Affairs. What he recommends be done about you, the Director is almost sure to decree. I warn you, Brenner, be careful!"

He regarded me a while before he obeyed. His next words were astonishing. "Did that girl who traveled with you, Laurie MacIver, did she ship out in the *Bering*?"

"Why yes."

"Too bad." He spoke softly, and for a moment laid his hand on my shoulder. "I think you want to help us, son, according to your lights. But she had something extra. You know the word *simpático*?"

I nodded. "She is that," I agreed.

We went ranging about, she and I, after a ground-effect car had been brought down and assembled. My thought was to interview as many Sibyllans as possible before they left. None were alive who had experienced the attack, but older ones might recollect what the generation before them had said, and might have noticed significant things in the bombed-out towns before salvage and erosion blurred the clues. Laurie accompanied me for several reasons. We didn't need a computer officer here, and you don't travel alone on another planet. But primarily, she understood people, she listened, and they talked freely because they sensed that she cared.

It is not true what the alleydwellers snigger, that spacewomen are nothing but a convenience for spacemen. They hold down responsible posts. And in the black ocean between stars, among the deaths that lair on every new world, on return to an Earth grown strange, you need someone very special.

Just the same, we had thin luck. Sunset handicapped us. Cumae hung low and went lower, casting an inflamed light that was hard to see by across the plateaus. But the air had cooled sufficiently for outdoor work, and everyone on those pitiful farms toiled till he dropped in his tracks. They must complete their daylight jobs—discing and sowing at the present season, plus hay harvest, livestock roundup, and I don't know what else—largely with muscle power. They could only illuminate a limited part of their holdings after the moonless dark came upon them, truck gardens and such that would fail otherwise. Metal and manpower were too scarce to produce the factories which could have produced the machines and energy sources they lacked.

To be sure, this was the last round for them. They were going to Earth. But you can't spaceload ten thousand human beings overnight. The Fleet was barely able to carry the rations they would need on their journey. They must feed themselves meanwhile, and they had no reserves. I was appalled at the wretched yields, the scrawny animals, the stunted timber. And, while most of the individuals I saw were whipcord tough, they were undersized, they had few living children, the graveyards were broad and filled.

"Terrene life is so marginal here," Laurie said as we drove. Her voice was muted with compassion. We had no logical need for a recital of the facts. We had known them since before we left Earth, when we studied the reports of communications from Sibylla. But those were words. Here she met the reality. She needed to put it back into words for herself, before she could reach beyond the anguish and think about practical ways to help.

"Not simply that the native species are poisonous to us," she said. "They poison the soil for our crops. You have to keep weeds, bacteria, everything out of a field for years before the rain's leached it to the point where you can begin building a useful ecology. And then it's apt to be attacked by something—new poisons seeping in, diseases, stormwinds—and at best, it never gets strongly established."

I nodded and listed the causes, to hold off the idea of a personally evil cosmos. "Long nights, weird seasons, shortage of several trace elements, ultraviolet poverty coupled with X-ray and particle irradiation, gravity tending to throw terrene fluid balances out of kilter, even the geological instability. Some of their best mines collapsed in earthquakes in the early days, did you know?—and never could be reopened. Oh, yes, it's a hard world for humans."

My fist struck the control panel and I said with a barren anger: "But so are others. There's nothing wrong here that men haven't found, and beaten. The wildlife is worse on Zion, the weight is heavier on Atlas, a full-fledged ice age is under way on Asgard, Lucifer is hotter and has a higher particle count—"

She turned in her seat to face me. Sundown light, streaming through the turret, changed her gold hair to copper against purple shadows. "But none of those were attacked," she said.

"Not yet," I said. "At least, as far as we know."

We should not have mentioned it. The thought had haunted us since we returned from our last voyage and got the news. It dwelt in the back of every mind on Earth. Perhaps it had done so since man first ventured beyond the Solar System. Our few score parsecs of exploring are no trail whatsoever into that wilderness which is the galaxy. Who can doubt that others prowl it, with longer legs and sharper fangs?

Why had they struck? How? Where else? *Who's next?*

The Sibyllans did their best to answer Laurie's questions and mine. But not only were they hard-pressed for time and dull-witted with exhaustion, their information was scant. I had now inspected the ruins, some photographs of ships in flight, eyewitness accounts, compiled histories. The basic narrative was in my brain.

The raiders could not hit everywhere at once. Josiah Brenner, Tom's father, President in his day, got most population centers evacuated before they went up in fireballs. A majority already lived on isolated farms, it took so many hectares to support one person. For the same reason, the former townsfolk scattered across the whole habitable planet afterward.

The result was that hardly anyone today knew anything that I did not. In fact, my picture of the catastrophe was clearer than most. The ordinary Sibyllan had neither time nor energy for studying the past. The educational level had plummeted; children generally left school to work before they were twelve Earth-years old. Folklore took the place of books.

The books themselves were vague. No real census or scholarship was possible. "Casualties were heavy," said the chroniclers, and told many tales of suffering and heroism. But the figures they gave were obvious guesswork, often contradicting someone else's. I believed I could make a better estimate myself on the basis of one fact. The Sibyllan population which the original colonizing scheme had projected for this decade was some two hundred thousand. The actual population was a twentieth of that.

After a while, Laurie and I quit. We could do more good back in Jimstown, helping prepare for the exodus. With facilities as primitive as they were here, that was going to be a harrowing job. Our crew would stay after the Fleet left and search for further clues. Besides, I didn't fancy traveling after dark.

We had to, though. Passing near a scarp, our car was struck by a boulder when the crust shivered and started a landslide. The damage took hours to fix—in that smoldering light and abominable wind. We could have called for a flitter, but that would have meant leaving the car till dawn. It might be totally wrecked, and it could ill be spared. We drove on.

Cumae went under the mountains. Night thickened as clouds lifted. Presently it was absolute, except where our headlights speared before us, picking out bushes that tossed in the wind and occasional three-eyed animals that slunk between them. The air grew louder, thrusting against the sides, making them quiver and resonate until the noise filled our skulls. Then the rain came, a cloudburst such as Earth has never seen, mixed with hail like knucklebones.

"We'd better take shelter!" I yelled. Laurie could barely hear me through the drumbeat and the howling. "High ground—get away from flash floods—" Lightning blinded me; the whole heaven was incandescent, again and again and again, and thunder picked me up and shook me. I strained over the charts, the inertial navigator, yes, this way, a farmstead…

We could not have made it on wheels. The ground effect held us above mudslides, water avalanches, flattened crops and splintered orchards. Barely, it held us, though the hurricane tried to fling us back into the rising river which had been a valley. I do not know how long it was before we found the cottage, save that it was long indeed.

The house stood. Like most dwellings on Sibylla, it was a fortress, rock walls, shuttered slit windows, ponderous doors, roof held down by cables. In thin air, driven by high temperature differentials and solar irradiations, you must expect murderous weather from time to time. The barns were smashed, there having been insufficient manpower and materials to build them as sturdily, and no doubt the cattle and crops were lost. But the house stood.

I reached its lee, threw out a couple of ground anchors, put the autopilot on standby, and opened the escape hatch. Laurie slipped, the wind caught her, she almost went downhill to her death. I grabbed her, though, got dragged into the mud but hung on somehow. Clinging together, we fought our way through a universe of storm to the house. The door was bolted from within. Our pounding was lost in the racket. I remembered about hurricane doors before the hail beat us unconscious. We found one on the south side, an airlock-type arrangement which could safely admit refugees. At that, I had hell's own time reclosing and dogging the outer door before we opened the inner.

We stumbled through, into a typical Sibyllan home. One room served for cooking, eating, sleeping, handcrafting, everything. Screens offered some pretense of privacy, but here they stood unused against the sooty, unornamented walls. A brick oven gave reasonable warmth, but the single lantern was guttering and demon-shaped shadows moved in every corner.

A man and his wife sat on a bench by a cradle that he must have made himself. She had her face against his breast, her arms around his neck, and wept, not loudly, only with a despair so complete that she had no strength left to curse God. He held her, murmuring, sometimes stroking her faded hair. With one foot he rocked the cradle.

They didn't notice us for a moment. Then he let her go and climbed erect, a burly man, his beard flecked with gray, his clothes clean but often patched. She remained seated, staring at us, trying to stop her tears and comprehend what we were.

Wind, rain, thunder invaded the stout walls. I heard the man say, slowly, "You're from Earth."

"Yes." I introduced us. He shook hands in an absentminded fashion and mumbled his own name too low for me to catch.

"You can stay here, sure," he added. "We got food in the cupboard till the storm passes. Afterward, Jimstown's walking distance."

"We can do better than that," I said, commanding a smile forth, trying to ignore our drowned-rat condition, for they needed whatever comfort was to be gotten. "We have a car."

Laurie went to the woman. "Don't cry, please, my dear," she murmured; somehow I heard her through the noise, and her head shone in the murk. "I know your farm's wiped out. But you're leaving soon anyway, and we'll see you're taken care of, you and your whole fam—Oh!" She stopped. Her teeth gleamed, catching at her lip.

The woman was not pregnant. But, craning my neck, I too saw that the cradle stood empty.

"I buried her around sundown," the man said, looking past me. His tone was flat and his face was stiff, but the scarred hands kept twisting together. "A little girl. She lived several weeks. We hoped—And now the rain must've washed her out. I did think Sibylla might have let her sleep. We wrapped her up snug, and gave her a doll I'd made, so she wouldn't be too lonesome after we were gone. But everything's scattered now, I reckon."

"I'm sorry," I groped. "Maybe…later—" Barely in time, I saw Laurie's furious headshake. "What a terrible thing."

Laurie sat down by the wife and whispered to her.

Once, on our way home, she told me what had been confided that night, hoping it would influence my report. This was the one child they had had, after five miscarriages. The birth was difficult and the doctor did not think any more were possible.

I told her it was no surprise. Standing by that cradle, I had recalled the few children elsewhere and the many graves. And at once, like a blow to the guts, wildly swearing to myself I must be wrong, I saw the face of the alien enemy.

Jules d'Indre sat behind his desk, a shriveled, fussily dressed man whom it was wise to respect. He nodded, quick dip of bald head, as Brenner and I came in. "Be seated, citizens," he did not invite, he ordered.

I found the edge of a chair. My pulse thuttered and my palms were wet. Brenner leaned back, meeting those eyes, faintly smiling. "How d'you do, sir?" he drawled.

"Let us not waste words," d'Indre said. "Perhaps you are not aware how uncommon a physical confrontation in line of business is on Earth. I would normally use a vidiphone three-way, and during working hours. Can you guess why I did otherwise?"

"Informality," Brenner said. "No record, no snoops, no commitments to anything. Suits me. We lived old-fashioned on Sibylla. Not that we wanted to, understand." His smile departed, his voice grew crisp, I had a sense of sparks flying. "It gave us some old-fashioned ideas, however, like about the rights of man."

D'Indre's schoolmaster accent did not alter. "Rights are forfeited when one perpetrates a felony."

"Who's done what and with which unto whom?"

"The Colonial Fleet has been tied up on a useless mission for almost seventy years. Billions of munits have been spent." D'Indre leaned forward. He tapped a pencil on the edge of the desk, *tick-tick* into an all-underlying silence. "The first thing I wish to know, Brenner, is how many were privy to the hoax."

The leather visage sought mine. "What made you report the attack was faked?" Brenner asked calmly, even amiably.

"I didn't want to," burst from me. "I tried—everything—my whole team did. We couldn't risk Earth being unprepared, if there was any chance a hostile fleet existed. And"—I noticed my hands reach toward him—"we didn't want to hurt you!"

"I know," he said, briefly serious. His tone lightened again: "But I've got a curiosity. The fake was arranged by some mighty smart men. Time must've faded the evidence What put you on?"

"Oh…any number of things," I forced myself to say "Close study of certain pictures turned up some unlikely perspectives in them. Analysis of crater material gave results that were consistent with the explosion of stationary plants, not of warheads. Any warhead we could think of needs a fission trigger, or it'd be too bulky. Analyzing the bones of supposed missile victims, we got clear indications that they'd died years earlier. Some of the diaries and correspondence, allegedly from the immediate post-attack period, contradict each other more than is reasonable when you apply symbolic logic. I could go on, but it's in the report. No single detail conclusive, but no doubt left after the whole jigsaw puzzle was fitted together."

I wet my lips. "Sir," I said to d'Indre, "our team discussed suppressing the facts. We decided we couldn't do that to Earth. But you should know we did seriously consider it. We were that sorry for these people."

Tick-tick. "You have not answered my question, Brenner."

"Hey?" The Sibyllan coughed. "How many were in on the conspiracy? Just a few key men that my dad recruited. Still fewer today. The least number necessary to keep things shuffled around so nobody who wasn't in on it would suspect."

"That has to be true, sir," I blurted. "Ten thousand ordinary mortals can't keep a secret or act a role."

"Obvious." *Tick-tick.* "How did you, or rather your predecessors, avoid massacring their own populace?"

"Well, everybody thanked his luck that he'd not been in a target area or was evacuated in time," Brenner said. "He heard about casualties, but they'd always happened somewhere else, in places where nobody lived that he knew. He couldn't check up, supposing it occurred to him. Sibylla never had global electronic communications, or fast transport except for some official flitters. What did exist—like a newspaper or three—was lost when the towns went. Took quite a spell even to re-establish a mail service. Meanwhile everything was confused, and refugees were getting relocated among strangers, and—The stunt wasn't easy, Dad told me. But it did come off. Later, histories and chronicles and such were written; and who had reason to suspect them? Everybody knew our numbers were way below the original forecasts, and dwindling. But accurate pre-disaster figures were filed only in certain heads now, that kept their mouths shut. And nobody had time to sit down and think hard. So it came to be taken for granted that the loss of people was mainly, if not entirely, due to the attack and its aftermath. I assure you, sir, nearly everyone among us honestly believes in the alien enemy."

His gaze challenged d'Indre. "Do what you like to me and my partners," he said. "We were ready for this, if the truth should come out. But you can't punish ten thousand who also got foxed!"

"Presumably the Director will not wish to do so," d'Indre said as if stating a theorem. "Nevertheless, the problem of assimilating them, so that they can make a living on this overcrowded world, may well prove insoluble. And individuals are apt to be subjected to mob violence. And it is politically impossible to send them to a different planet, when so many others desire that for themselves. Did the conspirators foresee this?"

"Yes," Brenner said. He sat straight. The big fists clenched on his knees. "But there was no mucking choice. We had to get off Sibylla. We—my father's group—didn't think Earth would fetch us just because we were slowly dying. We'd already gotten too many refusals of our pleas for help, only a little help. 'Too expensive,' we were told. 'They cope with the same problems elsewhere. Why can't you?' Unquote.

"Expensive!" The word ripped from him, together with a detonating obscenity. I started where I sat. D'Indre did not change expression, but he stopped tapping that pencil. Brenner clamped lips together, took a breath, and went doggedly on: "To be quite frank, sir, on the basis of what knowledge I have, I wouldn't put it past certain officials to fake incoming messages from a colony that stopped sending."

For the first time, I saw d'Indre lose color. The pencil broke in his fingers. Doubtless Brenner noticed too, for he paused through several still seconds before he finished: "Survival knows no law. My father and his men created a false enemy so their grandchildren could be saved from the real one."

"Which was?" d'Indre whispered.

"Sibylla, of course," Brenner said, almost as softly. "The world where everything was wrong. Where the sum total defeated us. Like a woman who wouldn't miscarry *too* often in high gravity, except that she never got enough ultraviolet or oxygen, and did get too many hard roentgens, and had a poor diet, and was overworked, and the very daylight wasn't the right color for easy vision…An entire world, fighting us on a hundred different fronts, never letting up. That was the alien enemy. We wouldn't have lasted another century."

I said into the silence which followed: "Earth has known some analogies. Like the Vikings, around the year 1000. They made themselves rulers of England, Ireland, Normandy, Russia. They ranged unbeatable through half of Europe. They settled Iceland, they discovered America. But they could not hold Greenland. They had a colony there, and it hung on for maybe four hundred years, always more isolated, poorer, smaller, hungrier, weaker. In the end it perished. When archaeologists dug up the skeletons of the last survivors, every one was dwarfed and deformed. Greenland had beaten them."

"I've read about it," Brenner said. "Men won in the end. Eskimos, who had the right technology for the place. Europeans, later, with sheer power of machinery. We, our race, we'll lick Sibylla yet, one way or another. But it's taken the first battle. In such cases, a good general retreats."

D'Indre had recovered his poise. "I also know the history," he said. "Captain Simić's report was exhaustive. I wished, however, to add a personal encounter to my data store before deciding what disposal of this affair I should advise."

Brenner folded his arms and waited.

"As a matter of fact," d'Indre said, "Captain Simić has already proposed a solution which seems viable to me. Parts of Earth remain empty because development has been economically unfeasible. The tropical deserts, for example, the Sahara or the Rub' al-Qali. Sand, stone, drought, low water table or none, fierce heat and light, no worthwhile minerals. Converting them by machine would tie up too much capital equipment and skilled personnel that are badly needed elsewhere. Theoretically, the task could be accomplished by minimal robotic and maximal hand labor. But who among the proles combines the necessary attitude and hardihood? It will be interesting to see if the Sibyllans do."

Briefly, humanness broke through him. "I am sorry, especially for the children," he said. "But under present circumstances, this is the best that anyone can give you."

Brenner remained steady. "I sort of expected it," he said. "The captain dropped a few hints on our way down here. What about us, uh, conspirators?"

D'Indre spread his hands. "Your colony will need leadership. I daresay the Director will rule that providing such leadership is an acceptable expiation."

Brenner's own right hand crashed on the desk. Laughter roared from him. "Why, man!" he cried. "After what we've been up against, you think a nice kind Earthside desert's going to be any problem?"

Discussion dragged on. I took small part. My mind wandered and wondered. I didn't speak, lest I jeopardize the solution that was being hammered out. But take these people, I thought. A world battled them for generations. What those now alive had experienced was of no importance compared to what their germ plasm had experienced. With that natural selection in their past, what would they do with their future?

Ten thousand of them among billions—set down in the worst lands on Earth—could make a difference? Nonsense!

I got rid of the notion. I took command of my ship and went off on a voyage. I came home after eighty-five years and found that I had not thought nonsense after all.

Eventide

Gone sunset amberful, the lake
Lies mirror-quiet for the pines
That ring it round with shadow heights
Through which a ghost of golden shines
To burnish blue those metal bits
Above the water, wing and wing,

Enough Rope

Hurulta, Arkazhik of Unzuvan, fitted his own personality. A magnificent specimen of Ulugani malehood, two and a half meters tall, so broad that he seemed shorter, he dwarfed the thin red-haired human before him. His robes were a barbaric shout of color, as if he were draped in fire and rainbows, and the volume of his speaking made the fine crystal ornaments in the audience chamber tremble and sing, ever so faintly. But the words were hard and steady and utterly cold.

"Our will in this matter is unshakable," he said curtly. "If the League wants to go to war over it, that will be the League's misfortune."

Wing Alak of Sol III and the Galactic League Patrol looked up into the hairless blue face and ventured an urbane smile. The Ulugani were humanoid to several degrees of classification—six fingers to a hand, clawed feet, pointed ears, and the rest meant little when you dealt with the fantastic variety of intelligent life making up Alak's compatriots. This race looked primitive—small head, beetling eyebrow ridges, flat nose and prognathous jaw—but inside, they were as bright as any other known species.

Too bright!

"It would be straining the obvious, your excellency," said Alak, "to point out that the Unzuvan Empire comprises just one planetary system of which only Ulugan is habitable, whereas the Galactic League embraces a good million stars. It cannot have been omitted from all calculation. But I must say that, under these circumstances, I am puzzled; perhaps your excellency would condescend to enlighten me with regard to your attitude on this disparity."

Hurulta snorted, showing a formidable mouthful of teeth. During the years in which Alak, as chief representative of the League and its Patrol, had been visiting Ulugan—off and on—and particularly during the past several months of mounting crisis during which Alak had been here continuously, he had learned to regard the Solarian as a weak, wordy, and pedantic bumbler. Now one huge blue fist crashed into the palm of the other hand and he grinned contemptuously.

"Let us not bandy words," he said. "The nearest border of the League is almost a thousand light-years away, which would make your lines of communication ridiculously long if you tried to attack. Also, in spite of this distance, we have had our own agents in your territory for years. We know that the temper of the League population is…well, let us not say decadent, let us be kindly and say pacific. It would not react favorably to a war which could only mean expense and grief for it. Moreover, the Patrol is a minimal force, designed merely to keep order within the bounds of the League itself. Policemen! We have built up a *war machine*."

He shrugged massively. "Why go on?" he rumbled. "It is only our intention to claim the natural rights of Ulugan. You go your way, we will go ours; we do not wish to fight you, but neither do we feel bound to respect the morals of an altogether different civilization. You can, at best, only be a nuisance if you try to stop us; and if the nuisance becomes too great, we are not afraid of fighting a thousand-year war to exterminate it. We are a warrior race and you are not: there is the essential difference, and mere statistics will not change it."

He sat down behind his desk and fiddled absently with a jeweled dagger. His voice was remote, uninterested. "You may inform your government that Ulugan is already commencing the occupation of Tukatan and the other planets in its system. That is all. You may go."

To dismiss an ambassador thus was like a slap. Alak had to fight himself for an instant before self-control came. Then his gaunt sharp face smoothed itself out, and his tone was unctuous.

"As your excellency wishes, so be it. Good day."

He bowed and backed out of the magnificent room.

Scene: An upper office in the League Patrol Intelligence—Sol Sector—building, Britn, Terra. A sparsely furnished room, a few relaxers, a desk, the control-studded board of a robofile. One wall is transparent, opening on a serene landscape of rolling, wooded hills, a few private dwelling-units, the distant bulk of a food factory. Overhead, the sky is full of white clouds and sunshine, now and then the metal gleam of an airboat. It all seems incredibly remote from the troubled world of Galactic politics.

Characters: Myrn Kaltro, sector chief, a big gray-haired man in the iridescent undress uniform of a human Patrol officer. Jorel Meinz, sociotechnic director of the Solar System, small, dark, intense, conservatively dressed in gold and crimson. Wing Alak, unattached field agent, enough of a dandy to wear the latest fashion in civilian clothes—plain gray and blue. But then, he has been away from home for a good many years.

Background: In a civilization embracing nearly a million separate intelligent races, most of them with independent governments of their own, a civilization which is growing almost daily, it is impossible for even a well-informed administrator to keep track of all significant events. Jorel Meinz has hardly heard the name "Ulugan" before today; now he is being asked to authorize an action which may change Galactic history.

He fumbled out a cigar and inhaled it into lighting. His words were quick, jerky, harsh. "What has Sol to do with this? It's a matter for the entire League Council."

"Which won't meet for another two years," said Kaltro. "As our friend Hurulta well knows. It would take six months just to get a quorum together for an emergency session. Oh, they timed it well, those Ulugani."

"Well, the high command of the Patrol can exercise broad discretion," Meinz grimaced. "Too broad. I don't mind saying I haven't liked all reports of your activities which have come to me. However, in this case—"

"The high command is prepared to act," said Kaltro. "I've contacted all members. Nevertheless, the situation is unprecedented. The Patrol was created to enforce peace within the League. Nothing was said about dealing with a power outside it. If we act against Ulugan, we'll be on legally shaky ground, and there may be a day of reckoning which would do a lot of harm. Many local politicians are spoiling to take a crack at the Patrol, push through constitutional amendments limiting its scope—if they can persuade enough beings that the Patrol has become an irresponsible machine capable of starting wars on its own initiative, they may succeed."

"I see. But what can I do?"

"Your influence can swing the Solar Parliament into authorizing the Patrol to act against Ulugan. In effect, Sol will say: 'As far as we're concerned, the Patrol can have emergency powers, and use them immediately.' Thereafter, we'll proceed."

"But one system can't do that. The Patrol belongs to the whole League!"

"Please." Kaltro lifted shaggy gray brows and smiled, creasing his face as if it were a stiff brown fabric. "You're a practical political engineer. You know as well as I do that Sol is still the leading system in the League. If it'll back us, enough other planets will follow that lead to put us in the clear when the business is brought up at the next Council. Technically, it'll be a *post facto* O.K. on what we'll already have done, but that'll suffice. It'll have to!"

"Well—" Meinz rolled his cigar between bony fingers, scowling at it. "Well, all right, I see your point. But you still haven't seen mine. *Why* should I help you take action against Ulugan?"

He held up a hand. "No, wait, let me finish. As I understand it, Ulugan is a one-system empire lying nearly a thousand light-years outside our territorial bounds. It wants to incorporate one other system into itself. The natives of that system object, to be sure, and ask us for help—but the hard-boiled League Patrol is, I am certain, the last organization in the universe to get interested in noble crusades. The operation of crushing Ulugan would be enormously expensive. The logistic difficulties alone would make it a project of many years—even if it could succeed, which is by no means certain. The Ulugani could, and certainly would, retaliate with raids on our territory, perhaps they could penetrate to Sol itself. After all, interstellar space is so huge that any kind of blockade or defense line is utterly impossible. And you know what horror and destruction even a raid can bring, what with the power of modern weapons.

"The League is *not* a nation, empire, or alliance. It was formed to arbitrate interstellar disputes and prevent future wars. Such other services as it performs are relatively minor; and its systems are, politically and commercially, so loosely knit that it could never evolve into a true federal government. In short, it is totally unable to put forth the united effort of a war. If Ulugan is as determined as Agent Alak says, it may be able to bring the League to terms even if it is one planet against a million. The League may not feel the game is worth the candle, you see. And the resentment at having been involved in a war of which ninety per cent of its citizens would never have heard before death rained on them from the sky—that resentment could destroy the League itself!"

He put the cigar back to his mouth and blew a huge cloud of smoke. "In short, gentlemen," he finished, "if you want my support for this project of yours, you're going to have to give me a pretty good reason."

Kaltro cocked an eye at Wing Alak. The field agent nodded slightly and took out a cigarette for himself. He waited till he had it going before he spoke:

"Let me recapitulate a little, director. Ulugan is a dense, metallic planet of a red dwarf sun. Terrestroid, which means a human can live there but not very comfortably—one-point-five Terran gravity, high air pressure, cold and stormy. The natives are a gifted species, but turbulent, not very polite or moral, all too ready to follow a leader blindly. Those are cultural rather than genetic traits, of course, but they've been pretty well drilled in by now. The history of Ulugan is one of mounting international wars, which pushed the technological development ahead fast but exhausted the natural resources of the planet. In short, a history not unlike ours prior to the Unification; but they never developed a true psychological technology, so their society still contains many archaisms.

"They invented the faster-than-light drive about two centuries ago and started exploring—and exploiting, quite ruthlessly—the nearer stars. They still had nations then, and quarreling over the spoils led to a slam-bang interstellar war. One nation, Unzuvan, finally conquered all the others and absorbed them into a racial empire. That was about thirty years back. It was shortly thereafter that a long-range exploration party from the League, off to study the starclouds near Galactic center, chanced on them. Naturally, even though they are remote from our integrated territory, they were invited to join us. All races of suitably high civilization are, and so far none had refused. They did. Quite rudely, too. Said they were perfectly capable of gaining everything we offered for themselves, and be damned if they'd give up any of their sovereignty."

"Um-m-m. Paranoid culture, then," said Meinz.

"Obviously. Well, the League…or rather, its agent the Patrol…did what it could. Sent embassies, cultural missions, and so on, in the hope of gradually converting them. I've been more or less in charge for the past fifteen years, though of course I could only get out there once in a while. Too much else to do. We had no luck, anyway, except—" Briefly, Alak grinned. "Well, we do have an efficient intelligence service."

"Spies, you mean?" asked Meinz impatiently.

"No, never! What, *never*? Hardly ever!" Alak's classical quotation was lost on Kaltro, who merely grunted, but Meinz smiled. "We weren't too interested in the military-political details of Ulugan," went on the field agent cryptically. "Mostly, we studied the neighboring stars. No one could object to scientific study of primitive planets, could they?

"I'll see that you get our complete dossier on Ulugani sociodynamics, but briefly, the set-up is simple. There's a hereditary emperor and a military aristocracy ruling a subservient class of peasants and workers. The aristocracy is hand in glove with the big commercial interests—it's a sort of monopoly capitalism, partly controlled by the state and partly controlling the state. No, that's a poor way to phrase it. Let's say that the industrial trusts and the military caste together *are* the state. The supreme power is, for all practical purposes, lodged in the Arkazhik, a kind of combined premier and war minister. Right now he's one Hurulta, an able, aggressive, ambitious being with some colorful dreams of glory."

"Very well. Ulugan, under Hurulta, wants to start conquering itself an empire. Specifically, they intend to annex Tukatan, a fertile planet with a backward population. In fact, by now, in the time it's taken me to get here, they have begun doing so. But you know they aren't going to stop there."

"No," said Meinz after a pause. "No, I suppose not." Then, briskly: "But after all, what does it concern us? A thousand light-years away—"

"That thousand light-years is shrinking," said Kaltro. "The League territory is expanding, through exploration, colonization, the joining of new systems. The Ulugani empire will also expand, toward us. Our analysts estimate that in a mere two hundred years, there will be contact. You know that an interstellar civilization can't be big merely in space; it has to be big in time, too. We have to think ahead."

"Um-m-m—" Meinz rubbed his chin.

"My guess is that if we don't stop Ulugan now, we won't even have those two centuries," said Alak. "They're spoiling for trouble. A real war would unite their still new empire like nothing else."

Meinz nodded. "A good point. But *can* you stop them? To try and then fail would be—catastrophic."

"We can only try," said Kaltro gravely. "I won't hide from you that the situation is, well, precarious. But I don't see how we can afford not to try."

"Still...war—" Meinz twisted his mouth, as if it held a sour taste. "The ruination of planets. The killing of a billion innocent civilians to get at a few guilty leaders. The legacy of hatred. The corrosive effects of victory on the so-called victors. The Patrol has always existed to prevent war. If it instigated one—"

"Our intention," said Kaltro, "is to stop Ulugan without starting a war."

"How?"

"I can't tell you that. We have to have our secrets."

"And if you do provoke them into declaring one—?"

Alak shrugged. "That," he said, "is the chance we have to take."

"I warn you," said Meinz; "if you get us into real trouble, the Council will have your personal hides."

To that, neither of the Patrolmen replied.

Presently the administrator left. He took with him a bulky file of reports and sociodynamic calculations, and he gave no definite promises. But Kaltro nodded gravely at his agent. "He'll agree," he said.

"He'd better," said Alak. "I tell you, the situation is worse than I can describe, You have to be on such a planet and *feel* the hate and tension building up. Like… well…It feels sticky. You want to go wash yourself."

"Can you handle the operation?" asked Kaltro. "I'll have to stay behind to fend off outraged citizens."

"I can try," said Alak. There was a bleakness on his lips.

"And look, Wing," said Kaltro, "this is an unprecedented situation, I know. We're acting outside the League, and you might feel free, in real emergency, to violate the Prime Directive. Don't."

"I know," said Alak. "Any Patrolman who does—mnemonic erasure and cashiering from the service. No reasons or excuses accepted. It will be observed in this operation, too. Even if it costs us the war."

He left after a while, to begin on the mountain of paper work which is the essence of a large-scale mission. Not bureaucratic red tape, but necessary organizational detail, and nothing glamorous about it. Nothing of jack-booted heroes, roaring warships, and flaming guns.

But then, the League Patrol had little to do with such matters anyway. They who would end war cannot resort to it themselves, or the injustice, butchery, and waste of it will provoke a hatred that must finally destroy them. The Patrol cultivated a wholly fictitious reputation as a terrible enemy, it cooked news releases about its battles and it maintained a number of impressive fighting ships. When sweet reasonableness failed to enforce the arbitration of the League, the Patrol used bluff; when that failed, it used bribery, blackmail, fomented revolution, any means that came to hand. But always and forever it held by the Prime Directive which was its own most closely watched secret.

Under no circumstances whatsoever may the Patrol or any unit thereof kill an intelligent being.

A thousand warships lanced through an interstellar night. In their van were the scouts, flanking them were the cruisers, riding magnificently at their center were the monstrous dreadnoughts each of which could annihilate all life on an ordinary-sized planet. They convoyed another thousand noncombatant vessels—transports, supply craft, flying workshops. Behind them lay the stars of the League, lost in a cold glory of constellations; before them were the swelling suns of the loose cluster holding Ulugan.

The task force found the particular star it was looking for, a yellow dwarf some ten light-years from Tumu—which is simply the Unzuvani word for "sun"—and took up an orbit around the clouded second planet. Scouts dropping down through the atmosphere used infrared scopes to see through the mists and the hot, spilling rains; geosonic probes tested a thousand kilometers of swamp and jungle and sullen tideless ocean before reporting a stable surface. Then the big workships began landing.

Wing Alak stood in the phosphorescent twilight of the sixth day looking at the labor that went on around him. Blasters had driven back the jungle, exposing a raw red scar. Now, under the white glare of floodlights, robotracs moved ponderously back and forth, laying the foundations of a landing field. He could not see through the dimness and the acrid mists to the prefab barracks which housed his workers.

The planet was humanly habitable—just barely. Alak's clothes hung wetly around him and he cursed in a tired voice and wished it weren't too humid for him to sweat. The ceaseless thin buzz of the sanitator about his neck, destroying air-borne molds and bacteria that would otherwise soon have destroyed him, was in a fair way to driving him crazy. *And to think,* he reflected in one corner of his soggy brain, *I could have been a food factory technician at home.*

The scaly, tentacled Sarrushian Patrolmen who made up most of his gang sloshed happily through the muck. This hellhole was almost like their own planet. Not quite—there were some dangerous animals around, you could hear them stamping and roaring out in the fever-mists. And a weird sort of tree that shot poisoned thorns had killed two of his men already.

Won't those stupid Ulugani ever catch on?

It was no coincidence that the message should have come just then, for Alak had had few other thoughts since he first landed. The lean, beak-faced Karkarian who was his chief aide came from the communications shack and saluted, awkward in the space armor which was necessary for him here. His voder spoke tonelessly: "Subspace call, sir. From Tumu."

"Oh, good!" Alak felt too miserable to do more than nod, but he followed the tall metallic shape with a tinge of energy. It began to rain, and he was soaked before he reached the shack. Not a very dignified spectacle for the eyes of the Ulugani in the screen.

He sat down and ran a hand through his fiery hair. That face—yes, by the First Cause, it was General Sevulan of Hurulta's personal staff; he'd met him a few times. Mustering all his cheerfulness, he said: "Hello." That was an insult in itself.

"Are you in charge of this expedition?" snapped Sevulan.

"More or less," said Alak.

"I demand an immediate and official explanation," said the Ulugani. "A scout ship noticed radiations and investigated. You fired on it, though it got away—"

"Too bad," said Alak, though the fire had missed by his orders.

"That is an act of war in itself," rapped Sevulan.

"Not at all," said Alak. "This is a military reservation. Your scout probed in despite radioed orders to stop."

"But you are building a military base—on Garvish II!"

"That is correct. What of it?"

"Garvish is—"

"Unclaimed territory," said Alak coldly. "If Ulugan can take over Tukatan against the natives' will, the League can surely annex an uninhabited planet."

"You are within ten light-years of Tumu. My government must regard this as an unfriendly act."

"Well," said Alak, "your government hasn't been exactly friendly toward us, you know. We're just taking precautions."

"This is an ultimatum," said Sevulan. "If the subspace radio would reach so far, we would call the League secretariat directly, to give it. As it is, I am delivering it to you. If you do not evacuate Garvish at once, Ulugan will consider your aggression a cause for war."

"Now look—" began Alak.

"A task force is on its way to force your evacuation, if you will not go peacefully," said Sevulan. "Take your choice."

Weakness flitted across Alak's well-trained features. "I...I am really not given such responsibility," he said slowly. "You must allow me time to communicate with my government—"

"No!"

"Well—"

"You have my message," said Sevulan. The screen blanked.

Alak stood up, hugged his aide, and danced around the shack.

Hurulta the Arkazhik leaned over his desk as if he meant to attack Sevulan. Then, slowly, his great fists unclenched and he sat back.

"They were gone, you say?" he repeated.

"Yes, lord," said the general. "When our task force landed, the planet—the whole system—was abandoned. Obviously they took fright when they realized our determination."

"But *where* did they go?"

Sevulan permitted himself a shrug. "A light-year is too big to imagine," he said. "They could be anywhere, lord. My best guess is, though, that they are running home with their tails between their legs."

"Still—to abandon a base which must have cost an enormous effort and sum to start—"

"Yes, lord, it was astonishingly far advanced. They must have employed some life-form adapted to Garvish II conditions as workers. They do have that advantage: among their citizens, they can always find a species which is at home on any possible world." Sevulan smiled. "I suggest, lord, that we complete the base ourselves and use it, since they were obliging enough to do all the real labor."

Hurulta stroked his massive chin. "We have no choice," he said thinly. "If we don't hold that system, they may come back any time—and it is dangerously close to our home, and as you say their men can function better there than ours." He muttered an oath. "It's a nuisance. We need most of our forces to complete the conquest of Tukatan in a swift and orderly manner. But there's no help for it."

"We were going to take Garvish eventually, lord," said Sevulan respectfully.

"Yes, yes, of course. Take this whole cluster—and after that, who knows how much more? Still—" Being a realist, Hurulta dismissed his own annoyance. "As you say, this will save us time and money in the long run."

"I—"

Sevulan was interrupted by the buzzing of the official telescreen. Hurulta switched it on. "Yes?" he growled.

"General Ulanho of Central Intelligence reporting, lord."

"I know who you are. "What is it?"

"Scout just came in, lord. The Patrol is on Shang V. Apparently they're building another base."

"Shang V—"

"Twelve-point-three light-years from here, lord."

"I know that! Stand by." Hurulta switched off again. There was something of a giant dynamo about him as he swung on Sevulan.

"What sort of planet is this Shang V?" he snarled.

"Little known, lord," faltered the officer. "A big world, as I recall. Twice our gravity, mostly hydrogen atmosphere—storms of unparalleled violence, volcanic upheavals, a hell planet! I don't see how they would dare—"

"They must be relying on sheer audacity," snapped Hurulta. "Well, they won't get away with it! No ultimatum this time—no message of any kind. You will organize a task force to go there at once and blow them off it!"

The Arkazhik was in an ugly mood, and his subordinates tried to make themselves invisible as he stamped past them. But then, the whole planet was foul-tempered and jumpy. The Garvish and Shang operations had been—still were—messy and costly enterprises which completely disrupted the schedule for Tukatan. That the Patrol fleet had been gone when the Ulugani arrived at Shang, saving them a battle, was small consolation, for it meant that the enemy was still at large, he could strike anywhere, any time, bringing death and ruin out of the big spaces. That meant an elaborate warning system around Tumu, tying up hundreds of thousands of trained spacemen; it meant the inconveniences of civilian defense, force-screens over all cities, transportation slowed, space-raid drills, spy scares, nervousness among the commoners that was not far from exploding into hysteria. It meant that the unrewarding Shang System must also be garrisoned, lest the Patrol sneak back there. It meant irritation, delay, expense, and a turbulent cabinet meeting in which Hurulta had needed all his personality to control the dissatisfied members.

He took a grav-shaft now, dropping through many levels to a corridor hewn out of the rock below the capitol. Along this he stalked, the boots of his guards slamming a hollow rhythm back from the walls, until he came to a certain door. This he entered, to find a colonel of Intelligence seated among his instruments. The colonel bowed low. The little being in the chair merely cowered.

"What planet is this from?" grunted Hurulta. "Nobody told me that."

The small one spoke up in a fluting voice that could not hide his terror. He was a skinny, four-armed, greenish being, with a bulging-eyed head that seemed too big for his body. "Please, lord, I am from—"

"I didn't ask you," barked Hurulta, snapping at him. The oversized head rocked back on the spindling neck, and the prisoner began to cry. "Well?"

"From Aldebaran VIII, lord," said the colonel. "A League planet. His name is Goln, and he is a trader who has operated in this sector for a number of years. We pulled him in, together with all other aliens, according to your orders, lord, two days ago. No physical duress was necessary—in panic, he submitted to the usual truth-finding procedures. It turned out that he is a Patrol agent."

"That much I have already been told," snorted Hurulta. "What of it? Why should that concern me? He hasn't learned anything of value, has he?"

"No, lord, not about us. He was a trader too, as he claimed. He merely reported to Wing Alak from time to time, telling him whatever he had learned anywhere. Under our questioning, he revealed a distinct impression that Alak is interested in Umung."

"Umung…hm-m-m-…the insectiles, aren't they? About thirty light-years off, on the edge of our cluster."

"Yes, lord. He has traded with them for many years. They are a completely organized race, with little individual personality, but the collective intelligence is high. They are also, perhaps, the most skillful workers in the galaxy."

"Yes. It comes back to me now, Did Alak intend to organize them against us?"

"Not as far as this Goln knows, lord. They are totally unwarlike, have too little initiative to make good soldiers. Goln's impression is that the Patrol would like to deal with them, secretly, trading raw materials difficult to obtain on their world for finished products. That would, obviously, simplify the enemy supply problem."

"So…it…would." Hurulta stood in thought for a moment. Then, whirling on Goln, he made his voice a roar: "All right, scum, how well do you know Umung?"

The Aldebaranian shrieked in utter panic. When he found his voice again, he gasped: "Well, most excellent lord. I know it w-w-well—"

"You'll obey us and be rewarded, or you'll be pulled apart cell by cell. Which shall it be?"

"I…obey, my lord. The ps-s-s-sychomachines w-will show how well I m-mean to obey—"

"Good. I want you to prepare a dossier on Umung. Use the machines to help you remember everything. Correlate it with all information available in Intelligence files. Submit the complete report to me within an eight-day.

"I…I will try, l-lord—"

Hurulta turned back toward the door. No one dared speak to him as he went down the corridor, but his mind was busy.

Umung—yes. It had real possibilities. From all he had heard of it, Umung was a treasure chest. He had to prevent Alak's using it, of course—

But the Patrol! As long as they were in this vicinity, he could not declare war on the League. That might be just the excuse they wanted. He'd fight them if he caught them, but until then it was safer to wait, consolidate his victories.

But it wouldn't take much to occupy Umung. Not if its natives were as docile as all reports had it. And then he could show some real progress to those fat money barons. Already the war would have begun to pay off, and they'd support him in further schemes, let him build up his own power and prestige until the day he turned on them and broke them.

Umung, yes. By all the hells, yes!

Imagine a creature somewhat like an ant—only in general outline, to be sure. It stands a meter tall on two horny legs whose cilia, rubbed together, are its voice organs. There is one pair of tentacles, ending in supple boneless fingers; above them are the true arms, and there is a small stalk on the wrist of each arm holding an eye with microscopic vision. The head is faceless, little more than a set of jaws and a pair of larger eye-stalks for normal seeing. The creature is utterly obedient to the mass-mind of its hivelike community, a patient, tireless, delicate worker. Apart from food and reproduction, its only need is work. Once you have persuaded the mass-mind—embodied in the queen—that it is to its advantage to do as you say, a hundred thousand little brown artisans are ready to slave to the death for you.

Umung is not a large planet. Its atmosphere is thin and dry, its landscape mostly dreary plains. The Ulugani soldiers stationed there grumbled about its dullness. But not many were needed, and soldiers have always complained; it is a healthy sign.

Technicians were required in large numbers, to educate the Umungi in the use of machine tools. But the hive dwellers learned fast. Goln of Aldebaran was invaluable, he knew the ins and outs of native ways. Before long, a good part of the entire planet was ready to start producing for Ulugan.

It produced!

"All right, colonel, don't just stand there! Give me your report."

"If it please you, lord, my scout squadron was investigating the Junnuzhik System as per orders—"

"I know! We have to watch every planet of this cluster now, we never know where the Patrol may sneak in next—Well, what is it? Don't tell me they're trying to build another base!"

"No, lord. Our intelligence unit captured some leading natives of Ilwar for questioning—"

"Ilwar! What do you mean? I can't remember every stinking native name for every worthless little area of a thousand inhabited planets."

"The world is Junnuzhik III, lord, the only inhabited one in the system. The natives are centauroids—big scaly fellows, beaked heads, crests—Oh, yes, I see that my lord remembers now. Well, Ilwar is the leading nation on the planet. They've attained a petroleum technology, are pretty good metallurgists, and so on. Under pressure, it was found out that the Patrol has been dickering with them. Wants them to supply several million troops, presumably for an invasion of our planet."

"Patrol have any luck?"

"Well, lord, the natives are thoroughly anti-Ulugan. They assume that if we aren't stopped, we'll conquer them."

"True enough. But…oh, and damn! We'll just have to take over the planet."

"They're tough warriors, lord."

"I know. And occupying a whole planet is a major operation. But we can't simply sterilize; we'll need it ourselves in the long run. And we must take over the entire world now, colonel. At the very least, we must garrison thousands of key points, or the Patrol ships can simply sneak in and pick up their recruits. At this time, too!"

"Lord—"

"Shut up: File a complete report. Now get out of here. Hello, hello, give me the General Staff building…Commander Tuac? Ready your planners, boy. We're going to invade still another world."

"Tuac? Listen and obey."

"Yes, lord."

"You know the planet Yarnaz IV?"

"Hm-m-m…let me think, lord."

"Don't. You're not capable of it—you and your planning section!"

"Lord, how could we know the Hwari would be such guerrilla fighters? Even under extreme difficulties, we're carrying all the conquest—it's just going more slowly than we had anticipated. If we could only have more troops, more supplies—"

"Shut up, I said! We haven't even finished with Tukatan itself, thanks to that Patrol. Junnuzhik will have to make do with what we can spare. Now listen, or I'll have your head. Yarnaz is a red dwarf sun about fifteen light-years from Tumu. Its fourth planet is trackless desert, poisonous air, venomous life. Nevertheless, our checkup reveals that the Patrol has been there. Not a base. They've been mining near the equator. *Why?*"

"Lord, I can't say. Unless they wanted supplies—fissionables, perhaps—"

"I checked up on that, idiot. Yarnaz IV is about as poor in natural resources as empty space itself."

"Could it be a camouflage, lord? A device to divert our attention from their real activities?"

"It may well be. But, we don't *know!* The Patrol seems to have studied the primitive planets of our cluster better than we have ourselves. Furthermore, they have the natives of a million worlds to choose from in making up their crews. Doubtless there is at least one race in the League to whom Yarnaz IV is just like home. We can't know where their real advantage lies."

"Well, lord, it…it looks as if we'll have to establish garrisons there."

"I'm glad you've seen that much. How soon can you send a force?"

"The planning—Lord, we're getting bogged down. There's just too much to handle. Even one world is a major problem in strategy, tactics, logistics—"

"Nevertheless, Yarnaz IV shall be occupied within one month. Or do you want your head adorning a pole in Market Square?"

Fear was cold along the spine of Hurulta as he looked at the being in the cage.

It seemed harmless enough—a small kangaroolike mammal, with big ears on its round, blunt-muzzled head. The sensitive four-fingered hands spoke of intelligence, the basic tool-making ability. There was no menace in the soft brown eyes.

Nevertheless Hurulta was afraid. It took all the discipline he had to face that creature and hold his own visage expressionless.

"It was caught on the fringes of Dengavash City, lord, just after the riots there," said the police officer. "Obviously it was the thing responsible. It creates an aura of terror."

Hurulta forced his tongue to shape coherent words. "Where's it from?"

"We checked up, lord. It's from Gyreion, as the explorers have named it—a planet not unlike ours, on the fringes of our cluster. This is one of the natives. They haven't been studied much, but seem to be a timid paleolithic race. Telepaths, though."

"I…see. And when they're frightened, as must happen rather easily, they radiate the fear-impulse and our minds pick it up."

"Yes, lord. We think a Patrol sneak-boat must have taken a few and dropped them here on Ulugan. We'll soon round up the others and we'll be sure."

"Um-m-m." Hurulta's heavy blue face contracted in a scowl. It was hard to think clearly, when he had to keep fighting down the germ of panic that screamed far down within him. "Yes. A good idea. But quantitatively insufficient. The Patrol can't possibly smuggle enough of them here to make any significant trouble."

"No, lord. Just nuisance value. Like everything they've done so far, isn't it…if I may make bold to speak."

Hurulta turned and walked out of the room. Gyreion—hm-m-m. A tough nut to crack, that world—but worth while. If enough of those hoppers could be turned loose on an enemy planet—why, it was the ultimate in psychological warfare!

The League planets—a decadent bunch. They couldn't stand up long to such fear. They'd be ready to surrender to the first warship that came along.

Meanwhile, it was necessary to cut off the Patrol's access to Gyreion. Wouldn't take too big a force for an effective occupation; the natives weren't fighters. Once their fears had been calmed, they would be quite harmless—to Ulugan.

This time, my friend, he thought with a savage glee, *this time you've finally overreached yourself!*

Wing Alak was getting bored. He didn't have much to do now but sit in his flagship and read the reports of his scouts and radio monitors. He welcomed the newcomer who had arrived with the last courier ship from home, even if it did mean a struggle.

Jorel Meinz entered the vessel and followed Alak down a long corridor. His nose wrinkled a bit at the many odors that filled it. The crew of the battlewagon all came from terrestroid planets, but they had their characteristic smells and their own styles of cooking; no ventilation system could quite purify the air. But then, he reminded himself, a Terran probably didn't smell any better to them.

Alak's cabin was a spacious one, sybaritically furnished. One large viewport showed the eerie hugeness of space, the rest of the room seemed devoted to human comfort just to offset that chilling spectacle. The Patrolman waited till he was alone with his guest before pouring out drinks.

"Scotch," he said. "It may not mean much to you, but out here it's a real luxury."

"The Patrol seems to do itself well," observed Meinz.

"Quite," nodded Alak. "When you're out for months or years at a time, surrounded by total alienness, every comfort means a lot. It's pure superstition that the being with a low standard of living is hardier." He lifted his glass and sipped appreciatively.

"Are you sure you won't be found out here?" asked Meinz. "I imagine the enemy is ripping holes in space, hunting for you."

Alak grinned, which made him more than ever resemble a fox. "No doubt they are," he said. "The harder they search, the better I like it, since it means a useless waste of their time, men, and matériel. Several thousand cubic light-years makes a pretty effective concealment. Anyway, if by some freak they should blunder across us, we need only run for it."

Meinz scowled. "That's what I'm here about," he said brusquely.

"Aren't they satisfied at home with my conduct of the operation?"

"Frankly, no. Now I'm on your side, Alak. I was the one who pushed that approval through Parliament. But that was almost a year ago, and so far you've reported no results at all. Your dispatches have been so much meaningless verbiage, Finally certain political groups hired an investigating force of their own. They sent out observers—"

"A wonder they weren't nabbed, Hurulta has an efficient Intelligence Service and Secret Police."

"Well, they weren't. They saw enough to send them hightailing back home, and the stink it's raised on Terra—"

"Ah-hah! That explains it. Hurulta must have foreseen that result and let the observers do as they pleased. He's a canny lad, that old blueface."

"Well, you must admit there's some justification for the complaints," said Meinz with a hint of bitterness. "The authorization was of doubtful legality in the first place, and could only be justified at the next Council meeting if there were solid results to show. Instead, you've dawdled out here, skulking I might say. You haven't fought one battle, not so much as a skirmish. You've let Ulugan occupy no less than seven planets besides Tukatan—"

"At last reports, it was about twenty," said Alak blandly. "We've got them scared, you see. They're grabbing everything that might conceivably be of value to us."

"In other words," said Meinz, "you're pushing them in exactly the direction they want to go."

"Correct."

"Now look, Alak, I came out here myself, and it's a long troublesome journey, to get your side of it. I have to tell them something at home, or they'll pass a recall order in spite of everything I can do. Now I'm not even sure if I would resist such a move."

"Give me credit for some sense," urged Alak. "I can't tell you everything. The real reason why we operate this way is a Patrol secret. Let's just say, which is true enough, that outright war is cruel and expensive, and that I don't even think we could win one."

"But what *are* you doing then, man?"

"Just sitting here," laughed Alak. "Sitting here drinking Scotch, and letting nature take its course."

The medical officer halted at the entrance to the tent. The steady, endless rain dripped off his shoulders and made a puddle about his muddy feet. By the one glaring lamp inside, he noticed that the fungus had begun to devour this tent, too. It would be a rag before the eight-day was out. And you couldn't live in the metal barracks left by the Patrolmen—they were bake-ovens, and air-conditioning units rotted and rusted too fast to be of help.

He saluted wearily. The commandant of Garvish Base looked up from his game of galanzu solitaire. "What is it?" he asked listlessly.

"Fifteen more men down with fever, sir," said the medical officer. "And ten of the earlier cases are dead."

The commandant nodded. Light gleamed off his wet bald head. The blue face was haggard, unhealthily flushed, and the smart uniform was a sodden ruin. "The sanitators don't work, eh?" he asked.

"Not against this stuff, sir," said the doctor. "It seems to be a virus which isn't bothered by the vibrations, but I haven't been able to isolate it yet."

"We just aren't built for this climate." The commandant wagged his head, and one shaky hand reached for a bottle. "We're cold-world dwellers."

A beast screamed out in the jungle. "Poison plants got several more this eight-day," said the doctor.

"I know. I've begged and pleaded with headquarters to send us air domes and space armor. But they claim it's needed elsewhere."

A faint hope flickered in the medical officer's eyes. "When that planet Umung really gets to producing—"

"Yes, yes. But we'll probably be dead then, you and I." The commandant shivered. "I feel cold." His voice was suddenly high and thin.

"Sir—" The doctor took a nervous step forward. "Sir, let me look at you—"

The commandant stood up. For a moment he leaned on the table, then something buckled within him and he went toppling to the floor.

There was forest, endless forest, and beyond it the plains and mountains and sea, and all of it was full of death.

The Patrol wound slowly through the woods. Every detector they had was straining itself—metal, mental pulses, the thermal radiation of living bodies. But still eyes were restless, shifting under the big square helmets, and hands strayed nervously toward guns.

In an armored car near the middle of the column, the Ulugani Patrol chief was sounding off to his aide. "It's no good," he said. "These Hwari are just too tough for us."

"They can't stand up to us, sir," said the aide. "Not in open battle."

"And they don't try. What can you do with a people who're willing to scorch their earth and evacuate their own dwellings before we get there? What's the point of silly little actions like this one—going out, burning a city in reprisal, what does the enemy care? It's just a chance for him to harass us some more."

"We'll teach them manners, sir," said the aide.

"Oh, in time, of course. In time. When we get enough troops and supplies here. But curse it, I can't *get* enough!"

An explosion cracked before them. The chief saw three men fall screaming from the grenade. A heavy machine gun began to clatter.

"Guerrillas!" he roared.

He glimpsed the big green forms dashing in out of the brush. They could gallop like the wind, those devils, and they could carry as much armament on their backs as a small truck. The war whoop sent a brief tingle of fear along his nerves.

The tanks began to speak, throwing flame and thunder at the enemy. One of the machines was suddenly wrapped in red smoke—a fire bomb. The Ulugani infantry had thrown themselves to the ground and were shooting up at the trampling, yelling centauroids.

"Drive 'em back!" screamed the chief. "Drive 'em back!"

The Patrol did, after a short interval of utter ferocity. But not before a bomb had struck the command car and incinerated its contents.

The colonel looked out of the thick plastic port and shivered. Beyond it, the landscape was one vast gloom. Poisonous mists curled between him and the unseen horizon, like a wall. He thought he could see the sudden red spouting of a volcano, somewhere in the fog. A moment later, the floor quivered under his feet.

"You fool!" he raged. "You utter imbecile!"

The base geologist stood his ground. "'We did our best, sir," he answered. "As far as we could tell, the terrain here was stable."

"One whole base has already been destroyed in a quake. Isn't that enough for you?"

The wind slapped monstrously at the dome. They had never seen such gales as blew endlessly across Shang V. A blind whirl of sleet—solid ammonia—hid the outside view.

"Sir," said the geologist, "this planet is utterly crazy. The probes gave readings that on any normal world would mean safe, solid ground."

"Nevertheless, one of our domes has just been cracked open. Every man within it died instantly. You and your team are due for court-martial."

The geologist nodded.

"As the colonel says. But may I suggest that we find another site? This one is obviously dangerous after all."

"And do you realize what it means, in terms of effort and materials, to break camp on this planet?"

"I can't help that, sir. I am officially proposing that we move."

"Headquarters will have my skin, too," said the colonel gloomily. He looked out again at the sinister land. "How could we know? How could anyone have foretold it would be like this?"

The Patrol knew! laughed his mind. *They knew! Now all I can do is submit a recommendation that we evacuate. The other commanders here will back me up. But that's an invitation to the enemy to return.*

The floor trembled. He heard a paperweight jump on his desk. Outside, not five meters off, a hole opened in the ground—slowly, hugely, with all the time in the universe to do its work. Fire spilled from it, and magma crawled forth toward the dome.

The Elgash family had come up the hard way, from the peasant stock of a conquered land; it had been ennobled only fifty years ago. For that, and for its owning the Munitions Trust, Hurulta despised it. But he did not underestimate the being who sat across from his desk. The present Elgash was fat and wheezy and dandified, but there was a hard drive and a cold brain in him.

"I speak for several others, your excellency," he said. "I need not mention their names."

"The money barons," replied Hurulta sullenly. "The industrialists and financiers. What of it?"

"Shall I speak plainly?" asked Elgash.

"Go ahead. We're alone."

"The group I represent is not at all satisfied with the conduct of the war."

"Oh? And you have constituted yourselves the new General Staff?"

"Spare the sarcasm, your excellency. It was understood that Tukatan would be subjugated within six months. Now, after almost a year, we are still fighting there."

"They could be bombarded from space," said Hurulta, "but as you well know, that would destroy the whole value of the planet. We have to go slowly. Then the Patrol appeared to complicate matters."

"I realize all that." The insolence was more marked than ever. "And rather than concentrate on Tukatan and the Patrol, and get them safely out of the way, your ministry has tried to take on the whole star cluster. You have blundered disastrously into planets we hardly knew a thing about."

"To keep the Patrol from using them against us." Hurulta checked his temper. "All right, I admit we've had our troubles. But we're making progress. The over-all timetable for the establishment of our hegemony has been accelerated enormously. In the long run, that will mean a saving."

"Will it now? Even your successes are dubious. Take that forsaken little pill of sand, Yarnaz IV. There's been no trouble in occupying it. But the expense of maintaining bases under such alien conditions is fantastic. The commoners are being taxed to the limit, and your new tax on the leading groups of society is outrageous."

"It has to be done. Or would you rather have the Patrol come in and run things?"

"Of course," said Elgash coldly, "your most inexcusable blunder was the occupation of Umung."

"*What?*" For a moment Hurulta could find no words. Slowly, then, he gulped down his rage, and when he spoke it was with thin precision. "That was the one operation which went off like clockwork. At a negligible cost in men and money, we have already doubled our war production. Inside another year, we can expect to quadruple it."

"I thought you were a realist, your excellency," said Elgash. "I thought you understood the economic foundation on which the empire rests. Or are you deliberately ruining my class?"

"Are you mad? First you complain about taxes, then when I find a way to increase production, a way that costs us hardly one crown, you—"

"Your excellency, we have only so many soldiers and there is a limit to the amount of war matériel they can use. When Umung is producing all of it, *what will become of Ulugan's factories?*"

Fear.

Shamuvaz, soldier of the empire, looked around him. He moved his head very slowly, lest he see something behind his back. There was only the landscape-distorted trees, murmuring reddish grass, a remote waterfall that echoed the furious clamor of his heart.

He felt ill. He wanted to vomit. Looking at the faces of his companions, he thought that they were impossibly alien. They were evil. They were made evil by the same horror that rode on him, and in their panic they might turn and tear him.

Shamuvaz whimpered, deep in his throat, and thought of his wife and children. They were so far away, so many centuries away, he would never see them again. He would rot on Gyreion, the wind would blow through his ribs and the small beasts of the field would nest in his empty, empty skull.

They said it was harmless. They said it was only that the natives—so thoroughly indoctrinated by the Patrol that there was no dealing with them…or was it that, being telepaths, they knew Ulugan meant them for pawns?—the natives were afraid, and you yourself heard their fear. Nothing to it. Ignore it. You are a soldier of the empire, and fear of nothingness is unworthy of you.

Only the generals didn't have to live with fear. They didn't have to torment themselves, night after night, to stay awake, for fear of the dreams; and when they finally did sleep, in spite of everything, they weren't brought up within minutes, screaming. They didn't see their comrades break, one by one, and be sent home muttering idiot words, and wonder when their turn would come.

Fear, panic, terror, blind howling horror. Shamuvaz groaned to himself.

When a hand touched his shoulder, he leaped up, cursing, and spun around. His pistol was out before he saw that it was only Armazan. Armazan had been his best friend once. But you couldn't trust anyone now. Shamuvaz held the gun leveled on Armazan's belly.

"Don't do that," he choked. "Don't ever do that again."

"Listen." Armazan spoke swiftly, a whisper that was blurred with his own trembling. "Listen, Sham, we're meeting after taps, down by the river. Sneak out of the barracks and join us."

"What, what, what? Go out after dark? You're crazy! This planet has driven you crazy."

"No, not that, not that. Listen, a lot of us have decided we aren't going to take any more of this. The empire can't ask it of us. It's too much. Can't trust those officers. Get them out of the way—a shot in the back, it's easy if we just stick together, and then we can grab the base spaceship—"

Hurulta had been sleeping poorly in the last month, and drugs no longer seemed to whip up his vitality. He clasped a ringing head in his hands and leaned on the desk.

"It's no use," he said aloud. "We'll have to pull out of Gyreion. Every regiment there has been ruined for service. It'll take months to restore them to usefulness."

"But the Patrol, lord—" faltered Sevulan.

"Patrol! We'll maintain a base on the neighboring planet, and a few orbital scouts around Gyreion itself. Should have done that in the first place."

"But then a strong attack could come in, wipe out our forces, take over the whole system—"

"I know. What of it? A chance we'll have to take. If only the busybodies would come out of hiding and fight! It's like shadowboxing, this."

"Lord, I understand the General Staff plans to overrule you and order the evacuation of Garvish and Shang. They say it's too costly to hold them, they're just consuming men badly needed elsewhere—"

"Don't tell me that!" shouted Hurulta. "I know it, you idiot! I know all of it! The blind, bloody fools! Shortsighted—aaargh!" His fists clamped together. "But by all the hells, we're hanging on to Umung. Let the moneybags squawk. I'll lodge treason charges if they say much more."

The telescreen buzzed. Hurulta flicked a switch, and the excited voice gabbled out.

"Lord, a report just came in from space. Patrol activity around Ustuban VII. They seem to be rendezvousing—"

"Ustuban VII! They can't! It's a giant planet. It's surrounded by a meteor belt. It…no!"

"Lord, the report says—"

"*Shut up!* Send me the full report at once." Hurulta whirled on the general. His eyes were feverish.

"Action," he gasped. "I think we're going to see some action. The populace has been complaining about our retreats, have they? Their morale is bad, is it?

All right, we'll give them something to talk about. We'll send the fleet and seize Ustuban VII, and just let the Patrol dare try to stop us!"

"Lord, it's impossible," whispered Sevulan. "We're spread so thin already that we could never mount such an undertaking. It's just a trick of theirs to lure us out—"

"We'll turn the trick on them!" Hurulta's bellow rattled between the walls. "I'm still the supreme commander here!"

Slowly, as he regarded his chief, Sevulan's eyes narrowed.

"We have, of course, been propagandizing Ulugan," said Wing Alak. "Radio, message-scattering robombs, and so on—the usual techniques. I think we've gotten it across to them that, while League membership means a loss of imperial glories, it means a definite gain in material comfort and security."

"For the commoners," said Jorel Meinz. He was annoyed; three days aboard ship, with Alak engaged in directing some obscure maneuver and parrying every significant question when the two men did meet, had worn down his nerves. "But it's the aristocrats and the industrialists who run things."

"To be sure. However, they aren't stupid. They just need a hard lesson to convince them that imperialism doesn't pay."

"They were all set to make it pay."

"Of course, till we interfered. But as long as there is a Patrol, conquest will mean a money loss. We'll see to that! Once they're convinced that it's to their advantage too to come to terms with us, they'll do it."

"I see your general strategy, of course," said Meinz. "You've led them into taking over one unprofitable planet after another. Except this Umung, now…I can't see where that could fail to pay off."

"Oh, that was my proudest achievement," said Alak smugly. "I planned that years in advance. I had a cowardly little part-time agent who got to know Umung quite well. As far as he could tell, I meant to use it for the Patrol's benefit. Ulugan got hold of him, as I thought they would, and learned this. So naturally Ulugan had to grab it first.

"But don't you see, I've studied their economy for years. It's an archaic form of capitalism, like Terra's during the First Industrial Revolution. It depends on buying cheap and selling dear—and it must sell manufactured goods. In short, a colony which can manufacture better and cheaper than the mother country is, in the long run, impossible; it must be abandoned or ruined, or else the homeland's economic system must be changed. After a while, Ulugan's financiers realized that. And they're a powerful element."

He lit a cigarette and leaned back in his chair. "If I might generalize a bit," he said, "history shows pretty conclusively that an empire must form a natural socioeconomic unit if it is to be stable. Most empires of the past grew slowly, by accretion; or if they were conquered fast, they had to be reorganized swiftly. We forced the Ulugani into taking on more real estate than they could handle, most of it more than useless; and we kept them off balance so that they couldn't get a chance to organize it properly. Result—an unstable situation which is now rapidly deteriorating."

"Do we *want* them within the League?" asked Meinz. "They look like a nest of troublemakers."

"They are. But in the long run, they can be integrated. Contact with other cultures will break down their paranoid attitude. Interstellar empires are economically unjustifiable anyway, more of a drain than a gain. If you've mastered faster-than-light travel, you are also able to produce just about everything you need at home, and trade for the rest. They'll come to see that too, eventually."

He glanced at the intercom. "I'm expecting a message hourly," he said. "My last scout ship brought some interesting political news from Ulugan."

"Eh?"

"Play me some chess, will you? I love dramatic revelations. You can allow me this one. It's been a rather dreary year."

It was only half an hour later that the ship's radioman announced a subspace broadcast, Ulugan calling the Patrol command. Alak made a leisurely way to the communications room, letting Meinz jitter behind him.

The blue face in the screen was trying hard to maintain its old arrogance, but not succeeding very well. "Hello, Sevulan," said Alak. "What's new?"

"There has been a change of government in the empire," said the Ulugani stiffly.

"Violent, I'm sure. Did you shoot Hurulta or just jail him?"

"The Arkazhik is—very ill. Frankly, we suspected he was a mental case. His rashness brought on many actions of which the new cabinet never did approve."

"Well," said Alak genially, "if you want to negotiate, here are my terms."

When he had finished, and sent a representative off to meet the Ulugani delegation, he yawned mightily. "I think that's that," he said. "There'll be a lot of dickering, of course, and cleaning up the military forces there will take time. But we've got what we were after."

"You mean—" Meinz chuckled dryly. This success wasn't going to hurt his own career a bit. "You mean you let them give you what you wanted."

"Oh, no," said Wing Alak. "I was the donor all along. I gave Hurulta all the rope he needed."

THE SHARING OF FLESH

1.

Moru understood about guns.
 At least the tall strangers had demonstrated to their guides what the things that each of them carried at his hip could do in a flash and a flameburst. But he did not realize that the small objects they often moved about in their hands, while talking in their own language, were audiovisual transmitters. Probably he thought they were fetishes.

Thus, when he killed Donli Sairn, he did so in full view of Donli's wife.

That was happenstance. Except for prearranged times at morning and evening of the planet's twenty-eight-hour day, the biologist, like his fellows, sent only to his computer. But because they had not been married long and were helplessly happy, Evalyth received his 'casts whenever she could get away from her own duties.

The coincidence that she was tuned in at that one moment was not great. There was little for her to do. As militech of the expedition—she being from a half barbaric part of Kraken where the sexes had equal opportunities to learn arts of combat suitable to primitive environments—she had overseen the building of a compound; and she kept the routines of guarding it under a close eye. However, the inhabitants of Lokon were as cooperative with the visitors from heaven as mutual mysteriousness allowed. Every instinct and experience assured Evalyth Sairn that their reticence masked nothing except awe, with perhaps a wistful hope of friendship. Captain Jonafer agreed. Her position having thus become rather a sinecure, she was trying to learn enough about Donli's work to be a useful assistant after he returned from the lowlands.

Also, a medical test had lately confirmed that she was pregnant. She wouldn't tell him, she decided, not yet, over all those hundreds of kilometers, but rather when they lay again together. Meanwhile, the knowledge that they had begun a new life made him a lodestar to her.

On the afternoon of his death she entered the bio-lab whistling. Outside, sunlight struck fierce and brass-colored on dusty ground, on prefab shacks huddled about the boat which had brought everyone and everything down from the orbit where *New Dawn* circled, on the parked flitters and gravsleds that took men around the big island that was the only habitable land on this globe, on the men and the women themselves. Beyond the stockade, plumy treetops, a glimpse of mud-brick buildings, a murmur of voices and mutter of footfalls, a drift of bitter woodsmoke, showed that a town of several thousand people sprawled between here and Lake Zelo.

The bio-lab occupied more than half the structure where the Sairns lived. Comforts were few, when ships from a handful of cultures struggling back to civilization ranged across the ruins of empire. For Evalyth, though, it sufficed that this was their home. She was used to austerity anyway. One thing that had first attracted her to Donli, meeting him on Kraken, was the cheerfulness with which he, a man from Atheia, which was supposed to have retained or regained almost as many amenities as Old Earth knew in its glory, had accepted life in her gaunt grim country.

The gravity field here was 0.77 standard, less than two-thirds of what she had grown in. Her gait was easy through the clutter of apparatus and specimens. She was a big young woman, good-looking in the body, a shade too strong in the features for most men's taste outside her own folk. She had their blondness and, on legs and forearms, their intricate tattoos; the blaster at her waist had come down through many generations. Otherwise she had abandoned Krakener costume for the plain coveralls of the expedition.

How cool and dim the shack was! She sighed with pleasure, sat down, and activated the receiver. As the image formed, three-dimensional in the air, and Donli's voice spoke, her heart sprang a little.

"—appears to be descended from a clover."

The image was of plants with green trilobate leaves, scattered low among the reddish native pseudo-grasses. It swelled as Donli brought the transmitter near so that the computer might record details for later analysis. Evalyth frowned, trying to recall what…Oh, yes. Clover was another of those life forms that man had brought with him from Old Earth, to more planets than anyone now remembered, before the Long Night fell. Often they were virtually unrecognizable; over thousands of years, evolution had fitted them to alien conditions, or mutation and genetic drift had acted on small initial populations in a nearly random fashion. No one on Kraken had known that pines and gulls and rhizobacteria were altered immigrants, until Donli's crew arrived and identified them. Not that he, or anybody from this part of the galaxy, had yet made it back to the mother world. But the Atheian data banks were packed with information; and, so was Donli's dear curly head—

And there was his hand, huge in the field of view, gathering specimens. She wanted to kiss it. *Patience, patience,* the officer part of her reminded the bride. *We're here to work. We've discovered one more lost colony, the most wretched one so far; sunken back to utter primitivism. Our duty is to advise the Board, whether a civilizing mission is worthwhile, or whether the slender resources that the Allied Planets can spare had better be used elsewhere, leaving these people in their misery for another two or three hundred years. To make an honest report, we must study them, their cultures, their world. That's why I'm in the barbarian highlands and he's down in the jungle among out-and-out savages.*

Please finish soon, darling.

She heard Donli speak in the lowland dialect. It was a debased form of Lokonese, which in turn was remotely descended from Anglic. The expedition's linguists had unraveled the language in a few intensive weeks. Then all personnel took a brain-feed in it. Nonetheless, she admired how quickly her man had become fluent in the woodsrunners' version, after mere days of conversation with them.

"Are we not coming to the place, Moru? You said the thing was close by our camp."

"We are nearly arrived, man-from-the-clouds."

A tiny alarm struck within Evalyth. What was going on? Donli hadn't left his companions to strike off alone with a native had he? Rogar of Lokon had warned them to beware of treachery in those parts. But, to be sure, only yesterday the guides had rescued Haimie Fiell when he tumbled into a swift-running river...at some risk to themselves...

The view bobbed as the transmitter swung in Donli's grasp. It made Evalyth a bit dizzy. From time to time, she got glimpses of the broader setting. Forest crowded about a game trail, rust-colored leafage, brown trunks and branches, shadows beyond, the occasional harsh call of something unseen. She could practically feel the heat and dank weight of the atmosphere, smell the unpleasant pungencies. This world—which no longer had a name, except World, because the dwellers upon it had forgotten what the stars really were—was ill suited to colonization. The life it had spawned was often poisonous, always nutritionally deficient. With the help of species they had brought along, men survived marginally. The original settlers doubtless meant to improve matters. But then the breakdown came—evidence was that their single town had been missiled out of existence, a majority of the people with it—and resources were lacking to rebuild; the miracle was that anything human remained except bones.

"Now here, man-from-the-clouds."

The swaying scene grew steady. Silence hummed from jungle to cabin. "I do not see anything," Donli said at length.

"Follow me. I show."

Donli put his transmitter in the fork of a tree. It scanned him and Moru while they moved across a meadow. The guide looked childish beside the space traveler, barely up to his shoulder; an old child, though, near-naked body seamed with scars and lame in the right foot from some injury of the past, face wizened in a great black bush of hair and beard. He, who could not hunt but could only fish and trap to support his family, was even more impoverished than his fellows. He must have been happy indeed when the flitter landed near their village and the strangers offered fabulous trade goods for a week or two of being shown around the countryside. Donli had projected the image of Moru's straw hut for

Evalyth—the pitiful few possessions, the woman already worn out with toil, the surviving sons who, at ages said to be about seven or eight, which would equal twelve or thirteen standard years, were shriveled gnomes.

Rogar seemed to declare—the Lokonese tongue was by no means perfectly understood yet—that the lowlanders would be less poor if they weren't such a vicious lot, tribe forever at war with tribe. *But really,* Evalyth thought, *what possible menace can they be?*

Moru's gear consisted of a loinstrap, a cord around his body for preparing snares, an obsidian knife, and a knapsack so woven and greased that it could hold liquids at need. The other men of his group, being able to pursue game and to win a share of booty by taking part in battles, were noticeably better off. They didn't look much different in person, however. Without room for expansion, the island populace must be highly inbred.

The dwarfish man squatted, parting a shrub with his hands. "Here," he grunted, and stood up again.

Evalyth knew well the eagerness that kindled in Donli. Nevertheless he turned around, smiled straight into the transmitter, and said in Atheian: "Maybe you're watching, dearest. If so, I'd like to share this with you. It may be a bird's nest."

She remembered vaguely that the existence of birds would be an ecologically significant datum. What mattered was what he had just said to her. "Oh, yes, oh, yes!" she wanted to cry. But his group had only two receivers with them, and he wasn't carrying either.

She saw him kneel in the long, ill-colored vegetation. She saw him reach with the gentleness she also knew, into the shrub, easing its branches aside.

She saw Moru leap upon his back. The savage wrapped legs about Donli's middle. His left hand seized Donli's hair and pulled the head back. The knife flew back in his right.

Blood spurted from beneath Donli's jaw. He couldn't shout, not with his throat gaping open; he could only bubble and croak while Moru haggled the wound wider. He reached blindly for his gun. Moru dropped the knife and caught his arms; they rolled over in that embrace, Donli threshed and flopped in the spouting of his own blood. Moru hung on. The brush trembled around them and hid them, until Moru rose red and dripping, painted, panting, and Evalyth screamed into the transmitter beside her, into the universe, and she kept on screaming and fought them when they tried to take her away from the scene in the meadow where Moru went about his butcher's work, until something stung her with coolness and she toppled into the bottom of the universe whose stars had all gone out forever.

2.

Haimie Fiell said through white lips: "No, of course we didn't know till you alerted us. He and that—creature were several kilometers from our camp. *Why* didn't you let us go after him right away?"

"Because of what we'd seen on the transmission," Captain Jonafer replied. "Sairn was irretrievably dead. You could've been ambushed, arrows in the back or something, pushing down those narrow trails. Best stay where you were, guarding each other, till we got a vehicle to you."

Fiell looked past the big gray-haired man, out the door of the command hut, to the stockade and the unpitying noon sky. "But what that little monster was doing meanwhile—" Abruptly he closed his mouth.

With equal haste, Jonafer said: "The other guides ran away, you have told me, as soon as they sensed you were angry. I've just had a report from Kallaman. His team flitted to the village. It's deserted. The whole tribe's pulled up stakes. Afraid of our revenge, evidently. Though it's no large chore to move, when you can carry your household goods on your back and weave a new house in a day."

Evalyth leaned forward. "Stop evading me," she said. "What did Moru do with Donli that you might have prevented if you'd arrived in time?"

Fiell continued to look past her. Sweat gleaned in droplets on his forehead. "Nothing, really," he mumbled. "Nothing that mattered...once the murder itself had been committed."

"I meant to ask you what kind of services you want for him, Lieutenant Sairn," Jonafer said to her. "Should the ashes be buried here, or scattered in space after we leave, or brought home?"

Evalyth turned her gaze full upon him. "I never authorized that he be cremated, Captain," she said slowly.

"No, but— Well, be realistic. You were first under anesthesia, then heavy sedation while we recovered the body. Time had passed. We've no facilities for, um, cosmetic repair, nor any extra refrigeration space, and in this heat—"

Since she had been let out of sickbay, there had been a kind of numbness in Evalyth. She could not entirely comprehend the fact that Donli was gone. It seemed as if at any instant yonder doorway would fill with him, sunlight across his shoulders, and he would call to her, laughing, and console her for a meaningless nightmare she had had. That was the effect of the psycho-drugs, she knew and damned the kindliness of the medic.

She felt almost glad to feel a slow rising anger. It meant the drugs were wearing off. By evening she would be able to weep.

"Captain," she said, "I saw him killed. I've seen deaths before, some of them quite messy. We do not mask the truth on Kraken. You've cheated me of my right to lay my man out and close his eyes. You will not cheat me of my right to obtain justice. I demand to know exactly what happened."

Jonafer's fists knotted on his desktop. "I can hardly stand to tell you."

"But you shall, Captain."

"All right! All right!" Jonafer shouted. The words leaped out like bullets. "We saw the thing transmitted. He stripped Donli, hung him up by the heels from a tree, bled him into that knapsack. He cut off the genitals and threw them in with the blood. He opened the body and took heart, lungs, liver, kidneys, thyroid, prostate, pancreas, and loaded them up too, and ran off into the woods. Do you wonder why we didn't let you see what was left?"

"The Lokonese warned us against the jungle dwellers," Fiell said dully. "We should have listened. But they seemed like pathetic dwarfs. And they did rescue me from the river. When Donli asked about the birds—described them, you know, and asked if anything like that was known—Moru said yes, but they were rare and shy; our gang would scare them off; but if one man would come along with him, he could find a nest and they might see the bird. A house he called it, but Donli thought he meant a nest. Or so he told us. It'd been a talk with Moru when they happened to be a ways offside, in sight but out of earshot. Maybe that should have alerted us, maybe we should have asked the other tribesmen. But we did not see any reason to—I mean, Donli was bigger, stronger, armed with a blaster. What savage would dare attack him? And anyway, they *had* been friendly, downright frolicsome after they got over their initial fear of us, and they'd shown as much eagerness for further contact as anybody here in Lokon has, and—" His voice trailed off.

"Did he steal tools or weapons?" Evalyth asked.

"No," Jonafer said. "I have everything your husband was carrying, ready to give you."

Fiell said: "I don't think it was an act of hatred. Moru must have had some superstitious reason."

Jonafer nodded. "We can't judge him by our standards."

"By whose, then?" Evalyth retorted. Supertranquilizer or no, she was surprised at the evenness of her own tone. "I'm from Kraken, remember. I'll not let Donli's child be born and grow up knowing he was murdered and no one tried to do justice for him."

"You can't take revenge on an entire tribe," Jonafer said.

"I don't mean to. But, Captain, the personnel of this expedition are from several different planets, each with its characteristic societies. The articles specifically state that the essential mores of every member shall be respected. I want to be relieved of my regular duties until I have arrested the killer of my husband and done justice upon him."

Jonafer bent his head. "I have to grant that," he said low.

Evalyth rose. "Thank you, gentlemen," she said. "If you will excuse me, I'll commence my investigation at once."

—While she was still a machine, before the drugs wore off.

3.

In the drier, cooler uplands, agriculture had remained possible after the colony otherwise lost civilization. Fields and orchards, painstakingly cultivated with neolithic tools, supported a scattering of villages and the capital town Lokon.

Its people bore a family resemblance to the forest dwellers. Few settlers indeed could have survived to become the ancestors of this world's humanity. But the highlanders were better nourished, bigger, straighter. They wore gaily dyed tunics and sandals. The well-to-do added jewelry of gold and silver. Hair was braided, chins kept shaven. Folk walked boldly, without the savages' constant fear of ambush, and talked merrily.

To be sure, this was only strictly true of the free. While *New Dawn*'s anthropologists had scarcely begun to unravel the ins and outs of the culture, it had been obvious from the first that Lokon kept a large slave class. Some were sleek household servants. More toiled meek and naked in the fields, the quarries, the mines, under the lash of overseers and the guard of soldiers whose spearheads and swords were of ancient Imperial metal. But none of the space travelers was unduly shocked. They had seen worse elsewhere. Historical data banks described places in olden time called Athens, India, America.

Evalyth strode down twisted, dusty streets, between the gaudily painted walls of cubical, windowless adobe houses. Commoners going about their tasks made respectful salutes. Although no one feared any longer that the strangers meant harm, she did tower above the tallest man, her hair was colored like metal and her eyes like the sky, she bore lightning at her waist and none knew what other godlike powers.

Today soldiers and noblemen also genuflected, while slaves went on their faces. Where she appeared, the chatter and clatter of everyday life vanished; the business of the market plaza halted when she passed the booths; children ceased their games and fled; she moved in silence akin to the silence in her soul. Under the sun and the snowcone of Mount Burus, horror brooded. For by now Lokon knew that a man from the stars had been slain by a lowland brute; and what would come of that?

Word must have gone ahead to Rogar, though, since he awaited her in his house by Lake Zelo next to the Sacred Place. He was not king or council president or high priest, but he was something of all three, and it was he who dealt most with the strangers.

His dwelling was the usual kind, larger than average but dwarfed by the adjacent walls. Those enclosed a huge compound, filled with buildings, where none of the outworlders had been admitted. Guards in scarlet robes and grotesquely carved wooden helmets stood always at its gates. Today their number was doubled, and others flanked Rogar's door. The lake shone like polished steel at their backs. The trees along the shore looked equally rigid.

Rogar's major-domo, a fat elderly slave, prostrated himself in the entrance as Evalyth neared. "If the heaven-borne will deign to follow this unworthy one, *Klev* Rogar is within—" The guards dipped their spears to her. Their eyes were wide and frightened.

Like the other houses, this turned inward. Rogar sat on a dais in a room opening on a courtyard. It seemed doubly cool and dim by contrast with the glare outside. She could scarcely discern the frescos on the walls or the patterns on the carpet; they were crude art anyway. Her attention focused on Rogar. He did not rise, that not being a sign of respect here. Instead, he bowed his grizzled head above folded hands. The major-domo offered her a bench and Rogar's chief wife set a bombilla of herb tea by her before vanishing.

"Be greeted, *Klev*," Evalyth said formally.

"Be greeted, heaven-borne." Alone now, shadowed from the cruel sun, they observed a ritual period of silence.

Then: "This is terrible what has happened, heaven-borne," Rogar said. "Perhaps you do not know that my white robe and bare feet signify mourning as for one of my own blood."

"That is well done," Evalyth said. "We shall remember."

The man's dignity faltered. "You understand that none of us had anything to do with the evil, do you not? The savages are our enemies too. They are vermin. Our ancestors caught some and made them slaves, but they are good for nothing else. I warned your friends not to go down among those we have not tamed."

"Their wish was to do so," Evalyth replied. "Now my wish is to get revenge for my man." She didn't know if this language included a word for justice. No matter. Because of the drugs, which heightened the logical faculties while they muffled the emotions, she was speaking Lokonese quite well enough for her purposes.

"We can get soldiers and help you kill as many as you choose," Rogar offered.

"Not needful. With this weapon at my side I alone can destroy more than your army might. I want your counsel and help in a different matter. How can I find him who slew my man?"

Rogar frowned. "The savages can vanish into trackless jungles, heaven-borne."

"Can they vanish from other savages, though?"

"Ah! Shrewdly thought, heaven-borne. Those tribes are endlessly at each other's throats. If we can make contact with one, its hunters will soon learn for you where the killer's people have taken themselves." His scowl deepened. "But he must have gone from them, to hide until you have departed our land. A single man might be impossible to find. Lowlanders are good at hiding, of necessity."

"What do you mean by necessity?"

Rogar showed surprise at her failure to grasp what was obvious to him. "Why, consider a man out hunting," he said. "He cannot go with companions after every kind of game or the noise and scent would frighten it away. So he is often alone in the jungle. Someone from another tribe may well set upon him. A man stalked and killed is just as useful as one slain in open war."

"Why this incessant fighting?"

Rogar's look of bafflement grew stronger. "How else shall they get human flesh?"

"But they do not live on that!"

"No, surely not, except as needed. But that need comes many times as you know. Their wars are their chief way of taking men; booty is good too, but not the main reason to fight. He who slays, owns the corpse, and naturally divides it solely among his close kin. Not everyone is lucky in battle. Therefore these who did not chance to kill in a war may well go hunting on their own, two or three of them together hoping to find a single man from a different tribe. And that is why a lowlander is good at hiding."

Evalyth did not move or speak. Rogar drew a long breath and continued trying to explain: "Heaven-borne, when I heard the evil news, I spoke long with men from your company. They told me what they had seen from afar by the wonderful means you command. Thus it is clear to me what happened. This guide—what is his name? Yes, Moru—he is a cripple. He had no hope of killing himself a man except by treachery. When he saw that chance, he took it."

He ventured a smile. "That would never happen in the highlands," he declared. "We do not fight wars, save when we are attacked, nor do we hunt our fellowmen as if they were animals. Like yours, ours is a civilized race." His lips drew back from startlingly white teeth. "But, heaven-borne, your man was slain. I propose we take vengeance, not simply on the killer if we catch him, but on his tribe, which we can certainly find as you suggested. That will teach all the savages to beware of their betters. Afterward we can share the flesh, half to your people, half to mine."

Evalyth could only know an intellectual astonishment. Yet she had the feeling somehow of having walked off a cliff. She stared through the shadows, into the grave old face, and after a long time she heard herself whisper: "You…also…here…eat men?"

"Slaves," Rogar said. "No more than required. One of them will do for four boys."

Her hand dropped to her gun. Rogar sprang up in alarm. "Heaven-borne," he exclaimed, "I told you we are civilized. Never fear attack from any of us! We—we—"

She rose too, high above him. Did he read judgment in her gaze? Was the terror that snatched him on behalf of his whole people? He cowered from her, sweating and shuddering. "Heaven-borne, believe me, you have no quarrel with Lokon—no, now, let me show you, let me take you into the Sacred Place, even if you are no initiate…for surely you are akin to the gods, surely the gods will not be offended— Come, let me show you how it is, let me prove we have no will and no *need* to be your enemies—"

There was the gate that Rogar opened for her in that massive wall. There were the shocked countenances of the guards and loud promises of many sacrifices to appease the Powers. There was the stone pavement beyond, hot and hollowly resounding underfoot. There were the idols grinning around a central temple. There was the house of the acolytes who did the work and who shrank in fear when they saw their master conduct a foreigner in. There were the slave barracks.

"See, heaven-borne, they are well treated, are they not? We do have to crush their hands and feet when we choose them as children for this service. Think now dangerous it would be otherwise, hundreds of boys and young men in here. But we treat them kindly unless they misbehave. Are they not fat? Their own Holy Food is especially honorable, bodies of men of all degree who have died in their full strength. We teach them that they will live on in those for whom they are slain. Most are content with that, believe me, heaven-borne. Ask them yourself…though remember, they grow dull-witted, with nothing to do year after year. We slay them quickly, cleanly, at the beginning of each summer—no more than we must for that year's crop of boys entering into manhood, one slave for four boys, no more than that. And it is a most beautiful rite, with days of feasting and merrymaking afterward. Do you understand now, heaven-borne? You have nothing to fear from us. We are not savages, warring and raiding and skulking to get our man-flesh. We are civilized—not godlike in your fashion, no, I dare not claim that, do not be angry—but civilized—surely worthy of your friendship, are we not? Are we not, heaven-borne?

4.

Chena Darnard, who headed the cultural anthropology team, told her computer to scan its data bank. Like the others, it was a portable, its memory housed in *New Dawn*. At the moment the spaceship was above the opposite hemisphere, and perceptible time passed while beams went back and forth along the strung-out relay units.

Chena leaned back and studied Evalyth across her desk. The Krakener girl sat so quietly. It seemed unnatural, despite the drugs in her bloodstream retaining some power. To be sure, Evalyth was of aristocratic descent in a warlike society. Furthermore, hereditary psychological as well as physiological differences might exist on the different worlds. Not much was known about that, apart from extreme cases like Gwydion—or this planet? Regardless, Chena thought, it would be better if Evalyth gave way to simple shock and grief.

"Are you quite certain of your facts, dear?" the anthropologist asked as gently as possible. "I mean, while this island alone is habitable, it's large, the topography is rugged, communications are primitive, my group has already identified scores of distinct cultures."

"I questioned Rogar for more than an hour," Evalyth replied in the same flat voice, looking out of the same flat eyes as before. "I know interrogation techniques, and he was badly rattled. He talked.

"The Lokonese themselves are not as backward as their technology. They've lived for centuries with savages threatening their borderlands. It's made them develop a good intelligence network. Rogar described its functioning to me in detail. It can't help but keep them reasonably well informed about everything that goes on. And, while tribal customs do vary tremendously, the cannibalism is universal. That is why none of the Lokonese thought to mention it to us. They took for granted that we had our own ways of providing human meat."

"People have, m-m-m, latitude in those methods?"

"Oh, yes. Here they breed slaves for the purpose. But most lowlanders have too skimpy an economy for that. Some of them use war and murder. Among others, they settle it within the tribe by annual combats. Or— Who cares? The fact is that, everywhere in this country, in whatever fashion it may be, the boys undergo a puberty rite that involves eating an adult male."

Chena bit her lip. "What in the name of chaos might have started it? Computer! Have you scanned?"

"Yes," said the machine voice out of the case on her desk. "Data on cannibalism in man are comparatively sparse, because it is a rarity. On all planets hitherto known to us it is banned and has been throughout their history, although it is sometimes considered forgivable as an emergency measure when no alternative means of preserving life is available. Very limited forms of what might be called ceremonial cannibalism have occurred, as for example the drinking of minute amounts of each other's blood in pledging oath brotherhood among the Falkens of Lochlanna—"

"Never mind that," Chena said. A tautness in her throat thickened her tone. "Only here, it seems, have they degenerated so far that— Or is it degeneracy? Reversion, perhaps? What about Old Earth?"

"Information is fragmentary. Aside from what was lost during the Long Night, knowledge is under the handicap that the last primitive societies there vanished before interstellar travel began. But certain data collected by ancient historians and scientists remain.

"Cannibalism was an occasional part of human sacrifice. As a rule, victims were left uneaten. But in a minority of religions, the bodies, or selected portions of them, were consumed, either by a special class, or by the community as a whole. Generally this was regarded as theophagy. Thus, the Aztecs of Mexico offered thousands of individuals annually to their gods. The requirement of doing this forced them to provoke wars and rebellions, which in turn made it easy for the eventual European conqueror to get native allies. The majority of prisoners were simply slaughtered, their hearts given directly to the idols. But in at least one cult the body was divided among the worshippers.

"Cannibalism could be a form of magic, too. By eating a person, one supposedly acquired his virtues. This was the principal motive of the cannibals of Africa and Polynesia. Contemporary observers did report that the meals were relished, but that is easy to understand, especially in protein-poor areas.

"The sole recorded instance of systematic non-ceremonial cannibalism was among the Carib Indians of America. They ate man because they preferred man. They were especially fond of babies and used to capture women from their tribes for breeding stock. Male children of these slaves were generally gelded to make them docile and tender. In large part because of strong aversion to such practices, the Europeans exterminated the Caribs to the last man."

The report stopped. Chena grimaced. "I can sympathize with the Europeans," she said.

Evalyth might once have raised her brows; but her face stayed as wooden as her speech. "Aren't you supposed to be an objective scientist?"

"Yes. Yes. Still, there is such a thing as value judgment. And they did kill Donli."

"Not they. One of them. I shall find him."

"He's nothing but a creature of his culture, dear, sick with his whole race." Chena drew a breath, struggling for calm. "Obviously, the sickness has become a behavioral basic," she said. "I daresay it originated in Lokon. Cultural radiation is practically always from the more to the less advanced peoples. And on a single island, after centuries, no tribe has escaped the infection. The Lokonese later elaborated and rationalized the practice. The savages left its cruelty naked. But highlander or lowlander, their way of life is founded on that particular human sacrifice."

"Can they be taught differently?" Evalyth asked without real interest.

"Yes. In time. In theory. But—well, I do know enough about what happened on Old Earth, and elsewhere, when advanced societies undertook to reform primitive ones. The entire structure was destroyed. It had to be.

"Think of the result, if we told these people to desist from their puberty rite. They wouldn't listen. They couldn't. They *must* have grandchildren. They *know* a boy won't become a man unless he has eaten part of a man. We'd have to conquer them, kill most, make sullen prisoners of the rest. And when the next crop of boys did in fact mature without the magic food…what then? Can you imagine the demoralization, the sense of utter inferiority, the loss of that tradition which is the core of every personal identity? It might be kinder to bomb this island sterile."

Chena shook her head. "No," she said harshly, "the single decent way for us to proceed would be gradually. We could send missionaries. By their precept and example, we could start the natives phasing out their custom after two or three generations…And we can't afford such an effort. Not for a long time to come. Not with so many other worlds in the galaxy, so much worthier of what little help we can give. I am going to recommend this planet be left alone."

Evalyth considered her for a moment before asking: "Isn't that partly because of your own reaction?"

"Yes," Chena admitted. "I cannot overcome my disgust. And I, as you pointed out, am supposed to be professionally broad-minded. So even if the Board tried to recruit missionaries, I doubt if they'd succeed." She hesitated. "You yourself, Evalyth—"

The Krakener rose. "My emotions don't matter," she said. "My duty does. Thank you for your help." She turned on her heel and went with military strides out of the cabin.

5.

The chemical barriers were crumbling. Evalyth stood for a moment before the little building that had been hers and Donli's, afraid to enter. The sun was low, so that the compound was filling with shadows. A thing leathery-winged and serpentine cruised silently overhead. From outside the stockade drifted sounds of feet, foreign voices, the whine of a wooden flute. The air was cooling. She shivered. Their home would be too hollow.

Someone approached. She recognized the person glimpsewise, Alsabeta Mondain from Nuevamerica. Listening to her well-meant foolish condolences would be worse than going inside. Evalyth took the last three steps and slid the door shut behind her.

Donli will not be here again. Eternally.

But the cabin proved not to be empty to him. Rather, it was too full. That chair where he used to sit, reading that worn volume of poetry which she could not understand and teased him about, that table across which he had toasted her and tossed kisses, that closet where his clothes hung, that scuffed pair of slippers, that bed—it screamed of him. Evalyth went fast into the laboratory section and drew the curtain that separated it from the living quarters. Rings rattled along the rod. The noise was monstrous in the twilight.

She closed her eyes and fists and stood breathing hard. *I will not go soft,* she declared. *You always said you loved me for my strength—among numerous other desirable features, you'd add with your slow grin, but I remember that yet—and I don't aim to let slip anything that you loved.*

I've got to get busy, she told Donli's child. *The expedition command is pretty sure to act on Chena's urging and haul mass for home. We've not many days to avenge your father.*

Her eyes snapped open. *What am I doing,* she thought, bewildered, *talking to a dead man and an embryo?*

She turned on the overflow fluoro and went to the computer. It was made no differently from the other portables. Donli had used it. But she could look away from the unique scratches and bumps on that square case, as she could not escape his microscope, chemanalyzers, chromosome tracer, biological specimens…She seated herself. A drink would have been very welcome, except that she needed clarity. "Activate!" she ordered.

The On light glowed yellow. Evalyth tugged her chin, searching for words. "The objective," she said at length, "is to trace a lowlander who has consumed several kilos of flesh and blood from one of this party, and afterward vanished into the jungle. The killing took place about sixty hours ago. How can he be found?"

The least hum answered her. She imagined the links; to the maser in the ferry, up past the sky to the nearest orbiting relay unit, to the next, to the next around the bloated belly of the planet, by ogre sun and inhuman stars, until the pulses reached the mother ship; then down to an unliving brain that routed the question to the appropriate data bank; then to the scanners, whose resonating energies flew from molecule to distorted molecule, identifying more bits of information than it made sense to number, data garnered from hundreds or thousands of entire worlds, data preserved through the wreck of Empire and the dark ages that followed, data going back to an Old Earth that perhaps no longer existed. She shied from the thought and wished herself back on dear, stern Kraken. *We will go there,* she promised Donli's child. *You will dwell apart from these too many machines and grow up as the gods meant you should.*

"Query," said the artificial voice. "Of what origin was the victim of this assault?"

Evalyth must wet her lips before she could reply: "Atheian. He was Donli Sairn, your master."

"In the event, the possibility of tracking the desired local inhabitant may exist. The odds will now be computed. In the interim, do you wish to know the basis of the possibility?"

"Y-yes."

"Native Atheian biochemistry developed in a manner quite parallel to Earth's," said the voice, "and the early colonists had no difficulty in introducing terrestrial species. Thus they enjoyed a friendly environment, where population soon grew sufficiently large to obviate the danger of racial change through mutation and/or genetic drift. In addition, no selection pressure tended to force change. Hence the modern Atheian human is little different from his ancestors of Earth, on which account his physiology and bio-chemistry are known in detail.

"This has been essentially the case on most colonized planets for which records are available. Where different breeds of men have arisen, it has generally been because the original settlers were highly selected groups. Randomness, and evolutionary adaptation to new conditions, have seldom produced radical changes in biotype. For example, the robustness of the average Krakener is a response to comparatively high gravity; his size aids him in resisting cold, his fair complexion is helpful beneath a sun poor in ultraviolet. But his ancestors, were people who already had the natural endowments for such a world. His deviations from their norm are not extreme. They do not preclude his living on more Earth-like planets or interbreeding with the inhabitants of these.

"Occasionally, however, larger variations have occurred. They appear to be due to a small original population or to unterrestroid conditions or both. The population may have been small because the planet could not support more, or have become small as the result of hostile action when the Empire fell. In the former case, genetic accidents had a chance to be significant; in the latter, radiation produced a high rate of mutant births among survivors. The variations are less apt to be in gross anatomy than in subtle endocrine and enzymatic qualities, which affect the physiology and psychology. Well known cases include the reaction of the Gwydiona to nicotine and certain indoles, and the requirement of the Ifrians for trace amounts of lead. Sometimes the inhabitants of two planets are actually intersterile because of their differences.

"While this world has hitherto received the sketchiest of examinations—" Evalyth was yanked out of a reverie into which the lecture had led her. "—certain facts are clear. Few terrestrial species have flourished; no doubt others were introduced originally, but died off after the technology to maintain them was lost. Man has thus been forced to depend on autochthonous life for the major part of his food. This life is deficient in various elements of human nutrition. For example, the only Vitamin C appears to be in immigrant plants; Sairn observed that the people consume large amounts of grass and leaves from those species, and that fluoroscopic pictures indicate this practice has measurably modified the digestive tract. No one would supply skin, blood, sputum, or similar samples, not even from corpses." *Afraid of magic,* Evalyth thought drearily, *yes, they're back to that too.* "But intensive analysis of the usual meat animals shows these to be under-supplied with three essential amino acids, and human adaptation to this must have involved considerable change on the cellular and sub-cellular levels. The probable type and extent of such change are computable."

"The calculations are now complete." As the computer resumed, Evalyth gripped the arms of her chair and could not breathe. "While the answer is subject to fair probability of success. In effect, Atheian flesh is alien here. It can be metabolized, but the body of the local consumer will excrete certain compounds, and these will import a characteristic odor to skin and breath as well as to urine and feces. The chance is good that it will be detectable by neo-Freeholder technique at distances of several kilometers, after sixty or seventy hours. But since the molecules in question are steadily being degraded and dissipated, speed of action is recommended."

I am going to find Donli's murderer. Darkness roared around Evalyth.

"Shall the organisms be ordered for you and given the appropriate search program?" asked the voice. "They can be on hand in an estimated three hours."

"Yes," she stammered. "Oh, please—Have you any other…other…advice?"

"The man ought not to be killed out of hand, but brought here for examination, if for no other reason, than in order that the scientific ends of the expedition may be served."

That's a machine talking, Evalyth cried. *It's designed to help research. Nothing more. But it was his.* And its answer was so altogether Donli that she could no longer hold back her tears.

6.

The single big moon rose nearly full, shortly after sundown. It drowned most stars; the jungle beneath was cobbled with silver and dappled with black; the snowcone of Mount Burus floated unreal at the unseen edge of the world. Wind slid around Evalyth where she crouched on her gravsled; it was full of wet acrid odors, and felt cold though it was not, and chuckled at her back. Somewhere something screeched, every few minutes, and something else cawed reply.

She scowled at her position indicators, aglow on the control panel. Curses and chaos, Moru had to be in this area! He could not have escaped from the valley on foot in the time available, and her search pattern had practically covered it. If she ran out of bugs before she found him, must she assume he was dead? They ought to be able to find his body regardless, ought they not? Unless it was buried deep. Here. She brought the sled to hover, took the next phial off the rack, and stood up to open it.

The bugs came out many and tiny, like smoke in the moonlight. Another failure?

No! Wait! Were not those motes dancing back together, into a streak barely visible under the moon, and vanishing downward? Heart fluttering, she turned to the indicator. Its neurodetector antenna was not aimlessly wobbling, but pointed straight west-northwest, declination thirty-two degrees below horizontal. Only a concentration of the bugs could make it believe like that. And only the particular mixture of molecules to which the bugs had been presensitized, in several parts per million or better, would make them converge on the source.

"Ya-a-ah!" She couldn't help the one hawk-yell. But thereafter she bit her lips shut—blood trickled unnoticed down her chin—and drove the sled in silence.

The distance was a mere few kilometers. She came to a halt above an opening in the forest. Pools of scummy water gleamed in its rank growth. The trees made a solid-seeming wall around. Evalyth clapped her night goggles down off her helmet and over her eyes. A lean-to became visible. It was hastily woven from vines and withes, huddled against a pair of the largest trees to let their branches hide it from the sky. The bugs were entering.

Evalyth lowered her sled to a meter off the ground and got to her feet again. A stun pistol slid from its sheath into her right hand. Her left rested on the blaster.

Moru's two sons groped from the shelter. The bugs whirled around them, a mist that blurred their outlines. *Of course,* Evalyth realized, nonetheless shocked into a higher hatred. *I should have known they did the actual devouring.* More than ever they resemble gnomes—skinny limbs, big heads, the pot bellies of undernourishment. Krakener boys of their age would have been twice their bulk and be noticeably on the way to becoming men. These nude bodies belonged to children, except that they had the grotesqueness of eld.

The parents followed them, ignored by the entranced bugs. The mother wailed. Evalyth identified a few words. "What is the matter, what are those things—oh, help—" But her gaze was locked upon Moru.

Limping out of the hutch, stooped to clear its entrance, he made her think of some huge beetle crawling from an offal heap. But she would know that bushy head though her brain were coming apart. He carried a stone blade, surely the one that had hacked up Donli. *I will take it away from him, and the hand with it,* Evalyth wept. *I will keep him alive while I dismantle him with these my own hands, and in between times he can watch me flay his repulsive spawn.*

The wife's scream broke through. She had seen the metal thing, and the giant that stood on its platform, with skull and eyes shimmering beneath the moon.

"I have come for you who killed my man," Evalyth said.

The mother screamed anew and cast herself before the boys. The father tried to run around in front of her, but his lame foot twisted under him, and he fell into a pool. As he struggled out of its muck, Evalyth shot the woman. No sound was heard; she folded and lay moveless.

"Run!" Moru shouted. He tried to charge the sled. Evalyth twisted a control stick. Her vehicle whipped in a circle, heading off the boys. She shot them from above, where Moru couldn't quite reach her.

He knelt beside the nearest, took the body in his arms and looked upward. The moonlight poured relentlessly across him. "What can you now do to me?" he called.

She stunned him too, landed, got off and quickly hogtied the four of them. Loading them aboard, she found them lighter than she had expected.

Sweat had sprung forth upon her, until her coverall stuck dripping to her skin. She began to shake, as if with fever. Her ears buzzed. "I would have destroyed you," she said. Her voice sounded remote and unfamiliar. A still more distant part wondered why she bothered speaking to the unconscious, in her own tongue at that. "I wish you hadn't acted the way you did. That made me remember what the computer said, about Donli's friends needing you for study.

"You're too good a chance, I suppose. After your doings, we have the right under Allied rules to make prisoners of you, and none of his friends are likely to get maudlin about your feelings.

"Oh, they won't be inhuman. A few cell samples, a lot of tests, anesthesia where necessary, nothing harmful, nothing but a clinical examination as thorough as facilities allow.

"No doubt you'll be better fed than at any time before, and no doubt the medics will find some pathologies they can cure for you. In the end, Moru, they'll release your wife and children."

She stared into his horrible face.

"I am pleased," she said, "that to you, who won't comprehend what is going on, it will be a bad experience. And when they are finished, Moru, I will insist on having you at least, back. They can't deny me that. Why, your tribe itself has, in effect, cast you out. Right? My colleagues won't let me do more than kill you, I'm afraid, but on this I will insist."

She gunned the engine and started toward Lokon, as fast as possible, to arrive while she felt able to be satisfied with that much.

7.

And the days without him and the days without him.

The nights were welcome. If she had not worked herself quite to exhaustion, she could take a pill. He rarely returned in her dreams. But she had to get through each day and would not drown him in drugs.

Luckily, there was a good deal of work involved in preparing to depart, when the expedition was short-handed and on short notice. Gear must be dismantled, packed, ferried to the ship, and stowed. *New Dawn* herself must be readied, numerous systems recommissioned and tested. Her militechnic training qualified Evalyth to double as mechanic, boat jockey, or loading gang boss. In addition, she kept up the routines of defense in the compound.

Captain Jonafer objected mildly to this. "Why bother, Lieutenant? The locals are scared blue of us. They've heard what you did—and this coming and going through the sky, robots and heavy machinery in action, floodlights after dark—I'm having trouble persuading them not to abandon their town!"

"Let them," she snapped. "Who cares?"

"We did not come here to ruin them, Lieutenant."

"No. In my judgment, though, Captain, they'll be glad to ruin us if we present the least opportunity. Imagine what special virtues *your* body must have."

Jonafer sighed and gave in. But when she refused to receive Rogar the next time she was planetside, he ordered her to do so and to be civil.

The *Klev* entered the biolab section—she would not have him in her living quarters—with a gift held in both hands, a sword of Imperial metal. She shrugged; no doubt a museum would be pleased to get the thing. "Lay it on the floor," she told him.

Because she occupied the single chair, he stood. He looked little and old in his robe. "I came," he whispered, "to say how we of Lokon rejoice that the heaven-borne has won her revenge."

"Is winning it," she corrected.

He could not meet her eyes. She stared moodily at his faded hair. "Since the heaven-borne could…easily…find those she wished…she knows the truth in the hearts of us of Lokon, that we never intended harm to her folk."

That didn't seem to call for an answer.

His fingers twisted together. Then why do you forsake us?" he went on. "When first you came, when we had come to know you and you spoke our speech, you said you would stay for many moons, and after you would come others to teach and trade. Our hearts rejoiced. It was not alone the goods you might someday let us buy, nor that your wisemen talked of ways to end hunger, sickness, danger, and sorrow. No, our jubilation and thankfulness were most for the wonders you opened. Suddenly the world was made great, that had been so narrow. And now you are going away. I have asked, when I dared, and those of your men who will speak to me say none will return. How have we offended you, and how may it be made right, heaven-borne?"

"You can stop treating your fellow men like animals," Evalyth got past her teeth.

"I have gathered…somewhat…that you from the stars say it is wrong what happens in the Sacred Place. But we only do it once in our lifetimes, heaven-borne, and because we must!"

"You have no need."

Rogar went on his hands and knees before her. "Perhaps the heaven-borne are thus," he pleaded, "but we are merely men. If our sons do not get the manhood, they will never beget children of their own, and the last of us will die alone in a world of death, with none to crack his skull and let the soul out—" He dared glance up at her. What he saw made him whimper and crawl backwards into the sun-glare.

Later Chena Darnard sought Evalyth. They had a drink and talked around the subject for a while, until the anthropologist plunged in: "You were pretty hard on the sachem, weren't you?"

"How'd you—Oh." The Krakener remembered that the interview had been taped, as was done whenever possible for later study. "What was I supposed to do, kiss his man-eating mouth?"

"No." Chena winced. "I suppose not."

"Your signature heads the list, on the official recommendation that we quit this planet."

"Yes. But—now I don't know. I was repelled. I am—However, I've been observing the medical team working on those prisoners of yours. Have you?"

"No."

"You should. The way they cringe and shriek and react to each other when they're strapped down in the lab and cling together afterward in their cell."

"They aren't suffering any pain or mutilation, are they?"

"Of course not. But can they believe it when their captors say they won't? They can't be tranquilized while under study, you know, if the results are to be valid. Their fear of the absolutely unknown— Well, Evalyth, I had to stop observing. I couldn't take any more." Chena gave the other a long stare. "You might, though."

Evalyth shook her head. "I don't gloat. I'll shoot the murderer because my family honor demands it. The rest can go free, even the boys. Even in spite of what they ate." She poured herself a stiff draught and tossed it off in a gulp. The liquor burned on the way down.

"I wish you wouldn't," Chena said. "Donli wouldn't have liked it. He had a proverb that he claimed was very ancient—he was from my city, don't forget, and I have known…I did know him longer than you, dear. I heard him say, twice or thrice, *Do I not destroy my enemies if it makes them my friends?*"

"Think of a venomous insect," Evalyth replied. "You don't make friends with it. You put it under your heel."

"But a man does what he does because of what he is, what his society has made him." Chena's voice grew urgent; she leaned forward to grip Evalyth's hand, which did not respond. "What is one man, one lifetime, against all who live around him and all who have gone before? Cannibalism wouldn't be found everywhere over the island, in every one of these otherwise altogether different groupings, if it weren't the most deeply rooted cultural imperative this race has got."

Evalyth grinned around a rising anger. "And what kind of race are they to acquire it? And how about according me the privilege of operating on my own cultural imperatives? I'm bound home, to raise Donli's child away from your gutless civilization. He will not grow up disgraced because his mother was too weak to exact justice for his father. Now if you will excuse me, I have to get up early and take another boatload to the ship and get it inboard."

That task required a while. Evalyth came back toward sunset of the next day. She felt a little more tired than usual, a little more peaceful. The raw edge of what had happened was healing over. The thought crossed her mind, abstract but not shocking, not disloyal: *I'm young. One year another man will come. I won't love you the less, darling.*

Dust scuffed under her boots. The compound was half stripped already, a corresponding number of personnel berthed in the ship. The evening reached quiet beneath a yellowing sky. Only a few of the expedition stirred among the machines and remaining cabins. Lokon lay as hushed as it had lately become. She welcomed the thud of her footfalls on the steps into Jonafer's office.

He sat waiting for her, big and unmoving behind his desk. "Assignment completed without incident," she reported.

"Sit down," he said.

She obeyed. The silence grew. At last he said, out of a stiff face: "The clinical team has finished with the prisoners."

Somehow it was a shock. Evalyth groped for words. "Isn't that too soon? I mean, well, we don't have a lot of equipment, and just a couple of men who can see the advanced stuff, and then without Donli for an expert on Earth biology—Wouldn't a good study, down to the chromosomal level if not further—something that the physical anthropologists could use—wouldn't it take longer?"

"That's correct," Jonafer said. "Nothing of major importance was found. Perhaps something would have been, if Uden's team had any inkling of what to look for. Given that, they could have made hypotheses and tested them in a whole-organism context and come to some understanding of their subjects as functioning beings. You're right, Donli Sairn had the kind of professional intuition that might have guided them. Lacking that, and with no particular clues, and no cooperation from those ignorant, terrified savages, they had to grope and probe almost at random. They did establish a few digestive peculiarities—nothing that couldn't have been predicted on the basis of ambient ecology."

"Then why have they stopped? We won't be leaving for another week at the earliest."

"They did so on my orders, after Uden had shown me what was going on and said he'd quit regardless of what I wanted."

"What—? Oh." Scorn lifted Evalyth's head. "You mean the psychological torture."

"Yes. I saw that scrawny woman secured to a table. Her head, her body were covered with leads to the meters that clustered around her and clicked and hummed and flickered. She didn't see me; her eyes were blind with fear. I suppose she imagined her soul was being pumped out. Or maybe the process was worse for being something she couldn't put a name to. I saw her kids in a cell, holding hands. Nothing else left for them to hold onto, in their total universe. They're just at puberty; what'll this do to their psychosexual development? I saw their father lying drugged beside them, after he'd tried to batter his way straight through the wall. Uden and his helpers told me how they'd tried to make friends and failed. Because naturally the prisoners know they're in the power of those who hate them with a hate that goes beyond the grave."

Jonafer paused. "There are decent limits to everything, Lieutenant," he ended, "including science and punishment. Especially when, after all, the chance of discovering anything else unusual is slight. I ordered the investigation terminated. The boys and their mother will be flown to their home area and released tomorrow."

"Why not today?" Evalyth asked, foreseeing his reply.

"I hoped," Jonafer said, "that you'd agree to let the man go with them."

"No."

"In the name of God—"

"Your God." Evalyth looked away from him. "I won't enjoy it, Captain. I'm beginning to wish I didn't have to. But it's not as if Donli's been killed in an honest war or feud—or he was slaughtered like a pig. That's the evil in cannibalism; it makes a man nothing but another meat animal. I won't bring him back, but

I will somehow even things, by making the cannibal nothing but a dangerous animal that needs shooting."

"I see." Jonafer too stared long out of the window. In the sunset light his face became a mask of brass. "Well," he said finally, coldly, "under the Charter of the Alliance and the articles of this expedition, you leave me no choice. But we will not have any ghoulish ceremonies, and you will not deputize what you have done. The prisoner will be brought to your place privately after dark. You will dispose of him at once and assist in cremating the remains."

Evalyth's palms grew wet. *I never killed a helpless man before!*
But he did, it answered. "Understood, Captain," she said.

"Very good, Lieutenant. You may go up and join the mess for dinner if you wish. No announcements to anyone. The business will be scheduled for—"Jonafer glanced at his watch, set to local rotation. "—2600 hours."

Evalyth swallowed around a clump of dryness. "Isn't that rather late?"

"On purpose," he told her. "I want the camp asleep." His glance struck hers. "And want you to have time to reconsider."

"No!" She sprang erect and went for the door.

His voice pursued her. "Donli would have asked you for that."

8.

Night came in and filled the room. Evalyth didn't rise to turn on the light. It was as if this chair, which had been Donli's favorite, wouldn't let her go.

Finally she remembered the psychodrugs. She had a few tablets left. One of them would make the execution easy to perform. No doubt Jonafer would direct that Moru be tranquilized—now, at last—before they brought him here. So why should she not give herself calmness?

It wouldn't be right.

Why not?

I don't know. I don't understand anything any longer.

Who does? Moru alone. He knows why he murdered and butchered a man who trusted him. Evalyth found herself smiling wearily into the darkness. *He has superstition for his sure guide. He's actually seen his children display the first signs of maturity. That ought to console him a little.*

Odd, that the glandular upheaval of adolescence should have commenced under frightful stress. One would have expected a delay instead. True, the captives had been getting a balanced diet for a change, and medicine had probably eliminated various chronic low-level infections. Nonetheless the fact was odd. Besides, normal children under normal conditions would not develop the outward signs beyond mistaking in this short a time. Donli would have puzzled over the matter. She could almost see him, frowning, rubbing his forehead, grinning one-sidedly with the pleasure of a problem.

"I'd like to have a go at this myself," she heard him telling Uden over a beer and a smoke. "Might turn up an angle."

"How?" the medic would have replied. "You're a general biologist. No reflection on you, but detailed human physiology is out of your line."

"Um-m-m…yes and no. My main job is studying species of terrestrial origin and how they've adapted to new planets. By a remarkable coincidence, man is included among them."

But Donli was gone, and no one else was competent to do his work—to be any part of him, but she fled from that thought and from the thought of what she must presently do. She held her mind tightly to the realization that none of Uden's team had tried to apply Donli's knowledge. As Jonafer remarked, a living Donli might well have suggested an idea, unorthodox and insightful, that would have led to the discovery of whatever was there to be discovered, if anything was. Uden and his assistants were routineers. They hadn't even thought to make Donli's computer ransack its data banks for possibly relevant information. Why should they, when they saw their problem as strictly medical? And, to be sure, they were not cruel. The anguish they were inflicting had made them avoid whatever might lead to ideas demanding further research. Donli would have approached the entire business differently from the outset.

Suddenly the gloom thickened. Evalyth fought for breath. Too hot and silent here; too long a wait; she must do something or her will would desert her and she would be unable to squeeze the trigger.

She stumbled to her feet and into the lab. The fluoro blinded her for a moment when she turned it on. She went to his computer and said: "Activate!"

Nothing responded but the indicator light. The windows were totally black. Clouds outside shut off moon and stars.

"What—" The sound was a curious croak. But that brought a releasing gall: *Take hold of yourself, you blubbering idiot, or you're not fit to mother the child you're carrying.* She could then ask her question. "What explanations in terms of biology can be devised for the behavior of the people on this planet?"

"Matters of that nature are presumably best explained in terms of psychology and cultural anthropology," said the voice.

"M-m-maybe," Evalyth said. "And maybe not." She marshaled a few thoughts and stood them firm amidst the others roiling in her skull. "The inhabitants could be degenerate somehow, not really human." *I want Moru to be.* "Scan every fact recorded about them, including the detailed clinical observations made on four of them in the past several days. Compare with basic terra data. Give me whatever hypotheses look reasonable." Sue hesitated. "Correction. I mean possible hypotheses—anything that does not flatly contradict established facts. We've used up the reasonable ideas already."

The machine hummed. Evalyth closed her eyes and clung to the edge of the desk. *Donli, please help me.*

At the other end of forever, the voice came to her:

"The sole behavioral element which appears to be not easily explicable by postulates concerning environment and accidental historical developments, is the cannibalistic puberty rite. According to the anthropological computer, this might well have originated as a form of human sacrifice. But that computer notes certain illogicalities in the idea as follows.

"On Old Earth, sacrificial religion was normally associated with agricultural societies, which were more vitally dependent on continued fertility and good weather than hunters. Even for them, the offering of humans proved disadvantageous in the long run, as the Aztec example most clearly demonstrates. Lokon has rationalized the practice to a degree, making it a part of the slavery system and thus minimizing its impact on the generality. But for the lowlanders it is a powerful evil, a source of perpetual danger, a diversion of effort and resources that are badly needed for survival. It is not plausible that the custom, if ever imitated from Lokon, should persist among every one of those tribes. Nevertheless it does. Therefore it must have some value and the problem is to find what.

"The method of obtaining victims varies widely, but the requirement always appears to be the same. According to the Lokonese, one adult male body is necessary and sufficient for the maturation of four boys. The killer of Donli Sairn was unable to carry off the entire corpse. What he did take of it is suggestive.

"Hence a dipteroid phenomenon may have appeared in man on this planet. Such a thing is unknown among higher animals elsewhere, but is conceivable. A modification of the Y chromosome would produce it. The test for that modification, and thus the test of the hypothesis, is easily made."

The voice stopped. Evalyth heard the blood slugging in her veins. "What are you talking about?"

"The phenomenon is found among lower animals on several worlds," the computer told her.

It is uncommon and so is not widely known. The name derives from the Diptera, a type of dung fly on Old Earth."

Lightning flickered. "Dung fly—good, yes!"

The machine went on to explain.

9.

Jonafer came along with Moru, The savage's hands were tied behind his back, and the spaceman loomed enormous over him. Despite that and the bruises he had inflicted on himself, he hobbled along steadily. The clouds were breaking and the moon shone ice-white. Where Evalyth waited, outside her door, she saw the compound reach bare to the saw-topped stockade and a crane stand above like a gibbet. The air was growing cold—the planet spinning toward an autumn—and a small wind had arisen to whimper behind the dust devils that stirred across the earth. Jonafer's footfalls rang loud.

He noticed her and stopped. Moru did likewise. "What did they learn?" she asked.

The captain nodded. "Uden got right to work when you called," he said. "The test is more complicated than your computer suggested—but then, it's for Donli's kind of skill, not Uden's. He'd never have thought of it unassisted. Yes, the notion is true."

"How?"

Moru stood waiting while the language he did not understand went to and fro around him.

"I'm no medic." Jonafer kept his altogether colorless. "But from what Uden told me, the chromosome defect means that the male gonads here can't mature spontaneously. They need an extra supply of hormones—he mentioned testosterone and androsterone, I forget what else—to start off the series of changes which bring on puberty. Lacking that, you'll get eunuchism. Uden thinks the surviving population was tiny after the colony was bombed out, and so poor that it resorted to cannibalism for bare survival, the first generation or two. Under those circumstances a mutation that would otherwise have eliminated itself got established and spread to every descendant."

Evalyth nodded. "I see."

"You understand want this means, I suppose," Jonafer said. "There'll be no problem to ending the practice. We'll simply tell we have a new and better Holy Food, and prove it with a few pills. Terrestrial-type meat animals can be reintroduced later and supply what's necessary. In the end, no doubt our geneticists can repair that faulty Y chromosome."

He could not stay contained any longer. His mouth opened, a gash across his half-seen face, and he rasped: "I should praise you for saving a whole people. I can't. Get your business over with, will you?"

Evalyth trod forward to stand before Moru. He shivered but met her eyes. Astonished, She said: "You haven't drugged him."

"No," Jonafer said. "I wouldn't help you." He spat.

"Well, I'm glad." She addressed Moru in his own language: "You killed my man. Is it right that I should kill you?"

"It is right," he answered, almost as levelly as she. "I thank that my woman and my sons are to go free." He was quiet for a second or two. "I have heard that your folk can preserve food for years without it rotting. I would be glad if you kept my body to give to your sons."

"Mine will not need it," Evalyth said. "Nor will the sons of your sons."

Anxiety tinged his words: "Do you know why I slew your man? He was kind to me, and like a god. But I am lame. I saw no other way to get what my sons must have; and they must have it soon, or it would be too late and they could never become men."

"He taught me," Evalyth said, "how much it is to be a man."

She turned to Jonafer, who stood tense and puzzled. "I had my revenge," she said in Donli's tongue.

"What?" His question was a reflexive noise.

"After I learned about the dipteroid phenomenon," she said. "All that was necessary was for me to keep silent. Moru, his children, his entire race would go on being prey for centuries, maybe forever. I sat for half an hour, I think, having my revenge."

"And then?" Jonafer asked.

"I was satisfied and could start thinking about justice," Evalyth said.

She drew a knife. Moru straightened his back. She stepped behind him and cut his bonds. "Go home," she said. "Remember him."

BARBAROUS ALLEN

All in the merry month of March,
When the tax collector's callin',
Sweet William took a club and went
To call on Barbarous Allen.

He bopped him once, he bonked him twice,
He barfed him three times runnin'.
Said Allen with a sad sweet smile:
"Young man, you're simply stunnin'."

He lived alone up in his eave
But by his pets was che-ered:
The bats that nested in his ears,
The buzzard in his be-ard.

Sweet William said: "You stole my gal.
Now give me back my Ellen!"
"I don't think you could carry her down
The hill," said Barbarous Allen.

And then he took a naily club
And whopped sweet William strongly.
His American blood flowed red, white, and blue.
(He never voted wrongly.)

Said William: "Now it is my turn.
Hold still, you Barbarous Allen."
He whonked him hard; his club was like
A redwood pine tree (for the sake of the meter) fallin'.

Then Allen bashed, and William smashed,
Until the sun was fallin'
And finally the hermit crashed
To earth, did Barbarous Allen.

Said William, speakin' to the cave:
"Come out, my gentle Ellen.
Go home with me, for now you're saved
From cruel Barbarous Allen."

And out she came, and whacked him good.
Go home, you rat," said Ellen.
"The whole damn township ain't as much
A (wow!) MAN as Barbarous Allen!"

Welcome

Barlow's first astonishment was at how little different the future seemed. He had thought that five hundred years would change every detail beyond imagination. To be sure, nothing was quite like the twentieth century United States; but contemporary Mexico had been a good deal more exotic than the North American Federation of the United World Republics looked.

Several persons awaited him when he emerged from the superenergy state. All but one were men, ranging from boyish to middle-aged: two Orientals, a Negro, the others white. They wore shirts, trousers, and fabric shoes, of synthetic material in subdued colors, cut much like Barlow's. One had a sleek pistol-like weapon in a holster, but left it there, unafraid of the newcomer. They all gathered around, made sympathetic noises in accented but recognizable English, led him to a couch and gave him a drink. The room was windowless, with a fluorescent ceiling and ventilator grilles. A workbench supported miscellaneous scientific equipment, most of which Barlow could identify.

"Heh, now, buddo, swallow this an' you'll feel better."

Barlow obeyed mechanically. He had a bad case of the shakes. A gentle, relaxing warmth spread through him. Within minutes he could regard his situation as calmly as if it were someone else's. He felt happy, his mind clearer and quicker than usual. And yet, he thought, this was not so different from the tranquilizers of his era.

"I guess he's 'kay now, Joe," said a young man.

The oldest, who appeared to be the leader, nodded. "How're you?" he smiled, offering his hand. "I'm Joe Grozen. Here's my primary daughter Amily. She 'nsisted on seeing you arrive. I won' ask you to 'member any other names right off."

"Tom Barlow." He was much taken with Amily, who was tall and well-formed, with dark hair falling past a heart-shaped blue-eyed face and halfway down her back. She wore sandals, shorts, a kind of tee shirt, and a friendly expression. "What, uh, what year is this?"

"Twen'y-four nine'y-seven," she replied.

"The twelfth April. Your calculations were very close. This place was readied special for your coming."

He had to ask it, with his heart in his throat despite all soothing drugs: "Is there any way for me to return?"

Joe Grozen's broad red visage grew sober. "No," he muttered. " 'Fraid not."

Barlow sighed. "Never mind. I didn't expect it. Travel into the past, an obvious absurdity. All I did was give myself a jolt of energy, a vector along the time axis rather than through space, and so increased my rate of existence several millionfold…But you know all about that." He fumbled after a cigarette.

"Oh, yes," said an Oriental. "The phenomenon's well un'erstood today." He bowed. "Though 's an honor to meet its first discoverer. So youthful you are, too."

"Sam's chief o' the technics department," explained Amily. "Natur'lly he'd be mos' in'erested in the science aspect. An' Phil here." She laid a hand briefly on the shoulder of the Negro. "He heads up the sociohist'ry section. He'll want to ask you all sorts o' questions 'bout the past."

"You'll have status all your life in my department, if you wish," Phil assured Barlow. "Special lecturer, consultant, whatever you want to call it. We're missing so much information about everything prior to the Atomic Wars."

"Shut up, you damn scientists," said Joe good-naturedly. "Our frien' Tom is first of all a free human being. You can quiz him later, but give the poor tovarsh time to get used to us first. How y' feeling now, Tom?"

"Okay." Barlow drew heavily on his cigarette. It might have been the drug, or simply the conviction, now proven, that his farewells in the twentieth century had been final. But whatever the cause, that era already seemed remote—though he had departed it less than half an hour ago, as far as his conscious mind knew. His fears had not materialized: emergence in a desert, or an Orwellian dictatorship, or something equally horrible. He'd gambled on finding a world where his own romantic advent would give him a head start in establishing himself. (Surely, even in the course of five hundred years, there had not been many time leapers. The messages he left, sealed into marked blocks of concrete, had been carefully designed to arouse the curiosity of future humankind about Thomas Barlow.) These easy-going, familiar-looking people dissolved the tension in him. His gamble had paid off.

"Sure, I'm fine," he said. "Tired, is all."

Joe nodded. "That I un'erstan'. We got a home all prepared for you. You can rest up there. I'd like to give you a welcoming banquet this evening, though. Lots o' people want to meet you."

"I don't need—" Barlow was interrupted as Amily took him by the hand.

"You come with me," she said. "I'll take you to your place. On the way I can give you a lining o' what the world's like these days."

"Now, wait," objected Phil.

"Wait yourself," she chuckled. "I know you, you ol' professor. You'd stuff him so full o' precise information he wouldn' know his charge from a Dirac hole. What he needs right now is facts, not data."

"An' someone to snuggle with," Sam teased.

She made a face at him. Joe grinned. What's the use o' being the Pres'dent's daughter, Tom, if she can' get to know you ahead of all the other girls?" he said. "You're going to be the most chased bachelor on this planet, in case you hadn' guessed."

As a matter of fact, Barlow had guessed, but it was pleasant to have his anticipations borne out.

There was a little more conversation, then he left the room with the young woman. They went through a very ordinary door and down a very ordinary hall to an underground garage. Gray-clad men, shaven-headed, bowed to Amily with extreme deference and wheeled forth a small, brightly colored, teardrop-shaped machine. The seats, within a transparent canopy, were luxurious. She punched controls and leaned back. Under some kind of automatic piloting, the vehicle whirred up a ramp and into the air.

From above, Barlow saw endless miles of buildings. The effect was more like Chicago than any futuristic megalopolis: drab, dirty cubicles, with nearly solid streams of pedestrians moving through the canyons between. Enormous vehicles, freight and passenger, rumbled on elevated ways which sometimes ducked below ground. Only a few private cars were to be seen, flitting like the one which bore him over the city.

"What's the population?" he asked slowly.

Amily shrugged. "Who knows? For the whole world, maybe fifteen billion."

He whistled. A fifth of that number had been obscene enough when he departed his own century. However, progress must have been made in food production: algae, ocean farming, and whatnot. He was pleased to note that the air was free of smog. Probably exhaustion of chemical fuels had forced total conversion to atomic-electrical power.

Still, fifteen billion! He asked about other planets, and was a trifle saddened, but not surprised, to hear that they were visited about as often and as significantly as Pago Pago or Antarctica had been in his day.

"What sort of government do you have?" he inquired.

Amily's laugh was as musical a sound as he had ever heard. "True scientist, you! First you find out 'bout Mars, then 'bout affairs at home! Well, if I 'member my hist'ry right, you had many sep'rate countries in the twentieth century. That was before the Atomic Wars, no? All one country now, the United World Republics. How else could fifteen billion people survive?"

"And I suppose all the races are equal?"

"What? I don' un'erstan'."

With some effort, he got across to her the idea that secondary physical characteristics had once been considered important. She was as startled and amused to hear of race riots as he had once been to learn of blood spilled by early Christians over the iota distinguishing homoousian from homoiousian.

"That's cheering," he said. "As I'd hoped." She regarded him closely, for minutes while the aircar whispered through an April sky the color of her eyes. "Your message was never clear as to why you left," she said.

He looked away, down to the brick and concrete earth, up again to clouds. "It's hard to explain. Disgust would be the simplest word. I had no close personal ties after my mother died. And I saw freedom being crushed in most of the world, rotted and vulgarized in my own country; I read interviews with allegedly sane leaders, who spoke calmly of incinerating some tens of millions of women and children, if national policy so demanded. What had I to lose?"

She grimaced. "You did wisely, Tom. I won'er why so few others did the same. But then, there were the Atomic Wars, an' all their aftermath. Not much chance for escape. Nowadays, not much incentive. Who, with access to a time accelerator, 'd want to leave this world?"

He watched her, healthy, serene, and beautiful, and thought: *Who, indeed? Of course he hadn't found any Utopia, but he hadn't been so naive as to expect that. It was enough to have found hope.* He took out another cigarette, offered her one, and was politely refused. "Very few people use tobacco," she said. "Maybe jus' 'cause how expensive 'tis. But if you want, 's your own affair."

"The supremely civilized art," he said. "Minding one's own business."

She gave him a long, sidewise look. "Could be my business too," she murmured. "You're a han'some buddo, Tom."

The drug didn't slow down his pulse much.

He steered the conversation toward herself. She told him she was interested in sports and theatricals. Another bit of semantic confusion straightened itself out after he realized that "amateur performances" would have been a redundant phrase. All art nowadays was amateur, in the sense of being done for love (and, admittedly, social prestige) by people who had no need to do it for money. The mass-produced entertainment of Barlow's birth century was long forgotten. He was not displeased to learn that scientific research, as opposed to technology and engineering, was classed among the arts. Amily voiced a few opinions on Shakespeare's real intent in Hamlet and Lear, which might be banal to her contemporaries but to Barlow were so novel and perceptive that he felt this would prove one of the great artistic eras.

"But I did expect more change," he said. "More inventions, especially. What I've seen looks less than fifty years in advance of my period. No offense," he hastened to add.

Her expression was puzzled rather than hurt. "Why should there be change? Isn' this aircar good enough?"

Perhaps these folk were only rationalizing a static technology forced on them by swollen population and dwindled resources. Obviously capitalism such as Barlow's America had known, with its inherent need to innovate, was extinct. But he didn't mind. So much so-called progress had been sheer hokum anyhow. Let the world take a thousand years to digest the authentic advances of the Industrial Revolution; give the simple graces of living a chance to catch up.

The car glided down to a platform on the fiftieth floor of a skyscraper. The surrounding buildings were as hideous as most of the continent-wide city; but this tower stood clean and proud, its starkness relieved by colorful beds of mutated flowers on each terrace. "So many men wanted to sponsor you, we set up a fund an' got a special place," said Amily. She squeezed his arm. "But I saw you first, 'member."

With that buildup, he was surprised at the modesty of the apartment: two smallish rooms, plus bath and kitchenette. Amily showed him how to operate the gadgets, which were little different from those he knew. He was more interested in the quiet good taste of the interior decoration. The bookshelves were filled with finer volumes than he was accustomed to, most of them handbound. He wouldn't have much trouble getting used to the spelling, he saw. A music library ranged from medieval chants to modern symphonies almost as foreign to his ear; but in between he found many old friends, and when he tried out part of the Beethoven Ninth, he had never heard it better performed.

"I think you're hungry," said the girl. She opened a built-in refrigerator. "Lemme make you a san'wich." The meat was exotic, the bread far tastier than that library paste sold under the name in Barlow's milieu. He ate with pleasure, downing a bottle of excellent beer.

"Might be best you nap now," she said. "Been a strain, I know."

"I feel fine," he said, rising.

"Tha's jus' the tranquistim," she warned. "Tonight'll be a big do. Last till all hours."

He edged closer. She stayed where she was. Her eyelashes fluttered, long and smoky against smooth sunbrowned cheeks. "I can rest tomorrow," he said.

"Sure. You're your own master here, Tom. Later Dad'll find some status position for you, but tha's nominal. An' no hurry 'bout it."

He stopped, struck by a thought. In all this bewilderment of newness, it hadn't occurred to him before. But if he really was such a wonder, he had been received with extraordinary quietness and informality. "What does your father do?" he asked.

"Why, Joe's the Pres'dent o' the world. Didn' you realize?" She laughed afresh. "I s'pose not. We all get so used to each other, all good frien's not standin' on ceremony, we plain forgot—Oh, yes, Joe's the Pres'dent. Sam Wong heads the World Department o' Technics, Phil Faubus is chief sociohistorian, Ivan—No matter."

He needed a while to shed his preconceptions. That the chief executive of fifteen billion people could be so human seemed almost a contradiction in terms. He noticed he'd stepped back from Amily.

She noticed too, seized both his hands and pulled him closer. "Don' be scared," she said merrily. "Jus' 'cause I'm the Pres'dent's daughter, I won't eat you. Got other plans."

Barlow decided to take things as they came. "I told you before," he said. "Please don't rush off."

"Well," she answered, low-voiced, "I'm not in that much of a hurry…"

An hour or two later, when she declared that now he did need a rest and he was inclined to agree, he asked casually if she had any brothers or sisters.

"Sure. Lots of 'em." She kept her eyes on the mirror, before which she sat combing her hair. "Rozh'd like to've met you when you came, but he's too busy studying. 'S not all fun, being President."

"Rozh? A brother? But you said your father—"

"Well, Joe won' live forever, you know. Rozh has to be prepared."

"But this—hey, wait!"

She gave him a direct glance. "Don' you un'erstan'? Rozh is Joe's oldes' son by his chief orthowife. So he'll be the next Pres'dent."

"Oh." Barlow sat for a while. At last: "Is the succession like that in all the other offices?"

"What else? It'd be an unnatural father who didn' han' on his position to his heirs, wouldn't it?" Amily finished combing her locks, sprang up, and blew him a kiss. "I mus' run. 'Bye, darling." She hurried from the room. A moment later he heard her aircar take off.

Alone, he fretted for a while. But after all, he told himself, in the total context of history, hereditary government was the norm, elective government the deviation. Given proper training…modern genetics also, no doubt, and medicine, so there were no defectives…the same family might provide wise rulers for hundreds of years.

He was too tired to think further. Sleep swooped on him.

Soft music awoke him at dusk. A man entered, bearing a tray with tea and cookies. He was a burly fellow, with shaven pate and gray clothes like the garage attendants. His face was expressionless. He set the tray on the bed and prostrated himself.

After he had lain there for a number of seconds, Barlow snapped nervously, "Well, what's the matter with you?"

"My owner hasn' commanded me t' arise," responded a dead voice.

"Huh?"

Another man drifted in. He was more gaily clad, in some kind of livery, but his skull was as bare as the other's. "If my owner please," he said, "his bath an' garments 're ready. It's soon time for the banquet."

Barlow swung his feet to the carpet. "Good Lord!" he exploded. His tea spilled on the prostrate man, and it was hot, but there was no stir or whimper.

When he had argued his way to comprehension—which was not easy, both his chattels being invincibly stupid—Barlow stood for a long while staring at the wall. Well, he told himself at last, in a remote fashion, when fifteen billion people are jammed together on one impoverished planet, they are bound to become a cheap commodity.

With the help of some more tranquilizer, he made a creditable entrance at the feasting place and chatted with many of Earth's rulers. Their total number was small, and he learned they were careful to restrict their own reproduction, lest the power they had be divided. However, they were no more conscious of tyrannizing the unfree than a rancher would be of unfairly dominating his cattle. Their welcome to Barlow was warm and genuine. When Amily took his arm and led the procession into the dining room, he began to feel that he had come home.

The hors d'oeuvres, soup, and salad were delicious. Then, proud and fond, Amily's father stood up to do the honors as the main course was brought in: roast suckling coolie.

FLIGHT TO FOREVER

Chapter 1
No Return

That morning it rained, a fine summer mist blowing over the hills and hiding the gleam of the river and the village beyond. Martin Saunders stood in the doorway letting the cool, wet air blow in his face and wondered what the weather would be like a hundred years from now.

Eve Lang came up behind him and laid a hand on his arm. He smiled down at her, thinking how lovely she was with the raindrops caught in her dark hair like small pearls. She didn't say anything; there was no need for it, and he felt grateful for silence.

He was the first to speak. "Not long now, Eve. And then, realizing the banality of it," he smiled. "Only why do we have this airport feeling? It's not as if I'll be gone long."

"A hundred years," she said.

"Take it easy, darling. The theory is foolproof. I've been on time jaunts before, remember? Twenty years ahead and twenty back. The projector works, it's been proven in practice. This is just a little longer trip, that's all."

"But the automatic machines, that went a hundred years ahead, never came back—"

"Exactly. Some damn fool thing or other went wrong with them. Tubes blew their silly heads off, or some such thing. That's why Sam and I have to go, to see what went wrong. We can repair our machine. We can compensate for the well-known perversity of vacuum tubes."

"But why the two of you? One would be enough. Sam—"

"Sam is no physicist. He might not be able to find the trouble. On the other hand, as a skilled mechanic he can do things I never could. We supplement each other." Saunders took a deep breath. Look, darling—"

Sam Hull's bass shout rang out to them. "All set, folks! Any time you want to go, we can ride!"

"Coming." Saunders took his time, bidding Eve a proper farewell, a little in advance. She followed him into the house and down to the capacious underground workshop.

The projector stood in a clutter of apparatus under the white radiance of fluorotubes. It was unimpressive from the outside, a metal cylinder some ten feet high and thirty feet long with the unfinished look of all experimental setups. The outer shell was simply protection for the battery banks and the massive dimensional projector within. A tiny space in the forward end was left for the two men.

Sam Hull gave them a gay wave. His massive form almost blotted out the gray smocked little body of MacPherson. "All set for a hundred years ahead," he exclaimed. "Two thousand seventy-three, here we come!"

MacPherson blinked owlishly at them from behind thick lenses. "It all tests out," he said. "Or so Sam here tells me. Personally, I wouldn't know an oscillograph from a klystron. You have an ample supply of spare parts and tools. There should be no difficulty."

"I'm not looking for any, Doc" said Saunders. "Eve here won't believe we aren't going to be eaten by monsters with stalked eyes and long fangs. I keep telling her all we're going to do is check your automatic machines, if we can find them, and make a few astronomical observations, and come back."

"There'll be people in the future," said Eve.

"Oh, well, if they invite us in for a drink we won't say no," shrugged Hull. "Which reminds me—" He fished a pint out of his capacious coverall pocket. We ought to drink a toast or something, huh?"

Saunders frowned a little. He didn't want to add to Eve's impression of a voyage into darkness. She was worried enough, poor kid, poor, lovely kid. "Hell," he said, "we've been back to nineteen fifty-three and seen the house standing. We've been ahead to nineteen ninety-three and seen the house standing. Nobody home at either time. These jaunts are too dull to rate a toast."

"Nothing," said Hull, "is too dull to rate a drink." He poured and they touched glasses, a strange little ceremony in the utterly prosaic laboratory. "Bon voyage!"

"Bon voyage." Eve tried to smile, but the hand that lifted the glass to her lips trembled a little.

"Come on," said Hull. "Let's go, Mart. Sooner we set out, the sooner we can get back."

"Sure." With a gesture of decision, Saunders put down his glass and swung toward the machine. "Good-bye, Eve. I'll see you in a couple of hours—after a hundred years or so."

"So long—Martin." She made the name a caress.

MacPherson beamed with avuncular approval.

Saunders squeezed himself into the forward compartment with Hull. He was a big man, long-limbed and wide-shouldered, with blunt, homely features under a shock of brown hair and wide-set gray eyes lined with crow's feet from much squinting into the sun. He wore only the plain blouse and slacks of his work, stained here and there with grease or acid.

The compartment was barely large enough for the two of them, and crowded with instruments—as well as the rifle and pistol they had along entirely to quiet Eve's fears. Saunders swore as the guns got in his way, and closed the door. The clang had in it an odd note of finality.

"Here goes," said Hull unnecessarily.

Saunders nodded and started the projector warming up. Its powerful thrum filled the cabin and vibrated in his bones. Needles flickered across gauge faces, approaching stable values.

Through the single porthole he saw Eve waving. He waved back and then, with an angry motion, flung down the main switch.

The machine shimmered, blurred, and was gone. Eve drew a shuddering breath and turned back to MacPherson.

Grayness swirled briefly before them, and the drone of the projectors filled the machine with an enormous song. Saunders watched the gauges, and inched back the switch which controlled their rate of time advancement. A hundred years ahead—less the number of days since they'd sent the first automatic, just so that no dunderhead in the future would find it and walk off with it.

He slapped down the switch, and the noise and vibration came to a ringing halt.

Sunlight streamed in through the porthole. "No house?" asked Hull.

"A century is a long time," said Saunders.

"Come on, let's go out and have a look."

They crawled through the door and stood erect. The machine lay in the bottom of a half-filled pit above which grasses waved. A few broken shards of stone projected from the earth. There was a bright blue sky overhead, with fluffy white clouds blowing across it.

"No automatics," said Hull, looking around. "That's odd. But maybe the ground-level adjustments—let's go topside. Saunders scrambled up the sloping walls of the pit.

It was obviously the half-filled basement of the old house, which must somehow have been destroyed in the eighty years since his last visit The ground-level machine in the projector automatically materialized it on the exact surface whenever it emerged. There would be no sudden falls or sudden burials under risen earth. Nor would there be disastrous materializations inside something solid; mass-sensitive circuits prevented the machine from halting whenever solid matter occupied its own space. Liquid or gas molecules could get out of the way fast enough.

Saunders stood in tall, wind-rippled grass and looked over the serene landscape of upper New York State. Nothing had changed, the river and the forested hills beyond it were the same, the sun was bright and clouds shone in the heavens.

No—no, before God! Where was the village?

House gone, town gone—what had happened? Had people simply moved away, or…

He looked back down to the basement. Only a few minutes ago—a hundred years in the past—he had stood there in a tangle of battered apparatus, and Doc and Eve—and now it was a pit with wild grass covering the raw earth. An odd desolation tugged at him.

Was *he* still alive today? Was—Eve? The gerontology of 1973 made it entirely possible, but one never knew. And he didn't want to find out.

"Must'a given the country back to the Indians," grunted Sam Hull.

The prosaic wisecrack restored a sense of balance. After all, any sensible man knew that things changed with time. There would be good and evil in the future as there had been in the past. "—And they lived happily ever after" was pure myth. The important thing was change, an unending flux out of which all could come. And right now there was a job to do.

They scouted around in the grass, but there was no trace of the small automatic projectors. Hull scowled thoughtfully. "You know," he said, "I think they started back and blew out on the way."

"You must be right," nodded Saunders. "We can't have arrived more than a few minutes after their return-point." He started back toward the big machine. "Let's take our observation and get out."

They set up their astronomical equipment and took readings on the declining sun. Waiting for night, they cooked a meal on a camp stove and sat while a cricket-chirring dusk deepened around them.

"I like this future," said Hull. "It's peaceful. Think I'll retire here—or now—in my old age."

The thought of transtemporal resorts made Saunders grin. But—who knew? Maybe!

The stars wheeled grandly overhead. Saunders jotted down figures on right ascension, declination and passage times. From that, they could calculate later, almost to the minute, how far the machine had taken them. They had not moved in space at all, of course, relative to the surface of the earth. "Absolute space" was an obsolete fiction, and as far as the projector was concerned Earth was the immobile center of the universe.

They waded through dew-wet grass back down to the machine. "We'll try ten-year stops, looking for the automatics, said Saunders. "If we don't find 'em that way, to hell with them. I'm hungry."

2063—it was raining into the pit.

2053—sunlight and emptiness.

2043—the pit was fresher now, and a few rotting timbers lay half buried in the ground.

Saunders scowled at the meters. "She's drawing more power than she should," he said.

2023—the house had obviously burned, charred stumps of wood were in sight. And the projector had roared with a skull-cracking insanity of power; energy drained from the batteries like water from a squeezed sponge; a resistor was beginning to glow.

They checked the circuits, inch by inch, wire by wire. Nothing was out of order.

"Let's go." Hull's face was white.

It was a battle to leap the next ten years, it took half an hour of bawling, thundering, tortured labor for the projector to fight backward. Radiated energy made the cabin unendurably hot.

2013—the fire-blackened basement still stood.

On its floor lay two small cylinders, tarnished with some years of weathering.

"The automatics got a little further back," said Hull. "Then they quit, and just lay here."

Saunders examined them. When he looked up from his instruments, his face was grim with the choking fear that was rising within him "Drained," he said. "Batteries completely dead. They used up all their energy reserves."

"What in the devil is this?" It was almost a snarl from Hull.

"I—don't—know. There seems to be some kind of resistance which increases the further back we try to go—"

"Come on!"

"But—"

"Come on, God damn it!"

Saunders shrugged hopelessly.

It took two hours to fight back five years. Then Saunders stopped the projector. His voice shook.

"No go, Sam. We've used up three quarters of our stored energy—and the farther back we go, the more we use per year. It seems to be some sort of high-order exponential function."

"So—"

"So we'd never make it. At this rate, our batteries will be dead before we get back another ten years." Saunders looked ill. "It's some effect the theory didn't allow for, some accelerating increase in power requirements the farther back into the past we go. For twenty-year hops or less, the energy increases roughly as the square of the number of years traversed. But it must actually be something like an exponential curve, which starts building up fast and furious beyond a certain point. We haven't enough power left in the batteries!"

"If we could recharge them—"

"We don't have such equipment with us. But maybe—"

They climbed out of the ruined basement and looked eagerly towards the river. There was no sign of the village. It must have been torn down or otherwise destroyed still further back in the past at a point they'd been through.

"No help there," said Saunders.

"We can look for a place. There must be people somewhere!"

"No doubt." Saunders fought for calm. "But we could spend a long time looking for them, you know. And—" His voice wavered. "Sam, I'm not sure even recharging at intervals would help. It looks very much to me as if the curve of energy consumption is approaching a vertical asymptote."

"Talk English, will you?" Hull's grin was forced.

"I mean that beyond a certain number of years an infinite amount of energy may be required. Like the Einsteinian concept of light as the limiting velocity. As you approach the speed of light, the energy needed to accelerate increases ever more rapidly. You'd need infinite energy to get beyond the speed of light—which is just a fancy way of saying you can't do it. The same thing may apply to time as well as space."

"You mean—we can't ever get back?"

"I don't know." Saunders looked desolately around at the smiling landscape. "I could be wrong. But I'm horribly afraid I'm right."

Hull swore. "What're we going to do about it?"

"We've got two choices," Saunders said.

"One, we can hunt for people, recharge our batteries, and keep trying. Two, we can go into the future."

"The future!"

"Uh-huh. Sometime in the future, they ought to know more about such things than we do. They may know a way to get around this effect. Certainly they could give us a powerful enough engine so that, if energy is all that's needed, we can get back. A small atomic generator, for instance."

Hull stood with bent head, turning the thought over in his mind. There was a meadowlark singing, somewhere, maddeningly sweet.

Saunders forced a harsh laugh. "But the very first thing on the agenda," he said, "is breakfast."

Chapter 2
Belgotai of Syrtis

The food was tasteless. They ate in a heavy silence, choking the stuff down. But in the end they looked at each other with a common resolution.

Hull grinned and stuck out a hairy paw. "It's a hell of a roundabout way to get home," he said, "but I'm for it."

Saunders clasped hands with him, wordlessly. They went back to the machine.

"And now where?" asked the mechanic.

"It's two thousand eight," said Saunders.

"How about—well—two thousand five hundred A.D.?"

"Okay. It's a nice round number. Anchors aweigh!"

The machine thrummed and shook. Saunders was gratified to notice the small power consumption as the years and decades fled by. At that rate, they had energy enough to travel to the end of the world.

Eve, Eve, I'll come back. I'll come back if I have to go ahead to Judgment Day...

2500 A.D. The machine blinked into materialization on top of a low hill—the pit had filled in during the intervening centuries. Pale, hurried sunlight flashed through wind-driven rain clouds into the hot interior.

"Come," said Hull. "We haven't got all day."

He picked up the automatic rifle.

"What's the idea?" exclaimed Saunders.

"Eve was right the first time," said Hull grimly. "Buckle on that pistol, Mart."

Saunders strapped the heavy weapon to his thigh. The metal was cold under his fingers.

They stepped out and swept the horizon.

Hull's voice rose in a shout of glee. "People!"

There was a small town beyond the river, near the site of old Hudson. Beyond it lay fields of ripening grain and clumps of trees. There was no sign of a highway. Maybe surface transportation was obsolete now.

The town looked—odd. It must have been there a long time, the houses were weathered. They were tall peak-roofed buildings, crowding narrow streets. A flashing metal tower reared some five hundred feet into the lowering sky, near the center of town.

Somehow, it didn't look the way Saunders had visualized communities of the future. It had an oddly stunted appearance, despite the high buildings and—sinister? He couldn't say. Maybe it was only his depression.

Something rose from the center of the town, a black ovoid that whipped into the sky and lined out across the river. *Reception committee,* thought Saunders. His hand fell on his pistol butt.

It was an airjet, he saw as it neared, an egg-shaped machine with stubby wings and a flaring tail. It was flying slowly now, gliding groundward toward them.

"Hallo, there!" bawled Hull. He stood erect with the savage wind tossing his flame-red hair, waving. "Hallo, people!"

The machine dove at them. Something stabbed from its nose, a line of smoke—tracers!

Conditioned reflex flung Saunders to the ground. The bullets whined over his head, exploding with a vicious crash behind him. He saw Hull blown apart.

The jet rushed overhead and banked for another assault. Saunders got up and ran, crouching low, weaving back and forth. The line of bullets spanged past him again, throwing up gouts of dirt where they hit. He threw himself down again.

Another try...Saunders was knocked off his feet by the bursting of a shell. He rolled over and hugged the ground, hoping the grass would hide him. Dimly, he thought that the jet was too fast for strafing a single man; it overshot its mark.

He heard it whine overhead, without daring to look up. It circled vulture-like, seeking him. He had time for a rising tide of bitter hate.

Sam—they'd killed him, shot him without provocation—Sam, red-haired Sam with his laughter and his comradeship, Sam was dead and they had killed him.

He risked turning over. The jet was settling to earth; they'd hunt him from the ground. He got up and ran again.

A shot wailed past his ear. He spun around the pistol in his hand, and snapped a return shot. There were men in black uniforms coming out of the jet. It was long range, but his gun was a heavy war model; it carried. He fired again and felt a savage joy at seeing one of the black-clad figures spin on its heels and lurch to the ground.

The time machine lay before him. No time for heroics; he had to get away—fast! Bullets were singing around him.

He burst through the door and slammed it shut. A slug whanged through the metal wall. Thank God the tubes were still warm!

He threw the main switch. As vision wavered he saw the pursuers almost on him. One of them was aiming something like a bazooka.

They faded into grayness. He lay back, shuddering. Slowly, he grew aware that his clothes were torn and that a metal fragment had scratched his hand.

And Sam was dead. Sam was dead.

He watched the dial creep upward. Let it be 3000 A.D. Five hundred years was not too much to put between himself and the men in black.

He chose nighttime. A cautious look outside revealed that he was among tall buildings with little if any light. Good!

He spent a few moments bandaging his injury and changing into the extra clothes Eve had insisted on providing—a heavy wool shirt and breeches, boots and a raincoat that should help make him relatively inconspicuous. The holstered pistol went along, of course, with plenty of extra cartridges. He'd have to leave the machine while he reconnoitered and chance its discovery. At least he could lock the door.

Outside he found himself standing in a small cobbled courtyard between high houses with shuttered and darkened windows. Overhead was utter night, the stars must be clouded, but he saw a vague red glow to the north, pulsing and flickering. After a moment, he squared his shoulders and started down an alley that was like a cavern of blackness.

Briefly, the incredible situation rose in his mind. In less than an hour he had leaped a thousand years past his own age, had seen his friend murdered and now stood in an alien city more alone than man had ever been. *And Eve, will I see you again?*

A noiseless shadow, blacker than the night, slipped past him. The dim light shone greenly from its eyes—an alley cat. At least man still had pets. But he could have wished for a more reassuring one.

Noise came from ahead, a bobbing light flashing around at the doors of houses. He dropped a hand through the slit in his coat to grasp the pistol butt.

Black against the narrowed skyline four men came abreast, filling the street. The rhythm of their footfalls was military. A guard of some kind. He looked around for shelter; he didn't want to be taken prisoner by unknowns.

No alleys to the side—he sidled backward.

The flashlight beam darted ahead, crossed his body, and came back. A voice shouted something, harsh and peremptory.

Saunders turned and ran. The voice cried again behind him. He heard the slam of boots after him. Someone blew a horn, raising echoes that hooted between the high dark walls.

A black form grew out of the night. Fingers like steel wires closed on his arm, yanking him to one side. He opened his mouth, and a hand slipped across it. Before he could recover balance, he was pulled down a flight of stairs in the street.

"In heah." The hissing whisper was taut in his ear. "Quickly."

A door slid open just a crack. They burst through, and the other man closed it behind them. An automatic lock clicked shut.

"Ih don' tink dey vised us," said the man grimly. "Dey better not ha'!"

Saunders stared at him. The other man was of medium height, with a lithe, slender build shown by the skin-tight gray clothes under his black cape. There was a gun at one hip, a pouch at the other. His face was sallow, with a yellowish tinge, and the hair was shaven. It was a lean, strong face, with high cheekbones and narrow jaw, straight nose with flaring nostrils, dark, slant eyes under Mephistophelean brows. The mouth, wide and self-indulgent, was drawn into a reckless grin that showed sharp white teeth. Some sort of white-Mongoloid half-breed, Saunders guessed.

"Who are *you*?" he asked roughly.

The stranger surveyed him shrewdly. "Belgotai of Syrtis," he said at last. "But yuh don' belong heah."

"I'll say I don't." Wry humor rose in Saunders. "Why did you snatch me that way?"

"Yuh didn' wanna fall into de Watch's hands, did yuh?" asked Belgotai. "Don' ask mih why Ih ressued a stranger. Ih happened to come out, see yuh running, figgered anybody running fro de Watch desuhved help, an' pulled yuh back in." He shrugged. "Of course, if yuh don' wanna be helped, go back upstaiahs."

"I'll stay here, of course," he said. "And—thanks for rescuing me."

"De nada," said Belgotai. "Come, le's ha' a drink."

It was a smoky, low-ceilinged room, with a few scarred wooden tables crowded about a small charcoal fire and big barrels in the rear—a tavern of some sort, an underworld hangout. Saunders reflected that he might have done worse. Crooks wouldn't be as finicky about his antecedents as officialdom might be. He could ask his way around, learn.

"I'm afraid I haven't any money," he said. "Unless—" He pulled a handful of coins from his pocket.

Belgotai looked sharply at them and drew a whistling breath between his teeth. Then his face smoothed into blankness. "Ih'll buy," he said genially. "Come, Hennaly, gi' us whissey."

Belgotai drew Saunders into a dark corner seat, away from the others in the room. The landlord brought tumblers of rotgut remotely akin to whiskey, and Saunders gulped his with a feeling of need.

"Wha' name do yuh go by?" asked Belgotai.

"Saunders. Martin Saunders."

"Glad to see yuh. Now—" Belgotai leaned closer, and his voice dropped to a whisper— "Now, Saunders, *when*'re yuh from?"

Saunders started. Belgotai smiled thinly. "Be frank," he said. "Dese're mih frien's heah. Dey'd think nawting of slitting yuh troat and dumping yuh in de alley. But Ih mean well."

With a sudden great weariness, Saunders relaxed. What the hell, it had to come out sometime. "Nineteen hundred seventy-three," he said.

"Eh? De future?"

"No—the past."

"Oh. Diff'ent chronning, den. How far back?"

"One thousand and twenty-seven years."

Belgotai whistled. "Long ways! But Ih were sure yuh mus' be from de past. Nobody eve' come fro' de future."

Sickly: "You mean—it's impossible?"

"Ih do' know." Belgotai's grin was wolfish. "Who'd visit dis era fro' de future, if dey could? But wha's yuh story?"

Saunders bristled. The whiskey was coursing hot in his veins now. "I'll trade information," he said coldly. "I won't give it."

"Faiah enawff. Blast away, Mahtin Saundahs."

Saunders told his story in a few words. At the end, Belgotai nodded gravely. "Yuh ran into de Fanatics, five hundred yeahs ago," he said. "Dey was deat' on time travelers. Or on most people, for dat matter."

"But what's happened? What sort of world is this, anyway?"

Belgotai's slurring accents were getting easier to follow. Pronunciation had changed a little, vowels sounded different, the "r" had shifted to something like that in twentieth-century French or Danish, other consonants were modified. Foreign words, especially Spanish, had crept in. But it was still intelligible. Saunders listened. Belgotai was not too well versed in history, but his shrewd brain had a grasp of the more important facts.

The time of troubles had begun in the twenty-third century with the revolt of the Martian colonists against the increasingly corrupt and tyrannical Terrestrial Directorate. A century later the folk of Earth were on the move, driven by famine, pestilence and civil war, a chaos out of which rose the religious enthusiasm of the Armageddonists—the Fanatics, as they were called later. Fifty years after the massacres on Luna, Huntry was the military dictator of Earth, and the rule of the Armageddonists endured for nearly three hundred years. It was a nominal sort of rule, vast territories were always in revolt and the planetary colonists were building up a power which kept the Fanatics out of space, but wherever they did have control they ruled with utter ruthlessness.

Among other things they forbade was time travel. But it had never been popular with anyone since the Time War, when a defeated Directorate army had leaped from the twenty-third to the twenty-fourth century and wrought havoc before their attempt at conquest was smashed. Time travelers were few anyway, the future was too precarious—they were apt to be killed or enslaved in one of the more turbulent periods.

In the late twenty-seventh century, the Planetary League and the African Dissenters had finally ended Fanatic rule. Out of the postwar confusion rose the Pax Africana, and for two hundred years man had enjoyed an era of comparative peace and progress which was wistfully looked back on as a golden age; indeed, modern chronology dated from the ascension of John Mteza I. Breakdown came through internal decay and the onslaughts of barbarians from the outer planets, the Solar System split into a multitude of small states and even independent cities. It was a hard, brawling period, not without a brilliance of its own, but it was drawing to a close now.

"Dis is one of de city-states," said Belgotai. "Liung-Wei, it's named—founded by Sinese invaders about tree centuries ago. It's under de dictatorship of Krausmann now, a stubborn old buzzard who'll no surrender dough de armies of de Atlantic Master're at ouah very gates now. Yuh see de red glow? Dat's deir projectors working on our energy screen. When dey break it down, day'll take de city and punish it for holding out so long. Nobody looks happily to dat day."

He added a few remarks about himself. Belgotai was of a dying age, the past era of small states who employed mercenaries to fight their battles. Born on Mars, Belgotai had hired out over the whole Solar System. But the little mercenary companies were helpless before the organized levies of the rising nations, and after the annihilation of his band Belgotai had fled to Earth where he dragged out a weary existence as thief and assassin. He had little to look forward to.

"Nobody wants a free comrade now," he said ruefully. "If de Watch don't catch me first, Ih'll hang when de Atlantics take de city."

Saunders nodded with a certain sympathy.

Belgotai leaned close with a gleam in his slant eyes. "But yuh can help me, Mahtin Saundahs," he hissed. "And help yuhself too."

"Eh?" Saunders blinked wearily at him.

"Sure, sure. Take me wid yuh, out of dis damned time. Dey can't help yuh here, dey know no more about time travel dan yuh do—most likely dey'll trow yuh in de calabozo and smash yuh machine. Yuh have to go on. Take me!"

Saunders hesitated, warily. What did he really know? How much truth was in Belgotai's story? How far could he trust—

"Set me off in some time when a free comrade can fight again. Meanwhile Ih'll help. Ih'm a good man wid gun or vibrodagger. Yuh can't go batting alone into de future."

Saunders wondered. But what the hell—it was plain enough that this period was of no use to him. And Belgotai had saved him, even if the Watch wasn't as bad as he claimed. And—well—he needed someone to talk to, if nothing else. Someone to help him forget Sam Hull and the gulf of centuries separating him from Eve.

Decision came. "Okay."

"Wonnaful! Yuh'll no be sorry, Mahtin." Belgotai stood up. "Come, le's be blasting off."

"Now?"

"De sooner de better. Someone may find yuh machine. Den it's too late."

"But—you'll want to make ready—say goodbye—"

Belgotai slapped his pouch. "All Ih own is heah." Bitterness underlay his reckless laugh. "Ih've none to say good-bye to, except mih creditors. Come!"

Half dazed, Saunders followed him out of the tavern. This time-hopping was going too fast for him, he didn't have a chance to adjust.

For instance, if he ever got back to his own time he'd have descendants in this age. At the rate at which lines of descent spread, there would be men in each army who had his own and Eve's blood, warring on each other without thought of the tenderness which had wrought their very beings. But then, he remembered wearily, he had never considered the common ancestors he must have with men he'd shot out of the sky in the war he once had fought.

Men lived in their own times, a brief flash of light ringed with an enormous dark, and it was not in their nature to think beyond that little span of years. He began to realize why time travel had never been common.

"Hist!" Belgotai drew him into the tunnel of an alley. They crouched there while four black-caped men of the Watch strode past. In the wan red light, Saunders had a glimpse of high cheekbones, half-Oriental features, the metallic gleam of guns slung over their shoulders.

They made their way to the machine where it lay between lowering houses crouched in a night of fear and waiting. Belgotai laughed again, a soft, joyous ring in the dark. "Freedom!" he whispered.

They crawled into it and Saunders set the controls for a hundred years ahead. Belgotai scowled. "Most like de world'll be very tame and quiet den," he said.

"If I get a way to return," said Saunders, "I'll carry you on whenever you want to go."

"Or yuh could carry me back a hundred years from now," said the warrior. "Blast away, den!"

3100 A.D. A waste of blackened, fused rock. Saunders switched on the Geiger counter and it clattered crazily. Radioactive! Some hellish atomic bomb had wiped Liung-Wei from existence. He leaped another century, shaking.

3200 A.D. The radioactivity was gone, but the desolation remained, a vast vitrified crater under a hot, still sky, dead and lifeless. There was little prospect of walking across it in search of man, nor did Saunders want to get far from the machine. If he should be cut off from it…

By 3500, soil had drifted back over the ruined land and a forest was growing. They stood in a drizzling rain and looked around them.

"Big trees," said Saunders. "This forest has stood for a long time without human interference."

"Maybe man went back to de caves?" suggested Belgotai.

"I doubt it. Civilization was just too widespread for a lapse into total savagery. But it may be a long ways to a settlement."

"Le's go ahead, den!" Belgotai's eyes gleamed with interest.

The forest still stood for centuries thereafter. Saunders scowled in worry. He didn't like this business of going farther and farther from his time, he was already too far ahead ever to get back without help. Surely, in all ages of human history—

4100 A.D. They flashed into materialization on a broad grassy sward where low, rounded buildings of something that looked like tinted plastic stood between fountains, statues, and bowers. A small aircraft whispered noiselessly overhead, no sign of motive power on its exterior.

There were humans around, young men and women who wore long colorful capes over light tunics. They crowded forward with a shout. Saunders and Belgotai stepped out, raising hands in a gesture of friendship. But the warrior kept his hands close to his gun.

The language was a flowing, musical tongue with only a baffling hint of familiarity. Had times changed that much?

They were taken to one of the buildings. Within its cool, spacious interior, a grave, bearded man in ornate red robes stood up to greet them. Someone else brought in a small machine reminiscent of an oscilloscope with microphone attachments. The man set it on the table and adjusted its dials.

He spoke again, his own unknown language rippling from his lips. But words came out of the machine—English!

"Welcome, travelers, to this branch of the American College. Please be seated."

Saunders and Belgotai gaped. The man smiled. "I see the psychophone is new to you. It is a receiver of encephalic emissions from the speech centers. When one speaks, the corresponding thoughts are taken by the machine, greatly amplified, and beamed to the brain of the listener, who interprets them in terms of his own language.

"Permit me to introduce myself. I am Hamalon Avard; dean of this branch of the College." He raised bushy gray eyebrows in polite inquiry.

They gave their names and Avard bowed ceremoniously. A slim girl, whose scanty dress caused Belgotai's eyes to widen, brought a tray of sandwiches and a beverage not unlike tea. Saunders suddenly realized how hungry and tired he was. He collapsed into a seat that molded itself to his contours and looked dully at Avard.

Their story came out, and the dean nodded. "I thought you were time travelers," he said. "But this is a matter of great interest. The archaeology departments will want to speak to you, if you will be so kind—"

"Can you help us?" asked Saunders bluntly. "Can you fix our machine so it will reverse?"

"Alas, no. I am afraid our physics holds no hope for you. I can consult the experts, but I am sure there has been no change in spatiotemporal theory since Priogan's reformulation. According to it, the energy needed to travel into the past increases tremendously with the period covered. The deformation of world lines, you see. Beyond a period of about seventy years, infinite energy is required."

Saunders nodded dully. "I thought so. Then there's no hope?"

"Not in this time, I am afraid. But science is advancing rapidly. Contact with alien culture in the Galaxy has proved an immense stimulant—"

"Yuh have interstellar travel?" exploded Belgotai. "Yuh can travel to de stars?"

"Yes, of course. The faster-than-light drive was worked out over five hundred years ago on the basis of Priogan's modified relativity theory. It involves warping through higher dimensions— But you have more urgent problems than scientific theories."

"Not Ih!" said Belgotai fiercely. "If Ih can get put among de stars—dere must be wars dere—"

"Alas, yes, the rapid expansion of the frontier has thrown the Galaxy into chaos. But I do not think you could get passage on a spaceship. In fact, the Council will probably order your temporal deportation as unintegrated individuals. The sanity of Sol will be in danger otherwise."

"Why, yuh—" Belgotai snarled and reached for his gun. Saunders clapped a hand on the warrior's arm.

"Take it easy, you bloody fool," he said furiously. "We can't fight a whole planet. Why should we? There'll be other ages."

Belgotai relaxed, but his eyes were still angry.

They stayed at the College for two days. Avard and his colleagues were courteous, hospitable, eager to hear what the travelers had to tell of their periods. They provided food and living quarters and much-needed rest. They even pleaded Belgotai's case to the Solar Council, via telescreen. But the answer was inexorable: the Galaxy already had too many barbarians. The travelers would have to go.

Their batteries were taken out of the machine for them and a small atomic engine with nearly limitless energy reserves installed in its place. Avard gave them a psychophone for communication with whoever they met in the future. Everyone was very nice and considerate. But Saunders found himself reluctantly agreeing with Belgotai. He didn't care much for these overcivilized gentlefolk. He didn't belong in this age.

Avard bade them grave good-bye. "It is strange to see you go," he said. "It is a strange thought that you will still be traveling long after my cremation, that you will see things I cannot dream of." Briefly, something stirred in his face. "In a way I envy you." He turned away quickly, as if afraid of the thought. "Good-bye and good fortune."

4300 A.D. The campus buildings were gone, but small, elaborate summerhouses had replaced them. Youths and girls in scanty rainbow-hued dress crowded around the machine.

"You are time travelers?" asked one of the young men, wide-eyed.

Saunders nodded, feeling too tired for speech. "Time travelers!" A girl squealed in delight. "I don't suppose you have any means of traveling into the past these days?" asked Saunders hopelessly.

"Not that I know of. But please come, stay for a while, tell us about your journeys. This is the biggest lark we've had since the ship came from Sirius."

There was no denying the eager insistence. The women, in particular, crowded around, circling them in a ring of soft arms, laughing and shouting and pulling them away from the machine. Belgotai grinned. "Le's stay de night," he suggested.

Saunders didn't feel like arguing the point. There was time enough, he thought bitterly. All the time in the world.

It was a night of revelry. Saunders managed to get a few facts. Sol was a Galactic backwater these days, stuffed with mercantile wealth and guarded by non-human mercenaries against the interstellar raiders and conquerors. This region was one of many playgrounds for the children of the great merchant families, living for generations off inherited riches. They were amiable kids, but there was a mental and physical softness over them, and a deep inward weariness from a meaningless round of increasingly stale pleasure. Decadence.

Saunders finally sat alone under a moon that glittered with the diamond-points of domed cities, beside a softly lapping artificial lake, and watched the constellations wheel overhead—the far suns that man had conquered without mastering himself. He thought of Eve and wanted to cry, but the hollowness in his breast was dry and cold.

Chapter 3
Trapped in the Time-Stream

Belgotai had a thumping hangover in the morning which a drink offered by one of the women removed. He argued for a while about staying in this age. Nobody would deny him passage this time; they were eager for fighting men out in the Galaxy. But the fact that Sol was rarely visited now, that he might have to wait years, finally decided him on continuing.

"Dis won' go on much longer," he said. "Sol is too tempting a prize, an' mercenaries aren' allays loyal. Sooner or later, dere'll be war on Eart' again."

Saunders nodded dispiritedly. He hated to think of the blasting energies that would devour a peaceful and harmless folk, the looting and murdering and enslaving, but history was that way. It was littered with the graves of pacifists.

The bright scene swirled into grayness. They drove ahead.

4400 A.D. A villa was burning, smoke and flame reaching up into the clouded sky. Behind it stood the looming bulk of a ray-scarred spaceship, and around it boiled a vortex of men, huge bearded men in helmets and cuirasses, laughing as they bore out golden loot and struggling captives. The barbarians had come!

The two travelers leaped back into the machine. Those weapons could fuse it to a glowing mass. Saunders swung the main-drive switch far over.

"We'd better make a longer jump," Saunders said, as the needle crept past the century mark. "Can't look for much scientific progress in a dark age. I'll try for five thousand A.D."

His mind carried the thought on: *Will there ever be progress of the sort we must have? Eve, will I ever see you again?* As if his yearning could carryover the abyss of millennia: *Don't mourn me too long, my dearest. In all the bloody ages of human history, your happiness is all that ultimately matters.*

As the needle approached six centuries, Saunders tried to ease down the switch. Tried!

"What's the matter?" Belgotai leaned over his shoulder.

With a sudden cold sweat along his ribs, Saunders tugged harder. The switch was immobile—the projector wouldn't stop.

"Out of order?" asked Belgotai anxiously.

"No—it's the automatic mass-detector. We'd be annihilated if we emerged in the same space with solid matter. The detector prevents the projector from stopping if it senses such a structure." Saunders grinned savagely. "Some damned idiot must have built a house right where we are!"

The needle passed its limit, and still they droned on through a featureless grayness. Saunders reset the dial and noted the first half millennium. It was nice, though not necessary, to know what year it was when they emerged.

He wasn't worried at first. Man's works were so horribly impermanent; he thought with a sadness of the cities and civilizations he had seen rise and spend their little hour and sink back into the night and chaos of time. But after a thousand years...

Two thousand...

Three thousand...

Belgotai's face was white and tense in the dull glow of the instrument panel. "How long to go?" he whispered.

"I—don't—know."

Within the machine, the long minutes passed while the projector hummed its song of power and two men stared with hypnotized fascination at the creeping record of centuries.

For twenty thousand years that incredible thing stood. In the year 25,296 A.D., the switch suddenly went down under Saunders' steady tug. The machine flashed into reality, tilted, and slid down a few feet before coming to rest. Wildly, they opened the door.

The projector lay on a stone block big as a small house, whose ultimate slipping from its place had freed them. It was halfway up a pyramid.

A monument of gray stone, a tetrahedron a mile to a side and a half a mile high. The outer casing had worn away, or been removed, so that the tremendous blocks stood naked to the weather. Soil had drifted up onto it, grass and trees grew on its titanic slopes. Their roots, and wind and rain and frost, were slowly crumbling the artificial hill to earth again, but still it dominated the landscape.

A defaced carving leered out from a tangle of brush. Saunders looked at it and looked away, shuddering. No human being had ever carved that thing.

The countryside around was altered; he couldn't see the old river and there was a lake glimmering in the distance which had not been there before. The hills seemed lower, and forest covered them. It was a wild, primeval scene, but there was a spaceship standing near the base, a monster machine with its nose rearing skyward and a sunburst blazon on its hull. And there were men working nearby.

Saunders' shout rang in the still air. He and Belgotai scrambled down the steep slopes of earth, clawing past trees and vines. Men!

No—not all men. A dozen great shining engines were toiling without supervision at the foot of the pyramid—robots. And of the group which turned to stare at the travelers, two were squat, blue-furred, with snouted faces and six-fingered hands.

Saunders realized with an unexpectedly eerie shock that he was seeing extraterrestrial intelligence. But it was to the men that he faced.

They were all tall, with aristocratically refined features and a calm that seemed inbred. Their clothing was impossible to describe, it was like a rainbow shimmer around them, never the same in its play of color and shape. So, thought Saunders, so must the old gods have looked on high Olympus, beings greater and more beautiful than man.

But it was a human voice that called to them, a deep, well-modulated tone in a totally foreign language. Saunders remembered exasperatedly that he had forgotten the psychophone. But one of the blue-furred aliens was already fetching a round, knob-studded globe out of which the familiar translating voice seemed to come: "…time travelers."

"From the very remote past, obviously," said another man. Damn him, damn them all, they weren't any more excited than at the bird which rose, startled, from the long grass. You'd think time travelers would at least be worth shaking by the hand.

"Listen," snapped Saunders, realizing in the back of his mind that his annoyance was a reaction against the awesomeness of the company, "we're in trouble. Our machine won't carry us back, and we have to find a period of time which knows how to reverse the effect. Can you do it?"

One of the aliens shook his animal head. "No," he said. "There is no way known to physics of getting farther back than about seventy years. Beyond that, the required energy approaches infinity and—"

Saunders groaned. "We know it," said Belgotai harshly.

"At least you must rest," said one of the men in a more kindly tone. "It will be interesting to hear your story."

"I've told it to too many people in the last few millennia," rasped Saunders. "Let's hear yours for a change."

Two of the strangers exchanged low-voiced words. Saunders could almost translate them himself: *"Barbarians—childish emotional pattern—well, humor them for a while."*

"This is an archaeological expedition, excavating the pyramid," said one of the men patiently. "We are from the Galactic Institute, Sarlan-sector branch. I am Lord Arsfel of Astracyr, and these are my subordinates. The nonhumans, as you may wish to know, are from the planet Quulhan, whose sun is not visible from Terra."

Despite himself, Saunders' awed gaze turned to the stupendous mass looming over them. "Who built it?" he breathed.

"The Ixchulhi made such structures on planets they conquered, no one knows why. But then, no one knows what they were, or where they came from, or where they ultimately went. It is hoped that some of the answers may be found in their pyramids."

The atmosphere grew more relaxed. Deftly, the men of the expedition got Saunders' and Belgotai's stories and what information about their almost prehistoric periods they cared for. In exchange, something of history was offered them.

After the Ixchulhi's ruinous wars the Galaxy had made a surprisingly rapid comeback. New techniques of mathematical psychology made it possible to unite the peoples of a billion worlds and rule them effectively. The Galactic Empire was egalitarian—it had to be, for one of its mainstays was the fantastically old and evolved race of the planet called Vro-Hi by men.

It was peaceful, prosperous, colorful with diversity of races and cultures, expanding in science and the arts. It had already endured for ten thousand years, and there seemed no doubt in Arsfel's calm mind that it could endure forever. The barbarians along the Galactic periphery and out in the Magellanic Clouds? Nonsense! The Empire would get around to civilizing them in due course; meanwhile they were only a nuisance.

But Sol could almost be called one of the barbarian suns, though it lay within the Imperial boundaries. Civilization was concentrated near the center of the Galaxy, and Sol lay up in what was actually a remote and thinly starred region of space. A few primitive landsmen still lived on its planets and had infrequent intercourse with the nearer stars, but they hardly counted. The human race had almost forgotten its ancient home.

Somehow the picture was saddening to the American. He thought of old Earth spinning on her lonely way through the emptiness of space, he thought of the great arrogant Empire and of all the mighty dominions which had fallen to dust through the millennia. But when he ventured to suggest that this civilization, too, was not immortal, he was immediately snowed under with figures, facts, logic, the curious paramathematical symbolism of modern mass psychology. It could be shown rigorously that the present setup was inherently stable—and already ten thousand years of history had given no evidence to upset that science…

"I give up," said Saunders. "I can't argue with you."

They were shown through the spaceship's immense interior, the luxurious apartments of the expedition, the looming intricate machinery which did its own thinking. Arsfel tried to show them his art, his recorded music, his psycho-books, but it was no use, they didn't have the understanding.

Savages! Could an Australian aborigine have appreciated Rembrandt, Beethoven, Kant, or Einstein? Could he have lived happily in sophisticated New York society?

"We'd best go," muttered Belgotai. "We don't belong heah."

Saunders nodded. Civilization had gone too far for them, they could never be more than frightened pensioners in its hugeness. Best to get on their way again.

"I would advise you to leap ahead for long intervals," said Arsfel. "Galactic civilization won't have spread out this far for many thousands of years, and certainly whatever native culture Sol develops won't be able to help you." He smiled. "It doesn't matter if you overshoot the time when the process you need is invented. The records won't be lost, I assure you. From here on, you are certain of encountering only peace and enlightenment…unless, of course, the barbarians of Terra get hostile, but then you can always leave them behind. Sooner or later, there will be true civilization here to help you."

"Tell me honestly," said Saunders. "Do you think the negative time machine will ever be invented?"

One of the beings from Quulhan shook his strange head. "I doubt it," he said gravely. "We would have had visitors from the future."

"They might not have cared to see your time," argued Saunders desperately. "They'd have complete records of it. So they'd go back to investigate more primitive ages, where their appearance might easily pass unnoticed."

"You may be right," said Arsfel. His tone was disconcertingly like that with which an adult comforts a child by a white lie.

"Le's go!" snarled Belgotai.

In 26,000 the forests still stood and the pyramid had become a high hill where trees nodded and rustled in the wind.

In 27,000 a small village of wood and stone houses stood among smiling grain fields.

In 28,000 men were tearing down the pyramid, quarrying it for stone. But its huge bulk was not gone before 30,000 A.D., and a small city had been built from it.

Minutes ago, thought Saunders grayly, they had been talking to Lord Arsfel of Astracyr, and now he was five thousand years in his grave.

In 31,000 they materialized on one of the broad lawns that reached between the towers of a high and proud city. Aircraft swarmed overhead and a spaceship, small beside Arsfel's but nonetheless impressive, was standing nearby.

"Looks like de Empire's got heah," said Belgotai.

"I don't know," said Saunders. "But it looks peaceful, anyway. Let's go out and talk to people."

They were received by tall, stately women in white robes of classic lines. It seemed that the Matriarchy now ruled Sol, and would they please conduct themselves as befitted the inferior sex? No, the Empire hadn't ever gotten out here; Sol paid tribute, and there was an Imperial legate at Sirius, but the actual boundaries of Galactic culture hadn't changed for the past three millennia. Solar civilization was strictly home-grown and obviously superior to the alien influence of the Vro-Hi.

No, nothing was known about time theory. Their visit had been welcome and all that, but now would they please go on? They didn't fit in with the neatly regulated culture of Terra.

"I don't like it," said Saunders as they walked back toward the machine. "Arsfel swore the Imperium would keep expanding its actual as well as its nominal sphere of influence. But it's gone static now. Why?"

"Ih tink," said Belgotai, "dat spite of all his fancy mathematics, yuh were right. Nawthing lasts forever."

"But—my God!"

Chapter 4
End of Empire

34,000 A.D. The Matriarchy was gone. The city was a tumbled heap of fire-blackened rocks. Skeletons lay in the ruins.

"The barbarians are moving again," said Saunders bleakly. "They weren't here so very long ago; these bones are still fresh, and they've got a long ways to go to dead center. An empire like this one will be many thousands of years in dying. But it's doomed already."

"What'll we do?" asked Belgotai.

"Go on," said Saunders tonelessly. "What else can we do?"

35,000 A.D. A peasant hut stood under huge old trees. Here and there a broken column stuck out of the earth, remnant of the city. A bearded man in coarsely woven garments fled wildly with his woman and brood of children as the machine appeared.

36,000 A.D. There was a village again, with a battered old spaceship standing hard by. There were half a dozen different races, including man, moving about, working on the construction of some enigmatic machine. They were dressed in plain, shabby clothes, with guns at their sides and the hard look of warriors in their eyes. But they didn't treat the new arrivals too badly.

Their chief was a young man in the cape and helmet of an officer of the Empire. But his outfit was at least a century old, and he was simply head of a small troop which had been hired from among the barbarian hordes to protect this part of Terra. Oddly, he insisted he was a loyal vassal of the Emperor.

The Empire! It was still a remote glory, out there among the stars. Slowly it waned, slowly the barbarians encroached while corruption and civil war tore it apart from the inside, but it was still the pathetic, futile hope of intelligent beings throughout the Galaxy. Some day it would be restored. Some day civilization would return to the darkness of the outer worlds, greater and more splendid than ever. Men dared not believe otherwise.

"But we've got a job right here," shrugged the chief. "Tautho of Sirius will be on Sol's necks soon. I doubt if we can stand him off for long."

"And what'll yuh do den?" challenged Belgotai.

The young-old face twisted in a bitter smile. "Die, of course. What else is there to do—these days?"

They stayed overnight with the troopers. Belgotai had fun swapping lies about warlike exploits, but in the morning he decided to go on with Saunders. The age was violent enough, but its hopelessness daunted even his tough soul.

Saunders looked haggardly at the control panel. "We've got to go a long ways ahead," he said. "A hell of a long ways."

50,000 A.D. They flashed out of the time drive and opened the door. A raw wind caught at them, driving thin sheets of snow before it. The sky hung low and gray over a landscape of high rocky hills where pine trees stood gloomily between naked crags. There was ice on the river that murmured darkly out of the woods.

Geology didn't work that fast; even fourteen thousand years wasn't a very long time to the slowly changing planets. It must have been the work of intelligent beings, ravaging and scoring the world with senseless wars of unbelievable forces.

A gray stone mass dominated the landscape. It stood enormous a few miles off, its black walls sprawling over incredible acres, its massive crenellated towers reaching gauntly into the sky. And it lay half in ruin, torn and tumbled stone distorted by energies that once made rock run molten, blurred by uncounted millennia of weather—old.

"Dead," Saunders voice was thin under the hooting wind. "All dead."

"No!" Belgotai's slant eyes squinted against the flying snow. "No, Mahtin, Ih tink Ih see a banner flying."

The wind blew bitterly around them, searing them with its chill. "Shall we go on?" asked Saunders dully.

"Best we go find out wha's happened," said Belgotai. "Dey can do no worse dan kill us, and Ih begin to tink dat's not so bad."

Saunders put on all the clothes he could find and took the psychophone in one chilled hand. Belgotai wrapped his cloak tightly about him. They started toward the gray edifice.

The wind blew and blew. Snow hissed around them, covering the tough gray-green vegetation that hugged the stony ground. Summer on Earth, 50,000 A.D.

As they neared the structure, its monster size grew on them. Some of the towers which still stood must be almost half a mile high, thought Saunders dizzily. But it had a grim, barbaric look; no civilized race had ever built such a fortress.

Two small, swift shapes darted into the air from that cliff-like wall. "Aircraft," said Belgotai laconically. The wind ripped the word from his mouth.

They were ovoidal, without external controls or windows, apparently running on the gravitic forces which had long ago been tamed. One of them hovered overhead, covering the travelers, while the other dropped to the ground. As it landed, Saunders saw that it was old and worn and scarred. But there was a faded sunburst on its side. Some memory of the Empire must still be alive.

Two came out of the little vessel and approached the travelers with guns in their hands. One was human, a tall well-built young man with shoulder-length black hair blowing under a tarnished helmet, a patched purple coat streaming from his cuirassed shoulders, a faded leather kilt and buskins. The other…

He was a little shorter than the man, but immensely broad of chest and limb. Four muscled arms grew from the massive shoulders, and a tufted tail lashed against his clawed feet. His head was big, broad-skulled, with a round half animal face and cat-like whiskers about the fanged mouth and the split-pupilled yellow eyes. He wore no clothes except a leather harness but soft blue-gray fur covered the whole great body.

The psychophone clattered out the man's hail: "Who comes?"

"Friends," said Saunders. "We wish only shelter and a little information."

"Where are you from?" There was a harsh, peremptory note in the man's voice. His face-straight, thin-boned, the countenance of a highly bred aristocrat—was gaunt with strain. "What do you want? What sort of spaceship is that you've got down there?"

"Easy, Vargor," rumbled the alien's bass. "That's no spaceship, you can see that."

"No," said Saunders. "It's a time projector."

"Time travelers!" Vargor's intense blue eyes widened. "I heard of such things once, but—time travelers!" Suddenly: "When are you from? Can you help us?"

"We're from very long ago," said Saunders pityingly. "And I'm afraid we're alone and helpless."

Vargor's erect carriage sagged a little. He looked away. But the other being stepped forward with an eagerness in him. "How far back?" he asked. "Where are you going?"

"We're going to hell, most likely. But can you get us inside? We're freezing."

"Of course. Come with us. You'll not take it amiss if I send a squad to inspect your machine? We have to be careful, you know."

The four squeezed into the aircraft and it lifted with a groan of ancient engines. Vargor gestured at the fortress ahead and his tone was a little wild. "Welcome to the hold of Brontothor! Welcome to the Galactic Empire!"

"The Empire?"

"Aye, this is the Empire, or what's left of it. A haunted fortress on a frozen ghost world, last fragment of the old Imperium and still trying to pretend that the Galaxy is not dying—that it didn't die millennia ago, that there is something left besides wild beasts howling among the ruins." Vargor's throat caught in a dry sob. "Welcome!"

The alien laid a huge hand on the man's shoulder. "Don't get hysterical, Vargor," he reproved gently. "As long as brave beings hope, the Empire is still alive—whatever they say."

He looked over his shoulder at the others.

"You really are welcome," he said. "It's a hard and dreary life we lead here. Taury and the Dreamer will both welcome you gladly." He paused. Then, unsurely, "But best you don't say too much about the ancient time, if you've really seen it. We can't bear too sharp a reminder, you know."

The machine slipped down beyond the wall, over a gigantic flagged courtyard to the monster bulk of the—the donjon, Saunders supposed one could call it. It rose up in several tiers, with pathetic little gardens on the terraces, toward a dome of clear plastic.

The walls, he saw, were immensely thick, with weapons mounted on them which he could see clearly through the drifting snow. Behind the donjon stood several long, barracks-like buildings, and a couple of spaceships which must have been held together by pure faith rested near what looked like an arsenal. There were guards on duty, helmeted men with energy rifles, their cloaks wrapped tightly against the wind, and other folk scurried around under the monstrous walls, men and women and children.

"There's Taury," said the alien, pointing to a small group clustered on one of the terraces. "We may as well land right there." His wide mouth opened in an alarming smile. "And forgive me for not introducing myself before. I'm Hunda of Haamigur, general of the Imperial armies, and this is Vargor Alfri, prince of the Empire."

"Yuh crazy?" blurted Belgotai. "What Empire ?"

Hunda shrugged. "It's a harmless game, isn't it? At that, you know, we are the Empire—legally. Taury is a direct descendant of Maurco the Doomer, last Emperor to be anointed according to the proper forms. Of course, that was five thousand years ago, and Maurco had only three systems left then, but the law is clear. These hundred or more barbarian pretenders, human and otherwise, haven't the shadow of a real claim to the title."

The vessel grounded and they stepped out. The others waited for them to come up. There were half a dozen old men, their long beards blowing wildly in the gale, there was a being with the face of a long-beaked bird and one that had the shape of a centauroid.

"The Court of the Empress Taury," said Bunda.

"Welcome." The answer was low and gracious.

Saunders and Belgotai stared dumbly at her. She was tall, tall as a man, but under her tunic of silver links and her furred cloak she was such a woman as they had dreamed of without ever knowing in life. Her proudly lifted head had something of Vargor's looks, the same clean-lined, high-cheeked face, but it was the countenance of a woman, from the broad clear brow to the wide, wondrously chiseled mouth and the strong chin. The cold had flushed the lovely pale planes of her cheeks. Her heavy bronze-red hair was braided about her helmet, with one rebellious lock tumbling softly toward the level, dark brows. Her eyes, huge and oblique and gray as northern seas, were serene on them.

Saunders found tongue. "Thank you, your majesty," he said in a firm voice.

"If it please you, I am Martin Saunders of America, some forty-eight thousand years in the past, and my companion is Belgotai, free companion from Syrtis about a thousand years later. We are at your service for what little we may be able to do."

She inclined her stately head, and her sudden smile was warm and human. "It is a rare pleasure," she said. "Come inside, please. And forget the formality. Tonight let us simply be alive."

They sat in what had been a small council chamber. The great hall was too huge and empty, a cavern of darkness and rustling relics of greatness, hollow with too many memories. But the lesser room had been made livable, hung with tapestries and carpeted with skins. Fluorotubes cast a white light over it, and a fire crackled cheerfully in the hearth. Had it not been for the wind against the windows, they might have forgotten where they were.

"—and you can never go back?" Taury's voice was sober. "You can never get home again?"

"I don't think so," said Saunders. "From our story, it doesn't look that way, does it?"

"No," said Hunda. "You'd better settle down in some time and make the best of matters."

"Why not with us?" asked Vargor eagerly.

"We'd welcome you with all our hearts," said Taury, "but I cannot honestly advise you to stay. These are evil times."

It was a harsh language they spoke, a ringing metallic tongue brought in by the barbarians. But from her throat, Saunders thought, it was utter music.

"We'll at least stay a few days," he said impulsively. "It's barely possible we can do something."

"I doubt that," said Hunda practically. "We've retrogressed, yes. For instance, the principle of the time projector was lost long ago. But still, there's a lot of technology left which was far beyond your own times."

"I know," said Saunders defensively. "But—well, frankly—we haven't fitted in any other time, as well."

"Will there ever be a decent age again?" asked one of the old courtiers bitterly.

The avian from Klakkahar turned his eyes on Saunders. "It wouldn't be cowardice for you to leave a lost cause which you couldn't possibly aid," he said in his thin, accented tones. "When the Anvardi come, I think we will all die."

"What is de tale of de Dreamer?" asked Belgotai. "You've mentioned some such."

It was like a sudden darkness in the room. There was silence, under the whistling wind, and men sat wrapped in their own cheerless thoughts. Finally Taury spoke.

"He is the last of the Vro-Hi, counselors of the Empire. That one still lives—the Dreamer. But there can never really be another Empire, at least not on the pattern of the old one. No other race is intelligent enough to coordinate it."

Hunda shook his big head, puzzled. "The Dreamer once told me that might be for the best," he said. "But he wouldn't explain."

"How did you happen to come here—to Earth, of all planets?" Saunders asked.

Taury smiled with a certain grim humor. "The last few generations have been one of the Imperium's less fortunate periods," she said. "In short, the most the Emperor ever commanded was a small fleet. My father had even that shot away from him. He fled with three ships, out toward the Periphery. It occurred to him that Sol was worth trying as a refuge."

The Solar System had been cruelly scarred in the dark ages. The great engineering works which had made the other planets habitable were ruined, and Earth herself had been laid waste. There had been a weapon used which consumed atmospheric carbon dioxide. Saunders, remembering the explanation for the Ice Ages offered by geologists of his own time, nodded in dark understanding. Only a few starveling savages lived on the planet now, and indeed the whole Sirius Sector was so desolated that no conqueror thought it worth bothering with.

It had pleased the Emperor to make his race's ancient home the capital of the Galaxy. He had moved into the ruined fortress of Brontothor, built some seven thousand years ago by the nonhuman Grimmani and blasted out of action a millennium later. Renovation of parts of it, installation of weapons and defensive works, institution of agriculture… "Why, he had suddenly acquired a whole planetary system!" said Taury with a half-sad little smile.

She took them down into the underground levels the next day to see the Dreamer. Vargor went along too, walking close beside her, but Hunda stayed topside; he was busy supervising the construction of additional energy screen generators.

They went through immense vaulted caverns hewed out of the rock, dank tunnels of silence where their footfalls echoed weirdly and shadows flitted beyond the dull glow of fluorospheres. Now and then they passed a looming monstrous bulk, the corroded hulk of some old machine. The night and loneliness weighed heavily on them, they huddled together and did not speak for fear of rousing the jeering echoes.

"There were slideways here once," remarked Taury as they started, "but we haven't gotten around to installing new ones. There's too much else to do."

Too much else—a civilization to rebuild, with these few broken remnants. How can they dare even to keep trying in the face of the angry gods? What sort of courage is it they have?

Taury walked ahead with the long, swinging stride of a warrior, a red lioness of a woman in the wavering shadows. Her gray eyes caught the light with a supernatural brilliance. Vargor kept pace, but he lacked her steadiness, his gaze shifted nervously from side to side as they moved down the haunted, booming length of the tunnels. Belgotai went cat-footed, his own restless eyes had merely the habitual wariness of his hard and desperate lifetime. Again Saunders thought, what a strange company they were, four humans from the dawn and the dusk of human civilization, thrown together at the world's end and walking to greet the last of the gods. His past life, Eve, MacPherson, the world of his time, were dimming in his mind, they were too remote from his present reality. It seemed as if he had never been anything but a follower of the Galactic Empress.

They came at last to a door. Taury knocked softly and swung it open—yes, they were even back to manual doors now.

Saunders had been prepared for almost anything, but nonetheless the appearance of the Dreamer was a shock. He had imagined a grave white-bearded man, or a huge-skulled spider-thing, or a naked brain pulsing in a machine-tended case. But the last of the Vro-Hi was—a monster.

No—not exactly. Not when you discarded human standards, then he even had a weird beauty of his own. The gross bulk of him sheened with iridescence, and his many seven-fingered hands were supple and graceful, and the eyes—the eyes were huge pools of molten gold, lambent and wise, a stare too brilliant to meet directly.

He stood up on his stumpy legs as they entered, barely four feet high though the head-body unit was broad and massive. His hooked beak did not open, and the psychophone remained silent, but as the long delicate feelers pointed toward him Saunders thought he heard words, a deep organ voice rolling soundless through the still air: "Greeting, your majesty. Greeting, your highness. Greeting, men out of time, and welcome!"

Telepathy—direct telepathy—so that was how it felt!

"Thank you…sir." Somehow, the thing rated the title, rated an awed respect to match his own grave formality. "But I thought you were in a trance of concentration till now. How did you know—" Saunders' voice trailed off and he flushed with sudden distaste.

"No, traveler, I did not read your mind as you think. The Vro-Hi always respected privacy and did not read any thoughts save those contained in speech addressed solely to them. But my induction was obvious."

"What were you thinking about in the last trance?" asked Vargor. His voice was sharp with strain. "Did you reach any plan?"

"No, your highness," vibrated the Dreamer. As long as the factors involved remain constant, we cannot logically do otherwise than we are doing. When new data appear, I will reconsider immediate necessities. No, I was working further on the philosophical basis which the Second Empire must have."

"What Second Empire?" sneered Vargor bitterly.

"The one which will come—some day," answered Taury quietly.

The Dreamer's wise eyes rested on Saunders and Belgotai. "With your permission," he thought, "I would like to scan your complete memory patterns, conscious, subconscious, and cellular. We know so little of your age." As they hesitated: "I assure you, sirs, that a nonhuman being half a million years old can keep secrets, and certainly does not pass moral judgments. And the scanning will be necessary anyway if I am to teach you the present language."

Saunders braced himself. "Go ahead," he said distastefully.

For a moment he felt dizzy, a haze passed over his eyes and there was an eerie thrill along every nerve of him. Taury laid an arm about his waist, bracing him.

It passed. Saunders shook his head, puzzled. "Is that *all?*"

"Aye, sir. A Vro-Hi brain can scan an indefinite number of units simultaneously." With a faint hint of a chuckle: "But did you notice what tongue you just spoke in?"

"I—eh—huh?" Saunders looked wildly at Taury's smiling face. The hard, open-voweled syllables barked from his mouth: "I—by the gods—I can speak Stellarian now!"

"Aye," thought the Dreamer. "The language centers are peculiarly receptive, it is easy to impress a pattern on them. The method of instruction will not work involving other faculties, but you must admit it is a convenient and efficient way to learn speech."

"Blast off wit me, den," said Belgotai cheerfully. "Ih allays was a dumkoff at languages."

When the Dreamer was through, he thought: "You will not take it amiss if I tell all that what I saw in both your minds was good—brave and honest, under the little neuroses which all beings at your level of evolution cannot help accumulating. I will be pleased to remove those for you, if you wish."

"No, thanks," said Belgotai. "I like my little neuroses."

"I see that you are debating staying here," went on the Dreamer. "You will be valuable, but you should be fully warned of the desperate position we actually are in. This is not a pleasant age in which to live."

"From what I've seen," answered Saunders slowly, "golden ages are only superficially better. They may be easier on the surface, but there's death in them. To travel hopefully, believe me, is better than to arrive."

"That has been true in all past ages, aye. It was the great mistake of the Vro-Hi. We should have known better, with ten million years of civilization behind us." There was a deep and tragic note in the rolling thought-pulse. "But we thought that since we had achieved a static physical state in which the new frontiers and challenges lay within our own minds, all beings at all levels of evolution could and should have developed in them the same ideal.

"With our help, and with the use of scientific psychodynamics and the great cybernetic engines, the coordination of a billion planets became possible. It was perfection, in a way—but perfection is death to imperfect beings, and even the Vro-Hi had many shortcomings. I cannot explain all the philosophy to you; it involves concepts you could not fully grasp, but you have seen the workings of the great laws in the rise and fall of cultures. I have proved rigorously that permanence is a self-contradictory concept. There can be no goal to reach, not ever."

"Then the Second Empire will have no better hope than decay and chaos again?" Saunders grinned humorlessly. "Why the devil do you want one?"

Vargor's harsh laugh shattered the brooding silence. "What indeed does it matter?" he cried. "What use to plan the future of the universe, when we are outlaws on a forgotten planet? The Anvardi are coming!" He sobered, and there was a set to his jaw which Saunders liked. "They're coming, and there's little we can do to stop it," said Vargor. "But we'll give them a fight. We'll give them such a fight as the poor old Galaxy never saw before!"

Chapter 5
Attack of the Anvardi

"Oh, no—oh no—oh no."

The murmur came unnoticed from Vargor's lips, a broken cry of pain as he stared at the image which flickered and wavered on the great interstellar communiscreen. And there was horror in the eyes of Taury, grimness to the set of Hunda's mighty jaws, a sadness of many hopeless centuries in the golden gaze of the Dreamer.

After weeks of preparation and waiting, Saunders realized matters were at last coming to a head.

"Aye, your majesty," said the man in the screen. He was haggard, exhausted, Worn out by strain and struggle and defeat. "Aye fifty-four shiploads of us, and the Anvardian fleet in pursuit."

"How far behind?" rapped Hunda.

"About half a light-year, sir, and coming up slowly. We'll be close to Sol before they can overhaul us."

"Can you fight them?" rapped Hunda.

"No sir, said the man. "We're loaded with refugees, women and children and unarmed peasants, hardly a gun on a ship—Can't you help?" It was a cry, torn by the ripping static that filled the interstellar void. "Can't you help us, your majesty? They'll sell us for slaves!"

"How did it happen?" asked Taury wearily.

"I don't know, your majesty. We heard you were at Sol through your agents, and secretly gathered ships. We don't want to be under the Anvardi, Empress; they tax the life from us and conscript our men and take our women and children…We only communicated by ultrawave; it can't be traced, and we only used the code your agents gave us. But as we passed Canopus, they called on us to surrender in the name of their king—and they have a whole war fleet after us!"

"How long before they get here?" asked Hunda.

"At this rate, sir, perhaps a week," answered the captain of the ship. Static snarled through his words.

"Well, keep on coming this way," said Taury wearily. "We'll send ships against them. You may get away during the battle. Don't go to Sol, of course, we'll have to evacuate that. Our men will try to contact you later."

"We aren't worth it, your majesty. Save all your ships."

"We're coming," said Taury flatly, and broke the circuit.

She turned to the others, and her red head was still lifted. "Most of our people can get away," she said. "They can flee into the Arlath cluster; the enemy won't be able to find them in that wilderness." She smiled, a tired little smile that tugged at one corner of her mouth. "We all know what to do, we've planned against this day. Munidor, Falz, Mico, start readying for evacuation. Hunda, you and I will have to plan our assault. We'll want to make it as effective as possible, but use a minimum of ships."

"Why sacrifice fighting strength uselessly?" asked Belgotai.

"It won't be useless. We'll delay the Anvardi, and give those refugees a chance to escape."

"If we had weapons," rumbled Hunda. His huge fists clenched. "By the gods, if we had decent weapons!"

The Dreamer stiffened. And before he could vibrate it, the same thought had leaped into Saunders' brain, and they stared at each other, man and Vro-Hian, with a sudden wild hope…

Space glittered and flared with a million stars, thronging against the tremendous dark, the Milky Way foamed around the sky in a rush of cold silver, and it was shattering to a human in its utter immensity. Saunders felt the loneliness of it as he had never felt it on the trip to Venus—for Sol was dwindling behind them, they were rushing out into the void between the stars.

There had only been time to install the new weapon on the dreadnought, time and facilities were so cruelly short, there had been no chance even to test it in maneuvers. They might, perhaps, have leaped back into time again and again, gaining weeks, but the shops of Terra could only turn out so much material in the one week they did have.

So it was necessary to risk the whole fleet and the entire fighting strength of Sol on this one desperate gamble. If the old *Vengeance* could do her part, the outnumbered Imperials would have their chance. But if they failed…

Saunders stood on the bridge, looking out at the stellar host, trying to discern the Anvardian fleet. The detectors were far over scale, the enemy was close, but you couldn't visually detect something that outran its own image.

Hunda was at the control central, bent over the cracked old dials and spinning the corroded signal wheels, trying to coax another centimeter per second from a ship more ancient than the Pyramids had been in Saunders' day. The Dreamer stood quietly in a corner, staring raptly out at the Galaxy. The others at the court were each in charge of a squadron, Saunders had talked to them over the inter-ship visiscreen—Vargor white-lipped and tense, Belgotai blasphemously cheerful, the rest showing only cool reserve.

"In a few minutes," said Taury quietly. "In just a few minutes, Martin."

She paced back from the viewport, lithe and restless as a tigress. The cold white starlight glittered in her eyes. A red cloak swirled about the strong, deep curves of her body, a Sunburst helmet sat proudly on her bronze-bright hair. Saunders thought how beautiful she was—by all the gods, how beautiful!

She smiled at him. "It is your doing, Martin," she said. "You came from the past just to bring us hope. It's enough to make one believe in destiny." She took his hand. "But of course it's not the hope you wanted. This won't get you back home."

"It doesn't matter," he said.

"It does, Martin. But—may I say it? I'm still glad of it. Not only for the sake of the Empire, but—"

A voice rattled over the bridge communicator: "Ultrawave to bridge. The enemy is sending us a message, your majesty. Shall I send it up to you?"

"Of course." Taury switched on the bridge screen.

A face leaped into it, strong and proud and ruthless, the Sunburst shining in the green hair. "Greeting, Taury of Sol," said the Anvardian. "I am Ruulthan, Emperor of the Galaxy."

"I know who you are," said Taury thinly, "but I don't recognize your assumed title."

"Our detectors report your approach with a fleet approximately one-tenth the size of ours. You have one Supernova ship, of course, but so do we. Unless you wish to come to terms, it will mean annihilation."

"What are your terms?"

"Surrender, execution of the criminals who led the attacks on Anvardian planets, and your own pledge of allegiance to me as Galactic Emperor." The voice was clipped, steel-hard.

Taury turned away in disgust. Saunders told Ruulthan in explicit language what to do with his terms, and then cut off the screen.

Taury gestured to the newly installed time-drive controls. "Take them, Martin," she said. "They're yours, really." She put her hands in his and looked at him with serious gray eyes. "And if we should fail in this—good-bye, Martin. "

"Good-bye," he said thickly.

He wrenched himself over the panel and sat down before its few dials. *Here goes nothing!*

He waved one hand, and Hunda cut off the hyperdrive. At low intrinsic velocity, the *Vengeance* hung in space while the invisible ships of her fleet flashed past toward the oncoming Anvardi.

Slowly then, Saunders brought down the time-drive switch. And the ship roared with power, atomic energy flowed into the mighty circuits which they had built to carry her huge mass through time—the lights dimmed, the giant machine throbbed and pulsed, and a featureless grayness swirled beyond the ports.

He took her back three days. They lay in empty space, the Anvardi were still fantastic distances away. His eyes strayed to the brilliant yellow spark of Sol. Right there, this minute, he was sweating his heart out installing the time projector which had just carried him back...

Bur no, that was meaningless, simultaneity was arbitrary. And there was a job to do right now.

The chief astrogator's voice came with a torrent of figures. They had to find the exact position in which the Anvardian flagship would be in precisely seventy-two hours. Hunda rang the signals to the robots in the engine room, and slowly, ponderously, the *Vengeance* slid across five million miles of space.

"All set," said Hunda. "Let's go!"

Saunders smiled, a mirthless skinning of teeth, and threw his main switch in reverse. Three days forward in time...

To lie alongside the Anvardian dreadnought! Frantically Hunda threw the hyperdrive back in, matching translight velocities. They could see the ship now, it loomed like a metal mountain against the stars. And every gun in the *Vengeance* cut loose!

Vortex cannon—blasters—atomic shells and torpedoes—gravity snatchers—all the hell which had ever been brewed in the tortured centuries of history vomited against the screens of the Anvardian flagship.

Under that monstrous barrage, filling space with raving energy till it seemed its very structure must boil, the screens went down, a flare of light searing like another nova. And through the solid matter of her hull those weapons bored, cutting, blasting, disintegrating. Steel boiled into vapor, into atoms, into pure devouring energy that turned on the remaining solid material. Through and through the hull that fury raged, a waste of flame that left not even ash in its track.

And now the rest of the Imperial fleet drove against the Anvardi. Assaulted from outside, with a devouring monster in its very midst, the Anvardian fleet lost the offensive, recoiled and broke up into desperately fighting units. War snarled between the silent white stars.

Still the Anvardi fought, hurling themselves against the ranks of the Imperials, wrecking ships and slaughtering men even as they went down. They still had the numbers, if not the organization, and they had the same weapons and the same bitter courage of their foes.

The bridge of the *Vengeance* shook and roared with the shock of battle. The lights darkened, flickered back, dimmed again. The riven air was sharp with ozone, and the intolerable energies loosed made her interior a furnace. Reports clattered over the communicator: "—Number Three screen down—Compartment Number Five doesn't answer—Vortex turret Five Hundred Thirty Seven out of action—"

Still she fought, still she fought, hurling metal and energy in an unending storm, raging and rampaging among the ships of the Anvardi. Saunders found himself manning a gun, shooting out at vessels he couldn't see, getting his aim by sweat-blinded glances at the instruments—and the hours dragged away in flame and smoke and racking thunder..."

"*They're fleeing!*"

The exuberant shout rang through every remaining compartment of the huge old ship. *Victory, victory, victory*—she had not heard such cheering for five thousand weary years.

Saunders staggered drunkenly back onto the bridge. He could see the scattered units of the Anvardi now that he was behind them, exploding out into the Galaxy in wild search of refuge, hounded and harried by the vengeful Imperial fleet.

And now the Dreamer stood up, and suddenly he was not a stump-legged little monster but a living god whose awful thought leaped across space, faster than light, to bound and roar through the skulls of the barbarians. Saunders fell to the floor under the impact of that mighty shout, he lay numbly staring at the impassive stars while the great command rang in his shuddering brain:

"*Soldiers of the Anvardi, your false emperor is dead and Taury the Red, Empress of the Galaxy, has the victory. You have seen her power. Do not resist it longer, for it is unstoppable.*

"*Lay down your arms. Surrender to the mercy of the Imperium. We pledge you amnesty and safe-conduct. And bear this word back to your planets:*

"*Taury the Red calls on all the chiefs of the Anvardian Confederacy to pledge fealty to her and aid her in restoring the Galactic Empire!*"

Chapter 6
Flight Without End

They stood on a balcony of Brontothor and looked again at old Earth for the first time in almost a year and the last time, perhaps, in their lives.

It was strange to Saunders, this standing again on the planet which had borne him after those months in the many and alien worlds of a Galaxy huger than he could really imagine. There was an odd little tug at his heart, for all the bright hope of the future. He was saying good-bye to Eve's world.

But Eve was gone, she was part of a past forty-eight thousand years dead, and he had *seen* those years rise and die, his one year of personal time was filled and stretched by the vision of history until Eve was a remote, lovely dream. God keep her, wherever her soul had wandered in these millennia—God grant she had had a happy life—but as for him, he had his own life to live, and a mightier task at hand than he had ever conceived.

The last months rose in his mind, a bewilderment of memory. After the surrender of the Anvardian fleet, the Imperials had gone under their escort directly to Canopus and thence through the Anvardian empire. And chief after chief, now that Ruulthan was dead and Taury had shown she could win a greater mastery than his, pledged allegiance to her.

Hunda was still out there with Belgotai, fighting a stubborn Anvardian earl. The Dreamer was in the great Polarian System, toiling at readjustment. It would be necessary, of course, for the Imperial capital to move from isolated Sol to central Polaris, and Taury did not think she would ever have time or opportunity to visit Earth again.

And so she had crossed a thousand starry light-years to the little lonely sun which had been her home. She brought ships, machines, troops. Sol would have a military base sufficient to protect it. Climate engineers would drive the glacial winter of Earth back to its poles and begin the resettlement of the other planets. There would be schools, factories, civilization. Sol would have cause to remember its Empress.

Saunders came along because he couldn't quite endure the thought of leaving Earth altogether without farewell. Vargor, grown ever more silent and moody, joined them, but otherwise the old comradeship of Brontothor was dissolving in the sudden fury of work and war and complexity which claimed them.

And so they stood again in the old ruined castle, Saunders and Taury, looking out at the night of Earth.

It was late, all others seemed to be asleep. Below the balcony, the black walls drooped dizzily to the gulf of night that was the main courtyard. Beyond it, a broken section of outer wall showed snow lying white and mystic under the moon. The stars were huge and frosty, flashing and glittering with cold crystal light above the looming pines, grandeur and arrogance and remoteness wheeling enormously across the silent sky. The moon rode high, its scarred old face the only familiarity from Saunders' age, its argent radiance flooding down on the snow to shatter in a million splinters.

It was quiet, sound seemed to have frozen to death in the bitter windless cold, Saunders had stood alone, wrapped in furs with his breath shining ghostly from his nostrils, looking out on the silent winter world and thinking his own thoughts, He had heard a soft footfall and turned to see Taury approaching.

"I couldn't sleep," she said.

She came out onto the balcony to stand beside him. The moonlight was white on her face, shimmering faintly from her eyes and hair, she seemed a dim goddess of the night.

"What were you thinking, Martin?" she asked after a while.

"Oh—I don't know," he said. "Just dreaming a little, I suppose. It's a strange thought to me, to have left my own time forever and now to be leaving even my own world."

She nodded gravely. "I know I feel the same way." Her low voice dropped to a whisper. "I didn't have to come back in person, you know. They need me more at Polaris. But I thought I deserved this last farewell to the days when we fought with our own hands, and fared between the stars, when we were a small band of sworn comrades whose dreams outstripped our strength. It was hard and bitter, yes, but I don't think we'll· have time for laughter anymore. When you work for a million stars, you don't have a chance to see one peasant's wrinkled face light with a deed of kindness you did, or hear him tell you what you did wrong—the world will all be strangers to us—"

For another moment, silence under the far cold stars, then, "Martin—I am so lonely now."

He took her in his arms. Her lips were cold against his, cold with the cruel silent chill of the night, but she answered him with a fierce yearning.

"I think I love you, Martin," she said after a very long time. Suddenly she laughed, a clear and lovely music echoing from the frosty towers of Brontothor. "Oh, Martin, I shouldn't have been afraid. We'll never be lonely, not ever again—"

The moon had sunk far toward the dark horizon when he took her back to her rooms. He kissed her good night and went down the booming corridor toward his own chambers.

His head was awhirl—he was drunk with the sweetness and wonder of it, he felt like singing and laughing aloud and embracing the whole starry universe. Taury, Taury, Taury!

"Martin."

He paused. There was a figure standing before his door, a tall slender form wrapped in a dark cloak. The dull light of a fluoroglobe threw the face into sliding shadow and tormented highlights. Vargor.

"What is it?" he asked.

The prince's hand came up, and Saunders saw the blunt muzzle of a stun pistol gaping at him. Vargor smiled, lopsidedly and sorrowfully, "I'm sorry, Martin," he said.

Saunders stood paralyzed with unbelief. Vargor—why, Vargor had fought beside him; they'd saved each other's lives, laughed and worked and lived together—Vargor!

The gun flashed. There was a crashing in Saunders' head and he tumbled into illimitable darkness.

He awoke very slowly, every nerve tingling with the pain of returning sensation. Something was restraining him. As his vision cleared, he saw that he was lying bound and gagged on the floor of his time projector.

The time machine—he'd all but forgotten it, left it standing in a shed while he went out to the stars; he'd never thought to have another look at it. The time machine!

Vargor stood in the open door, a fluoroglobe in one hand lighting his haggard face. His hair fell in disarray past his tired, handsome features, and his eyes were as wild as the low words that spilled from his mouth.

"I'm sorry, Martin, really I am. I like you, and you've done the Empire such a service as it can never forget, and this is as low a trick as one man can ever play on another. But I have to. I'll be haunted by the thought of this night all my life, but I have to."

Saunders tried to move, snarling incoherently through his gag. Vargor shook his head. "Oh, no, Martin, I can't risk letting you make an outcry. If I'm to do evil, I'll at least do a competent job of it.

"I love Taury, you see. I've loved her ever since I first met her, when I came from the stars with a fighting fleet to her father's court and saw her standing there with the frost crackling through her hair and those gray eyes shining at me. I love her so it's like a pain in me. I can't be away from her, I'd pull down the cosmos for her sake. And I thought she was slowly coming to love me.

"And tonight I saw you two on the balcony, and knew I'd lost. Only I can't give up! Our breed has fought the Galaxy for a dream, Martin—it's not in us ever to stop fighting while life is in us. Fighting by any means, for whatever is dear and precious—but fighting!"

Vargor made a gesture of deprecation. "I don't want power, Martin, believe me. The consort's job will be hard and unglamorous, galling to a man of spirit— but if that's the only way to have her, then so be it. And I do honestly believe, right or wrong, that I'm better for her and for the Empire than you. You don't really belong here, you know. You don't have the tradition, the feeling, the training—you don't even have the biological heritage of five thousand years. Taury may care for you now, but think twenty years ahead!"

Vargor smiled wryly. "I'm taking a chance, of course. If you do find a means of negative time travel and come back here, it will be disgrace and exile for me. It would be safer to kill you. But I'm not quite that much of a scoundrel. I'm giving you your chance. At worst, you should escape into the time when the Second Empire is in its glorious bloom, a happier age than this. And if you do find a means to come back—well, remember what I said about your not belonging, and try to reason with clarity and kindness. Kindness to Taury, Martin."

He lifted the fluoroglobe, casting its light over the dim interior of the machine. "So it's goodbye, Martin, and I hope you won't hate me too much. It should take you several thousand years to work free and stop the machine. I've equipped it with weapons, supplies, everything I think you may need for any eventuality. But I'm sure you'll emerge in a greater and more peaceful culture, and be happier there."

His voice was strangely tender, all of a sudden. "Good-bye, Martin my comrade. And—good luck!"

He opened the main-drive switch and stepped out as the projector began to warm up. The door clanged shut behind him.

Saunders writhed on the floor, cursing with a brain that was a black cauldron of bitterness. The great drone of the projector rose, he was on his way—*Oh no—stop the machine, God, set me free before it's too late!*

The plastic cords cut his wrists. He was lashed to a stanchion, unable to reach the switch with any part of his body. His groping fingers slid across the surface of a knot, the nails clawing for a hold. The machine roared with full power, driving ahead through the vastness of time.

Vargor had bound him skillfully. It took him a long time to get free. Toward the end he went slowly, not caring, knowing with a dull knowledge that he was already more thousands of irretrievable years into the future than his dials would register.

He climbed to his feet, plucked the gag from his mouth, and looked blankly out at the faceless gray. The century needle was hard against its stop. He estimated vaguely that he was some ten thousand years into the future already.

Ten thousand years!

He yanked down the switch with a raging burst of savagery.

It was dark outside. He stood stupidly for a moment before he saw water seeping into the cabin around the door. Water—he was under water—short circuits! Frantically, he slammed the switch forward again.

He tasted the water on the floor. It was salt. Sometime in that ten thousand years, for reasons natural or artificial, the sea had come in and covered the site of Brontothor.

A thousand years later he was still below its surface. Two thousand, three thousand, ten thousand…

Taury, Taury! For twenty thousand years she had been dust on an alien planet. And Belgotai was gone with his wry smile, Hunda's staunchness, even the Dreamer must long ago have descended into darkness. The sea rolled over dead Brontothor, and he was alone.

He bowed his head on his arms and wept.

For three million years the ocean layover Brontothor's land. And Saunders drove onward.

He stopped at intervals to see if the waters had gone. Each time the frame of the machine groaned with pressure and the sea poured in through the crack of the door. Otherwise he sat dully in the throbbing loneliness, estimating time covered by his own watch and the known rate of the projector, not caring anymore about dates or places.

Several times he considered stopping the machine, letting the sea burst in and drown him. There would be peace in its depths, sleep and forgetting. But no, it wasn't in him to quit that easily. Death was his friend, death would always be there waiting for his call.

But Taury was dead.

Time grayed to its end. In the four millionth year, he stopped the machine and discovered that there was dry air around him.

He was in a city. But it was not such a city as he had ever seen or imagined, he couldn't follow the wild geometry of the titanic structures that loomed about him and they were never the same. The place throbbed and pulsed with incredible forces, it wavered and blurred in a strangely unreal light. Great devastating energies flashed and roared around him—lightning had come to Earth. The air hissed and stung with their booming passage.

The thought was a shout filling his skull, blazing along his nerves, too mighty a thought for his stunned brain to do more than grope after meaning:

CREATURE FROM OUT OF TIME, LEAVE THIS PLACE AT ONCE OR THE FORCES WE USE WILL DESTROY YOU!

Through and through him that mental vision seared, down to the very molecules of his brain, his life lay open to Them in a white flame of incandescence.

Can you help me? he cried to the gods. *Can you send me back through time?*

MAN, THERE IS NO WAY TO TRAVEL FAR BACKWARD IN TIME, IT IS INHERENTLY IMPOSSIBLE. YOU MUST GO ON TO THE VERY END OF THE UNIVERSE, AND BEYOND THE END, BECAUSE THAT WAY LIES—

He screamed with the pain of unendurably great thought and concept filling his human brain.

GO ON, MAN, GO ON! BUT YOU CANNOT SURVIVE IN THAT MACHINE AS IT IS. I WILL CHANGE IT FOR YOU…GO!

The time projector started again by itself. Saunders fell forward into a darkness that roared and flashed.

Grimly, desperately, like a man driven by demons, Saunders hurtled into the future.

There could be no gainsaying the awful word which had been laid on him. The mere thought of the gods had engraved itself on the very tissue of his brain. Why he should go on to the end of time, he could not imagine, nor did he care. But go on he must!

The machine had been altered. It was airtight now, and experiment showed the window to be utterly unbreakable. Something had been done to the projector so that it hurled him forward at an incredible rate, millions of years passed while a minute or two ticked away within the droning shell.

But what had the gods been?

He would never know. Beings from beyond the Galaxy, beyond the very universe—the ultimately evolved descendants of man—something at whose nature he could not even guess—there was no way of telling. This much was plain: whether it had become extinct or had changed into something else, the human race was gone. Earth would never feel human tread again.

I wonder what became of the Second Empire? I hope it had a long and good life. Or—could that have been its unimaginable end product?

The years reeled past, millions, billions mounting on each other while Earth spun around her star and the Galaxy aged. Saunders fled onward.

He stopped now and then, unable to resist a glimpse of the world and its tremendous history.

A hundred million years in the future, he looked out on great sheets of flying snow. The gods were gone. Had they too died, or abandoned Earth—perhaps for an altogether different plane of existence? He would never know.

There was a being coming through the storm. The wind flung the snow about him in whirling, hissing clouds. Frost was in his gray fur. He moved with a lithe, unhuman grace, carrying a curved staff at whose tip was a blaze like a tiny sun.

Saunders hailed him through the psychophone, letting his amplified voice shout through the blizzard: "Who are you? What are you doing on Earth?"

The being carried a stone ax in one hand and wore a string of crude beads about his neck. But he stared with bold yellow eyes at the machine and the psychophone brought his harsh scream: "You must be from the far past, one of the earlier cycles."

"They told me to go on, back almost a hundred million years ago. They told me to go to the end of time!"

The psychophone hooted with metallic laughter. "If *They* told you so—then go!"

The being walked on into the storm.

Saunders flung himself ahead. There was no place on Earth for him anymore, he had no choice but to go on.

A billion years in the future there was a city standing on a plain where grass grew that was blue and glassy and tinkled with a high crystalline chiming as the wind blew through it. But the city had never been built by humans, and it warned him away with a voice he could not disobey.

Then the sea came, and for a long time thereafter he was trapped within a mountain; he had to drive onward till it had eroded back to the ground.

The sun grew hotter and whiter as the hydrogen-helium cycle increased its intensity. Earth spiraled slowly closer to it, the friction of gas and dust clouds in space taking their infinitesimal toll of its energy over billions of years.

How many intelligent races had risen on Earth and had their day, and died, since the age when man first came out of the jungle? *At least,* he thought tiredly, *we were the first.*

A hundred billion years in the future, the sun had used up its last reserves of nuclear reactions. Saunders looked out on a bare mountain scene, grim as the Moon—but the Moon had long ago fallen back toward its parent world and exploded into a meteoric rain. Earth faced its primary now; its day was as long as its year. Saunders saw part of the sun's huge blood-red disc shining wanly.

So good-bye, Sol, he thought. *Good-bye, and thank you for many million years of warmth and light. Sleep well, old friend.*

Some billions of years beyond, there was nothing but the elemental dark. Entropy had reached a maximum, the energy sources were used up, the universe was dead.

The universe was dead!

He screamed with the graveyard terror of it and flung the machine onward. Had it not been for the gods' command, he might have let it hang there, might have opened the door to airlessness and absolute zero to die. But he had to go on. He had reached the end of all things, but he had to go on. *Beyond the end of time—*

Billions upon billions of years fled. Saunders lay in his machine, sunk into an apathetic coma. Once he roused himself to eat, feeling the sardonic humor of the situation—the last living creature, the last free energy in all the cindered cosmos, fixing a sandwich.

Many billions of years in the future, Saunders paused again. He looked out into blackness. But with a sudden shock he discerned a far faint glow, the vaguest imaginable blur of light out in the heavens.

Trembling, he jumped forward another billion years. The light was stronger now, a great sprawling radiance swirling inchoately in the sky.

The universe was re-forming.

It made sense, thought Saunders, fighting for self-control. Space had expanded to some kind of limit, now it was collapsing in on itself to start the cycle anew— the cycle that had been repeated none knew how many times in the past. The universe was mortal, but it was a phoenix which would never really die.

But he was disturbingly mortal, and suddenly he was free of his death wish. At the very least he wanted to see what the next time around looked like. But the universe would, according to the best theories of twentieth-century cosmology, collapse to what was virtually a point-source, a featureless blaze of pure energy out of which the primal atoms would be reformed. If he wasn't to be devoured in that raging furnace, he'd better leap a long ways ahead. A hell of a long ways!

He grinned with sudden reckless determination and plunged the switch forward.

Worry came back. How did he know that a planet would be formed under him? He might come out in open space, or in the heart of a sun… Well, he'd have to risk that. The gods must have foreseen and allowed for it.

He came out briefly—and flashed back into time-drive. The planet was still molten!

Some geological ages later, he looked out at a spuming gray rain, washing with senseless power from a hidden sky, covering naked rocks with a raging swirl of white water. He didn't go out; the atmosphere would be unbreathable until plants had liberated enough oxygen.

On and on! Sometimes he was under seas, sometimes on land. He saw strange jungles like overgrown ferns and mosses rise and wither in the cold of a glacial age and rise again in altered life-form.

A thought nagged at him, tugging at the back of his mind as he rode onward. It didn't hit him for several million years, then: *The moon! Oh, my God, the moon!*

His hands trembled too violently for him to stop the machine. Finally, with an effort, he controlled himself enough to pull the switch. He skipped on, looking for a night of full moon.

Luna. The same old face—*Luna!*

The shock was too great to register. Numbly, he resumed his journey. And the world began to look familiar, there were low forested hills and a river shining in the distance…

He didn't really believe it till he saw the village. It was the same—Hudson, New York.

He sat for a moment, letting his physicist's brain consider the tremendous fact. In Newtonian terms, it meant that every particle newly formed in the Beginning had exactly the same position and velocity as every corresponding particle formed in the previous cycle. In more acceptable Einsteinian language, the continuum was spherical in all four dimensions. In any case—if you traveled long enough, through space of time, you got back to your starting point.

He could go home!

He ran down the sunlit hill, heedless of his foreign garments, ran till the breath sobbed in raw lungs and his heart seemed about to burst from the ribs. Gasping, he entered the village, went into a bank, and looked at the tear-off calendar and the wall clock.

June 17, 1936, 1:30 P.M From that, he could figure his time of arrival in 1973 to the minute.

He walked slowly back, his legs trembling under him, and started the time machine again. Grayness was outside—for the last time.

1973.

Martin Saunders stepped out of the machine. Its moving in space, at Brontothor, had brought it outside MacPherson's house; it lay halfway up the hill at the top of which the rambling old building stood.

There came a flare of soundless energy. Saunders sprang back in alarm and saw the machine dissolve into molten metal—into gas—into a nothingness that shone briefly and was gone.

The gods must have put some annihilating device into it. They didn't want its devices from the future loose in the twentieth century.

But there was no danger of that, thought Saunders as he walked slowly up the hill through the rain-wet grass. He had seen too much of war and horror ever to give men knowledge they weren't ready for. He and Eve and MacPherson would have to suppress the story of his return around time—for that would offer a means of travel into the past, remove the barrier which would keep man from too much use of the machine for murder and oppression. The Second Empire and the Dreamer's philosophy lay a long time in the future.

He went on. The hill seemed strangely unreal, after all that he had seen from it, the whole enormous tomorrow of the cosmos. He would never quite fit into the little round of days that lay ahead.

Taury—her bright lovely face floated before him, he thought he heard her voice whisper in the cool wet wind that stroked his hair like her strong, gentle hands.

"Good-bye," he whispered into the reaching immensity of time. "Good-bye, my dearest."

He went slowly up the steps and in the front door. There would be Sam to mourn. And then there would be the carefully censored thesis to write, and a life spent in satisfying work with a girl who was sweet and kind and beautiful even if she wasn't Taury. It was enough for a mortal man.

He walked into the living room and smiled at Eve and MacPherson. "Hello," he said. "I guess I must be a little early."

Barnacle Bull

The *Hellik Olav* was well past Mars, acceleration ended, free-falling into the Asteroid Belt on a long elliptical orbit, when the interior radiation count began to rise. It wasn't serious, and worried none of the four men aboard. They had been so worried all along that a little extra ionization didn't seem to matter.

But as the days passed, the Geigers got still more noisy.

And then the radio quit.

This was bad! No more tapes were being made of signals received—Earth to one of the artificial satellites to Phobos to a cone of space which a rather smug-looking computer insisted held the *Hellik Olav*—for later study by electronics engineers. As for the men, they were suddenly bereft of their favorite programs. Adam Langnes, captain, no longer got the beeps whose distortions gave him an idea of exterior conditions and whose Doppler frequency gave him a check on his velocity. Torvald Winge, astronomer, had no answers to his requests for data omitted from his handbook and computations too elaborate for the ship's digital. Per Helledahl, physicist, heard no more sentimental folk songs nor the recorded babblings of his youngest child. And Erik Bull, engineer, couldn't get the cowboy music sent from the American radio satellite. He couldn't even get the Russians' Progressive jazz.

Furthermore, and still more ominous, the ship's transmitter also stopped working.

Helledahl turned from its disassembled guts. Despite all he could do with racks, bags, magnetic boards, he was surrounded by a zero gravity halo of wires, resistances, transistors, and other small objects. His moon face peered through it with an unwonted grimness. "I can find nothing wrong," he said. "The trouble must be outside, in the boom."

Captain Langnes, tall and gaunt and stiff of manner, adjusted his monocle. "I dare say we can repair the trouble," he said. "Can't be too serious, can it?"

"It can like the devil, if the radar goes out too," snapped Helledahl.

"Oh, heavens!" exclaimed Winge. His mild, middle-aged features registered dismay. "If I can't maintain my meteorite count, what am I out here for?"

"If we can't detect the big meteorites in time for the autopilot to jerk us off a collision course, you won't be out here very long," said Bull. "None of us will, except as scrap metal and frozen hamburger."

Helledahl winced. "Must you, Erik?"

"Your attitude is undesirable, Herr Bull," Captain Langnes chided. "Never forget, gentlemen, the four of us, crowded into one small vessel for possibly two years, under extremely hazardous conditions, can only survive by maintaining order, self-respect, morale."

"How can I forget?" muttered Bull. "You repeat it every thirty-seven hours and fourteen minutes by the clock." But he didn't mutter very loudly.

"You had best have a look outside, Herr Bull," went on the captain.

"I was afraid it'd come to that," said the engineer dismally. "Hang on, boys, here we go again."

Putting on space armor is a tedious job at best, requiring much assistance. In a cramped air-lock chamber—for lack of another place—and under free fall, it gets so exasperating that one forgets any element of emergency. By the time he was through the outer valve, Bull had invented three new verbal obscenities, the best of which took four minutes to enunciate.

He was a big, blocky, redhaired and freckle-faced young man, who hadn't wanted to come on this expedition. It was just a miserable series of accidents, he thought. As a boy, standing at a grisly hour on a cliff above the Sognefjord to watch the first Sputnik rise, he had decided to be a spaceship engineer. As a youth, he got a scholarship to the Massachusetts Institute of Technology, and afterward worked for two years on American interplanetary projects. Returning home, he found himself one of the few Norwegians with that kind of experience. But he also found himself thoroughly tired of it. The cramped quarters, tight discipline, reconstituted food and reconstituted air and reconstituted conversation, were bad enough. The innumerable petty nuisances of weightlessness, especially the hours a day spent doing ridiculous exercises lest his very bones atrophy, were worse. The exclusively male companionship was still worse: especially when that all-female Russian satellite station generally called the Nunnery passed within view.

"In short," Erik Bull told his friends, "if I want to take vows of poverty, chastity, and obedience, I'd do better to sign up as a Benedictine monk. I'd at least have something drinkable on hand."

Not that he regretted the time spent, once it was safely behind him. With judicious embroidering, he had a lifetime supply of dinner-table reminiscences. More important, he could take his pick of Earthside jobs. Such as the marine reclamation station his countrymen were building off Svalbard, with regular airbus service to Trondheim and Oslo. *There* was a post!

Instead of which, he was now spinning off beyond Mars, hell for leather into a volume of space that had already swallowed a score of craft without trace.

He emerged on the hull, made sure his life line was fast, and floated a few minutes to let his eyes adjust. A tiny heatless sun, too brilliant to look close to, spotted puddles of undiffused glare among coalsack shadows. The stars, unwinking, needle bright, were so many that they swamped the old familiar constellations in their sheer number. He identified several points as asteroids, some twinkling as rotation exposed their irregular surfaces, some so close that their relative motion was visible. His senses did not react to the radiation, which the ship's magnetic field was supposed to ward off from the interior but which sharply limited his stay outside. Bull imagined all those particles zipping through him, each drilling a neat submicroscopic hole, and wished he hadn't.

The much-touted majestic silence of space wasn't evident either. His air pump made too much noise. Also, the suit stank.

Presently he could make sense out of the view. The ship was a long cylinder, lumpy where meteor bumpers protected the most vital spots. A Norwegian flag, painted near the bows, was faded by solar ultraviolet, eroded by micrometeoric impacts. The vessel was old, though basically sound. The Russians had given it to Norway for a museum piece, as a propaganda gesture. But then the Americans had hastily given Norway the parts needed to renovate. Bull himself had spent six dreary months helping do that job. He hadn't been too unhappy about it, though. He liked the idea of his country joining in the exploitation of space. Also, he was Americanized enough to feel a certain malicious pleasure when the *Ivan Pavlov* was rechristened in honor of St. Olav.

However, he had not expected to serve aboard the thing!

"O.K., O.K.," he sneered in English, "hold still, Holy Ole, and we'll have a look at your latest disease."

He drew himself back along the line and waddled forward over the hull in stickum boots. Something on the radio transceiver boom…what the devil? He bent over. The motion pulled his boots loose. He upended and went drifting off toward Andromeda. Cursing in a lackluster voice, he came back hand over hand. But as he examined the roughened surface he forgot even to be annoyed.

He tried unsuccessfully to pinch himself.

An hour convinced him. He made his laborious way below again. Captain Langnes, who was Navy insisted that you went "below" when you entered the ship, even in free fall. When his spacesuit was off, with only one frost burn suffered from touching the metal, he faced the others across a cluttered main cabin.

"Well?" barked Helledahl. "What is it?"

"As the lady said when she saw an elephant eating cabbages with what she thought was his tail," Bull answered slowly, "if I told you, you wouldn't believe me."

"Of course I would!" said Langnes. "Out with it!"

"Well, skipper…we have barnacles."

A certain amount of chemical and biological apparatus had been brought along to study possible effects of the whatever-it-was that seemed to forbid spacecraft crossing the Asteroid Belt. The equipment was most inadequate, and between them the four men had only an elementary knowledge of its use. But then, all equipment was inadequate in zero gravity, and all knowledge was elementary out here.

Work progressed with maddening slowness. And meanwhile the *Hellik Olav* fell outward and outward, on an orbit which would not bend back again until it was three Astronomical Units from the sun. And the ship was out of communication. And the radar, still functional but losing efficiency all the time, registered an ever thicker concentration of meteorites. And the 'tween-decks radiation count mounted, slowly but persistently.

"I vote we go home," said Helledahl. Sweat glistened on his forehead, where he sat in his tiny bunk cubicle without touching the mattress.

"Second the motion," said Bull at once. "Any further discussion? I move the vote. All in favor, say, *'Ja.'* All opposed, shut up."

"This is no time for jokes, Herr Bull," said Captain Langnes.

"I quite agree, sir. And this trip is more than a joke, it's a farce. Let's turn back!"

"Because of an encrustation on the hull?"

Surprisingly, gentle Torvald Winge supported the skipper with almost as sharp a tone. "Nothing serious has yet happened," he said. "We have now shielded the drive tubes so that the barnacle growth can't advance to them. As for our communications apparatus, we have spare parts in ample supply and can easily repair it once we're out of this fantastic zone. Barnacles can be scraped off the radar arms, as well as the vision parts. What kind of cowards will our people take us for, if we give up at the first little difficulty?"

"Live ones," said Helledahl.

"You see," Bull added, "we're not in such bad shape now, but what'll happen if this continues? Just extrapolate the radiation. I did. We'll be dead men on the return orbit."

"You assume the count will rise to a dangerous level," said Winge. "I doubt that. Time enough to turn back, if it seems we have no other hope. But what you don't appreciate, Erik, is the very real, unextrapolated danger of such a course."

"Also, we seem to be on the track of an answer to the mystery—the whole purpose of this expedition," said Langnes. "Given a little more data, we should find out what happened to all the previous ships."

"Including the Chinese?" asked Bull.

Silence descended. They sat in mid-air, reviewing a situation which familiarity did nothing to beautify.

Observations from the Martian moons had indicated the Asteroid Belt was much fuller than astronomers had believed. Of course, it was still a rather hard vacuum…but one through which sand, gravel, and boulders went flying with indecent speed and frequency. Unmanned craft were sent in by several nations. Their telemetering instruments confirmed the great density of cosmic debris, which increased as they swung further in toward the central zone. But then they quit sending. They were never heard from again. Manned ships stationed near the computed orbits of the robot vessels, where these emerged from the danger area, detected objects with radar, panted to match velocities, and saw nothing but common or garden variety meteorites.

Finally the Chinese People's Republic sent three craft with volunteer crews, toward the Belt. One ship went off course and landed in the Pacific Ocean near San Francisco. After its personnel explained the unique methods by which they had been persuaded to volunteer, they were allowed to stay. The scientists got good technical jobs, the captain started a restaurant, and the political commissar went on the lecture circuit.

But the other two ships continued as per instructions.

Their transmission stopped at about the same distance as the robot radios had, and they were never seen again either.

After that, the big nations decided there was no need for haste in such expensive undertakings. But Norway had just outfitted her own spaceship, and all true Norwegians are crazy. The *Hellik Olav* went out.

Winge stirred. "I believe I can tell you what happened to the Chinese," he said.

"Sure," said Bull. "They stayed on orbit till it was too late. Then the radiation got them."

"No. They saw themselves in our own situation, panicked, and started back."

"So?"

"The meteorites got them."

"Excuse me," said Langnes, obviously meaning it the other way around. "You know better than that, Professor Winge. The hazard isn't that great. Even at the highest possible density of material, the probability of impact with anything of considerable mass is so low—"

"I am not talking about that, captain," said the astronomer. "Let me repeat the facts *ab initio*, to keep everything systematic, even if you know most of them already.

"Modern opinion holds that the asteroids, and probably most meteorites throughout the Solar System, really are the remnants of a disintegrated world. I am inclined to suspect that a sudden phase change in its core caused the initial explosion—this can happen at a certain planetary mass and then Jupiter's attraction gradually broke up the larger pieces. Prior to close-range study, it was never believed the asteroidean planet could have been large enough for this to happen. But today we know it must have been roughly as big as Earth. The total mass was not detectable at a distance, prior to space flight, because so much of it consists of small dark particles. These, I believe, were formed when the larger chunks broke up into lesser ones which abraded and shattered each other in collisions, before gravitational forces spread them too widely apart."

"What has this to do with the mess we're in?" asked Bull.

Winge looked startled. "Why...that is—" He blushed. "Nothing, I suppose." To cover his embarrassment, he began talking rapidly, repeating the obvious at even greater length:

"We accelerated from Earth, and a long way beyond, thus throwing ourselves into an eccentric path with a semi-major axis of two Astronomical Units. But this is still an ellipse, and as we entered the danger zone, our velocity gained more and more of a component parallel to the planetary orbits. At our aphelion, which will be in the very heart of the Asteroid Belt, we will be moving substantially with the average meteorite. Relative velocity will be very small, or zero. Hence collisions will be rare, and mild when they do occur. Then we'll be pulled back sunward. By the time we start accelerating under power toward Earth, we will again be traveling at a large angle to the natural orbits. But by that time, also, we will be back out of the danger zone.

"Suppose, however, we decided to turn back at this instant. We would first have to decelerate, spending fuel to kill an outward velocity which the sun would otherwise have killed for us. Then we must accelerate inward. We can just barely afford the fuel. There will be little left for maneuvers. *And…*we'll be cutting almost perpendicularly across the asteroidal orbits. Their full density and velocity will be directed almost broadside to us.

"Oh, we still needn't worry about being struck by a large object. The probability of that is quite low. But what we will get is the fifteen kilometer-per-second sandblast of the uncountable small particles. I have been computing the results of my investigations so far, and arrive at a figure for the density of this cosmic sand which is, well, simply appalling. Far more than was hitherto suspected. I don't believe our hull can stand such a prolonged scouring, meteor bumpers or no."

"Are you certain?" gulped Helledahl.

"Of course not," said Winge testily. "What is certain, out here? I believe it highly probably, though. And the fact that the Chinese never came back would seem to lend credence to my hypothesis."

The barnacles had advanced astoundingly since Bull last looked at them. Soon the entire ship would be covered, except for a few crucial places toilfully kept clean.

He braced his armored self against the reactive push of his cutting torch. It was about the only way to get a full-grown barnacle loose. The things melded themselves with the hull. The flame drowned the sardonic stars in his vision but illuminated the growths.

They looked quite a bit like the Terrestrial marine sort. Each humped up in a hard conoidal shell of blackish-brown material. Beneath them was a layer of excreted metal, chiefly ferrous, plated onto the aluminum hull.

I'd hate to try landing through an atmosphere, thought Bull. Of course, that wouldn't be necessary. We would go into orbit around Earth and call for someone to lay alongside and take us off…But heading back sunward, we'll have one sweet time controlling internal temperature…No, I can simply slap some shiny paint on. That should do the trick. I'd have to paint anyway, to maintain constant radiation characteristics when micrometeorites are forever scratching our metal. Another chore. Space flight is nothing but one long round of chores. The next poet who recites in my presence an ode to man's conquest of the universe can take that universe—every galaxy and every supernova through every last, long light-year—and put…

If we get home alive.

He tossed the barnacle into a metal canister for later study. It was still red hot, and doubtless the marvelously intricate organism within the shell had suffered damage. But the details of the lithophagic metabolism could be left for professional biologists to figure out. All they wanted aboard Holy Ole was enough knowledge to base a decision on.

Before taking more specimens, Bull made a circuit of the hull. There were many hummocks on it, barnacles growing upon barnacles. The foresection had turned into a hill of shells, under which the radio transceiver boom lay buried. Another could be built when required for Earth approach. The trouble was, with the interior radiation still mounting—while a hasty retreat seemed impossible—Bull had started to doubt he ever would see Earth again.

He scrubbed down the radar, then paused to examine the spot where he had initially cut off a few dozen samples. New ones were already burgeoning on the ferroplate left by their predecessors—little fellows with delicate glasslike shells which would soon grow and thicken, becoming incredibly tough. Whatever that silicate material was, study of it should repay Terrestrial industry. Another bonanza from the Asteroid Belt, the modern Mother Lode.

"Ha!" said Bull.

It had sounded very convincing. The proper way to exploit space was not to mine the planets, where you must grub deep in the crust to find a few stingy ore pockets, then spend fabulous amounts of energy hauling your gains home. No, the asteroids had all the minerals man would ever need, in developing his extraterrestrial colonies and on Earth herself. Freely available minerals, especially on the metallic asteroids from the core of the ancient planet. Just land and help yourself. No elaborate apparatus needed to protect you from your environment. Just the spaceship and space armor you had to have anyway. No gravitational well to back down into and climb back out of. Just a simple thrust of minimum power.

Given free access to the asteroids, even a small nation like Norway could operate in space, with all the resulting benefits to her economy, politics, and prestige. And there was the *Hellik Olav,* newly outfitted, with plenty of volunteers—genuine ones—for an exploratory mission and to hell with the danger.

"Ha!" repeated Bull.

He had been quite in favor of the expedition, provided somebody else went. But he was offered a berth and made the mistake of telling his girl.

"Ohhhh, Erik!" she exclaimed, enormous-eyed.

After six months in space helping to rig and test the ship, Bull could have fallen in love with the Sea Hag. However, this had not been necessary. When he had returned to Earth, swearing a mighty oath never to set foot above the stratosphere again, he met Marta. She was small and blond and deliciously shaped. She adored him right back. The only flaw he could find in her was a set of romantic notions about the starry universe and the noble Norwegian destiny therein.

"Oh, oh," he said, recognizing the symptoms. In haste: "Don't get ideas, now. I told you I'm a marine reclamation man, from here on forever."

"But this, darling! This chance! To be one of the conquerors! To make your name immortal!"

"The trouble is, I'm still mortal myself."

"The service you can do—to our country!"

"Uh, apart from everything else, do you realize that, uh, even allowing for acceleration under power for part of the distance, I'd be gone for more than two years?"

"I'll wait for you."

"But—"

"Are you *afraid,* Erik?"

"Well, no. But—"

"Think of the Vikings! Think of Fridtjof Nansen! Think of Roald Amundsen!"

Bull dutifully thought of all these gentlemen. "What about them?" he asked.

But it was a light summer night, and Marta couldn't imagine any true Norwegian refusing such a chance for deathless glory, and one thing sort of led to another. Before he recovered his wits, Bull had accepted the job.

There followed a good deal of work up in orbit, readying the ship, and a shakedown cruise lasting some weeks. When he finally got pre-departure leave, Bull broke every known traffic law and a few yet to be invented, on the way to Marta's home. She informed him tearfully that she was so sorry and she hoped they would always be good friends, but she had been seeing so little of him and had met someone else but she would always follow his future career with the greatest interest. The someone else turned out to be a bespectacled writer who had just completed a three-volume novel about King Harald Hardcounsel (1015-1066). Bull didn't remember the rest of his furlough very clearly.

A shock jarred through him. He bounced from the hull, jerked to a halt at the end of his life line, and waited for the dizziness to subside. The stars leered.

"Hallo! Hallo, Erik! Are you all right?"

Bull shook his head to clear it. Helledahl's voice, phoned across the life line, was tinny in his earphones. "I think so. What happened?"

"A small meteorite hit us, I suppose. It must have had an abnormal orbit to strike so hard. We can't see any damage from inside, though. Will you check the outer hull?"

Bull nodded, though there was no point in doing so. After he hauled himself back, he needed a while to find the spot of impact. The pebble had collided near the waist of the ship, vaporizing silicate shell material to form a neat little crater in a barnacle hummock. It hadn't quite penetrated to the ferroplate. A fragment remained, trapped between the rough lumps.

Bull shivered. Without that overgrowth, the hull would have been pierced. Not that that mattered greatly in itself. There was enough patching aboard to repair several hundred such holes. But the violence of impact was an object lesson. Torvald Winge was almost certainly right. Trying to cut straight across the Asteroid Belt would be as long a chance as men had ever taken. The incessant bombardment of particles, mostly far smaller than this but all possessing a similar speed, would wear down the entire hull. When it was thin enough to rip apart under stress, no meteor bumpers or patches would avail.

His eyes sought the blue-green glint of Earth, but couldn't find it among so many stars. *You know,* he told himself, *I don't even mind the prospect of dying* out here as much as I do the dreariness of it. If we turned around now and somehow survived, I'd be home by Christmas. I'd only have wasted one extra year in space, instead of more than three—counting in the preparations for this arduous cruise. I'd find me a girl, no, a dozen girls. And a hundred bottles. I'd make up for that year in style, before settling down to do work I really enjoy.

But we aren't likely to survive, if we turn around now.

But how likely is our survival if we keep going—with the radiation shield failing us? And an extra two years on Holy Ole? I'd go nuts!

Judas priest! Was ever a man in such an ugh situation?

Langnes peered at the sheaf of papers in his hand. "I have drafted a report of our findings with regard to the, ah, space barnacles," he said. "I would like you gentlemen to criticize it as I read aloud. We have now accounted for the vanishing of the previous ships—"

Helledahl mopped his brow. Tiny beads of sweat broke loose and glittered in the air. "That doesn't do much good if we also vanish," he pointed out.

"Quite," Langnes looked irritated. "Believe me, I am more than willing to turn home at once. But that is impracticable, as Professor Winge has shown and the unfortunate Chinese example has confirmed."

"I say it's just as impracticable to follow the original orbit," declared Bull.

"I understand you don't like it here," said Winge, "but really, courting an almost certain death in order to escape two more years of boredom seems a trifle extreme."

"The boredom will be all the worse, now that we don't have anything to work toward," said Bull.

The captain's monocle glared at him. "Ahem!" said Langnes. "If you gentlemen are quite through, may I have the floor?"

"Sure," said Bull. "Or the wall or the ceiling, if you prefer. Makes no difference here."

"I'll skip the preamble of the report and start with our conclusions. 'Winge believes the barnacles originated as a possibly mutant life form on the ancient planet before it was destroyed. The slower breakup of the resulting super-asteroidal masses gave this life time to adapt to spatial conditions. The organism itself is not truly protoplasmic. Instead of water, which would either boil or freeze in vacuo at this distance from the sun, the essential liquid is some heavy substance we have not been able to identify except as an aromatic compound.' "

"Aromatic is too polite," said Bull, wrinkling his nose.

The air purifiers had still not gotten all the chemical stench out.

Langnes proceeded unrelenting: " 'The basic chemistry does remain that of carbon, of proteins, albeit with an extensive use of complex silicon compounds. We theorize the life cycle as follows. The adult form ejects spores which drift freely through space. Doubtless most are lost, but such wastefulness is characteristic of nature on Earth, too. When a spore does chance on a meteorite or an asteroid it can use, it develops rapidly. It requires silicon and carbon, plus traces of other elements; hence it must normally flourish only on stony meteorites, which are, however, the most abundant sort. Since the barnacle's powerful, pseudo-enzymatic digestive processes—deriving their ultimate energy from sunlight—also extract metals where these exist, it must eliminate same, which it does by laying down a plating, molecule by molecule, under its shell. Research into the details of this process should interest both biologists and metallurgists.

"'The shell serves a double function. To some extent, it protects against ionizing radiation of solar or cosmic origin. Also, being a nonconductor, it can hold a biologically generated static charge, which will cause nearby dust to drift down upon it. Though this is a slow method of getting the extra nourishment, the barnacle is exceedingly long-lived, and can adjust its own metabolic and reproductive rates to the exigencies of the situation. Since the charge is not very great, and he himself is encased in metal, a spaceman notices no direct consequences.

"'One may well ask why this life form has never been observed before. First, it is doubtless confined to the Asteroid Belt, the density of matter being too low elsewhere. We have established that it is poisoned by water and free oxygen, so no spores could survive on any planet man has yet visited, even if they did drift there. Second, if a meteorite covered with such barnacles does strike an atmosphere, the surface vaporization as it falls will destroy all evidence. Third, even if barnacle-crusted meteorites have been seen from spaceships, they look superficially like any other stony objects. No one has captured them for closer examination.'"

He paused to drink water from a squeeze bottle. "Hear, hear," murmured Bull, pretending the captain stood behind a lectern.

"That's why the unmanned probe ships never were found," said Helledahl. "They may well have been seen, more or less on their predicted orbits, but they weren't recognized."

Langnes nodded. "Of course. That comes next in the report. Then I go on to say: 'The reason that radio transmission ceased in the first place is equally obvious. Silicon components are built into the boom, as part of a transistor system. The barnacles ate them.

"'The observed increase in internal irradiation is due to the plating of heavy metals laid down by the barnacles. First, the static charges and the ferromagnetic atoms interfere with the powerful external magnetic fields which are generated to divert ions from the ship. Second, primary cosmic rays coming through that same plating produce showers of secondary particles.

"'Some question may be raised as to the explosive growth rate of barnacles on our hull, even after all the silicon available in our external apparatus had been consumed. The answer involves consideration of vectors. The ordinary member of the Asteroid Belt, be it large or small, travels in an orbit roughly parallel to the orbits of all other members. There are close approaches and occasional collisions, but on the whole, the particles are thinly scattered by Terrestrial standards, isolated from each other. Our ship, however, is slanting across those same orbits, thus exposing itself to a veritable rain of bodies, ranging in size from microscopic to sand granular. Even a single spore, coming in contact with our hull, could multiply indefinitely.'"

"That means we're picking up mass all the time," groaned Bull. "Which means we'll accelerate slower and get home even later than I'd feared."

"Do you think we'll get home at all?" fretted Helledahl. "We can expect the interference with our radiation shield, and the accumulation of heavy atoms, to get worse all the time. Nobody will ever be able to cross the Belt!"

"Oh, yes, they will," said Captain Langnes. "Ships must simply be redesigned. The magnetic screens must be differently heterodyned, to compensate. The radio booms must be enclosed in protective material. Or perhaps—"

"I know," said Bull in great weariness. "Perhaps antifouling paint can be developed. Or spaceships can be careened, God help us. Oh, yes. All I care about is how we personally get home. I can't modify our own magnetic generators. I haven't the parts or the tools, even if I knew precisely how. We'll spin on and on, the radiation worse every hour, till—"

"Be quiet!" snapped Langnes.

"The Chinese turned around, and look what happened to them," underlined Winge. "We must try something different, however hopeless it too may look."

Bull braced his heavy shoulders. "See here, Torvald," he growled, "what makes you so sure the Chinese did head back under power?"

"Because they were never seen again. If they had been on the predicted orbit, or even on a completed free-fall ellipse, one of the ships watching for them in the neighborhood of Earth would have—Oh."

"Yes," said Bull through his teeth. "Would have seen them? How do you know they weren't seen? I think they were. I think they plugged blindly on as they'd been ordered to, and the radiation suddenly started increasing on a steep curve—as you'd expect, when a critical point of fouling up was passed. I think they died, and came back like comets, sealed into spaceships so crusted they looked like ordinary meteorites!"

The silence thundered.

"So we may as well turn back," said Bull at last. "If we don't make it, our death'll be a quicker and cleaner one than those poor devils had."

Again the quietude. Until Captain Langnes shook his head. "No. I'm sorry, gentlemen. But we go on."

"What?" screamed Helledahl.

The captain floated in the air, a ludicrous parody of officerlike erectness. But there was an odd dignity to him all the same.

"I'm sorry," he repeated. "I have a family too, you know. I would turn about if it could be done with reasonable safety. But Professor Winge has shown that that is impossible. We would die anyhow—and our ship would be a ruin, a few bits of worn and crumpled metal, all our results gone. If we proceed, we can prepare specimens and keep records which will be of use to our successors. Us they will find, for we can improvise a conspicuous feature on the hull that the barnacles won't obliterate."

He looked from one to another.

"Shall we do less for our country's honor than the Chinese did for theirs?" he finished.

Well, if you put it that way, thought Bull, *yes.*

But he couldn't bring himself to say it aloud. Maybe they all thought the same, including Langnes himself, but none was brave enough to admit it. *The trouble with us moral cowards,* thought Bull, *is that we make heroes of ourselves.*

I suppose Marta will shed some pretty, nostalgic tears when she gets the news. Ech! It's bad enough to croak out here; but if that bluestocking memorializes me with a newspaper poem about my Viking spirit—

Maybe that's what we should rig up on the hull, so they won't ignore this poor barnacled derelict as just another flying boulder Make the Holy Ole into a real, old-fashioned, Gokstad type ship. Dragon figurehead, oars, sail…shields hung along the side…hey, yes! Imagine some smug Russian on an Earth satellite, bragging about how his people were the first into space—and then along comes this Viking ship—

I think I'll even paint the shields. A face on each one, with its tongue out and a thumb to its nose—

Holy hopping Ole!

"Shields!" roared Bull.

"What?" said Langnes through the echoes.

"We're shielded! We can turn back! Right now!"

When the hubbub had died down and a few slide rule calculations had been made, Bull addressed the others.

"It's really quite simple," he said. "All the elements of the answer were there all the time. I'm only surprised that the Chinese never realized it; but then, I imagine they used all their spare moments for socialist self-criticism.

"Anyhow, we know our ship is a space barnacle's paradise. Even our barnacles have barnacles. Why? Because it picks up so much sand and gravel. Now what worried us about heading straight home was not an occasional meteorite big enough to punch clear through the skin of the ship—we've patching to take care of that—no, we were afraid of a sandblast wearing the entire hull paper thin. But we're protected against precisely that danger! The more such little particles that hit us, the more barnacles we'll have. They can't be eroded away, because they're alive. They renew themselves from the very stuff that strikes them. Like a stone in a river, worn away by the current, while the soft moss is always there.

"We'll get back out of the Belt before the radiation level builds up to anything serious. Then, if we want to, we can chisel off the encrustation. But why bother, really? We'll soon be home."

"No argument there," smiled Langnes.

"I'll go check the engines prior to starting up," said Bull. "Will you and Torvald compute us an Earthward course?"

He started for the doorway, paused, and added slowly: "Uh, I kind of hate to say this, but those barnacles are what will really make the Asteroid Belt available to men."

"What?" said Helledahl.

"Sure," said Bull. "Simple. Naturally, we'll have to devise protection for the radio, and redesign the radiation screen apparatus, as the skipper remarked. But under proper control, the barnacles make a self-repairing shield against sandblast. It shouldn't be necessary to go through the Belt on these tedious elliptical orbits. The space miners can take hyperbolic paths, as fast as they choose, in any direction they please.

"I," he finished with emphasis, "will not be among them."

"Where will you be?" asked Winge.

But Erik Bull was already headed aft to his work. A snatch of song, bawled from powerful lungs, came back to the others. They all knew English, but it took them a moment to get the drift.

> " '...Who's that knocking at my door?'
> Said the fair young maiden.
> 'Oh, it's only me, from over the sea,'
> Said Barnacle Bill the sailor.
> 'I've sailed the seas from shore to shore,
> I'll never sail the seas no more.
> Now open up this blank-blank door!'
> Said Barnacle Bill the sailor."

To Jack Williamson

> Judge this: the gathering of dreams that grew
> Across the span of half a century,
> Called out of space and time by one who knew—
> Knew well, and knows—what miracles must be
> Where stars and stars hold back the outer night
> In radiance, begetting worlds and souls.
> Longed has his vision raised beyond our sight,
> Light-years, to find adventures, hopes and goals.
> Imagination likewise dares the deeps
> And danger of our future and our past,
> Man's fate; and if man laughs or shouts or weeps,
> Still in these tales we see ourselves at last.
> On Earth, from which the questing ships depart,
> No bard among us bears a higher heart.

Time Heals

Hart followed the doctor down a long corridor where they were the only two in sight and their footsteps had a hollow echo. The fluorescent lights were almost pitilessly bright, and the hall was silent. Silent and empty as—death? No, as the Crypt at its end, as timelessness.

Hart's lips were dry, his throat felt tight, and his heart beat with a rapid violence that dinned faintly in his ears. He was frightened. Why not admit it? The feeling was utterly illogical, but he was scared silly.

He asked inanely, as if he and all the rest of the world didn't know, "There won't be any sensation at all?"

"None," replied the doctor with a patience suggesting he had led many down this hallway. "You'll stand on a plate between the field coils, I'll throw the main switch and—as far as you're concerned—you'll be in the future. Time simply does not exist, as a 'flow' at any rate, in a level-entropy field."

Hart licked his lips. "It's like dying," he said.

The doctor nodded. "In a way, it is death," he replied. "You'll be leaving everything behind you—family, friends, the whole world in which you have lived. You can't go back. When you're released from the field—ten, fifty, a hundred, a thousand years hence maybe—you'll be irrevocably in the future." He shrugged. "But, of course, you'll live, whereas your only choice in this era is death."

"Don't get me wrong," said Hart. "I'm nervous sure but I'm not scared. I have every confidence in your machine. It's just that I never did understand the principles of it, and of course one is naturally skittish in the face of the unknown."

"It's very simple," said the doctor. "The newspapers have, as usual, made a horrible mess of trying to explain it to the public, and all the legal and moral argument it's stirred up have further confused the issue. But the scientific basis is very simple indeed." He adopted a lecturing tone: "Time, of course, is a fourth dimension in a more or less rigid continuum—that's putting it very crudely, of course, but it shows that simple relativity gives no reason why time should flow, or if it flows, why it should do so in one direction only. That difficulty was resolved by suggesting that the increase of time was the general increase of entropy throughout the universe with respect to the 'rigid' time dimension. Again, that's a clumsy way of putting it, but you get my general idea. I don't pretend to understand the details of it myself.

"Anyway, just a couple of years ago, in 1950 I believe, Seaton found an effect, a field, in which entropy was held level. An object in such a field could not experience any time flow—for it, time would not exist. The generation of such a field turned out to be fairly simple once the basic principles were discovered, so that before long we had the Crypt."

Hart nodded—although he didn't understand it even now. Science had bored him; he regarded himself as a natural-born aesthete and observer of man, a pursuit which a medium-sized independent income made possible. He wrote a little, painted a little, played the piano a little, went to all the exhibitions and concerts, chose his friends and occasional mistresses primarily on a basis of conversational ability, and in general had a pretty good time.

The fundamental idea of the Crypt was hardly new to him. He had read the old legends—the Seven Sleepers, the tales of Herla, Frederik Barbarossa, and Holger Danske—of men for whom time had stopped until the remote future date when they awoke. Only last night, his last night in this world, he had played the whole *Tannhäuser* in an orgy of sentimentality.

There was always a catch. But he had very little to lose. A cancer which had metastasized to the lymph glands meant a short and unpleasant life, perhaps prolonged by operations hopelessly carving away more and more of his flesh—better to take some poison and go out like a gentleman.

Or, better yet, go into the future when they would have worked out some sure and easy cure for his sickness. And perhaps, he thought, a cure for the political cancers which ate at his own society, a cure for war and poverty and misery. Utopia was not inherently unattainable, to a close approximation anyway…For a moment he was almost looking forward to the adventure, but the tightness and the heavy pulse wouldn't leave him. He liked his present existence, and the future would have to be pretty good to make up for his present.

Though I'm lucky, he thought. *I have no really close ties, none who'll really miss me or whom I can't live without. And I have a high I.Q. and adaptability, I can get along with almost anybody. I won't suffer.*

He asked, "Are there any people besides those with diseases at present incurable going into the Crypt?"

"No," answered the doctor, "except, of course, husbands and wives who wish to accompany their sick spouses, and a few other special cases like that. We just don't have room for any more.

"Naturally," he went on, "we're swamped with applications from people who want to escape the tribulations of the present for a presumably happier future. But those we ignore. There's been talk of developing level-entropy units which can be used for everyday purposes like preserving food or other perishables, or even in the household. Imagine cooking a chicken dinner, putting it in the field, and taking it out piping hot whenever needed, maybe twenty years hence! But the manufacturers are very careful about releasing stasis generators, precisely because too many people would try to take a one-way ride into tomorrow. What would become of the present—and would the future want our neurotic escapists?

"Several state legislatures have already tried to regulate the use of the Seaton effect, and Congress is arguing about a Federal law. Meanwhile, the Crypt staff uses it simply to save lives which are lost to the present anyway."

"If you can be sure they are saved—" murmured Hart. "Of course, we can give no hundred-percent guarantee," said the doctor with elaborate patience, "but I think it's a very safe bet. The Crypt is in an underground vault well away from any area which might be presumable atomic-bomb targets. Not that even an atom bomb could penetrate a stasis field. Once the fields are set up, they're self-maintaining until neutralized from outside. Information about the Crypt is diffused throughout the world by now, even if something should happen to the permanent staff, which is unlikely. Whenever a cure for a specific disease is found, we will consult our records and release those suffering from it."

"Yes, yes, I know all that," said Hart. "But what kind of future—?"

"Who knows?" The doctor shrugged. "But I don't think it will be too hard to adjust. I rather imagine that a smart Roman or Elizabethan Englishman, say, could do very well for himself in the present. Besides, at the rate medical science is advancing, I don't think anyone will be in here longer than fifty or a hundred years."

"And making a living—"

"You invested all your money as safely as possible before coming here, didn't you? You'll still have it when you awake, then, or the equivalent of it if they change the fiscal system. The Crypt staff will see to that if it isn't taken care of automatically. You'll also have quite a bit of accumulated interest."

Hart nodded his sleek dark head. "It seems as sound a proposition as human ingenuity can make it," he said. He added wryly, "Anyway, there's no point in quibbling, not when the old man with the scythe is so close."

"Quite so," said the doctor.

They came to the end of the passage, where a great vault door sealed off the Crypt itself. The doctor worked the multiple combination lock, remarking idly, "Even if this whole place should be destroyed, the sleepers would be safe. Literally nothing from outside except a neutralizing field can penetrate the stasis. You could be buried under ten tons of earth without its making any difference—till they dug you out and opened your field."

"There are things worse than death," muttered Hart, and then added quickly, "but hardly worse than death by cancer."

"Quite." The doctor started the little motor which opened the huge door. "In a way," he said, "I envy you. You'll wake up rich, in a society which is better than ours—it must be, it couldn't be much worse—and has all the great new adventures we're just beginning to glimpse—the planets, the stars…" He shrugged. "I may see you again, of course. They're working hard on the cancer problem right now. But I'll be a pretty old man then."

Hart nodded. "Benjamin Franklin once said he wished that, after he was dead, somebody would wake him every hundred years and tell him what happened. I see his point."

They entered the Crypt. The room was a huge one, cold in steel and concrete and the white fluorescent lighting. There was little about to suggest the sensation it was arousing in the outer world. It looked much like a burial vault—a sinister thought, that, and one which Hart did his best to abolish—with its long row on row of steel caskets sliding into the walls. Each box, Hart noticed, had a complete case history engraved on its end.

The doctor followed his eye. "Those supplement our other records, in case they get lost," he said. "The future physicians can read directly what is the matter with each patient. And just in case something should happen to the Crypt itself, everyone takes another case history into stasis with him, like the one you're carrying now. So if it should become necessary, if nothing else survived, you could always be 'wakened' for the sole purpose of reexamination. But all those precautions are more for the benefit of worriers than because we think they'll ever be needed."

"The patients are actually in those—coffins?"

"Yes. The Seaton generator throws an almost cubical field about the subject. You've seen pictures or movies of it—a totally reflecting region, six or seven feet on a side. This field is, as I said, inherently self-maintaining. I heard Seaton himself lecture once, and he said something like the field requiring finite time in which to break down—only there is no time in it. Anyway, we find it most convenient to store those, uh, blocks of frozen time in the vaults you see."

Hart licked his lips again. He had always had a touch of necrophobia, and his hands were damp and cold now. To be frozen in time like a fish in a chunk of ice; and stowed away in a steel box for no one knew how long…He had a morbid desire to see his own coffin, but did not indulge it. That would not have fitted the picture he had of himself, which was somewhere between Epicure and Stoic.

They came into a smaller room at the end of the Crypt. It was crowded with apparatus which was meaningless to Hart. A couple of technicians stood by, smoking and talking and most infernally casual about it all.

"Well," said the doctor, a little awkwardly, "I guess this is it. Are you sure you don't want to leave any farewell messages or—?"

"No," said Hart. "I hate good-byes. I've said mine, and don't want that railway-platform waiting at the end. Let's get it over with."

"Okay. Mount that plate over there, please, between those four big coils. And—good luck." The doctor extended his hand and Hart shook it, thinking to himself that it was a wholly unnecessary gesture. Maybe they'd have better taste in the future.

He climbed up onto the silvery disk and stood looking out between coils that were taller than he was. His knees were a little weak—almost, he was tempted to shout to call a halt—but that would be silly, of course.

The technicians busied themselves about the generator with that casual competence he had always found irritating in their breed. He heard the list of instrument readings called out, someone else said, "Check," and he thought briefly and wildly, *Maybe it's also mate.* A switch slammed down and a blue glow hovered over the coils. He heard a low, rising hum.

It faded. "Alri, no," said the doctor. "Du can downstep no."

Hart had a moment where his mind wobbled, where he thought wildly that it hadn't worked after all. Great Heaven he was still in the world, still at home—

What had happened to the doctor? Where were the technicians? These weren't the same men they had been an instant ago!

An instant—no, an age. There was no time flow in the stasis field—he was in the future.

He had thought himself mentally prepared. But it was too sudden. The shock was too blurringly great—shattering, devastating shock of suddenly alien men, alien speech, alien world. He staggered a little, and the doctor stepped up on the platform to support him.

Hart leaned on the man's arm—a big, solid fellow, which was somehow reassuring—and let the soft, lilting words slide over the surface of his mind. Almost, they were familiar. For a moment he couldn't follow the speech at all, then he caught words and recognized the changes in accent. Except for the foreign terms and the slang, he could follow the language. Certainly he could get the drift of it.

Only—how long would it take to modify the tongue so much?

He almost croaked the question. The doctor said slowly, "Dis are yaar 2837, du would say. But bay chronomizing nos, are yaar 2841."

"What on earth—?" The sheer incongruity of it jerked Hart from his daze. He might have accepted a wholly different chronology, but—four years' difference! "How the hell did that ever happen?"

"Hell?" For a moment, the doctor was puzzled, then his face cleared. "Oh, yes, medyaeval belief." He smiled. "Skood du raaly ask huw de Heaven. See du, in su-named Second Dark Ages Americas waar under rule of de Kyirk of de Second Coming. Dey waar religio-fanatics whuw held dat chronomizing skood be set up four yaars since dey claimed Christ waar rally borned in 4 B.C. bay uwld chronomizing. Bay time yoke of de Kyirk waar overthruwn, everybody waar used to new style."

Hart nodded, a little overwhelmed. "I…see…"

It didn't matter, though. It didn't matter. The…the Church of the Second Coming was in the past now, the dusty buried past which had still been in the future—ten minutes ago!

Almost nine hundred years. Nine hundred years!

"Here." The doctor gave him a little flask. "Drink du dis."

He gulped the liquid. It was tasteless, but it seemed to lay a great calm hand on him; his mind steadied and the trembling went out of his knees. He looked around him.

The chamber was different. The Crypt was not nearly so full, and it bore signs of extensive repair work. Many must have been released, many…But lymphatic cancer was really a tough disease, it would have taken time to work out the cure and if ages of barbarism had intervened—

His eyes swung to the men. There were, as before, two technicians and a doctor. (And the three men of his time were dust these many centuries.) They were large, well-shaped fellows, with dark hair and skin, eyes with a hint of obliquity, high cheekbones—but, clearly, the Caucasoid strain still predominated, however great an admixture there had been. They looked curiously alike, as if they were brothers, and were dressed almost identically—sandals, kilt, and tunic of some faintly iridescent material, with a curious involved pattern reminiscent of Scottish tartans on the left breast. There must have been immense folk wanderings during the dark ages, thought Hart vaguely, fantastic interbreeding and a rise of composite types of man.

He said aloud, slowly, "You have a cure for my case?"

"Of cuwrse, Tov Hart. De uwld records did not survive, but de Crypt and traditions abuwt it did. Su alsuw did de case histories engraved on de metal. We are ready for du no. De meditechnics have bee-an perfected uwnly in de last fifty yaars, and of cuwrse we wanted to be shoor we waar right before waking any of de 'sleepers.' "

"I seem to be one of the last. "

"Indeed, Tov Hart, du are. Case duurs proved more difficult dan had bee-an antsipated. But we have a quick and aisy treating no."

"Well…" It might only have been the stimulant, or maybe the words, but Hart felt immensely braced. He was going to live! And in a superscientific world of friendly people, he should be able to make his way. His money would hardly have survived all the changes of history, but—well, there must be some provision made for the "sleepers. "

The world wasn't such a bad place. Even in the far future, it wasn't bad.

"I'm afraid you have the better of me," he said to the doctor. At his puzzled look, he added: "With regard to names, I mean."

"Oh. Pardon, Tov. We are all Rostoms here. I are Waldor Rostom Chang, here are Hallan Rostom Duwgal and Olwar Rostom Serwitch."

The three men bowed formally. Hart tried to return the gesture, but couldn't quite imitate the slight knee bend and the position of hands and head. "Philip Bronson Hart," he said. "But the middle name isn't the family name, the last is."

"As wit us," said the doctor, Waldor Chang. "Family name nos come last, group name in middle, gived name in front. But dey had not de groupings in time duurs, did dey?" He smiled. "Come du no, towarish, above ground. De clinic are quite nea-ar, and we will suwn have du well."

The landscape hadn't changed much, there were still the same hills and trees, the far shining thread of a river, and the wind cool and fresh on their faces. White clouds walked overhead through a sky of sunny blue, and a thrush was singing in a little thicket.

But there were few signs of man. The little village which had once been visible down beside the river had long since moldered into the earth, and the buildings of the Crypt center were gone, replaced with a single-roomed frame hut over the vault itself. Above the trees Hart could see a structure of stone and sun-flashing glass which must be the clinic, but otherwise there was no trace of civilization.

"This region must have become pretty well depopulated in the time since I went to 'sleep,' " he remarked.

"Why, nuw. It are raader heawily settled," replied Chang. "Dere must be-a, oh, all of a million people witin a radyus of a tousand kilometers."

"But—that's less than—How many people are there in the country?"

"About tirty million in Nort America. Or on all Eart, abuwt haaf a billion. Of cuwrse, dere must be-a a good ten million on de oder planets of de Solsystem, and perhaps anoder haaf billion in Centaari and elsewhaar—but little are knuwed abuwt dat."

"But—in my time, there were over two billion people on Earth!"

Chang gave Hart a quizzical look. "Su I have heared," he said slowly. "But times have cha-enged, Tov. It may taak du some while to reelayze huw much dey have cha-enged."

They entered the clinic. A blond young woman who was apparently a nurse stood waiting for them. She wore a crisp white skirt, and nothing else, and she was gorgeous.

She and Chang gave their patient an examination which for thoroughness surpassed anything in his time. He didn't pretend to understand the machines that buzzed and clicked and glowed around him, the serological tests and the curious symbolic notation. But he hadn't expected to—naturally, medicine would be far advanced, and he hadn't troubled himself to learn the details even of the past techniques.

"Very good," said the doctor at last. "Satisfactry reactions tuw virus Beta, good Delta coefficient—yes, we skood suwn have du well, Tov Hart."

"What's the cure?" he asked idly. "In my time they were beginning to think there'd never be a specific for cancer."

"Dere aren't, but dere are specifics for de difrent kinds. Artficial diseases have bee-an developed which attack uwnly de disorganized cancer cells. Frinstance, for cancer of de liver we inject a disease of de liver, but one which healthy tissue can resist. De sick cells are eaten away sluwly enough so dat normal tissue grows back to replace dem as dey disappear. It are more complex dan dat, of cuwrse, but dat give du de genral idea-a." He smiled. "A mont or su in hospital skood suffice for du, and we ran give du de oder tests in de mea-anwhile."

"The…other—?" It sounded faintly ominous.

"Classficating and su on. Worry du not abuwt it no."

"Come du," said the nurse. "I will taak du to ruwm duurs."

Hart followed her to an elevator. It went up with a pleasingly low acceleration, but his pulse went a little fast just the same. She was exciting!

"What's your name, please?" he asked. He put on the smile which had usually worked in the past. "We'll be seeing a lot of each other, I hope."

The girl frowned, then seemed to make an allowance for him. "Mara Sorens Haalwor."

"This is a pleasure…you're not married?" Hart edged closer.

"Mayried? Oh, de uwld style. Nuw, but—" She backed away. Her face bore an expression of distaste, barely covered by politeness. "Please du, Tov Hart—"

"Oh. Sorry." Hart moved from her, a little chapfallen. Oh, well.

He had a room to himself—he found out later that all hospital patients did—which delighted him. It was large and sunny, more like a living room than anything else. The furniture was curious, rather hard and low-legged—Asiatic influence during the Dark Ages?—but he could get used to that. There was a set of buttons on the wall which he learned how to use when he wanted to read. Central "libraries" had all the books and music in existence, no one owned volumes or records privately anymore. To read anything in existence, one simply called the nearest "library" and asked for it; automatically, the books—actually, record tapes—were flashed onto a screen, the speed being regulated by the reader. Likewise, any music was played directly into the citizen's own room. There were enough copies of all record tapes to take care of any reasonable number of simultaneous requests, and if a local "library" didn't happen to have a certain item, it would be relayed from one which did.

Curiously, there were no movie records, and no regular radio or television programs. Hart was too busy catching up with history and language at first to wonder why.

His synthetic disease and the physiological strain of growing new tissue left him a little weak. He stayed close to his room and only went out in the hospital gardens on orders of the staff. Nor did he have any visitors except the medical workers. After a while, he began to be lonely.

He was put through a series of psychological tests more exhaustive than the physical checkups. Here, too, he was baffled by the intricacy of a science evolved immensely beyond the older one which itself had puzzled him. Some of it was recognizable—word-association, elaborate questionnaires much of which seemed to be completely irrelevant, long informal talks with a psychiatrist. And the huge machines which studied him seemed remote descendants of the electroencephalographs he had known. But he went through completely bewildering processes—hypnotism, drugging, physical exercises.

"What's the idea?" he demanded, a little indignantly. "You seem to want to know me better than I know myself. Why?"

"Psychoclassificating," said the tester. "All citizens undergo it, with periodic rechecks."

That sounded ominous. *What kind of totalitarian state have I landed in?* "What do you do with the results?"

"Counsel, advise, straighten uwt conflicts. And, of cuwrse, arra-enge introductions." The psychiatrist looked troubled. He kept looking at the elaborate data sheets in his hand, as if he couldn't quite believe what he saw. "Suwcial integrating of individual depend on what psychotype he are, Tov Hart. No, if du will excoose me, must study dese results ⸺"

Hart went back to his reading. He was having trouble finding out what kind of world he lived in. There were plenty of histories, but they said little about the details of daily life, and they grew remarkably uneventful as they neared the present time. There were also plenty of sociological texts, but these were written in a technical language that left his head whirling—much of the material, indeed, was mathematical. He recognized the symbology as descended from the symbolic logic and calculus of statement of his own time, but since his acquaintance with those had been completely superficial, that didn't help much.

But manners, customs, family relations, all the million little details which make up life—rather than the abstractions of life, such as history and sociology—were nowhere explicitly described. After all, why should a people concern itself with its own mores? Such things are learned in childhood, are absorbed unconsciously as the individual grows through life. Had any twentieth century anthropologist ever described the habits and customs and beliefs of New York as carefully and objectively as he did those of the upper Congo? Hart found himself in the curious position of having learned more about the social organization of the natives of Procyon IV than those of Sol III.

He went back to history. That he could learn objectively, and with such a background feel his way around contemporary Earth until he learned the social ropes.

But it was not part of the matrix which had produced him. The Church of the Second Coming, the Asiatic invasion of America, the mechaniolatry of the Australian Reformers, the invasion of Luna by the weirdly changed descendants of Earth's old Martian colonists, the Scientific State, the Overthrow, the retirement of the Dissenters, the evolution of the family groups…Well, what was it? A story, a dream which had passed by while he slept, the thoughts and deeds and struggles of men unthought of in his own age.

Napoleon had been an almost living reality to Hart. He had read Emil Ludwig, he had listened to *Die Beiden Grenadiere*, he had heard all the tired old jokes about crazy men with hands in their coats, he had been subjected to the wistful reminiscences of old men who had grown up in that forever lost world which came between the Congress of Vienna and the murder at Sarajevo—he had, without being unusually interested in the Corsican, lived in a world where the little man had been a dominating influence even a century after his death. Napoleon was as much a part of his background, part of the complex of events which had, *inter alia,* produced Philip Hart, as the sun or the moon or the banging canyons of New York.

But could an imperial Roman transported to the twentieth century *feel* that a defeated dictator of a hundred years ago had existed? Would Napoleon be more than a dusty fiction? Would the Roman consider it logical that Frenchmen should be below the average European height, that the French law should be completely revised, that the Louisiana Territory should be American and Haiti independent, that the Nelson column should rise in London, that the whole existing world should *be,* all because of one little *condottiere?* The Roman might realize the fact, with the top of his mind, but it would not look reasonable to him. Because *he* would not be one of those inevitable results.

Hart gave up trying to make more than superficial sense out of all that had happened since the twentieth century, and simply learned the salient facts. He got a rough outline of the present political and economic status of man.

Earth—and the Lunar cave-cities—were under one rule. The colonists on Venus, Mars, and the outer planet satellites had evolved their own societies, often radically different from that of the mother world; man himself had had to become modified before he could settle the reaches of space, an evolution which had been carried out by the eugenics of the Scientific State with ruthless completeness. There was still regular interplanetary contact, but it was infrequent. The different branches of man had too little in common by now. Once in a great while there would be a ship from one of the colonies on the nearer stars, but distances were too great; even Alpha Centauri was fifty years away, and social evolution was diverging out there.

But could it be said that Earth was—ruled? Not in any traditional sense. The social organization was uniform, and a single council did what little administrative work the planet required. But there was nothing like a real government. History—wars, social changes, migrations, important new discoveries and concepts, events of any great significance—had been slowing for the last three centuries, ever since the family-group society had gained the ascendancy. For the last hundred years or so, nothing had really happened to mankind as a whole. *Nothing!*

It might be called a philosophical anarchy. Superficially, there was perfect freedom. The general law had almost no regulations on individual behavior. There was, apparently, universal content.

Decadent? No, not in the usual sense. These people were too magnificently healthy, too full of life and laughter. But they were certainly not progressive.

Hart tried to make friends with the nurses, and failed completely. They were all frigidly polite. The male staff members were cordial enough, but there was an inward reserve which increased with the days. Hart wondered what was the matter. His unhappiness waxed with his returning strength.

Chang came in at last. "I think du can leave clinic no," he said cheerily. "Du have best undergo periodic checkups for a yaar or twuw, but all medics are shoor du are guwing to recover completely." He handed the patient a set of clothes like his own, but without the group insigne.

Hart got out of the hospital robe and climbed into the garments. "And now what?" he asked. "I've tried to plump everybody on what I'm supposed to do, but they're all so evasive I haven't really learned a thing."

Chang looked uncomfortable. "We have place for du," he said. "It have taak unusually long time to analyze psychometric results duurs. Dey are su very different from ordinary."

"Well…" Hart waited impatiently. They'd been stalling him long enough.

Chang explained as well as he could. Psychometry and preventive psychiatry were really the basis of society. The fundamental personality of the individual was determined at an early age and he was "developed" throughout life in accordance with that—conditioned to society, but not in such a rigid fashion as to interfere with really basic urges. Vocations, recreations, social life were all planned in accordance with psychometric data.

"Planned?" exclaimed Hart. "How on earth can you plan everything?"

Well, not exactly planned either. Guided. An individual had such and such an I.Q., his main interests were so and so, his personality factors were as follows—it all went into a great electronic "file," in the powerful psychosymbology of the time. And any citizen had access to that file, with technicians to help him in its use. Thus you could find your likes, your associates, wherever they might happen to live, rather than leave it to chance encounters. It was scientifically predictable whether a friendship, a marriage, a business association, would be really of mutual profit. Naturally, everyone made use of the service, and adjusted his life accordingly.

"But—ye gods! You mean *anyone* can find out all about you at any time? What kind of privacy is that?"

Privacy? Chang was puzzled now. The word still remained in the language, but it had come to mean simply solitude. Why should you care whether or not anyone else knew just what you were? It didn't make you any better or worse, did it? You could find your kind in the world—those whose company was most pleasing to you. You could know yourself, and set your goals accordingly; you could change most really undesirable characteristics, with the help of psychiatry or even endocrinology and surgery.

The "groups," originally simply clans formed for mutual protection, were increasingly becoming endogamous associations of similar people. It was the group which was the real unit of society. Business, social life-all were integrated with the needs of the group, and of the world as a whole.

For instance, it was desirable that population be limited. Overpopulation was probably the most basic cause of misery in past history. Thus the group council regulated how many children there should be in a given family. It decided how long a marriage—family association was the term now—should last; a person might have children by three or four different people, if that seemed to be for the good of human evolution.

"But suppose your individual doesn't want to obey? I noticed nothing in the law compelling him to."

"Obedience are customary, and psychoconditioning in childhood delibraatly plants reflexes of conformity wit custom. No sane person *wants* to do oderwise."

"But—but—talk about tyrannies!"

"Why, nuw." Chang was taken aback at Hart's violent reaction. "All societies in past conditioned young. Waar du not told to obey law and worship flag—dey still had flag-worship in time duurs, did dey not?—and how it are wrong to kill and steal? But such conditioning waar superficial, it did not always affect basic impulses, so dat dere waar tragic conflicts between individual needs and desires and de laws and customs. Frustrating, crime, insanity? No wonder de dark ages came. Today we simply condition so thoroughly—and de inculcated desires do not conflict wit basic instincts—dat no one wants to break rules which fit him su perfectly."

"Everyone?"

"Well, dere are exceptions, ewen today. If dey cannot be adjusted, or will not be—since noting is legally compulsory—dey must eider be sent to space colonies or struggle though an unhappy life on Eart, witout friends or marriage, witout ewen a group. But numbers deys gruw less all de time."

"Hm-m-m...well..."

"Ewerybody have his place in society. Ewerybody happy wit life, nobody have conflicts wit felluw man—dat are goal nos. And we are close to it."

"It sounds nice," muttered Hart. He shrugged. "Not much I can do about it, anyway." His eyes swung back to the doctor's. "Now what about me?"

"Well..." Chang was obviously steeling himself. He smiled with a false geniality. "Well, we have seweral possibilities. Dere are a weader station in Greenland, or a small farm in Brazil, or—"

"Hold on!" Hart reached out and grabbed the doctor's tunic. His throat choked with a sudden rage and, under that, a gathering horrible dismay. "What do you think you're doing? Am I going to be stuck somewhere out of the sight of man and forgotten?"

"I—"

"Come on, " snarled Hart. The fist he lifted was shaking. "Spit out the truth, or you'll be spitting out your teeth"

Chang disengaged himself and held the smaller man with an effortless strength. His face was twisted. "I—I are sorry, Tov Hart," he said, very quietly. "It waar raally a cruel kindness to wake du. But I are afraid dat—du are right. "

Hart sagged, the anger draining from him and leaving only a vast hollow void. Dimly, he heard Chang's voice: "Du have nuw place in world. Du belong to nuw famly or group. Du have no traits wort perpetuating—indeed, we would not want children wit cancer tendency duurs. Psychotests show du as unstable, egocentric, unable to adjust to cityless world, to close familial relationship, to—anything. No one would want to associate wit completely unintegrated, hopelessly neurotic—foreigner.

"Best du find a quiet place where du can serve—out of sight."

Hart rebelled. Bitterly, desperately, he tried to escape.

There must be something. He had been the admired leader of his little clique. Broad knowledge, sardonic humor, a way with women, ready money, all had combined to impress and delight. Surely the world had not changed so much!

No compulsion was put on him. He went where and when he chose; he spent a good three months prowling this new Earth, riding the free public transport and using an unlimited government credit card to buy necessities. And he found that the world had indeed changed.

The tall, healthy, serene folk were polite to him, and no more. But they had nothing in common with him. He belonged to no group and, for eugenic and other reasons, could not be adopted into one, and all social functions were within such alliances. He did not follow their jokes, his manners were gauche compared to the formality now accepted; his learning and background were from a period too remote to interest any but scholars. There was no underworld, no demimonde. Morality was somewhat changed, but it was never violated.

For his part, Hart began to be bored. It was not entirely a subjective attitude rising out of resentment at inferiority. These people were slow-speaking, formal, calm; they lacked the tension and the acrid mirth of the twentieth century. They were not weaklings in any sense, but they were—innocent.

There was no entertainment except what groups provided for themselves—singing, dancing, amateur showmanship, a great deal of hobbycraft. The reason for the absence of professional entertainment was basically the same as that for the lack of large-scale industry. The group society was deliberately throwing the individual and the family on their own resources. Now that there were no external challenges of war, poverty, famine, disease, now that history had slowed almost to a standstill, man must return to a degree of primitive self-sufficiency and independence if he was not to become the glorified termite inhabiting a purposeless machine city.

Hart saw the reasoning, but it seemed puritanical to him. And he could not sympathize with a people who deliberately submitted to it. A man who plowed his own fields when science had advanced to the point where everyone could eat out of cans was a fool. To be sure, the man was conditioned to like it, and certainly the food was better than the sterilized pap of twentieth century canneries, but even so...

Hart tried to leave Earth altogether. But he lacked the physique and the technical skill which would justify a spaceship in hauling him. And from what he read of the spatial colonies, he was likely to find a still more alien society out there.

In the end, desperately, he took the weather-station job.

For a while that was better. He was alone, away from the subtler and crueler isolation of strangers' company, and he was not entirely useless. The vast windswept snowfields, the far mysterious glimmer of northern lights wavering over enormous mountains, the snug hut which had access to the books and music of all history, were all somehow comforting. He barely spoke to the pilot of the occasional supply rocket, and refused to be relieved.

He couldn't go back to a world which had no use for him. He could stay here and dream of what had been, out here in the wind-whining loneliness, alone in the dark with the ghosts of his own time whispering to him...

They muttered in the dark corners, they wavered in the auroras and the pale cold sunlight, ghosts of the past, calling to him over a gulf of time. Time began to be meaningless, and space. In this unreal landscape of ice and snow and dark, wind blowing up between the frosty stars, it was hard to say where the solid world left off and the dreams began.

Hart realized vaguely that he was slipping. But it didn't matter. Certainly he couldn't return to the politeness of the world, more cold and remote than the flying haggard moon, he couldn't leave his old friends here...Why, his relief would sweep the dust out of the cabin, dust which had once been human, dust which had once lain in his arms or laughed at his humor...Now the wind laughed, hooting around the house and rattling the shutters in appreciation of Hart's jokes.

Waldor Rostom Chang looked, with horror creeping behind his eyes, at the thing which mumbled on the floor of the airjet. Hart was almost· completely catatonic now.

"If we had knuwed!" said the doctor. "If we had uwnly knuwed!"

"How skood we?" asked the pilot, a weather-service technician. "De job waar just 'made' work, to give de poor felluw someting to do. Reports his waar filed in de wastebasket. And he had bee-an su unsuwciable dat de supply pilots simply left stuff his witout ewen seeing him. It waar uwnly when he had quit reporting for sewral days dat we got alarmed."

"I newwer drea-amed he would go crazy, ewen when he had bee-an dere two yaars witout relief," said Chang. "After all, a modem man could stand it easily. And de twentyet century mind waar too strange to mind nos, completely unintegrated as it waar, for de psychotechnics to spot de instability in him."

"And nuw what will we do wit him?"

"We cannot help de poor jorp. Psychiatry nos are preventive, mental disease su long forgetted dat we have no real curative technique—teories, records of old cure metods, yes, but nuw experenced mental doctors." Chang shrugged. "All we can do is put Hart back in de Crypt till such day as psychiatry have evolved cure for su extreme a case as his. And dere are su little need for psychocuring today dat I fear it will be a long, long time befuwere Hart can be outtaken again."

The pilot grinned mirthlessly. "By den," he said, "society may be su alien dat Hart, once cured, will relapse into insanity too deep for dem to handle—so dey will have to put him back in de Crypt…" He spied his goal and sent the airjet slanting downward.

MacCannon

MacCannon was a Fireball man. That rambling rocketeer
Could lift off into orbit on a single keg of beer.
The whisky that he much preferred was made not for the meek
Unless you were a Scot, it would ground you for a week.

MacCannon was a macho man, a brawling, balling Celt.
For EVA he needed just a helmet and his pelt
His lady friends expressed their love in moans and groans and pants
And made remarks among themselves concerning elephants.

Its clouds sulfuric acid, high above the CO_2(½ down)
So hot and thick down underneath that lead itself would stew,
The atmosphere of Venus is as poisonously ripe
As the air became around us when MacCannon lit his pipe.

His ship once had an argument while passing thru the void,
Alone, about the right of way, with one big asteroid.
Adrift, he used the time to make a large discovery,
The art of shooting craps to win in zero gravity.

The devil knocked upon the lock and said, "You're doomed to die.
Come down with me." MacCannon spat some whisy in his eye.
The sizzle and the reaction sent the devil with a yell
On a hyperbolic orbit that would take him back to hell.

MacCannon then decided his diabled boat should boost.
He ate himself a mighty meal of beans and set himself to roost
Upon a mass ejector tube far sternward in his craft,
And the ship went leaping forward from the thunders booming aft.

THE MARTIAN CROWN JEWELS

The signal was picked up when the ship was still a quarter million miles away, and recorded voices summoned the technicians. There was no haste, for the ZX28749, otherwise called the *Jane Brackney*, was right on schedule; but landing an unmanned spaceship is always a delicate operation. Men and machines prepared to receive her as she came down, but the control crew had the first order of business.

Yamagata, Steinmann, and Ramanowitz were in the GCA tower, with Hollyday standing by for an emergency. If the circuits *should* fail—they never had, but a thousand tons of cargo and nuclear-powered vessel, crashing into the port, could empty Phobos of human life. So Hollyday watched over a set of spare assemblies, ready to plug in whatever might be required.

Yamagata's thin fingers danced over the radar dials. His eyes were intent on the screen. "Got her," he said. Steinmann made a distance reading and Ramanowitz took the velocity off the Dopplerscope. A brief session with a computer showed the figures to be almost as predicted.

"Might as well relax," said Yamagata, taking out a cigarette. "She won't be in control range for a while yet."

His eyes roved over the crowded room and out its window. From the tower he had a view of the spaceport: unimpressive, most of its shops and sheds and living quarters being underground. The smooth concrete field was chopped off by the curvature of the tiny satellite. It always faced Mars, and the station was on the far side, but he could remember how the planet hung enormous over the opposite hemisphere, soft ruddy disc blurred with thin air, hazy greenish-brown mottlings of heath and farmland. Though Phobos was clothed in vacuum, you couldn't see the hard stars of space: the sun and the floodlamps were too bright.

There was a knock on the door. Hollyday went over, almost drifting in the ghostly gravity, and opened it. "Nobody allowed in here during a landing," he said. Hollyday was a stocky blond man with a pleasant, open countenance, and his tone was less peremptory than his words.

"Police." The newcomer, muscular, round-faced and earnest, was in plain clothes, tunic and pajama pants, which was expected; everyone in the tiny settlement knew Inspector Gregg. But he was packing a gun, which was not usual, and look harried.

Yamagata peered out again and saw the port's four constables down on the field in official spacesuits, watching the ground crew. They carried weapons. "What's the matter?" he asked.

"Nothing...I hope." Gregg came in and tried to smile. "But the *Jane* has a very unusual cargo this trip."

"Hm?" Ramanowitz's eyes lit up in his broad plump visage. "Why weren't we told?"

"That was deliberate. Secrecy. The Martian crown jewels are aboard." Gregg fumbled a cigarette from his tunic.

Hollyday and Steinmann nodded at each other. Yamagata whistled. "On a robot ship?" he asked.

"Uh-huh. A robot ship is the one form of transportation from which they could not be stolen. There were three attempts made when they went to Earth on a regular liner, and I hate to think how many while they were at the British Museum. One guard lost his life. Now my boys are going to remove them before anyone else touches that ship and scoot 'em right down to Sabaeus."

"How much are they worth?" wondered Ramanowitz.

"Oh...they could be fenced on Earth for maybe half a billion UN dollars," said Gregg. "But the thief would do better to make the Martians pay to get them back...no, Earth would have to, I suppose, since it's our responsibility." He blew nervous clouds. "The jewels were secretly put on the *Jane*, last thing before she left on her regular run. I wasn't even told till a special messenger on this week's liner gave me the word. Not a chance for any thief to know they're here, till they're safely back on Mars. And that'll be *safe!*"

Ramanowitz shuddered. All the planets knew what guarded the vaults at Sabaeus.

"Some people did know, all along," said Yamagata thoughtfully. "I mean the loading crew back at Earth."

"Uh-huh, there is that." Gregg smiled. "Several of them have quit since then, the messenger said, but of course, there's always a big turnover among spacejacks—they're a restless bunch." His gaze drifted across Steinmann and Hollyday, both of whom had last worked at Earth Station and come to Mars a few ships back. The liners went on a hyperbolic path and arrived in a couple of weeks; the robot ships followed the more leisurely and economical Hohmann A orbit and needed 258 days. A man who knew what ship was carrying the jewels could leave Earth, get to Mars well ahead of the cargo, and snap up a job here—Phobos was always shorthanded.

"Don't look at me!" said Steinmann, laughing. "Chuck and I knew about this—of course—but we were under security restrictions. Haven't told a soul."

"Yeah. I'd have known it if you had," nodded Gregg. "Gossip travels fast here. Don't resent this, please, but I'm here to see that none of you boys leaves this tower till the jewels are aboard our own boat."

"Oh, well. It'll mean overtime pay."

"If I want to get rich fast, I'll stick to prospecting," added Hollyday.

"When are you going to quit running around with that Geiger in your free time?" asked Yamagata. "Phobos is nothing but iron and granite."

"I have my own ideas about that," said Hollyday stoutly.

"Hell, everybody needs a hobby on this God-forsaken clod," declared Ramanowitz. "I might try for those sparklers myself, just for the excitement—" He stopped abruptly, aware of Gregg's eyes.

"All right," snapped Yamagata. "Here we go. Inspector, please stand back out of the way, and for your life's sake don't interrupt us."

The *Jane* was drifting in, her velocity on the carefully precalculated orbit almost identical with that of Phobos. Almost, but not quite—there had been the inevitable small disturbing factors, which the remote-controlled jets had to compensate, and then there was the business of landing her. The team got a fix and were frantically busy.

In free fall, the *Jane* approached within a thousand miles of Phobos—a spheroid 500 feet in radius, big and massive, but lost against the incredible bulk of the satellite. And yet Phobos is an insignificant airless pill, negligible even beside its seventh-rate planet. Astronomical magnitudes are simply and literally incomprehensible.

When the ship was close enough, the radio directed her gyros to rotate her, very, very gently, until her pickup antenna was pointing directly at the field. Then her jets were cut in, a mere whisper of thrust. She was nearly above the spaceport, her path tangential to the moon's curvature. After a moment Yamagata slapped the keys hard, and the rockets blasted furiously, a visible red streak up in the sky. He cut them again, checked his data, and gave a milder blast.

"Okay," he grunted. "Let's bring her in."

Her velocity relative to Phobos's orbit and rotation was now zero, and she was falling. Yamagata slewed her around till the jets were pointing vertically down. Then he sat back and mopped his face while Ramanowitz took over; the job was too nerve-stretching for one man to perform in its entirety. Ramanowitz sweated the awkward mass to within a few yards of the cradle. Steinmann finished the task, easing her into the berth like an egg into a cup. He cut the jets and there was silence.

"Whew! Chuck, how about a drink?" Yamagata held out unsteady fingers and regarded them with an impersonal stare.

Hollyday smiled and fetched a bottle. It went happily around. Gregg declined. His eyes were locked to the field, where a technician was checking for radioactivity. The verdict was clean, and he saw his constables come soaring over the concrete, to surround the great ship with guns. One of them went up, opened the manhatch, and slipped inside.

It seemed a very long while before he emerged. Then he came running. Gregg cursed and thumbed the tower's radio board. "Hey, there! Ybarra! What's the matter?"

The helmet set shuddered a reply: "Señor…Señor Inspector…the crown jewels are gone."

* * *

The Martian Crown Jewels

Sabaeus is, of course, a purely human name for the old city nestled in the Martian tropics, at the juncture of the "canals", Phison and Euphrates. Terrestrial mouths simply cannot form the syllables of High Chlannach, though rough approximations are possible. Nor did humans ever build a town exclusively of towers broader at the top than the base, or inhabit one for twenty thousand years. If they had, though, they would have encouraged an eager tourist influx; but Martians prefer more dignified ways of making a dollar, even if their parsimonious fame has long replaced that of Scotchmen. The result is that though interplanetary trade is brisk and Phobos a treaty port, a human is still a rare sight in Sabaeus.

Hurrying down the avenues between the stone mushrooms, Gregg felt conspicuous. He was glad the airsuit muffled him. Not that the grave Martians stared; they varkled, which is worse.

The Street of Those Who Prepare Nourishment in Ovens is a quiet one, given over to handicrafters, philosophers, and residential apartments. You won't see a courtship dance or a parade of the Lesser Halberdiers on it: nothing more exciting than a continuous four-day argument on the relativistic nature of the null class or an occasional gunfight. The latter are due to the planet's most renowned private detective, who nests here.

Gregg always found it eerie to be on Mars, under the cold deep-blue sky and the shrunken sun, among noises muffled by the thin oxygen-deficient air. But for Syaloch he had a good deal of affection, and when he had gone up the ladder and shaken the rattle outside the second-floor apartment and had been admitted, it was like escaping from nightmare.

"Ah, Krech!" The investigator laid down the stringed instrument on which he had been playing and towered gauntly over his visitor. "An unexbectet bleassure to see hyou. Come in, my tear chab, to come in." He was proud of his English—but simple misspellings will not convey the whistling, clicking Martian accent. Gregg had long ago fallen into the habit of translating it into a human pronunciation as he listened.

The Inspector felt a cautious way into the high, narrow room. The glowsnakes which illuminated it after dark were coiled asleep on the stone floor, in a litter of papers, specimens, and weapons; rusty sand covered the sills of the Gothic windows. Syaloch was not neat except in his own person. In one corner was a small chemical laboratory. The rest of the walls were taken up with shelves, the criminological literature of three planets—Martian books, Terrestrial micros, Venusian talking stones. At one place, patriotically, the glyphs representing the reigning Nestmother had been punched out with bullets. An Earthling could not sit on the trapezelike native furniture, but Syaloch had courteously provided chairs and tubs as well; his clientèle was also triplanetary. Gregg found a scarred Duncan Phyfe and lowered himself, breathing heavily into his oxygen tubes.

"I take it you are here on official but confidential business." Syaloch got out a big-bowled pipe. Martians have happily adopted tobacco, though in their atmosphere it must include potassium permanganate. Gregg was thankful he didn't have to breathe the blue fog.

He started. "How the hell do you know that?"

"Elementary, my dear fellow. Your manner is most agitated, and I know nothing but a crisis in your profession would cause that in a good stolid bachelor. Yet you come to me rather than the Homeostatic Corps…so it must be a delicate affair."

Gregg laughed wryly. He himself could not read any Martian's expression—what corresponds to a smile or a snarl on a totally nonhuman face? But this overgrown stork—

No. To compare the species of different planets is merely to betray the limitations of language. Syaloch was a seven-foot biped of vaguely storklike appearance. But the lean, crested, red-beaked head at the end of the sinuous neck was too large, the yellow eyes too deep; the white feathers were more like a penguin's than a flying bird's, save at the blue-plumed tail; instead of wings there were skinny red arms ending in four-fingered hands. And the overall posture was too erect for a bird.

Gregg jerked back to awareness. God in Heaven! The city lay gray and quiet; the sun was slipping westward over the farmlands of Sinus Sabaeus and the desert of the Aeria; he could just make out the rumble of a treadmill cart passing beneath the windows—and he sat here with a story which could blow the Solar System apart!

His hands, gloved against the chill, twisted together. "Yes, it's confidential, all right. If you can solve this case, you can just about name your own fee." The gleam in Syaloch's eyes made him regret that, but he stumbled on: "One thing, though. Just how do you feel about us Earthlings?"

"I have no prejudices. It is the brain that counts, not whether it is covered by feathers or hair or bony plates."

"No, I realize that. But some Martians resent us. We do disrupt an old way of life—we can't help it, if we're to trade with you—"

"*K'teh*. The trade is on the whole beneficial. Your fuel and machinery—and tobacco, yesss—for our kantz and snull. Also, we were getting too…stale. And of course space travel has added a whole new dimension to criminology. Yes, I favor Earth."

"Then you'll help us? And keep quiet about something which could provoke your planetary federation into kicking us off Phobos?"

The third eyelids closed, making the long-beaked face a mask. "I make no promises yet, Gregg."

"Well…damn it, all right, I'll have to take the chance." The policeman swallowed hard. "You know about your crown jewels, of course."

"They were lent to Earth for exhibit and scientific study."

"After years of negotiation. There's no more priceless relic on all Mars—and you were an old civilization when we were hunting mammoths. All right. They've been stolen."

Syaloch opened his eyes, but his only other movement was to nod.

"They were put on a robot ship at Earth Station. They were gone when that ship reached Phobos. We've damn near ripped the boat apart trying find them—we did take the other cargo to pieces, bit by bit—and they aren't there!"

Syaloch rekindled his pipe, an elaborate flint-and-steel process on a world where matches won't burn. Only when it was drawing well did he suggest: "Is it possible the ship was boarded en route?"

"No. It isn't possible. Every spacecraft in the System is registered, and its whereabouts are known at any time. Furthermore, imagine trying to find a speck in hundreds of millions of cubic miles, and match velocities with it...no vessel ever built could carry that much fuel. And mind you, it was never announced that the jewels were going back this way. Only the UN police and the Earth Station crew *could* know till the ship had actually left—by which time it'd be too late to catch her."

"Most interesting." Syaloch puffed hard.

"If word of this gets out," said Gregg miserably, "you can guess the results. I suppose we'd still have a few friends left in your Parliament—"

"In the House of Actives, yesss...a few. Not in the House of Philosophers, which is of course the upper chamber."

"It could mean a twenty-year hiatus in Earth-Mars traffic—maybe a permanent breaking off of relations. Damn it, Syaloch, you've *got* to find those stones!"

"Hm-m-m. I pray your pardon. This requires thought." The Martian picked up his crooked instrument and plucked a few tentative chords. Gregg sighed and attempted to relax. He knew the Chlannach temperament; he'd have to listen to an hour of minor-key caterwauling.

The colorless sunset was past, night had fallen with the unnerving Martian swiftness, and the glowsnakes were emitting blue radiance when Syaloch put down the demifiddle.

"I fear I shall have to visit Phobos in person," he said. "There are too many unknowns for analysis, and it is never well to theorize before all the data have been gathered." A bony hand clapped Gregg's shoulder. "Come, come, old chap. I am really most grateful to you. Life was becoming infernally dull. Now, as my famous Terrestrial predecessor would say, the game's afoot...and a very big game indeed!"

A Martian in an Earthlike atmosphere is not much hampered, needing only an hour in a compression chamber and a filter on his beak to eliminate excess oxygen and moisture. Syaloch walked freely about the port clad in filter, pipe, and *tirstokr* cap, grumbling to himself at the heat and humidity. He noticed that all the humans but Gregg were reserved, almost fearful, as they watched him—they were sitting on a secret which could unleash red murder.

He donned a spacesuit and went out to inspect the *Jane Brackney*. The vessel had been shunted aside to make room for later arrivals, and stood by a raw crag at the edge of the field, glimmering in the hard spatial sunlight. Gregg and Yamagata were with him.

"I say, you *have* been thorough," remarked the detective. "The outer skin is quite stripped off."

The spheroid resembled an egg which had tangled with a waffle iron; an intersecting grid of girders and braces above a thin aluminum hide. The jets, hatches, and radio mast were the only breaks in the checkerboard pattern, whose depth was about a foot and whose squares were a yard across at the "equator."

Yamagata laughed in a strained fashion. "No, the cops fluoroscoped every inch of her, but that's the way these cargo ships always look. They never land on Earth, you know, or any place where there's air, so streamlining would be unnecessary. And since nobody is aboard in transit, we don't have to worry about insulation or airtightness. Perishables are stowed in sealed compartments."

"I see. Now where were the crown jewels kept?"

"They were supposed to be in a cupboard near the gyros," said Gregg. "They were in a locked box, about six inches high, six inches wide, and a foot long." He shook his head, finding it hard to believe that so small a box could contain so much potential death.

"Ah…but *were* they placed there?"

"I radioed Earth and got a full account," said Gregg. "The ship was loaded as usual at the satellite station, then shoved a quarter mile away till it was time for her to leave—to get her out of the way, you understand. She was still in the same free-fall orbit, attached by a light cable— perfectly standard practice. At the last minute, without anyone being told beforehand, the crown jewels were brought up from Earth and stashed aboard."

"By a special policeman, I presume?"

"No. Only licensed technicians are allowed to board a ship in orbit, unless there's a life-and-death emergency. One of the regular station crew—fellow named Carter—was told where to put them. He was watched by the cops as he pulled himself along the cable and in through the manhatch." Gregg pointed to a small door near the radio mast. "He came out, closed it, and returned on the cable. The police immediately searched him and his spacesuit, just in case, and he positively did not have the jewels. There was no reason to suspect him of anything—good steady worker—though I'll admit he's disappeared since then. The *Jane* blasted a few minutes late and her jets were watched till they cut off and she went into free fall. And that's the last anyone saw of her till she got here—without the jewels."

"And right on orbit," added Yamagata. "If by some freak she had been boarded, it would have thrown her off enough for us to notice as she came in. Transference of momentum between her and the other ship."

"I see." Behind his faceplate, Syaloch's beak cut a sharp black curve across heaven. "Now then, Gregg, were the jewels actually in the box when it was delivered?"

"At Earth Station, you mean? Oh, yes. There are four UN Chief Inspectors involved, and HQ says they're absolutely above suspicion. When I sent back word of the theft, they insisted on having their own quarters an so on searched, and went under scop voluntarily."

"And your own constables on Phobos?"

"Same thing," said the policeman grimly. "I've slapped on an embargo—nobody but me has left this settlement since the loss was discovered. I've had every room and tunnel and warehouse searched." He tried to scratch his head, a frustrating attempt when one is in a spacesuit. "I can't maintain those restrictions much longer. Ships are coming in and the consignees want their freight."

"*Hnachla*. That puts us under a time limit, then." Syaloch nodded to himself. "Do you know, this is a fascinating variation of the old locked room problem. A robot ship in transit is a locked room in the most classic sense." He drifted off into a reverie.

Gregg stared bleakly across the savage horizon, naked rock tumbling away under his feet, and then back over the field. Odd how tricky your vision became in airlessness, even when you had bright lights. That fellow crossing the field there, under the full glare of sun and floodlamps, was merely a stipple of shadow and luminance…what the devil was he doing, tying a shoe of all things? No, he was walking quite normally—

"I'd like to put everyone on Phobos under scop," said Gregg with a violent note, "but the law won't allow it unless the suspect volunteers—and only my own men have volunteered."

"Quite rightly, my dear fellow," said Syaloch. "One should at least have the privilege of privacy in his own skull. And it would make the investigation unbearably crude."

"I don't give a fertilizing damn how crude it is," snapped Gregg. "I just want that box with the crown jewels safe inside."

"Tut-tut! Impatience has been the ruin of many a promising young police officer, as I seem to recall my spiritual ancestor of Earth pointing out to a Scotland Yard man who—hm—may even have been a physical ancestor of yours, Gregg. It seems we must try another approach. Are there any people on Phobos who might have known the jewels were aboard this ship?"

"Yes. Two men only. I've pretty well established that they never broke security and told anyone else till the secret was out."

"And who are they?"

"Technicians, Hollyday and Steinmann. They were working at Earth Station when the *Jane* was loaded. They quit soon after—not at the same time—and came here by liner and got jobs. You can bet that *their* quarters have been searched!"

"Perhaps," murmured Syaloch, "it would be worthwhile to interview the gentlemen in question."

Steinmann, a thin redhead, wore truculence like a mantle; Hollyday merely looked worried. It was no evidence of guilt—everyone had been rubbed raw of late. They sat in the police office, with Gregg behind the desk and Syaloch leaning against the wall, smoking and regarding them with unreadable yellow eyes.

"Damn it, I've told this over and over till I'm sick of it!" Steinmann knotted his fists and gave the Martian a bloodshot stare. "I never touched the things and I don't know who did. Hasn't any man a right to change jobs?"

"Please," said the detective mildly. "The better you help the sooner we can finish this work. I take it you were acquainted with the man who actually put the box aboard the ship?"

"Sure. Everybody knew John Carter. Everybody knows everybody else on a satellite station." The Earthman stuck out his jaw. "That's why none of us'll take scop. We won't blab out all our thoughts to guys we see fifty times a day. We'd go nuts!"

"I never made such a request," said Syaloch.

"Carter was quite a good friend of mine," volunteered Hollyday.

"Uh-huh," grunted Gregg. "And he quit too, about the same time you fellows did, and went Earthside and hasn't been seen since. HQ told me you and he were thick. What'd you talk about?"

"The usual." Hollyday shrugged. "Wine, women, and song. I haven't heard from him since I left Earth."

"Who says Carter stole the box?" demanded Steinmann. "He just got tired of living in space and quit his job. He *couldn't* have stolen the jewels—he was searched, remember?"

"Could he have hidden it somewhere for a friend to get at this end?" inquired Syaloch.

"Hidden it? Where? Those ships don't have secret compartments." Steinmann spoke wearily. "And he was only aboard the *Jane* a few minutes, just long enough to put the box where he was supposed to." His eyes smoldered at Gregg. "Let's face it: the only people anywhere along the line who ever had a chance to lift it were our own dear cops."

The Inspector reddened and half rose. "Look here, you—"

"We've got *your* word that you're innocent," growled Steinmann. "Why should it be any better than mine?"

Syaloch waved both men back. "If you please. Brawls are unphilosophic." His beak opened and clattered, the Martian equivalent of a smile. "Has either of you, perhaps, a theory? I am open to all ideas."

There was a stillness. Then Hollyday mumbled: "Yes. I have one."

Syaloch hooded his eyes and puffed quietly, waiting.

Hollyday's grin was shaky. "Only if I'm right, you'll never see those jewels again."

Gregg sputtered.

"I've been around the Solar System a lot," said Hollyday. "It gets lonesome out in space. You never know how big and lonesome it is till you've been there, all by yourself. And I've done just that—I'm an amateur uranium prospector, not a lucky one so far. I can't believe we know everything about the universe, or that there's only vacuum between the planets."

"Are you talking about the cobblies?" snorted Gregg.

"Go ahead and call it superstition. But if you're in space long enough...well, somehow, you *know*. There are beings out there—gas beings, radiation beings, whatever you want to imagine, there's *something* living in space."

"And what use would a box of jewels be to a cobbly?"

Hollyday spread his hands. "How can I tell? Maybe we bother them, scooting through their own dark kingdom with our little rockets. Stealing the crown jewels would be a good way to disrupt the Mars trade, wouldn't it?"

Only Syaloch's pipe broke the inward-pressing silence. But its burbling seemed quite irreverent.

"Well—" Gregg fumbled helplessly with a meteoric paperweight. "Well, Mr. Syaloch, do you want to ask any more questions?"

"Only one." The third lids rolled back, and coldness looked out at Steinmann. "If you please, my good man, what is your hobby?"

"Huh? Chess. I play chess. What's it to you?" Steinmann lowered his head and glared sullenly.

"Nothing else?"

"What else is there?"

Syaloch glanced at the Inspector, who nodded confirmation, and then replied gently: "I see. Thank you. Perhaps we can have a game sometime. I have some small skill of my own. That is all for now, gentlemen."

They left, moving like things of dream through the low gravity.

"Well?" Gregg's eyes pleaded with Syaloch. "What next?"

"Very little. I think…yesss, while I am here I should like to watch the technicians at work. In my profession, one needs a broad knowledge of all occupations."

Gregg sighed.

Ramanowitz showed the guest around. The *Kim Brackney* was in and being unloaded. They threaded through a hive of spacesuited men.

"The cops are going to have to raise that embargo soon," said Ramanowitz. "Either that or admit why they've clamped it on. Our warehouses are busting."

"It would be politic to do so," nodded Syaloch. "Ah, tell me…is this equipment standard for all stations?"

"Oh, you mean what the boys are wearing and carrying around? Sure. Same issue everywhere."

"May I inspect it more closely?"

"Hm?" *Lord, deliver me from visiting firemen!* thought Ramanowitz. He waved a mechanic over to him. "Mr. Syaloch would like you to explain your outfit," he said with ponderous sarcasm.

"Sure. Regular spacesuit here, reinforced at the seams." The gauntleted hands moved about, pointing. "Heating coils powered from this capacitance battery. Ten-hour air supply in the tanks. These buckles, you snap your tools into them, so they won't drift around in free fall. This little can at my belt holds paint that I spray out through this nozzle."

"Why must spaceships be painted?" asked Syaloch. "There is nothing to corrode the metal."

"Well, sir, we just call it paint. It's really gunk, to seal any leaks in the hull till we can install a new plate, or to mark any other kind of damage. Meteor punctures and so on." The mechanic pressed a trigger and a thin, almost invisible stream jetted out, solidifying as it hit the ground.

"But it cannot readily be seen, can it?" objected the Martian. "I, at least, find it difficult to see clearly in airlessness."

"That's right, Light doesn't diffuse, so…well, anyhow, the stuff is radioactive—not enough to be dangerous, just enough so that the repair crew can spot the place with a Geiger counter."

"I understand. What is the half-life?"

"Oh, I'm not sure. Six months, maybe? It's supposed to remain detectable for a year."

"Thank you." Syaloch stalked off. Ramanowitz had to jump to keep up with those long legs.

"Do you think Carter may have hid the box in his paint can?" suggested the human.

"No, hardly. The can is too small, and I assume he was searched thoroughly." Syaloch stopped and bowed. "You have been very kind and patient. Mr. Ramanowitz. I am finished now, and can find the Inspector myself."

"What for?"

"To tell him he can lift the embargo, of course." Syaloch made a harsh sibilance. "And then I must get the next boat to Mars. If I hurry, I can attend the concert in Sabaeus tonight." His voice grew dreamy. "They will be premiering Hanyech's *Variations on a Theme by Mendelssohn,* transcribed to the Royal Chlannach scale. It should be most unusual."

It was three days afterward that the letter came. Syaloch excused himself and kept an illustrious client squatting while he read it. Then he nodded to the other Martian. "You will be interested to know, sir, that the Estimable Diadems have arrived at Phobos and are being returned at this moment."

The client, a Cabinet Minister from the House of Actives, blinked. "Pardon, Freehatched Syaloch, but what have you to do with that?"

"Oh…I am a friend of the Featherless police chief. He thought I might like to know."

"*Hraa.* Were you not on Phobos recently?"

"A minor case." The detective folded the letter carefully, sprinkled it with salt, and ate it. Martians are fond of paper, especially official Earth stationery with high rag content. "Now, sir, you were saying—?"

The parliamentarian responded absently. He would not dream of violating privacy—no, never—but if he had X-ray vision he would have read:

Dear Syaloch,

You were absolutely right. Your locked room problem is solved. We've got the jewels back, everything is in fine shape, and the same boat which brings you this letter will deliver them to the vaults. It's too bad the public can never know the facts—two planets ought to be grateful to you—but I'll supply that much thanks all by myself, and insist that any bill you care to send be paid in full. Even if the Assembly had to make a special appropriation, which I'm afraid it will.

"I admit your idea of lifting the embargo at once looked pretty wild to me, but it worked. I had our boys out, of course, scouring Phobos with Geigers, but Hollyday found the box before we did. Which saved us a lot of trouble, to be sure. I arrested him as he came back into the settlement, and he had the box among his ore samples. He has confessed, and you were right all along the line.

"What was that thing you quoted at me, the saying of that Earthman you admire so much? 'When you have eliminated the impossible, whatever remains, however improbable, must be true.' Something like that. It certainly applies to this case.

"As you decided, the box must have been taken to the ship at Earth Station and left there—no other possibility existed. Carter figured it out in half a minute when he was ordered to take the thing out and put it aboard the *Jane*. He went inside, all right, but still had the box when he emerged. In that uncertain light nobody saw him put it 'down' between four girders right next to the hatch. Or as you remarked, if the jewels are not *in* the ship, and yet not *away* from the ship, they must be *on* the ship. Gravitation would hold them in place. When the *Jane* blasted off, acceleration pressure slid the box back, but of course the waffle-iron pattern kept it from being lost; it fetched up against the after rib and stayed there. All the way to Mars! But the ship's gravity held it securely enough even in free fall, since both were on the same orbit.

"Hollyday says that Carter told him all about it. Carter couldn't go to Mars himself without being suspected and watched every minute once the jewels were discovered missing. He needed a confederate. Hollyday went to Phobos and took up prospecting as a cover for the search he'd later be making for the jewels.

"As you showed me, when the ship was within a thousand miles of this dock, Phobos gravity would be stronger than her own. Every spacejack knows that the robot ships don't start decelerating till they're quite close; that they are then almost straight above the surface; and that the side with the radio mast and manhatch—the side on which Carter had placed the box—is rotated around to face the station. The centrifugal force of rotation threw the box away from the ship, and was in a direction toward Phobos rather than away from it. Carter knew that this rotation is slow and easy, so the force wasn't enough to accelerate the box to escape velocity and lose it in space. It would have to fall down toward the satellite. Phobos Station being on the side opposite Mars, there was no danger that the loot would keep going till it hit the planet.

"So the crown jewels tumbled onto Phobos, just as you deduced. Of course Carter had given the box a quick radioactive spray as he laid it in place, and Hollyday used that to track it down among all those rocks and crevices. In point of fact, its path curved clear around this moon, so it landed about five miles from the station.

"Steinmann has been after me to know why you quizzed him about his hobby. You forgot to tell me that, but I figured it out for myself and told him. He or Hollyday had to be involved, since nobody else knew about the cargo, and the guilty person had to have some excuse to go out and look for the box. Chess playing doesn't furnish that kind of alibi. Am I right? At least, my deduction proves I've been studying the same canon you go by. Incidentally, Steinmann asks if you'd care to take him on the next time he has planet leave.

"Hollyday knows where Carter is hiding, and we've radioed the information back to Earth. Trouble is, we can't prosecute either of them without admitting the facts. Oh, well, there are such things as blacklists.

"Will have to close this now to make the boat. I'll be seeing you soon—not professionally, I hope!"

Admiring regards,
Inspector Gregg

But as it happened, the Cabinet minister did not possess X-ray eyes. He dismissed unprofitable speculation and outlined his problem. Somebody, somewhere in Sabaeus, was farniking the krats, and there was an alarming zaksnautry among the hyukus. It sounded to Syaloch like an interesting case.

Then Death Will Come

To tell you of the ending of the day.
And you will see her tallness with surprise,
And looking into gentled, shadowed eyes,
Protest: it's not that late, you have to stay
Awake a minute more, just one, to play
With yonder ball. But nonetheless you rise
So they won't hear her say, :"A baby cries
But you are big. Put all your toys away."

She lets you a shabby bear in bed,
Though fairly doubting that you two can go
Through dream-shared living rooms or wingless flight.
She tucks the blankets close beneath your head
And smooths your hair, and kisses you, and so
Goes out, turns off the light. "Good night. Sleep tight."

PROPHECY

Ambassadors are rarely, if ever, met by the head of the nation to which they come. They go to him. But this case was an exception to every established precedent, and the President of the United States, Philip Brackney, felt no loss in dignity as he came to the spaceship.

It was, he thought, really a lovely machine, with all the beauty of perfect functionalism—and something more than that, a touch of the haunting indefinable splendor of a clipper ship or a Greek temple. The five-hundred-foot pylon towered over the green Iowan plain, a blinding metallic dazzle in the sunlight, a spearhead poised at infinity. Its gleaming height dwarfed the buildings on the farm on which it had descended.

As the presidential car and its attendants swept up the dirt road—it was in extremely poor condition after the thousands of sightseers who had used it in the past month—the chief of Brackney's secret service guards said nervously: "For the last time, sir, are you sure this is wise?"

"Of course," he answered, a little irritable with excitement. "Any other procedure would be madness!"

"But…if they have bad intentions—"

"Listen, Mr. Dickson, if they meant to do anything hostile, they'd do it. That one ship has more power than all this planet's combined military forces." The awe of it swept over Brackney, he breathed almost religiously: "A spaceship from the stars—and *men* aboard—"

The Secretary of Defense spoke slowly: "You know, every night for the past month I've gone down on my knees—and am not ashamed to admit it—to thank God that ship landed here. Not in some potential enemy's camp, but here—with us."

"It wouldn't have made any difference," said the President. "The visitors have been all over Earth in their lifeboats, seeing for themselves, taking almost all the printed matter they could get back. They probably have a better overall picture of Earth than we do."

He said, as the car swung up the driveway: "This is by rights not a matter for us at all. The United Nations alone should handle it, and they must take over soon. But—it was never set up to deal with ambassadors. I have to make the first official approach, for lack of anyone else."

The farmer stood nervously waiting. Since that rainy night a month gone when the ship landed in his pasture, he had lived in such a glare of publicity as to become a bit blasé about it. But after all—the President—

"I think they're waiting, sir," he mumbled.

"Very well. Come along, gentlemen." Brackney led the way.

A ramp had been lowered from the entrance lock, a hundred feet above ground. The party stepped on it and it rose smoothly up, with an uncanny, almost living flexibility.

For a moment, Brackney's throat was dry. A spaceship from the stars—*Don't be a fool!* he reproached himself sharply. *The Taithans have emphasized their friendliness a hundred times. They aren't conquistadores, they are representatives of a culture a thousand years ahead of ours—a culture that must have outgrown war, or the race would destroy itself with the weapons it has.*

The crew of the ship stood waiting at the lock. There were not many of them, a score or so, and nearly all of these were scientists. The ship, they had said, practically ran itself. Nor were they at all spectacular. They looked like very ordinary human beings of a curiously mixed race—dark skin, Mongoloid eyes of a light shade, thin Caucasoid noses, woolly hair. They wore robes of a shimmering blue material, and had no outward insignia of rank.

"Greetings, gentlemen," said one, in accented but ready-flowing English, "Permit me to introduce myself—Gor Haml, the one of us who learned your language. The others, of course, have learned other tongues of your planet."

"I am Philip Brackney—" Introductions went around, acknowledged by the Taithans with grave bows. Thereafter Gor Haml led the way along a bare metal corridor and into a small—well, living room, thought Brackney, who was no sailor. It was furnished with chairs and tables of a comfortable, massive style, and there were some uncannily three-dimensional pictures on the walls. As the party sat down, they felt the chairs mold themselves to the body contours.

"I take it that the visit of such high dignitaries may be considered official?" asked Gor Haml.

"Certainly," replied Brackney. "But—may I ask if your own visit is in the nature of a formal embassy? Your refusal to admit anyone to your ship, or to hold other than the most academic discourse with those you met, until your invitation to me yesterday—that suggests you are on an official mission yourselves."

"Yes and no," answered the Taithan. "We are travelers, exploring this section of the Galaxy, but we are representatives of the Taithan people too, empowered to decide policy with regard to any world we visit."

"But why did you hold yourselves so aloof?" The Secretary of State looked worried. "All Earth was ready to welcome you. Nearly all churches held thanksgiving services that you had come. Every government has besieged you with official congratulations and invitations."

Gor Haml seemed a little unhappy. "We have met great courtesy everywhere," he said, "but it is a rule of the exploration service not to perform any policy-making act until the new planet is—classified."

"I should hardly think a month would suffice for that," ventured Brackney.

Gor Haml rubbed a hand over his weary eyes. "It is grueling work," he admitted, "but it can be done, due to a combination of the highly evolved Taithan psychotechnology and certain phenomena of evolution and history. We have a very exact technique for dealing with human races."

"*Human* races!"

"Yes! It seems strange, but the fact is that in three hundred years of Galactic exploration the Taithans have never found an Earth-like world which was not inhabited by a human race. Oh, there are differences, of course, and even races which look and think exactly alike could hardly be so similar as to make interbreeding possible—but by and large, the similarities exceed the differences."

"I should think the random element—"

"There is none, not if you agree that like causes produce like effects. All planets are produced by the same basic process, and so every Sol-type star *must* have a system like this one. And every Earth-type planet *must* produce the same general forms of life—because two processes beginning with the same initial conditions must run the same course."

"But how can the initial conditions be so much alike?"

"They are, in at least half the cases. There are deviations of greater or less degree, but over half the G0-type stars explored so far have been found to have planets similar to Taitha inhabited by an intelligent race similar to our own—and Earth is such a one." Gor Haml's eyes rested speculatively on the President: "We were astonished at this ourselves, when we first began exploring, but the fact was there. Now we know the reasons and see that such similarity is inevitable in this universe, but I cannot explain the philosophy to you. A thousand years from now, Earthlings should be able to understand it—but not at your present stage of development."

"I begin to see how you were able to learn about us so quickly," said Brackney. "You knew just about what to expect and what to look for."

"That is part of it, to be sure. Also, we have the benefits of a psychological science evolved to a point that might seem miraculous to you. It includes all human knowledge, which is after all only a function of the human organism, and integrates it according to principles your scientists and philosophers have not yet imagined. You have the germ of it in your experimental and analytical psychology, in semantics and symbolic logic, in physical and biological sciences, yes, and in some of your philosophical speculations. But you have not begun to exploit the potentialities of your own nervous systems. Taithans have no more inherent intelligence than Earthlings, but they know how to use it; just as a caveman was inherently capable of using, say, tensor analysis, but the knowledge did not exist for him. Thus we can perform such apparent feats of legerdemain as understanding and classifying a planet in a month's hard work."

"I see," nodded Brackney. "I can even guess your main line of approach—simply reading tons of written material of every kind, at some fantastic speed, and analyzing the information, both direct and indirect, it contains."

"That is one important line, at least," smiled the Taithan. "I might add that history books are the leading source of the knowledge we are after."

There was a moment of silence. The Earthlings sat looking at the strangers, seeking some sign of foreignness or of godlike power or anything, rather than the score of weary-looking, ordinary men before them. Brackney, with a politician's sensitivity to moods, could not, escape the nagging conviction that the Taithans were depressed. *They look at us as if they felt sorry for us!*

He said, more to break that awkward stillness than for any other reason: "I suppose this is a rather meaningless question, but how far ahead of our civilization is yours? I mean…well, of course we're contemporaries, but what time equivalent separates us—?" He stopped, acutely aware of his own lack of terminology.

"The question is not meaningless," replied Gor Haml. "We are about fifteen hundred years ahead of you—in actual time. Our recorded and archeological history is longer than yours by that many years. Indeed, that is the only significant difference between our races."

"That's quite encouraging," smiled the Secretary of State. "I was beginning to fear you were the sort of supermen the fiction writers love—completely alien to us. But if you help us get started, we should be able to catch up with you in a generation or two."

"That…yes, that is why I have been so thankful," exclaimed Brackney. "Here on Earth we die of disease and war, we impoverish ourselves and go in fear and ignorance, we are bound to this one little planet—worse yet, to our own archaic superstitions and hates. Taithan science means things like spaceships and limitless energy sources and disease-free men, yes, and that's what all the world has been so jubilant about. But to me, it is the enlightenment and the freedom from our old heritage of cave and beast which is the great gift—" He stopped, a little embarrassed at his own loquacity. He heard his own blood beating in his arteries, and his face was hot.

Gor Haml smiled. It was a very weary smile, with no humor in it, and his lined gaunt visage was not brightened by it. He said quietly:

"The histories of Earth and Taitha run as parallel as the histories of nearly all human races known to us. The only important difference is that ours is some fifteen hundred years older—but that difference is enormous. In the Galaxy so far, we have found human races in every stage from pure savagery to our own level, but in nearly every case—and your own among them—the only variation seems to be when they got started. Once under way, they follow the same patterns."

"But—hold on!" exploded Brackney. "You don't mean to say that on every planet there was an ancient Egypt and Rome, or a United States—?"

"Oh, no." Gor Haml's smile twitched with the faintest hint of amusement. "Indeed, the superficial differences—language, dress, religion, laws and customs, almost everything which an untrained observer would notice—are usually radical. I am, however, speaking in a deeper sense. There is a parallelism in mental and, well, spiritual evolution which transcends outward appearances."

At their evident puzzlement, he went on: "I suppose some of you, at least, are familiar with such philosophers of history as Spengler and Toynbee. They have the beginnings of the truth, in their analysis of history into distinct cultures. And be it noted, those cultures follow a cycle of genesis in barbaric folk-wanderings, growth and expression of innate tendencies in the people, breakdown, time of troubles, stiffening into a 'universal state' statism, and ultimate extinction. The cycle has a time scale which varies by no more than ten or twenty years from the norm for each distinct stage.

"There is no reason to invoke a mysterious 'Destiny' to explain this fact. The casual law is sufficient. Under similar conditions, human beings react similarly. For instance, the nature myths of primitive peoples who never heard of each other are so alike that your own anthropologists have been able to classify them according to type, and to enunciate the unspoken beliefs underlying magic rites everywhere. In like manner, what is more natural than that outlying barbarians should invade a decadent empire and, coming under its influence, generate a new civilization—or that the miseries of a time of troubles should be forcibly ended by the imposition of a universal state? I am, of course, much oversimplifying, but I believe you can see in a rough way why Earth-type planets must evolve human races and why these races must have similar cycles of history."

"But history isn't all cyclic," objected Brackney.

"No, no, of course not. It is, indeed, an irreversible process only one of whose components, so to speak, is cyclic. For instance, the progress in technology is almost a direct line. Likewise, when a planet has advanced far enough, it is able to break out of the cycle of wars and other social evils—as Taitha has done. But the time of that achievement is governed by casual laws, not by wishful thinking or futile attempts at interference."

"*Wait a minute*—" A sudden fear, dim and inchoate, all the more ghastly for that, crawled coldly along Brackney's spine. "Wait! Aren't you assuming that conditions remain the same? For instance, your arrival on Earth is a factor which, I suppose, has no parallel on Taitha—"

"That is true." Suddenly Gar Haml's eyes were bright—with tears? "But when we depart, our brief visit will have had no long-range significance. Men tend to thrust unpleasant facts out of their minds, and the existence of planets immensely beyond Earth will prove unpleasant to most humans."

"Not…oh, no!" Brackney started out of his chair. "But you…you're going to stay! You're going to guide us, help us become truly civilized—"

"No, Mr. Brackney. We have classified Earth, and it is well below the stage of development at which prolonged contact with superior culture would be safe for either side. We leave immediately."

He stood up, and laid a hand on the President's shoulder. His face was bleak and stern and sorrowful. "Your assumption that we, whose intentions are admittedly benevolent, will give you guidance, is based on my own statement that Earthlings are intellectually capable of learning all that Taithans know. But man is not entirely, or even primarily, an intellectual animal. He has to *feel* his knowledge, if he is not to make hideous misuse of it. A wise man is not necessarily a good man, and intellect turns as readily to destructive as to useful ends. Do not forget the example of Japan, which your own people forced from feudalism to industrialism without changing the inherent structure of society—thus loosing a fanatical menace on the world."

"But…you *would* change our society—wouldn't you?"

"Never. It would leave Earthlings pensioners, with no sense of cultural continuity—worse off than primitive aborigines forced into modern factories."

The grave, implacable voice seemed to come from enormous distances, gulfs of space and time and evolution. "Man must win his own salvation. He must learn, not only with his brain but with bitter and horrible and unforgettable experience, branded so deep as to be almost an instinct, that he is part of a whole, and that misuse of wisdom recoils a thousand fold.

"I am afraid that there is nothing we can do for you until you have had your atomic wars. We will be back in a thousand years. Good-by, gentlemen."

Sea Burial

Wise shall you wander, at one with the world,
Ever the all of you eagerly errant:
Spirit in sunlight and spindrift and sea-surge,
Flesh in the fleetness of fish and of fowl,
Back to the Bearer your bone and your blood-salt.
Beloved:
The sky take you.
The sea take you.
And we will remember you in the wind.

Einstein's Distress

$\Delta p \Delta x$,
Werner K. Heisenberg
Claimed that our knowledge of
Atoms has gaps.
Einstein, distressed by such
Discontinuity,
Said that the Almighty
Does not shoot craps.

Kings Who Die

Luckily, Diaz was facing the other way when the missile exploded. It was too far off to blind him permanently, but the retinal burns would have taken a week or more to heal. He saw the glare reflected in his view lenses. As a ground soldier he would have hit the rock and tried to claw himself a hole. But there was no ground here, no up or down, concealment or shelter, on a fragment of spaceship orbiting through the darkness beyond Mars. Diaz went loose in his armor. Countdown: brow, jaw, neck, shoulders, back, chest, belly... No blast came, to slam him against the end of his lifeline and break any bones whose muscles were not relaxed. So it had not been a shaped charge shell, firing a cone of atomic-powered concussion through space. Or if it was, he had not been caught in the danger zone. As for radiation, he needn't worry much about that. Whatever particles and gamma photons he got at this distance should not be too big a dose for the anti-X in his body to handle the effects.

He drew a breath which was a good deal shakier than the Academy satorist would have approved of. ("If your nerves twitch, cadet-san, then you know yourself alive and they need not twitch. Correct?" To hell with that, except as a technique.) Slowly, he hauled himself in until his boots made magnetic contact and he stood, so to speak, upon his raft. Then he turned about for a look.

"*Nombre de Dios,*" he murmured, a hollow noise in the helmet. Forgotten habit came back, with a moment's recollection of his mother's face. He crossed himself.

Against blackness and a million wintry stars, a gas cloud expanded. It glowed in many soft hues, the center still bright, edges fading into vacuum. Shaped explosions did not behave like that, thought the calculator part of Diaz; this had been a standard fireball type. But the cloud was nonspherical. Hence a ship had been hit, a big ship, but whose?

Most of him stood in wonder. A few years ago he'd spent a furlough at Antarctic Lodge. He and some girl had taken a snowcat out to watch the aurora, thinking it would make a romantic background. But when they saw the sky, they forgot about each other for a long time. There was only the aurora.

The same awesome silence was here, as that incandescence which had been a ship and her crew swelled and vanished into space.

The calculator in his head proceeded with its business. Of those American vessels near the *Argonne* when first contact was made with the enemy, only the *Washington* was sufficiently massive to go out in a blast of yonder size and shape. If that was the case Captain Martin Diaz of the United States Astromilitary Corps was a dead man. The other ships of the line were too distant, traveling on vectors too unlike his own, for their scout boats to come anywhere close. On the other hand, it might well have been a Unasian battlewagon. Diaz had small information on the dispositions of the enemy fleet. He'd had his brain full just directing the torp launchers under his immediate command. If that had indeed been a hostile dreadnaught that got clobbered, surely none but the *Washington* could have delivered the blow, and its boats would be near—

There!

For half a second Diaz was too stiffened by the sight to react. The boat ran black across waning clouds, accelerating on a streak of its own fire. The wings and sharp shape that were needed in atmosphere made him think of a marlin he had once hooked off Florida, blue lightning under the sun…Then a flare was in his hand, he squeezed the igniter and radiance blossomed.

Just an attention-getting device, he thought, and laughed unevenly as he and Bernie Sternthal had done, acting out the standard irreverences of high school students toward the psych course. But Bernie had left his bones on Ganymede, three years ago, and in this hour Diaz's throat was constricted and his nostrils full of his own stench. He skyhooked the flare and hunkered in its harsh illumination by his radio transmitter. Clumsy in their gauntlets, his fingers adjusted controls, set the revolving beams on SOS. If he had been noticed, and if it was physically possible to make the velocity changes required, a boat would come for him. The Corps looked after its own.

Presently the flare guttered out. The pyre cloud faded to nothing. The raft deck was between Diaz and the shrunken sun. But the stars that crowded on every side gave ample soft light. He allowed his gullet, which felt like sandpaper, a suck from his one water flask. Otherwise he had several air bottles, an oxygen reclaim unit, and a ridiculously large box of Q rations. His raft was a section of inner plating, torn off when the *Argonne* encountered the ball storm. She was only a pursuit cruiser, unarmored against such weapons. At thirty miles per second, relative, the little steel spheres tossed in her path by some Unasian gun had not left much but junk and corpses. Diaz had found no other survivors. He'd lashed what he could salvage onto this raft, including a shaped torp charge that rocketed him clear of the ruins. This far spaceward he didn't need screen fields against solar particle radiation. So he had had a small hope of rescue. Maybe bigger than small, now.

Unless an enemy craft spotted him first. His scalp crawled with that thought. His right arm, where the thing he might use in the event of capture lay buried, began to itch. But no, he told himself, don't be sillier than regulations require. That scoutboat was positively American. The probability of a hostile vessel being in detection range of his flare and radio—or able to change vectors fast enough—or giving a damn about him in any event—approached so close to zero as made no difference.

"Wish I'd found our bottle in the wreckage," he said aloud. He was talking to Carl Bailey, who'd helped him smuggle the Scotch aboard at Shepard Field when the fleet was alerted for departure. The steel balls had chewed Carl to pieces, some of which Diaz had seen. "It gripes me not to empty that bottle. On behalf of us both, I mean. Maybe," his voice wandered on, "a million years hence, it'll drift into another planetary system and owl-eyed critters will pick it up in boneless fingers, eh, Carl, and put it in a museum." He realized what he was doing and snapped his mouth shut. But his mind continued. *The trouble is, those critters won't know about Carl Bailey, who collected antique jazz tapes, and played a rough game of poker, and had a D.S.M. and a gimpy leg from rescuing three boys whose patroller crashed on Venus, and went on the town with Martin Diaz one evening not so* long ago when—*What did happen that evening, anyhow?*

There was a joint down in the Mexican section of San Diego which Diaz remembered was fun. So they caught a giro outside the Hotel Kennedy, where the spacemen were staying—they could afford swank, and felt they owed it to the Corps—and where they had bought their girls dinner. Diaz punched the cantina's name. The autopilot searched its directory and swung the cab onto the Embarcadero-Balboa skyrail.

Sharon sighed and snuggled into the curve of his arm. "How beautiful," she said. "How nice of you to show me this." He felt she meant a little more than polite banality. The view through the bubble really was great tonight. The city winked and blazed, a god's hoard of jewels, from horizon to horizon. Only in one direction was there anything but light: westward, where the ocean lay aglow. A nearly full moon stood high in the sky. He pointed out a tiny glitter on its dark edge.

"Vladimir Base."

"Ugh," said Sharon. "Unasians." She stiffened a trifle.

"Oh, they're decent fellows," Bailey said from the rear seat.

"How do you know?" asked his own date, Naomi, a serious-looking girl and quick on the uptake.

"I've visited them a time or two," he shrugged.

"What?" Sharon exclaimed. "When we're at *war?*"

"Why not?" Diaz said. "The ambassador of United Asia gave a party for our President just yesterday. I watched on the newscreen. Big social event."

"But that's different," Sharon protested. "The war goes on in space, not on Earth, and—"

"We don't blow up each other's Lunar bases, either," Bailey said. "Too close to home. So once in a while we have occasion to, uh, parley is the official word. Actually, the last time I went over—couple years ago now—it was to return a crater-bug we'd borrowed and bring some alga-blight antibiotic they needed. They poured me full of excellent vodka."

"I'm surprised you admit this so openly," said Naomi.

"No secret, my dear," purred Diaz in his best grandee manner, twirling an imaginary mustache. "The newscreens simply don't mention it. Wouldn't be popular, I suppose."

"Oh, people wouldn't care, seeing it was the Corps," Sharon said.

"That's right," Naomi smiled. "The Corps can do no wrong."

"Why, thankee kindly." Diaz grinned at Sharon, chucked her under the chin and kissed her. She held back an instant, having met him only this afternoon. But of course she knew what a date with a Corpsman usually meant, and he knew she knew, and she knew he knew she knew, so before long she relaxed and enjoyed it.

The giro stopped those proceedings by descending to the street and rolling three blocks to the cantina. They entered a low, noisy room hung with bullfight posters and dense with smoke. Diaz threw a glance around and wrinkled his nose. *"Sanamabiche!"* he muttered. "The tourists have discovered it."

"Uh-huh," Bailey answered in the same disappointed *sotto voce*. "Loud tunics, lard faces, 3V, and a juke wall. But let's have a couple drinks, at least, seeing we're here."

"That's the trouble with being in space two or three years at a time," Diaz said. "You lose track. Well…" They found a booth.

The waiter recognized him, even after so long a lapse, and called the proprietor. The old man bowed nearly to the floor and begged they accept tequila from his private stock. *"No, no, Señor Capitán, conserva el dinero, por favor."* The girls were delighted—picturesqueness seemed harder to come by each time Diaz made Earthfall—and the evening was off to a good start in spite of everything.

But then someone paid the juke. The wall came awake with a scrawny blonde fourteen-year-old, the latest fashion in sex queens, wearing a grass skirt and three times life size.

> *Bingle-jingle-jungle-bang-POW!*
> *Bingle-jingle-jangle-bang-UGH!*
> *Uh'm uh redhot Congo gal an' Uh'm lookin' fuh a pal*
> *Tuh share muh bingle-jingle-bangle-jungle-ugh-YOW!*

"What did you say?" Sharon called through the saxophones.

"Never mind," Diaz grunted. "They wouldn't've included it in your school Spanish anyway."

"Those things make me almost wish World War Four would start," Naomi said bitterly.

Bailey's mouth tightened. "Don't talk like that," he said. "Wasn't Number Three a close enough call for the race? Without even accomplishing its aims, for either side. I've seen—Any war is too big."

Lest they become serious, Diaz said thoughtfully above the racket: "You know, it should be possible to do something about those Kallikak walls. Like, maybe, an oscillator. They've got oscillators these days which'll even goof a solid-state apparatus at close range."

"The FCC wouldn't allow that," Bailey said. "Especially since it'd interfere with local 3V reception."

"That's bad? Besides, you could miniaturize the oscillator so it'd be hard to find. Make it small enough to carry in your pocket. Or in your body, if you could locate a doctor who'd, uh, perform an illegal operation. I've seen uplousing units no bigger than—"

"You could strew 'em around town," Bailey said, getting interested. "Hide 'em in obscure corners and—"

Ugga-wugga-wugga, hugga-hugga me, do!

"I *wish* it would stop," Naomi said. "I came here to get to know you, Carl, not that thing."

Bailey sat straight. One hand, lying on the table, shaped a fist. "Why not?" he said.

"Eh?" Diaz asked.

Bailey rose. "Excuse me a minute." He bowed to the girls and made his way through the dancers to the wall control. There he switched the record off.

Silence fell like a meteor. For a moment, voices were stilled, too. Then a large tourist came barreling off his bar stool and yelled, "Hey, wha'd'you think you're—"

"I'll refund your money, sir," Bailey said mildly. "But the noise bothers the lady I'm with."

"Huh? Hey, who d'yuh think yuh are, you—"

The proprietor came from around the bar. "If the lady weeshes it off," he declared, "off it stays."

"What kinda discrimination is this?" roared the tourist. Several other people growled with him.

Diaz prepared to go help, in case things got rough. But his companion pulled up the sleeve of his mufti tunic. The ID bracelet gleamed into view. "First Lieutenant Carl H. Bailey, United States Astromilitary Corps, at your service," he said; and a circular wave of quietness expanded around him. "Please forgive my action. I'll gladly stand the house a round if—"

But that wasn't necessary. The tourist fell all over himself apologizing and begged to buy the drinks. Someone else bought them next, and someone after him. Nobody ventured near the booth, where the spacemen obviously wanted privacy. But from time to time, when Diaz glanced out, he got many smiles and a few shy waves. It was almost embarrassing.

"I was afraid for a minute we'd have a fight," he said.

"N-no," Bailey answered. "I've watched our prestige develop exponentially, being Stateside while my leg healed. I doubt if there's an American alive who'd lift a finger against a Corpsman these days. But I admit I was afraid of a scene. That wouldn't've done the name of the Corps any good. As things worked out, though…"

"We came off too bloody well," Diaz finished. "Now there's not even any pseudolife in this place. Let's haul mass. We can catch the transpolar shuttle to Paris if we hurry."

But at that moment the proprietor's friends and relations, who also remembered him, began to arrive. They must have been phoned the great news. Pablo was there, Manuel, Carmen with her castanets, Juan with his guitar, Tio Rico waving a bottle in each enormous fist; and they welcomed Diaz back with embraces, and soon there was song and dancing, and the fiesta ended in the rear courtyard watching the moon set before dawn, and everything was like the old days, for Señor Capitán Diaz's sake. That had been a hell of a good furlough.

Another jet splashed fire across the Milky Way. Closer this time, and obviously reducing relative speed. Diaz croaked out a cheer. He had spent weary hours waiting. The hugeness and aloneness had eaten farther into his defenses than he wished to realize. He had begun to understand why some people were disturbed to see the stars on a clear mountain night. (Where wind went soughing through Jeffrey pines whose bark smelled like vanilla if you laid your head close, and a river flowed cold and loud over stones—oh, Christ, how beautiful Earth was!) He shoved such matters aside and reactivated his transmitter.

The streak winked out and the stars crowded back into his eyes. But that was all right, it meant the boat had decelerated as much as necessary, and soon a scooter would be homing on his beam, and water and food and sleep, and a new ship and eventually certain letters to write. That would be the worst part—but not for months or years yet, not till one side or the other conceded the present phase of the war. Diaz found himself wishing most for a cigarette.

He hadn't seen the boat's hull this time, of course; no rosy cloud had existed to silhouette its blackness. Nor did he see the scooter until it was almost upon him. That jet was very thin, since it need only drive a few hundred pounds of mass on which two spacesuited men sat. They were little more than a highlight and a shadow. Diaz's pulse filled the silence. "Hallo!" he called in his helmet mike. "Hallo, yonder!"

They didn't reply. The scooter matched velocities a few yards off. One man tossed a line with a luminous bulb at the end. Diaz caught it and made fast. The line was drawn taut. Scooter and raft bumped together and began gently rotating.

Diaz recognized those helmets.

He snatched for a sidearm he didn't have. A Unasian sprang to one side, lifeline unreeling. His companion stayed mounted, a chucker gun cradled in his arms. The sun rose blindingly over the raft edge.

There was nothing to be done. Yet. Diaz fought down a physical nausea of defeat, "raised" his hands and let them hang free. The other man came behind him and deftly wired his wrists together. Both Unasians spent a few minutes inspecting the raft. The man with the gun tuned in on the American band. "You make very clever salvage, sir," he said.

"Thank you," Diaz whispered.

"Come, please." He was lashed to the carrier rack. Weight tugged at him as the scooter accelerated.

They took an hour or more to rendezvous. Diaz had time to adjust his emotions. The first horror passed into numbness; then he identified a sneaking relief, that he would get a reasonably comfortable vacation from war until the next prisoner exchange; and then he remembered the new doctrine, which applied to all commissioned officers on whom there had been time to operate.

I may never get the chance, he thought frantically. *They told me not to waste myself on anything less than a cruiser; my chromosomes and several million dollars spent in training me make me that valuable to the country, at least. I may go straight to Pallas, or wherever their handiest prison base is, in a lousy scoutboat or cargo ship.*

But I may get a chance to strike a blow that'll hurt. Have I got the guts? I hope so. No, I don't even know if I hope it. This is a cold place to die.

The feeling passed. Emotional control, drilled into him at the Academy and practiced at every refresher course, took over. It was essentially psychosomatic, a matter of using conditioned reflexes to bring muscles and nerves and glands back toward normal. If the fear symptoms, tension, tachycardia, sweat, decreased salivation, and the rest, were alleviated, then fear itself was. Far down under the surface, a four-year-old named Martin woke from nightmare and screamed for his mother, who did not come; but Diaz grew able to ignore him.

The boat became visible, black across star clouds. No, not a boat. A small ship…abnormally large jets and light guns, a modified Panyushkin…what had the enemy been up to in his asteroid shipyards? Some kind of courier vessel, maybe. Recognition signals must be flashing back and forth. The scooter passed smoothly through a lock that closed again behind it. Air was pumped in, and Diaz went blind as frost condensed on his helmet. Several men assisted him out of the armor. They hadn't quite finished when an alarm rang, engines droned, and weight came back. The ship was starting off at about half a gee.

Short bodies in green uniforms surrounded Diaz. Their immaculate appearance reminded him of his own unshaven filthiness, how much he ached, and how sandy his brain felt. "Well," he mumbled, "where's your interrogation officer?"

"You go more high, Captain," answered a man with colonel's insignia. "Forgive us we do not attend your needs at once, but he says very important."

Diaz bowed to the courtesy, remembering what had been planted in his arm and feeling rather a bastard. Though it looked as if he wouldn't have occasion to use the thing. Dazed by relief and weariness, he let himself be escorted along corridors and tubes until he stood before a door marked with great black Cyrillic warnings and guarded by two soldiers. Which was almost unheard of aboard a spaceship, he thought joltingly.

There was a teleye above the door. Diaz barely glanced at it. Whoever sat within the cabin must be staring through it, at him. He tried to straighten his shoulders. "Martin Diaz," he croaked, "Captain, USAC, serial number—"

Someone yelled from the loudspeaker beside the pickup. Diaz half understood. He whirled about. His will gathered itself and surged. He began to think the impulses that would destroy the ship. A guard tackled him. A rifle butt came down on his head. And that was that.

They told him forty-eight hours passed while he was in sickbay. "I wouldn't know," he said dully. "Nor care." But he was again in good physical shape. Only a bandage sheathing his lower right arm, beneath the insigneless uniform given him, revealed that surgeons had been at work. His mind was sharply aware of its environment—muscle play beneath his skin, pastel bulkheads and cold fluorescence, faint machine-quiver underfoot, gusts from ventilator grilles, odors of foreign cooking, and always the men, with alien faces and carefully expressionless voices, who had caught him.

At least he suffered no abuse. They might have been justified in resenting his attempt to kill them. Some would call it treacherous. But they gave him the treatment due an officer and, except for supplying his needs, left him alone in his tiny bunk cubicle. Which was worse, in some respects, than punishment. Diaz was actually glad when he was at last summoned for an interview.

They brought him to the guarded door and gestured him through. It closed behind him.

For a moment Diaz noticed only the suite itself. Even a fleet commander didn't get such space and comfort. The ship had long ceased accelerating, but spin provided a reasonable weight. The suite was constructed within a rotatable shell, so that the same deck was "down" as when the jets were in operation. Diaz stood on a Persian carpet, looking past low-legged furniture to a pair of arched doorways. One revealed a bedroom, lined with microspools—ye gods, there must be ten thousand volumes! The other showed part of an office, a desk, and a great enigmatic control panel and—

The man seated beneath the Monet reproduction got up and made a slight bow. He was tall for a Unasian, with a lean mobile face whose eyes were startlingly blue against a skin as white as a Swedish girl's. His undress uniform was neat but carelessly worn. No rank insignia were visible, for a gray hood, almost a coif, covered his head and fell over the shoulders.

"Good day, Captain Diaz," he said, speaking English with little accent. "Permit me to introduce myself: General Leo Ilyitch Rostock, Cosmonautical Service of the People of United Asia."

Diaz went through the rituals automatically. Most of him was preoccupied with how quiet this place was, how vastly quiet…But the layout was serene. Rostock must be fantastically important if his comfort rated this much mass. Diaz's gaze flickered to the other man's waist. Rostock bore a sidearm. More to the point, though, one loud holler would doubtless be picked up by the teleye mike and bring in the guards from outside.

Diaz tried to relax. *If they haven't kicked my teeth in so far, they don't plan to. I'm going to live.* But he couldn't believe that. Not here, in the presence of this hooded man. Still more so, in this drawing room. Its existence beyond Mars was too eerie. "No, sir, I have no complaints," he heard himself saying. "You run a good ship. My compliments."

"Thank you." Rostock had a charming, almost boyish smile. "Although this is not my ship, actually. Colonel Sumoro commands the *Ho Chi Minh*. I shall convey your appreciation to him."

"You may not be called the captain," Diaz said bluntly, "but the vessel is obviously your instrument."

Rostock shrugged. "Will you not sit down?" he invited, and resumed his own place on the couch. Diaz took a chair across the table from him, feeling knobby and awkward. Rostock pushed a box forward. "Cigarette?"

"Thank you." Diaz struck and inhaled hungrily.

"I hope your arm does not bother you."

Diaz's belly muscles tightened. "No. It's all right."

"The surgeons left the metal ulna bone in place, as well as its nervous and muscular connections. Complete replacement would have required more hospital equipment than a spaceship can readily carry. We did not want to cripple you by removing the bone. After all, we were only interested in the cartridge."

Diaz gathered courage and snapped: "The more I see of you, General, the sorrier I am that it didn't work. You're big game."

Rostock chuckled. "Perhaps. I wonder, though, if you are as sorry as you would like to feel you are. You would have died too, you realize."

"Uh-huh."

"Do you know what the weapon embedded in you was?"

"Yes. *We* tell our people such things. A charge of isotopic explosive, with a trigger activated by a particular series of motor nerve pulses. Equivalent to about ten tons of TNT." Diaz gripped the chair arms, leaned forward and said harshly: "I'm not blabbing anything you don't now know. I daresay you consider it a violation of the customs of war. Not me! I gave no parole—"

"Certainly, certainly." Rostock waved a deprecating hand. "We hold…what is your idiom?…no hard feelings. The device was ingenious. We have already dispatched a warning to our Central, whence the word can go out through the fleet, so your effort, the entire project, has gone for nothing. But it was a rather a gallant attempt."

He leaned back, crossed one long leg over the other, and regarded the American candidly. "Of course, as you implied, we would have proceeded somewhat differently," he said. "Our men would not have known what they carried, and the explosion would have been triggered posthypnotically, by some given class of situations, rather than consciously. In that way, there would be less chance of betrayal."

"How did you know, anyway?" Diaz sighed.

Rostock gave him an impish grin. "As the villain of this particular little drama, I shall only say that I have my methods." Suddenly he was grave. "One reason we made so great an effort to pick you up before your own rescue party arrived, was to gather data on what you have been doing, you people. You know how comparatively rare it is to get a prisoner in space warfare; and how hard to get spies into an organization of high morale which maintains its own laboratories and factories off Earth. Divergent developments can go far these days, before the other side is aware of them. The miniaturization involved in your own weapon, for example, astonished our engineers."

"I can't tell you anything else," Diaz said.

"Oh, you could," Rostock answered gently. "You know as well as I what can be done with a shot of babble juice. Not to mention other techniques—nothing melodramatic, nothing painful or disabling, merely applied neurology—in which I believe Unasia is ahead of the Western countries. But don't worry, Captain. I shall not permit any such breach of military custom.

"However, I do want you to understand how much trouble we went to, to get you. When combat began, I reasoned that the ships auxiliary to a dreadnaught would be the likeliest to suffer destruction of the type which leaves a few survivors. From the pattern of action in the first day, I deduced the approximate orbits and positions of several American capital ships. Unasia tactics throughout the second day were developed with two purposes: to inflict damage, of course, but also to get the *Ho* so placed that we would be likely to detect any distress signals. This cost us the *Genghis*—a calculated risk that did not pay off—I am not omniscient. But we did hear your call.

"You are quite right about the importance of this ship here. My superiors will be horrified at my action. But of necessity, they have given me carte blanche. And since the *Ho* itself takes no direct part in any engagement if we can avoid it, the probability of our being detected and attacked was small."

Rostock's eyes held Diaz's. He tapped the table, softly and repeatedly, with one fingernail. "Do you appreciate what all this means, Captain?" he asked "Do you see how badly you were wanted?"

Diaz could only wet his lips and nod.

"Partly," Rostock said, smiling again, "there was the desire I have mentioned, to…er…check up on American activities during the last cease-fire period. But partly, too, there was a wish to bring you up to date on what we have been doing."

"Huh?" Diaz half scrambled from his chair, sagged back and gaped.

"The choice is yours, Captain," Rostock said. "You can be transferred to a cargo ship when we can arrange it, and so to an asteroid camp, and in general receive the normal treatment of a war prisoner. Or you may elect to hear what I would like to discuss with you. In the latter event, I can guarantee nothing. Obviously I can't let you go home in a routine prisoner exchange with a prime military secret of ours. You will have to wait until it is no longer a secret—until American intelligence has learned the truth and we know that they have. That may take years. It may take forever, because I have some hope that the knowledge will change certain of your own attitudes.

"No, no, don't answer now. Think it over. I will see you again tomorrow. In twenty-four hours, that is to say."

Rostock's eyes shifted past Diaz, as if to look through the bulkheads. His tone dropped to a whisper. "Have you ever wondered, like me, why we carry Earth's rotation period to space with us? Habit; practicality; but is there not also an element of magical thinking? A hope that somehow we can create our own sunrises? The sky is very black out there. We need all the magic we can invent. Do we not?"

Several hours later, alarms sounded, voices barked over the intercoms, spin was halted but weight came quickly back as the ship accelerated. Diaz knew just enough Mandarin to understand from what he overheard that radar contact had been made with American units and combat would soon resume. The guard who brought him dinner in his cubicle confirmed it, with many a bow and hissing smile. Diaz had gained enormous face by his audience with the man in the suite.

He couldn't sleep, though the racket soon settled down to a purposeful murmur with few loud interruptions. Restless in his bunk harness, he tried to reconstruct a total picture from the clues he had. The primary American objective was the asteroid base system of the enemy. But astromilitary tactics were too complicated for one brain to grasp. A battle might go on for months, flaring up whenever hostile units came near enough in their enormous orbitings to exchange fire. Eventually, Diaz knew, if everything went well—that is, didn't go too badly haywire—Americans would land on the Unasian worldlets. That would be the rough part. He remembered ground operations on Mars and Ganymede far too well.

As for the immediate situation, though, he could only make an educated guess. The leisurely pace at which the engagement was developing indicated that ships of dreadnaught mass were involved. Therefore no mere squadron was out there, but an important segment of the American fleet, perhaps the task force headed by the *Alaska*. But if this was true, then the *Ho Chi Minh* must be directing a flotilla of comparable size.

Which wasn't possible! Flotillas and subfleets were bossed from dreadnaughts. A combat computer and its human staff were too big and delicate to be housed in anything less. And the *Ho* was not even as large as the *Argonne* had been.

Yet what the hell was this but a command ship? Rostock had hinted as much. The activity aboard was characteristic: the repeated sound of courier boats coming and going, intercom calls, technicians hurrying along the corridors, but no shooting.

Nevertheless...

Voices jabbered beyond the cell door. Their note was triumphant. Probably they related a hit on an American vessel. Diaz recalled brushing aside chunks of space-frozen meat that had been his Corps brothers. Sammy Yoshida was in the *Utah Beach,* which was with the *Alaska*—Sammy who'd covered for him back at the Academy when he crawled in dead drunk hours after taps, and some years later had dragged him from a shell-struck foxhole on Mars and shared oxygen till a rescue squad happened by. Had the *Utah Beach* been hit? Was that what they were giggling about out there?

Prisoner exchange, in a year or two or three, will get me back for the next round of the war, Diaz thought in darkness. But I'm only one man. And I've goofed somehow, spilled a scheme which might've cost the Unies several ships before they tumbled. It's hardly conceivable I could smuggle out whatever information Rostock wants to give me. But there'd be some tiny probability that I could, somehow, sometime. Wouldn't there?

I don't want to. Dios mio, *how I don't want to! Let me rest a while, and then be swapped, and go back for a long furlough on Earth, where anything I ask for is mine and mainly I ask for sunlight and ocean and flowering trees. But Carl liked those things too, didn't he?*

A lull came in the battle. The fleets had passed each other, decelerating as they fired. They would take many hours to turn around and get back within combat range. A great quietness descended on the *Ho*. Walking down the passageways, which thrummed with rocket blast, Diaz saw how the technicians slumped at their posts. The demands on them were as hard as those on a pilot or gunner or missile chief. Evolution designed men to fight with their hands, not with computations and pushbuttons. Maybe ground combat wasn't the worst kind at that.

The sentries admitted Diaz through the door of the warning. Rostock sat at the table again. His coifed features looked equally drained, and his smile was automatic. A samovar and two teacups stood before him.

"Be seated, Captain," he said tonelessly. "Pardon me if I do not rise. This has been an exhausting time."

Diaz accepted a chair and a cup. Rostock drank noisily, eyes closed and forehead puckered. There might have been an extra stimulant in his tea, for before long he appeared more human. He refilled the cups, passed out cigarettes, and leaned back on his couch with a sigh.

"You may be pleased to know," he said, "that the third pass will be the final one. We shall refuse further combat and proceed instead to join forces with another flotilla near Pallas."

"Because that suits your purposes better," Diaz said.

"Well, naturally. I compute a higher likelihood of ultimate success if we followed a strategy of…no matter now."

Diaz leaned forward. His heart slammed. "So this *is* a command ship," he exclaimed "I thought so."

The blue eyes weighed him with care. "If I give any further information," Rostock said—softly, but the muscles tightened along his jaw—"you must accept the conditions I set forth."

"I do," Diaz got out.

"I realize that you do so in the hope of passing on the secret to your countrymen," Rostock said. "You may as well forget about that. You won't get the chance."

"Then why do you want to tell me? You won't make a Unie out of me, General." The words sounded too stuck up, Diaz decided. "That is, I respect your people and so forth, but…uh…my loyalties lie elsewhere"

"Agreed. I don't hope or plan to change them. At least, not in an easterly direction." Rostock drew hard on his cigarette, let smoke stream from his nostrils, and squinted through it. "The microphone is turned down," he remarked. "We cannot be overheard unless we shout. I must warn you, if you make any attempt to reveal what I am about to say to you to any of my own people, I shall not merely deny it but order you sent out the airlock. It is that important."

Diaz rubbed his hands on his trousers. The palms were wet. "Okay," he said.

"Not that I mean to browbeat you, Captain," said Rostock hastily. "What I offer is friendship. In the end, maybe, peace." He sat a while longer, looking at the wall, before his glance shifted back to Diaz. Suppose you begin the discussion. Ask me what you like."

"Uh…" Diaz floundered about, as if he'd been leaning on a door that was thrown open. "Uh…well, was I right? Is this a command ship?"

"Yes. It performs every function of a flag dreadnaught, except that it seldom engages in direct combat. The tactical advantages are obvious. A smaller, lighter vessel can get about much more readily, hence be a correspondingly more effective directrix. Furthermore, if due caution is exercised, we are not likely to be detected and fired at. The massive armament of a dreadnaught is chiefly to stave off the missiles that can annihilate the command post within. Ships of this class avoid that whole problem by avoiding attack in the first place."

"But your computer! You, you must have developed a combat computer as…small and rugged as an autopilot… I thought miniaturization was our specialty."

Rostock laughed.

"And you'd still need a large human staff," Diaz protested. "Bigger than the whole crew of this ship!

"Wouldn't you?" he finished weakly.

Rostock shook his head. "No." His smile faded. "Not under this new system. I am the computer."

"What?"

"Look." Rostock pulled off his hood.

The head beneath was hairless, not shaved but depilated. A dozen silvery plates were set into it, flush with the scalp; in them were plug outlets. Rostock pointed toward the office. "The rest of me is in there," he said. "I need only set the jacks into the appropriate points of myself, and I become…no, not part of the computer. It becomes part of me."

He fell silent again, gazing now at the floor. Diaz hardly dared move, until his cigarette burned his fingers and he had to stub it out. The ship pulsed around them. Monet's picture of sunlight caught in young leaves was like something seen at the far end of a tunnel.

"Consider the problem," Rostock said at last, low. "In spite of much loose talk about giant brains, computers do not think, except perhaps on an idiot level. They simply perform logical operations, symbol-shuffling, according to instructions given them. It was shown long ago that there are infinite classes of problems that no computer can solve: the classes dealt with in Gödel's theorem, that can only be solved by the nonlogical process of creating a metalanguage. Creativity is not logical and computers do not create.

"In addition, as you know, the larger a computer becomes, the more staff it requires, to perform such operations as data coding, programming, retranslation of the solutions into practical terms, and adjustment of the artificial answer to the actual problems. Yet your own brain does this sort of thing constantly…because it is creative. Moreover, the advanced computers are heavy, bulky, fragile things. They use cryogenics and all the other tricks, but that involves elaborate ancillary apparatus. Your brain weighs a kilogram or so, is quite adequately protected in the skull, and needs less than a hundred kilos of outside equipment—your body.

"I am not being mystical. There is no reason why creativity cannot someday be duplicated in an artificial structure. But I think that structure will look very much like a living organism; will, indeed, be one. Life has had a billion years to develop these techniques.

"Now if the brain has so many advantages, why use a computer at all? Obviously, to do the uncreative work, for which the brain is not specifically designed. The brain visualizes a problem of, say, orbits, masses, and tactics, and formulates it as a set of matrix equations; then the computer goes swiftly through the millions of idiot counting operations needed to produce a numerical solution. What we have developed here, we Unasians, is nothing but a direct approach. We eliminate the middle man, as you Americans would say.

"In yonder office is a highly specialized computer. It is built from solid-state units, analogous to neurons, but in spite of being able to treat astromilitary problems, it is comparatively small, simple, and sturdy device. Why? Because it is used in connection with my brain, which directs it. The normal computer must have its operational patterns built in. Mine develops synapse pathways as needed, just as a man's lower brain can develop skills under the direction of the cerebral cortex. And these pathways are modifiable by experience; the system is continually restructuring itself. The normal computer must have elaborate failure detection systems and arrangements for rerouting. I in the hookup here sense any trouble directly, and am no more disturbed by the temporary disability of some region than you are disturbed by the fact that most of your brain cells at any given time are resting.

"The human staff becomes superfluous here. My technicians bring me the data, which need not be reduced to standardized format. I link myself to the machine and…think about it…there are no words. The answer is worked out in no more time than any other computer would require. But it comes to my consciousness not as a set of figures, but in practical terms, decisions about what to do. Furthermore, the solution is modified by my human awareness of those factors too complex to go into mathematical form—like the physical condition of men and equipment, morale, long-range questions of logistics and strategy and ultimate goals. You might say this is a computer system with common sense. Do you understand, Captain?"

Diaz sat still for a long time before he said, "Yes. I think I do."

Rostock had gotten a little hoarse. He poured himself a fresh cup of tea and drank half, struck another cigarette and said earnestly: "The military value is obvious. Were that all, I would never have revealed this to you. But something else developed as I practiced and increased my command of the system. Something quite unforeseen. I wonder if you will comprehend." He finished his cup. "The repeated experience has…changed me. I am no longer human. Not really."

The ship whispered, driving through darkness.

"I suppose a hookup like that would affect the emotions," Diaz ventured. "How does it feel?"

"There are no words," Rostock repeated, "except those I have made for myself." He rose and walked restlessly across the subdued rainbows in the carpet, hands behind his back, eyes focused on nothing Diaz could see. "As a matter of fact, the emotional effect may be a simple intensification. Although…there are myths about mortals who became gods. How did it feel to them? I think they hardly noticed the palaces and music and feasting on Olympus. What mattered was how, piece by piece, as he mastered his new capacities, the new god won a god's understanding. His perception, involvement, detachment, totalness…there *are* no words."

Back and forth he paced, feet noiseless but metal and energies humming beneath his low and somehow troubled voice. "My cerebrum directs the computer," he said, "and the relationship becomes reciprocal. True, the computer part has no creativity of its own; but it endows mine with a speed and sureness you cannot imagine. After all, a great part of original thought consists merely in proposing trial solutions—the scientist hypothesizes, the artist draws a charcoal line, the poet scribbles a phrase—and testing them to see if they work. By now, to me, this mechanical aspect of imagination is back down on the subconscious level where it belongs. What my awareness senses is the final answer, springing to life almost simultaneously with the question, and yet with a felt reality to it such as comes only from having pondered and tested the issue thousands of times.

"Also, the amount of sense data I can handle is fantastic. Oh, I am blind and deaf and numb away from my machine half! So you will realize that over the months I have tended to spend more and more time in the linked state. When there was no immediate command problem to solve, I would sit and savor total awareness. Or I would think."

In a practical tone: "That is how I perceived that you were about to sabotage us, Captain. Your posture alone betrayed you. I guessed the means at once and ordered the guards to knock you unconscious. I think, also, that I detected in you the potential I need. But that demands closer examination. Which is easily given. When I am linked, you cannot lie to me. The least insincerity is written across your whole organism."

He paused, to stand a little slumped, looking at the bulkhead. For a moment Diaz's legs tensed. *Three jumps and I can be there and get his gun!* But no, Rostock wasn't any brainheavy dwarf. The body in that green uniform was young and trained. Diaz took another cigarette. "Okay," he said. "What do you propose?"

"First," Rostock said, turning about—and his eyes kindled—"I want you to understand what you and I are. What the spacemen of both factions are."

"Professional soldiers," Diaz grunted uneasily. Rostock waited. Diaz puffed hard and plowed on, since he was plainly expected to, "The last soldiers left. You can't count those ornamental regiments on Earth, nor the guys sitting by the big missiles. Those missiles will never be fired. World War Three was a large enough dose of nucleonics. Civilization was lucky to survive. Terrestrial life would be lucky to survive, next time around. So war has moved into space. Uh…professionalism…the old traditions of mutual respect and so forth have naturally revived." He made himself look up. "What more clichés need I repeat?"

"Suppose your side completely annihilated our ships," Rostock said. "What would happen?"

"Why…that's been discussed theoretically…by damn near every political scientist, hasn't it? The total command of space would not mean total command of Earth. We could destroy the whole Eastern Hemisphere without being touched. But we wouldn't, because Unasia would fire its cobalt weapons while dying, and we'd have no Western Hemisphere to come home to, either. Not that that situation will ever arise. Space is too big; there are too many ships and fortresses scattered around; combat is too slow a process. Neither fleet can wipe out the other."

"Since we have this perpetual stalemate, then," Rostock pursued, "why do we have perpetual war?"

"Um…well, not really. Cease-fires—"

"Breathing spells! Come now, Captain, you are too intelligent to believe that rigmarole. If victory cannot be achieved, why fight?"

"Well, uh, partial victories are possible. Like our capture of Mars, or your destruction of three dreadnaughts in one month, on different occasions. The balance of power shifts. Rather than let its strength continue being whittled down, the side which is losing asks for a parley. Negotiations follow, which end to the relative advantage of the stronger side. Meanwhile the arms race continues. Pretty soon a new dispute arises, the cease-fire ends, and maybe the other side is lucky that time."

"Is this situation expected to be eternal?"

"No!" Diaz stopped, thought a minute, and grinned with one corner of his mouth. "That is, they keep talking about an effective international organization. Trouble is, the two cultures are too far apart by now. They can't live together."

"I used to believe that myself," Rostock said. "Lately I have not been sure. A world federalism could be devised which would let both civilizations keep their identities. Many such proposals have in fact been made, as you know. None has gotten beyond the talking stage. None ever will. Because you see, what maintains the war is not the difference between our two cultures, but their similarity."

"Whoa, there!" Diaz bristled. "I resent that."

"Please," Rostock said. "I pass no moral judgments. For the sake of argument, at least, I can concede you the moral superiority, remarking only in parenthesis that Earth holds billions of people who not only fail to comprehend what you mean by freedom but would not like it if you gave it to them. The similarity I am talking about is technological. Both civilizations are based on the machine, with all the high organization and dynamism which this implies."

"So?"

"So war is a necessity—Wait! I am not talking about 'merchants of death,' or 'dictators needing an outside enemy,' or whatever the current propaganda lines are. I mean that conflict is built into the culture. There *must* be an outlet for the destructive emotions generated in the mass of the people by the type of life they lead. A type of life for which evolution never designed them.

"Have you ever heard about L. F. Richardson? No? He was an Englishman in the last century, a Quaker, who hated war but, being a scientist, realized the phenomenon must be understood clinically before it can be eliminated. He performed some brilliant theoretical and statistical analyses which showed, for example, that the rate of deadly quarrels was nearly constant over the decades. There could be many small clashes or a few major ones, but the result was the same. Why were the United States and the Chinese Empire so peaceful during the nineteenth century? The answer is that they were not; they had their Civil War and Taiping Rebellion, which devastated them as much as required. I need not multiply examples. We can discuss this later in detail. I have carried Richardson's work a good deal further and more rigorously. I say to you now only that civilized societies must have a certain rate of immolations."

Diaz listened to silence for a minute before he said: "Well, I've sometimes thought the same. I suppose you mean we spacemen are the goats these days?"

"Exactly. War fought out here does not menace the planet. By our deaths we keep Earth alive."

Rostock sighed. His mouth drooped. "Magic works, you know," he said, "on the emotions of the people who practice it. If a primitive witch doctor told a storm to go away, the storm did not hear, but the tribe did and took heart. The ancient analogy to us, though, is the sacrificial king in the early agricultural societies; a god in mortal form, who was regularly slain so that the fields might bear fruit. This was not mere superstition. You must realize that. It worked—on the people. The rite was essential to the operation of their culture, to their sanity and hence to their survival.

"Today the machine age has developed its own sacrificial kings. We are the chosen of the race, the best it can offer. None gainsays us. We may have what we choose, pleasure, luxury, women, adulation—only not the simple pleasures of wife and child and hope, for we must die that the people may live."

Again silence, until: "Do you seriously mean that's why the war goes on?" Diaz breathed.

Rostock nodded.

"But nobody...I mean, people wouldn't—"

"They do not reason these things out, of course. Traditions develop blindly. The ancient peasant did not elaborate logical reasons why the king must die. He merely knew this was so, and left the syllogism for modern anthropologists to expound. I did not see the process going on today until I had had the chance to...to become more perceptive than I had been," Rostock said humbly.

Diaz couldn't endure sitting any longer. He jumped to his feet. "Assuming you're right," he snapped, "and you may be, what of it? What can be done?"

"Much," Rostock said. Calm descended on his face like a mask. "I am not being mystical about this, either. The sacrificial king has reappeared as the end product of a long chain of cause and effect. There is no reason inherent in natural law why this must be. Richardson was right in his basic hope, that when war becomes understood, as a phenomenon, it can be eliminated. This would naturally involve restructuring the entire terrestrial culture—gradually, subtly. Remember—" His hand shot out, seized Diaz's shoulder and gripped painfully hard. "There is a new element in history today. Us. The kings. We are not like those who spend their lives under Earth's sky. In some ways we are more, in other ways less, but always we are different. You and I are more akin to each other than to our planet-dwelling countrymen. Are we not?

"In the time and loneliness granted me, I have used all my new powers to think about this. Not only think; this is so much more than cold reason. I have tried to feel. To love what is, as the Buddhists say. I believe a nucleus of spacemen like us, slowly and secretly gathered, wishing the good of everyone on Earth and the harm of none, gifted with powers and insights they cannot really imagine at home—I believe we may accomplish something. If not us, then our sons. Men ought not to kill each other, when the stars are waiting."

He let go, turned away and looked at the deck. "Of course," he mumbled, "I, in my peculiar situation, must first destroy a number of your brothers."

They had given Diaz a whole pack of cigarettes, an enormous treasure out here, before they locked him into his cubicle for the duration of the second engagement. He lay in harness, hearing clang and shout and engine roar through the vibrating bulkheads, stared at blackness, and smoked until his tongue was foul. Sometimes the *Ho* accelerated, mostly it ran free and he floated. Once a tremor went through the entire hull, near miss by a shaped charge. Doubtless gamma rays, ignoring the magnetic force screens, sleeted through the men and knocked another several months off their life expectancies. Not that that mattered; spacemen rarely lived long enough to worry about degenerative diseases. Diaz hardly noticed.

Rostock's not lying. Why should he? What could he gain? He may be a nut, of course. But he doesn't act like a nut either. He wants me to study his statistics and equations, satisfy myself that he's right. And he must be damn sure I will be convinced, to tell me what he has.

How many are there like him? Few, I'm sure. The man-machine symbiosis is obviously new, or we'd've had some inkling ourselves. This is the first field trial of the system. I wonder if the others have reached the same conclusions as Rostock. No, he said he doubts that; their minds impressed him as being more deeply channeled than his. He's a lucky accident.

Lucky? Now how can I tell? I'm only a man. I've never experienced an I.Q. of a thousand, or whatever the figure may be. A god's purposes aren't necessarily what a man would elect.

An eventual end to war? Well, other institutions had been ended, at least in the Western countries: judicial torture, chattel slavery, human sacrifice—no, wait, according to Rostock human sacrifice had been revived.

"But is our casualty rate high enough to fit your equations?" Diaz had argued. "Space forces aren't as big as old-time armies. No country could afford that."

"Other elements than death must be taken into account," Rostock answered. "The enormous expense is one factor. Taxpaying is a form of symbolic self-mutilation. It also tends to direct civilian resentments and aggressions against their own governments, thus taking some pressure off international relations.

"Chiefly, though, there is the matter of emotional intensity. A spaceman does not simply die, he usually dies horribly; and that moment is the culmination of a long period under grisly conditions. His groundling brothers, administrative and service personnel, suffer vicariously: 'sweat it out,' as your idiom so well expresses the feeling. His kinfolk, friends, women, are likewise racked. When Adonis dies—or Osiris, Tammuz, Baldur, Christ, Tlaloc, whichever of his hundred names you choose—the people must in some degree share his agony. That is part of the sacrifice."

Diaz had never thought about it in quite that way. Like most Corpsmen, he had held the average civilian in thinly disguised contempt. But…from time to time, he remembered, he'd been glad his mother died before he enlisted. And why did his sister hit the bottle so hard? Then there had been Lois, she of the fire-colored hair and violet eyes, who wept as if she would never stop weeping when he left for duty. He'd promised to get in touch with her on his return, but of course he knew better.

Which did not erase memories of men whose breath and blood came exploding from burst helmets; who shuddered and vomited and defecated in the last stages of radiation sickness; who stared without immediate apprehension at a red spurt which a second ago had been an arm or a leg; who went insane and must be gassed because psychoneurosis is catching on a six months' orbit beyond Saturn; who—Yeah, Carl had been lucky.

You could talk as much as you wished about Corps brotherhood, honor, tradition, and gallantry. It remained sentimental guff…No, that was unjust. The Corps had saved the people, their lives and liberties. There could be no higher achievement—for the Corps. But knighthood had once been a noble thing, too; then, lingering after its day, it became a yoke and eventually a farce. The warrior virtues were not ends in themselves. If the warrior could be made obsolete…

Could he? How much could one man, even powered by a machine, hope to do? How much could he even hope to understand?

The moment came upon Diaz. He lay as if blinded by shellburst radiance.

As consciousness returned, he knew first, irrelevantly, what it meant to get religion.

"By God," he told the universe, "we're going to try!"

The battle would resume shortly. At any moment, in fact, some scoutship leading the American force might fire a missile. But when Diaz told his guard he wanted to speak with General Rostock, he was take there within minutes.

The door closed behind him. The living room lay empty, altogether still except for the machine throb, which was not loud since the *Ho* was running free. Because acceleration might be needful on short notice, there was no spin. Diaz hung weightless as fog. And the Monet flung into his eyes all Earth's sunlight and summer forests.

"Rostock?" he called uncertainly.

"Come," said a voice, almost too low to hear. Diaz gave a shove with his foot and flew toward the office.

He stopped himself by grasping the doorjamb. A semicircular room lay before him, the entire side taken up by controls and meters. Lights blinked, needles wavered on dials, buttons and switches and knobs reached across black paneling. But none of that was important. Only the man at the desk mattered, who free-sat with wires running from his head to the wall.

Rostock seemed to have lost weight. Or was that an illusion? The skin was drawn taut across his high cheekbones and gone a dead, glistening white. His nostrils were flared and the colorless lips held tense. Diaz looked into his eyes, once, and away again. He could not meet them. He could not even think about them. He drew a shaken breath and waited.

"You made your decision quickly," Rostock whispered. "I had not awaited you until after the engagement."

"I...I didn't think you would see me till then."

"This is more important." Diaz felt as if he were being probed with knives. He could not altogether believe it was his imagination. He stared desperately at paneled instruments. Their nonhumanness was like a comforting hand. *They must be for the benefit of maintenance techs,* he thought in a distant part of himself. *The brain doesn't need them.* "You are convinced," Rostock said in frank surprise.

"Yes," Diaz answered.

"I had not expected that. I hoped for little more than your reluctant agreement to study my work." Rostock regarded him for a still century. "You were ripe for a new faith," he decided. "I had not taken you for the type. But then, the mind can only use what data are given it, and I have hitherto had small opportunity to meet Americans. Never since I became what I am. You have another psyche from ours."

"I need to understand your findings, sir," Diaz said. "Right now I can only believe. That isn't enough, is it?"

Slowly, Rostock's mouth drew into a smile of quite human warmth. "Correct. But given the faith, intellectual comprehension should be swift."

"I...I shouldn't be taking your time...now, sir," Diaz stammered. "How should I begin? Should I take some books back with me?"

"No." Acceptance had been reached; Rostock spoke resonantly, a master to his trusted servant. "I need your help here. Strap into yonder harness. Our first necessity is to survive the battle upon us. You realize that this means sacrificing many of your comrades. I know how that will hurt you. Afterward we shall spend our lives repaying our people...both our peoples. But today I shall ask you questions about your fleet. Any information is valuable, especially details of construction and armament which our intelligence has not been able to learn."

Doña mía. Diaz let go the door, covered his face and fell free, endlessly. *Help me.*

"It is not betrayal," said the superman. "It is the ultimate loyalty you can offer."

Diaz made himself look at the cabin again. He shoved against the bulkhead and stopped by the harness near the desk.

"You cannot lie to me," said Rostock. "Do not deny the pain I am giving you." Diaz glimpsed his fists clamping together. "Each time I look at you, I share what you feel."

Diaz clung to his harness. There went an explosion through him.

NO, BY GOD!

Rostock screamed.

"Don't," Diaz sobbed. "I don't want—" But wave after wave ripped outward. Rostock flopped about in his harness and shrieked. The scene came back, ramming home like a bayonet.

"We like to put an extra string on our bow," the psych officer said. Lunar sunlight, scarcely softened by the dome, blazed off his bronze eagles, wings and beaks. "You know that your right ulna will be replaced with a metal section which contains a nerve-triggered nuclear cartridge. But that may not be all, gentlemen."

He bridged his fingers. The young men seated on the other side of his desk stirred uneasily. "In this country," the psych officer said, "we don't believe humans should be turned into puppets. Therefore you will have voluntary control of your bombs; no posthypnosis, Pavlov reflex, or any such insult. However, those of you who are willing will receive a rather special extra treatment, and that fact will be buried from the consciousness of everyone of you.

"Our reasoning is that if and when the Unasians learn about the prisoner weapon, they'll remove the cartridge by surgery but leave the prosthetic bone in place. And they will, we hope, not examine it in microscopic detail. Therefore they won't know that it holds an oscillator, integrated with the crystal structure. Nor will you; because what you don't know, you can't babble under anesthesia.

"The opportunity may come, if you are captured and lose your bomb, to inflict damage by this reserve means. You may find yourself near a crucial electronic device, for example a spaceship's autopilot. At short range, the oscillator will do an excellent job of bollixing it. Which will at least discomfit the enemy, and may give you a chance to escape.

"The posthypnotic command will be such that you'll remember about this oscillator when conditions seem right for using it. Not before. Of course, the human mind is a damned queer thing; it twists and turns and bites its own tail. In order to make an opportunity to strike this blow, your subconscious may lead you down strange paths—may even have you seriously contemplating treason, if treason seems the only way of getting access to what you can wreck. Don't let that bother you afterward, gentlemen. Your superiors will know what happened.

"Nevertheless, the experience may be painful. And posthypnosis is, at best humiliating to a free man. So this aspect of the program is strictly volunteer. Does anybody want to go for broke?"

The door flung open. The guards burst in. Diaz was already behind the desk, next to Rostock. He yanked out the general's sidearm and fired at the soldiers. Free-fall recoil sent him back against the computer panel. He braced himself, fired again, and used his left elbow to smash the nearest meter face.

Rostock clawed at the wires in his head. For a moment Diaz guessed what it must be like to have random oscillations in your brain, amplified by an electronic engine that was part of you. He laid the pistol to the screaming man's temple and fired once more.

Now to get out! He shoved hard, arrowing past the sentries, who rolled through the air in a crimson galaxy of blood globules. Confusion boiled in the corridor beyond. Someone snatched at him. He knocked the fellow aside and dove along a tubeway. Somewhere hereabouts should be a scooter locker—there, and nobody around!

He didn't have time to get on a spacesuit, even if a Unasian one would have fitted, but he slipped an air dome over the scooter. That, with the heater unit and oxy reclaim, would serve. He didn't want to get off anywhere en route; not before he'd steered the machine through an American hatch.

With luck, he'd do that. Their command computer gone, the enemy were going to get smeared. American ships would close in as the slaughter progressed. Eventually one should come within range of the scooter's little radio.

He set the minilock controls, mounted the saddle, dogged the air dome, and waited for ejection. It came none too soon. Three soldiers had just appeared down the passageway. Diaz applied full thrust and jetted away from the *Ho*. Its blackness was soon lost among the star clouds.

Battle commenced. The first Unasian ship to be destroyed must have been less than fifty miles distant. Luckily, Diaz was facing the other way when the missile exploded.

Ochlan

Oh, would the stars might mourn for this our comrade,
    Weep tears of light across a riven sky,
Or that the rain which falls upon his homeland
    Were bidding him a long last goodbye,
Or at the least, a blossom drop to kiss him
    From off a tree where springtime breezes blow;
For then we'd not be all alone in grieving.
    The world would sorrow too, the world that he loved so.

But silence reigns among the suns and planets.
    The leaves are dumb, the weather's deaf and blind.
We've only us to keen for this our comrade
    And know that he was bright and strong and kind.
Ochone, ochone! He's gone like any sunrise.
    Ochone, ochone! He laughed while he was here.
Ochone, ochone! He is no more forever.
    What's left for us lies still, yet still is very dear.

Starfog

"From another universe. Where space is a shining cloud, two hundred light-years across, roiled by the red stars that number in the many thousands, and where the brighter suns are troubled and cast forth great flames. Your spaces are dark and lonely."

Daven Laure stopped the recording and asked for an official translation. A part of *Jaccavrie's* computer scanned the molecules of a plugged-in memory cylinder, identified the passage, and flashed the Serievan text onto a reader screen. Another part continued the multitudinous tasks of planetary approach. Still other parts waited for the man's bidding, whatever he might want next. A Ranger of the Commonalty traveled in a very special ship.

And even so, every year, a certain number did not come home from their missions.

Laure nodded to himself. Yes, he'd understood the woman's voice correctly. Or, at least, he interpreted her sentences approximately the same way as did the semanticist who had interviewed her and her fellows. And this particular statement was as difficult, as ambiguous as any which they had made. Therefore: (a) Probably the linguistic computer on Serieve had done a good job of unraveling their basic language. (b) It had accurately encoded its findings—vocabulary, grammar, tentative reconstruction of the underlying world-view—in the cylinders which a courier had brought to Sector HQ. (c) The reencoding, into his own neurones, which Laure underwent on his way here, had taken well. He had a working knowledge of the tongue which—among how many others?—was spoken on Kirkasant.

"Wherever that may be," he muttered.

The ship weighed his words for a nanosecond or two, decided no answer was called for, and made none.

Restless, Laure got to his feet and prowled from the study cabin, down a corridor to the bridge. It was so called largely by courtesy. *Jaccavrie* navigated, piloted, landed, lifted, maintained, and, if need be, repaired and fought herself. But the projectors here offered a full outside view. At the moment, the bulkheads seemed cramped and barren. Laure ordered the simulacrum activated.

The bridge vanished from his eyes. Had it not been for the G-field underfoot, he might have imagined himself floating in space. A crystal night enclosed him, unwinking stars scattered like jewels, the frosty glitter of the Milky Way. Large and near, its radiance stopped down to preserve his retinas, burned the yellow sun of Serieve. The planet itself was a growing crescent, blue banded with white, rimmed by a violet sky. A moon stood opposite, worn golden coin.

But Laure's gaze strayed beyond, toward the deeps and then, as if in search of comfort, the other way, toward Old Earth. There was no comfort, though. They still named her Home, but she lay in the spiral arm behind this one, and Laure had never seen her. He had never met anyone who had. None of his ancestors had, for longer than their family chronicles ran. Home was a half-remembered myth; reality was here, these stars on the fringes of this civilization.

Serieve lay near the edge of the known. Kirkasant lay somewhere beyond.

"Surely not outside of spacetime," Laure said.

"If you've begun thinking aloud, you'd like to discuss it," *Jaccavrie* said.

He had followed custom in telling the ship to use a female voice and, when practical, idiomatic language. The computer had soon learned precisely what pattern suited him best. That was not identical with what he liked best; such could have got disturbing on a long cruise. He found himself more engaged, inwardly, with the husky contralto that had spoken in strong rhythms out of the recorder than he was with the mezzo-soprano that now reached his ears.

"Well…maybe so," he said. "But you already know everything in the material we have aboard."

"You need to set your thoughts in order. You've spent most of our transit time acquiring the language."

"All right, then, let's run barefoot through the obvious." Laure paced a turn around the invisible deck. He felt its hardness, the vibration back through his sandals, he sensed the almost subliminal beat of driving energies, he caught a piny whiff of air as the ventilators shifted to another part of their odor-temperature-ionization cycle; but still the stars blazed about him, and their silence seemed to enter his bones. Abruptly, harshly, he said: "Turn that show off."

The ship obeyed. "Would you like a planetary scene?" she asked. "You haven't yet looked at those tapes from the elf castles on Jair that you bought—"

"Not now." Laure flung himself into a chair web and regarded the prosaic metal, instruments, manual override controls that surrounded him. "This will do."

"Are you feeling well? Why not go in the diagnoser and let me check you out? We've time before we arrive."

The tone was anxious. Laure didn't believe that emotion was put on. He refrained from anthropomorphizing his computer, just as he did those nonhuman sophonts he encountered. At the same time, he didn't go along with the school of thought which claimed that human-sensibility terms were absolutely meaningless in such connections. An alien brain, or a cybernetic one like *Jaccavrie's*, could think; it was aware; it had conation. Therefore it had analogies to his.

Quite a few Rangers were eremitic types, sane enough but basically schizoid. That was their way of standing the gaff. It was normal for them to think of their ships as elaborate tools. Daven Laure, who was young and outgoing, naturally thought of his as a friend.

"No, I'm all right," he said. "A bit nervous, nothing else. This could turn out to be the biggest thing I…you and I have tackled yet. Maybe one of the biggest anyone has, at least on this frontier. I'd've been glad to have an older man or two along." He shrugged. "None available. Our service should increase its personnel, even if it means raising dues. We're spread much too thin across—how many stars?"

"The last report in my files estimated ten million planets with a significant number of Commonalty members on them. As for how many more there may be with which these have reasonably regular contact—"

"Oh, for everything's sake, come off it!" Laure actually laughed, and wondered if the ship had planned things that way. But, regardless, he could begin to talk of this as a problem rather than a mystery.

"Let me recapitulate," he said, "and you tell me if I'm misinterpreting matters. A ship comes to Serieve, allegedly from far away. It's like nothing anybody has ever seen, unless in historical works. (They haven't got the references on Serieve to check that out, so we're bringing some from HQ.) Hyperdrive, gravity control, electronics, yes, but everything crude, archaic, bare-bones. Fission instead of fusion power, for example…and human piloting!

"That is, the crew seem to be human. We have no record of their anthropometric type, but they don't look as odd as people do after several generations on some planets I could name. And the linguistic computer, once they get the idea that it's there to decipher their language and start cooperating with it, says their speech appears to have remote affinities with a few that we know, like ancient Anglic. Preliminary semantic analysis suggests their abstractions and constructs aren't quite like ours, but do fall well inside the human psych range. All in all, then, you'd assume they're explorers from distant parts."

"Except for the primitive ship," *Jaccavrie* chimed in. "One wouldn't expect such technological backwardness in any group which had maintained any contact, however tenuous, with the general mass of the different human civilizations. Nor would such a slow, underequipped vessel pass through them without stopping, to fetch up in this border region."

"Right. So…if it isn't a fake…their gear bears out a part of their story. Kirkasant is an exceedingly old colony…yonder." Laure pointed toward unseen stars. "Well out in the Dragon's Head sector, where we're barely beginning to explore. Somehow, somebody got that far, and in the earliest days of interstellar travel. They settled down on a planet and lost the trick of making spaceships. Only lately have they regained it."

"And come back, looking for the companionship of their own kind." Laure had a brief, irrational vision of *Jaccavrie* nodding. Her tone was so thoughtful. She would be a big, calm, dark-haired woman, handsome in middle age though getting somewhat plump…"What the crew themselves have said, as communication got established, seems to bear out this idea. Beneath a great many confused mythological motifs, I also get the impression of an epic voyage, by a defeated people who ran as far as they could."

"But Kirkasant!" Laure protested. "The whole situation they describe. It's impossible."

"Might not that Vandange be mistaken? I mean, we know so little. The Kirkasanters keep talking about a weird home environment. Ours appears to have stunned and bewildered them. They simply groped on through space till they happened to find Serieve. Thus might their own theory, that somehow they blundered in from an altogether different continuum, might it not conceivably be right?"

"Hm-m-m. I guess you didn't see Vandange's accompanying letter. No, you haven't, it wouldn't've been plugged into your memory. Anyway he claims his assistants examined that ship down to the bolt heads. And they found nothing, no mechanism, no peculiarity, whose function and behavior weren't obvious. He really gets indignant. Says the notion of interspace-time transference is mathematically absurd. I don't have quite his faith in mathematics, myself, but I must admit he has one common-sense point. If a ship could somehow flip from one entire cosmos to another…why, in five thousand years of interstellar travel, haven't we gotten some record of it happening?"

"Perhaps the ships to which it occurs never come back."

"Perhaps. Or perhaps the whole argument is due to misunderstanding. We don't have any good grasp of the Kirkasanter language. Or maybe it's a hoax. That's Vandange's opinion. He claims there's no such region as they say they come from. Not anywhere. Neither astronomers nor explorers have ever found anything like a…a space like a shining fog, crowded with stars—"

"But why should these wayfarers tell a falsehood?" *Jaccavrie* sounded honestly puzzled.

"I don't know. Nobody does. That's why the Serievan government decided it'd better ask for a Ranger."

Laure jumped up and started pacing again. He was a tall young man, with the characteristic beardlessness, fair hair and complexion, slightly slanted blue eyes of the Fireland mountaineers on New Vixen. But since he had trained at Starborough, which is on Aladir not far from Irontower City, he affected a fashionably simple gray tunic and blue hose. The silver comet of his calling blazoned his left breast.

"I don't know," he repeated. There rose in him a consciousness of that immensity which crouched beyond this hull. "Maybe they are telling the sober truth. We don't dare not know."

When a few score million people have an entire habitable world to themselves, they do not often build high. That comes later, along with formal wilderness preservation, disapproval of fecundity, and inducements to emigrate. Pioneer towns tend to be low and rambling. (Or so it is in that civilization wherein the Commonalty operates. We know that other branches of humanity have their distinctive ways, and hear rumors of yet stranger ones. But so vast is the galaxy—these two or three spiral arms, a part of which our race has to date thinly occupied—so vast, that we cannot even keep track of our own culture, let alone anyone else's.)

Pelogard, however, was founded on an island off the Branzan mainland, above Serieve's arctic circle: which comes down to almost 56°. Furthermore, it was an industrial center. Hence most of its buildings were tall and crowded. Laure, standing by the outer wall of Ozer Vandange's office and looking forth across the little city, asked why this location had been chosen.

"You don't know?" responded the physicist. His inflection was a touch too elaborately incredulous.

"I'm afraid not," Laure confessed. "Think how many systems my service has to cover, and how many individual places within each system. If we tried to remember each, we'd never be anywhere but under the neuroinductors."

Vandange, seated small and bald and prim behind a large desk, pursed his lips. "Yes, yes," he said. "Nevertheless, I should not think an *experienced* Ranger would dash off to a planet without temporarily mastering a few basic facts about it."

Laure flushed. An experienced Ranger would have put this conceited old dustbrain in his place. But he himself was too aware of youth and awkwardness. He managed to say quietly, "Sir, my ship has complete information. She needed only scan it and tell me no precautions were required here. You have a beautiful globe and I can understand why you're proud of it. But please understand that to me it has to be a way station. My job is with those people from Kirkasant, and I'm anxious to meet them."

"You shall, you shall," said Vandange, somewhat mollified. "I merely thought a conference with you would be advisable first. As for your question, we need a city here primarily because upwelling ocean currents make the arctic waters mineral-rich. Extractor plants payoff better than they would farther south."

Despite himself, Laure was interested. "You're getting your minerals from the sea already? At so early a stage of settlement?"

"This sun and its planets are poor in heavy metals. Most local systems are. Not surprising. We aren't far, here, from the northern verge of the spiral arm. Beyond is the halo—thin gas, little dust, ancient globular clusters very widely scattered. The interstellar medium from which stars form has not been greatly enriched by earlier generations."

Laure suppressed his resentment at being lectured like a child. Maybe it was just Vandange's habit. He cast another glance through the wall. The office was high in one of the buildings. He looked across soaring blocks of metal, concrete, glass, and plastic, interlinked with trafficways and freight cables, down to the waterfront. There bulked the extractor plants, warehouses, and skydocks. Cargo craft moved ponderously in and out. Not many passenger vessels flitted between. Pelogard must be largely automated.

The season stood at late spring. The sun cast brightness across a gray ocean that a wind rumpled. Immense flocks of seabirds dipped and wheeled. Or were they birds? They had wings, anyhow, steely blue against a wan sky. Perhaps they cried or sang, into the wind skirl and wave rush; but Laure couldn't hear it in this enclosed place.

"That's one reason I can't accept their yarn," Vandange declared.

"Eh?" Laure came out of his reverie with a start.

Vandange pressed a button to opaque the wall. "Sit down. Let's get to business."

Laure eased himself into a lounger opposite the desk. "Why am I conferring with you?" he counterattacked. "Whoever was principally working with the Kirkasanters had to be a semanticist. In short, Paeri Ferand. He consulted specialists on your university faculty, in anthropology, history, and so forth. But I should think your own role as a physicist was marginal. Yet you're the one taking up my time. Why?"

"Oh, you can see Ferand and the others as much as you choose," Vandange said. "You won't get more from them than repetitions of what the Kirkasanters have already told. How could you? What else have they got to go on? If nothing else, an underpopulated world like ours can't maintain staffs of experts to ferret out the meaning of every datum, every inconsistency, every outright lie. I had hoped, when our government notified your sector headquarters, the Rangers would have sent a real team, instead of—" He curbed himself. "Of course, they have many other claims on their attention. They would not see at once how important this is."

"Well," Laure said in his annoyance, "if you're suspicious, if you think the strangers need further investigation, why bother with my office? It's just an overworked little outpost. Send them on to a heart world, like Samac, where the facilities and people really can be had."

"It was urged," Vandange said. "I, and a few others who felt as I do, fought the proposal bitterly. In the end, as a compromise, the government decided to dump the whole problem in the lap of the Rangers. Who turn out to be, in effect, you. Now I must persuade you to be properly cautious. Don't you see, if those…beings…have some hostile intent, the very worst move would be to send them on—let them spy out our civilization—let them, perhaps, commit nuclear sabotage on a vital center, and then vanish back into space." His voice grew shrill. "That's why we've kept them here so long, on one excuse after the next, here on our home planet. We feel responsible to the rest of mankind!"

"But what—" Laure shook his head. He felt a sense of unreality. "Sir, the League, the troubles, the Empire, its fall, the Long Night…every such thing—behind us. In space and time alike. The people of the Commonalty don't get into wars."

"Are you quite certain?"

"What makes *you* so certain of any menace in one antiquated ship. Crewed by a score of men and women. Who came here openly and peacefully. Who, by every report, have been struggling to get past the language and culture barriers and communicate with you in detail—what in cosmos' name makes you worry about them?"

"The fact that they are liars."

Vandange sat awhile, gnawing his thumb, before he opened a box, took out a cigar and puffed it into lighting. He didn't offer Laure one. That might be for fear of poisoning his visitor with whatever local weed he was smoking. Scattered around for many generations on widely differing planets, populations did develop some odd distributions of allergy and immunity. But Laure suspected plain rudeness.

"I thought my letter made it clear," Vandange said. "They insist they are from another continuum. One with impossible properties, including visibility from ours. Conveniently on the far side of the Dragon's Head, so that we don't see it here. Oh, yes," he added quickly, "I've heard the arguments. That the whole thing is a misunderstanding due to our not having an adequate command of their language. That they're really trying to say they came from—well, the commonest rationalization is a dense star cluster. But it won't work, you know. It won't work at all."

"Why not?" Laure asked.

"Come, now. Come, now. You must have learned some astronomy as part of your training. You must know that some things simply do not occur in the galaxy."

"Uh—"

"They showed us what they alleged were lens-and-film photographs taken from, ah, inside their home universe." Vandange bore down heavily on the sarcasm. "You saw copies, didn't you? Well, now, where in the real universe do you find that kind of nebulosity—so thick and extensive that a ship can actually lose its bearings, wander around lost, using up its film among other supplies, until it chances to emerge in clear space? For that matter, assuming there were such a region, how could anyone capable of building a hyperdrive be so stupid as to go beyond sight of his beacon stars?"

"Uh...I thought of a cluster, heavily hazed, somewhat like the young clusters of the Pleiades type."

"So did many Serievans," Vandange snorted. "Please use your head. Not even Pleiadic clusters contain that much gas and dust. Besides, the verbal description of the Kirkasanters sounds like a globular cluster, insofar as it sounds like anything. But not much. The ancient red suns are there, crowded together, true. But they speak of far too many younger ones.

"And of far too much heavy metal at home. Which their ship demonstrates. Their use of alloying elements like aluminum and beryllium is incredibly parsimonious. On the other hand, electrical conductors are gold and silver, the power plant is shielded not with lead but with inert-coated osmium, and it burns plutonium which the Kirkasanters assert was mined!

"They were astonished that Serieve is such a light-metal planet. Or claimed they were astonished. I don't know about that. I do know that this whole region is dominated by light elements. That its interstellar spaces are relatively free of dust and gas, the Dragon's Head being the only exception and it merely in transit through our skies. That all this is even more true of the globular clusters, which formed in an ultratenuous medium, mostly before the galaxy had condensed to its present shape—which, in fact, practically don't *occur* in the main body of the galaxy, but are off in the surrounding halo!"

Vandange stopped for breath and triumph.

"Well." Laure shifted uneasily in his seat and wished *Jaccavrie* weren't ten thousand kilometers away at the only spaceport. "You have a point. There are contradictions, aren't there? I'll bear what you said in mind when I, uh, interview the strangers themselves."

"And you will, I trust, be wary of them," Vandange said.

"Oh, yes. Something queer does seem to be going on."

In outward appearance, the Kirkasanters were not startling. They didn't resemble any of the human breeds that had developed locally, but they varied less from the norm than some. The fifteen men and five women were tall, robust, broad in chest and shoulders, slim in waist. Their skins were dark coppery reddish, their hair blue-black and wavy; males had some beard and mustache which they wore neatly trimmed. Skulls were dolichocephalic, faces disharmonically wide, noses straight and thin, lips full. The total effect was handsome. Their eyes were their most arresting feature, large, long-lashed, luminous in shades of gray, or green, or yellow.

Since they had refused—with an adamant politeness they well knew how to assume—to let cell samples be taken for chromosome analysis, Vandange had muttered to Laure about nonhumans in surgical disguise. But that the Ranger classed as the fantasy of a provincial who'd doubtless never met a live xeno. You couldn't fake so many details, not and keep a viable organism. Unless, to be sure, happenstance had duplicated most of those details for you in the course of evolution…

Ridiculous, Laure thought. *Coincidence isn't that energetic.*

He walked from Pelogard with Demring Lodden, captain of the *Makt,* and Demring's daughter, navigator Graydal. The town was soon behind them. They found a trail that wound up into steeply rising hills, among low, gnarly trees which had begun to put forth leaves that were fronded and colored like old silver. The sun was sinking, the air noisy and full of salt odors. Neither Kirkasanter appeared to mind the chill.

"You know your way here well," Laure said clumsily.

"We should," Demring answered, "for we have been held on this sole island, with naught to do but ramble it when the *reyad* takes us."

"*Reyad?*" Laure asked.

"The need to…search," Graydal said. "To track beasts, or find what is new, or be alone in wild places. Our folk were hunters until not so long ago. We bear their blood."

Demring wasn't to be diverted from his grudge. "Why are we thus confined?" he growled. "Each time we sought an answer, we got an evasion. Fear of disease, need for us to learn what to expect—Ha, by now I'm half minded to draw my gun, force my way to our ship, and depart for aye!"

He was erect, grizzled, deeply graven of countenance and bleak of gaze. Like his men, he wore soft boots, a knee-length gown of some fine-scaled leather, a cowled cloak, a dagger and an energy pistol at his belt. On his forehead sparkled a diamond that betokened authority.

"Well, but, Master," Graydal said, "here today we deal with no village witchfinders. Daven Laure is a king's man, with power to act, knowledge and courage to act rightly. Has he not gone off alone with us because you said you felt stifled and spied on in the town? Let us talk as freefolk with him."

Her smile, her words in the husky voice that Laure remembered from his recordings, were gentle. He felt pretty sure, though, that as much steel underlay her as her father, and possibly whetted sharper. She almost matched his height, her gait was tigerish, she was herself weaponed and diademmed. Unlike Laure's close cut or Demring's short bob, her hair passed through a platinum ring and blew free at full length. Her clothes were little more than footgear, fringed shorts, and thin blouse. However attractive, the sight did not suggest seductive femininity to the Ranger—when she wasn't feeling the cold that struck through his garments. Besides, he had already learned that the sexes were mixed aboard the *Makt* for no other reason than that women were better at certain jobs than men. Every female was accompanied by an older male relative. The Kirkasanters were not an uncheeerful folk on the whole, but some of their ideals looked austere.

Nonetheless, Graydal had lovely strong features, and her eyes, under the level brows, shone amber.

"Maybe the local government was overcautious," Laure said, "but don't forget, this is a frontier settlement. Not many light-years hence, in that part of the sky you came from, begins the unknown. It's true the stars are comparatively thin in these parts—average distance between them about four parsecs—but still, their number is too great for us to do more than feel our way slowly forward. Especially when, in the nature of the case, planets like Serieve must devote most of their effort to developing themselves. So, when one is ignorant, one does best to be careful."

He flattered himself that was a well-composed conciliatory speech. It wasn't as oratorical as one of theirs, but they had lung capacity for a thinner atmosphere than this. He was disappointed when Demring said scornfully, "*Our* ancestors were not so timid."

"Or else their pursuers were not," Graydal laughed.

The captain looked offended. Laure hastily asked: "Have you no knowledge of what happened?"

"No," said the girl, turned pensive. "Not in truth. Legends, found in many forms across all Kirkasant, tell of battle, and a shipful of people who fled far until at last they found haven. A few fragmentary records—but those are vague, save the Baorn Codex; and it is little more than a compendium of technical information which the wisemen of Skribent preserved. Even in that case"—she smiled again—"the meaning of most passages was generally obscure until after our modern scientists had invented the thing described for themselves."

"Do you know what records remain in Homeland?" Demring asked hopefully.

Laure sighed and shook his head. "No. Perhaps none, by now. Doubtless, in time, an expedition will go from us to Earth. But after five thousand trouble-filled years—And your ancestors may not have started from there. They may have belonged to one of the first colonies."

In a dim way, he could reconstruct the story. There had been a fight. The reasons—personal, familial, national, ideological, economic, whatever they were—had dropped into the bottom of the millennia between then and now. (A commentary on the importance of any such reasons.) But someone had so badly wanted the destruction of someone else that one ship, or one fleet, hounded another almost a quarter way around the galaxy.

Or maybe not, in a literal sense. It would have been hard to do. Crude as they were, those early vessels could have made the trip, if frequent stops were allowed for repair and resupply and refilling of the nuclear converters. But to this day, a craft under hyperdrive could only be detected within approximately a light-year's radius by the instantaneous "wake" of space-pulses. If she lay doggo for a while, she was usually unfindable in the sheer stupendousness of any somewhat larger volume. That the hunter should never, in the course of many months, either have overhauled his quarry or lost the scent altogether, seemed conceivable but implausible.

Maybe pursuit had not been for the whole distance. Maybe the refugees had indeed escaped after a while, but—in blind panic, or rage against the foe, or desire to practice undisturbed a brand of utopianism, or whatever the motive was—they had continued as far as they possibly could, and hidden themselves as thoroughly as nature allowed.

In any case, they had ended in a strange part of creation: so strange that numerous men on Serieve did not admit it existed. By then, their ship must have been badly in need of a complete overhaul, amounting virtually to a rebuilding. They settled down to construct the necessary industrial base. (Think, for example, how much plant you must have before you make your first transistor.) They did not have the accumulated experience of later generations to prove how impossible this was.

Of course they failed. A few score—a few hundred at absolute maximum, if the ship had been rigged with suspended-animation lockers—could not preserve a full-fledged civilization while coping with a planet for which man was never meant. And they had to content themselves with that planet. Once into the Cloud Universe, even if their vessel could still wheeze along for a while, they were no longer able to move freely about, picking and choosing.

Kirkasant was probably the best of a bad lot. And Laure thought it was rather a miracle that man had survived there. So small a genetic pool, so hostile an environment...but the latter might well have saved him from the effects of the former. Natural selection must have been harsh. And, seemingly, the radiation background was high, which led to a corresponding mutation rate. Women bore from puberty to menopause, and buried most of their babies. Men struggled to keep them alive. Often death harvested adults, too, entire families. But those who were fit tended to survive. And the planet did have an unfilled ecological niche: the one reserved for intelligence. Evolution galloped. Population exploded. In one or two millennia, man was at home on Kirkasant. In five, he crowded it and went looking for new planets.

Because culture had never totally died. The first generation might be unable to build machine tools, but could mine and forge metals. The next generation might be too busy to keep public schools, but had enough hard practical respect for learning that it supported a literate class. Succeeding generations, wandering into new lands, founding new nations and societies, might war with each other, but all drew from a common tradition and looked to one goal: reunion with the stars.

Once the scientific method had been created afresh, Laure thought, progress must have been more rapid than on Earth. For the natural philosophers knew certain things were possible, even if they didn't know how, and this was half the battle. They must have got some hints, however oracular from the remnants of ancient texts. They actually had the corroded hulk of the ancestral ship for their studying. Given this much, it was not too surprising that they leaped in a single lifetime from the first moon rockets to the first hyperdrive craft—and did so on a basis of wildly distorted physical theory, and embarked with such naïveté that they couldn't find their way home again!

All very logical. Unheard of, outrageously improbable, but in this big a galaxy the strangest things are bound to happen now and again. The Kirkasanters could be absolutely honest in their story.

If they were.

"Let the past tend the past," Graydal said impatiently. "We've tomorrow to hunt in."

"Yes," Laure said, "but I do need to know a few things. It's not clear to me how you found us. I mean, you crossed a thousand light-years or more of wilderness. How did you come on a speck like Serieve?"

"We were asked that before," Demring said, "but then we could not well explain, few words being held in common. Now you show a good command of the Hobrokan tongue, and for our part, albeit none of these villagers will take the responsibility of putting one of us under your educator machine…in talking with technical folk we've gained various technical words of yours."

He was silent awhile, collecting phrases. The three people continued up the trail. It was wide enough for them to walk abreast, somewhat muddy with rain and melted snow. The sun was so far down that the woods walled it off; twilight smoked from the ground and from either side, though the sky was still pale. The wind was dying but the chill deepening. Somewhere behind those dun trunks and ashy-metallic leaves, a voice went "K-kr-r-r-*rukl*" and, above and ahead, the sound of a river became audible.

Demring said with care: "See you, when we could not find our way back to Kirkasant's sun, and at last had come out in an altogether different cosmos, we thought our ancestors might have originated there. Certain traditional songs hinted as much, speaking of space as dark, for instance; and surely darkness encompassed us now, and immense loneliness between the stars. Well, but in which direction might Homeland lie? Casting about with telescopes, we spied afar a black cloud, and thought, if the ancestors had been in flight from enemies, they might well have gone through such, hoping to break their trail."

"The Dragon's Head Nebula," Laure nodded.

Graydal's wide shoulders lifted and fell. "At least it gave us something to steer by," she said.

Laure stole a moment's admiration of her profile. "You had courage," he said. "Quite aside from everything else, how did you know this civilization had not stayed hostile to you?"

"How did we know it ever was in the first place?" she chuckled. "Myself, insofar as I believe the myths have any truth, I suspect our ancestors were thieves or bandits, or—"

"Daughter!" Demring hurried on, in a scandalized voice: "When we had fared thus far, we found the darkness was dust and gas such as pervade the universe at home. There was simply an absence of stars to make it shine. Emerging on the far side, we tuned our neutrino detectors. Our reasoning was that a highly developed civilization would use a great many nuclear power plants. Their neutrino flux should be detectable above the natural noise level—in this comparatively empty cosmos—across several score light-years or better, and we could home on it."

First they sound like barbarian bards, Laure thought, *and then like radionicians. No wonder a dogmatist like Vandange can't put credence in them.*

Can I?

"We soon began to despair," Graydal said. "We were nigh to the limit—"

"No matter," Demring interrupted.

She looked steadily first at one man, then the other, and said, "I dare trust Daven Laure." To the Ranger: "Belike no secret anyhow, since men on Serieve must have examined our ship with knowledgeable eyes. We were nigh to our limit of travel without refueling or refurbishing. We were about to seek for a planet not too unlike Kirkasant where—But then, as if by Valfar's Wings, came the traces we sought, and we followed them here.

"And here were humans!

"Only of late has our gladness faded as we begin to see how they temporize and keep us half prisoner. Wholly prisoner, maybe, should we try to depart. Why will they not rely on us?"

"I tried to explain that when we talked yesterday," Laure said. "Some important men don't see how you could be telling the truth."

She caught his hand in a brief, impulsive grasp. Her own was warm, slender, and hard. "But you are different?"

"Yes." He felt helpless and alone. "They've, well, they've called for me. Put the entire problem in the hands of my organization. And my fellows have so much else to do that, well, I'm given broad discretion."

Demring regarded him shrewdly. "You are a young man," he said. "Do not let your powers paralyze you."

"No. I will do what I can for you. It may be little."

The trail rounded a thicket and they saw a rustic bridge across the river, which ran seaward in foam and clangor. Halfway over, the party stopped, leaned on the rail and looked down. The water was thickly shadowed between its banks, and the woods were becoming a solid black mass athwart a dusking sky. The air smelled wet.

"You realize," Laure said "it won't be easy to retrace your route. You improvised your navigational coordinates. They can be transformed into ours on this side of the Dragon's Head, I suppose. But once beyond the nebula, I'll be off my own charts, except for what few listed objects are visible from either side. No one from this civilization has been there, you see, what with millions of suns closer to our settlements. And the star sights you took can't have been too accurate."

"You are not going to take us to Homeland, then," Demring said tonelessly.

"Don't you understand? Homeland, Earth, it's so far away that I myself don't know what it's like anymore!"

"But you must have a nearby capital, a more developed world than this. Why do you not guide us thither that we may talk with folk wiser than these wretched Serievans?"

"Well…uh…Oh, many reasons. I'll be honest, caution is one of them. Also, the Commonalty does not have anything like a capital, or—But yes, I could guide you to the heart of civilization. Any of numerous civilizations in this galactic arm." Laure took a breath and slogged on. My decision, though, under the circumstances is that first I'd better see your world Kirkasant. After that…well, certainly, if everything is all right, we'll establish regular contacts, and invite your people to visit ours and—Don't you like the plan? Don't you want to go home?"

"How shall we, ever?" Graydal asked low.

Laure cast her a surprised glance. She stared ahead of her and down, into the river. A fish—some kind of swimming creature—leaped. Its scales caught what light remained in a gleam that was faint but startling against those murky waters. She didn't seem to notice, though she cocked her head instinctively toward the splash that followed.

"Have you not listened?" she said. "Did you not hear us? How long we searched in the fog, through that forest of suns, until at last we left our whole small bright universe and came into this great one that has so much blackness in it—and thrice we plunged back into our own space, and groped about, and came forth without having found trace of any star we knew—" Her voice lifted the least bit. "We are lost, I tell you, eternally lost. Take us to your home, Daven Laure, that we may try to make ours there."

He wanted to stroke her hands, which had clenched into fists on the bridge rail. But he made himself say only: "Our science and resources are more than yours. Maybe we can find a way where you cannot. At any rate, I'm duty bound to learn as much as I can, before I make report and recommendation to my superiors."

"I do not think you are kind, forcing my crew to return and look again on what has gone from them," Demring said stiffly. "But I have scant choice save to agree." He straightened. "Come, best we start back toward Pelogard. Night will soon be upon us."

"Oh, no rush," Laure said, anxious to change the subject. "An arctic zone, at this time of year—We'll have no trouble."

"Maybe you will not," Graydal said. "But Kirkasant after sunset is not like here."

They were on their way down when dusk became night, a light night where only a few stars gleamed and Laure walked easily through a clear gloaming. Graydal and Demring must needs use their energy guns at minimum intensity for flashcasters. And even so, they often stumbled.

Makt was three times the size of *Jaccavrie*, a gleaming torpedo. shape whose curve was broken by boat housings and weapon turrets. The Ranger vessel looked like a gig attending her. In actuality, *Jaccavrie* could have outrun, outmaneuvered, or outfought the Kirkasanter with ludicrous ease. Laure didn't emphasize that fact. His charges were touchy enough already. He had suggested hiring a modern carrier for them, and met a glacial negative. This craft was the property and bore the honor of the confederated clans that had built her. She was not to be abandoned.

Modernizing her would have taken more time than increased speed would save. Besides, while Laure was personally convinced of the good intentions of Demring's people, he had no right to present them with up-to-date technology until he had proof they wouldn't misuse it.

One could not accurately say that he resigned himself to accompanying them in his ship at the plodding pace of theirs. The weeks of travel gave him a chance to get acquainted with them and their culture. And that was not only his duty but his pleasure. Especially, he found, when Graydal was involved.

Some time passed before he could invite her to dinner *à deux*. He arranged it with what he felt sure was adroitness. Two persons, undisturbed, talking socially, could exchange information of the subtle kind that didn't come across in committee. Thus he proposed a series of private meetings with the officers of *Makt*. He began with the captain, naturally; but after a while came the navigator's turn.

Jaccavrie phased in with the other vessel, laid alongside and made air-lock connections in a motion too smooth to feel. Graydal came aboard and the ships parted company again. Laure greeted her according to the way of Kirkasant, with a handshake. The clasp lasted a moment. "Welcome," he said.

"Peace between us." Her smile offset her formalism. She was in uniform—another obsolete aspect of her society—but it shimmered gold and molded itself to her.

"Won't you come to the saloon for a drink before we eat?"

"I shouldn't. Not in space."

"No hazard," said the computer in an amused tone. "I operate everything anyway."

Graydal had tensed and clapped hand to gun at the voice. She relaxed and tried to laugh. "I'm sorry. I am not used to…you." She almost bounded on her way down the corridor with Laure. He had set the interior weight at one standard G. The Kirkasanters maintained theirs fourteen percent higher, to match the pull of their home world.

Though she had inspected this ship several times already, Graydal looked wide-eyed around her. The saloon was small but sybaritic. "You do yourself proud," she said amidst the draperies, music, perfumes, and animations.

He guided her to a couch. "You don't sound quite approving," he said.

"Well—"

"There's no virtue in suffering hardships."

"But there is in the ability to endure them." She sat too straight for the form-fitter cells to make her comfortable.

"Think I can't?"

Embarrassed, she turned her gaze from him toward the viewscreen, on which flowed a color composition. Her lips tightened. "Why have you turned off the exterior scene?"

"You don't seem to like it, I've noticed." He sat down beside her. "What will you have? We're fairly well stocked."

"Turn it on."

"What?"

"The outside view." Her nostrils dilated. "It shall not best me."

He spread his hands. The ship saw his rueful gesture and obliged. Space leaped into the screen, star-strewn except where the storm-cloud mass of the dark nebula reared ahead. He heard Graydal suck in a breath and said quickly, "Uh, since you aren't familiar with our beverages, I suggest daiquiris. They're tart, a little sweet—"

Her nod was jerky. Her eyes seemed locked to the screen. He leaned close, catching the slight warm odor of her, not quite identical with the odor of other women he had known, though the difference was too subtle for him to name. "Why does that sight bother you?" he asked.

"The strangeness. The aloneness. It is so absolutely alien to home. I feel forsaken and—" She filled her lungs, forced detachment on herself, and said in an analytical manner: "Possibly we are disturbed by a black sky because we have virtually none of what you call night vision." A touch of trouble returned. "What else have we lost?"

"Night vision isn't needed on Kirkasant, you tell me," Laure consoled her. "And evolution there worked fast. But you must have gained as well as atrophied. I know you have more physical strength, for instance, than your ancestors could've had." A tray with two glasses extended from the side. "Ah, here are the drinks."

She sniffed at hers. "It smells pleasant," she said. "But are you sure there isn't something I might be allergic to?"

"I doubt that. You didn't react to anything you tried on Serieve, did you?"

"No, except for finding it overly bland."

"Don't worry," he grinned. "Before we left, your father took care to present me with one of your saltshakers. It'll be on the dinner table."

Jaccavrie had analyzed the contents. Besides sodium and potassium chloride—noticeably less abundant on Kirkasant than on the average planet, but not scarce enough to cause real trouble—the mixture included a number of other salts. The proportion of rare earths and especially arsenic was surprising. An ordinary human who ingested the latter element at that rate would lose quite a few years of life expectancy. Doubtless the first refugee generations had, too, when something else didn't get them first. But by now their descendants were so well adapted that food didn't taste right without a bit of arsenic trioxide.

"We wouldn't have to be cautious—we'd know in advance what you can and cannot take—if you'd permit a chromosome analysis," Laure hinted. "The laboratory aboard this ship can do it."

Her cheeks turned more than ever coppery. She scowled. "We refused before," she said.

"May I ask why?"

"It…violates integrity. Humans are not to be probed into."

He had encountered that attitude before, in several guises. To the Kirkasanter—at least, to the Hobrokan clansman; the planet had other cultures—the body was a citadel for the ego, which by right should be inviolable. The feeling, so basic that few were aware of having it, had led to the formation of reserved, often rather cold personalities. It had handicapped if not stopped the progress of medicine. On the plus side, it had made for dignity and self-reliance; and it had caused this civilization to be spared professional gossips, confessional literature, and psychoanalysis.

"I don't agree," Laure said. "Nothing more is involved than scientific information. What's personal about a DNA map?"

"Well…maybe. I shall think on the matter." Graydal made an obvious effort to get away from the topic. She sipped her drink, smiled, and said, "Mm-m-m, this *is* a noble flavor."

"Hoped you'd like it. I do. We have a custom in the Commonalty—" He touched glasses with her.

"Charming. Now we, when good friends are together, drink half what's in our cups and then exchange them."

"May I?"

She blushed again, but with pleasure. "Certainly. You honor me."

"No, the honor is mine." Laure went on, quite sincere: "What your people have done is tremendous. What an addition to the race you'll be!"

Her mouth drooped. "If ever my folk may be found."

"Surely—"

"Do you think we did not try?" She tossed off another gulp of her cocktail. Evidently it went fast to her unaccustomed head. "We did not fare forth blindly.

Understand that *Makt* is not the first ship to leave Kirkasant's sun. But the prior ones went to nearby stars, stars that can be seen from home. They are many. We had not realized how many more are in the Cloud Universe, hidden from eyes and instruments, a few light-years farther on. We, our ship, we intended to take the next step. Only the next step. Barely beyond that shell of suns we could see from Kirkasant's system. We could find our way home again without trouble. Of course we could! We need but steer by those suns that were already charted on the edge of instrumental perception. Once we were in their neighborhood, our familiar part of space would be visible."

She faced him, gripping his arm painfully hard, speaking in a desperate voice. "What we had not known, what no one had known, was the imprecision of that charting. The absolute magnitudes, therefore the distances and relative positions of those verge-visible stars…had not been determined as well as the astronomers believed. Too much haze, too much shine, too much variability. Do you understand? And so, suddenly, our tables were worthless. We thought we could identify some suns. But we were wrong. Flitting toward them, we must have bypassed the volume of space we sought…and gone on and on, more hopelessly lost each day, each endless day—"

"What makes you think you can find our home?"

Laure, who had heard the details before, had spent the time admiring her and weighing his reply. He sipped his own drink, letting the sourness glide over his palate and the alcohol slightly, soothingly burn him, before he said: "I can try. I do have instruments your people have not yet invented. Inertial devices, for example, that work under hyperdrive as well as at true velocity. Don't give up hope." He paused. "I grant you, we might fail. Then what will you do?"

The blunt question, which would have driven many women of his world to tears, made her rally. She lifted her head and said—haughtiness rang through the words: "Why, we will make the best of things, and I do not think we will do badly."

Well, he thought, *she's descended from nothing but survivor types. Her nature is to face trouble and whip it.*

"I'm sure you will succeed magnificently," he said. "You'll need time to grow used to our ways, and you may never feel quite easy in them, but—"

"What are your marriages like?" she asked.

"Uh?" Laure fitted his jaw back into place.

She was not drunk, he decided. A bit of drink, together with these surroundings, the lilting music, odors and pheromones in the air, had simply lowered her inhibitions. The huntress in her was set free, and at once attacked whatever had been most deeply perturbing her. The basic reticence remained. She looked straight at him, but she was fiery-faced, as she said:

"We ought to have had an equal number of men and women along on *Makt*. Had we known what was to happen, we would have done so. But now ten men shall have to find wives among foreigners. Do you think they will have much difficulty?"

"Uh, why no. I shouldn't think they will," he flundered. "They're obviously superior types, and then, being exotic—glamorous…"

"I speak not of amatory pleasure. But…what I overheard on Serieve, a time or two…did I miscomprehend? Are there truly women among you who do not bear children?"

"On the older planets, yes, that's not uncommon. Population control—"

"We shall have to stay on Serieve, then, or worlds like it." She sighed. "I had hoped we might go to the pivot of your civilization, where your real work is done and our children might become great."

Laure considered her. After a moment, he understood. Adapting to the uncountably many alienesses of Kirkasant had been a long and cruel process. No blood line survived which did not do more than make up its own heavy losses. The will to reproduce was a requirement of existence. It, too, became an instinct.

He remembered that, while Kirkasant was not a very fertile planet, and today its population strained its resources, no one had considered reducing the birthrate. When someone on Serieve had asked why, Demring's folk had reacted strongly. The idea struck them as obscene. They didn't care for the notion of genetic modification or exogenetic growth either. And yet they were quite reasonable and non-compulsive about most other aspects of their culture.

Culture, Laure thought. *Yes. That's mutable. But you don't change your instincts; they're built into your chromosomes. Her people* must *have children.*

"Well," he said, "you can find women who want large families on the central planets, too. If anything, they'll be eager to marry your friends. They have a problem finding men who feel as they do, you see."

Graydal dazzled him with a smile and held out her glass. "Exchange?" she proposed.

"Hoy, you're way ahead of me." He evened the liquid levels. "Now."

They looked at each other throughout the little ceremony. He nerved himself to ask, "As for you women, do you necessarily have to marry within your ship?"

"No," she said. "It would depend on…whether any of your folk…might come to care for one of us."

"That I can guarantee!"

"I would like a man who travels," she murmured, "if I and the children could come along."

"Quite easy to arrange," Laure said.

She said in haste: "But we are buying grief, are we not? You told me perhaps you can find our planet for us."

"Yes. I hope, though, if we succeed, that won't be the last I see of you."

"Truly it won't."

They finished their drinks and went to dinner. *Jaccavrie* was also an excellent cook. And the choice of wines was considerable. What was said and laughed at over the table had no relevance to anyone but Laure and Graydal.

Except that, at the end, with immense and tender seriousness she said: "If you want a cell sample from me…for analysis…you may have it."

He reached across the table and took her hand. "I wouldn't want you to do anything you might regret later," he said.

She shook her head. The tawny eyes never left him. Her voice was slow, faintly slurred, but bespoke complete awareness of what she was saying. "I have come to know you. For you to do this thing will be no violation."

Laure explained eagerly: "The process is simple and painless as far as you're concerned. We can go right down to the lab. The computer operates everything. It'll give you an anesthetic spray and remove a small sample of flesh, so small that tomorrow you won't be sure where the spot was. Of course, the analysis will take a long while. We don't have all possible equipment aboard. And the computer does have to devote most of her—most of its attention to piloting and interior work. But at the end, we'll be able to tell you—"

"Hush." Her smile was sleepy. "No matter. If you wish this, that's enough. I ask only one thing."

"What?"

"Do not let a machine use the knife, or the needle, or whatever it is. I want you to do that yourself."

"…Yes. Yonder is our home sky." The physicist Hirn Oran's son spoke slow and hushed. Cosmic interference seethed across his radio voice, nigh drowning it in Laure's and Graydal's earplugs.

"No," the Ranger said. "Not off there. We're already in it."

"What?" Silvery against rock, the two space-armored figures turned to stare at him. He could not see their expressions behind the faceplates, but he could imagine how astonishment flickered above awe.

He paused, arranging words in his mind. The star noise in his receivers was like surf and fire. The landscape overwhelmed him.

Here was no simple airless planet. No planet is ever really simple, and this one had a stranger history than most. Eons ago it was apparently a subjovian, with a cloudy hydrohelium and methane atmosphere and an immense shell of ice and frozen gases around the core; for it orbited its sun at a distance of almost a billion and a half kilometers, and though that primary was bright, at this remove it could be little more than a spark.

Until stellar evolution—hastened, Laure believed, by an abnormal infall of cosmic material—took the star off the main sequence. It swelled, surface cooling to red but total output growing so monstrous that the inner planets were consumed. On the farther ones, like this, atmosphere fled into space. Ice melted; the world-ocean boiled; each time the pulsations of the sun reached a maximum, more vapor escaped. Now nothing remained except a ball of metal and rock, hardly larger than a terrestrial-type globe. As the pressure of the top layers was removed, frightful tectonic forces must have been liberated. Mountains—the younger ones with crags like sharp teeth, the older ones worn by meteorite and thermal erosion—rose from a cratered plain of gloomy stone. Currently at a minimum, but nonetheless immense, a full seven degrees across, blue core surrounded and dimmed by the tenuous ruddy atmosphere, the sun smoldered aloft.

Its furnace light was not the sole illumination. Another star was passing sufficiently near at the time that it showed a perceptible disk…in a stopped-down viewscreen, because no human eye could directly confront that electric cerulean intensity. The outsider was a B_8, newborn out of dust and gas, blazing with an intrinsic radiance of a hundred Sols.

Neither one helped in the shadows cast by the pinnacled upthrust which Laure's party was investigating. Flashcasters were necessary.

But more was to see overhead, astride the dark. Stars in thousands powdered the sky, brilliant with proximity. And they were the mere fringes of the cluster. It was rising as the planet turned, partly backgrounding and partly following the sun. Laure had never met a sight to compare. For the most part, the individuals he could pick out in that enormous spheroidal cloud of light were themselves red: long-lived dwarfs, dying giants like the one that brooded over him. But many glistened exuberant golden, emerald, sapphire. Some could not be older than the blue which wandered past and added its own harsh hue to this land. All those stars were studded through a soft glow that pervaded the entire cluster, a nacreous luminosity into which they faded and vanished, the fog wherein his companions had lost their home but which was a shining beauty to behold.

"You live in a wonder," Laure said

Graydal moved toward him. She had had no logical reason to come down out of *Makt*'s orbit with him and Hirn. The idea was simply to break out certain large ground-based instruments that *Jaccavrie* carried, for study of their goal before traveling on. Any third party could assist. But she had laid her claim first, and none of her shipmates argued. They knew how often she and Laure were in each other's company.

"Wait until you reach our world," she said low. "Space is eldritch and dangerous. But once on Kirkasant—We will watch the sun go down in the Rainbow Desert; suddenly in that thin air, night has come, our shimmering star-crowded night, and the auroras dance and whisper above the stark hills. We will see great flying flocks rise from dawn mists over the salt marshes, hear their wings thunder and their voices flute. We will stand on the battlements of Ey under the banners of those very knights who long ago rid the land of the firegarms, and watch the folk dance welcome to a new year—"

"If the navigator pleases," said Hirn, his voice sharpened by an unadmitted dauntedness, "we will save our dreams for later and attend now to the means of realizing them. At present, we are supposed to choose a good level site for the observing apparatus. But, ah, Ranger Laure may I ask what you meant by saying we are already back in the Cloud Universe?"

Laure was not as annoyed to have Graydal interrupted as he might normally have been. She'd spoken of Kirkasant so often that he felt he had almost been there himself. Doubtless it had its glories, but by his standards it was a grim, dry, storm-scoured planet where he would not care to stay for long at a time. Of course, to her it was beloved home; and he wouldn't mind making occasional visits if—No, chaos take it, there was work on hand!

Part of his job was to make explanations. He said: "In your sense of the term, Physicist Hirn, the Cloud Universe does not exist."

The reply was curt through the static. "I disputed that point on Serieve already, with Vandange and others. And I resented their implication that we of *Makt* were either liars or incompetent observers."

"You're neither," Laure said quickly. "But communication had a double barrier on Serieve. First, an imperfect command of your language. Only on the way here, spending most of my time in contact with your crew, have I myself begun to feel a real mastery of Hobrokan. The second barrier, though, was in some ways more serious: Vandange's stubborn preconceptions, and your own."

"I was willing to be convinced."

"But you never got a convincing argument. Vandange was so dogmatically certain that what you reported having seen was impossible, that he didn't take a serious look at your report to see if it might have an orthodox explanation after all. You naturally got angry at this and cut the discussions off short. For your part, you had what you had always been taught was a perfectly good theory, which your experiences had confirmed. You weren't going to change your whole concept of physics just because the unlovable Ozer Vandange scoffed at it."

"But we were mistaken," Graydal said. "You've intimated as much, Daven, but never made your meaning clear."

"I wanted to see the actual phenomenon for myself, first," Laure said. "We have a proverb—so old that it's reputed to have originated on Earth—'It is a capital mistake to theorize in advance of the data.' But I couldn't help speculating, and what I see shows my speculations were along the right lines."

"Well?" Hirn challenged.

"Let's start with looking at the situation from your viewpoint," Laure suggested. "Your people spent millennia on Kirkasant. You lost every hint, except a few ambiguous traditions, that things might be different elsewhere. To you, it was natural that the night sky should be like a gently shining mist, and stars should crowd thickly around. When you developed the scientific method again, not many generations back, perforce you studied the universe you knew. Ordinary physics and chemistry, even atomistics and quantum theory, gave you no special problems. But you measured the distances of the visible stars as light-months—at most, a few light-years—after which they vanished in the foggy background. You measured the concentration of that fog, that dust and fluorescing gas. And you had no reason to suppose the interstellar medium was not equally dense everywhere. Nor had you any hint of receding galaxies.

"So your version of relativity made space sharply curved by the mass packed together throughout it. The entire universe was two or three hundred light-years across. Stars condensed and evolved—you could witness every stage of that—but in a chaotic fashion, with no particular overall structure. It's a wonder to me that you went on to gravities and hyperdrive. I wish I were scientist enough to appreciate how different some of the laws and constants must be in your physics. But you did plow ahead. I guess the fact you knew these things were possible was important to your success. Your scientists would keep fudging and finagling, in defiance of theoretical niceties, until they made something work."

"Um-m-m…as a matter of fact, yes," Hirn said in a slightly abashed tone. Graydal snickered.

"Well, then *Makt* lost her way, and emerged into the outer universe, which was totally strange," Laure said. "You had to account somehow for what you saw. As any scientists, you stayed with accepted ideas as long a feasible—a perfectly correct principle which my people call the razor of Occam. I imagine that the notion of continuous space-times with varying properties looks quite logical if you're used to thinking of a universe with an extremely small radius. You may have been puzzled by how you managed to get out of one 'bubble' and into the next, but I daresay you cobbled together a tentative explanation."

"I did," Hirn said. "If we postulate a multidimensional—"

"Never mind," Laure said. "That's no longer needful. We can account for the facts much more simply."

"How? I have been pondering it. I think I can grasp the idea of a universe billions of light-years across, in which the stars form galaxies. But our home space—"

"Is a dense star cluster. And as such, it has no definite boundaries. That's what I meant by saying we are already in it. In the thin verge at least." Laure pointed to the diffuse, jeweled magnificence that was rising higher above these wastes in the wake of the red and blue suns. "Yonder's the main body, and Kirkasant is somewhere there. But this system here is associated. I've checked proper motions and I know."

"I could have accepted some such picture while on Serieve," Hirn said. "But Vandange was so insistent that a star cluster like this cannot be." Laure visualized the sneer behind his faceplate. "I thought that he, belonging to the master civilization, would know whereof he spoke."

"He does. He's merely rather unimaginative," Laure said. "You see, what we have here is a globular cluster. That's a group made up of stars close together in a roughly spherical volume of space. I'd guess you have a quarter million, packed into a couple of hundred light-years' diameter.

"But globular clusters haven't been known like this one. The ones we do know lie mostly well off the galactic plane. The space within them is much clearer than in the spiral arms, almost a perfect vacuum. The individual members are red. Any normal stars of greater than minimal mass have gone off the main sequence long ago. The survivors are metal-poor. That's another sign of extreme age. Heavy elements are formed in stellar cores, you know, and spewed back into space. So it's the younger suns, coalescing out of the enriched interstellar medium, that contain a lot of metal. All in all, everything points to the globular clusters being relics of an embryo stage in the galaxy's life.

"Yours, however—! Dust and gas so thick that not even a giant can be seen across many parsecs. Plenty of mainsequence stars, including blues which cannot be more than a few million years old, they burn out so fast. Spectra, not to mention planets your explorers visited, showing atomic abundances far skewed toward the high end of the periodic table. A background radiation too powerful for a man like me to dare take up permanent residence in your country.

"Such a cluster shouldn't be!"

"But it is," Graydal said.

Laure made bold to squeeze her hand, though little of that could pass through the gauntlets. "I'm glad," he answered.

"How do you explain the phenomenon?" Hirn asked. "Oh, that's obvious... now that I've seen the things and gathered some information on its path," Laure said. "An improbable situation, maybe unique, but not impossible. This cluster happens to have an extremely eccentric orbit around the galactic center of mass,. Once or twice a gigayear, it passes through the vast thick clouds that surround that region. By gravitation, it sweeps up immense quantities of stuff. Meanwhile, I suppose, perturbation causes some of its senior members to drift off. You might say it's periodically rejuvenated.

"At present, it's on its way out again. Hasn't quite left our spiral arm. It passed near the galactic, midpoint just a short while back, cosmically speaking; I'd estimate less than fifty million years. The infall is still turbulent, still condensing out into new stars like that blue giant shining on us. Your home sun and its planets must be a product of an earlier sweep. But there've been twenty or thirty such since the galaxy formed, and each one of them was responsible for several generations of giant stars. So Kirkasant has a lot more heavy elements than the normal planet, even though it's not much younger than Earth. Do you follow me?"

"Hm-m-m...perhaps. I shall have to think." Hirn walked off, across the great tilted block on which the party stood to its edge where he stopped and looked down into the shadows below. They were deep and knife sharp. The mingled light of red and blue suns, stars, starfog played eerie across the stone land. Laure grew aware of what strangeness and what silence—under the hiss in his ears—pressed in on him.

Graydal must have felt the same, for she edged until their armors clinked together. He would have liked to see her face. She said: "Do you truly believe we can enter that realm and conquer it?"

"I don't know,'" he said, slow and blunt. "The sheer number of stars may beat us."

"A large enough fleet could search them, one by one."

"If it could navigate. We have yet to find out whether that's possible."

"Suppose. Did you guess a quarter million suns in the cluster? Not all are like ours. Not even a majority. On the other coin side with visibility as low as it is, space must be searched back and forth, light-year by light-year. We of *Makt* could die of eld before a single vessel chanced on Kirkasant."

"I'm afraid that's true."

"Yet an adequate number of ships, dividing the task, could find our home in a year or two."

"That would be unattainably expensive, Graydal."

He thought he sensed her stiffening. "I've come on this before," she said coldly, withdrawing from his touch. "In your Commonalty they count the cost and the profit first. Honor, adventure, simple charity must run a poor second."

"Be reasonable," he said. "Cost represents labor skill and resources. The gigantic fleet that would go looking for Kirkasant must be diverted from other jobs. Other people would suffer need as a result. Some might suffer sharply."

"Do you mean a civilization as big, as productive as yours could not spare that much effort for a while without risking disaster?"

She's quick on the uptake, Laure thought. *Knowing what machine technology can do on her single impoverished world, she can well guess what it's capable of with millions of planets to draw on. But how can I make her realize that matters aren't that simple?*

"Please, Graydal," he said. "Won't you believe I'm working for you? I've come this far, and I'll go as much farther as need be, if something doesn't kill us."

He heard her gulp. "Yes. I offer apology. *You* are different."

"Not really. I'm a typical Commonalty member. Later maybe, I can show you how our civilization works and what an odd problem in political economy we've got if Kirkasant is to be rediscovered. But first we have to establish that locating it is physically possible. We have to make long-term observations from here, and then enter those mists, and—One trouble at a time, I beg you!"

She laughed gently. "Indeed, my friend. And you will find a way." The mirth faded. It had never been strong. "Won't you?" The reflection of clouded stars glistened on her faceplate like tears.

Blindness was not dark. It shone.

Standing on the bridge, amidst the view of space, Laure saw nimbus and thunderheads. They piled in cliffs, they eddied. and streamed, their color was a sheen of all colors overlying white—mother-of-pearl—but here and there they darkened with shadows and grottoes; here and there they glowed dull red as they reflected a nearby sun. For the stars were scattered about in their myriads, dominantly ruby and ember, some yellow or candent, green or blue. The nearest were clear to the eye, a few showing tiny disks, but the majority were fuzzy glows rather than light-points. Such shimmers grew dim with distance until the mist engulfed them entirely and nothing remained but mist.

A crackling noise beat out of that roiling formlessness, like flames. Energies pulsed through his marrow. He remembered the old, old myth of the Yawning Gap, where fire and ice arose and out of them the Nine Worlds, which were doomed in the end to return to fire and ice; and he shivered.

"Illusion" said *Jaccavrie's* voice out of immensity.

"What?'" Laure started. It was as if a mother goddess had spoken.

She chuckled. Whether deity or machine, she had the greatest strength of ordinariness in her. "You're rather transparent to an observer who knows you well," she said. "I could practically read your mind."

Laure swallowed. "The sight, well, a big, marvelous, dangerous thing, maybe unique in the galaxy. Yes, I admit I'm impressed."

"We have much to learn here."

"Have you been doing so?"

"At a near-capacity rate, since we entered the denser part of the cluster." *Jacccavrie* shifted to primness. "If you'd been less immersed in discussions with the Kirkasanter navigation officer, you might have got running reports from me."

"Destruction!" Laure swore. "I was studying her notes from their trip outbound, trying to get some idea of what configuration to look for, once we've learned how to make allowances for what this material does to starlight—Never mind. We'll have our conference right now, just as you requested. What'd you mean by 'an illusion'?"

"The view outside," answered the computer. "The concentration of mass is not really as many atoms per cubic centimeter as would be found in a vaporous planetary atmosphere. It is only that, across lightyears, their absorption and reflection effects are cumulative. The gas and dust do, indeed, swirl, but not with anything like the velocity we think we perceive. That is due to our being under hyperdrive. Even at the very low. pseudospeed at which we are feeling our way, we pass swiftly through various densities. Space itself is not actually shining; excited atoms are fluorescing. Nor does space roar at you. What you hear is the sound of radiation counters and other instruments which I've activated. There are no real, tangible currents working on our hull, making it quiver. But when we make quantum microjumps across strong interstellar magnetic fields, and those fields vary according to an extraordinary complex pattern, we're bound to interact noticeably with them.

"Admittedly the stars are far thicker than appears. My instruments can detect none beyond a few parsecs. But what data I've gathered of late leads me to suspect the estimate of a quarter million total is conservative. To be sure, most are dwarfs—"

"Come off that!" Laure barked. "I don't need you to explain what I knew the minute I saw this place."

"You need to be drawn out of your fantasizing," *Jaccavrie* said. "Though you recognize your daydreams for what they are, you can't afford them. Not now."

Laure tensed. He wanted to order the view turned off but checked himself, wondered if the robot followed that chain of his impulses too, and said in a harshened voice: "When you go academic on me like that, it means you're postponing news you don't want to give me. We have troubles."

"We can soon have them, at any rate," *Jaccavrie* said. "My advice is to turn back at once."

"We can't navigate," Laure deduced. Though it was not unexpected, he nonetheless felt smitten.

"No. That is, I'm having difficulties already, and conditions ahead of us are demonstrably worse."

"What's the matter?"

"Optical methods are quite unsuitable. We knew that from the experience of the Kirkasanters. But nothing else works, either. You recall, you and I discussed the possibility of identifying supergiant stars through the clouds and using them for beacons. Though their light be diffused and absorbed, they should produce other effects—they should be powerful neutrino sources, for instance—that we could use."

"Don't they?"

"Oh, yes. But the effects are soon smothered. Too much else is going on. Too many neutrinos from too many different sources, to name one thing. Too many magnetic effects. The stars are so close together, you see; and so many of them are double, triple, quadruple, hence revolving rapidly and twisting the force lines;

and irradiation keeps a goodly fraction of the interstellar medium in the plasma state. Thus we get electromagnetic action of every sort, plus synchrotron and betatron radiation plus nuclear collisions, plus—"

"Spare me the complete list," Laure broke in. "Just say the noise level is too high for your instruments."

"And for any instruments that I can extrapolate as buildable," *Jaccavrie* replied. "The precision their filters would require seems greater than the laws of atomistics would allow."

"What about your inertial system? Bollixed up, too?"

"It's beginning to be. That's why I asked you to come take a good look at what's around us and what we're headed into, while you listen to my report." The robot was not built to know fear, but Laure wondered if she didn't spring back to pedantry as a refuge: "Inertial navigation would work here at kinetic velocities. But we can't traverse parsecs except under hyperdrive. Inertial and gravitational mass being identical, too rapid a change of gravitational potential will tend to cause uncontrollable precession and nutation. We can compensate for that in normal parts of space. but not here. With so many stars so closely packed, moving among each other on paths too complex for me to calculate, the variation rate is becoming too much."

"In short," Laure said slowly, "if we go deeper into this stuff, we'll be flying blind."

"Yes. Just as *Makt* did."

"We can get out into clear space any time, can't we? You can follow a more or less straight line till we emerge."

"True. I don't like the hazards. The cosmic ray background is increasing considerably."

"You have screen fields."

"But I'm considering the implications. Those particles have to originate somewhere. Magnetic acceleration will only account for a fraction of their intensity. Hence the rate of nova production in this cluster, and of supernovae in the recent past, must be enormous. This in turn indicates vast numbers of lesser bodies—neutron stars, rogue planets, large meteoroids, thick dust banks—things that might be undetectable before we blunder into them."

Laure smiled at her unseen scanner. "If anything goes wrong, you'll react fast," he said. "You always do."

"I can't guarantee we won't run into trouble I can't deal with."

"Can you estimate the odds on that for me?"

Jaccavrie was silent. The air sputtered and sibilated. Laure found his vision drowning in the starfog. He needed a minute to realize he had not been answered. "Well?" he said.

"The parameters are too uncertain." Overtones had departed from her voice. "I can merely say that the probability of disaster is high in comparison to the value for travel through normal regions of the galaxy."

"Oh, for chaos' sake!" Laure's laugh was uneasy. "That figure is almost too small to measure. We knew before we entered this nebula that we'd be taking a risk. Now what about coherent radiation from natural sources?"

"My judgment is that the risk is out of proportion to the gain," *Jaccavrie* said. "At best, this is a place for scientific study. You've other work to do. Your basic—and dangerous—fantasy is that you can satisfy the emotional cravings of a few semibarbarians."

Anger sprang up in Laure. He gave it cold shape: "My order was that you report on coherent radiation."

Never before had he pulled the rank of his humanness on her.

She said like dead metal: "I have detected some in the visible and short infrared, where certain types of star excite pseudoquasar processes in the surrounding gas. It is dissipated as fast as any other light."

"The radio bands are clear?"

"Yes, of that type of wave, although—"

"Enough. We'll proceed as before, toward the center of the cluster. Cut this view and connect me with *Makt*."

The hazy suns vanished. Laure was alone in a metal compartment. He took a seat and glowered at the outercom screen before him. What had gotten into *Jaccavrie*, anyway? She'd been making her disapproval of this quest more and more obvious over the last few days. She wanted him to turn around, report to HQ, and leave the Kirkasanters there for whatever they might be able to make of themselves in a lifetime's exile. Well…her judgments were always conditioned by the fact that she was a Ranger vessel, built for Ranger work. But couldn't she see that his duty, as well as his desire, was to help Graydal's people?

The screen flickered. The two ships were so differently designed that it was hard for them to stay in phase for any considerable time, and thus hard to receive the modulation imposed on space-pulses. After a while the image steadied to show a face. "I'll switch you to Captain Demring," the communications officer said at once. In his folk, such lack of ceremony was as revealing of strain as haggardness and dark-rimmed eyes.

The image wavered again and became the Old Man's. He was in his cabin, which had direct audiovisual connections, and the background struck Laure anew with outlandishness. What history had brought forth the artistic conventions of that bright-colored, angular-figured tapestry? What song was being sung on the player, in what language, and on what scale? What was the symbolism behind the silver mask on the door?

Worn but indomitable, Demring looked forth and said, "Peace between us. What occasions this call?"

"You should know what I've learned," Laure said. "Uh, can we make this a three-way with your navigator?"

"Why?" The question was machine steady.

"Well, that is, her duties—"

"She is to help carry out decisions," Demring said. "She does not make them. At maximum, she can offer advice in discussion." He waited before adding, with a thrust: "And you have been having a great deal of discussion already with my daughter, Ranger Laure."

"No...I mean, yes, but—" The younger man rallied. He did have psych training to call upon, although its use had not yet become reflexive in him. "Captain," he said, "Graydal has been helping me understand your ethos. Our two cultures have to see what each other's basics are if they're to cooperate, and that process begins right here, among these ships. Graydal can make things clearer to me, and I believe grasps my intent better, than anyone else of your crew."

"Why is that?" Demring demanded.

Laure suppressed pique at his arrogance—he was her father—and attempted a smile. "Well, sir, we've gotten acquainted to a degree, she and I. We can drop formality and just be friends."

"That is not necessarily desirable," Demring said.

Laure recollected that, throughout the human species, sexual customs are among the most variable. And the most emotionally charged. He put himself inside Demring's prejudices and said with what he hoped was the right slight note of indignation: "I assure you nothing improper has occurred."

"No, no." The Kirkasanter made a brusque, chopping gesture. "I trust her. And you, I am sure. Yet I must warn that close ties between members of radically different societies can prove disastrous to everyone involved."

Laure might have sympathized as he thought, *He's afraid to let down his mask—is that why their art uses the motif so much!—but underneath, he is a father worrying about his little girl.* He felt too harassed. First his computer, now this! He said coolly, "I don't believe our cultures are that alien. They're both rational-technological, which is a tremendous similarity to begin with. But haven't we got off the subject? I wanted you to hear the findings this ship has made."

Demring relaxed. The unhuman universe he could cope with. "Proceed at will, Ranger."

When he had heard Laure out, though, he scowled, tugged his beard, and said without trying to hide distress: "Thus we have no chance of finding Kirkasant by ourselves."

"Evidently not," Laure said. "I'd hoped that one of my modem locator systems would work in this cluster. If so, we could have zigzagged rapidly between the stars, mapping them, and had a fair likelihood of finding the group you know within months. But as matters stand, we can't establish an accurate enough grid, and we have nothing to tie any such grid to. Once a given star disappears in the fog, we can't find it again. Not even by straight-line backtracking, because we don't have the navigational feedback to keep on a truly straight line."

"Lost." Demring stared down at his hands, clenched on the desk before him. When he looked up again, the bronze face was rigid with pain. "I was afraid of this," he said. "It is why I was reluctant to come back at all. I feared the effect of disappointment on my crew. By now you must know one major respect in which we differ from you. To us, home, kinfolk, ancestral graves are not mere pleasures. They are an important part of our identities. We are prepared to explore and colonize, but not to be totally cut off." He straightened in his seat and turned the confession into a strategic datum by finishing dry-voiced: "Therefore, the sooner we leave this degree of familiarity behind us and accept with physical renunciation the truth of what has happened to us—the sooner we get out of this cluster—the better for us."

"No," Laure said. "I've given a lot of thought to your situation. There *are* ways to navigate here."

Demring did not show surprise. He, too, must have dwelt on contingencies and possibilities. Laure sketched them nevertheless:

"Starting from outside the cluster, we can establish a grid of artificial beacons. I'd guess fifty thousand, in orbit around selected stars, would do. If each has its distinctive identifying signal, a spaceship can locate herself and lay a course. I can imagine several ways to make them. You want them to emit something that isn't swamped by natural noise. Hyperdrive drones, shuttling automatically back and forth, would be detectable in a light-year's radius. Coherent radio broadcasters on the right bands should be detectable at the same distance or better. Since the stars hereabouts are only light-weeks or light-months apart, an electromagnetic network wouldn't take long to complete its linkups. No doubt a real engineer, turned loose on the problem, would find better answers than these."

"I know" Demring said. "We on *Makt* have discussed the matter and reached similar conclusions. The basic obstacle is the work involved first in producing that number of beacons, then—more significantly—in planting them. Many man-years, much shipping, must go to that task, if it is to be accomplished in a reasonable time."

"Yes."

"I like to think," said Demring, "that the clans of Hobrok would not haggle over who was to pay the cost. But I have talked with men on Serieve. I have taken heed of what Graydal does and does not relay of her conversations with you. Yours is a mercantile civilization."

"Not exactly," Laure said. "I've tried to explain—"

"Don't bother. We shall have the rest of our lives to learn about your Commonalty. Shall we turn about, now, and end this expedition?"

Laure winced at the scorn but shook his head. "No, best we continue. We can make extraordinary findings here. Things that'll attract scientists. And with a lot of ships buzzing around—"

Demring's smile had no humor. "Spare me, Ranger. There will never be that many scientists come avisting. And they will never plant beacons throughout the cluster. Why should they? The chance of one of their vessels stumbling on Kirkasant is negligible. They will be after unusual stars and planets, information on magnetic fields and plasmas and whatever else is readily studied. Not even the anthropologists will have any strong impetus to search out our world. They have many others to work on, equally strange to them, far more accessible."

"I have my own obligations," Laure said. "It was a long trip here. Having made it, I should recoup some of the cost to my organization by gathering as much data as I can before turning home."

"No matter the cost to my people?" Demring said slowly. "That they see their own sky around them, but nonetheless are exiles—for weeks longer?"

Laure lost his patience. "Withdraw if you like Captain," he snapped. "'I've no authority to stop you. But I'm going on. To the middle of the cluster, in fact."

Demring retorted in a cold flare: "Do you hope to find something that will make you personally rich, or only personally famous?" He reined himself in at once. "This is no place for impulsive acts. Your vessel is undoubtedly superior to mine. I am not certain, either, that *Makt's* navigational equipment is equal to finding that advanced base where we must refuel her. If you continue, I am bound in simple prudence to accompany you, unless the risks you take become gross. But I urge that we confer again."

"Any time, Captain." Laure cut his circuit.

He sat then, for a while, fuming. The culture barrier couldn't be that high. Could it? Surely the Kirkasanters were neither so stupid—nor so perverse as not to see what he was trying to do for them. Or were they? Or was it his fault? He'd concentrated more on learning about them than on teaching them about him. Still, Graydal, at least, should know him by now.

The ship sensed an incoming call and turned Laure's screen back on. And there she was. Gladness lifted in him until he saw her expression.

She said without greeting, winter in the golden gaze: "We officers have just been given a playback of your conversation with my father. What is your" (outphasing occurred, making the image into turbulence, filling the voice with static-like ugliness, but he thought he recognized) "intention?" The screen blanked.

"Maintain contact," Laure told *Jaccavrie*.

"Not easy, in these gravitic fields," the ship said.

Laure jumped to his feet, cracked fist in palm, and shouted, "Is everything trying to brew trouble for me? Bung her back or so help me, I'll scrap you!"

He got a picture again, though it was blurred and wavery and the voice was streaked with buzzes and whines as if he called to Graydal. across light-years of swallowing starfog. She said—was it a little more kindly?—"We're puzzled. I was deputed to inquire further, since I am most…familiar…with you. If our two craft can't find Kirkasant by themselves, why are we going on?"

Laure understood her so well, after the watches when they talked, dined, drank, played music, laughed together, that he saw the misery behind her armor. For her people—for herself—this journey among mists was crueler than it would have been for him had he originated here. He belonged to a civilization of travelers; to him, no one planet could be the land of lost content. But in them would always stand a certain ridge purple against sunset, marsh at dawn, ice cloud walking over wind-gnawed desert crags, ancient castle, wingbeat in heaven…and always, always, the dear bright nights that no other place in man's universe knew.

They were a warrior folk They would not settle down to be pitied; they would forge something powerful for themselves in their exile. But he was not helping them forget their uprootedness.

Thus he almost gave her his true reason. He halted in time and, instead, explained in more detail what he had told Captain Demring. His ship represented a considerable investment, to be amortized over her service life. Likewise, with his training, did he. The time he had spent coming hither was, therefore, equivalent to a large sum of money. And to date, he had nothing to show for that expense except confirmation of a fairly obvious guess about the nature of Kirkasant's surroundings.

He had broad discretion—while he was in service. But he could be discharged. He would be, if his career, taken as a whole didn't seem to be returning a profit. In this particular case, the profit would consist of detailed information about a unique environment. You could prorate that in such terms as: scientific knowledge, with its potentialities for technological progress; spacefaring experience; public relations—

Graydal regarded him in a kind of horror. "You cannot mean…we go on… merely to further your private ends," she whispered. Interference gibed at them both.

"No!" Laure protested. "Look, only look, I want to help you. But you, too, have to justify yourselves economically. You're the reason I came so far in the first place. If you're to work with the Commonalty, and it's to help you make a fresh start, you have to show that that's worth the commonalty's while. Here's where we start providing it. By going on. Eventually, by bringing them a bookful of knowledge they didn't have before."

Her gaze upon him calmed but remained aloof. "Do you think that is right?"

"It's the way things are, anyhow," he said. "Sometimes I wonder if my attempts to explain my people to you haven't glided right off your brain."

"You have made it clear that they think of nothing but their own good," she said thinly.

"If so, I've failed to make anything clear." Laure slumped in his chair web. Some days hit a man with one club after the next. He forced himself to sit erect again and say:

"We have a different ideal from you. Or no, that's not correct. We have the same set of ideals. The emphases are different. You believe the individual ought to be free and ought to help his fellowman. We do, too. But you make the service basic, you give it priority. We have the opposite way. You give a man, or a woman, duties to the clan and the country from birth. But you protect his individuality by frowning on slavishness and on anyone who doesn't keep a strictly private side to his life. We give a person freedom, within a loose framework of common-sense prohibitions. And then we protect his social aspect by frowning on greed, selfishness, callousness."

"I know," she said. "You have—"

"But maybe you haven't thought how we *must* do it that way," he pleaded. "Civilization's gotten too big out there for anything but freedom to work. The Commonalty isn't a government. How would you govern ten million planets? It's a private, voluntary, mutual-benefit society, open to anyone anywhere who meets the modest standards. It maintains certain services for its members, like my own space rescue work. The services are widespread and efficient enough that local planetary governments also like to hire them. But I don't speak for my civilization. Nobody does. You've made a friend of me. But how do you make friends with ten million times a billion individuals?"

"You've told me before," she said.

And it didn't register. Not really. Too new an idea for you, I suppose, Laure thought. He ignored her remark and went on:

"In the same way, we can't have a planned interstellar economy. Planning breaks down under the sheer mass of detail when it's attempted for a single continent. History is full of cases. So we rely on the market, which operates as automatically as gravitation. Also as efficiently, as impersonally, and sometimes as ruthlessly—but we didn't make this universe. We only live in it."

He reached out his hands, as if to touch her through the distance and the distortion. "Can't you see? I'm not able to help your plight. Nobody is. No individual quadrillionaire, no foundation, no government, no consortium could pay the cost of finding your home for you. It's not a matter of lacking charity. It's a matter of lacking resources for that magnitude of effort. The resources are divided among too many people, each of whom has his own obligations to meet first.

"Certainly, if each would contribute a pittance, you could buy your fleet. But the tax mechanism for collecting that pittance doesn't exist and can't be made to exist. As for free-will donations—how do we get your message across to an entire civilization, that big, that diverse, that busy with its own affairs?—which include cases of need far more urgent than yours.

"Graydal, we're not greedy where I come from. We're helpless."

She studied him at length. He wondered, but could not see through the ripplings, what emotions passed across her face. Finally she spoke, not altogether urgently, though helmeted again in the reserve of her kindred, and he could not hear anything of it through the buzzings except: "…proceed, since we must. For a while, anyhow. Good watch, Ranger."

The screen blanked. This time he couldn't make the ship repair the connection for him.

At the heart of the great cluster, where the nebula was so thick as to be a nearly featureless glow, pearl-hued and shot with rainbows, the stars were themselves so close that thousands could be seen. The spaceships crept forward like frigates on unknown seas of ancient Earth. For here was more than fog; here were shoals, reefs, and riptides. Energies travailed in the plasma. Drifts of dust, loose planets, burnt-out suns lay in menace behind the denser clouds. Twice *Makt* would have met catastrophe had not *Jaccavrie* sensed the danger with keener instruments and cried a warning to sheer off.

After Demring's subsequent urging had failed, Graydal came aboard in person to beg Laure that he turn homeward. That she should surrender her pride to such an extent bespoke how worn down she and her folk were. "What are we gaining worth the risk?" she asked shakenly.

"We're proving that this is a treasure house of absolutely unique phenomena," he answered. He was also hollowed, partly from the long travel and the now constant tension, partly from the half estrangement between him and her. He tried to put enthusiasm in his voice. Once we've reported, expeditions are certain to be organized. I'll bet the foundations of two or three whole new sciences will get laid here."

"I know. Everything astronomical, in abundance close together and interacting." Her shoulders drooped. "But our task isn't research. We can go back now, we could have gone back already, and carried enough details with us. Why do we not?"

"I want to investigate several planets yet, on the ground, in different systems," he told her. "Then we'll call a halt."

"What do they matter to you?"

"Well, local stellar spectra are freakish. I want to know if the element abundances in solid bodies correspond."

She stared at him. "I do not understand you," she said. "I thought I did, but I was wrong. You have no compassion. You led us, you lured us so far in that we can't escape without your ship for a guide. You don't care how tired and tormented we are. You can't, or won't, understand why we are anxious to live."

"I am myself," he tried to grin. "I enjoy the process."

The dark head shook. "I said you won't understand. We do not fear death for ourselves. But most of us have not yet had children. We do fear death for our bloodlines. We *need* to find a home, forgetting Kirkasant, and begin our families. You, though, you keep us on this barren search—why? For your own glory?"

He should have explained then. But the strain and weariness in him snapped: "You accepted my leadership. That makes me responsible for you, and I can't be responsible if I don't have command. You can endure another couple of weeks. That's all it'll take."

And she should have answered that she knew his motives were good and wished simply to hear his reasons. But being the descendant of hunters and soldiers, she clicked heels together and flung back at him: "Very well, Ranger. I shall convey your word to my captain."

She left, and did not again board *Jaccavrie*.

Later, after a sleepless "night," Laure said, "Put me through to *Makt's* navigator."

"I wouldn't advise that," said the woman-voice of his ship.

"Why not?"

"I presume you want to make amends. Do you know how she—-or her father, or her young male shipmates that must be attracted to her—how they will react? They are alien to you, and under intense strain."

"They're human!"

Engines pulsed. Ventilators whispered. "Well?" said Laure.

"I'm not designed to compute about emotions, except on an elementary level," *Jaccavrie* said. "But please recollect the diversity of mankind. On Reith, for example, ordinary peaceful men can fall into literally murderous rages. It happens so often that violence under those circumstances is not a crime in their law. A Talatto will be patient and cheerful in adversity, up to a certain point: after which he quits striving, contemplates his God, and waits to die. You can think of other cultures. And they are within the ambience of the Commonalty. How foreign might not the Kirkasanters be?"

"Um-m-m—"

"I suggest you obtrude your presence on them as little as possible. That makes for the smallest probability of provoking some unforeseeable outburst. Once our task is completed, once we are bound home, the stress will be removed and you can safely behave toward them as you like."

"Well…you may be right." Laure stared dull-eyed at a bulkhead. "I don't know. I just don't know!"

Before long, he was too busy to fret much. *Jaccavrie* went at his direction, finding planetary systems that belonged to various stellar types. In each, he landed on an airless body, took analytical readings and mineral samples, and gave the larger worlds a cursory inspection from a distance.

He did not find life. Not anywhere. He had expected that. In fact, he was confirming his whole guess about the inmost part of the cluster.

Here gravitation had concentrated dust and gas till the rate of star production became unbelievable. Each time the cluster passed through the clouds around galactic center and took on a new load of material, there must have been a spate of supernovae, several per century for a million years or more. He could not visualize what fury had raged; he scarcely dared put his estimate in numbers. Probably radiation had sterilized every abode of life for fifty light-years around. Kirkasant must therefore lie farther out—which fitted in with what he had been told, that the interstellar medium was much denser in this core region than in the neighborhood of the vanished world.

Nuclei had been cooked in stellar interiors, not the two, three, four star-generations which have preceded the majority of the normal galaxy—here, a typical atom might well have gone through a dozen successive supernova explosions. Transformation built on transformation. Hydrogen and helium remained the commonest elements, but only because of overwhelming initial abundance. Otherwise the lighter substances had mostly become rare. Planets were like nothing ever known before. Giant ones did not have thick shells of frozen water, nor did smaller ones have extensive silicate crusts. Carbon, oxygen, nitrogen, sodium, aluminum, calcium were all but lost among…iron, gold, mercury, tungsten, bismuth, uranium and transuranics—On some little spheres Laure dared not land. They radiated too fiercely. A heavily armored robot might someday set foot on them, but never a living organism.

The crew of *Makt* didn't offer to help him. Irrational in his hurt, he didn't ask them. *Jaccavrie* could carry on any essential communication with their captain and navigator. He toiled until he dropped, woke, fueled his body, and went back to work. Between stars, he made detailed analyses of his samples. That was tricky enough to keep his mind off Graydal. Minerals like these could have formed nowhere but in this witchy realm.

Finally the ships took orbit around a planet that had atmosphere. "Do you indeed wish to make entry there?" the computer asked. "I would not recommend it."

"You never recommend anything I want to do," Laure grunted. "I know air adds an extra factor to reckon with. But I want to get some idea of element distribution at the surface of objects like that." He rubbed bloodshot eyes. "It'll be the last. Then we go home."

"As you wish." Did the artificial voice actually sigh?

"But after this long a time in space, you'll have to batten things down for an aerodynamic landing."

"No, I won't. I'm taking the sled as usual. You'll stay put."

"You are being reckless. This isn't an airless globe where I can orbit right above the mountaintops and see everything that might happen to you. Why, if I haven't misgauged, the ionosphere is so charged that the sled radio can't reach me."

"Nothing's likely to go wrong," Laure said. "But should it, you can't be spared. The Kirkasanters need you to conduct them safely out."

"I—"

"You heard your orders." Laure proceeded to discuss certain basic precautions. Not that he felt they were necessary. His objective looked peaceful—dry, sterile, a stone spinning around a star.

Nevertheless, when he departed the main hatch and gunned his gravity sled to kill velocity, the view caught at his breath.

Around him reached the shining fog. Stars and stars were caught in it, illuminating caverns and tendrils, aureoled with many-colored fluorescences. Even as he looked, one such point, steely blue, multiplied its brilliance until the intensity hurt his eyes. Another nova. Every stage of stellar evolution was so richly represented that it was as if time itself had been compressed—cosmos, what an astrophysical laboratory!

(For unmanned instruments, as a general rule. Human flesh couldn't stand many months in a stretch of the cosmic radiation that sleeted through these spaces, the synchrotron and betatron and Cerenkov quanta that boiled from particles hurled in the gas across the intertwining magnetism of atoms and suns. Laure kept glancing at the cumulative exposure meter on his left wrist.)

The solar disk was large and lurid orange. Despite thermostating in the sled, Laure felt its heat strike at him through the bubble and his own armor. A step-down viewer revealed immense prominences licking flame-tongues across the sky, and a heartstoppingly beautiful corona. A Type K shouldn't be that spectacular, but there were no normal stars in sight—not with this element distribution and infall.

Once the planet he was approaching had been farther out. But friction with the nebula, over gigayears, was causing it to spiral inward. Surface temperature wasn't yet excessive, about 50° C, because the atmosphere was thin, mainly noble gases. The entire world hadn't sufficient water to fill a decent lake. It rolled before him as a gloom little relieved by the reddish blots of gigantic dust storms. Refracted light made its air a fiery ring.

His sled struck that atmosphere, and for a while he was busy amidst thunder and shudder, helping the autopilot bring the small craft down. In the end he hovered above a jumbled plain. Mountains bulked bare on the near horizon. The rock was black and brown and darkly gleaming. The sun stood high in a deep purple heaven. He checked with an induction probe, confirmed that the ground was solid—in fact, incredibly hard—and landed.

When he stepped out, weight caught at him. The planet had less diameter than the least of those on which men live, but was so dense that gravity stood at 1.22 standard G. An unexpectedly strong wind shoved at him. Though thin, the air was moving fast. He heard it wail through his helmet. From afar came a rumble, and a quiver entered his boots and bones. Landslide? Earthquake? Unseen volcano? He didn't know what was or was not possible here. Nor, he suspected, did the most expert planetologist. Worlds like this had not hitherto been trodden.

Radiation from the ground was higher than he liked. Better do his job quickly. He lugged forth apparatus. A power drill for samples—he set it up and let it work while he assembled a pyroanalyzer and fed it a rock picked off the chaotic terrain. Crumbled between alloy jaws, flash heated to vapor, the mineral gave up its fundamental composition to the optical and mass spectrographs. Laure studied the printout and nodded in satisfaction. The presence of atmosphere hadn't changed matters. This place was loaded with heavy metals and radioactives. He'd need a picture of molecular and crystalline structures before being certain that they were as easily extractable as he'd found them to be on the other planets; but he had no reason to doubt it.

Well, he thought, aware of hunger and aching feet, *let's relax awhile in the cab, catch a meal and a nap then go check a few other spots, just to make sure they're equally promising; and then—*

The sky exploded.

He was on his belly, faceplate buried in arms against that flash, before his conscious mind knew what had happened. Rangers learn about nuclear weapons. When, after a minute, no shock wave had hit him, no sound other than a rising wind, he dared sit up and look.

The sky had turned white. The sun was no longer like an orange lantern but molten brass. He couldn't squint anywhere near it. Radiance crowded upon him, heat mounted even as he climbed erect. *Nova,* he thought in his rocking reality, and caught Graydal to him for the moment he was to become a wisp of gas.

But he remained alive, alone, on a plain that now shimmered with light and mirage. The wind screamed louder still. He felt how it pushed him, and how the mass of the planet pulled, and how his mouth was dry and his muscles tautened for a leap. The brilliance pained his eyes, but was not unendurable behind a self-adapting faceplate and did not seem to be growing greater. The infrared brought forth sweat on his skin, but he was not being baked.

Steadiness came. Something almighty strange was happening. It hadn't killed him yet, though. As a check, with no hope of making contact, he tuned his radio. Static brawled in his earplugs.

His heart thudded. He couldn't tell whether he was afraid or exhilarated. He was, after all, quite a young man. But the coolness of his training came upon him. He didn't stop feeling. Wildness churned beneath self-control. But he did methodically begin to collect his equipment, and to reason while he acted.

Not a nova burst. Main sequence stars don't go nova. They don't vary in seconds, either…but then, every star around here is abnormal. Perhaps, if I'd checked the spectrum of this one, I'd have seen indications that it was about to move into another phase of a jagged output cycle. Or perhaps I wouldn't have known what the indications meant. Who's studied astrophysics in circumstances like these?

What had occurred might be akin to the Wolf-Rayet phenomenon, he thought. The stars around him did not evolve along ordinary lines. They had strange compositions to start with. And then matter kept falling into them, changing that composition, increasing their masses. That must produce instability. Each spectrum he had taken in this heart of the cluster showed enormous turbulence in the surface layers. So did the spots, flares, prominences, coronas he had seen. Well, the turbulence evidently went deeper than the photospheres. Actual stellar cores and their nuclear furnaces might be affected. Probably every local sun was a violent variable.

Even in the less dense regions, stars must have peculiar careers. The sun of Kirkasant had apparently been stable for five thousand years—or several million, more likely, since the planet had well-developed native life. But who could swear it would stay thus? Destruction! The place had to be found, had to, so that the people could be evacuated if need arose. You can't let little children fry—

Laure checked his radiation meter. The needle climbed ominously fast up the dial. Yonder sun was spitting X rays, in appreciable quantity, and the planet had no ozone layer to block them. He'd be dead if he didn't get to shelter—for choice, his ship and her forcescreens—before the ions arrived. Despite its density, the globe had no magnetic field to speak of, either, to ward them off. Probably the core was made of stuff like osmium and uranium. Such a weird blend might well be solid rather than molten. *I don't know about that. I do know I'd better get my tail out of here.*

The wind yelled. It began driving ferrous dust against him, borne from somewhere else. He saw the particles scud in darkling whirls and heard them click on his helmet. Doggedly he finished loading his gear. When at last he entered the sled cab and shut the air lock, his vehicle was trembling under the blast and the sun was reddened and dimmed by haze.

He started the motor and lifted. No sense in resisting the wind. He was quite happy to be blown toward the night side. Meanwhile he'd gain altitude, then get above the storm, collect orbital velocity and—

He never knew what happened. The sled was supposedly able to ride out more vicious blows than any this world could produce. But who could foretell what this world was capable of? The atmosphere, being thin, developed high velocities. Perhaps the sudden increased irradiation had triggered paroxysm in a cyclone cell. Perhaps the dust, which was conductive, transferred energy into such a vortex at a greater rate than one might believe. Laure wasn't concerned about meteorological theory.

He was concerned with staying alive, when an instant blindness clamped down upon him with a shriek that nigh tore the top off his skull, and he was whirled like a leaf and cast against a mountainside.

The event was too fast for awareness, for anything but reaction. His autopilot and he must somehow have got some control. The crash ruined the sled, ripped open its belly, scattered its cargo, but did not crumple the cab section. Shock harness kept the man from serious injury. He was momentarily unconscious, but came back with no worse than an aching body and blood in his mouth.

Wind hooted. Dust went hissing and scouring. The sun was a dim red disk, though from time to time a beam of pure fire struck through the storm and blazed off metallic cliffsides.

Laure fumbled with his harness and stumbled out. Half seen, the slope on which he stood caught at his feet with cragginess. He had to take cover. The beta particles would arrive at any moment, the protons within hours, and they bore his death.

He was dismayed to learn the stowed equipment was gone. He dared not search for it. Instead, he made his clumsy way into the murk.

He found no cave—not in this waterless land—but by peering and calculating (odd how calm you can grow when your life depends on your brain) he discovered in what direction his chances were best, and was rewarded. A onetime landslide had piled great slabs of rock on each other. Among them was a passage into which he could crawl.

Then nothing to do but lie in that narrow space and wait.

Light seeped around a bend, with the noise of the storm. He could judge thereby how matters went outside. Periodically he crept to the entrance of his dolmen and monitored the radiation level. Before long it had reached such a count that—space armor, expert therapy, and all—an hour's exposure would kill him.

He must wait.

Jaccavrie knew the approximate area where he intended to set down. She'd come looking as soon as possible. Flitting low, using her detectors, she'd find the wrecked sled. More than that she could not do unaided. But he could emerge and call her. Whether or not they actually saw each other in this mountainscape, he could emit a radio signal for her to home on. She'd hover, snatch him with a forcebeam, and reel him in.

But...this depended on calm weather. *Jaccavrie* could overmaster any wind. But the dust would blind both her and him. And deafen and mute them; it was conductive, radio could not get through. Laure proved that to his own satisfaction by experimenting with the miniradar built into his armor.

So everything seemed to depend on which came first, the end of the gale or the end of Laure's powerpack. His air renewer drew on it. About thirty hours' worth of charge remained before he choked on his own breath. If only he'd been able to grab a spare accumulator or two, or better still, a hand-cranked recharger! They might have rolled no more than ten meters off. But he had decided not to search the area. And by now, he couldn't go back. Not through the radiation.

He sighed, drank a bit from his water nipple, ate a bit through his chow lock, wished for a glass of beer and a comfortable bed, and went to sleep.

When he awoke, the wind had dropped from a full to a half gale; but the dust drift was so heavy as to conceal the glorious starfog night that had fallen. It screened off some of the radiation, too, though not enough to do him any good. He puzzled over why the body of the planet wasn't helping more. Finally he decided that ions, hitting the upper air along the terminator, produced secondaries and cascades which descended everywhere.

The day-side bombardment must really have got fierce!

Twenty hours left. He opened the life-support box he had taken off his shoulder rack, pulled out the sanitary unit, and attached it. Men don't die romantically, like characters on a stage. Their bodies are too stubborn.

So are their minds. He should have been putting his thoughts in order, but he kept being disturbed by recollections of his parents, of Graydal, of a funny little tavern he'd once visited, of a gaucherie he'd rather forget, of some money owing to him, of Graydal—He ate again, and drowsed again, and the wind filled the air outside with dust, and time closed in like a hand.

Ten hours left. No more?

Five. Already?

What a stupid way to end. Fear fluttered at the edge of his perception. He beat it off. The wind yammered. How long can a dust storm continue, anyhow? Where'd it come from? Daylight again, outside his refuge, colored like blood and brass. The charged particles and X rays were so thick that some diffused in to him. He shifted cramped muscles, and drank the stench of his unwashed skin, and regretted everything he had wanted and failed to do.

A shadow cast on the cornering rock. A rustle and slither conducted to his ears. A form, bulky and awkward as his own, crawling around the tunnel bend. Numb, shattered, he switched on his radio. The air was fairly clear in here and he heard her voice through the static: "…you are, you are alive! Oh, Valfar's Wings upbear us, you live!"

He held her while she sobbed, and he wept, too. "You shouldn't have," he stammered. "I never meant for *you* to risk yourself—"

"We dared not wait," she said when they were calmer. "We saw, from space, that the storm was enormous. It would go on in this area for days. And we didn't know how long you had to live. We only knew you were in trouble, or you'd have been back with us. We came down. I almost had to fight my father, but I won and came. The hazard wasn't so great for me. Really, no, believe me. She protected me till we found your sled. Then I did have to go out afoot with a metal detector to find you. Because you were obviously sheltered somewhere, and so you could only be detected at closer range than she can come. But the danger wasn't that great, Daven. I can stand much more radiation than you. I'm still well inside my tolerance, won't even need any drugs. Now I'll shoot off this flare and she'll see, and come so close that we can make a dash—You are all right, aren't you? You swear it?"

"Oh, yes," he said slowly. "I'm fine. Better off than ever in my life." Absurdly, he had to have the answer, however footling all questions were against the fact that she had come after him and was here and they were both alive. "We? Who's your companion?"

She laughed and clinked her faceplate against his. *"Jaccavrie,* of course. Who else? You didn't think your womenfolk were about to leave you alone, did you?"

The ships began their trek homeward. They moved without haste. Best to be cautious until they had emerged from the nebula, seen where they were, and aimed themselves at the Dragon's Head.

"My people and I are pleased at your safety," said Demring's image in the outercom screen. He spoke under the obligation to be courteous, and could not refrain from adding: "We also approve your decision not to investigate that planet further."

"For the first, thanks," Laure answered. "As for the second—" He shrugged. "No real need. I was curious about the effects of an atmosphere, but my computer has just run off a probability analysis of the data I already have, which proves that no more are necessary for my purposes."

"May one inquire what your purposes are?"

"I'd like to discuss that first with your navigator. In private."

The green gaze studied Laure before Demring said, unsmiling: You have the right of command. And by our customs she having been instrumental in saving your life, a special relationship exists. But again I counsel forethought."

Laure paid no attention to that last sentence. His pulse was beating too gladly. He switched off as soon as possible and ordered the best dinner his ship could provide.

Are you certain you want to make your announcement through her?" the voice asked him. "And to her in this manner?"

"I am. I think I've earned the pleasure. Now I'm off to make myself presentable for the occasion. Carry on." Laure went whistling down the corridor.

But when Graydal boarded, he took both her hands and they looked long in silence at each other. She had strewn jewels in her tresses, turning them to a starred midnight. Her clothes were civilian, a deep blue that offset coppery skin, amber eyes, and suppleness. And did he catch the least woodsy fragrance of perfume?

"Welcome," was all he could say at last.

"I am so happy," she answered.

They went to the saloon and sat down on the couch together. Daiquiris were ready for them. They touched glasses. "Good voyage," he made the old toast, and merry landing."

"For me, yes." Her smile faded. "And I hope for the rest. How I hope."

"Don't you think they can get along in the outside worlds?"

"Yes, undoubtedly." The incredible lashes fluttered. "But they will never be as fortunate as…as I think I may be."

"You have good prospects yourself?" The blood roared in his temples.

"I am not quite sure," she replied shyly.

He had intended to spin out his surprise at length, but suddenly he couldn't let her stay troubled, not to any degree. He cleared his throat and said, "I have news."

She tilted her head and waited with that relaxed alertness he liked to see. He wondered how foolish the grin was on his face. Attempting to recover dignity, he embarked on a roundabout introduction.

"You wondered why I insisted on exploring the cluster center, and in such detail. Probably I ought to have explained myself from the beginning. But I was afraid of raising false hopes. I'd no guarantee that things would turn out to be the way I'd guessed. Failure, I thought, would be too horrible for you, if you knew what success could mean. But I was working on your behalf, nothing else.

"You see, because my civilization is founded on individualism, it makes property rights quite basic. In particular, if there aren't any inhabitants or something like that, discoverers can claim ownership within extremely broad limits.

"Well, we...you...our expedition has met the requirements of discovery as far as those planets are concerned. We've been there, we've proven what they're like, we've located them as well as might be without beacons—"

He saw how she struggled not to be too sanguine. "That isn't a true location," she said. "I can't imagine how we will ever lead anybody back to precisely those stars."

"Nor can I," he said. "And it doesn't matter. Because, well, we took an adequate sample. We can be sure now that practically every star in the cluster heart has planets that are made of heavy elements. So it isn't necessary, for their exploitation, to go to any particular system. In addition, we've learned about hazards and so forth, gotten information that'll be essential to other people. And therefore"—he chuckled—"I guess we can't file a claim on your entire Cloud Universe. But any court will award you...us...a fair share. Not specific planets, since they can't be found right away. Instead, a share of everything. Your crew will draw royalties on the richest mines in the galaxy. On millions of them."

She responded with thoughtfulness rather than enthusiasm, "Indeed? We did wonder, on *Makt,* if you might not be hoping to find abundant metals. But we decided that couldn't be. For why would anyone come here for them? Can they not be had more easily, closer to home?"

Slightly dashed, he said, "No. Especially when most worlds in this frontier are comparatively metal-poor. They do have some veins of ore, yes. And the colonists can extract anything from the oceans, as on Serieve. But there's a natural limit to such a process. In time, carried out on the scale that'd be required when population has grown...it'd be releasing so much heat that planetary temperature would be affected."

"That sounds farfetched."

"No. A simple calculation will prove it. According to historical records, Earth herself ran into the problem, and not terribly long after the industrial era began. However, quite aside from remote prospects, people will want to mine these cluster worlds immediately. True, it's a long haul, and operations will have to be totally automated. But the heavy elements that are rare elsewhere are so abundant here as to more than make up for those extra costs." He smiled. "I'm afraid you can't escape your fate. You're going to be…not wealthy. To call you 'wealthy' would be like calling a supernova 'luminous.' You'll command more resources than many whole civilizations have done."

Her look upon him remained grave. "You did this for us? You should not have. What use would riches be to us if we lost you?"

He remembered that he couldn't have expected her to carol about this. In her culture, money was not unwelcome, but neither was it an important goal. So what she had just said meant less than if a girl of the Commonalty had spoken. Nevertheless, joy kindled in him. She sensed that, laid her hand across his, and murmured, "But your thought was noble."

He couldn't restrain himself any longer. He laughed aloud. "Noble?" he cried. "I'd call it clever. Fiendishly clever. Don't you see? I've given you Kirkasant back!"

She gasped.

He jumped up and paced exuberant before her. "You could wait a few years till your cash reserves grow astronomical and buy as big a fleet as you want to search the cluster. But it isn't needful. When word gets out, the miners will come swarming. They'll plant beacons, they'll have to. The grid will be functioning within one year, I'll bet. As soon as you can navigate, identify where you are and where you've been, you can't help finding your home—in weeks!"

She joined him, then, casting herself into his arms, laughing and weeping. He had known of emotional depth in her, beneath the schooled reserve. But never before now had he found as much warmth as was hers.

Long, long afterward, air locks linked and she bade him good night. "Until tomorrow," she said.

"Many tomorrows, I hope."

"And I hope. I promise."

He watched the way she had gone until the locks closed again and the ships parted company. A little drunkenly, not with alcohol, he returned to the saloon for a nightcap.

"Turn off that color thing," he said. "Give me an outside view."

The ship obeyed. In the screen appeared stars, and the cloud from which stars were being born. "Her sky," Laure said. He flopped on to the couch and admired.

"I might as well start getting used to it," he said. "I expect I'll spend a lot of vacation time, at least, on Kirkasant."

"Daven," said *Jaccavrie*.

She was not in the habit of addressing him thus, and so gently. He started. "Yes?"

"I have been—" Silence hummed for a second. "I have been wondering how to tell you. Any phrasing, any inflection, could strike you as something I computed to produce an effect. I am only a machine."

Though unease prickled him, he leaned forward to touch a bulkhead. It trembled a little with her engine energy. "And I, old girl," he said. "Or else you also are an organism. We're both people."

"Thank you," said the ship, almost too low to be heard.

Laure braced himself. "What did you have to tell me?"

She forgot about keeping her voice humanized. The words clipped forth: "I finished the chromosome analysis some time ago. Thereafter I tried to discourage certain tendencies I noticed in you. But now I have no way to avoid giving you the plain truth. They are not human on that planet."

"What?" he yelled. The glass slipped from his hand and splashed red wine across the deck. "You're crazy! Records, traditions, artifacts, appearance, behavior—"

The ship's voice came striding across his. "Yes, they are human descended. But their ancestors had to make an enormous adaptation. The loss of night vision is merely indicative. The fact that they can, for example, ingest heavy metals like arsenic unharmed might be interpreted as simple immunity. But you will recall that they find unarsenated food tasteless. Did that never suggest to you that they have developed a metabolic requirement for the element? And you should have drawn a conclusion from their high tolerance for ionizing radiation. It cannot be due to their having stronger proteins, can it? No, it must be because they have evolved a capacity for extremely rapid and error-free repair of chemical damage from that source. This in turn is another measure of how different their enzyme system is from yours.

"Now the enzymes, of course, are governed by the DNA of the cells, which is the molecule of heredity—"

"Stop," Laure said. His speech was as flat as hers. "I see what you're at. You are about to report that your chromosome study proved the matter. My kind of people and hers can't reproduce with each other."

"Correct," *Jaccavrie* said.

Laure shook himself, as if he were cold. He continued to look at the glowing fog. "You can't call them nonhuman on that account."

"A question of semantics. Hardly an important one. Except for the fact that Kirkasanters apparently are under an instinctual compulsion to have children."

"I know," Laure said.

And after a time: "Good thing, really. They're a high-class breed. We could use a lot of them."

"Your own genes are above average," *Jaccavrie* said.

"Maybe. What of it?"

Her voice turned alive again. "I'd like to have grandchildren," she said wistfully.

Laure laughed. "All right," he said. "No doubt one day you will." The laughter was somewhat of a victory.

Acknowledgements

Two names appear as the editors of this book. While we each did a lot of work, this page is for the many other people without whose labors, the book would never have been published.

Technical help was provided by Dave Grubbs, Alice Lewis, Tony Lewis, Mark Olson and Geri Sullivan.

Proofreading was done by Bonnie Atwood, Ann Broomhead, Jim Burton, Gay Ellen Dennett, Pam Fremon, Tony Lewis, Mark Olson, Lis Pfeffer, Sharon Sbarsky, and Tim Szczesuil.

Ann Crimmins and Dave Grubbs independently checked the book for errors previously missed. Many were found.

Alice Lewis then did her magic in producing the dust jacket.

Special thanks to Greg Bear for his introduction to the book and supplying that wonderful picture of Karen and Poul.

For those interested, the original proposal to Karen Anderson was made at the L.A. Worldcon in 2006. These books do take time to produce.

Rick Katze
Lis Carey
November 2008

Superlative SF Available from the NESFA Press

Major Ingredients by Eric Frank Russell..........................$29
Entities by Eric Frank Russell...$29

Works of Art by James Blish...$29

Brother in Arms by Lois McMaster Bujold $25

From These Ashes by Fredric Brown................................$29
*A New Dawn: The Don A. Stuart Stories
of John W. Campbell, Jr.* $26

Years in the Making by L. Sprague de Camp $25
The Mathematics of Magic
by L. Sprague de Camp & Fletcher Pratt.........................$26

The Masque of Mañana by Robert Sheckley.....................$29
Dimensions of Sheckley by Robert Sheckley......................$29

Here Comes Civilization by William Tenn $29
Immodest Proposals: The Short SF of William Tenn $29
Dancing Naked by William Tenn $29

Transfinite: The Essential A. E. van Vogt $29

All titles are hardback unless otherwise noted, and printed on long-life acid-free paper. NESFA Press accepts payment by mail, check, money order, MasterCard, or Visa. Please add $5 postage ($10 for multiple books) for each order. Massachusetts residents please add 5% sales tax. Fax orders (Visa/MC only): (617) 776-3243. Write for our free catalog, or check out our online catalog by directing your Internet web browser to: www.nesfapress.com.

NESFA Press

Post Office Box 809
Framingham, MA 01701
www.nesfa.org/press
2009